OFF THE MAIN SEQUENCE

Books by Robert A. Heinlein

Novels

Beyond This Horizon (1948)
Sixth Column (1949)
The Puppet Masters (1951)
Double Star (1956)
The Door Into Summer (1957)
Methuselah's Children (1958)
Starship Troopers (1959)
Stranger in a Strange Land (1961)
Glory Road (1963)
Orphans of the Sky (1963)
Farnham's Freehold (1964)
The Moon Is a Harsh Mistress (1966)
I Will Fear No Evil (1970)
Time Enough for Love (1973)
The Number of the Beast (1980)
Friday (1982)
Job: A Comedy of Justice (1984)
The Cat Who Walks Through Walls (1985)
To Sail Beyond the Sunset (1987)
For Us, The Living (2003)

Juvenile Novels

Rocket Ship Galileo (1947)
Space Cadet (1948)
Red Planet (1949)
Farmer in the Sky (1950)
Between Planets (1951)
The Rolling Stones (1952)
Starman Jones (1953)
The Star Beast (1954)
Tunnel in the Sky (1955)
Time for the Stars (1956)
Citizen of the Galaxy (1957)
Have Space Suit — Will Travel (1958)
Podkayne of Mars (1963)

Short Fiction & Miscellaneous

The Man Who Sold the Moon (1950)
Waldo and Magic, Inc. (1950)
The Green Hills of Earth (1951)
Revolt in 2100 (1953)
Assignment in Eternity (1953)
The Menace From Earth (1959)
The Unpleasant Profession of Jonathan Hoag (1959)
The Worlds of Robert A. Heinlein (1966)
The Past Through Tomorrow (1967)
Expanded Universe (1980)
Grumbles from the Grave (1989)
Requiem: New Collected Works (1992)
Tramp Royale (1992)
The Fantasies of Robert A. Heinlein (1999)

OFF THE MAIN SEQUENCE

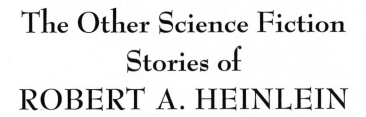

The Other Science Fiction
Stories of
ROBERT A. HEINLEIN

Edited by Andrew Wheeler
Introduction by Greg Bear
Foreword by Michael Cassutt

SCIENCE
FICTION

First SFBC Science Fiction Printing: October 2005

Published by arrangement with
The Robert A. and Virginia Heinlein Prize Trust
c/o Spectrum Literary Agency
320 Central Park West, Suite 1D
New York, NY 10025

Visit The SFBC online at http://www.sfbc.com
Visit the Heinlein Society at http://www.heinleinsociety.org

ISBN: 1-58288-184-7

Printed in the United States of America.

❖ CONTENTS ❖

❖ INTRODUCTION ❖

by Greg Bear

RE-READING THESE WONDERFUL stories leaves me with the feeling that I have been present at the creation. There are so many ideas buried in here that may never have been thought of before—by human beings, at any rate. What a treat to have them all in one volume—and what a bargain, as well!

Here you will find "Universe" and "Common Sense," both published in 1941—the first definitive stories about a generation starship, where entire cultures live and die on a massive craft cruising the unimaginable distances between the stars. (They were combined and published as the short novel *Orphans of the Sky* in 1963.) You're about to meet the two-headed mutant Joe-Jim, smartest man on a very big ship, and his microcephalic and cannibalistic pal Bobo . . . both of whom prove, in their perverse and charming ways, that Heinlein was an equal opportunity kind of writer. (Note that Heinlein never actually *shows* Joe-Jim and Bobo snatching and eating babies.)

Here also is "They" (1941), in which solipsistic paranoia is fully justified—and "By His Bootstraps" (also 1941—a banner year for Heinlein), which takes time travel paradoxes to a twisty new level— and "—All You Zombies—" (1959), which adds another turn of the screw that probably could not have been published in the period of "By His Bootstraps." And then there's "—And He Built a Crooked House—" (1941), in which a 1940s black and white screwball comedy is combined with some Technicolor math and architecture to create the wackiest building ever conceived of—in California, which is saying a lot. (Imagine Cary Grant, Carole Lombard, and Cecil Kellaway in the starring roles . . .)

This volume perfectly complements an earlier omnibus of Robert Heinlein's stories called *The Past Through Tomorrow*. That volume collected all of Heinlein's so-called Future History stories, which fit within a timeline. Heinlein was not the first to create a future history timeline—that credit probably goes to Neil R. Jones for his Professor Jameson series, for a multi-story sequence, or to H. G. Wells and Olaf

Stapledon for single-volume works. But Heinlein was the first to spread the idea to a significant population of modern science fiction readers by actually printing his timeline in *Astounding Science Fiction,* and later in the collection "The Man Who Sold the Moon." (It's also reprinted in the collections *Revolt in 2100* and *The Past Through Tomorrow.*)

The Future History stories and novels are ground-breaking, to be sure, but the "Off the Main Sequence" tales in this collection are every bit as influential—and more wide-ranging.

A few highlights:

"Solution Unsatisfactory" (1941) is Heinlein's latter-day response to H. G. Wells' "The World Set Free." Heinlein dispassionately tells a future history of atomic poison and Cold War stalemate leading to a compulsory world state—which is no one's desired solution. With chilling verisimilitude and political savvy, Heinlein lays out a prescient view of the next twenty years of human history. Like Wells, Heinlein gets the spirit of the future right, if not the details. Anyone who lived through the Cold War and Mutual Assured Destruction will shiver with recognition.

"Gulf" (1949) is a novella of espionage, competing supermen, semantics, another Ultimate Weapon—and ultimate sacrifice. It's a wild-ass tale bursting with didactic discussion and ideas, seemingly designed to fit right in with the then-current notion that science fiction readers—fans—were Slans, like A. E. van Vogt's superhuman mutants. In fact, "Gulf" reads like a tribute to A. E. van Vogt. Along with van Vogt, Heinlein was a student of the then-in-vogue Alfred Korzybski, creator of General Semantics. (Look it up—naturally, there's a great deal of material about Korzybski and his philosophy on the Web.) I also sense a touch of Hitchcock—a McGuffin and a conspiratorial ranch house straight out of *Saboteur* (1942). Heinlein paid a great deal of attention to contemporary films; his characters' speech patterns, romantic relationships, and can-do attitude mirror those found in movies more closely even than most pulp stories, and that certainly contributed to his success and readability—but today, these patterns may seem dated. To appreciate "Gulf," origins, models, and Heinlein's contemporary readership must be kept in mind.

Which leads us to Heinlein's actual film work . . .

"Destination Moon" (1950) is the story that resulted from Heinlein's participation in the George Pal film of the same name, the most technically accurate science fiction film since *Things to Come* (1936), and until *2001: A Space Odyssey* (1968). The movie's ending is different, however—Heinlein allowed himself an ambiguous but probably apocalyptic conclusion. (There's a concluding commemorative plaque here, as well as in "Gulf" . . .) George Pal, who firmly believed in relatively happy endings and box office receipts, apparently thought this might be too strong for the audiences of the day. Keep in mind, however, that a few years later, the movie version of James A. Michener's *The Bridges at Toko-Ri* (1955) ends with the pilot's death. Following the disillusionment of the Korean War, dark endings became a vogue, some much less heroic. Heinlein, as usual, was ahead of the curve.

It should be fairly chilling to read "The Year of the Jackpot" (1952), a brilliant, talky, and moving tale of statistics and final disaster. Chilling, because Heinlein mentions a Chief Justice Roberts, and in this year, 2005, we're likely to have a Chief Justice by that name appointed to preside over the U.S. Supreme Court. Worth paying attention to in a number of Heinlein's stories is the depth of his understanding of American culture and pop psychology—so much of what he describes in "Year of the Jackpot" could just as easily be transplanted into a story written today. In the context of grim statistical curves piling one upon another, the otherwise hokey romance and marriage—and bravery—of Potiphar Breen and Meade Barstow actually makes my eyes grow moist—and that shows how much Heinlein understood my psychology, as well.

Incidentally, Robert Heinlein has become a doyen to many modern conservatives, particularly Libertarians. "Year of the Jackpot" will provide both comfort and aggravation to rugged individualists. Heinlein was an equal opportunity charmer and puller of mustaches. You can never be certain what he will do or say next. To my mind, Heinlein's three most controversial novels, *Starship Troopers* (1959), *Stranger in a Strange Land* (1961), and *Farnham's Freehold* (1965)—are just such tweaks of the common American mustache. Heinlein loved to throw out philosophical tough steak—giving us all something substantial to chew on. Stuffed shirts on both sides of the political divide can spit gristle and huff and puff all they wish—that would delight Heinlein no end, I think.

Then there are the Lyle Monroe stories—puckish, a bit like L. Sprague de Camp, a bit like Thorne Smith, but with logical and science fictional touches that make them pure Heinlein. They remain a delight to read—trips back to a gentler sense of humor out of a deeply troubled but valiant and coping age.

Each of these stories has its own historical and science fictional delights. I've picked just a few . . . and I'm sure you'll have your favorites, and your own judgments—for that was what Robert Heinlein's stories inspired: joy, reflection, sense of wonder, doubt, affection, anger, and controversy in equal measure.

And all very far away from anyone's definition of the main sequence.

—September 13, 2005

❖ FOREWORD ❖

by Michael Cassutt

IN THE SPRING of 1939, a disabled young former naval officer— recently an unsuccessful candidate for California State Assembly—sat down at his typewriter in a small house in the Hollywood Hills, and began to write a science fiction story. Four days later it was finished; he submitted it to *Astounding Science Fiction*, the best-paying magazine in the field, where editor John Campbell read it, and bought it.

The $70 payment (the equivalent of $1,500 in twenty-first-century dollars) not only improved the young politician's bank balance, it gave him a career. Within two years Robert A. Heinlein would be considered the best, and most influential, science fiction writer in the world. Following a hiatus caused by World War II, he would expand his audience from the SF pulps to slick magazines like the *Saturday Evening Post* . . . to movies (George Pal's *Destination Moon*) . . . television (*Tom Corbett, Space Cadet*) . . . young adult novels (the fantastically successful and influential Scribner juveniles) . . . and controversial, even shocking adult works like *Stranger in a Strange Land*.

His stories not only entertained millions of readers around the world, they inspired an entire generation of engineers and rocket scientists, as well as social experimenters on opposite ends of the political spectrum.

Robert Anson Heinlein was born July 7, 1907, in the small town of Butler, Missouri, the third child of a family that eventually numbered seven. His father, Rex, soon moved the family to Kansas City, where he became a clerk for various companies over the years.

Young Robert grew up in a city that was a growing commercial center—as the Rodgers and Hammerstein song later put it, "Everything's up to date in Kansas City." To earn money, he sold magazines, was an office boy for Aetna Insurance, and had a paper route. (Two families on his route were those of actors William Powell and Jean Harlow.)

He was a bright youngster—learning to play chess when he was four. He grew interested in astronomy and mathematics, and became an omnivorous reader. Encountering Darwin's *Origin of the Species* and the works of T. H. Huxley at the age of thirteen, he became a "free-thinker," privately rejecting his family's Bible Belt fundamentalism.

He also discovered the adventure novels of Tom Swift and Frank Reade, as well as the speculations of Jules Verne and the writer who would most shape his life and career, H. G. Wells. He enjoyed the fantasies of Rudyard Kipling, Jack London, Olaf Stapledon, and Edgar Rice Burroughs.

But it was with the discovery of Hugo Gernsback's *Electrical Experimenter* magazine at age sixteen that he became a fan of modern science fiction. In his high school yearbook, a classmate would write that "he thinks in terms of the fifth dimension, never stopping at the fourth."

Heinlein's family couldn't afford to send the children to college. One older brother had enlisted in the Army during World War I. The next oldest, Rex, Jr., had earned an appointment to Annapolis.

Robert wanted an appointment, too, to either West Point or Annapolis (though he preferred the naval academy because of his interests in aviation and astronomy). Two successive appointments from the same family were out of the question. Robert found himself attending Kansas City Junior College for a year while continuing to solicit support for an appointment from Senator James A. Reed.

A member of the naval academy class of 1929, Robert prospered academically, ultimately graduating twentieth in a class of 243— marked down for "offenses against military discipline," or he would have stood fifth. He was a member of the academy's fencing team, and was poised for service in naval aviation.

He entered the U.S. Navy at a time of great change—the service was in the middle of the painful process of evolving from a battleship-based fleet to one that integrated "aeroplanes."

Ensign Heinlein was assigned to the U.S.S. *Lexington*, the third carrier commissioned by the navy, serving under Captain Ernest J. King, later the Chief of Naval Operations in World War II. Here Heinlein was exposed to the latest developments in gunnery, communications, aircraft, and even deep-sea diving. All of this experience would eventually shape his fiction.

Transferred to destroyer duty in 1932, Heinlein's military career began to founder: weakened by seasickness, he was stricken with tuberculosis and in 1933 was hospitalized at a sanitarium in Monrovia, California. (His older brother, Rex, had suffered the same fate—indeed, was hospitalized at the same sanitarium at the same time.)

Heinlein's T.B. was "arrested," but the recovery did not allow him to return to active duty. He was removed from active duty in August 1934 with the rank of lieutenant, junior grade, and given a small disability pension.

However, 1934 was the depth of the Depression. There were few jobs of any kind, certainly very few for young men with shaky health. Heinlein had a small pension; in 1932 he had married Leslyn MacDonald, an actress who later had a job in the music department at Columbia Pictures. He tried to sell real estate and to work in architecture. He also sat in on classes in physics and astronomy at UCLA. But because of his health, he was unable to find sustained employment, or to remain in school.

Always politically active and motivated—as were many young people in the 1930s—to encourage social change, Heinlein joined the End Poverty in California movement founded by activist writer Upton Sinclair.

Sinclair had run for governor of California in 1934, and been defeated in a notoriously ruthless campaign. But his movement lived on, aligning itself with the mainstream Democratic Party.

Heinlein first did volunteer legwork for the movement, then joined the staff of its newspaper, ultimately becoming deputy publisher of the *EPIC News*, with a circulation of two million. EPIC and its successors, Heinlein proudly reported, "recalled a mayor, kicked out a district attorney, replaced the governor with one of our choice," all between 1934 and 1938.

There was one notable failure in the EPIC-Democrat movement— that of Heinlein's political campaign. He ran for the 59th Assembly seat in the Hollywood Hills and Beverly Hills—his campaign contributors included the writer Dorothy Parker—against incumbent Charles Lyon, but was defeated in the August 1938 primary.

"There's no prize for place or show in politics," Heinlein would write years later. But there is a *price*: he had taken out a mortgage of $1,000 on his house. In defeat . . . physically worn down . . . with jobs hard to find . . . the mortgage a burden to a man supported only by a small naval disability pension . . . Heinlein turned to writing.

Although he would later declare that he had suddenly been inspired to attempt a fiction-writing career by ill-health and indebtedness only in the spring of 1939, Heinlein had made attempts at fiction as early as 1930, composing a mainstream story set at the naval academy. In the fall of 1938 he wrote an entire novel titled *For Us, the Living*, which was submitted to and rejected by at least two major publishers. This utopian fantasy about a young naval aviator who is killed in a car crash, then resurrected in the future, espoused a then-shocking mixture of casual nudity, radical economic theories, and even simplified spelling. Ideas aside, *For Us, the Living* was not a compelling story. Heinlein seems to have realized this, and put it aside.

Feeling that he had a better chance at making money with shorter lengths, in a few weeks in March and April 1939, he wrote two stories in this collection, " 'My Object All Sublime' " and " 'Let There Be Light,' " as well as "Lifeline."

"Light" and "Lifeline" were set in the near future—as we now know, a future largely imagined in *For Us, the Living*, in which global wars of the 1940s isolate the United States from Europe, with the U.S. developing startling new technologies such as free and unlimited power, rolling roads, and "antipodal" rockets. The United States reaches the moon in the late twentieth century, and begins to colonize the solar system. But a fundamentalist religious dictatorship fomented by a television evangelist named Nehemiah Scudder leads to a new "dark age" in the U.S., thrown off only by a revolution late in the twenty-first century, followed by the "first mature human civilization."

Using the model of Sinclair Lewis, who created maps and character biographies for his fictional state of Zenith, USA, Heinlein designed his own "Future History" chart, a wall-sized document that showed characters, inventions, and social upheavals to come—pencilling the titles of stories where they belonged. "Lifeline" was set in the present; " 'Let There Be Light' " took place around in 1980.

But not all of his stories fit that chart. On the heels of his success with "Lifeline" and another Future History tale, "Misfit," Heinlein composed a short-short written at the request of a young SF fan named Ray Bradbury, for publication in his fanzine *Futuria Fantasia*. Originally titled "Heil!," it would languish in obscurity for thirty years, until reprinted in the Sam Moskowitz anthology *Futures to Tomorrow* (1970). Heinlein himself collected it under a new title, "Successful Operation," a decade after that.

In that magical summer of 1939, Heinlein composed several fantasies ("Pied Piper"), political satires ("Beyond Doubt"), and even screwball comedies ("—And He Built a Crooked House—").

Campbell rejected most of these early attempts. The fantasies weren't quite right for his fantasy publication, *Unknown*, and the stories aimed at *Astounding* had other problems: " 'Let There Be Light' " was considered to be too racy. "The science fiction readers have shown a consistent distaste for . . . feminine scenery in science-fiction stories," Campbell wrote in his rejection letter. Of Heinlein's smart-mouth, sexy heroine, Mary Lou Martin, he said, "She's much more nicely handled than the average woman in science-fiction, but I'm still afraid of her.")

"Beyond Doubt" is interesting because it's Heinlein's only formal fictional collaboration. Elma Wentz was not only the wife of Heinlein's EPIC friend, Roby Wentz, she was Upton Sinclair's secretary. On a dare at a party, Heinlein composed a three-page story outline on the spot . . . Wentz then wrote a first draft, which Heinlein later revised and cut, then sold.

What propelled Heinlein to the first rank of SF writers was his clean storytelling style, characters whose psychological makeup was more mature and complex, and settings that felt "real." Before Heinlein, most SF writers were either scientists or engineers by profession . . . professional pulp writers translating other stories into SF settings . . . or brilliant teenagers who, for all their nascent storytelling skills, still lived with their parents.

Heinlein's engineering training gave astonishing verisimilitude to his imagined gadgets. His experiences in the military, in politics, and business made his future worlds much more believable. (He was undoubtedly the first SF writer to use a notary public in a story.) He was familiar with Boy Scout camps and fraternal lodges, with smoke-filled political meeting rooms and Hollywood parties. And he had apparently read most of the SF published to that time, from Wells to the authors who came to prominence in the pulps, notably E. E. Smith, Murray Leinster, and Campbell himself.

Even in person he was not the typical science fiction writer. Tall, formal, "theatrically handsome" (in the words of L. Sprague de Camp), he was a compelling presence, by turns gracious and icy. He quickly claimed a dominant role in the Los Angeles SF writing community, holding monthly salons at his home in Laurel Canyon for what he called the Mañana Literary Society, a group intended "to permit young writers to talk out their stories to each other in order to get them off their minds and thereby save themselves the trouble of writing them down."

MLS was more than a club, however. It was a way for Heinlein to communicate his—and Campbell's—ideas on their new approach to SF and fantasy. It also allowed Heinlein, who often dismissed his own stories as "hackwork," and made no secret of his plans to give up writing once he was out of debt, to recruit new writers for Campbell against the day he would retire. Even other professional writers came under Heinlein's spell, too: Edmond Hamilton, Henry Kuttner, and Jack Williamson. "I used to feel he was the most truly civilized person I'd ever known," Williamson wrote years later.

As several stories in this collection show, Heinlein also had a mystical streak and was fascinated by ideas outside the bounds of known science. He was familiar with the pioneering parapsychological research of J. B. Rhine . . . the memory training of Samuel Renshaw . . . the unexplained events collected in the books of Charles Fort . . . and especially Alfred Korzybski's General Semantics. And, of course (as many of his titles and character names will show), the King James Bible as read by Bible Belt Methodists.

Feeling bound by the Future History—he would later call it a "Procrustean Bed"—he would unleash his wilder speculations and fantasy in stories such as "Elsewhen" and especially "Lost Legacy."

In the summer of 1940, emboldened by his success, his mortgage paid off, and planning to attend the Democratic National Convention in Chicago, Heinlein and Leslyn traveled east, where Heinlein met Campbell face-to-face.

During their discussions, Heinlein showed Campbell the Future History chart. Campbell wanted more of those stories. Heinlein was happy to write them, but on one condition: he would write for Campbell until the editor bounced a story. "Now that I know you personally," he says he told Campbell, "it would be too traumatic to have you reject one."

So he and Campbell concocted a new pen name that Heinlein could use on "non-Future History" work published in *Astounding*—"Anson MacDonald," using Heinlein's own middle name and Leslyn's maiden name.

The first "Anson MacDonald" story was a commission from Campbell, who had an unfinished novella in his files about an Asian invasion of the United States. He told Heinlein the story in person. Heinlein wrote the text in a few weeks, as he and Leslyn traveled to Chicago for the Democratic National Convention. It was during this trip that he also wrote one of his most daring fantasies, "They."

Returning to Los Angeles, energized by Campbell's encouragement, and as much creative freedom as a writer could hope to have, Heinlein plunged into a year of intense writing that produced the Anson MacDonald stories "Solution Unsatisfactory," "By His Bootstraps," "Universe," and "Common Sense," "—We Also Walk Dogs—," and several others, in addition to the Future History novel *Methuselah's Children*.

He also began to sell the stories Campbell had rejected, using the pen name "Lyle Monroe," to such lower-paying markets as *Super Science* and *Future*. (Heinlein had invented it in 1939—using names from his mother's side of the family—for Bradbury's fanzine, and other fan-related pieces over the next year. He bragged to Campbell that "Monroe" had "a phony address, fully divorced from the RAH persona.")

This magical year culminated in Heinlein's appearance at the third World Science Fiction Convention in Denver on the July 4th weekend, where he delivered an address called "The Discovery of the Future." Returning to Los Angeles, he wrote a new "Anson MacDonald" story called "Creation Took Eight Days," a dark drama drawing on the works of Charles Fort, and sent it to Campbell—

—Who rejected it. Heinlein reported an initial disappointment, then glee. "School was out." Free to return to his gentlemanly ways, to contemplate such arcane works as a book on monetary theory, he spent several days on long-delayed household construction projects, then found himself feeling "jittery" and absent-minded . . . signs, he thought, of a recurrence of T.B.

When Campbell learned that Heinlein had "retired," he suggested minor changes in "Creation." Sitting down to make the revisions, Heinlein discovered that his symptoms disappeared. "I was hooked on writing."

"Creation Took Eight Days" became "Goldfish Bowl."

Heinlein immediately plunged into a new "Anson MacDonald" serial, *Beyond This Horizon*, perhaps his most heartfelt work, in which he returned to the utopian methods of his failed *For Us, the Living*, but with the experience of two years of commercial writing. He pressed to complete *Horizon* by early December 1941 (having predicted a Japanese attack on Pearl Harbor for Sunday, December 7, in a letter to Campbell mailed a week before that date).

Heinlein presented himself to the navy at San Pedro Monday, December 8, 1941, volunteering for a return to active duty. In this he was to be disappointed—he was judged too disabled even for a staff position. Further inquiries went nowhere. The navy did not want him in uniform.

A former class- and ship-mate, Lt. Cmdr. Albert B. "Buddy" Scoles, had been assigned as head of the Naval Air Materiel Center in Philadelphia. He hired Heinlein as an aeronautical engineer.

While staying with Campbell in New Jersey, just prior to reporting to Philadelphia, Heinlein wrote his last two pre-war stories. (He needed money to pay for an operation for his wife, Leslyn.)

For the next three years, Heinlein worked on such mundane but important projects as de-icing for high-altitude cockpit windows and pressure suits. He served an important role as an intermediary between military and civilian personnel at the plant. He recruited talented engineers and scientists such as L. Sprague de Camp and Isaac Asimov, from the SF world, and other young engineers who went on to work on Project Apollo twenty years later.

His writing was limited to letters, occasional book reviews for Campbell, and technical reports.

❖

The detonation of two atomic bombs over Japan in August 1945 brought a quick end to Heinlein's engineering career. Within days of the Japanese surrender, he and Leslyn were on their way back to Los Angeles—including a detour to attempt to visit the Trinity Site in New Mexico. (They were unable to reach it.)

The existence of the atomic bomb—and the looming nuclear stalemate he had foreseen in "Solution Unsatisfactory"—hit Heinlein as hard as Pearl Harbor. The rules of conventional warfare no longer applied. Countries could now rain death on cities from across an ocean.

Heinlein decided that it was his mission to use his writing skills to "help explain the world of atomic power" to the public. He would no longer write pulp science fiction—the name "Anson MacDonald" was retired.

Now Heinlein would write articles for slick magazines . . . a handbook on politics for post-war leaders . . . young adult fiction for a new generation of Americans.

During his time in Philadelphia, Westminster Press, a well-known publisher of juvenile books, had solicited a science fiction novel from Heinlein, only to reject it in March 1946 as too "far fetched." By now, however, Heinlein was represented by agent Lurton Blassingame, who sold *Young Atomic Engineers* to the prestigious house of Charles Scribner's and Sons, where it was published as *Rocketship "Galileo,"* becoming the first of a fabulously successful series of books for boys that ran for the next twelve years.

By 1946, Heinlein had returned to writing adult fiction—but not for the SF pulps. His first post-war short story wasn't even SF, but a mystery eventually published as "They Do It with Mirrors" (under the name "Simon York").

Heinlein's post-war SF shorts were aimed at a higher market—the *Saturday Evening Post*. In October 1946, Blassingame sold Heinlein's "The Green Hills of Earth" there, the first of four to appear in its pages. In all, there would be ten Heinlein works in the slicks over the next few years, including "Water Is for Washing," in *Argosy*.

Not all of his stories hit the mark, however. For one thing, the slick magazines rarely used science fiction. So stories like "Free Men," "Columbus Was A Dope," "On the Slopes of Vesuvius," and "Jerry Was a Man" were laid off on pulps like *Thrilling Wonder Stories* (where "Columbus" marked the last appearance of Heinlein's "Lyle Monroe" pen name) or went into the trunk for decades.

Heinlein's growing popularity as a writer of juveniles led to a contribution to *Boys' Life*, "Nothing Ever Happens on the Moon," beginning a fruitful association with that magazine that persisted for two decades.

In the fall of 1948, *Astounding* editor John Campbell published a humorous letter of comment from a fan named Richard Hoen—rating the stories of the November *1949* issue of the magazine, featuring purported works by Theodore Sturgeon, A. E. van Vogt, Lester del Rey, and L. Sprague de Camp, and the serial novel "Gulf" by "Anson MacDonald." At this time, Heinlein and Campbell were occasionally chatting long-distance via ham radio, Heinlein from his home in Colorado Springs, Campbell from New Jersey. It was Heinlein who jokingly suggested to Campbell that he try to make the November 1949 issue a reality, offering to write a story titled "Gulf." Campbell was taken with the idea and set out to make it happen.

Heinlein and his wife, Virginia, whom he had married in October 1948, following a divorce from Leslyn, brainstormed several ideas. Her first suggestion—"Why don't you write a Mowgli story?"

Heinlein was so fired up by the SF possibility of a human raised by wolves . . . or Martians . . . that he disappeared into his study and wrote several single-spaced pages of notes. He showed the idea to Campbell, who agreed that it was fascinating, but too big for a relatively short serial in his magazine. (Written over the course of a dozen years, the Mowgli story was eventually published in 1961 as *Stranger in a Strange Land*, Heinlein's most famous work.)

Setting the notes aside, Heinlein found another story to fit the title "Gulf"—the gulf between ordinary humans, and the "new men" who will ultimately replace them.

The story and theme remained close to Heinlein's heart—he would resurrect the concept and even plot points for a failed 1964 television project called *XXII Century*, and would eventually write a sequel novel, *Friday* (1982).

Shortly after the completion of "Gulf," Heinlein and Virginia returned to Hollywood: a script he had written the year before had found a producer (George Pal) and funding. It was to be filmed as *Destination Moon*, with Heinlein on set as technical adviser.

Released in June 1950, *Destination Moon* was the first movie to portray space travel realistically. Heinlein was asked to "novelize" the script, turning it into the novelette of the same title published in *Short Story* magazine.

By this time, Heinlein and Virginia had returned to Colorado Springs, where they designed and built a futuristic home near the Broadmoor hotel. Heinlein needed cash for the construction, which, thanks to materials shortages caused by the Korean War, went wildly over his budget. He returned to writing adult novels (*The Puppet Masters*) as well as his last flurry of short stories.

All three showed Heinlein at the peak of his storytelling powers, and touched on concepts dear to him: the brutal realities of space flight that resulted in a heart-breaking human sacrifice ("Sky Lift") . . . the uses military minds would make of ESP in the Cold War ("Project Nightmare") . . . and the utter futility of human aspirations in the face of the universe's cold mathematics ("The Year of the Jackpot").

Although he had great success in selling to slick markets, he and Blassingame could see that the market was disappearing. And those fewer outlets were not publishing science fiction: these stories earned top rates from the best SF magazines, such as *Amazing* and *Galaxy*, but these were no longer competitive with Heinlein's earnings from novels, the Scribner juveniles, and television.

The whole world of professional storytelling was changing, and Heinlein changed with it. From pure pulp markets he expanded to the slick magazines, to books from small presses and major publishers, to mass market paperbacks, to film and television.

Throughout the late 1950s, he continued to write the occasional short story. But, pressed by commitments to Scribner's, Doubleday, and the SF presses, not to mention requests for magazine articles, speeches, and television scripts, there was simply very little time. "A Tenderfoot in Space" was written because the editor of *Boys' Life* asked for more from Heinlein.

One day in the summer of 1958, taking a break from the difficult novel that would become *Stranger in a Strange Land*, Heinlein composed, in a single day, the marvelous "—All You Zombies—." In a letter to Blassingame, he called it "the furthest south in time travel stories." It's hard to see how a character could be more knotted up in time than Heinlein's "Jane."

Intended for the "fancy rates" of *Playboy* magazine, it was rejected, but quickly bought by *The Magazine of Fantasy & Science Fiction*.

With the exception of a piece commissioned by an ad agency in 1962, Heinlein's career as a writer of short fiction was over.

His greatest acclaim was still to come, of course. *Stranger in a Strange Land* would be published in 1961 and ultimately be known as one of the most popular and controversial novels of the decade. He would battle ill health and too much acclaim. He would travel the world, and hole up behind an electrified "hippie-proof" fence. He would become a hero of the counterculture of the 1960s, and the emerging "new right" (thanks to the Libertarian ideas in his 1966 novel, *The Moon Is a Harsh Mistress*).

He would struggle artistically, but he would continue publishing until 1987, eight months before his death in Carmel, California, from emphysema on May 8, 1988, widely hailed as the most influential and accomplished science fiction writer since Wells, and as the author of these dark, funny, disturbing, intriguing stories written and published "off the main sequence."

—Los Angeles, 2005

❖ EDITOR'S NOTE ❖
by Andrew Wheeler

THIS BOOK WAS conceived as a companion to *The Past Through Tomorrow,* the monumental collection of Heinlein's "Future History" stories. Because of this, *Off the Main Sequence* contains none of the stories in the earlier book, though it does include a few stories left out of *Past*—such as " 'Let There Be Light' "—that are generally considered part of the "Future History."

Off the Main Sequence does overlap somewhat with the third major Heinlein collection, *The Fantasies of Robert A. Heinlein,* with stories such as "—And He Built a Crooked House—" and "—All You Zombies—." These stories are included here because I considered them science fiction rather than fantasy, or at least thought their categorization was debatable. But this book does not contain any stories that seemed to me unequivocally fantasy—such as "Magic, Inc." and "The Unpleasant Profession of Jonathan Hoag." Adding them would have pushed this book to an even greater, and possibly unfeasible, size. Heinlein additionally wrote a few mainstream stories—available in the miscellaneous collections *Requiem* and *Expanded Universe*—that are not included here.

What this book *does* have is twenty-seven SF stories, including some of the best works by perhaps the best, and certainly the most influential, American SF writer ever. The stories are arranged in order of first publication, except for two short pieces—"Free Men" and "On the Slopes of Vesuvius"—written in 1947 but not published until decades later. Those two stories are placed together at the beginning of Heinlein's post-war stories.

My thanks go out to Heinlein scholar Bill Patterson for his help finding and determining the correct texts of these stories, and for his arguments on the SF/Fantasy split. This book also literally would not exist without Eleanor Wood, the agent for Heinlein's estate, and I thank her for her support for the SFBC and our Heinlein projects over the years. SFBC's Editor-in-Chief Ellen Asher was also invaluable, as a colleague, a mentor, and a friend. The actual production and layout of this book was shepherded by Kathy Kiernan and Lisa Thornbloom, without whom these words would look like a badly word-processed memo. And the wonderful cover was art-directed by SFBC's talented Nicholas Sica and painted by Bruce Jensen, who has now done a half-dozen great Heinlein covers for the club. But my greatest thanks must go to the Dean of Science Fiction, the late Robert A. Heinlein—if he hadn't written these stories in the first place, none of us would be here.

OFF THE MAIN SEQUENCE

SUCCESSFUL OPERATION

Futuria Fantasia #4, Summer 1940

as "Heil!" by Lyle Monroe

"HOW DARE YOU make such a suggestion!"
The State Physician doggedly stuck by his position. "I would not make it, sire, if your life were not at stake. There is no other surgeon in the Fatherland who can transplant a pituitary gland but Doctor Lans."
"You will operate!"
The medico shook his head. "You would die, Leader. My skill is not adequate."
The Leader stormed about the apartment. He seemed about to give way to one of the girlish bursts of anger that even the inner state clique feared so much. Surprisingly he capitulated.
"Bring him here!" he ordered.

Doctor Lans faced the Leader with inherent dignity, a dignity and presence that three years of "protective custody" had been unable to shake. The pallor and gauntness of the concentration camp lay upon him, but his race was used to oppression. "I see," he said. "Yes, I see . . . I can perform that operation. What are your terms?"
"Terms?" The Leader was aghast. "Terms, you filthy swine? You are being given a chance to redeem in part the sins of your race!"
The surgeon raised his brows. "Do you not think that I *know* that you would not have sent for me had there been any other course available to you? Obviously, my services have become valuable."
"You'll do as you are told! You and your kind are lucky to be alive."
"Nevertheless I shall not operate without my fee."
"I said you are lucky to be alive—" The tone was an open threat.
Lans spread his hands, did not answer.
"Well—I am informed that you have a family . . ."
The surgeon moistened his lips. His Emma—they would hurt

3

his Emma . . . and his little Rose. But he must be brave, as Emma would have him be. He was playing for high stakes—for all of them. "They cannot be worse off dead," he answered firmly, "than they are now."

It was many hours before the Leader was convinced that Lans could not be budged. He should have known—the surgeon had learned fortitude at his mother's breast.

"What is your fee?"

"A passport for myself and my family."

"Good riddance!"

"My personal fortune restored to me—"

"Very well."

"—to be paid in gold before I operate!"

The Leader started to object automatically, then checked himself. Let the presumptuous fool think so! It could be corrected after the operation.

"And the operation to take place in a hospital on foreign soil."

"Preposterous!"

"I must insist."

"You do not trust me?"

Lans stared straight back into his eyes without replying. The Leader struck him, hard, across the mouth. The surgeon made no effort to avoid the blow, but took it, with no change of expression. . . .

"You are willing to go through with it, Samuel?" The younger man looked at Doctor Lans without fear as he answered,

"Certainly, Doctor."

"I can not guarantee that you will recover. The Leader's pituitary gland is diseased; your younger body may or may not be able to stand up under it—that is the chance you take."

"I know it—but I am out of the concentration camp!"

"Yes. Yes, that is true. And if you do recover, you are free. And I will attend you myself, until you are well enough to travel."

Samuel smiled. "It will be a positive joy to be sick in a country where there are no concentration camps!"

"Very well, then. Let us commence."

They returned to the silent, nervous group at the other end of the room. Grimly, the money was counted out, every penny that the famous surgeon had laid claim to before the Leader had decided that men of his religion had no need for money. Lans placed half of the gold in a money belt and strapped it around his waist. His wife concealed the other half somewhere about her ample person.

It was an hour and twenty minutes later that Lans put down the last instrument, nodded to the surgeons assisting him, and commenced to strip off operating gloves. He took one last look at his two patients before he left the room. They were anonymous under the sterile gowns and dressings. Had he not known, he could not have told dictator from oppressed. Come to think about it, with the exchange of those two tiny glands there was something of the dictator in his victim, and something of the victim in the dictator.

Doctor Lans returned to the hospital later in the day, after seeing his wife and daughter settled in a first class hotel. It was an extravagance, in view of his uncertain prospects as a refugee, but they had enjoyed no luxuries for years back *there*—he did not think of it as his home country—and it was justified this once.

He enquired at the office of the hospital for his second patient. The clerk looked puzzled. "But he is not here."

"Not here?"

"Why, no. He was moved at the same time as His Excellency— back to your country."

Lans did not argue. The trick was obvious; it was too late to do anything for poor Samuel. He thanked his God that he had had the foresight to place himself and his family beyond the reach of such brutal injustice before operating. He thanked the clerk and left.

The Leader recovered consciousness at last. His brain was confused—then he recalled the events before he had gone to sleep. The operation!—it must be over! And he was alive! He had never admitted to anyone how terribly frightened he had been at the prospect. But he had lived—he had lived!

He groped around for the bell cord, and, failing to find it, gradually forced his eyes to focus on the room. What outrageous nonsense was this? This was no sort of a room for the Leader to convalesce in. He took in the dirty white-washed ceiling, and the bare wooden floor with distaste. And the bed! It was no more than a cot!

He shouted. Someone came in, a man wearing the uniform of a trooper in his favorite corps. He started to give him the tongue-lashing of his life, before having him arrested. But he was cut short.

"Cut out that racket, you unholy pig!"

At first he was too astounded to answer, then he shrieked, "Stand at attention when you address your Leader! Salute!"

The man looked dumbfounded, then guffawed. "Like this, maybe?" He stepped to the side of the cot, struck a pose with his right arm raised in salute. He carried a rubber truncheon in it. "Hail to the Leader!" he shouted, and brought his arm down smartly. The truncheon crashed into the Leader's cheekbone.

Another trooper came in to see what the noise was while the first was still laughing at his witticism. "What's up, Jon? Say, you'd better not handle that monkey too rough—he's still carried on the hospital list." He glanced casually at the Leader's bloody face.

"Him? Didn't you know?" He pulled him to one side and whispered.

The second's eyes widened; he grinned. "So? They don't want him to get well, eh? Well, I could use some exercise this morning—"

"Let's get Fats," the other suggested. "He always has such amusing ideas."

"Good idea." He stepped to the door, and bellowed, "Hey, Fats!"

They didn't really start in on him until Fats was there to help.

"LET THERE BE LIGHT"

Super Science Stories, May 1940

as by Lyle Monroe

ARCHIBALD DOUGLAS, SC. D., Ph.D., B.S., read the telegram with unconcealed annoyance.

"ARRIVING CITY LATE TODAY STOP DESIRE CONFERENCE COLD LIGHT YOUR LABORATORY TEN P M (signed) DR. M. L. MARTIN"

He was, was he? He did, did he? What did he think this lab was; a hotel? And did Martin think that his time was at the disposal of any Joe Doakes who had the price of a telegram? He had framed in his mind an urbanely discouraging reply when he noticed that the message had been filed at a midwestern airport. Very well, let him arrive. Douglas had no intention of meeting him.

Nevertheless, his natural curiosity caused him to take down his copy of *Who's Who in Science,* and look up the offender. There it was: Martin, M. L., bio-chemist and ecologist, P.D.Q., X.Y.Z., N.R.A., C.I.O.—enough degrees for six men. Hmmm—director Guggenheim Orinoco Fauna Survey, Author: *Co-Lateral Symbiosis of the Boll Weevil,* and so on, through three inches of fine print. The old boy seemed to be a heavyweight.

A little later Douglas surveyed himself in the mirror of the laboratory washroom. He took off a dirty laboratory smock, removed a comb from his vest pocket, and put a careful polish on his sleek black hair. An elaborately tailored checked jacket, a snap-brim hat and he was ready for the street. He fingered the pale scar that stenciled the dark skin of one cheek. Not bad, he thought, in spite of the scar. If it weren't for the broken nose he would look O.K.

The restaurant where he dined alone was only partly filled. It wouldn't become lively until after the theatres were out, but Douglas appreciated the hot swing band and the good food. Toward the end of his meal, a young woman walked past his table and sat down, facing him, one table away. He sized her up with care. Pretty fancy! Figure like a dancer, lots of corn-colored hair, nice complexion, and great big soft eyes. Rather dumb pan, but what could you expect?

He decided to invite her over for a drink. If things shaped up, Dr. Martin could go to the devil. He scribbled a note on the back of a menu, and signalled the waiter.

"Who is she, Leo? One of the entertainers?"

"No, m'sieur. I have not seen her before."

Douglas relaxed, and waited for results. He knew the come-hither look when he saw it, and he was sure of the outcome. The girl read his note and glanced over at him with a little smile. He returned it with interest. She borrowed a pencil from the waiter, and wrote on the menu. Presently Leo handed it to him.

"Sorry,"—it read—"and thanks for the kind offer, but I am otherwise engaged."

Douglas paid his bill, and returned to the laboratory.

His laboratory was located on the top floor of his father's factory. He left the outer door open and the elevator down in anticipation of Doctor Martin's arrival, then he busied himself by trying to locate the cause of an irritating vibration in his centrifuge. Just at ten o'clock he heard the whir of the elevator. He reached the outer door of his office just as his visitor arrived.

Facing him was the honey-colored babe he had tried to pick up in the restaurant.

He was immediately indignant. "How did you get here? Follow me?"

She froze up at once. "I have an appointment with Doctor Douglas. Please tell him that I am here."

"The devil you have. What kind of a game is this?"

She controlled herself, but her face showed the effort. "I think Doctor Douglas is the best judge of that. Tell him I'm here—at once."

"You're looking at him. I'm Doctor Douglas."

"You! I don't believe it. You look more like a—a gangster."

"I am, nevertheless. Now cut out the clowning, sister, and tell me what the racket is. What's your name?"

"I am Doctor M. L. Martin."

He looked completely astounded, then bellowed his amusement. "No foolin'? You wouldn't kid your country cousin, would you? Come in, doc, come in."

She followed him, suspicious as a strange dog, ready to fight at any provocation. She accepted a chair, then addressed him again. "Are you really Doctor Douglas?"

He grinned at her. "In the flesh—and I can prove it. How about you? I still think this is some kind of a badger game."

She froze up again. "What do you want—my birth certificate?"

"You probably murdered Doctor Martin in the elevator, and stuffed the old boy's body down the shaft."

She arose, gathered up her gloves and purse, and prepared to leave. "I came fifteen hundred miles for this meeting. I am sorry I bothered. Good evening, Doctor Douglas."

He was instantly soothing. "Aw, don't get sore—I was just needling you. It just tickled me that the distinguished Doctor Martin should look so much like Marilyn Monroe. Now sit back down"—he gently disengaged her hands from her gloves—"and let me buy you that drink you turned down earlier."

She hesitated, still determined to be angry, then her natural good nature came to his aid, and she relaxed. "O.K., Butch."

"That's better. What'll it be; Scotch or bourbon?"

"Make mine bourbon—and not too much water."

By the time the drinks were fixed and cigarets lighted the tension was lifted. "Tell me," he began, "to what do I owe this visit? I don't know anything about biology."

She blew a smoke ring and poked a carmine fingernail through it. "You remember that article you had in the April *Physical Review*? The one about cold light, and possible ways of achieving it?"

He nodded. "*Electroluminescence vs. Chemiluminescence*: not much in that to interest a biologist."

"Nevertheless I've been working on the same problem."

"From what angle?"

"I've been trying to find out how a lightning bug does the trick. I saw some gaudy ones down in South America, and it got me to thinking."

"Hmm—maybe you got something. What have you found out?"

"Not much that wasn't already known. As you probably know, the firefly is an almost incredibly efficient source of light—at least 96 percent efficient. Now how efficient would you say the ordinary commercial tungsten-filament incandescent lamp is?"

"Not over two percent at the best."

"That's fair enough. And a stupid little beetle does fifty times as well without turning a hair. We don't look so hot, do we?"

"Not very," he acknowledged. "Go on about the bug."

"Well, the firefly has in his tummy an active organic compound—very complex—called luciferin. When this oxidizes in the presence of a catalyst, luciferase, the entire energy of oxidation is converted into green light—no heat. Reduce it with hydrogen and it's ready to go again. I've learned how to do it in the laboratory."

9

"What! Congratulations! You don't need me. I can close up shop."

"Not so fast. It isn't commercially feasible; it takes too much gear to make it work; it's too messy; and I can't get an intense light. Now I came to see you to see if we might combine forces, pool our information, and work out something practical."

Three weeks later at four in the morning Doctor M. L. Martin—Mary Lou to her friends—was frying an egg over a bunsen burner. She was dressed in a long rubber shop apron over shorts and a sweater. Her long corn-colored hair hung in loose ripples. The expanse of shapely leg made her look like something out of a cheesecake magazine.

She turned to where Douglas lay sprawled, a wretched exhausted heap, in a big arm chair. "Listen, Ape, the percolator seems to have burnt out. Shall I make the coffee in the fractional distillator?"

"I thought you had snake venom in it."

"So I have. I'll rinse it out."

"Yikes, woman! Don't you care what chances you take with yourself?—or with me?"

"Pooh—snake venom wouldn't hurt you even if you did drink it—unless that rotgut you drink has given your stomach ulcers. Soup's on!"

She chucked aside the apron, sat down and crossed her legs.

"Mary Lou, why don't you wear some clothes around the shop? You arouse my romantic nature."

"Nonsense. You haven't any. Let's get down to cases. Where do we stand?"

He ran a hand through his hair and chewed his lip. "Up against a stone wall, I think. Nothing we've tried so far seems to offer any promise."

"The problem seems to be essentially one of confining radiant energy to the visible band of frequency."

"You make it sound so simple, bright eyes."

"Stow the sarcasm. That is, nevertheless, where the loss comes in with ordinary electric light. The filament is white hot, maybe two percent of the power is turned into light, the rest goes into infra-red and ultra-violet."

"So beautiful. So true."

"Pay attention, you big ape. I know you're tired, but listen to mama. There should be some way of sharply tuning the wave length. How about the way they do it in radio?"

He perked up a little. "Wouldn't apply to the case. Even if you could manage to work out an inductance-capacitance circuit with a natural resonant frequency within the visual band, it would require too much gear for each lighting unit, and if it got out of tune, it wouldn't give any light at all."

"Is that the only way frequency is controlled?"

"Yes—well, practically. Some transmitting stations, especially amateurs, use a specially cut quartz crystal that has a natural frequency of its own to control wave length."

"Then why can't we cut a crystal that would have a natural frequency in the octave of visible light?"

He sat up very straight. "Great Scott, kid!—I think you've hit it."

He got up, and strode up and down, talking as he went.

"They use ordinary quartz crystal for the usual frequencies, and tourmaline for short wave broadcasting. The frequency of vibration depends directly on the way the crystal is cut. There is a simple formula—" He stopped, and took down a thick Indiapaper handbook. "Hmm—yes, here it is. For quartz, every millimeter of thickness of the crystal gives one hundred meters of wave length. Frequency is, of course, the reciprocal of wave length. Tourmaline has a similar formula for shorter wave lengths."

He continued to read. " 'These crystals have the property of flexing when electric charges are applied to them, and, vice versa, show an electric charge when flexed. The period of flexure is an inherent quality of the crystal, depending on its geometrical proportions. Hooked into a radio transmitting circuit, such a crystal requires the circuit to operate at one, and only one, frequency, that of the crystal.' That's it, kid, that's it! Now if we can find a crystal that can be cut to vibrate at the frequency of visible light, we've got it—a way to turn electrical energy into light without heat losses!"

Mary Lou cluck-clucked admiringly. "Mama's *good* boy. Mama knew he could do it, if he would only *try*."

Nearly six months later Douglas invited his father up to the laboratory to see the results. He ushered the mild, silver-haired old gentleman into the sanctum sanctorum and waved to Mary Lou to draw the shades. Then he pointed to the ceiling.

"There it is, Dad—cold light—at a bare fraction of the cost of ordinary lighting."

The elder man looked up and saw, suspended from the ceiling, a grey screen, about the size and shape of the top of a card table. Then Mary Lou threw a switch. The screen glowed brilliantly, but not dazzlingly, and exhibited a mother-of-pearl iridescence. The room was illuminated by strong white light without noticeable glare.

The young scientist grinned at his father, as pleased as a puppy who expects a pat. "How do you like it, Dad? One hundred candle power—that'd take a hundred watts with ordinary bulbs, and we're doing it with two watts—half an ampere at four volts."

The old man blinked absent-mindedly at the display. "Very nice, son, very nice indeed. I'm pleased that you have perfected it."

"Look, Dad—do you know what that screen up there is made out of? Common, ordinary clay. It's a form of aluminum silicate; cheap and easy to make from any clay, or ore, that contains aluminum. I can use bauxite, or cryolite, or most anything. You can gather up the raw materials with a steam shovel in any state in the union."

"Is your process all finished, son, and ready to be patented?"

"Why, yes, I think so, Dad."

"Then let's go into your office, and sit down. I've something I must discuss with you. Ask your young lady to come, too."

Young Douglas did as he was told, his mood subdued by his father's solemn manner. When they were seated, he spoke up.

"What's the trouble, Dad? Can I help?"

"I wish you could, Archie, but I'm afraid not. I'm going to have to ask you to close your laboratory."

The younger man took it without flinching. "Yes, Dad?"

"You know I've always been proud of your work, and since your mother passed on my major purpose has been to supply you with the money and equipment you needed for your work."

"You've been very generous, Dad."

"I wanted to do it. But now a time has come when the factory won't support your research any longer. In fact, I may have to close the doors of the plant."

"As bad as that, Dad? I thought that orders had picked up this last quarter."

"We do have plenty of orders, but the business isn't making a profit on them. Do you remember I mentioned something to you about the public utilities bill that passed at the last session of the legislature?"

"I remember it vaguely, but I thought the Governor vetoed it."

"He did, but they passed it over his veto. It was as bold a case of corruption as this state has ever seen—the power lobbyists had both houses bought, body and soul." The old man's voice trembled with impotent anger.

"And just how does it affect us, Dad?"

"This bill pretended to equalize power rates according to circumstances. What it actually did was to permit the commission to discriminate among consumers as they saw fit. You know what that commission is—I've always been on the wrong side of the fence politically. Now they are forcing me to the wall with power rates that prevent me from competing."

"But good heavens, Dad—they can't do that. Get an injunction!"

"In this state, son?" His white eyebrows raised.

"No, I guess not." He got to his feet and started walking the floor. "There *must* be something we can do."

His father shook his head. "The thing that really makes me bitter is that they can do this with power that actually belongs to the people. The federal government's program has made plenty of cheap power possible—the country should be rich from it—but these local pirates have gotten hold of it, and use it as a club to intimidate free citizens."

After the old gentleman had left, Mary Lou slipped over and laid a hand on Douglas' shoulder and looked down into his face.

"You poor boy!"

His face showed the upset he had concealed from his father. "Cripes, Mary Lou. Just when we were going good. But I mind it most for Dad."

"Yes, I know."

"And not a thing I can do about it. It's politics, and those pot-bellied racketeers own this state."

She looked disappointed and faintly scornful. "Why, Archie Douglas, you great big panty-waist! You aren't going to let those mugs get away with this without a fight, are you?"

He looked up at her dully. "No, of course not. I'll fight. But I know when I'm licked. This is way out of my field."

She flounced across the room. "I'm surprised at you. You've invented one of the greatest things since the dynamo, and you talk about being licked."

"Your invention, you mean."

"Nuts! Who worked out the special forms? Who blended them to get the whole spectrum? And besides, you aren't out of your field. What's the problem? Power! They're squeezing you for power. You're a physicist. Dope out some way to get power without buying from them."

"What would you like? Atomic power?"

"Be practical. You aren't the Atomic Energy Commission."

"I might stick a windmill on the roof."

"That's better, but still not good. Now get busy with that knot in the end of your spinal cord. I'll start some coffee. This is going to be another all night job."

He grinned at her. "O.K., Carrie Nation. I'm coming."

She smiled happily at him. "That's the way to talk."

He rose and went over to her, slipped an arm about her waist and kissed her. She relaxed to his embrace, but when their lips parted, she pushed him away.

As the first light of dawn turned their faces pale and sickly, they were rigging two cold light screens face to face. Archie adjusted them until they were an inch apart.

"There now—practically all the light from the first screen should strike the second. Turn the power on the first screen, Sex Appeal."

She threw the switch. The first screen glowed with light, and shed its radiance on the second.

"Now to see if our beautiful theory is correct." He fastened a voltmeter across the terminals of the second screen and pressed the little black button in the base of the voltmeter. The needle sprang over two volts.

She glanced anxiously over his shoulder. "How about it, guy?"

"It works! There's no doubt about it. These screens work both ways. Put juice in 'em; out comes light. Put light in 'em; out comes electricity."

"What's the power loss, Archie?"

"Just a moment." He hooked in an ammeter, read it, and picked up his slide rule. "Let me see—Loss is about thirty percent. Most of that would be the leakage of light around the edges of the screens."

"The sun's coming up, Archie. Let's take screen number two up on the roof, and try it out in the sunlight."

Some minutes later they had the second screen and the electrical measuring instruments on the roof. Archie propped the screen up against a sky-light so that it faced the rising sun, fastened the voltmeter across its terminals and took a reading. The needle sprang at once to two volts.

Mary Lou jumped up and down. "It works!"

"Had to work," commented Archie. "If the light from another screen will make it pour out juice, then sunlight is bound to. Hook in the ammeter. Let's see how much power we get."

The ammeter showed 18.7 amperes.

Mary Lou worked out the result on the slide rule. "Eighteen-point-seven times two gives thirty-seven-point-four watts or about five hundredths of a horsepower. That doesn't seem like very much. I had hoped for more."

"That's as it should be, kid. We are using only the visible light rays. As a light source the sun is about fifteen percent efficient; the other eighty-five percent are infra-red and ultra-violet. Gimme that slipstick." She passed him the slide rule. "The sun pours out about a horsepower and a half, or one and one eighth kilowatts on every square yard of surface on the earth that is faced directly towards the sun. Atmospheric absorption cuts that down about a third, even at high noon over the Sahara desert. That would give one horsepower per square yard. With the sun just rising we might not get more than one-third horsepower per square yard here. At fifteen percent efficiency that would be about five hundredths of a horsepower. It checks—Q.E.D.—what are you looking so glum about?"

"Well—I had hoped that we could get enough sunpower off the roof to run the factory, but if it takes twenty square yards to get one horsepower, it won't be enough."

"Cheer up, Baby Face. We doped out a screen that would vibrate only in the band of visible light; I guess we can dope out another that will be atonic—one that will vibrate to any wave length. Then it will soak up any radiant energy that hits it, and give it up again as electrical power. With this roof surface we can get maybe a thousand horsepower at high noon. Then we'll have to set up banks of storage batteries so that we can store power for cloudy days and night shifts."

She blinked her big blue eyes at him. "Archie, does your head ever ache?"

Twenty minutes later he was back at his desk, deep in the preliminary calculations, while Mary Lou threw together a scratch breakfast.

He looked up. "Never mind the creative cookery, Doctor Martin."

She turned around and brandished the skillet at him. "To hear is to obey, my Lord. However, Archie, you are an over-educated Neanderthal, with no feeling for the higher things of life."

"I won't argue the point. But take a gander at this. I've got the answer—a screen that vibrates all down the scale."

"No foolin', Archie?"

"No foolin', kid. It was already implied in our earlier experiments, but we were so busy trying to build a screen that wouldn't vibrate at random, we missed it. I ran into something else, too."

"Tell mamma!"

"We can build screens to radiate in the infra-red just as easily as cold light screens. Get it? Heating units of any convenient size or shape, economical and with no high wattage or extreme temperatures to make 'em fire hazards or dangerous to children. As I see it, we can design these screens to, one"—he ticked the points off on his fingers—"take power from the sun at nearly one hundred percent efficiency; two, deliver it as cold light; or three, as heat; or four, as electrical power. We can bank 'em in series to get any required voltage; we can bank in parallel to get any required current, and the power is absolutely free, except for the installation costs."

She stood and watched him in silence for several seconds before speaking. "All that from trying to make a cheaper light. Come eat your breakfast, Steinmetz. You men can't do your work on mush."

They ate in silence, each busy with new thoughts. Finally Douglas spoke. "Mary Lou, do you realize just how big a thing this is?"

"I've been thinking about it."

"It's enormous. Look, the power that can be tapped is incredible. The sun pours over two hundred and thirty trillion horsepower onto the earth all the time and we use almost none of it."

"As much as that, Archie?"

"I didn't believe my own figures when I worked it out, so I looked it up in Richardson's Astronomy. Why, we could recover more than twenty thousand horsepower in any city block. Do you know what that means? Free power! Riches for everybody! It's the greatest thing since the steam engine." He stopped suddenly, noticing her glum face. "What's the matter, kid, am I wrong someplace?"

She fiddled with her fork before replying. "No, Archie—you're not wrong. I've been thinking about it, too. Decentralized cities, labor-saving machinery for everybody, luxuries—it's all possible, but I've a feeling that we're staring right into a mess of trouble. Did you ever hear of 'Breakages Ltd.'?"

"What is it, a salvage concern?"

"Not by a long sight. You ought to read something besides the 'Proceedings of the American Society of Physical Engineers.' George Bernard Shaw, for instance. It's from the preface of *Back to Methuselah,* and is a sardonic way of describing the combined power of corporate industry to resist any change that might threaten their dividends. You threaten the whole industrial set-up, son, and you're in danger right where you're sitting. What do you think happened to atomic power?"

He pushed back his chair. "Oh, surely not. You're just tired and jumpy. Industry welcomes invention. Why, all the big corporations have their research departments, with some of the best minds in the country working in them. And they are in atomics up to their necks."

"Sure—and any bright young inventor can get a job with them. And then he's a kept man—the inventions belong to the corporation, and only those that fit into the pattern of the powers-that-be ever see light. The rest are shelved. Do you really think that they'd let a free lance like you upset investments of billions of dollars?"

He frowned, then relaxed and laughed. "Oh, forget it, kid, it's not that serious."

"That's what you think. Did you ever hear of celanese voile? Probably not. It's a synthetic dress material used in place of chiffon. But it wore better and was washable, and it only cost about forty cents a yard, while chiffon costs four times as much. You can't buy it any more.

"And take razor blades. My brother bought one about five years ago that never had to be re-sharpened. He's still using it, but if he ever loses it, he'll have to go back to the old kind. They took 'em off the market.

"Did you ever hear of guys who had found a better, cheaper fuel than gasoline? One showed up about four years ago and proved his claims—but he drowned a couple of weeks later in a swimming accident. I don't say that he was murdered, but it's damn funny that they never found his formula.

"And that reminds me—I once saw a clipping from the *Los Angeles Daily News*. A man bought a heavy standard make car in San Diego, filled her up and drove her to Los Angeles. He only used two gallons. Then he drove to Agua Caliente and back to San Diego, and only used three gallons. About a week later the sales company found him and bribed him to make an exchange. By mistake they had let him have a car that wasn't to be sold—one with a trick carburetor.

"Do you know any big heavy cars that get seventy miles to the gallon? You're not likely to—not while 'Breakages Ltd.' rules the roost. But the story is absolutely kosher—you can look it up in the files.

"And of course, everybody knows that automobiles aren't built to wear, they're build to wear out, so you will buy a new one. They build 'em just as bad as the market will stand. Steamships take a worse beating than a car, and *they* last thirty years or more."

Douglas laughed it off. "Cut out the gloom, Sweetie Pie. You've got a persecution complex. Let's talk about something more cheerful—you and me, for instance. You make pretty good coffee. How about us taking out a license to live together?"

She ignored him.

"Well, why not. I'm young and healthy. You could do worse."

"Archie, did I ever tell you about the native chief that got a yen for me down in South America?"

"I don't think so. What about him?"

"He wanted me to marry him. He even offered to kill off his seventeen current wives and have them served up for the bridal feast."

"What's that got to do with my proposition?"

"I should have taken him up. A girl can't afford to turn down a good offer these days."

Archie walked up and down the laboratory, smoking furiously. Mary Lou perched on a workbench and watched him with troubled eyes. When he stopped to light another cigaret from the butt of the last, she bid for attention.

"Well, Master Mind, how does it look to you now?"

He finished lighting his cigaret, burned himself, cursed in a monotone, then replied, "Oh, you were right, Cassandra. We're in more trouble than I ever knew existed. First, when we build an electric runabout that gets its power from the sun, while it's parked at the curb, somebody pours kerosene over it and burns it up. I didn't mind that so much—it was just a side issue. But when I refuse to sell out to them, they slap all those phony law suits on us, and tie us up like a kid with the colic."

"They haven't a legal leg to stand on."

"I know that, but they've got unlimited money and we haven't. They can run these suits out for months—maybe years—only we can't last that long."

"What's our next move? Do you keep this appointment?"

"I don't want to. They'll try to buy me off again, and probably threaten me, in a refined way. I'd tell 'em to go jump, if it wasn't for Dad. Somebody's broken into his house twice now, and he's too old to stand that sort of thing."

"I suppose all this labor trouble in the plant worries him, too."

"Of course it does. And since it dates from the time we started manufacturing the screens on a commercial scale, I'm sure it's part of the frame-up. Dad never had any labor trouble before. He always ran a union shop and treated his men like members of his own family. I don't blame him for being nervous. I'm getting tired of being followed everywhere I go, myself. It makes me jumpy."

Mary Lou puffed out a cloud of smoke. "I've been tailed the past couple of weeks."

"The heck you have! Mary Lou, that tears it. I'm going to settle this thing today."

"Going to sell out?"

"No." He walked over to his desk, opened a side drawer, took out a .38 automatic, and slipped it in his pocket. Mary Lou jumped down from the bench and ran to him. She put her hands on his shoulders, and looked up at him, fear in her face.

"Archie!"

He answered gently. "Yes, kid."

"Archie, don't do anything rash. If anything happened to you, you know I couldn't get along with a normal man."

He patted her hair. "Those are the best words I've heard in weeks, kid."

Douglas returned about one P.M. Mary Lou met him at the elevator. "Well?"

"Same old song-and-dance. Nothing done in spite of my brave promises."

"Did they threaten you?"

"Not exactly. They asked me how much life insurance I carried."

"What did you tell them?"

"Nothing. I reached for my handkerchief and let them see that I was carrying a gun. I thought it might cause them to revise any immediate plans they might have in mind. After that the interview sort of fizzled out and I left. Mary's little lamb followed me home, as usual."

"Same plug-ugly that shadowed you yesterday?"

"Him, or his twin. He couldn't be a twin, though, come to think about it. They'd have both died of fright at birth."

"True enough. Have you had lunch?"

"Not yet. Let's ease down to the shop lunch room and take on some groceries. We can do our worrying later."

The lunch room was deserted. They talked very little. Mary Lou's blue eyes stared vacantly over his head. At the second cup of coffee she reached out and touched him.

"Relax—that's what we've got to do."

"Speak English."

"I'll give you a blueprint. Why are we under attack?"

"We've got something they want."

"Not at all. We've got something they want to quarantine—they don't want anyone else to have it. So they try to buy you off, or scare you into quitting. If these don't work, they'll try something stronger. Now you're dangerous to them and in danger from them because you've got a secret. What happens if it isn't a secret? Suppose everybody knows it?"

"They'd be sore as hell."

"Yes, but what would they do? Nothing. Those big tycoons are practical men. They won't waste a dime on heckling you if it no longer serves their pocketbooks."

"What do you propose that we do?"

"Give away the secret. Tell the world how it's done. Let anybody manufacture power screens and light screens who wants to. The heat process on the mix is so simple that any commercial chemist can duplicate it once you tell 'em how, and there must be a thousand factories, at least, that could manufacture them with their present machinery from materials at their very doorsteps."

"But, good Lord, Mary Lou, we'd be left in the lurch."

"What can you lose? We've made a measly couple of thousand dollars so far, keeping the process secret. If you turn it loose, you still hold the patent, and you charge a nominal royalty—one that it wouldn't be worthwhile trying to beat, say ten cents a square yard on each screen manufactured. There would be millions of square yards turned out the first year—hundreds of thousands of dollars to you the first year, and big income for life. You can have the finest research laboratory in the country."

He slammed his napkin down on the table. "Kid, I believe you're right."

"Don't forget, too, what you'll be doing for the country. There'll be factories springing up right away all over the Southwest—every place where there's lots of sunshine. Free power! You'll be the new emancipator."

He stood up, his eyes shining. "Kid, we'll do it! Half a minute while I tell Dad our decision, then we'll beat it for town."

Two hours later the teletype in every news service office in the country was clicking out the story. Douglas insisted that the story included the technical details of the process as a condition of releasing it. By the time he and Mary Lou walked out of the Associated Press building the first extra was on the street: "GENIUS GRANTS GRATIS POWER TO PUBLIC." Archie bought one and beckoned to the muscle man who was shadowing him.

"Come here, Sweetheart. You can quit pretending to be a fireplug. I've an errand for you." He handed the lunk the newspaper. It was accepted uneasily. In all his long and unsavory career he had never had the etiquette of shadowing treated in so cavalier a style. "Take this paper to your boss and tell him Archie Douglas sent him a valentine. Don't stand there staring at me! Beat it, before I break your fat head!"

As Archie watched him disappear in the crowd, Mary Lou slipped a hand in his. "Feel better, son?"

"Lots."

"All your worries over?"

"All but one." He grabbed her shoulders and swung her around. "I've got an argument to settle with you. Come along!" He grabbed her wrist and pulled her out into the crosswalk.

"What the hell, Archie! Let go my wrist."

"Not likely. You see that building over there? That's the court house. Right next to the window where they issue dog licenses, there's one where we can get a wedding permit."

"I'm not going to marry you!"

"Oh, yes, you are—or I'll start to scream right here in the street."

"This is blackmail!"

As they entered the building, she was still dragging her feet—but not too hard.

—AND HE BUILT A
CROOKED HOUSE—

Astounding Science Fiction, February 1941

AMERICANS ARE CONSIDERED crazy anywhere in the world.

They will usually concede a basis for the accusation but point to California as the focus of the infection. Californians stoutly maintain that their bad reputation is derived solely from the acts of the inhabitants of Los Angeles County. Angelenos will, when pressed, admit the charge but explain hastily, "It's Hollywood. It's not our fault—we didn't ask for it; Hollywood just grew."

The people in Hollywood don't care; they glory in it. If you are interested, they will drive you up Laurel Canyon "—where we keep the violent cases." The Canyonites—the brown-legged women, the trunks-clad men constantly busy building and rebuilding their slap-happy unfinished houses—regard with faint contempt the dull creatures who live down in the flats, and treasure in their hearts the secret knowledge that they, and only they, know how to live.

Lookout Mountain Avenue is the name of a side canyon which twists up from Laurel Canyon. The other Canyonites don't like to have it mentioned; after all, one must draw the line somewhere!

High up on Lookout Mountain at number 8775, across the street from the Hermit—the original Hermit of Hollywood—lived Quintus Teal, graduate architect.

Even the architecture of southern California is different. Hot dogs are sold from a structure built like and designated "The Pup." Ice cream cones come from a giant stucco ice cream cone, and neon proclaims "Get the Chili Bowl Habit!" from the roofs of buildings which are indisputably chili bowls. Gasoline, oil, and free road maps are dispensed beneath the wings of tri-motored transport planes, while the certified rest rooms, inspected hourly for your comfort, are located in the cabin of the plane itself. These things may surprise, or amuse, the tourist, but the local residents, who walk bareheaded in the famous California noonday sun, take them as a matter of course.

Quintus Teal regarded the efforts of his colleagues in architecture as faint-hearted, fumbling, and timid.

"What is a house?" Teal demanded of his friend, Homer Bailey.

"Well—" Bailey admitted cautiously, "speaking in broad terms, I've always regarded a house as a gadget to keep off the rain."

"Nuts! You're as bad as the rest of them."

"I didn't say the definition was complete—"

"Complete! It isn't even in the right direction. From that point of view we might just as well be squatting in caves. But I don't blame you," Teal went on magnanimously, "you're no worse than the lugs you find practicing architecture. Even the Moderns—all they've done is to abandon the Wedding Cake School in favor of the Service Station School, chucked away the gingerbread and slapped on some chromium, but at heart they are as conservative and traditional as a county courthouse. Neutra! Schindler! What have those bums got? What's Frank Lloyd Wright got that I haven't got?"

"Commissions," his friend answered succinctly.

"Huh? Wha' d'ju say?" Teal stumbled slightly in his flow of words, did a slight double take, and recovered himself. "Commissions. Correct. And why? Because I don't think of a house as an upholstered cave; I think of it as a machine for living, a vital process, a live dynamic thing, changing with the mood of the dweller—not a dead, static, oversized coffin. Why should we be held down by the frozen concepts of our ancestors? Any fool with a little smattering of descriptive geometry can design a house in the ordinary way. Is the static geometry of Euclid the only mathematics? Are we to completely disregard the Picard-Vessiot theory? How about modular systems?—to say nothing of the rich suggestions of stereochemistry. Isn't there a place in architecture for transformation, for homomorphology, for actional structures?"

"Blessed if I know," answered Bailey. "You might just as well be talking about the fourth dimension for all it means to me."

"And why not? Why should we limit ourselves to the—Say!" He interrupted himself and stared into distances. "Homer, I think you've really got something. After all, why not? Think of the infinite richness of articulation and relationship in four dimensions. What a house, what a house—" He stood quite still, his pale bulging eyes blinking thoughtfully.

Bailey reached up and shook his arm. "Snap out of it. What the hell are you talking about, four dimensions? Time is the fourth dimension; you can't drive nails into *that*."

Teal shrugged him off. "Sure. Sure. Time is *a* fourth dimension, but I'm thinking about a fourth spatial dimension, like length, breadth, and thickness. For economy of materials and convenience of arrangement you couldn't beat it. To say nothing of the saving of ground space—you could put an eight-room house on the land now occupied by a one-room house. Like a tesseract—"

"What's a tesseract?"

"Didn't you go to school? A tesseract is a hypercube, a square figure with four dimensions to it, like a cube has three, and a square has two. Here, I'll show you." Teal dashed out into the kitchen of his apartment and returned with a box of toothpicks which he spilled on the table between them, brushing glasses and a nearly empty Holland gin bottle carelessly aside. "I'll need some plasticine. I had some around here last week." He burrowed into a drawer of the littered desk which crowded one corner of his dining room and emerged with a lump of oily sculptor's clay. "Here's some."

"What are you going to do?"

"I'll show you." Teal rapidly pinched off small masses of the clay and rolled them into pea-sized balls. He stuck toothpicks into four of these and hooked them together into a square. "There! That's a square."

"Obviously."

"Another one like it, four more toothpicks, and we make a cube." The toothpicks were now arranged in the framework of a square box, a cube, with the pellets of clay holding the corners together. "Now we make another cube just like the first one, and the two of them will be two sides of the tesseract."

Bailey started to help him roll the little balls of clay for the second cube, but became diverted by the sensuous feel of the docile clay and started working and shaping it with his fingers.

"Look," he said, holding up his effort, a tiny figurine, "Gypsy Rose Lee."

"Looks more like Gargantua; she ought to sue you. Now pay attention. You open up one corner of the first cube, interlock the second cube at the corner, and then close the corner. Then take eight more toothpicks and join the bottom of the first cube to the bottom of the second, on a slant, and the top of the first to the top of the second, the same way." This he did rapidly, while he talked.

"What's that supposed to be?" Bailey demanded suspiciously.

"That's a tesseract, eight cubes forming the sides of a hypercube in four dimensions."

"It looks more like a cat's cradle to me. You've only got two cubes there anyhow. Where are the other six?"

"Use your imagination, man. Consider the top of the first cube in relation to the top of the second; that's cube number three. Then the two bottom squares, then the front faces of each cube, the back faces, the right hand, the left hand—eight cubes." He pointed them out.

"Yeah, I see 'em. But they still aren't cubes; they're what-chamucallems—prisms. They are not square, they slant."

"That's just the way you look at it, in perspective. If you drew a picture of a cube on a piece of paper, the side squares would be slaunchwise, wouldn't they? That's perspective. When you look at a four-dimensional figure in three dimensions, naturally it looks crooked. But those are all cubes just the same."

"Maybe they are to you, brother, but they still look crooked to me."

Teal ignored the objections and went on. "Now consider this as the framework of an eight-room house; there's one room on the ground floor—that's for service, utilities, and garage. There are six rooms opening off it on the next floor, living room, dining room, bathroom, bedrooms, and so forth. And up at the top, completely enclosed and with windows on four sides, is your study. There! How do you like it?"

"Seems to me you have the bathtub hanging out of the living room ceiling. Those rooms are interlaced like an octopus."

"Only in perspective, only in perspective. Here, I'll do it another way so you can see it." This time Teal made a cube of toothpicks, then made a second of halves of toothpicks, and set it exactly in the center of the first by attaching the corners of the small cube to the large cube by short lengths of toothpick. "Now—the big cube is your ground floor, the little cube inside is your study on the top floor. The six cubes joining them are the living rooms. See?"

Bailey studied the figure, then shook his head. "I still don't see but two cubes, a big one and a little one. Those other six things, they look like pyramids this time instead of prisms, but they still aren't cubes."

"Certainly, certainly, you are seeing them in different perspective. Can't you see that?"

"Well, maybe. But that room on the inside, there. It's completely surrounded by the thingamujigs. I thought you said it had windows on four sides."

"It has—it just looks like it was surrounded. That's the grand feature about a tesseract house, complete outside exposure for every room, yet every wall serves two rooms and an eight-room house requires only a one-room foundation. It's revolutionary."

"That's putting it mildly. You're crazy, bud; you can't build a house like that. That inside room is on the inside, and there she stays."

Teal looked at his friend in controlled exasperation. "It's guys like you that keep architecture in its infancy. How many square sides has a cube?"

"Six."

"How many of them are inside?"

"Why, none of 'em. They're all on the outside."

"All right. Now listen—a tesseract has eight cubical sides, *all on the outside*. Now watch me. I'm going to open up this tesseract like you can open up a cubical pasteboard box, until it's flat. That way you'll be able to see all eight of the cubes." Working very rapidly he constructed four cubes, piling one on top of the other in an unsteady tower. He then built out four more cubes from the four exposed faces of the second cube in the pile. The structure swayed a little under the loose coupling of the clay pellets, but it stood, eight cubes in an inverted cross, a double cross, as the four additional cubes stuck out in four directions. "Do you see it now? It rests on the ground floor room, the next six cubes are the living rooms, and there is your study, up at the top."

Bailey regarded it with more approval than he had the other figures. "At least I can understand it. You say that is a tesseract, too?"

"That is a tesseract unfolded in three dimensions. To put it back together you tuck the top cube onto the bottom cube, fold those side cubes in till they meet the top cube and there you are. You do all this folding through a fourth dimension of course; you don't distort any of the cubes, or fold them into each other."

Bailey studied the wobbly framework further. "Look here," he said at last, "why don't you forget about folding this thing up through a fourth dimension—you can't anyway—and build a house like this?"

"What do you mean, I can't? It's a simple mathematical problem—"

"Take it easy, son. It may be simple in mathematics, but you could never get your plans approved for construction. There isn't any fourth dimension; forget it. But this kind of a house—it might have some advantages."

Checked, Teal studied the model. "Hm-m-m—Maybe you got something. We could have the same number of rooms, and we'd save the same amount of ground space. Yes, and we would set that middle cross-shaped floor northeast, southwest, and so forth, so that every room would get sunlight all day long. That central axis lends itself nicely to central heating. We'll put the dining room on the northeast and the kitchen on the southeast, with big view windows in every room. O.K., Homer, I'll do it! Where do you want it built?"

"Wait a minute! Wait a minute! I didn't say you were going to build it for me—"

"Of course I am. Who else? Your wife wants a new house; this is it."

"But Mrs. Bailey wants a Georgian house—"

"Just an idea she has. Women don't know what they want—"

"Mrs. Bailey does."

"Just some idea an out-of-date architect has put in her head. She drives a new car, doesn't she? She wears the very latest styles—why should she live in an eighteenth century house? This house will be even later than this year's model; it's years in the future. She'll be the talk of the town."

"Well—I'll have to talk to her."

"Nothing of the sort. We'll surprise her with it. Have another drink."

"Anyhow, we can't do anything about it now. Mrs. Bailey and I are driving up to Bakersfield tomorrow. The company's bringing in a couple of wells tomorrow."

"Nonsense. That's just the opportunity we want. It will be a surprise for her when you get back. You can just write me a check right now, and your worries are over."

"I oughtn't to do anything like this without consulting her. She won't like it."

"Say, who wears the pants in your family anyhow?"

The check was signed about halfway down the second bottle.

Things are done fast in southern California. Ordinary houses there are usually built in a month's time. Under Teal's impassioned heckling the tesseract house climbed dizzily skyward in days rather than weeks, and its cross-shaped second story came jutting out at the four corners of the world. He had some trouble at first with the inspectors over these four projecting rooms but by using strong girders and folding money he had been able to convince them of the soundness of his engineering.

By arrangement, Teal drove up in front of the Bailey residence the morning after their return to town. He improvised on his two-tone horn. Bailey stuck his head out the front door. "Why don't you use the bell?"

"Too slow," answered Teal cheerfully. "I'm a man of action. Is Mrs. Bailey ready? Ah, there you are, Mrs. Bailey! Welcome home, welcome home. Jump in, we've got a surprise for you!"

"You know Teal, my dear," Bailey put in uncomfortably.

Mrs. Bailey sniffed. "I know him. We'll go in our own car, Homer."

"Certainly, my dear."

"Good idea," Teal agreed; " 'sgot more power than mine; we'll get there faster. I'll drive, I know the way." He took the keys from Bailey, slid into the driver's seat, and had the engine started before Mrs. Bailey could rally her forces.

"Never have to worry about my driving," he assured Mrs. Bailey, turning his head as he did so, while he shot the powerful car down the avenue and swung onto Sunset Boulevard, "it's a matter of power and control, a dynamic process, just my meat—I've never had a serious accident."

"You won't have but one," she said bitingly. "Will you *please* keep your eyes on the traffic?"

He attempted to explain to her that a traffic situation was a matter, not of eyesight, but intuitive integration of courses, speeds, and probabilities, but Bailey cut him short. "Where is the house, Quintus?"

"House?" asked Mrs. Bailey suspiciously. "What's this about a house, Homer? Have you been up to something without telling me?"

Teal cut in with his best diplomatic manner. "It certainly is a house, Mrs. Bailey. And what a house! It's a surprise for you from a devoted husband. Just wait till you see it—"

"I shall," she agreed grimly. "What style is it?"

"This house sets a new style. It's later than television, newer than next week. It must be seen to be appreciated. By the way," he went on rapidly, heading off any retort, "did you folks feel the earthquake last night?"

"Earthquake? What earthquake? Homer, was there an earthquake?"

"Just a little one," Teal continued, "about two A.M. If I hadn't been awake, I wouldn't have noticed it."

Mrs. Bailey shuddered. "Oh, this awful country! Do you hear that, Homer? We might have been killed in our beds and never have known it. Why did I ever let you persuade me to leave Iowa?"

"But my dear," he protested hopelessly, "you wanted to come out to California; you didn't like Des Moines."

"We needn't go into that," she said firmly. "You are a man; you should anticipate such things. Earthquakes!"

"That's one thing you needn't fear in your new home, Mrs. Bailey," Teal told her. "It's absolutely earthquake-proof; every part is in perfect dynamic balance with every other part."

"Well, I hope so. Where is this house?"

"Just around this bend. There's the sign now." A large arrow sign of the sort favored by real estate promoters, proclaimed in letters that were large and bright even for southern California:

THE HOUSE OF THE FUTURE!!!

COLOSSAL—AMAZING—

REVOLUTIONARY

See How Your Grandchildren Will Live!

Q. Teal, Architect

"Of course that will be taken down," he added hastily, noting her expression, "as soon as you take possession." He slued around the corner and brought the car to a squealing halt in front of the House of the Future. *"Voilá!"* He watched their faces for response.

Bailey stared unbelievingly, Mrs. Bailey in open dislike. They saw a simple cubical mass, possessing doors and windows, but no other architectural features, save that it was decorated in intricate mathematical designs. "Teal," Bailey asked slowly, "what have you been up to?"

Teal turned from their faces to the house. Gone was the crazy tower with its jutting second-story rooms. No trace remained of the seven rooms above ground floor level. Nothing remained but the single room that rested on the foundations. "Great jumping cats!" he yelled, "I've been robbed!"

He broke into a run.

But it did him no good. Front or back, the story was the same: the other seven rooms had disappeared, vanished completely. Bailey caught up with him, and took his arm. "Explain yourself. What is this about being robbed? How come you built anything like this—it's not according to agreement."

"But I didn't. I built just what we had planned to build, an eight-room house in the form of a developed tesseract. I've been sabotaged; that's what it is! Jealousy! The other architects in town didn't dare let me finish this job; they knew they'd be washed up if I did."

"When were you last here?"

"Yesterday afternoon."

"Everything all right then?"

"Yes. The gardeners were just finishing up."

Bailey glanced around at the faultlessly manicured landscaping. "I don't see how seven rooms could have been dismantled and carted away from here in a single night without wrecking this garden."

Teal looked around, too. "It doesn't look it. I don't understand it."

Mrs. Bailey joined them. "Well? Well? Am I to be left to amuse myself? We might as well look it over as long as we are here, though I'm warning you, Homer, I'm not going to like it."

"We might as well," agreed Teal, and drew a key from his pocket with which he let them in the front door. "We may pick up some clues."

The entrance hall was in perfect order, the sliding screens that separated it from the garage space were back, permitting them to see the entire compartment. "This looks all right," observed Bailey. "Let's go up on the roof and try to figure out what happened. Where's the staircase? Have they stolen that, too?"

"Oh, no," Teal denied, "look—" He pressed a button below the light switch; a panel in the ceiling fell away and a light, graceful flight of stairs swung noiselessly down. Its strength members were the frosty silver of duralumin, its treads and risers transparent plastic. Teal wriggled like a boy who has successfully performed a card trick, while Mrs. Bailey thawed perceptibly.

It was beautiful.

"Pretty slick," Bailey admitted. "Howsomever it doesn't seem to go any place—"

"Oh, that—" Teal followed his gaze. "The cover lifts up as you approach the top. Open stair wells are anachronisms. Come on." As predicted, the lid of the staircase got out of their way as they climbed the flight and permitted them to debouch at the top, but not, as they had expected, on the roof of the single room. They found themselves standing in the middle one of the five rooms which constituted the second floor of the original structure.

For the first time on record Teal had nothing to say. Bailey echoed him, chewing on his cigar. Everything was in perfect order. Before them, through open doorway and translucent partition lay the kitchen, a chef's dream of up-to-the-minute domestic engineering, monel metal, continuous counter space, concealed lighting, functional arrangement. On the left the formal, yet gracious and hospitable dining room awaited guests, its furniture in parade-ground alignment.

Teal knew before he turned his head that the drawing room and lounge would be found in equally substantial and impossible existence.

"Well, I must admit this *is* charming," Mrs. Bailey approved, "and the kitchen is just *too* quaint for words—though I would never have guessed from the exterior that this house had so much room upstairs. Of course *some* changes will have to be made. That secretary now—if we moved it over *here* and put the settle over *there*—"

"Stow it, Matilda," Bailey cut in brusquely. "Wha'd' yuh make of it, Teal?"

"Why, Homer Bailey! The very id—"

"Stow it, I said. Well, Teal?"

The architect shuffled his rambling body. "I'm afraid to say. Let's go on up."

"How?"

"Like this." He touched another button; a mate, in deeper colors, to the fairy bridge that had let them up from below offered them access to the next floor. They climbed it, Mrs. Bailey expostulating in the rear, and found themselves in the master bedroom. Its shades were drawn, as had been those on the level below, but the mellow lighting came on automatically. Teal at once activated the switch which controlled still another flight of stairs, and they hurried up into the top floor study.

"Look, Teal," suggested Bailey when he had caught his breath, "can we get to the roof above this room? Then we could look around."

"Sure, it's an observatory platform." They climbed a fourth flight of stairs, but when the cover at the top lifted to let them reach the level above, they found themselves, not on the roof, but *standing in the ground floor room where they had entered the house.*

Mr. Bailey turned a sickly gray. "Angels in heaven," he cried, "this place is haunted. We're getting out of here." Grabbing his wife he threw open the front door and plunged out.

Teal was too much preoccupied to bother with their departure. There was an answer to all this, an answer that he did not believe. But he was forced to break off considering it because of hoarse shouts from somewhere above him. He lowered the staircase and rushed upstairs. Bailey was in the central room leaning over Mrs. Bailey, who had fainted. Teal took in the situation, went to the bar built into the lounge, and poured three fingers of brandy, which he returned with and handed to Bailey. "Here—this'll fix her up."

Bailey drank it.

"That was for Mrs. Bailey," said Teal.

"Don't quibble," snapped Bailey. "Get her another." Teal took the precaution of taking one himself before returning with a dose earmarked for his client's wife. He found her just opening her eyes.

"Here, Mrs. Bailey," he soothed, "this will make you feel better."

"I never touch spirits," she protested, and gulped it.

"Now tell me what happened," suggested Teal. "I thought you two had left."

"But we did—we walked out the front door and found ourselves up here, in the lounge."

"The hell you say! Hm-m-m—wait a minute." Teal went into the lounge. There he found that the big view window at the end of the room was open. He peered cautiously through it. He stared, not out at the California countryside, but into the ground floor room—or a reasonable facsimile thereof. He said nothing, but went back to the stair well which he had left open and looked down it. The ground floor room was still in place. Somehow, it managed to be in two different places at once, on different levels.

He came back into the central room and seated himself opposite Bailey in a deep, low chair, and sighted him past his upthrust bony knees. "Homer," he said impressively, "do you know what has happened?"

"No, I don't—but if I don't find out pretty soon, something is going to happen and pretty drastic, too!"

"Homer, this is a vindication of my theories. This house is a real tesseract."

"What's he talking about, Homer?"

"Wait, Matilda—now Teal, that's ridiculous. You've pulled some hanky-panky here and I won't have it—scaring Mrs. Bailey half to death, and making me nervous. All I want is to get out of here, with no more of your trapdoors and silly practical jokes."

"Speak for yourself, Homer," Mrs. Bailey interrupted, "I was *not* frightened; I was just took all over queer for a moment. It's my heart; all of my people are delicate and high-strung. Now about this tessy thing—explain yourself, Mr. Teal. Speak up."

He told her as well as he could in the face of numerous interruptions the theory back of the house. "Now as I see it, Mrs. Bailey," he concluded, "this house, while perfectly stable in three dimensions, was not stable in four dimensions. I had built a house in the shape of an unfolded tesseract; something happened to it, some jar or side thrust, and it collapsed into its normal shape—it folded up." He snapped his fingers suddenly. "I've got it! The earthquake!"

"Earthquake?"

"Yes, yes, the little shake we had last night. From a four-dimensional standpoint this house was like a plane balanced on edge. One little push and it fell over, collapsed along its natural joints into a stable four-dimensional figure."

"I thought you boasted about how safe this house was."

"It *is* safe—three-dimensionally."

"I don't call a house safe," commented Bailey edgily, "that collapses at the first little temblor."

"But look around you, man!" Teal protested. "Nothing has been disturbed, not a piece of glassware cracked. Rotation through a fourth dimension can't effect a three-dimensional figure any more than you can shake letters off a printed page. If you had been sleeping in here last night, you would never have awakened."

"That's just what I'm afraid of. Incidentally, has your great genius figured out any way for us to get out of this booby trap?"

"Huh? Oh, yes, you and Mrs. Bailey started to leave and landed back up here, didn't you. But I'm sure there is no real difficulty—we came in, we can go out. I'll try it." He was up and hurrying downstairs before he had finished talking. He flung open the front door, stepped through, and found himself staring at his companions, down the length of the second floor lounge. "Well, there does seem to be some slight problem," he admitted blandly. "A mere technicality, though—we can always go out a window." He jerked aside the long drapes that covered the deep French windows set in one side wall of the lounge. He stopped suddenly.

"Hm-m-m," he said, "this is interesting—very."

"What is?" asked Bailey, joining him.

"This." The window stared directly into the dining room, instead of looking outdoors. Bailey stepped back to the corner where the lounge and the dining room joined the central room at ninety degrees.

"But that can't be," he protested, "that window is maybe fifteen, twenty feet from the dining room."

"Not in a tesseract," corrected Teal. "Watch." He opened the window and stepped through, talking back over his shoulder as he did so.

From the point of view of the Baileys he simply disappeared.

But not from his own viewpoint. It took him some seconds to catch his breath. Then he cautiously disentangled himself from the rosebush to which he had become almost irrevocably wedded, making a mental note the while never again to order landscaping which involved plants with thorns, and looked around him.

He was outside the house. The massive bulk of the ground floor room thrust up beside him. Apparently he had fallen off the roof.

He dashed around the corner of the house, flung open the front door and hurried up the stairs. "Homer!" he called out, "Mrs. Bailey! I've found a way out!"

Bailey looked annoyed rather than pleased to see him. "What happened to you?"

"I fell out. I've been outside the house. You can do it just as easily—just step through those French windows. Mind the rosebush, though—we may have to build another stairway."

"How did you get back in?"

"Through the front door."

"Then we shall leave the same way. Come, my dear." Bailey set his hat firmly on his head and marched down the stairs, his wife on his arm.

Teal met them in the lounge. "I could have told you that wouldn't work," he announced. "Now here's what we have to do: As I see it, in a four-dimensional figure a three-dimensional man has two choices every time he crosses a line of juncture, like a wall or a threshold. Ordinarily he will make a ninety-degree turn through the fourth dimension, only he doesn't feel it with his three dimensions. Look." He stepped through the very window that he had fallen out of a moment before. Stepped through and arrived in the dining room, where he stood, still talking.

"I watched where I was going and arrived where I intended to." He stepped back into the lounge. "The time before I didn't watch and I moved on through normal space and fell out of the house. It must be a matter of subconscious orientation."

"I'd hate to depend on subconscious orientation when I step out for the morning paper."

"You won't have to; it'll become automatic. Now to get out of the house this time—Mrs. Bailey, if you will stand here with your back to the window, and jump backward, I'm pretty sure you will land in the garden."

Mrs. Bailey's face expressed her opinion of Teal and his ideas. "Homer Bailey," she said shrilly, "are you going to stand there and let him suggest such—"

"But Mrs. Bailey," Teal attempted to explain, "we can tie a rope on you and lower you down eas—"

"Forget it, Teal," Bailey cut him off brusquely. "We'll have to find a better way than that. Neither Mrs. Bailey nor I are fitted for jumping."

Teal was temporarily nonplused; there ensued a short silence. Bailey broke it with, "Did you hear that, Teal?"

"Hear what?"

"Someone talking off in the distance. D'you s'pose there could be someone else in the house, playing tricks on us, maybe?"

"Oh, not a chance. I've got the only key."

"But I'm sure of it," Mrs. Bailey confirmed. "I've heard them ever since we came in. Voices. Homer, I can't stand much more of this. Do something."

"Now, now, Mrs. Bailey," Teal soothed, "don't get upset. There can't be anyone else in the house, but I'll explore and make sure. Homer, you stay here with Mrs. Bailey and keep an eye on the rooms on this floor." He passed from the lounge into the ground floor room and from there to the kitchen and on into the bedroom. This led him back to the lounge by a straight-line route, that is to say, by going straight ahead on the entire trip he returned to the place from which he started.

"Nobody around," he reported. "I opened all of the doors and windows as I went—all except this one." He stepped to the window opposite the one through which he had recently fallen and thrust back the drapes.

He saw a man with his back toward him, four rooms away. Teal snatched open the French window and dived through it, shouting, "There he goes now! Stop thief!"

The figure evidently heard him; it fled precipitately. Teal pursued, his gangling limbs stirred to unanimous activity, through drawing room, kitchen, dining room, lounge—room after room, yet in spite of Teal's best efforts he could not seem to cut down the four-room lead that the interloper had started with.

He saw the pursued jump awkwardly but actively over the low sill of a French window and in so doing knock off his hat. When he came up to the point where his quarry had lost his headgear, he stopped and picked it up, glad of an excuse to stop and catch his breath. He was back in the lounge.

"I guess he got away from me," he admitted. "Anyhow, here's his hat. Maybe we can identify him."

Bailey took the hat, looked at it, then snorted, and slapped it on Teal's head. It fitted perfectly. Teal looked puzzled, took the hat off, and examined it. On the sweat band were the initials "Q.T." It was his own.

Slowly comprehension filtered through Teal's features. He went back to the French window and gazed down the series of rooms through which he had pursued the mysterious stranger. They saw him wave his arms semaphore fashion. "What are you doing?" asked Bailey.

"Come see." The two joined him and followed his stare with their own. Four rooms away they saw the backs of three figures, two male and one female. The taller, thinner of the men was waving his arms in a silly fashion.

Mrs. Bailey screamed and fainted again.

Some minutes later, when Mrs. Bailey had been resuscitated and somewhat composed, Bailey and Teal took stock. "Teal," said Bailey, "I won't waste any time blaming you; recriminations are useless and I'm sure you didn't plan for this to happen, but I suppose you realize we are in a pretty serious predicament. How are we going to get out of here? It looks now as if we would stay until we starve; every room leads into another room."

"Oh, it's not that bad. I got out once, you know."

"Yes, but you can't repeat it—you tried."

"Anyhow we haven't tried all the rooms. There's still the study."

"Oh, yes, the study. We went through there when we first came in, and didn't stop. Is it your idea that we might get out through its windows?"

"Don't get your hopes up. Mathematically, it ought to look into the four side rooms on this floor. Still we never opened the blinds; maybe we ought to look."

" 'Twon't do any harm anyhow. Dear, I think you had best just stay here and rest—"

"Be left alone in this horrible place? I should say not!" Mrs. Bailey was up off the couch where she had been recuperating even as she spoke.

They went upstairs. "This is the inside room, isn't it, Teal?" Bailey inquired as they passed through the master bedroom and climbed on up toward the study. "I mean it was the little cube in your diagram that was in the middle of the big cube, and completely surrounded."

"That's right," agreed Teal. "Well, let's have a look. I figure this window ought to give into the kitchen." He grasped the cords of Venetian blinds and pulled them.

It did not. Waves of vertigo shook them. Involuntarily they fell to the floor and grasped helplessly at the pattern on the rug to keep from falling. "Close it! Close it!" moaned Bailey.

Mastering in part a primitive atavistic fear, Teal worked his way back to the window and managed to release the screen. The window had looked *down* instead of *out,* down from a terrifying height.

Mrs. Bailey had fainted again.

Teal went back after more brandy while Bailey chafed her wrists. When she had recovered, Teal went cautiously to the window and raised the screen a crack. Bracing his knees, he studied the scene. He turned to Bailey. "Come look at this, Homer. See if you recognize it."

"You stay away from there, Homer Bailey!"

"Now, Matilda, I'll be careful." Bailey joined him and peered out.

"See up there? That's the Chrysler Building, sure as shooting. And there's the East River, and Brooklyn." They gazed straight down the sheer face of an enormously tall building. More than a thousand feet away a toy city, very much alive, was spread out before them. "As near as I can figure it out, we are looking down the side of the Empire State Building from a point just above its tower."

"What is it? A mirage?"

"I don't think so—it's too perfect. I think space is folded over through the fourth dimension here and we are looking past the fold."

"You mean we aren't really seeing it?"

"No, we're seeing it all right. I don't know what would happen if we climbed out this window, but I for one don't want to try. But what a view! Oh, boy, what a view! Let's try the other windows."

They approached the next window more cautiously, and it was well that they did, for it was even more disconcerting, more reason-shaking, than the one looking down the gasping height of the skyscraper. It was a simple seascape, open ocean and blue sky—but the ocean was where the sky should have been, and contrariwise. This time they were somewhat braced for it, but they both felt seasickness about to overcome them at the sight of waves rolling overhead; they lowered the blind quickly without giving Mrs. Bailey a chance to be disturbed by it.

Teal looked at the third window. "Game to try it, Homer?"

"Hrrumph—well, we won't be satisfied if we don't. Take it easy." Teal lifted the blind a few inches. He saw nothing, and raised it a little more—still nothing. Slowly he raised it until the window was fully exposed. They gazed out at—nothing.

Nothing, nothing at all. What color is nothing? Don't be silly! What shape is it? Shape is an attribute of *something*. It had neither depth nor form. It had not even blackness. It was *nothing*.

Bailey chewed at his cigar. "Teal, what do you make of that?"

Teal's insouciance was shaken for the first time. "I don't know, Homer, I don't rightly know—but I think that window ought to be walled up." He stared at the lowered blind for a moment. "I think maybe we looked at a place where space *isn't*. We looked around a fourth-dimensional corner and there wasn't anything there." He rubbed his eyes. "I've got a headache."

They waited for a while before tackling the fourth window. Like an unopened letter, it might *not* contain bad news. The doubt left hope. Finally the suspense stretched too thin and Bailey pulled the cord himself, in the face of his wife's protests.

It was not so bad. A landscape stretched away from them, right side up, and on such a level that the study appeared to be a ground floor room. But it was distinctly unfriendly.

A hot, hot sun beat down from lemon-colored sky. The flat ground seemed burned a sterile, bleached brown and incapable of supporting life. Life there was, strange stunted trees that lifted knotted, twisted arms to the sky. Little clumps of spiky leaves grew on the outer extremities of these misshapen growths.

"Heavenly day," breathed Bailey, "where is that?"

Teal shook his head, his eyes troubled. "It beats me."

"It doesn't look like anything on Earth. It looks more like another planet—Mars, maybe."

"I wouldn't know. But, do you know, Homer, it might be worse than that, worse than another planet, I mean."

"Huh? What's that you say?"

"It might be clear out of our space entirely. I'm not sure that that is our sun at all. It seems too bright."

Mrs. Bailey had somewhat timidly joined them and now gazed out at the outré scene. "Homer," she said in a subdued voice, "those hideous trees—they frighten me."

He patted her hand.

Teal fumbled with the window catch.

"What are you doing?" Bailey demanded.

"I thought if I stuck my head out the window I might be able to look around and tell a bit more."

"Well—all right," Bailey grudged, "but be careful."

"I will." He opened the window a crack and sniffed. "The air is all right, at least." He threw it open wide.

His attention was diverted before he could carry out his plan. An uneasy tremor, like the first intimation of nausea, shivered the entire building for a long second, and was gone.

"Earthquake!" They all said it at once. Mrs. Bailey flung her arms around her husband's neck.

Teal gulped and recovered himself, saying:

"It's all right, Mrs. Bailey. This house is perfectly safe. You know you can expect settling tremors after a shock like last night." He had just settled his features into an expression of reassurance when the second shock came. This one was no mild shimmy but the real seasick roll.

In every Californian, native born or grafted, there is a deep-rooted primitive reflex. An earthquake fills him with soul-shaking claustrophobia which impels him blindly to *get outdoors!* Model Boy Scouts will push aged grandmothers aside to obey it. It is a matter of record that Teal and Bailey landed on top of Mrs. Bailey. Therefore, she must have jumped through the window first. The order of precedence cannot be attributed to chivalry; it must be assumed that she was in readier position to spring.

They pulled themselves together, collected their wits a little, and rubbed sand from their eyes. Their first sensations were relief at feeling the solid sand of the desert land under them. Then Bailey noticed something that brought them to their feet and checked Mrs. Bailey from bursting into the speech that she had ready.

"Where's the house?"

It was gone. There was no sign of it at all. They stood in the center of flat desolation, the landscape they had seen from the window. But, aside from the tortured, twisted trees there was nothing to be seen but the yellow sky and the luminary overhead, whose furnacelike glare was already almost insufferable.

Bailey looked slowly around, then turned to the architect. "Well, Teal?" His voice was ominous.

Teal shrugged helplessly. "I wish I knew. I wish I could even be sure that we were on Earth."

"Well, we can't stand here. It's sure death if we do. Which direction?"

"Any, I guess. Let's keep a bearing on the sun."

They had trudged on for an undetermined distance when Mrs. Bailey demanded a rest. They stopped. Teal said in an aside to Bailey, "Any ideas?"

"No . . . no, none. Say, do you hear anything?"

Teal listened. "Maybe—unless it's my imagination."

"Sounds like an automobile. Say, it *is* an automobile!"

They came to the highway in less than another hundred yards. The automobile, when it arrived, proved to be an elderly, puffing light truck, driven by a rancher. He crunched to a stop at their hail. "We're stranded. Can you help us out?"

"Sure. Pile in."

"Where are you headed?"

"Los Angeles."

"Los Angeles? Say, where is this place?"

"Well, you're right in the middle of the Joshua-Tree National Forest."

The return was as dispiriting as the Retreat from Moscow. Mr. and Mrs. Bailey sat up in front with the driver while Teal bumped along in the body of the truck, and tried to protect his head from the sun. Bailey subsidized the friendly rancher to detour to the tesseract house, not because they wanted to see it again, but in order to pick up their car.

At last the rancher turned the corner that brought them back to where they had started. But the house was no longer there.

There was not even the ground floor room. It had vanished. The Baileys, interested in spite of themselves, poked around the foundations with Teal.

"Got any answers for this one, Teal?" asked Bailey.

"It must be that on that last shock it simply fell through into another section of space. I can see now that I should have anchored it at the foundations."

"That's not all you should have done."

"Well, I don't see that there is anything to get downhearted about. The house was insured, and we've learned an amazing lot. There are possibilities, man, possibilities! Why, right now I've got a great new revolutionary idea for a house—"

Teal ducked in time. He was always a man of action.

BEYOND DOUBT

Astonishing Stories, April 1941

as by Lyle Monroe and Elma Wentz

From the June number of The Science Review

SAVANT SOLVES SECRET OF EASTER ISLAND IMAGES

"According to Professor J. Howard Erlenmeyer, Sc.D., Ph.D., F. R. S., director of the Archeological Society's Easter Island Expedition. Professor Erlenmeyer was quoted as saying, 'There can no longer be any possible doubt as to the significance of the giant monolithic images which are found in Easter Island. When one considers the primary place held by religious matters in all primitive cultures, and compares the design of these images with artifacts used in the rites of present day Polynesian tribes, the conclusion is inescapable that these images have a deep esoteric religious significance. Beyond doubt, their large size, their grotesque exaggeration of human form, and the seemingly aimless, but actually systematic, distribution gives evidence of the use for which they were carved, to wit; the worship of. . . .' "

WARM, AND INCREDIBLY golden, the late afternoon sun flooded the white-and-green city of Nuria, gilding its maze of circular criss-crossed streets. The Towers of the Guardians, rising high above the lushly verdant hills, gleamed like translucent ivory. The hum from the domed buildings of the business district was muted while merchants rested in the cool shade of luxuriant, moistly green trees, drank refreshing okrada, and gazed out at the great hook-prowed green-and-crimson ships riding at anchor in the harbor—ships from Hindos, from Cathay, and from the far-flung colonies of Atlantis.

In all the broad continent of Mu there was no city more richly beautiful than Nuria, capital of the province of Lac.

But despite the smiling radiance of sun, and sea, and sky, there was an undercurrent of atmospheric tenseness—as though the air itself were a tight coil about to be sprung, as though a small spark would set off a cosmic explosion.

Through the city moved the sibilant whispering of a name—the name was everywhere, uttered in loathing and fear, or in high hope, according to the affiliations of the utterer,—but in any mouth the name had the potency of thunder.

The name was Talus.

Talus, apostle of the common herd; Talus, on whose throbbing words hung the hopes of a million eager citizens; Talus, candidate for governor of the province of Lac.

In the heart of the tenement district, near the smelly waterfront, between a narrow side street and a garbage alley was the editorial office of Mu Regenerate, campaign organ of the Talus-for-Governor organization. The office was as quiet as the rest of Nuria, but with the quiet of a spent cyclone. The floor was littered with twisted scraps of parchment, overturned furniture, and empty beer flagons. Three young men were seated about a great, round, battered table in attitudes that spoke their gloom. One of them was staring cynically at an enormous poster which dominated one wall of the room. It was a portrait of a tall, majestic man with a long curling white beard. He wore a green toga. One hand was raised in a gesture of benediction. Over the poster, under the crimson-and-purple of crossed Murian banners, was the legend:

TALUS FOR GOVERNOR!

The one who stared at the poster let go an unconscious sigh. One of his companions looked up from scratching at a sheet of parchment with a stubby stylus. "What's eating on you, Robar?"

The one addressed waved a hand at the wall. "I was just looking at our white hope. Ain't he beautiful? Tell me, Dolph, how can anyone look so noble, and be so dumb?"

"God knows. It beats me."

"That's not quite fair, fellows," put in the third, "the old boy ain't really dumb; he's just unworldly. You've got to admit that the Plan is the most constructive piece of statesmanship this country has seen in a generation."

Robar turned weary eyes on him. "Sure. Sure. And he'd make a good governor, too. I won't dispute that; if I didn't think the Plan would work, would I be here, living from hand to mouth and breaking my heart on this bloody campaign? Oh, he's noble all right. Sometimes he's so noble it gags me. What I mean is: Did you ever work for a candidate that was so bull-headed stupid about how to get votes and win an election?"

"Well . . . no."

"What gets me, Clevum," Robar went on, "is that he could be elected so easily. He's got everything; a good sound platform that you can stir people up with, the correct background, a grand way of speaking, and the most beautiful appearance that a candidate ever had. Compared with Old Bat Ears, he's a natural. It ought to be just one-two-three. But Bat Ears will be re-elected, sure as shootin'."

"I'm afraid you're right," mourned Clevum. "We're going to take such a shellacking as nobody ever saw. I thought for a while that we would make the grade, but now—Did you see what the *King's Men* said about him this morning?"

"That dirty little sheet—What was it?"

"Besides some nasty cracks about Atlantis gold, they accused him of planning to destroy the Murian home and defile the sanctity of Murian womanhood. They called upon every red-blooded one hundred percent Murian to send this subversive monster back where he came from. Oh, it stank! But the yokels were eating it up."

"Sure they do. That's just what I mean. The governor's gang slings mud all the time, but if we sling any mud about Governor Vortus, Talus throws a fit. His idea of a news story is a nifty little number about comparative statistics of farm taxes in the provinces of Mu . . . What are you drawing now, Dolph?"

"This." He held up a ghoulish caricature of Governor Vortus himself, with his long face, thin lips, and high brow, atop of which rested the tall crimson governor's cap. Enormous ears gave this sinister face the appearance of a vulture about to take flight. Beneath the cartoon was the simple caption:

BAT EARS FOR GOVERNOR

"There!" exclaimed Robar, "that's what this campaign needs. Humor! If we could plaster that cartoon on the front page of *Mu Regenerate* and stick one under the door of every voter in the province, it 'ud be a landslide. One look at that mug and they'd laugh themselves sick— and vote for our boy Talus!"

He held the sketch at arms length and studied it, frowning: Presently he looked up. "Listen, dopes—Why not do it? Give me one last edition with some guts in it. Are you game?"

Clevum looked worried. "Well . . . I don't know . . . What are you going to use for money? Besides, even if Oric would crack loose from the dough, how would we get an edition of that size distributed that well? And even if we did get it done, it might boomerang on us—the opposition would have the time and money to answer it."

Robar looked disgusted. "That's what a guy gets for having ideas in this campaign—nothing but objections, objections!"

"Wait a minute, Robar," Dolph interposed. "Clevum's kicks have some sense to them, but maybe you got something. The idea is to make Joe Citizen laugh at Vortus, isn't it? Well, why not fix up some dodgers of my cartoon and hand 'em out at the polling places on election day?"

Robar drummed on the table as he considered this. "Umm, no, it wouldn't do. Vortus' goon squads would beat the hell out of our workers and high jack our literature."

"Well, then how about painting some big banners with old Bat Ears on them? We could stick them up near each polling place where the voters couldn't fail to see them."

"Same trouble. The goon squads would have them down before the polls open."

"Do you know what, fellows," put in Clevum, "what we need is something big enough to be seen and too solid for Governor's plug-uglies to wreck. Big stone statues about two stories high would be about right."

Robar looked more pained than ever. "Clevum, if you can't be helpful, why not keep quiet? Sure, statues would be fine—if we had forty years and ten million simoleons."

"Just think, Robar," Dolph jibed, with an irritating smile, "if your mother had entered you for the priesthood, you could integrate all the statues you want—no worry, no trouble, no expense."

"Yeah, wise guy, but in that case I wouldn't be in politics—Say!"

" 'S trouble?"

"Integration! Suppose we *could* integrate enough statues of old Picklepuss—"

"How?"

"Do you know Kondor?"

"The moth-eaten old duck that hangs around the Whirling Whale?"

"That's him. I'll bet he could do it!"

"That old stumblebum? Why, he's no adept; he's just a cheap unlicensed sorcerer. Reading palms in saloons and a little jackleg horoscopy is about all he's good for. He can't even mix a potent love philtre: I know; I've tried him."

"Don't be too damn certain you know all about him. He got all tanked up one night and told me the story of his life. He used to be a priest back in Ægypt."

"Then why isn't he now?"

"That's the point. He didn't get along with the high priest. One night he got drunk and integrated a statue of the high priest right where it would show up best and too big to be missed—only he stuck the head of the high priest on the body of an animal."

"Whew!"

"Naturally when he sobered up the next morning and saw what he had done all he could do was to run for it. He shipped on a freighter in the Red Sea and that's how come he's here."

Clevum's face had been growing longer and longer all during the discussion. He finally managed to get in an objection. "I don't suppose you two red hots have stopped to think about the penalty for unlawful use of priestly secrets?"

"Oh, shut up, Clevum. If we win the election, Talus'll square it. If we lose the election—Well, if we lose, Mu won't be big enough to hold us whether we pull this stunt or not."

Oric was hard to convince. As a politician he was always affable; as campaign manager for Talus, and consequently employer of Robar, Dolph, and Clevum, the boys had sometimes found him elusive, even though chummy.

"Ummm, well, I don't know—" he had said, "I'm afraid Talus wouldn't like it."

"Would he need to know until it's all done?"

"Now, boys, really, ah, you wouldn't want me to keep him in ignorance . . ."

"But, Oric, you know perfectly well that we are going to lose unless we do something, and do it quick."

"Now, Robar, you are too pessimistic." Oric's pop eyes radiated synthetic confidence.

"How about that straw poll? We didn't look so good; we were losing two to one in the back country."

"Well . . . perhaps you are right, my boy." Oric laid a hand on the younger man's shoulder. "But suppose we do lose this election; Mu wasn't built in a day. And I want you to know that we appreciate the hard, unsparing work that you boys have done, regardless of the outcome. Talus won't forget it, and neither shall, uh, I . . . It's young men like you three who give me confidence in the future of Mu—"

"We don't want appreciation; we want to win this election."

"Oh, to be sure! To be sure! So do we all—none more than myself. Uh—how much did you say this scheme of yours would cost?"

"The integration won't cost much. We can offer Kondor a contingent fee and cut him in on a spot of patronage. Mostly we'll need to keep him supplied with wine. The big item will be getting the statues to the polling places. We had planned on straight commercial apportation."

"Well, now, that will be expensive."

"Dolph called the temple and got a price—"

"Good heavens, you haven't told the priests what you plan to do?"

"No, sir. He just specified tonnage and distances."

"What was the bid?"

Robar told him. Oric looked as if his first born were being ravaged by wolves. "Out of the question, out of the question entirely," he protested.

But Robar pressed the matter. "Sure it's expensive—but it's not half as expensive as a campaign that is just good enough to lose. Besides—I know the priesthood isn't supposed to be political, but isn't it possible with your connections for you to find one who would do it on the side for a smaller price, or even on credit? It's a safe thing for him; if we go through with this we'll *win*—it's a cinch."

Oric looked really interested for the first time. "You might be right. Mmmm—yes." He fitted the tips of his fingers carefully together. "You boys go ahead with this. Get the statues made. Let me worry about the arrangements for apportation." He started to leave, a preoccupied look on his face.

"Just a minute," Robar called out, "we'll need some money to oil up old Kondor."

Oric paused. "Oh, yes, yes. How stupid of me." He pulled out three silver pieces and handed them to Robar. "Cash, and no records, eh?" He winked.

"While you're about it, sir," added Clevum, "how about my salary? My landlady's getting awful temperamental."

Oric seemed surprised. "Oh, haven't I paid you yet?" He fumbled at his robes. "You've been very patient; most patriotic. You know how it is—so many details on my mind, and some of our sponsors haven't been prompt about meeting their pledges." He handed Clevum one piece of silver. "See me the first of the week, my boy. Don't let me forget it." He hurried out.

The three picked their way down the narrow crowded street, teeming with vendors, sailors, children, animals, while expertly dodging refuse of one kind or another, which was unceremoniously tossed from balconies. The Whirling Whale tavern was apparent by its ripe, gamey odor some little distance before one came to it. They found Kondor draped over the bar, trying as usual to cadge a drink from the seafaring patrons.

He accepted their invitation to drink with them with alacrity. Robar allowed several measures of beer to mellow the old man before he brought the conversation around to the subject. Kondor drew himself up with drunken dignity in answer to a direct question.

"Can I integrate simulacra? My son you are looking at the man who created the Sphinx." He hiccoughed politely.

"But can you still do it, here and now?" Robar pressed him, and added, "For a fee, of course."

Kondor glanced cautiously around. "Careful, my son. Some one might be listening . . . Do you want original integration, or simply re-integration?"

"What's the difference?"

Kondor rolled his eyes up, and inquired of the ceiling, "What do they teach in these modern schools? Full integration requires much power, for one must disturb the very heart of the aether itself; re-integration is simply a re-arrangement of the atoms in a predetermined pattern. If you want stone statues, any waste stone will do."

"Re-integration, I guess. Now here's the proposition—"

"That will be enough for the first run. Have the porters desist." Kondor turned away and buried his nose in a crumbling roll of parchment, his rheumy eyes scanning faded hieroglyphs. They were assembled in an abandoned gravel pit on the rear of a plantation belonging to Dolph's uncle. They had obtained the use of the pit without argument, for, as Robar had reasonably pointed out, if the old gentleman did not know that his land was being used for illicit purposes, he could not possibly have any objection.

Their numbers had been augmented by six red-skinned porters from the Land of the Inca—porters who were not only strong and untiring but possessed the desirable virtue of speaking no Murian. The porters had filled the curious ventless hopper with grey gravel and waited impassively for more toil to do. Kondor put the parchment away somewhere in the folds of his disreputable robe, and removed from the same mysterious recesses a tiny instrument of polished silver.

"Your pattern, son."

Dolph produced a small waxen image, modelled from his cartoon of Bat Ears. Kondor placed it in front of him, and stared through the silver instrument at it. He was apparently satisfied with what he saw, for he commenced humming to himself in a tuneless monotone, his bald head weaving back and forth in time.

Some fifty lengths away, on a stone pedestal, a wraith took shape. First was an image carved of smoke. The smoke solidified, became translucent. It thickened, curdled. Kondor ceased his humming and surveyed his work. Thrice as high as a man stood an image of Bat Ears— good honest stone throughout. "Clevum, my son," he said, as he examined the statue, "will you be so good as to hand me that jug?"

The gravel hopper was empty.

Oric called on them two days before the election. Robar was disconcerted to find that he had brought with him a stranger who was led around through the dozens of rows of giant statues. Robar drew Oric to one side before he left, and asked in a whisper, "Who is this chap?"

Oric smiled reassuringly. "Oh, he's all right. Just one of the boys— a friend of mine."

"But can he be trusted? I don't remember seeing him around campaign headquarters."

"Oh, sure! By the way, you boys are to be congratulated on the job of work you've done here. Well, I must be running on—I'll drop in on you again."

"Just a minute, Oric. Are you all set on the apportation?"

"Oh, yes. Yes indeed. They'll all be distributed around to the polling places in plenty of time—every statue."

"When are you going to do it?"

"Why don't you let me worry about those details, Robar?"

"Well . . . you are the boss, but I still think I ought to know when to be ready for the apportation."

"Oh, well, if you feel that way, shall we say, ah, midnight before election day?"

"That's fine. We'll be ready."

Robar watched the approach of the midnight before election with a feeling of relief. Kondor's work was all complete, the ludicrous statues were lined up, row on row, two for every polling place in the province of Lac, and Kondor himself was busy getting reacquainted with the wine jug. He had almost sobered up during the sustained effort of creating the statues.

Robar gazed with satisfaction at the images. "I wish I could see the Governor's face when he first catches sight of one of these babies. Nobody could possibly mistake who they were. Dolph, you're a genius; I never saw anything sillier looking in my life."

"That's high praise, pal," Dolph answered. "Isn't it about time the priest was getting here? I'll feel easier when we see our little dollies flying through the air on their way to the polling places."

"Oh, I wouldn't worry. Oric told me positively that the priest would be here in plenty of time. Besides, apportation is fast. Even the images intended for the back country and the far northern peninsula will get there in a few minutes—once he gets to work."

But as the night wore on it became increasingly evident that something was wrong. Robar returned from his thirteenth trip to the highway with a report of no one in sight on the road from the city.

"What'll we do?" Clevum asked.

"I don't know. Something's gone wrong; that's sure."

"Well, we've got to do something. Let's go back to the temple and try to locate him."

"We can't do that; we don't know what priest Oric hired. We'll have to find Oric."

They left Kondor to guard the statues and hurried back into town. They found Oric just leaving campaign headquarters. With him was the visitor he had brought with him two days before. He seemed surprised to see them. "Hello boys. Finished with the job so soon?"

"He never showed up," Robar panted.

"Never showed up? Well, imagine that! Are you sure?"

"Of course we're sure; we were there!"

"Look," put in Dolph, "what is the name of the priest you hired to do this job? We want to go up to the temple and find him."

"His name? Oh, no, don't do that. You might cause all sorts of complications. I'll go to the temple myself."

"We'll go with you."

"That isn't necessary," he told them testily. "You go on back to the gravel pit, and be sure everything is ready."

"Good grief, Oric, everything has been ready for hours. Why not take Clevum along with you to show the priest the way?"

"I'll see to that. Now get along with you."

Reluctantly they did as they were ordered. They made the trip back in moody silence. As they approached their destination Clevum spoke up, "You know, fellows—"

"Well? Spill it."

"That fellow that was with Oric—wasn't he the guy he had out here, showing him around?"

"Yes; why?"

"I've been trying to place him. I remember now—I saw him two weeks ago, coming out of Governor Vortus' campaign office."

After a moment of stunned silence Robar said bitterly, "Sold out. There's no doubt about it; Oric has sold us out."

"Well, what do we do about it?"

"What can we do?"

"Blamed if I know."

"Wait a minute, fellows," came Clevum's pleading voice, "Kondor used to be a priest. Maybe he can do apportation."

"Say! There's a chance! Let's get going."

But Kondor was dead to the world.

They shook him. They poured water in his face. They walked him up and down. Finally they got him sober enough to answer questions.

Robar tackled him. "Listen, pop, this is important: Can you perform apportation?"

"Huh? Me? Why, of course. How else did we build the pyramids?"

"Never mind the pyramids. Can you move these statues here tonight?"

Kondor fixed his interrogator with a bloodshot eye. "My son, the great Arcane laws are the same for all time and space. What was done in Ægypt in the Golden Age can be done in Mu tonight."

Dolph put in a word. "Good grief, pop, why didn't you tell us this before."

The reply was dignified and logical. "No one asked me."

Kondor set about his task at once, but with such slowness that the boys felt they would scream just to watch him. First, he drew a large circle in the dust. "This is the house of darkness," he announced solemnly, and added the crescent of Astarte. Then he drew another large circle tangent to the first. "And this is the house of light." He added the sign of the sun god.

When he was done, he walked widder-shins about the whole three times the wrong way. His feet nearly betrayed him twice, but he recovered, and continued his progress. At the end of the third lap he hopped to the center of the house of darkness and stood facing the house of light.

The first statue on the left in the front row quivered on its base, then rose into the air and shot over the horizon to the east.

The three young men burst out with a single cheer, and tears streamed down Robar's face.

Another statue rose up. It was just poised for flight when old Kondor hiccoughed. It fell, a dead weight, back to its base, and broke into two pieces. Kondor turned his head.

"I am truly sorry," he announced; "I shall be more careful with the others."

And try he did—but the liquor was regaining its hold. He wove to and fro on his feet, his aim with the images growing more and more erratic. Stone figures flew in every direction, but none travelled any great distance. One group of six flew off together and landed with a high splash in the harbor. At last, with more than three fourths of the images still untouched he sank gently to his knees, keeled over, and remained motionless.

Dolph ran up to him and shook him. There was no response. He peeled back one of Kondor's eyelids and examined the pupil. "It's no good," he admitted. "He won't come to for hours."

Robar gazed heartbrokenly at the shambles around him. There they are, he thought, worthless! Nobody will ever see them—just so much left over campaign material, wasted! My biggest idea!

Clevum broke the uncomfortable silence. "Sometimes," he said, "I think what this country needs is a good earthquake."

> "... *the worship of their major deity.*
>
> *Beyond doubt, while errors are sometimes made in archeology, this is one case in which no chance of error exists. The statues are clearly religious in significance. With that sure footing on which to rest the careful scientist may deduce with assurance the purpose of* ..."

THEY

Unknown, April 1941

THEY WOULD NOT let him alone.

They would never let him alone. He realized that that was part of the plot against him—never to leave him in peace, never to give him a chance to mull over the lies they had told him, time enough to pick out the flaws, and to figure out the truth for himself.

That damned attendant this morning! He had come busting in with his breakfast tray, waking him, and causing him to forget his dream. If only he could remember that dream—

Someone was unlocking the door. He ignored it.

"Howdy, old boy. They tell me you refused your breakfast?" Dr. Hayward's professionally kindly mask hung over his bed.

"I wasn't hungry."

"But we can't have that. You'll get weak, and then I won't be able to get you well completely. Now get up and get your clothes on and I'll order an eggnog for you. Come on, that's a good fellow!"

Unwilling, but still less willing at that moment to enter into any conflict of wills, he got out of bed and slipped on his bathrobe. "That's better," Hayward approved. "Have a cigarette?"

"No, thank you."

The doctor shook his head in a puzzled fashion. "Darned if I can figure you out. Loss of interest in physical pleasures does not fit your type of case."

"What is my type of case?" he inquired in flat tones.

"Tut! Tut!" Hayward tried to appear roguish. "If medicos told their professional secrets, they might have to work for a living."

"What is my type of case?"

"Well—the label doesn't matter, does it? Suppose you tell me. I really know nothing about your case as yet. Don't you think it is about time you talked?"

"I'll play chess with you."

"All right, all right." Hayward made a gesture of impatient concession. "We've played chess every day for a week. If you will talk, I'll play chess."

What could it matter? If he was right, they already understood perfectly that he had discovered their plot; there was nothing to be gained by concealing the obvious. Let them try to argue him out of it. Let the tail go with the hide! To hell with it!

He got out the chessmen and commenced setting them up. "What do you know of my case so far?"

"Very little. Physical examination, negative. Past history, negative. High intelligence, as shown by your record in school and your success in your profession. Occasional fits of moodiness, but nothing exceptional. The only positive information was the incident that caused you to come here for treatment."

"To be brought here, you mean. Why should it cause comment?"

"Well, good gracious, man—if you barricade yourself in your room and insist that your wife is plotting against you, don't you expect people to notice?"

"But she was plotting against me—and so are you. White, or black?"

"Black—it's your turn to attack. Why do you think we are plotting against you?"

"It's an involved story, and goes way back into my early childhood. There was an immediate incident, however—" He opened by advancing the white king's knight to KB3. Hayward's eyebrows raised.

"You make a piano attack?"

"Why not? You know that it is not safe for me to risk a gambit with you."

The doctor shrugged his shoulders and answered the opening. "Suppose we start with your early childhood. It may shed more light than more recent incidents. Did you feel that you were being persecuted as a child?"

"No!" He half rose from his chair. "When I was a child I was sure of myself. I knew then, I tell you; I knew! Life was worthwhile, and I knew it. I was at peace with myself and my surroundings. Life was good and I was good and I assumed that the creatures around me were like myself."

"And weren't they?"

"Not at all! Particularly the children. I didn't know what viciousness was until I was turned loose with other children. The little devils! And I was expected to be like them and play with them."

The doctor nodded. "I know. The herd compulsion. Children can be pretty savage at times."

"You've missed the point. This wasn't any healthy roughness; these creatures were different—not like myself at all. They looked like me, but they were not like me. If I tried to say anything to one of them about anything that mattered to me, all I could get was a stare and a scornful laugh. Then they would find some way to punish me for having said it."

Hayward nodded. "I see what you mean. How about grown-ups?"

"That is somewhat different. Adults don't matter to children at first—or, rather they did not matter to me. They were too big, and they did not bother me, and they were busy with things that did not enter into my considerations. It was only when I noticed that my presence affected them that I began to wonder about them."

"How do you mean?"

"Well, they never did the things when I was around that they did when I was not around."

Hayward looked at him carefully. "Won't that statement take quite a lot of justifying? How do you know what they did when you weren't around?"

He acknowledged the point. "But I used to catch them just stopping. If I came into a room, the conversation would stop suddenly, and then it would pick up about the weather or something equally inane. Then I took to hiding and listening and looking. Adults did not behave the same way in my presence as out of it."

"Your move, I believe. But see here, old man—that was when you were a child. Every child passes through that phase. Now that you are a man, you must see the adult point of view. Children are strange creatures and have to be protected—at least, we do protect them—from many adult interests. There is a whole code of conventions in the matter that—"

"Yes, yes," he interrupted impatiently, "I know all that. Nevertheless, I noticed enough and remembered enough that was never clear to me later. And it put me on my guard to notice the next thing."

"Which was?" He noticed that the doctor's eyes were averted as he adjusted a castle's position.

"The things I saw people doing and heard them talking about were never of any importance. They must be doing something else."

"I don't follow you."

"You don't choose to follow me. I'm telling this to you in exchange for a game of chess."

"Why do you like to play chess so well?"

"Because it is the only thing in the world where I can see all the factors and understand all the rules. Never mind—I saw all around me this enormous plant, cities, farms, factories, churches, schools, homes, railroads, luggage, roller coasters, trees, saxophones, libraries, people, and animals. People that looked like me and who should have felt very much like me, if what I was told was the truth. But what did they appear to be doing? 'They went to work to earn the money to buy the food to get the strength to go to work to earn the money to buy the food to get the strength to go to work to get the strength to buy the food to earn the money to go to—' until they fell over dead. Any slight variation in the basic pattern did not matter, for they always fell over dead. And everybody tried to tell me that I should be doing the same thing. I knew better!"

The doctor gave him a look apparently intended to denote helpless surrender and laughed. "I can't argue with you. Life does look like that, and maybe it is just that futile. But it is the only life we have. Why not make up your mind to enjoy it as much as possible?"

"Oh, no!" He looked both sulky and stubborn. "You can't peddle nonsense to me by claiming to be fresh out of sense. How do I know? Because all this complex stage setting, all these swarms of actors, could not have been put here just to make idiot noises at each other. Some other explanation, but not that one. An insanity as enormous, as complex, as the one around me had to be planned. I've found the plan!"

"Which is?"

He noticed that the doctor's eyes were again averted.

"It is a play intended to divert me, to occupy my mind and confuse me, to keep me so busy with details that I will not have time to think about the meaning. You are all in it, every one of you." He shook his finger in the doctor's face. "Most of them may be helpless automatons, but you're not. You are one of the conspirators. You've been sent in as a troubleshooter to try to force me to go back to playing the role assigned to me!"

He saw that the doctor was waiting for him to quiet down.

"Take it easy," Hayward finally managed to say. "Maybe it is all a conspiracy, but why do you think that you have been singled out for special attention? Maybe it is a joke on all of us. Why couldn't I be one of the victims as well as yourself?"

"Got you!" He pointed a long finger at Hayward. "That is the essence of the plot. All of these creatures have been set up to look like me in order to prevent me from realizing that I was the center of the arrangements. But I have noticed the key fact, the mathematically inescapable fact, that I am unique. Here am I, sitting on the inside. The world extends outward from me. I am the center—"

"Easy, man, easy! Don't you realize that the world looks that way to me, too. We are each the center of the universe—"

"Not so! That is what you have tried to make me believe, that I am just one of millions more just like me. Wrong! If they were like me, then I could get into communication with them. I can't. I have tried and tried and I can't. I've sent out my inner thoughts, seeking some one other being who has them, too. What have I gotten back? Wrong answers, jarring incongruities, meaningless obscenity. I've tried. I tell you. God!—how I've tried! But there is nothing out there to speak to me—nothing but emptiness and otherness!"

"Wait a minute. Do you mean to say that you think there is nobody home at my end of the line? Don't you believe that I am alive and conscious?"

He regarded the doctor soberly. "Yes, I think you are probably alive, but you are one of the others—my antagonists. But you have set thousands of others around me whose faces are blank, not lived in, and whose speech is a meaningless reflex of noise."

"Well, then, if you concede that I am an ego, why do you insist that I am so very different from yourself?"

"Why? Wait!" He pushed back from the chess table and strode over to the wardrobe, from which he took out a violin case.

While he was playing, the lines of suffering smoothed out of his face and his expression took a relaxed beatitude. For a while he recaptured the emotions, but not the knowledge, which he had possessed in dreams. The melody proceeded easily from proposition to proposition with inescapable, unforced logic. He finished with a triumphant statement of the essential thesis and turned to the doctor. "Well?"

"Hm-m-m." He seemed to detect an even greater degree of caution in the doctor's manner. "It's an odd bit, but remarkable. 'S pity you didn't take up the violin seriously. You could have made quite a reputation. You could even now. Why don't you do it? You could afford to, I believe."

He stood and stared at the doctor for a long moment, then shook his head as if trying to clear it. "It's no use," he said slowly, "no use at all. There is no possibility of communication. I am alone." He replaced the instrument in its case and returned to the chess table. "My move, I believe?"

"Yes. Guard your queen."

He studied the board. "Not necessary. I no longer need my queen. Check."

The doctor interposed a pawn to parry the attack.

He nodded. "You use your pawns well, but I have learned to anticipate your play. Check again—and mate, I think."

The doctor examined the new situation. "No," he decided, "no—not quite." He retreated from the square under attack. "Not checkmate—stalemate at the worst. Yes, another stalemate."

He was upset by the doctor's visit. He couldn't be wrong, basically, yet the doctor had certainly pointed out logical holes in his position. From a logical standpoint the whole world might be a fraud perpetrated on everybody. But logic meant nothing—logic itself was a fraud, starting with unproved assumptions and capable of proving anything. The world is what it is!—and carries its own evidence of trickery.

But does it? What did he have to go on? Could he lay down a line between known facts and everything else and then make a reasonable interpretation of the world, based on facts alone—an interpretation free from complexities of logic and no hidden assumptions of points not certain. Very well—

First fact, himself. He knew himself directly. He existed.

Second facts, the evidence of his "five senses," everything that he himself saw and heard and smelled and tasted with his physical senses. Subject to their limitations, he must believe his senses. Without them he was entirely solitary, shut up in a locker of bone, blind, deaf, cutoff, the only being in the world.

And that was not the case. He knew that he did not invent the information brought to him by his senses. There had to be something else out there, some otherness that produced the things his senses recorded. All philosophies that claimed that the physical world around him did not exist except in his imagination were sheer nonsense.

But beyond that, what? Were there any third facts on which he could rely? No, not at this point. He could not afford to believe anything that he was told, or that he read, or that was implicitly assumed to be true about the world around him. No, he could not believe any of it, for the sum total of what he had been told and read and been taught in school was so contradictory, so senseless, so wildly insane that none of it could be believed unless he personally confirmed it.

Wait a minute—The very telling of these lies, these senseless contradictions, was a fact in itself, known to him directly. To that extent they were data, probably very important data.

The world as it had been shown to him was a piece of unreason, an idiot's dream. Yet it was on too mammoth a scale to be without some reason. He came wearily back to his original point: Since the world could not be as crazy as it appeared to be, it must necessarily have been arranged to appear crazy in order to deceive him as to the truth.

Why had they done it to him? And what was the truth behind the sham? There must be some clue in the deception itself. What thread ran through it all? Well, in the first place he had been given a superabundance of explanations of the world around him, philosophies, religions, "common sense" explanations. Most of them were so clumsy, so obviously inadequate, or meaningless, that they could hardly have expected him to take them seriously. They must have intended them simply as misdirection.

But there were certain basic assumptions running through all the hundreds of explanations of the craziness around him. It must be these basic assumptions that he was expected to believe. For example, there was the deepseated assumption that he was a "human being," essentially like millions of others around him and billions more in the past and the future.

That was nonsense! He had never once managed to get into real communication with all those things that looked so much like him but were so different. In the agony of his loneliness, he had deceived himself that Alice understood him and was a being like him. He knew now that he had suppressed and refused to examine thousands of little discrepancies because he could not bear the thought of returning to complete loneliness. He had needed to believe that his wife was a living, breathing being of his own kind who understood his inner thoughts. He had refused to consider the possibility that she was simply, a mirror, an echo—or something unthinkably worse.

He had found a mate, and the world was tolerable, even though dull, stupid, and full of petty annoyance. He was moderately happy and had put away his suspicions. He had accepted, quite docilely, the treadmill he was expected to use, until a slight mischance had momentarily cut through the fraud—then his suspicions had returned with impounded force; the bitter knowledge of his childhood had been confirmed.

He supposed that he had been a fool to make a fuss about it. If he had kept his mouth shut they would not have locked him up. He should have been as subtle and as shrewd as they, kept his eyes and ears open and learned the details of and the reasons for the plot against him. He might have learned how to circumvent it.

But what if they had locked him up—the whole world was an asylum and all of them his keepers.

A key scraped in the lock, and he looked up to see an attendant entering with a tray. "Here's your dinner, sir."

"Thanks, Joe," he said gently. "Just put it down."

"Movies tonight, sir," the attendant went on. "Wouldn't you like to go? Dr. Hayward said you could—"

"No, thank you. I prefer not to."

"I wish you would, sir." He noticed with amusement the persuasive intentness of the attendant's manner. "I think the doctor wants you to. It's a good movie. There's a Mickey Mouse cartoon—"

"You almost persuade me, Joe," he answered with passive agreeableness. "Mickey's trouble is the same as mine, essentially. However, I'm not going. They need not bother to hold movies tonight."

"Oh, there will be movies in any case, sir. Lots of our other guests will attend."

"Really? Is that an example of thoroughness, or are you simply keeping up the pretense in talking to me? It isn't necessary, Joe, if it's any strain on you. I know the game. If I don't attend, there is no point in holding movies."

He liked the grin with which the attendant answered this thrust. Was it possible that this being was created just as he appeared to be— big muscles, phlegmatic disposition, tolerant, doglike? Or was there nothing going on behind those kind eyes, nothing but robot reflex? No, it was more likely that he was one of them, since he was so closely in attendance on him.

The attendant left and he busied himself at his supper tray, scooping up the already-cut bites of meat with a spoon, the only implement provided. He smiled again at their caution and thoroughness. No danger of that—he would not destroy this body as long it served him in investigating the truth of the matter. There were still many different avenues of research available before taking that possibly irrevocable step.

After supper he decided to put his thoughts in better order by writing them; he obtained paper. He should start with a general statement of some underlying postulate of the credos that had been drummed into him all his "life." Life? Yes, that was a good one. He wrote:

"I am told that I was born a certain number of years ago and that I will die a similar number of years hence. Various clumsy stories have been offered me to explain to me where I was before birth and what becomes of me after death, but they are rough lies, not intended to deceive, except as misdirection. In every other possible way the world around me assures me that I am mortal, here but a few years, and a few years hence gone completely—nonexistent.

"WRONG—I am immortal. I transcend this little time axis; a seventy-year span on it is but a casual phase in my experience. Second only to the prime datum of my own existence is the emotionally convincing certainty of my own continuity. I may be a closed curve, but, closed or open, I neither have a beginning nor an end. Self-awareness is not relational; it is absolute, and cannot be reached to be destroyed, or created. Memory, however, being a relational aspect of consciousness, may be tampered with and possibly destroyed.

"It is true that most religions which have been offered me teach immortality, but note the fashion in which they teach it. The surest way to lie convincingly is to tell the truth unconvincingly. They did not wish me to believe.

"Caution: Why have they tried so hard to convince me that I am going to die in a few years? There must be a very important reason. I infer that they are preparing me for some sort of a major change. It may be crucially important for me to figure out their intentions about this— probably I have several years in which to reach a decision. Note: Avoid using the types of reasoning they have taught me."

The attendant was back. "Your wife is here, sir."

"Tell her to go away."

"Please, sir—Dr. Hayward is most anxious that you should see her."

"Tell Dr. Hayward that I said that he is an excellent chess player."

"Yes, sir." The attendant waited for a moment. "Then you won't see her, sir?"

"No, I won't see her."

He wandered around the room for some minutes after the attendant had left, too distrait to return to his recapitulation. By and large they had played very decently with him since they had brought him here. He was glad that they had allowed him to have a room alone, and he certainly had more time free for contemplation than had ever been possible on the outside. To be sure, continuous effort to keep him busy and to distract him was made, but, by being stubborn, he was able to circumvent the rules and gain some hours each day for introspection.

But, damnation!—he did wish they would not persist in using Alice in their attempts to divert his thoughts. Although the intense terror and revulsion which she had inspired in him when he had first rediscovered the truth had now aged into a simple feeling of repugnance and distaste for her company, nevertheless it was emotionally upsetting to be reminded of her, to be forced into making decisions about her.

After all, she had been his wife for many years. Wife? What was a wife? Another soul like one's own, a complement, the other necessary pole to the couple, a sanctuary of understanding and sympathy in the boundless depths of aloneness. That was what he had thought, what he had needed to believe and had believed fiercely for years. The yearning need for companionship of his own kind had caused him to see himself reflected in those beautiful eyes and had made him quite uncritical of occasional incongruities in her responses.

He sighed. He felt that he had sloughed off most of the typed emotional reactions which they had taught him by precept and example, but Alice had gotten under his skin, 'way under, and it still hurt. He had been happy—what if it had been a dope dream? They had given him an excellent, a beautiful mirror to play with—the more fool he to have looked behind it!

Wearily he turned back to his summing up:

"The world is explained in either one of two ways; the common-sense way which says that the world is pretty much as it appears to be and that ordinary human conduct and motivations are reasonable, and the religio-mystic solution which states that the world is dream stuff, unreal, insubstantial, with reality somewhere beyond.

"WRONG—both of them. The common-sense scheme has no sense to it of any sort. Life is short and full of trouble. Man born of woman is born to trouble as the sparks fly upward. His days are few and they are numbered. All is vanity and vexation. Those quotations may be jumbled and incorrect, but that is a fair statement of the common-sense world is-as-it-seems in its only possible evaluation. In such a world, human striving is about as rational as the blind darting of a moth against a light bulb. The common-sense world is a blind insanity, out of nowhere, going nowhere, to no purpose.

"As for the other solution, it appears more rational on the surface, in that it rejects the utterly irrational world of common sense. But it is not a rational solution, it is simply a flight from reality of any sort, for it refuses to believe the results of the only available direct communication between the ego and the Outside. Certainly the 'five senses' are poor enough channels of communication, but they are the only channels."

He crumpled up the paper and flung himself from the chair. Order and logic were no good—his answer was right because it smelled right. But he still did not know all the answer. Why the grand scale to the deception, countless creatures, whole continents, an enormously involved and minutely detailed matrix of insane history, insane tradition, insane culture? Why bother with more than a cell and a strait jacket?

It must be, it had to be, because it was supremely important to deceive him completely, because a lesser deception would not do. Could it be that they dare not let him suspect his real identity no matter how difficult and involved the fraud?

He had to know. In some fashion he must get behind the deception and see what went on when he was not looking. He had had one glimpse; this time he must see the actual workings, catch the puppet masters in their manipulations.

Obviously the first step must be to escape from this asylum, but to do it so craftily that they would never see him, never catch up with him, not have a chance to set the stage before him. That would be hard to do. He must excel them in shrewdness and subtlety.

Once decided, he spent the rest of the evening in considering the means by which he might accomplish his purpose. It seemed almost impossible—he must get away without once being seen and remain in strict hiding. They must lose track of him completely in order that they would not know where to center their deceptions. That would mean going without food for several days. Very well—he could do it. He must not give them any warning by unusual action or manner.

The lights blinked twice. Docilely he got up and commenced preparations for bed. When the attendant looked through the peephole he was already in bed, with his face turned to the wall.

❖

Gladness! Gladness everywhere! It was good to be with his own kind, to hear the music swelling out of every living thing, as it always had and always would—good to know that everything was living and aware of him, participating in him, as he participated in them. It was good to be, good to know the unity of many and the diversity of one. There had been one bad thought—the details escaped him—but it was gone—it had never been; there was no place for it.

The early-morning sounds from the adjacent ward penetrated the sleepladen body which served him here and gradually recalled him to awareness of the hospital room. The transition was so gentle that he carried over full recollection of what he had been doing and why. He lay still, a gentle smile on his face, and savored the uncouth, but not un-pleasant, languor of the body he wore. Strange that he had ever forgotten despite their tricks and stratagems. Well, now that he had recalled the key, he would quickly set things right in this odd place. He would call them in at once and announce the new order. It would be amusing to see old Glaroon's expression when he realized that the cycle had ended—

The click of the peephole and the rasp of the door being unlocked guillotined his line of thought. The morning attendant pushed briskly in with the breakfast tray and placed it on the tip table. "Morning, sir. Nice, bright day—want it in bed, or will you get up?"

Don't answer! Don't listen! Suppress this distraction! This is part of their plan—But it was too late, too late. He felt himself slipping, falling, wrenched from reality back into the fraud world in which they had kept him. It was gone, gone completely, with no single association around him to which to anchor memory. There was nothing left but the sense of heart-breaking loss and the acute ache of unsatisfied catharsis.

"Leave it where it is. I'll take care of it."

"Okey-doke." The attendant bustled out, slamming the door, and noisily locked it.

He lay quite still for a long time, every nerve end in his body screaming for relief.

At last he got out of bed, still miserably unhappy, and attempted to concentrate on his plans for escape. But the psychic wrench he had received in being recalled so suddenly from his plane of reality had left him bruised and emotionally disturbed. His mind insisted on rechewing its doubts, rather than engage in constructive thought. Was it possible that the doctor was right, that he was not alone in his miserable dilemma? Was he really simply suffering from paronoia, delusions of self-importance?

Could it be that each unit in this yeasty swarm around him was the prison of another lonely ego—helpless, blind, and speechless, condemned to an eternity of miserable loneliness? Was the look of suffering which he had brought to Alice's face a true reflection of inner torment and not simply a piece of play acting intended to maneuver him into compliance with their plans?

A knock sounded at the door. He said "Come in," without looking up. Their comings and goings did not matter to him.

"Dearest—" A well-known voice spoke slowly and hesitantly.

"Alice!" He was on his feet at once, and facing her. "Who let you in here?"

"Please, dear, please—I had to see you."

"It isn't fair. It isn't fair." He spoke more to himself than to her. Then: "Why did you come?"

She stood up to him with a dignity he had hardly expected. The beauty of her childlike face had been marred by line and shadow, but it shone with an unexpected courage. "I love you," she answered quietly. "You can tell me to go away, but you can't make me stop loving you and trying to help you."

He turned away from her in an agony of indecision. Could it be possible that he had misjudged her? Was there, behind that barrier of flesh and sound symbols, a spirit that truly yearned toward his? Lovers whispering in the dark—*"You do understand, don't you?"*

"Yes, dear heart, I understand."

"Then nothing that happens to us can matter, as long as we are together and understand—" Words, words, rebounding hollowly from an unbroken wall—

No, he couldn't be wrong! Test her again—"Why did you keep me on that job in Omaha?"

"But I didn't make you keep that job. I simply pointed out that we should think twice before—"

"Never mind. Never mind." Soft hands and a sweet face preventing him with mild stubbornness from ever doing the thing that his heart told him to do. Always with the best of intentions, the best of intentions, but always so that he had never quite managed to do the silly, unreasonable things that he knew were worthwhile. Hurry, hurry, hurry, and strive, with an angel-faced jockey to see that you don't stop long enough to think for yourself—

"Why did you try to stop me from going back upstairs that day?"

She managed to smile, although her eyes were already spilling over with tears. "I didn't know it really mattered to you. I didn't want us to miss the train."

It had been a small thing, an unimportant thing. For some reason not clear even to him he had insisted on going back upstairs to his study when they were about to leave the house for a short vacation. It was raining, and she had pointed out that there was barely enough time to get to the station. He had surprised himself and her, too, by insisting on his own way in circumstances in which he had never been known to be stubborn.

He had actually pushed her to one side and forced his way up the stairs. Even then nothing might have come of it had he not—quite unnecessarily—raised the shade of the window that faced toward the rear of the house.

It was a very small matter. It had been raining, hard, out in front. From this window the weather was clear and sunny, with no sign of rain.

He had stood there quite a long while, gazing out at the impossible sunshine and rearranging his cosmos in his mind. He re-examined long-suppressed doubts in the light of this one small but totally unexplainable discrepancy. Then he had turned and had found that she was standing behind him.

He had been trying ever since to forget the expression that he had surprised on her face.

"What about the rain?"

"The rain?" she repeated in a small, puzzled voice. "Why, it was raining, of course. What about it?"

"But it was not raining out my study window."

"What? But of course it was. I did notice the sun break through the clouds for a moment, but that was all."

"Nonsense!"

"But darling, what has the weather to do with you and me? What difference does it make whether it rains or not—to us?" She approached him timidly and slid a small hand between his arm and side. "Am I responsible for the weather?"

"I think you are. Now please go."

She withdrew from him, brushed blindly at her eyes, gulped once, then said in a voice held steady: "All right. I'll go. But remember—you can come home if you want to. And I'll be there, if you want me." She waited a moment, then added hesitantly: "Would you . . . would you kiss me good-bye?"

He made no answer of any sort, neither with voice nor eyes. She looked at him, then turned, fumbled blindly for the door, and rushed through it.

The creature he knew as Alice went to the place of assembly without stopping to change form. "It is necessary to adjourn this sequence. I am no longer able to influence his decisions."

They had expected it, nevertheless they stirred with dismay.

The Glaroon addressed the First for Manipulation. "Prepare to graft the selected memory track at once."

Then, turning to the First for Operations, the Glaroon said: "The extrapolation shows that he will tend to escape within two of his days. This sequence degenerated primarily through your failure to extend that rainfall all around him. Be advised."

"It would be simpler if we understood his motives."

"In my capacity as Dr. Hayward, I have often thought so," commented the Glaroon acidly, "but if we understood his motives, we would be part of him. Bear in mind the Treaty! He almost remembered."

The creature known as Alice spoke up. "Could he not have the Taj Mahal next sequence? For some reason he values it."

"You are becoming assimilated!"

"Perhaps. I am not in fear. Will he receive it?"

"It will be considered."

The Glaroon continued with orders: "Leave structures standing until adjournment. New York City and Harvard University are now dismantled. Divert him from those sectors.

"Move!"

SOLUTION UNSATISFACTORY

Astounding Science Fiction, May 1941

as by Anson MacDonald

IN 1903 THE Wright brothers flew at Kitty Hawk.

In December, 1938, in Berlin, Dr. Hahn split the uranium atom.

In April, 1943, Dr. Estelle Karst, working under the Federal Emergency Defense Authority, perfected the Karst-Obre technique for producing artificial radioactives.

So American foreign policy had to change.

Had to. *Had to*. It is very difficult to tuck a bugle call back into a bugle. Pandora's Box is a one-way proposition. You can turn pig into sausage, but not sausage into pig. Broken eggs stay broken. "All the King's horses and all the King's men can't put Humpty together again."

I ought to know—I was one of the King's men.

By rights I should not have been. I was not a professional military man when World War II broke out, and when Congress passed the draft law I drew a high number, high enough to keep me out of the army long enough to die of old age.

Not that very many died of old age that generation!

But I was the newly appointed secretary to a freshman congressman; I had been his campaign manager and my former job had left me. By profession, I was a high-school teacher of economics and sociology—school boards don't like teachers of social subjects actually to deal with social problems—and my contract was not renewed. I jumped at the chance to go to Washington.

My congressman was named Manning. Yes, *the* Manning, Colonel Clyde C. Manning, U.S. Army retired—Mr. Commissioner Manning. What you may not know about him is that he was one of the Army's No. 1 experts in chemical warfare before a leaky heart put him on the shelf. I had picked him, with the help of a group of my political associates, to run against the two-bit chiseler who was the incumbent in our district. We needed a strong liberal candidate and Manning was tailor-made for the job. He had served one term in the grand jury, which cut his political eye teeth, and had stayed active in civic matters thereafter.

Being a retired army officer was a political advantage in vote-getting among the more conservative and well-to-do citizens, and his record was O.K. for the other side of the fence. I'm not primarily concerned with vote-getting; what I liked about him was that, though he was liberal, he was tough-minded, which most liberals aren't. Most liberals believe that water runs downhill, but, praise God, it'll never reach the bottom.

Manning was not like that. He could see a logical necessity and act on it, no matter how unpleasant it might be.

We were in Manning's suite in the House Office Building, taking a little blow from that stormy first session of the Seventy-eighth Congress and trying to catch up on a mountain of correspondence, when the War Department called. Manning answered it himself.

I had to overhear, but then I was his secretary. "Yes," he said, "speaking. Very well, put him on. Oh . . . hello, General . . . Fine, thanks. Yourself?" Then there was a long silence. Presently, Manning said, "But I can't do that, General, I've got this job to take care of. . . . What's that? . . . Yes, who is to do my committee work and represent my district? . . . I think so." He glanced at his wrist watch. "I'll be right over."

He put down the phone, turned to me, and said, "Get your hat, John. We are going over to the War Department."

"So?" I said, complying.

"Yes," he said with a worried look, "the Chief of Staff thinks I ought to go back to duty." He set off at a brisk walk, with me hanging back to try to force him not to strain his bum heart. "It's impossible, of course." We grabbed a taxi from the stand in front of the office building and headed for the Department.

But it *was* possible, and Manning agreed to it, after the Chief of Staff presented his case. Manning had to be convinced, for there is no way on earth for anyone, even the President himself, to order a congressman to leave his post, even though he happens to be a member of the military service, too.

The Chief of Staff had anticipated the political difficulty and had been forehanded enough to have already dug up an opposition congressman with whom to pair Manning's vote for the duration of the emergency. This other congressman, the Honorable Joseph T. Brigham, was a reserve officer who wanted to go to duty himself—or was willing to; I never found out which. Being from the opposite political party, his vote in the House of Representatives could be permanently paired against Manning's and neither party would lose by the arrangement.

There was talk of leaving me in Washington to handle the political details of Manning's office, but Manning decided against it, judging that his other secretary could do that, and announced that I must go along as his adjutant. The Chief of Staff demurred, but Manning was in a position to insist, and the Chief had to give in.

A chief of staff can get things done in a hurry if he wants to. I was sworn in as a temporary officer before we left the building; before the day was out I was at the bank, signing a note to pay for the sloppy service uniforms the Army had adopted and to buy a dress uniform with a beautiful shiny belt—a dress outfit which, as it turned out, I was never to need.

We drove over into Maryland the next day and Manning took charge of the Federal nuclear research laboratory, known officially by the hush-hush title of War Department Special Defense Project No. 347. I didn't know a lot about physics and nothing about modern atomic physics, aside from the stuff you read in the Sunday supplements. Later, I picked up a smattering, mostly wrong, I suppose, from associating with the heavyweights with whom the laboratory was staffed.

Colonel Manning had taken an Army p.g. course at Massachusetts Tech and had received a master of science degree for a brilliant thesis on the mathematical theories of atomic structure. That was why the Army had to have him for this job. But that had been some years before; atomic theory had turned several cartwheels in the meantime; he admitted to me that he had to bone like the very devil to try to catch up to the point where he could begin to understand what his highbrow charges were talking about in their reports.

I think he overstated the degree of his ignorance; there was certainly no one else in the United States who could have done the job. It required a man who could direct and suggest research in a highly esoteric field, but who saw the problem from the standpoint of urgent military necessity. Left to themselves, the physicists would have reveled in the intellectual luxury of an unlimited research expense account, but, while they undoubtedly would have made major advances in human knowledge, they might never have developed anything of military usefulness, or the military possibilities of a discovery might be missed for years.

It's like this: It takes a smart dog to hunt birds, but it takes a hunter behind him to keep him from wasting time chasing rabbits. And the hunter needs to know nearly as much as the dog.

No derogatory reference to the scientists is intended—by no means! We had all the genius in the field that the United States could produce, men from Chicago, Columbia, Cornell, M.I.T., Cal Tech, Berkeley, every radiation laboratory in the country, as well as a couple of broad-A boys lent to us by the British. And they had every facility that ingenuity could think up and money could build. The five-hundred-ton cyclotron which had originally been intended for the University of California was there, and was already obsolete in the face of the new gadgets these brains had thought up, asked for, and been given. Canada supplied us with all the uranium we asked for—tons of the treacherous stuff—from Great Bear Lake, up near the Yukon, and the fractional-residues technique of separating uranium isotope 235 from the commoner isotope 238 had already been worked out, by the same team from Chicago that had worked up the earlier expensive mass spectrograph method.

Someone in the United States government had realized the terrific potentialities of uranium 235 quite early and, as far back as the summer of 1940, had rounded up every atomic research man in the country and had sworn them to silence. Atomic power, if ever developed, was planned to be a government monopoly, at least till the war was over. It might turn out to be the most incredibly powerful explosive ever dreamed of, and it might be the source of equally incredible power. In any case, with Hitler talking about secret weapons and shouting hoarse insults at democracies, the government planned to keep any new discoveries very close to the vest.

Hitler had lost the advantage of a first crack at the secret of uranium through not taking precautions. Dr. Hahn, the first man to break open the uranium atom, was a German. But one of his laboratory assistants had fled Germany to escape a pogrom. She came to this country, and told us about it.

We were searching, there in the laboratory in Maryland, for a way to use U235 in a controlled explosion. We had a vision of a one-ton bomb that would be a whole air raid in itself, a single explosion that would flatten out an entire industrial center. Dr. Ridpath, of Continental Tech, claimed that he could build such a bomb, but that he could not guarantee that it would not explode as soon as it was loaded and as for the force of the explosion—well, he did not believe his own figures; they ran out to too many ciphers.

The problem was, strangely enough, to find an explosive which would be weak enough to blow up only one county at a time, and stable enough to blow up only on request. If we could devise a really practical rocket fuel at the same time, one capable of driving a war rocket at a thousand miles an hour, or more, then we would be in a position to make most anybody say "uncle" to Uncle Sam.

We fiddled around with it all the rest of 1943 and well into 1944. The war in Europe and the troubles in Asia dragged on. After Italy folded up, England was able to release enough ships from her Mediterranean fleet to ease the blockade of the British Isles. With the help of the planes we could now send her regularly and with the additional over-age destroyers we let her have, England hung on somehow, digging in and taking more and more of her essential defense industries underground. Russia shifted her weight from side to side as usual, apparently with the policy of preventing either side from getting a sufficient advantage to bring the war to a successful conclusion. People were beginning to speak of "permanent war."

I was killing time in the administrative office, trying to improve my typing—a lot of Manning's reports had to be typed by me personally—when the orderly on duty stepped in and announced Dr. Karst. I flipped the interoffice communicator. "Dr. Karst is here, chief. Can you see her?"

"Yes," he answered, through his end.

I told the orderly to show her in.

Estelle Karst was quite a remarkable old girl and, I suppose, the first woman ever to hold a commission in the Corps of Engineers. She was an M.D. as well as an Sc.D. and reminded me of the teacher I had had in fourth grade. I guess that was why I always stood up instinctively when she came into the room—I was afraid she might look at me and sniff. It couldn't have been her rank; we didn't bother much with rank.

She was dressed in white coveralls and a shop apron and had simply thrown a hooded cape over herself to come through the snow. I said, "Good morning, ma'am," and led her into Manning's office.

The Colonel greeted her with the urbanity that had made him such a success with women's clubs, seated her, and offered her a cigarette.

"I'm glad to see you, Major," he said. "I've been intending to drop around to your shop."

I knew what he was getting at; Dr. Karst's work had been primarily physiomedical; he wanted her to change the direction of her research to something more productive in a military sense.

"Don't call me 'major,' " she said tartly.

"Sorry, Doctor—"

"I came on business, and must get right back. And I presume you are a busy man, too. Colonel Manning, I need some help."

"That's what we are here for."

"Good. I've run into some snags in my research. I think that one of the men in Dr. Ridpath's department could help me, but Dr. Ridpath doesn't seem disposed to be cooperative."

"So? Well, I hardly like to go over the head of a departmental chief, but tell me about it; perhaps we can arrange it. Whom do you want?"

"I need Dr. Obre."

"The spectroscopist. Hm-m-m. I can understand Dr. Ridpath's reluctance, Dr. Karst, and I'm disposed to agree with him. After all, the high-explosives research is really our main show around here."

She bristled and I thought she was going to make him stay in after school at the very least. "Colonel Manning, do you realize the importance of artificial radioactives to modern medicine?"

"Why, I believe I do. Nevertheless, Doctor, our primary mission is to perfect a weapon which will serve as a safeguard to the whole country in time of war—"

She sniffed and went into action. "Weapons—fiddlesticks! Isn't there a medical corps in the Army? Isn't it more important to know how to heal men than to know how to blow them to bits? Colonel Manning, you're not a fit man to have charge of this project! You're a . . . you're a, a warmonger, that's what you are!"

I felt my ears turning red, but Manning never budged. He could have raised Cain with her, confined her to her quarters, maybe even have court-martialed her, but Manning isn't like that. He told me once that every time a man is court-martialed, it is a sure sign that some senior officer hasn't measured up to his job.

"I am sorry you feel that way, Doctor," he said mildly, "and I agree that my technical knowledge isn't what it might be. And, believe me, I do wish that healing were all we had to worry about. In any case, I have not refused your request. Let's walk over to your laboratory and see what the problem is. Likely there is some arrangement that can be made which will satisfy everybody."

He was already up and getting out his greatcoat. Her set mouth relaxed a trifle and she answered, "Very well. I'm sorry I spoke as I did."

"Not at all," he replied. "These are worrying times. Come along, John."

I trailed after them, stopping in the outer office to get my own coat and to stuff my notebook in a pocket.

By the time we had trudged through mushy snow the eighth of a mile to her lab they were talking about gardening!

Manning acknowledged the sentry's challenge with a wave of his hand and we entered the building. He started casually on into the inner lab, but Karst stopped him. "Armor first, Colonel."

We had trouble finding overshoes that would fit over Manning's boots, which he persisted in wearing, despite the new uniform regulations, and he wanted to omit the foot protection, but Karst would not hear of it. She called in a couple of her assistants who made jury-rigged moccasins out of some soft-lead sheeting.

The helmets were different from those used in the explosives lab, being fitted with inhalers. "What's this?" inquired Manning.

"Radioactive dust guard," she said. "It's absolutely essential."

We threaded a lead-lined meander and arrived at the workroom door which she opened by combination. I blinked at the sudden bright illumination and noticed the air was filled with little shiny motes.

"Hm-m-m—it *is* dusty," agreed Manning. "Isn't there some way of controlling that?" His voice sounded muffled from behind the dust mask.

"The last stage has to be exposed to air," explained Karst. "The hood gets most of it. We could control it, but it would mean a quite expensive new installation."

"No trouble about that. We're not on a budget, you know. It must be very annoying to have to work in a mask like this."

"It is," acknowledged Karst. "The kind of gear it would take would enable us to work without body armor, too. That would be a comfort."

I suddenly had a picture of the kind of thing these researchers put up with. I am a fair-sized man, yet I found that armor heavy to carry around. Estelle Karst was a small woman, yet she was willing to work maybe fourteen hours, day after day, in an outfit which was about as comfortable as a diving suit. But she had not complained.

Not all the heroes are in the headlines. These radiation experts not only ran the chance of cancer and nasty radioaction burns, but the men stood a chance of damaging their germ plasm and then having their wives present them with something horrid in the way of offspring—no chin, for example, and long hairy ears. Nevertheless, they went right ahead and never seemed to get irritated unless something held up their work.

Dr. Karst was past the age when she would be likely to be concerned personally about progeny, but the principle applies.

I wandered around, looking at the unlikely apparatus she used to get her results, fascinated as always by my failure to recognize much that reminded me of the physics laboratory I had known when I was an undergraduate, and being careful not to touch anything. Karst started explaining to Manning what she was doing and why, but I knew that it was useless for me to try to follow that technical stuff. If Manning wanted notes, he would dictate them. My attention was caught by a big boxlike contraption in one corner of the room. It had a hopperlike gadget on one side and I could hear a sound from it like the whirring of a fan with a background of running water. It intrigued me.

I moved back to the neighborhood of Dr. Karst and the Colonel and heard her saying, "The problem amounts to this, Colonel: I am getting a much more highly radioactive end product than I want, but there is considerable variation in the half-life of otherwise equivalent samples. That suggests to me that I am using a mixture of isotopes, but I haven't been able to prove it. And frankly, I do not know enough about that end of the field to be sure of sufficient refinement in my methods. I need Dr. Obre's help on that."

I think those were her words, but I may not be doing her justice, not being a physicist. I understood the part about "half-life." All radioactive materials keep right on radiating until they turn into something else, which takes theoretically forever. As a matter of practice their periods, or "lives," are described in terms of how long it takes the original radiation to drop to one-half strength. That time is called a "half-life" and each radioactive isotope of an element has its own specific characteristic half-lifetime.

One of the staff—I forget which one—told me once that any form of matter can be considered as radioactive in some degree; it's a question of intensity and period, or half-life.

"I'll talk to Dr. Ridpath," Manning answered her, "and see what can be arranged. In the meantime you might draw up plans for what you want to reequip your laboratory."

"Thank you, Colonel."

I could see that Manning was about ready to leave, having pacified her; I was still curious about the big box that gave out the odd noises.

"May I ask what that is, Doctor?"

"Oh, that? That's an air conditioner."

"Odd-looking one. I've never seen one like it."

"It's not to condition the air of this room. It's to remove the radioactive dust before the exhaust air goes outdoors. We wash the dust out of the foul air."

"Where does the water go?"

"Down the drain. Out into the bay eventually, I suppose."

I tried to snap my fingers, which was impossible because of the lead mittens. "That accounts for it, Colonel!"

"Accounts for what?"

"Accounts for those accusing notes we've been getting from the Bureau of Fisheries. This poisonous dust is being carried out into Chesapeake Bay and is killing the fish."

Manning turned to Karst. "Do you think that possible, Doctor?"

I could see her brows draw together through the window in her helmet. "I hadn't thought about it," she admitted. "I'd have to do some figuring on the possible concentrations before I could give you a definite answer. But it is possible—yes. However," she added anxiously, "it would be simple enough to divert this drain to a sink hole of some sort."

"Hm-m-m—yes." He did not say anything for some minutes, simply stood there, looking at the box.

Presently he said, "This dust is pretty lethal?"

"Quite lethal, Colonel." There was another long silence.

At last I gathered he had made up his mind about something for he said decisively, "I am going to see to it that you get Obre's assistance, Doctor—"

"Oh, good!"

"—but I want you to help me in return. I am very much interested in this research of yours, but I want it carried on with a little broader scope. I want you to investigate for maxima both in period and intensity as well as for minima. I want you to drop the strictly utilitarian approach and make an exhaustive research along lines which we will work out in greater detail later."

She started to say something but he cut in ahead of her. "A really thorough program of research should prove more helpful in the long run to your original purpose than a more narrow one. And I shall make it my business to expedite every possible facility for such a research. I think we may turn up a number of interesting things."

He left immediately, giving her no time to discuss it. He did not seem to want to talk on the way back and I held my peace. I think he had already gotten a glimmering of the bold and drastic strategy this was to lead to, but even Manning could not have thought out that early the inescapable consequences of a few dead fish—otherwise he would never have ordered the research.

No, I don't really believe that. He would have gone right ahead, knowing that if he did not do it, someone else would. He would have accepted the responsibility while bitterly aware of its weight.

1944 wore along with no great excitement on the surface. Karst got her new laboratory equipment and so much additional help that her department rapidly became the largest on the grounds. The explosives research was suspended after a conference between Manning and Ridpath, of which I heard only the end, but the meat of it was that there existed not even a remote possibility at that time of utilizing U235 as an explosive. As a source of power, yes, sometime in the distant future when there had been more opportunity to deal with the extremely ticklish problem of controlling the nuclear reaction. Even then it seemed likely that it would not be a source of power in prime movers such as rocket motors or mobiles, but would be used in vast power plants at least as large as the Boulder Dam installation.

After that Ridpath became a sort of co-chairman of Karst's department and the equipment formerly used by the explosives department was adapted or replaced to carry on research on the deadly artificial radioactives. Manning arranged a division of labor and Karst stuck to her original problem of developing techniques for tailor-making radioactives. I think she was perfectly happy, sticking with a one-track mind to the problem at hand. I don't know to this day whether or not Manning and Ridpath ever saw fit to discuss with her what they intended to do.

As a matter of fact, I was too busy myself to think much about it. The general elections were coming up and I was determined that Manning should have a constituency to return to, when the emergency was over. He was not much interested, but agreed to let his name be filed as a candidate for re-election. I was trying to work up a campaign by remote control and cursing because I could not be in the field to deal with the thousand and one emergencies as they arose.

I did the next best thing and had a private line installed to permit the campaign chairman to reach me easily. I don't think I violated the Hatch Act, but I guess I stretched it a little. Anyhow, it turned out all right; Manning was elected as were several other members of the citizen-military that year. An attempt was made to smear him by claiming that he was taking two salaries for one job, but we squelched that with a pamphlet entitled "For Shame!" which explained that he got *one* salary for *two* jobs. That's the Federal law in such cases and people are entitled to know it.

It was just before Christmas that Manning first admitted to me how much the implications of the Karst-Obre process were preying on his mind. He called me into his office over some inconsequential matter, then did not let me go. I saw that he wanted to talk.

"How much of the K-O dust do we now have on hand?" he asked suddenly.

"Just short of ten thousand units," I replied. "I can look up the exact figures in half a moment." A unit would take care of a thousand men, at normal dispersion. He knew the figure as well as I did, and I knew he was stalling.

We had shifted almost imperceptibly from research to manufacture, entirely on Manning's initiative and authority. Manning had never made a specific report to the Department about it, unless he had done so orally to the Chief of Staff.

"Never mind," he answered to my suggestion, then added, "Did you see those horses?"

"Yes," I said briefly.

I did not want to talk about it. I like horses. We had requisitioned six broken-down old nags, ready for the bone yard, and had used them experimentally. We knew now what the dust would do. After they had died, any part of their carcasses would register on a photographic plate and tissue from the apices of their lungs and from the bronchia glowed with a light of its own.

Manning stood at the window, staring out at the dreary Maryland winter for a minute or two before replying, "John, I wish that radioactivity had never been discovered. Do you realize what that devilish stuff amounts to?"

"Well," I said, "it's a weapon, about like poison gas—maybe more efficient."

"Rats!" he said, and for a moment I thought he was annoyed with me personally. "That's about like comparing a sixteen-inch gun with a bow and arrow. We've got here the first weapon the world has ever seen against which there is no defense, none whatsoever. It's death itself, C.O.D.

"Have you seen Ridpath's report?" he went on.

I had not. Ridpath had taken to delivering his reports by hand to Manning personally.

"Well," he said, "ever since we started production I've had all the talent we could spare working on the problem of a defense against the dust. Ridpath tells me and I agree with him that there is no means whatsoever to combat the stuff, once it's used."

"How about armor," I asked, "and protective clothing?"

"Sure, sure," he agreed irritatedly, "provided you never take it off to eat, or to drink or for any purpose whatever, until the radioaction has ceased, or you are out of the danger zone. That is all right for laboratory work; I'm talking about war."

I considered the matter. "I still don't see what you are fretting about, Colonel. If the stuff is as good as you say it is, you've done just exactly what you set out to do—develop a weapon which would give the United States protection against aggression."

He swung around. "John, there are times when I think you are downright stupid!"

I said nothing. I knew him and I knew how to discount his moods. The fact that he permitted me to see his feelings is the finest compliment I have ever had.

"Look at it this way," he went on more patiently; "this dust, as a weapon, is not just simply sufficient to safeguard the United States, it amounts to a loaded gun held at the head of every man, woman, and child on the globe!"

"Well," I answered, "what of that? It's our secret, and we've got the upper hand. The United States can put a stop to this war, and any other war. We can declare a *Pax Americana,* and enforce it."

"Hm-m-m—I wish it were that easy. But it won't remain our secret; you can count on that. It doesn't matter how successfully we guard it; all that anyone needs is the hint given by the dust itself and then it is just a matter of time until some other nation develops a technique to produce it. You can't stop brains from working, John; the reinvention of the method is a mathematical certainty, once they know what it is they are looking for. And uranium is a common enough substance, widely distributed over the globe—don't forget that!

"It's like this: Once the secret is out—and it will be out if we ever use the stuff!—the whole world will be comparable to a room full of men, each armed with a loaded .45. They can't get out of the room and each one is dependent on the good will of every other one to stay alive. All offense and no defense. See what I mean?"

I thought about it, but I still didn't guess at the difficulties. It seemed to me that a peace enforced by us was the only way out, with precautions taken to see that we controlled the sources of uranium. I had the usual American subconscious conviction that our country would never use power in sheer aggression. Later, I thought about the Mexican War and the Spanish-American War and some of the things we did in Central America, and I was not so sure—

It was a couple of weeks later, shortly after inauguration day, that Manning told me to get the Chief of Staff's office on the telephone. I heard only the tail end of the conversation. "No, General, I won't," Manning was saying. "I won't discuss it with you, or the Secretary, either. This is a matter the Commander in Chief is going to have to decide in the long run. If he turns it down, it is imperative that no one else ever knows about it. That's my considered opinion. . . . What's that? . . . I took this job under the condition that I was to have a free hand. You've got to give me a little leeway this time. . . . Don't go brass hat on me. I knew you when you were a plebe. . . . O.K., O.K., sorry. . . . If the Secretary of War won't listen to reason, you tell him

I'll be in my seat in the House of Representatives tomorrow, and that I'll get the favor I want from the majority leader. . . . All right. Good-bye."

Washington rang up again about an hour later. It was the Secretary of War. This time Manning listened more than he talked. Toward the end, he said, "All I want is thirty minutes alone with the President. If nothing comes of it, no harm has been done. If I convince him, then you will know all about it. . . . No. sir, I did not mean that you would avoid responsibility. I intended to be helpful. . . . Fine! Thank you, Mr. Secretary."

The White House rang up later in the day and set a time.

We drove down to the District the next day through a nasty cold rain that threatened to turn to sleet. The usual congestion in Washington was made worse by the weather; it very nearly caused us to be late in arriving. I could hear Manning swearing under his breath all the way down Rhode Island Avenue. But we were dropped at the west wing entrance to the White House with two minutes to spare. Manning was ushered into the Oval Office almost at once and I was left cooling my heels and trying to get comfortable in civilian clothes. After so many months of uniform they itched in the wrong places.

The thirty minutes went by.

The President's reception secretary went in, and came out very promptly indeed. He stepped on out into the outer reception room and I heard something that began with, "I'm sorry, Senator, but—" He came back in, made a penciled notation, and passed it out to an usher.

Two more hours went by.

Manning appeared at the door at last and the secretary looked relieved. But he did not come out, saying instead, "Come in, John. The President wants to take a look at you."

I fell over my feet getting up.

Manning said, "Mr. President, this is Captain DeFries." The President nodded, and I bowed, unable to say anything. He was standing on the hearth rug, his fine head turned toward us, and looking just like his pictures—but it seemed strange for the President of the United States not to be a tall man.

I had never seen him before, though, of course, I knew something of his record the two years he had been in the Senate and while he was Mayor before that.

The President said, "Sit down, DeFries. Care to smoke?" Then to Manning, "You think he can do it?"

"I think he'll have to. It's Hobson's choice."

"And you are sure of him?"

"He was my campaign manager."

"I see."

The President said nothing more for a while and God knows I didn't!—though I was bursting to know what they were talking about. He commenced again with, "Colonel Manning, I intend to follow the procedure you have suggested, with the changes we discussed. But I will be down tomorrow to see for myself that the dust will do what you say it will. Can you prepare a demonstration?"

"Yes, Mr. President,"

"Very well, we will use Captain DeFries unless I think of a better procedure." I thought for a moment that they planned to use me for a guinea pig! But he turned to me and continued, "Captain, I expect to send you to England as my representative."

I gulped. "Yes, Mr. President." And that is every word I had to say in calling on the President of the United States.

After that, Manning had to tell me a lot of things he had on his mind. I am going to try to relate them as carefully as possible, even at the risk of being dull and obvious and of repeating things that are common knowledge.

We had a weapon that could not be stopped. Any type of K-O dust scattered over an area rendered that area uninhabitable for a length of time that depended on the half-life of the radioactivity.

Period. Full stop.

Once an area was dusted there was nothing that could be done about it until the radioactivity had fallen off to the point where it was no longer harmful. The dust could not be cleaned out; it was everywhere. There was no possible way to counteract it—burn it, combine it chemically; the radioactive isotope was still there, still radioactive, still deadly. Once used on a stretch of land, for a predetermined length of time that piece of earth *would not tolerate life*.

It was extremely simple to use. No complicated bomb-sights were needed, no care need be taken to hit "military objectives." Take it aloft in any sort of aircraft, attain a position more or less over the area you wish to sterilize, and drop the stuff. Those on the ground in the contaminated area are dead men, dead in an hour, a day, a week, a month, depending on the degree of the infection—but *dead*.

Manning told me that he had once seriously considered, in the middle of the night, recommending that every single person, including himself, who knew the Karst-Obre technique be put to death, in the interests of all civilization. But he had realized the next day that it had been sheer funk; the technique was certain in time to be rediscovered by someone else.

Furthermore, it would not do to wait, to refrain from using the grisly power, until someone else perfected it and used it. The only possible chance to keep the world from being turned into one huge morgue was for us to use the power first and drastically—get the upper hand and keep it.

We were not at war, legally, yet we had been in the war up to our necks with our weight on the side of democracy since 1940. Manning had proposed to the President that we turn a supply of the dust over to Great Britain, under conditions we specified, and enable them thereby to force a peace. But the terms of the peace would be dictated by the United States—for we were not turning over the secret.

After that, the *Pax Americana*.

The United States was having power thrust on it, willy-nilly. We had to accept it and enforce a worldwide peace, ruthlessly and drastically, or it would be seized by some other nation. There could not be co-equals in the possession of this weapon. The factor of time predominated.

I was selected to handle the details in England because Manning insisted, and the President agreed with him, that every person technically acquainted with the Karst-Obre process should remain on the laboratory reservation in what amounted to protective custody— imprisonment. That included Manning himself. I could go because I did not have the secret—I could not even have acquired it without years of schooling—and what I did not know I could not tell, even under, well, drugs. We were determined to keep the secret as long as we could to consolidate the *Pax;* we did not distrust our English cousins, but they were Britishers, with a first loyalty to the British Empire. No need to tempt them.

I was picked because I understood the background if not the science, and because Manning trusted me. I don't know why the President trusted me, too, but then my job was not complicated.

We took off from the new field outside Baltimore on a cold, raw afternoon which matched my own feelings. I had an all-gone feeling in my stomach, a runny nose, and, buttoned inside my clothes, papers appointing me a special agent of the President of the United States. They were odd papers, papers without precedent; they did not simply give me the usual diplomatic immunity; they made my person very nearly as sacred as that of the President himself.

At Nova Scotia we touched ground to refuel, the F.B.I. men left us, we took off again, and the Canadian transfighters took their stations around us. All the dust we were sending was in my plane; if the President's representative were shot down, the dust would go to the bottom with him.

No need to tell of the crossing. I was airsick and miserable, in spite of the steadiness of the new six-engined jobs. I felt like a hangman on the way to an execution, and wished to God that I were a boy again, with nothing more momentous than a debate contest, or a track meet, to worry me.

There was some fighting around us as we neared Scotland, I know, but I could not see it, the cabin being shuttered. Our pilot-captain ignored it and brought his ship down on a totally dark field, using a beam, I suppose, though I did not know nor care. I would have welcomed a crash. Then the lights outside went on and I saw that we had come to rest in an underground hangar.

I stayed in the ship. The Commandant came to see me to his quarters as his guest. I shook my head. "I stay here," I said. "Orders. You are to treat this ship as United States soil, you know."

He seemed miffed, but compromised by having dinner served for both of us in my ship.

There was a really embarrassing situation the next day. I was commanded to appear for a Royal audience. But I had my instructions and I stuck to them. I was sitting on that cargo of dust until the President told me what to do with it. Late in the day I was called on by a member of Parliament—nobody admitted out loud that it was the Prime Minister—and a Mr. Windsor. The M.P. did most of the talking and I answered his questions. My other guest said very little and spoke slowly with some difficulty. But I got a very favorable impression of him. He seemed to be a man who was carrying a load beyond human strength and carrying it heroically.

There followed the longest period in my life. It was actually only a little longer than a week, but every minute of it had that split-second intensity of imminent disaster that comes just before a car crash. The President was using the time to try to avert the need to use the dust. He had two face-to-face television conferences with the new Fuehrer. The President spoke German fluently, which should have helped. He spoke three times to the warring peoples themselves, but it is doubtful if very many on the Continent were able to listen, the police regulations there being what they were.

The Ambassador from the Reich was given a special demonstration of the effect of the dust. He was flown out over a deserted stretch of Western prairie and allowed to see what a single dusting would do to a herd of steers. It should have impressed him and I think that it did— *nobody* could ignore a visual demonstration!—but what report he made to his leader we never knew.

The British Isles were visited repeatedly during the wait by bombing attacks as heavy as any of the war. I was safe enough but I heard about them, and I could see the effect on the morale of the officers with whom I associated. Not that it frightened them—it made them coldly angry. The raids were not directed primarily at dockyards or factories, but were ruthless destruction of anything, particularly villages.

"I don't see what you chaps are waiting for," a flight commander complained to me. "What the Jerries need is a dose of their own *shrecklichkeit,* a lesson in their own Aryan culture."

I shook my head. "We'll have to do it our own way."

He dropped the matter, but I knew how he and his brother officers felt. They had a standing toast, as sacred as the toast to the King: "Remember Coventry!"

Our President had stipulated that the R.A.F. was not to bomb during the period of negotiation, but their bombers were busy nevertheless. The continent was showered, night after night, with bales of leaflets, prepared by our own propaganda agents. The first of these called on the people of the Reich to stop a useless war and promised that the terms of peace would not be vindictive. The second rain of pamphlets showed photographs of that herd of steers. The third was a simple direct warning to get out of cities and to stay out.

As Manning put it, we were calling "Halt!" three times before firing. I do not think that he or the President expected it to work, but we were morally obligated to try.

The Britishers had installed for me a televisor, of the Simonds-Yarley nonintercept type, the sort whereby the receiver must "trigger" the transmitter in order for the transmission to take place at all. It made assurance of privacy in diplomatic rapid communication for the first time in history, and was a real help in the crisis. I had brought along my own technician, one of the F.B.I.'s new corps of specialists, to handle the scrambler and the trigger.

He called to me one afternoon. "Washington signaling."

I climbed tiredly out of the cabin and down to the booth on the hangar floor, wondering if it were another false alarm.

It was the President. His lips were white. "Carry out your basic instructions, Mr. DeFries."

"Yes, Mr. President!"

❖

The details had been worked out in advance and, once I had accepted a receipt and token payment from the Commandant for the dust, my duties were finished. But, at our instance, the British had invited military observers from every independent nation and from the several provisional governments of occupied nations. The United States Ambassador designated me as one at the request of Manning.

Our task group was thirteen bombers. One such bomber could have carried all the dust needed, but it was split up to insure most of it, at least, reaching its destination. I had fetched forty percent more dust than Ridpath calculated would be needed for the mission and my last job was to see to it that every canister actually went on board a plane of the flight. The extremely small weight of dust used was emphasized to each of the military observers.

We took off just at dark, climbed to twenty-five thousand feet, refueled in the air, and climbed again. Our escort was waiting for us, having refueled thirty minutes before us. The flight split into thirteen groups, and cut the thin air for middle Europe. The bombers we rode had been stripped and hiked up to permit the utmost maximum of speed and altitude.

Elsewhere in England, other flights had taken off shortly before us to act as a diversion. Their destinations were every part of Germany; it was the intention to create such confusion in the air above the Reich that our few planes actually engaged in the serious work might well escape attention entirely, flying so high in the stratosphere.

The thirteen dust carriers approached Berlin from different directions, planning to cross Berlin as if following the spokes of a wheel. The night was appreciably clear and we had a low moon to help us. Berlin is not a hard city to locate, since it has the largest square-mile area of any modern city and is located on a broad flat alluvial plain. I could make out the River Spree as we approached it, and the Havel. The city was blacked out, but a city makes a different sort of black from open country. Parachute flares hung over the city in many places, showing that the R.A.F. had been busy before we got there and the A.A. batteries on the ground helped to pick out the city.

There was fighting below us, but not within fifteen thousand feet of our altitude as nearly as I could judge.

The pilot reported to the captain, "On line of bearing!" The chap working the absolute altimeter steadily fed his data into the fuse pots of the canister. The canisters were equipped with a light charge of black powder, sufficient to explode them and scatter the dust at a time after release predetermined by the fuse pot setting. The method used was no more than an efficient expedient. The dust would have been almost as effective had it simply been dumped out in paper bags, although not as well distributed.

The Captain hung over the navigator's board, a slight frown on his thin sallow face. "Ready one!" reported the bomber.

"Release!"

"Ready two!"

The Captain studied his wristwatch. "Release!"

"Ready three!"

"Release!"

When the last of our ten little packages was out of the ship we turned tail and ran for home.

No arrangements had been made for me to get home; nobody had thought about it. But it was the one thing I wanted to do. I did not feel badly; I did not feel much of anything. I felt like a man who has at last screwed up his courage and undergone a serious operation; it's over now, he is still numb from shock but his mind is relaxed. But I wanted to go home.

The British Commandant was quite decent about it; he serviced and manned my ship at once and gave me an escort for the offshore war zone. It was an expensive way to send one man home, but who cared? We had just expended some millions of lives in a desperate attempt to end the war; what was a money expense? He gave the necessary orders absentmindedly.

I took a double dose of nembutal and woke up in Canada. I tried to get some news while the plane was being serviced, but there was not much to be had. The government of the Reich had issued one official news bulletin shortly after the raid, sneering at the much vaunted "secret weapon" of the British and stating that a major air attack had been made on Berlin and several other cities, but that the raiders had been driven off with only minor damage. The current Lord Haw-Haw started one of his sarcastic speeches but was unable to continue it. The announcer said that he had been seized with a heart attack, and substituted some recordings of patriotic music. The station cut off in the middle of the "Horst Wessel" song. After that there was silence.

I managed to promote an Army car and a driver at the Baltimore field which made short work of the Annapolis speedway. We almost overran the turnoff to the laboratory.

Manning was in his office. He looked up as I came in, said, "Hello,

John," in a dispirited voice, and dropped his eyes again to the blotter pad. He went back to drawing doodles.

I looked him over and realized for the first time that the chief was an old man. His face was gray and flabby, deep furrows framed his mouth in a triangle. His clothes did not fit.

I went up to him and put a hand on his shoulder. "Don't take it so hard, chief. It's not your fault. We gave them all the warning in the world."

He looked up again. "Estelle Karst suicided this morning."

Anybody could have anticipated it, but nobody did. And somehow I felt harder hit by her death than by the death of all those strangers in Berlin. "How did she do it?" I asked.

"Dust. She went into the canning room, and took off her armor."

I could picture her—head held high, eyes snapping, and that set look on her mouth which she got when people did something she disapproved of. One little old woman whose lifetime work had been turned against her.

"I wish," Manning added slowly, "that I could explain to her why we *had* to do it."

We buried her in a lead-lined coffin, then Manning and I went on to Washington.

While we were there, we saw the motion pictures that had been made of the death of Berlin. You have not seen them; they never were made public, but they were of great use in convincing the other nations of the world that peace was a good idea. I saw them when Congress did, being allowed in because I was Manning's assistant.

They had been made by a pair of R.A.F. pilots, who had dodged the *Luftwaffe* to get them. The first shots showed some of the main streets the morning after the raid. There was not much to see that would show up in telephoto shots, just busy and crowded streets, but if you looked closely you could see that there had been an excessive number of automobile accidents.

The second day showed the attempt to evacuate. The inner squares of the city were practically deserted save for bodies and wrecked cars, but the streets leading out of town were boiling with people, mostly on foot, for the trams were out of service. The pitiful creatures were fleeing, not knowing that death was already lodged inside them. The plane swooped down at one point and the cinematographer had his telephoto lens pointed directly into the face of a young woman for several seconds. She stared back at it with a look too woebegone to forget, then stumbled and fell.

She may have been trampled. I hope so. One of those six horses had looked like that when the stuff was beginning to hit his vitals.

The last sequence showed Berlin and the roads around it a week after the raid. The city was dead; there was not a man, a woman, a child—nor cats, nor dogs, not even a pigeon. Bodies were all around, but they were safe from rats. There were no rats.

The roads around Berlin were quiet now. Scattered carelessly on shoulders and in ditches, and to a lesser extent on the pavement itself, like coal shaken off a train, were the quiet heaps that had been the citizens of the capital of the Reich. There is no use in talking about it.

But, so far as I am concerned, I left what soul I had in that projection room and I have not had one since.

The two pilots who made the pictures eventually died—systemic, cumulative infection, dust in the air over Berlin. With precautions it need not have happened, but the English did not believe, as yet, that our extreme precautions were necessary.

The Reich took about a week to fold up. It might have taken longer if the new Fuehrer had not gone to Berlin the day after the raid to "prove" that the British boasts had been hollow. There is no need to recount the provisional governments that Germany had in the following several months; the only one we are concerned with is the so-called restored monarchy which used a cousin of the old Kaiser as a symbol, the one that sued for peace.

Then the trouble started.

When the Prime Minister announced the terms of the private agreement he had had with our President, he was met with a silence that was broken only by cries of "Shame! Shame! Resign!" I suppose it was inevitable; the Commons reflected the spirit of a people who had been unmercifully punished for four years. They were in a mood to enforce a peace that would have made the Versailles Treaty look like the Beatitudes.

The vote of no confidence left the Prime Minister no choice. Forty-eight hours later the King made a speech from the throne that violated all constitutional precedent, for it had not been written by a Prime Minister. In this greatest crisis in his reign, his voice was clear and unlabored; it sold the idea to England and a national coalition government was formed.

I don't know whether we would have dusted London to enforce our terms or not; Manning thinks we would have done so. I suppose it depended on the character of the President of the United States, and there is no way of knowing about that since we did not have to do it.

The United States, and in particular the President of the United States, was confronted by two inescapable problems. First, we had to consolidate our position at once, use our temporary advantage of an overwhelmingly powerful weapon to insure that such a weapon would not be turned on us. Second, some means had to be worked out to stabilize American foreign policy so that it could handle the tremendous power we had suddenly had thrust upon us.

The second was by far the most difficult and serious. If we were to establish a reasonably permanent peace—say a century or so—through a monopoly on a weapon so powerful that no one dare fight us, it was imperative that the policy under which we acted be more lasting than passing political administrations. But more of that later—

The first problem had to be attended to at once—time was the heart of it. The emergency lay in the very simplicity of the weapon. It required nothing but aircraft to scatter it and the dust itself, which was easily and quickly made by anyone possessing the secret of the Karst-Obre process and having access to a small supply of uranium-bearing ore.

But the Karst-Obre process was simple and might be independently developed at any time. Manning reported to the President that it was Ridpath's opinion, concurred in by Manning, that the staff of any modern radiation laboratory should be able to work out an equivalent technique in six weeks, working from the hint given by the events in Berlin alone, and should then be able to produce enough dust to cause major destruction in another six weeks.

Ninety days—ninety days *provided* they started from scratch and were not already halfway to their goal. Less than ninety days—perhaps no time at all—

By this time Manning was an unofficial member of the Cabinet; "Secretary of Dust," the President called him in one of his rare jovial moods. As for me, well, I attended Cabinet meetings, too. As the only layman who had seen the whole show from beginning to end, the President wanted me there.

I am an ordinary sort of man who, by a concatenation of improbabilities, found himself shoved into the councils of the rulers. But I found that the rulers were ordinary men, too, and frequently as bewildered as I was.

But Manning was no ordinary man. In him ordinary hard sense had been raised to the level of genius. Oh, yes, I know that it is popular to blame everything on him and to call him everything from traitor to mad dog, but I still think he was both wise and benevolent. I don't care how many second-guessing historians disagree with me.

"I propose," said Manning, "that we begin by immobilizing all aircraft throughout the world."

The Secretary of Commerce raised his brows. "Aren't you," he said, "being a little fantastic, Colonel Manning?"

"No, I'm not," answered Manning shortly. "I'm being realistic. The key to this problem is aircraft. Without aircraft the dust is an inefficient weapon. The only way I see to gain time enough to deal with the whole problem is to ground all aircraft and put them out of operation. All aircraft, that is, not actually in the service of the United States Army. After that we can deal with complete world disarmament and permanent methods of control."

"Really now," replied the Secretary, "you are not proposing that commercial airlines be put out of operation. They are an essential part of world economy. It would be an intolerable nuisance."

"Getting killed is an intolerable nuisance, too," Manning answered stubbornly. "I do propose just that. All aircraft. *All.*"

The President had been listening without comment to the discussion. He now cut in. "How about aircraft on which some groups depend to stay alive, Colonel, such as the Alaskan lines?"

"If there are such, they must be operated by American Army pilots and crews. No exceptions."

The Secretary of Commerce looked startled. "Am I to infer from that last remark that you intended this prohibition to apply to the *United States* as well as other nations?"

"Naturally."

"But that's impossible. It's unconstitutional. It violates civil rights."

"Killing a man violates his civil rights, too," Manning answered stubbornly.

"You can't do it. Any Federal Court in the country would enjoin you in five minutes."

"It seems to me," said Manning slowly, "that Andy Jackson gave us a good precedent for that one when he told John Marshall to go fly a kite." He looked slowly around the table at faces that ranged from undecided to antagonistic. "The issue is sharp, gentlemen, and we might as well drag it out in the open. We can be dead men, with everything in due order, constitutional, and technically correct; or we can do what has to be done, stay alive, and try to straighten out the legal aspects later." He shut up and waited.

The Secretary of Labor picked it up. "I don't think the Colonel has any corner on realism. I think I see the problem, too, and I admit it is a serious one. The dust must never be used again. Had I known about it soon enough, it would never have been used on Berlin. And I agree that some sort of worldwide control is necessary. But where I differ with the Colonel is in the method. What he proposes is a military dictatorship imposed by force on the whole world. Admit it, Colonel. Isn't that what you are proposing?"

Manning did not dodge it. "That is what I am proposing."

"Thanks. Now we know where we stand. I, for one, do not regard democratic measures and constitutional procedure as of so little importance that I am willing to jettison them any time it becomes convenient. To me, democracy is more than a matter of expediency, it is a faith. Either it works, or I go under with it."

"What do you propose?" asked the President.

"I propose that we treat this as an opportunity to create a worldwide democratic commonwealth! Let us use our present dominant position to issue a call to all nations to send representatives to a conference to form a world constitution."

"League of Nations," I heard someone mutter.

"No!" he answered the side remark. "Not a League of Nations. The old League was helpless because it had no real existence, no power. It was not implemented to enforce its decisions; it was just a debating society, a sham. This would be different *for we would turn over the dust to it!*"

Nobody spoke for some minutes. You could see them turning it over in their minds, doubtful, partially approving, intrigued but dubious.

"I'd like to answer that," said Manning.

"Go ahead," said the President.

"I will. I'm going to have to use some pretty plain language and I hope that Secretary Larner will do me the honor of believing that I speak so from sincerity and deep concern and not from personal pique.

"I think a world democracy would be a very fine thing and I ask that you believe me when I say I would willingly lay down my life to accomplish it. I also think it would be a very fine thing for the lion to lie down with the lamb, but I am reasonably certain that only the lion would get up. If we try to form an actual world democracy, we'll be the lamb in the setup.

"There are a lot of good, kindly people who are internationalists these days. Nine out of ten of them are soft in the head and the tenth is ignorant. If we set up a worldwide democracy, what will the electorate be? Take a look at the facts: Four hundred million Chinese with no more concept of voting and citizen responsibility than a flea; three hundred million Hindus who aren't much better indoctrinated; God knows how many in the Eurasian Union who believe in God knows what; the entire continent of Africa only semicivilized; eighty million Japanese who really believe that they are Heaven-ordained to rule; our Spanish-American friends who might trail along with us and might not, but who don't understand the Bill of Rights the way we think of it; a quarter of a billion people of two dozen different nationalities in Europe, all with revenge and black hatred in their hearts.

"No, it won't wash. It's preposterous to talk about a world democracy for many years to come. If you turn the secret of the dust over to such a body, you will be arming the whole world to commit suicide."

Larner answered at once. "I could resent some of your remarks, but I won't. To put it bluntly, I consider the source. The trouble with you, Colonel Manning, is that you are a professional soldier and have no faith in people. Soldiers may be necessary, but the worst of them are martinets and the best are merely paternalistic." There was quite a lot more of the same.

Manning stood it until his turn came again. "Maybe I am all those things, but you haven't met my argument. *What are you going to do about the hundreds of millions of people who have no experience in, nor love for, democracy?* Now, perhaps, I don't have the same concept of democracy as yourself, but I do know this: Out West there are a couple of hundred thousand people who sent me to Congress; I am *not* going to stand quietly by and let a course be followed which I think will result in their deaths or utter ruin.

"Here is the probable future, as I see it, potential in the smashing of the atom and the development of lethal artificial radioactives. Some power makes a supply of the dust. They'll hit us first to try to knock us out and give them a free hand. New York and Washington overnight, then all of our industrial areas while we are still politically and economically disorganized. But our army would not be in those cities; we would have planes and a supply of dust somewhere where the first dusting wouldn't touch them. Our boys would bravely and righteously proceed to poison their big cities. Back and forth it would go until the organization of each country had broken down so completely that they were no longer able to maintain a sufficiently high level of industrialization to service planes and manufacture dust. That presupposes starvation and plague in the process. You can fill in the details.

"The other nations would get in the game. It would be silly and suicidal, of course, but it doesn't take brains to take a hand in this. All it takes is a very small group, hungry for power, a few airplanes and a supply of dust. *It's a vicious circle that cannot possibly be stopped until the entire planet has dropped to a level of economy too low to support the techniques necessary to maintain it.* My best guess is that such a point would be reached when approximately three-quarters of the world's population were dead of dust, disease, or hunger, and culture reduced to the peasant-and-village type.

"Where is your Constitution and your Bill of Rights if you let that happen?"

I've shortened it down, but that was the gist of it. I can't hope to record every word of an argument that went on for days.

The Secretary of the Navy took a crack at him next. "Aren't you getting a bit hysterical, Colonel? After all, the world has seen a lot of weapons which were going to make war an impossibility too horrible to contemplate. Poison gas, and tanks, and airplanes—even firearms, if I remember my history."

Manning smiled wryly. "You've made a point, Mr. Secretary. 'And when the wolf *really* came, the little boy shouted in vain.' I imagine the Chamber of Commerce in Pompeii presented the same reasonable argument to any early vulcanologist so timid as to fear Vesuvius. I'll try to justify my fears. The dust differs from every earlier weapon in its deadliness and ease of use, but most importantly in that we have developed no defense against it. For a number of fairly technical reasons, I don't think we ever will, at least not this century."

"Why not?"

"Because there is no way to counteract radioactivity short of putting a lead shield between yourself and it, an *airtight* lead shield. People might survive by living in sealed underground cities, but our characteristic American culture could not be maintained."

"Colonel Manning," suggested the Secretary of State, "I think you have overlooked the obvious alternative."

"Have I?"

"Yes—to keep the dust as our own secret, go our own way, and let the rest of the world look out for itself. That is the only program that fits our traditions." The Secretary of State was really a fine old gentleman, and not stupid, but he was slow to assimilate new ideas.

"Mr. Secretary," said Manning respectfully, "I wish we could afford to mind our own business. I do wish we could. But it is the best opinion of all the experts that we can't maintain control of this secret except by rigid policing. The Germans were close on our heels in nuclear research; it was sheer luck that we got there first. I ask you to imagine Germany a year hence—with a supply of dust."

The Secretary did not answer, but I saw his lips form the word Berlin.

They came around. The President had deliberately let Manning bear the brunt of the argument, conserving his own stock of goodwill to coax the obdurate. He decided against putting it up to Congress; the dusters would have been overhead before each senator had finished his say. What he intended to do might be unconstitutional, but if he failed to act there might not be any Constitution shortly. There was precedent—the Emancipation Proclamation, the Monroe Doctrine, the

Louisiana Purchase, suspension of habeas corpus in the War between the States, the Destroyer Deal.

On February 22nd the President declared a state of full emergency internally and sent his Peace Proclamation to the head of every sovereign state. Divested of its diplomatic surplusage, it said: *The United States is prepared to defeat any power, or combination of powers, in jig time. Accordingly, we are outlawing war and are calling on every nation to disarm completely at once. In other words, "Throw down your guns, boys; we've got the drop on you!"*

A supplement set forth the procedure: All aircraft capable of flying the Atlantic were to be delivered in one week's time to a field, or rather a great stretch of prairie, just west of Fort Riley, Kansas. For lesser aircraft, a spot near Shanghai and a rendezvous in Wales were designated. Memoranda would be issued later with respect to other war equipment. Uranium and its ores were not mentioned; that would come later.

No excuses. Failure to disarm would be construed as an act of war against the United States.

There were no cases of apoplexy in the Senate; why not, I don't know.

There were only three powers to be seriously worried about, England, Japan, and the Eurasian Union. England had been forewarned, we had pulled her out of a war she was losing, and she—or rather her men in power—knew accurately what we could and would do.

Japan was another matter. They had not seen Berlin and they did not really believe it. Besides, they had been telling each other for so many years that they were unbeatable, they believed it. It does not do to get too tough with a Japanese too quickly, for they will die rather than lose face. The negotiations were conducted very quietly indeed, but our fleet was halfway from Pearl Harbor to Kobe, loaded with enough dust to sterilize their six biggest cities, before they were concluded. Do you know what did it? This never hit the newspapers but it was the wording of the pamphlets we proposed to scatter before dusting.

The Emperor was pleased to declare a New Order of Peace. The official version, built up for home consumption, made the whole matter one of collaboration between two great and friendly powers, with Japan taking the initiative.

The Eurasian Union was a puzzle. After Stalin's unexpected death in 1941, no western nation knew very much about what went on in there. Our own diplomatic relations had atrophied through failure to replace men called home nearly four years before. Everybody knew, of course, that the new group in power called themselves Fifth Internationalists, but what that meant, aside from ceasing to display the pictures of Lenin and Stalin, nobody knew.

But they agreed to our terms and offered to cooperate in every way. They pointed out that the Union had never been warlike and had kept out of the recent world struggle. It was fitting that the two remaining great powers should use their greatness to insure a lasting peace.

I was delighted; I had been worried about the E.U.

They commenced delivery of some of their smaller planes to the receiving station near Shanghai at once. The reports on the number and quality of the planes seemed to indicate that they had stayed out of the war through necessity; the planes were mostly of German make and in poor condition, types that Germany had abandoned early in the war.

Manning went west to supervise certain details in connection with immobilizing the big planes, the transoceanic planes, which were to gather near Fort Riley. We planned to spray them with oil, then dust from a low altitude, as in crop dusting, with a low concentration of one-year dust. Then we could turn our backs on them and forget them, while attending to other matters.

But there were hazards. The dust must not be allowed to reach Kansas City, Lincoln, Wichita—any of the nearby cities. The smaller towns roundabout had been temporarily evacuated. Testing stations needed to be set up in all directions in order that accurate tab on the dust might be kept. Manning felt personally responsible to make sure that no bystander was poisoned.

We circled the receiving station before landing at Fort Riley. I could pick out the three landing fields which had hurriedly been graded. Their runways were white in the sun, the twenty-four-hour cement as yet undirtied. Around each of the landing fields were crowded dozens of parking fields, less perfectly graded. Tractors and bulldozers were still at work on some of them. In the easternmost fields, the German and British ships were already in place, jammed wing to body as tightly as planes on the flight deck of a carrier—save for a few that were still being towed into position, the tiny tractors looking from the air like ants dragging pieces of leaf many times larger than themselves.

Only three flying fortresses had arrived from the Eurasian Union. Their representatives had asked for a short delay in order that a supply of high-test aviation gasoline might be delivered to them. They claimed a shortage of fuel necessary to make the long flight over the Arctic safe. There was no way to check the claim and the delay was granted while a shipment was routed from England.

We were about to leave, Manning having satisfied himself as to safety precautions, when a dispatch came in announcing that a flight of

E.U. bombers might be expected before the day was out. Manning wanted to see them arrive; we waited around for four hours. When it was finally reported that our escort of fighters had picked them up at the Canadian border, Manning appeared to have grown fidgety and stated that he would watch them from the air. We took off, gained altitude, and waited.

There were nine of them in the flight, cruising in column of echelons and looking so huge that our little fighters were hardly noticeable. They circled the field and I was admiring the stately dignity of them when Manning's pilot, Lieutenant Rafferty, exclaimed, "What the devil! They are preparing to land downwind!"

I still did not tumble, but Manning shouted to the copilot, "Get the field!"

He fiddled with his instruments and announced, "Got 'em, sir!"

"General alarm! Armor!"

We could not hear the sirens, naturally, but I could see the white plumes rise from the big steam whistle on the roof of the Administration Building—three long blasts, then three short ones. It seemed almost at the same time that the first cloud broke from the E.U. planes.

Instead of landing, they passed low over the receiving station, jam-packed now with ships from all over the world. Each echelon picked one of three groups centered around the three landing fields and streamers of heavy brown smoke poured from the bellies of the E.U. ships. I saw a tiny black figure jump from a tractor and run toward the nearest building. Then the smoke screen obscured the field.

"Do you still have the field?" demanded Manning.

"Yes, sir."

"Cross connect to the chief safety technician. Hurry!"

The copilot cut in the amplifier so that Manning could talk directly. "Saunders? This is Manning. How about it?"

"Radioactive, chief. Intensity seven point four."

They had paralleled the Karst-Obre research.

Manning cut him off and demanded that the communication office at the field raise the Chief of Staff. There was nerve-stretching delay, for it had to be routed over land wire to Kansas City, and some chief operator had to be convinced that she should commandeer a trunk line that was in commercial use. But we got through at last and Manning made his report. "It stands to reason," I heard him say, "that other flights are approaching the border by this time. New York, of course, and Washington. Probably Detroit and Chicago as well. No way of knowing."

The Chief of Staff cut off abruptly, without comment. I knew that the U.S. air fleets, in a state of alert for weeks past, would have their orders in a few seconds, and would be on their way to hunt out and down the attackers, if possible before they could reach the cities.

I glanced back at the field. The formations were broken up. One of the E.U. bombers was down, crashed, half a mile beyond the station. While I watched, one of our midget dive bombers screamed down on a behemoth E.U. ship and unloaded his eggs. It was a center hit, but the American pilot had cut it too fine, could not pull out, and crashed before his victim.

There is no point in rehashing the newspaper stories of the Four-Days War. The point is that we should have lost it, and we would have, had it not been for an unlikely combination of luck, foresight, and good management. Apparently, the nuclear physicists of the Eurasian Union were almost as far along as Ridpath's crew when the destruction of Berlin gave them the tip they needed. But we had rushed them, forced them to move before they were ready, because of the deadline for disarmament set forth in our Peace Proclamation.

If the President had waited to fight it out with Congress before issuing the proclamation, there would not be any United States.

Manning never got credit for it, but it is evident to me that he anticipated the possibility of something like the Four-Days War and prepared for it in a dozen different devious ways. I don't mean military preparation; the Army and the Navy saw to that. But it was no accident that Congress was adjourned at the time. I had something to do with the vote-swapping and compromising that led up to it, and I know.

But I put it to you—would he have maneuvered to get Congress out of Washington at a time when he feared that Washington might be attacked if he had had dictatorial ambitions?

Of course, it was the President who was back of the ten-day leaves that had been granted to most of the civil-service personnel in Washington and he himself must have made the decision to take a swing through the South at that time, but it must have been Manning who put the idea in his head. It is inconceivable that the President would have left Washington to escape personal danger.

And then, there was the plague scare. I don't know how or when Manning could have started that—it certainly did not go through my notebook—but I simply do not believe that it was accidental that a completely unfounded rumor of bubonic plague caused New York City to be semideserted at the time the E.U. bombers struck.

At that, we lost over eight hundred thousand people in Manhattan alone.

Of course, the government was blamed for the lives that were lost

and the papers were merciless in their criticism at the failure to anticipate and force an evacuation of all the major cities.

If Manning anticipated trouble, why did he not ask for evacuation?

Well, as I see it, for this reason:

A big city will not be, never has been, evacuated in response to rational argument. London never was evacuated on any major scale and
we failed utterly in our attempt to force the evacuation of Berlin. The
people of New York City had considered the danger of air raids since
1940 and were long since hardened to the thought.

But the fear of a nonexistent epidemic of plague caused the most
nearly complete evacuation of a major city ever seen.

And don't forget what we did to Vladivostok and Irkutsk and
Moscow—those were innocent people, too. War isn't pretty.

I said luck played a part. It was bad navigation that caused one of
our ships to dust Ryazan instead of Moscow, but that mistake knocked
out the laboratory and plant which produced the only supply of military
radioactives in the Eurasian Union. Suppose the mistake had been the
other way around—suppose that one of the E.U. ships in attacking
Washington, D.C., by mistake had included Ridpath's shop forty-five
miles away in Maryland?

Congress reconvened at the temporary capital in St. Louis, and
the American Pacification Expedition started the job of pulling the
fangs of the Eurasian Union. It was not a military occupation in the
usual sense; there were two simple objectives: to search out and dust
all aircraft, aircraft plants, and fields, and to locate and dust radiation
laboratories, uranium supplies, and lodes of carnotite and pitch-
blende. No attempt was made to interfere with, or to replace, civil
government.

We used a two-year dust, which gave a breathing spell in which to
consolidate our position. Liberal rewards were offered to informers, a
technique which worked remarkably well not only in the E.U., but in
most parts of the world.

The "weasel," an instrument to smell out radiation, based on the
electroscope-discharge principle and refined by Ridpath's staff, greatly
facilitated the work of locating uranium and uranium ores. A grid of
weasels, properly spaced over a suspect area, could locate any important mass of uranium almost as handily as a direction-finder can spot a
radio station.

But, notwithstanding the excellent work of General Bulfinch and
the Pacification Expedition as a whole, it was the original mistake of
dusting Ryazan that made the job possible of accomplishment.

Anyone interested in the details of the pacification work done in
1945–6 should see the "Proceedings of the American Foundation for

Social Research" for a paper entitled *A Study of the Execution of the American Peace Policy from February, 1945*. The *de facto* solution of the problem of policing the world against war left the United States with the much greater problem of perfecting a policy that would insure that the deadly power of the dust would never fall into unfit hands.

The problem is as easy to state as the problem of squaring the circle and almost as impossible of accomplishment. Both Manning and the President believed that the United States must of necessity keep the power for the time being, until some permanent institution could be developed fit to retain it. The hazard was this: Foreign policy is lodged jointly in the hands of the President and the Congress. We were fortunate at the time in having a good President and an adequate Congress, but that was no guarantee for the future. We have had unfit Presidents and power-hungry Congresses—oh, yes! Read the history of the Mexican War.

We were about to hand over to future governments of the United States the power to turn the entire globe into an empire, our empire. And it was the sober opinion of the President that our characteristic and beloved democratic culture would not stand up under the temptation. Imperialism degrades both oppressor and oppressed.

The President was determined that our sudden power should be used for the absolute minimum of maintaining peace in the world—the simple purpose of outlawing war and nothing else. It must not be used to protect American investments abroad, to coerce trade agreements, for any purpose but the simple abolition of mass killing.

There is no science of sociology. Perhaps there will be, some day, when a rigorous physics gives a finished science of colloidal chemistry and that leads in turn to a complete knowledge of biology, and from there to a definitive psychology. After that we may begin to know something about sociology and politics. Sometime around the year 5000 A.D., maybe—if the human race does not commit suicide before then.

Until then, there is only horse sense and rule of thumb and observational knowledge of probabilities. Manning and the President played by ear.

The treaties with Great Britain, Germany, and the Eurasian Union, whereby we assumed the responsibility for world peace and at the same time guaranteed the contracting nations against our own misuse of power, were rushed through in the period of relief and goodwill that immediately followed the termination of the Four-Days War. We followed the precedents established by the Panama Canal treaties, the Suez Canal agreements, and the Philippine Independence policy.

But the purpose underneath was to commit future governments of the United States to an irrevocable benevolent policy.

The act to implement the treaties by creating the Commission of World Safety followed soon after, and Colonel Manning became Mr. Commissioner Manning. Commissioners had a life tenure and the intention was to create a body with the integrity, permanence, and freedom from outside pressure possessed by the Supreme Court of the United States. Since the treaties contemplated an eventual joint trust, commissioners need not be American citizens—and the oath they took was to *preserve the peace of the world.*

There was trouble getting the clause past the Congress! Every other similar oath had been to the Constitution of the United States.

Nevertheless the Commission was formed. It took charge of world aircraft, assumed jurisdiction over radioactives, natural and artificial, and commenced the long slow task of building up the Peace Patrol.

Manning envisioned a corps of world policemen, an aristocracy which, through selection and indoctrination, could be trusted with unlimited power over the life of every man, every woman, every child on the face of the globe. For the power *would* be unlimited; the precautions necessary to insure the unbeatable weapon from getting loose in the world again made it axiomatic that its custodians would wield power that is safe only in the hands of Deity. There would be no one to guard those selfsame guardians. Their own characters and the watch they kept on each other would be all that stood between the race and disaster.

For the first time in history, supreme political power was to be exerted with no possibility of checks and balances from the outside. Manning took up the task of perfecting it with a dragging subconscious conviction that it was too much for human nature.

The rest of the Commission was appointed slowly, the names being sent to the Senate after long joint consideration by the President and Manning. The director of the Red Cross, an obscure little professor of history from Switzerland, Dr. Igor Rimski who had developed the Karst-Obre technique independently and whom the A.P.F. had discovered in prison after the dusting of Moscow—those three were the only foreigners. The rest of the list is well known.

Ridpath and his staff were of necessity the original technical crew of the Commission; United States Army and Navy pilots its first patrolmen. Not all of the pilots available were needed; their records were searched, their habits and associates investigated, their mental processes and emotional attitudes examined by the best psychological research methods available—which weren't good enough. Their final acceptance for the Patrol depended on two personal interviews, one with Manning, one with the President.

Manning told me that he depended more on the President's feeling for character than he did on all the association and reaction tests the psychologists could think up. "It's like the nose of a bloodhound," he said. "In his forty years of practical politics he has seen more phonies than you and I will ever see and each one was trying to sell him something. He can tell one in the dark."

The long-distance plan included the schools for the indoctrination of cadet patrolmen, schools that were to be open to youths of any race, color, or nationality, and from which they would go forth to guard the peace *of every country but their own*. To that country a man would never return during his service. They were to be a deliberately expatriated band of Janizaries, with an obligation only to the Commission and to the race, and welded together with a carefully nurtured esprit de corps.

It stood a chance of working. Had Manning been allowed twenty years without interruption, the original plan might have worked.

The President's running mate for re-election was the result of a political compromise. The candidate for Vice President was a confirmed isolationist who had opposed the Peace Commission from the first, but it was he or a party split in a year when the opposition was strong. The President sneaked back in but with a greatly weakened Congress; only his power of veto twice prevented the repeal of the Peace Act. The Vice President did nothing to help him, although he did not publicly lead the insurrection. Manning revised his plans to complete the essential program by the end of 1952, there being no way to predict the temper of the next administration.

We were both overworked and I was beginning to realize that my health was gone. The cause was not far to seek; a photographic film strapped next to my skin would cloud in twenty minutes. I was suffering from cumulative minimal radioactive poisoning. No well-defined cancer that could be operated on, but a systemic deterioration of function and tissue. There was no help for it, and there was work to be done. I've always attributed it mainly to the week I spent sitting on those canisters before the raid on Berlin.

February 17, 1951. I missed the televue flash about the plane crash that killed the President because I was lying down in my apartment. Manning, by that time, was requiring me to rest every afternoon after lunch, though I was still on duty. I first heard about it from my secretary when I returned to my office, and at once hurried into Manning's office.

There was a curious unreality to that meeting. It seemed to me that we had slipped back to that day when I returned from England, the day that Estelle Karst died. He looked up. "Hello, John," he said.

I put my hand on his shoulder. "Don't take it so hard, chief," was all I could think of to say.

Forty-eight hours later came the message from the newly sworn-in President for Manning to report to him. I took it in to him, an official despatch which I decoded. Manning read it, face impassive.

"Are you going, chief?" I asked.

"Eh? Why, certainly."

I went back into my office, and got my topcoat, gloves, and briefcase.

Manning looked up when I came back in. "Never mind, John," he said. "You're not going." I guess I must have looked stubborn, for he added, "You're not to go because there is work to do here. Wait a minute."

He went to his safe, twiddled the dials, opened it and removed a sealed envelope which he threw on the desk between us. "Here are your orders. Get busy."

He went out as I was opening them. I read them through and got busy. There was little enough time.

The new President received Manning standing and in the company of several of his bodyguards and intimates. Manning recognized the senator who had led the movement to use the Patrol to recover expropriated holdings in South America and Rhodesia, as well as the chairman of the committee on aviation with whom he had had several unsatisfactory conferences in an attempt to work out a *modus operandi* for reinstituting commercial airlines.

"You're prompt, I see," said the President. "Good."

Manning bowed.

"We might as well come straight to the point," the Chief Executive went on. "There are going to be some changes of policy in the administration. I want your resignation."

"I am sorry to have to refuse, sir."

"We'll see about that. In the meantime, Colonel Manning, you are relieved from duty."

"Mr. Commissioner Manning, if you please."

The new President shrugged. "One or the other, as you please. You are relieved, either way."

"I am sorry to disagree again. My appointment is for life."

"That's enough," was the answer. "This is the United States of America. There can be no higher authority. You are under arrest."

I can visualize Manning staring steadily at him for a long moment, then answering slowly, "You are physically able to arrest me, I will concede, but I advise you to wait a few minutes." He stepped to the window. "Look up into the sky."

Six bombers of the Peace Commission patrolled over the Capitol. "None of those pilots is American born," Manning added slowly. "If you confine me, none of us here in this room will live out the day."

There were incidents thereafter, such as the unfortunate affair at Fort Benning three days later, and the outbreak in the wing of the Patrol based in Lisbon and its resultant wholesale dismissals, but for practical purposes, that was all there was to the *coup d'etat*.

Manning was the undisputed military dictator of the world.

Whether or not any man as universally hated as Manning can perfect the Patrol he envisioned, make it self-perpetuating and trustworthy, I don't know, and—because of that week of waiting in a buried English hangar—I won't be here to find out. Manning's heart disease makes the outcome even more uncertain—he may last another twenty years; he may keel over dead tomorrow—and there is no one to take his place. I've set this down partly to occupy the short time I have left and partly to show there is another side to any story, even world dominion.

Not that I would like the outcome, either way. If there is anything to this survival-after-death business, I am going to look up the man who invented the bow and arrow and take him apart with my bare hands. For myself, I can't be happy in a world where any man, or group of men, has the power of death over you and me, our neighbors, every human, every animal, every living thing. I don't like anyone to have that kind of power.

And neither does Manning.

UNIVERSE

Astounding Science Fiction, May 1941

The Proxima Centauri Expedition, sponsored by the Jordan Foundation in 2119, was the first recorded attempt to reach the nearer stars of this galaxy. Whatever its unhappy fate we can only conjecture. . . .

—Quoted from *The Romance of Modern Astrography,* by Franklin Buck, published by Lux Transcriptions, Ltd., 3.50 cr.

"THERE'S A MUTIE! Look out!"

At the shouted warning, Hugh Hoyland ducked, with nothing to spare. An egg-sized iron missile clanged against the bulkhead just above his scalp with force that promised a fractured skull. The speed with which he crouched had lifted his feet from the floor plates. Before his body could settle slowly to the deck, he planted his feet against the bulkhead behind him and shoved. He went shooting down the passageway in a long, flat dive, his knife drawn and ready.

He twisted in the air, checked himself with his feet against the opposite bulkhead at the turn in the passage from which the mutie had attacked him, and floated lightly to his feet. The other branch of the passage was empty. His two companions joined him, sliding awkwardly across the floor plates.

"Is it gone?" demanded Alan Mahoney.

"Yes," agreed Hoyland. "I caught a glimpse of it as it ducked down that hatch. A female, I think. Looked like it had four legs."

"Two legs or four, we'll never catch it now," commented the third man.

"Who the Huff wants to catch it?" protested Mahoney. "*I* don't."

"Well, I do, for one," said Hoyland. "By Jordan, if its aim had been two inches better, I'd be ready for the Converter."

"Can't either one of you two speak three words without swearing?" the third man disapproved. "What if the Captain could hear you?" He touched his forehead reverently as he mentioned the Captain.

"Oh, for Jordan's sake," snapped Hoyland, "don't be so stuffy, Mort Tyler. You're not a scientist yet. I reckon I'm as devout as you are—there's no grave sin in occasionally giving vent to your feelings. Even the scientists do it. I've heard 'em."

Tyler opened his mouth as if to expostulate, then apparently thought better of it.

Mahoney touched Hoyland on the arm. "Look, Hugh," he pleaded, "let's get out of here. We've never been this high before. I'm jumpy—I want to get back down to where I can feel some weight on my feet."

Hoyland looked longingly toward the hatch through which his assailant had disappeared while his hand rested on the grip of his knife, then he turned to Mahoney. "O.K., kid," he agreed, "it's a long trip down anyhow."

He turned and slithered back toward the hatch, whereby they had reached the level where they now were, the other two following him. Disregarding the ladder by which they had mounted, he stepped off into the opening and floated slowly down to the deck fifteen feet below, Tyler and Mahoney close behind him. Another hatch, staggered a few feet from the first, gave access to a still lower deck. Down, down, down, and still farther down they dropped, tens and dozens of decks, each silent, dimly lighted, mysterious. Each time they fell a little faster, landed a little harder. Mahoney protested at last.

"Let's walk the rest of the way, Hugh. That last jump hurt my feet."

"All right. But it will take longer. How far have we got to go? Anybody keep count?"

"We've got about seventy decks to go to reach farm country," answered Tyler.

"How do you know?" demanded Mahoney suspiciously.

"I counted them, stupid. And as we came down I took one away for each deck."

"You did not. Nobody but a scientist can do numbering like that. Just because you're learning to read and write you think you know everything."

Hoyland cut in before it could develop into a quarrel. "Shut up, Alan. Maybe he can do it. He's clever about such things. Anyhow, it feels like about seventy decks—I'm heavy enough."

"Maybe he'd like to count the blades on my knife."

"Stow it, I said. Dueling is forbidden outside the village. That is the Rule." They proceeded in silence, running lightly down the stairways until increasing weight on each succeeding level forced them to a more pedestrian pace. Presently they broke through into a level that was quite brilliantly lighted and more than twice as deep between decks as the ones above it. The air was moist and warm; vegetation obscured the view.

"Well, down at last," said Hugh. "I don't recognize this farm; we must have come down by a different line than we went up."

"There's a farmer," said Tyler. He put his little fingers to his lips and whistled, then called, "Hey! Shipmate! Where are we?"

The peasant looked them over slowly, then directed them in reluctant monosyllables to the main passageway which would lead them back to their own village.

A brisk walk of a mile and a half down a wide tunnel moderately crowded with traffic—travelers, porters, an occasional pushcart, a dignified scientist swinging in a litter borne by four husky orderlies and preceded by his master-at-arms to clear the common crew out of the way—a mile and a half of this brought them to the common of their own village, a spacious compartment three decks high and perhaps ten times as wide. They split up and went their own ways, Hugh to his quarters in the barracks of the cadets—young bachelors who did not live with their parents. He washed himself, and went thence to the compartments of his uncle, for whom he worked for his meals. His aunt glanced up as he came in, but said nothing, as became a woman.

His uncle said, "Hello, Hugh. Been exploring again?"

"Good eating, Uncle. Yes."

His uncle, a stolid, sensible man, looked tolerantly amused. "Where did you go and what did you find?"

Hugh's aunt had slipped silently out of the compartment, and now returned with his supper which she placed before him. He fell to—it did not occur to him to thank her. He munched a bite before replying.

"Up. We climbed almost to the level-of-no-weight. A mutie tried to crack my skull."

His uncle chuckled. "You'll find your death in those passageways, lad. Better you should pay more attention to my business against the day when I'll die and get out of your way."

Hugh looked stubborn. "Don't you have any curiosity, Uncle?"

"Me? Oh, I was prying enough when I was a lad. I followed the main passage all the way around and back to the village. Right through the Dark Sector I went, with muties tagging my heels. See that scar?"

Hugh glanced at it perfunctorily. He had seen it many times before and heard the story repeated to boredom. Once around the Ship—*pfui!* He wanted to go everywhere, see everything, and find out the why of things. Those upper levels now—if men were not intended to climb that high, why had Jordan created them?

But he kept his own counsel and went on with his meal. His uncle changed the subject. "I've occasion to visit the Witness. John Black claims I owe him three swine. Want to come along?"

"Why, no, I guess not—Wait—I believe I will."

"Hurry up, then."

They stopped at the cadets' barracks, Hugh claiming an errand. The Witness lived in a small, smelly compartment directly across the Common from the barracks, where he would be readily accessible to any who had need of his talents. They found him sitting in his doorway, picking his teeth with a fingernail. His apprentice, a pimply-faced adolescent with an intent nearsighted expression, squatted behind him.

"Good eating," said Hugh's uncle.

"Good eating to you, Edard Hoyland. D'you come on business, or to keep an old man company?"

"Both," Hugh's uncle returned diplomatically, then explained his errand.

"So?" said the Witness. "Well—the contract's clear enough:

> "Black John delivered ten bushels of oats,
> Expecting his pay in a pair of shoats;
> Ed brought his sow to breed for pig;
> John gets his pay when the pigs grow big.

"How big are the pigs now, Edard Hoyland?"

"Big enough," acknowledged Hugh's uncle, "but Black claims three instead of two."

"Tell him to go soak his head. 'The Witness has spoken.' "

He laughed in a thin, high cackle.

The two gossiped for a few minutes, Edard Hoyland digging into his recent experiences to satisfy the old man's insatiable liking for details. Hugh kept decently silent while the older men talked. But when his uncle turned to go he spoke up. "I'll stay awhile, Uncle."

"Eh? Suit yourself. Good eating, Witness."

"Good eating, Edard Hoyland."

"I've brought you a present, Witness," said Hugh, when his uncle had passed out of hearing.

"Let me see it."

Hugh produced a package of tobacco which he had picked up from his locker at the barracks. The Witness accepted it without acknowledgment, then tossed it to his apprentice, who took charge of it.

"Come inside," invited the Witness, then directed his speech to his apprentice. "Here, you—fetch the cadet a chair."

"Now, lad," he added as they sat themselves down, "tell me what you have been doing with yourself."

Hugh told him, and was required to repeat in detail all the incidents of his more recent explorations, the Witness complaining the meanwhile over his inability to remember exactly everything he saw.

"You youngsters have no capacity," he pronounced. "No capacity. Even that lout"—he jerked his head toward the apprentice—"he has none, though he's a dozen times better than you. Would you believe it, he can't soak up a thousand lines a day, yet he expects to sit in my seat when I am gone. Why, when I was apprenticed, I used to sing myself to sleep on a mere thousand lines. Leaky vessels—that's what you are."

Hugh did not dispute the charge, but waited for the old man to go on, which he did in his own time.

"You had a question to put to me, lad?"

"In a way, Witness."

"Well—out with it. Don't chew your tongue."

"Did you ever climb all the way up to no-weight?"

"Me? Of course not. I was a Witness, learning my calling. I had the lines of all the Witnesses before me to learn, and no time for boyish amusements."

"I had hoped you could tell me what I would find there."

"Well, now, that's another matter. I've never climbed, but I hold the memories of more climbers than you will ever see. I'm an old man. I knew your father's father, and his grandsire before that. What is it you want to know?"

"Well—" What was it he wanted to know? How could he ask a question that was no more than a gnawing ache in his breast? Still—"What is it all for, Witness? Why are there all those levels above us?"

"Eh? How's that? Jordan's name, son—I'm a Witness, not a scientist."

"Well—I thought you must know. I'm sorry."

"But I do know. What you want is the Lines from the Beginning."

"I've heard them."

"Hear them again. All your answers are in there, if you've the wisdom to see them. Attend me. No—this is a chance for my apprentice to show off his learning. Here, you! The Lines from the Beginning—and mind your rhythm."

The apprentice wet his lips with his tongue and began:

"In the Beginning there was Jordan, thinking His lonely thoughts alone.

In the Beginning there was darkness, formless, dead, and Man
    unknown.

Out of the loneness came a longing, out of the longing came a
    vision,

Out of the dream there came a planning, out of the plan there
    came decision—

Jordan's hand was lifted and the Ship was born!

Mile after mile of snug compartments, tank by tank for the
    golden corn,

Ladder and passage, door and locker, fit for the needs of the yet
    unborn.

He looked on His work and found it pleasing, meet for a race
    that was yet to be.

He thought of Man—Man came into being—checked his thought
    and searched for the key.

Man untamed would shame his Maker, Man unruled would spoil
    the Plan;

So Jordan made the Regulations, orders to each single man,

Each to a task and each to a station, serving a purpose beyond
    their ken,

Some to speak and some to listen—order came to the ranks of
    men.

Crew He created to work at their stations, scientists to guide the
    Plan.

Over them all He created the Captain, made him judge of the
    race of Man.

Thus it was in the Golden Age!

Jordan is perfect, all below him lack perfection in their deeds.

Envy, Greed, and Pride of Spirit sought for minds to lodge their
    seeds.

One there was who gave them lodging—accursed Huff, the first
    to sin!

His evil counsel stirred rebellion, planted doubt where it had not
    been;

Blood of martyrs stained the floor plates, Jordan's Captain made
    the Trip.

Darkness swallowed up—"

The old man gave the boy the back of his hand, sharp across the
mouth. "Try again!"

"From the beginning?"

"No! From where you missed."

The boy hesitated, then caught his stride:

"Darkness swallowed ways of virtue, Sin prevailed throughout
the Ship . . ."

The boy's voice droned on, stanza after stanza, reciting at great
length but with little sharpness of detail the old, old story of sin, rebellion, and the time of darkness. How wisdom prevailed at last and the
bodies of the rebel leaders were fed to the Converter. How some of the
rebels escaped making the Trip and lived to father the muties. How a
new Captain was chosen, after prayer and sacrifice.

Hugh stirred uneasily, shuffling his feet. No doubt the answers to
his questions were there, since these were the Sacred Lines, but he
had not the wit to understand them. Why? What was it all about? Was
there really nothing more to life than eating and sleeping and finally
the long Trip? Didn't Jordan intend for him to understand? Then why
this ache in his breast? This hunger that persisted in spite of good eating?

While he was breaking his fast after sleep an orderly came to the
door of his uncle's compartments. "The scientist requires the presence
of Hugh Hoyland," he recited glibly.

Hugh knew that the scientist referred to was Lieutenant Nelson, in
charge of the spiritual and physical welfare of the Ship's sector which
included Hugh's native village. He bolted the last of his breakfast and
hurried after the messenger.

"Cadet Hoyland!" he was announced. The scientist looked up from
his own meal and said:

"Oh, yes. Come in, my boy. Sit down. Have you eaten?"

Hugh acknowledged that he had, but his eyes rested with interest
on the fancy fruit in front of his superior. Nelson followed his glance.
"Try some of these figs. They're a new mutation—I had them brought
all the way from the far side. Go ahead—a man your age always has
somewhere to stow a few more bites."

Hugh accepted with much self-consciousness. Never before had he
eaten in the presence of a scientist. The elder leaned back in his chair,
wiped his fingers on his shirt, arranged his beard, and started in.

"I haven't seen you lately, son. Tell me what you have been doing
with yourself." Before Hugh could reply he went on: "No, don't tell
me—I will tell you. For one thing you have been exploring, climbing,
without too much respect for the forbidden areas. Is it not so?" He held
the young man's eye. Hugh fumbled for a reply.

But he was let off again. "Never mind. I know, and you know that I
know. I am not too displeased. But it has brought it forcibly to my attention that it is time that you decided what you are to do with your life.
Have you any plans?"

"Well—no definite ones, sir."

"How about that girl, Edris Baxter? D'you intend to marry her?"

"Why—uh—I don't know, sir. I guess I want to, and her father is willing, I think. Only—"

"Only what?"

"Well—he wants me to apprentice to his farm. I suppose it's a good idea. His farm together with my uncle's business would make a good property."

"But you're not sure?"

"Well—I don't know."

"Correct. You're not for that. I have other plans. Tell me, have you ever wondered why I taught you to read and write? Of course, you have. But you've kept your own counsel. That is good.

"Now attend me. I've watched you since you were a small child. You have more imagination than the common run, more curiosity, more go. And you are a born leader. You were different even as a baby. Your head was too large, for one thing, and there were some who voted at your birth inspection to put you at once into the Converter. But I held them off. I wanted to see how you would turn out.

"A peasant life is not for the likes of you. You are to be a scientist."

The old man paused and studied his face. Hugh was confused, speechless. Nelson went on: "Oh, yes. Yes, indeed. For a man of your temperament, there are only two things to do with him: Make him one of the custodians, or send him to the Converter."

"Do you mean, sir, that I have nothing to say about it?"

"If you want to put it that bluntly—yes. To leave the bright ones among the ranks of the Crew is to breed heresy. We can't have that. We had it once and it almost destroyed the human race. You have marked yourself out by your exceptional ability; you must now be instructed in right thinking, be initiated into the mysteries, in order that you may be a conserving force rather than a focus of infection and a source of trouble."

The orderly reappeared loaded down with bundles which he dumped on the deck. Hugh glanced at them, then burst out, "Why, those are my things!"

"Certainly," acknowledged Nelson. "I sent for them. You're to sleep here henceforth. I'll see you later and start you on your studies—unless you have something more on your mind?"

"Why, no, sir. I guess not. I must admit I am a little confused. I suppose—I suppose this means you don't want me to marry?"

"Oh, *that*," Nelson answered indifferently. "Take her if you like—her father can't protest now. But let me warn you you'll grow tired of her."

❖

Hugh Hoyland devoured the ancient books that his mentor permitted him to read, and felt no desire for many, many sleeps to go climbing, or even to stir out of Nelson's cabin. More than once he felt that he was on the track of the secret—a secret as yet undefined, even as a question—but again he would find himself more confused than ever. It was evidently harder to reach the wisdom of scientisthood than he had thought.

Once, while he was worrying away at the curious twisted characters of the ancients and trying to puzzle out their odd rhetoric and unfamiliar terms, Nelson came into the little compartment that had been set aside for him, and, laying a fatherly hand on his shoulder, asked, "How goes it, boy?"

"Why, well enough, sir, I suppose," he answered, laying the book aside. "Some of it is not quite clear to me—not clear at all, to tell the truth."

"That is to be expected," the old man said equably. "I've let you struggle along by yourself at first in order that you may see the traps that native wit alone will fall into. Many of these things are not to be understood without instruction. What have you there?" He picked up the book and glanced at it. It was inscribed *Basic Modern Physics*. "So? This is one of the most valuable of the sacred writings, yet the uninitiate could not possibly make good use of it without help. The first thing that you must understand, my boy, is that our forefathers, for all their spiritual perfection, did not look at things in the fashion in which we do.

"They were incurable romantics, rather than rationalists, as we are, and the truths which they handed down to us, though strictly true, were frequently clothed in allegorical language. For example, have you come to the Law of Gravitation?"

"I read about it."

"Did you understand it? No, I can see that you didn't."

"Well," said Hugh defensively, "it didn't seem to *mean* anything. It just sounded silly, if you will pardon me, sir."

"That illustrates my point. You were thinking of it in literal terms, like the laws governing electrical devices found elsewhere in this same book. 'Two bodies attract each other directly as the product of their masses and inversely as the square of their distance.' It sounds like a rule for simple physical facts, does it not? Yet it is nothing of the sort; it was the poetical way the old ones had of expressing the rule of propinquity which governs the emotion of love. The bodies referred to are human bodies, mass is their capacity for love. Young people have a greater capacity for love than the elderly; when they are thrown together, they fall in love, yet when they are separated they soon get over it. 'Out of sight, out of mind.' It's as simple as that. But you were seeking some deep meaning for it."

Hugh grinned. "I never thought of looking at it that way. I can see that I am going to need a lot of help."

"Is there anything else bothering you just now?"

"Well, yes, lots of things, though I probably can't remember them offhand. I mind one thing: Tell me, Father, can muties be considered as being people?"

"I can see you have been listening to idle talk. The answer to that is both yes and no. It is true that the muties originally descended from people but they are no longer part of the Crew—they cannot now be considered as members of the human race, for they have flouted Jordan's Law.

"This is a broad subject," he went on, settling down to it. "There is even some question as to the original meaning of the word 'mutie.' Certainly they number among their ancestors the mutineers who escaped death at the time of the rebellion. But they also have in their blood the blood of many of the mutants who were born during the dark age. You understand, of course, that during that period our present wise rule of inspecting each infant for the mark of sin and returning to the Converter any who are found to be mutations was not in force. There are strange and horrible things crawling through the dark passageways and lurking in the deserted levels."

Hugh thought about it for a while, then asked, "Why is it that mutations still show up among us, the people?"

"That is simple. The seed of sin is still in us. From time to time it still shows up, incarnate. In destroying those monsters we help to cleanse the stock and thereby bring closer the culmination of Jordan's Plan, the end of the Trip at our heavenly home, Far Centaurus."

Hoyland's brow wrinkled again. "That is another thing that I don't understand. Many of these ancient writings speak of the Trip as if it were an actual *moving,* a going-somewhere—as if the Ship itself were no more than a pushcart. How can that be?"

Nelson chuckled. "How can it, indeed? How can that move which is the background against which all else moves? The answer, of course, is plain. You have again mistaken allegorical language for the ordinary usage of everyday speech. Of course, the Ship is solid, immovable, in a physical sense. How can the whole universe move? Yet, it *does* move, in a spiritual sense. With every righteous act we move closer to the sublime destination of Jordan's Plan."

Hugh nodded. "I think I see."

"Of course, it is conceivable that Jordan could have fashioned the world in some other shape than the Ship, had it suited His purpose. When man was younger and more poetical, holy men vied with one another in inventing fanciful worlds which Jordan might have created. One school invented an entire mythology of a topsy-turvy world of endless reaches of space, empty save for pinpoints of light and bodiless mythological monsters. They called it the heavenly world, or heaven, as if to contrast it with the solid reality of the Ship. They seemed never to tire of speculating about it, inventing details for it, and of making pictures of what they conceived it to be like. I suppose they did it to the greater glory of Jordan, and who is to say that He found their dreams unacceptable? But in this modern age we have more serious work to do."

Hugh was not interested in astronomy. Even his untutored mind had been able to see in its wild extravagance an intention not literal. He turned to problems nearer at hand.

"Since the muties are the seed of sin, why do we make no effort to wipe them out? Would not that be an act that would speed the Plan?"

The old man considered a while before replying. "That is a fair question and deserves a straight answer. Since you are to be a scientist you will need to know the answer. Look at it this way: There is a definite limit to the number of Crew the Ship can support. If our numbers increase without limit, there comes a time when there will not be good eating for all of us. Is it not better that some should die in brushes with the muties than that we should grow in numbers until we killed each other for food?

"The ways of Jordan are inscrutable. Even the muties have a part in His Plan."

It seemed reasonable, but Hugh was not sure.

But when Hugh was transferred to active work as a junior scientist in the operation of the Ship's functions, he found there were other opinions. As was customary, he put in a period serving the Converter. The work was not onerous; he had principally to check in the waste materials brought in by porters from each of the villages, keep books of their contributions, and make sure that no reclaimable metal was introduced into the first-stage hopper. But it brought him into contact with Bill Ertz, the Assistant Chief Engineer, a man not much older than himself.

He discussed with him the things he had learned from Nelson, and was shocked at Ertz's attitude.

"Get this through your head, kid," Ertz told him. "This is a practical job for practical men. Forget all that romantic nonsense. Jordan's Plan! That stuff is all right to keep the peasants quiet and in their place, but don't fall for it yourself. There is no Plan—other than our own plans for looking out for ourselves. The Ship has to have light and heat and power for cooking and irrigation. The Crew can't get along without those things and that makes us boss of the Crew.

"As for this softheaded tolerance toward the muties, you're going to see some changes made! Keep your mouth shut and string along with us."

It impressed on him that he was expected to maintain a primary loyalty to the bloc of younger men among the scientists. They were a well-knit organization within an organization and were made up of practical, hardheaded men who were working toward improvement of conditions throughout the Ship, as they saw them. They were well-knit because an apprentice who failed to see things their way did not last long. Either he failed to measure up and soon found himself back in the ranks of the peasants, or, as was more likely, suffered some mishap and wound up in the Converter.

And Hoyland began to see that they were right.

They were realists. The Ship was the Ship. It was a fact, requiring no explanation. As for Jordan—who had ever seen Him, spoken to Him? What was this nebulous Plan of His? The object of life was living. A man was born, lived his life, and then went to the Converter. It was as simple as that, no mystery to it, no sublime Trip and no Centaurus. These romantic stories were simply hangovers from the childhood of the race before men gained the understanding and the courage to look facts in the face.

He ceased bothering his head about astronomy and mystical physics and all the other mass of mythology he had been taught to revere. He was still amused, more or less, by the Lines from the Beginning and by all the old stories about Earth—what the Huff was "Earth," anyhow?—but now realized that such things could be taken seriously only by children and dullards.

Besides, there was work to do. The younger men, while still maintaining the nominal authority of their elders, had plans of their own, the first of which was a systematic extermination of the muties. Beyond that, their intentions were still fluid, but they contemplated making full use of the resources of the Ship, including the upper levels. The young men were able to move ahead with their plans without an open breach with their elders because the older scientists simply did not bother to any great extent with the routine of the Ship. The present Captain had grown so fat that he rarely stirred from his cabin; his aide, one of the young men's bloc, attended to affairs for him.

Hoyland never laid eyes on the Chief Engineer save once, when he showed up for the purely religious ceremony of manning landing stations.

The project of cleaning out the muties required reconnaissance of the upper levels to be done systematically. It was in carrying out such scouting that Hugh Hoyland was again ambushed by a mutie.

This mutie was more accurate with his slingshot. Hoyland's companions, forced to retreat by superior numbers, left him for dead.

Joe-Jim Gregory was playing himself a game of checkers. Time was when they had played cards together, but Joe, the head on the right, had suspected Jim, the left-hand member of the team, of cheating. They had quarreled about it, then given it up, for they both learned early in their joint career that two heads on one pair of shoulders must necessarily find ways of getting along together.

Checkers was better. They could both see the board, and disagreement was impossible.

A loud metallic knocking at the door of the compartment interrupted the game. Joe-Jim unsheathed his throwing knife and cradled it, ready for quick use. "Come in!" roared Jim.

The door opened, the one who had knocked backed into the room—the only safe way, as everyone knew, to enter Joe-Jim's presence. The newcomer was squat and ruggedly powerful, not over four feet in height. The relaxed body of a man hung across one shoulder and was steadied by a hand.

Joe-Jim returned the knife to its sheath. "Put it down, Bobo," Jim ordered.

"And close the door," added Joe. "Now what have we got here?"

It was a young man, apparently dead, though no wound appeared on him. Bobo patted a thigh. "Eat 'im?" he said hopefully. Saliva spilled out of his still-opened lips.

"Maybe," temporized Jim. "Did you kill him?"

Bobo shook his undersized head.

"Good Bobo," Joe approved. "Where did you hit him?"

"Bobo hit him *there*." The microcephalic shoved a broad thumb against the supine figure in the area between the umbilicus and the breastbone.

"Good shot," Joe approved. "We couldn't have done better with a knife."

"Bobo *good* shot," the dwarf agreed blandly. "Want see?" He twitched his slingshot invitingly.

"Shut up," answered Joe, not unkindly. "No, we don't want to see; we want to make him talk."

"Bobo fix," the short one agreed, and started with simple brutality to carry out his purpose.

Joe-Jim slapped him away, and applied other methods, painful but considerably less drastic than those of the dwarf. The younger man jerked and opened his eyes.

"Eat 'im?" repeated Bobo.

"No," said Joe. "When did you eat last?" inquired Jim.

Bobo shook his head and rubbed his stomach, indicating with graphic pantomime that it had been a long time—too long. Joe-Jim went over to a locker, opened it, and withdrew a haunch of meat. He held it up. Jim smelled it and Joe drew his head away in nose-wrinkling disgust. Joe-Jim threw it to Bobo, who snatched it happily out of the air. "Now, get out," ordered Jim.

Bobo trotted away, closing the door behind him. Joe-Jim turned to the captive and prodded him with his foot. "Speak up," said Jim. "Who the Huff are you?"

The young man shivered, put a hand to his head, then seemed suddenly to bring his surroundings into focus, for he scrambled to his feet, moving awkwardly against the low weight conditions of this level, and reached for his knife.

It was not at his belt.

Joe-Jim had his own out and brandished it. "Be good and you won't get hurt. What do they call you?"

The young man wet his lips, and his eyes hurried about the room. "Speak up," said Joe.

"Why bother with him?" inquired Jim. "I'd say he was only good for meat. Better call Bobo back."

"No hurry about that," Joe answered. "I want to talk to him. What's your name?"

The prisoner looked again at the knife and muttered, "Hugh Hoyland."

"That doesn't tell us much," Jim commented. "What d'you do? What village do you come from? And what were you doing in mutie country?"

But this time Hoyland was sullen. Even the prick of the knife against his ribs caused him only to bite his lips. "Shucks," said Joe, "he's only a stupid peasant. Let's drop it."

"Shall we finish him off?"

"No. Not now. Shut him up."

Joe-Jim opened the door of a small side compartment, and urged Hugh in with the knife. He then closed and fastened the door and went back to his game. "Your move, Jim."

The compartment in which Hugh was locked was dark. He soon satisfied himself by touch that the smooth steel walls were entirely featureless save for the solid, securely fastened door. Presently he lay down on the deck and gave himself up to fruitless thinking.

He had plenty of time to think, time to fall asleep and awaken more than once. And time to grow very hungry and very, very thirsty.

When Joe-Jim next took sufficient interest in his prisoner to open the door of the cell, Hoyland was not immediately in evidence. He had planned many times what he would do when the door opened and his chance came, but when the event arrived, he was too weak, semi-comatose. Joe-Jim dragged him out.

The disturbance roused him to partial comprehension. He sat up and stared around him.

"Ready to talk?" asked Jim.

Hoyland opened his mouth but no words came out.

"Can't you see he's too dry to talk?" Joe told his twin. Then to Hugh: "Will you talk if we give you some water?"

Hoyland looked puzzled, then nodded vigorously.

Joe-Jim returned in a moment with a mug of water. Hugh drank greedily, paused, and seemed about to faint.

Joe-Jim took the mug from him. "That's enough for now," said Joe. "Tell us about yourself."

Hugh did so. In detail, being prompted from time to time.

Hugh accepted a *de facto* condition of slavery with no particular resistance and no great disturbance of soul. The word "slave" was not in his vocabulary, but the condition was a commonplace in everything he had ever known. There had always been those who gave orders and those who carried them out—he could imagine no other condition, no other type of social organization. It was a fact of nature.

Though naturally he thought of escape.

Thinking about it was as far as he got. Joe-Jim guessed his thoughts and brought the matter out into the open. Joe told him, "Don't go getting ideas, youngster. Without a knife you wouldn't get three levels away in this part of the Ship. If you managed to steal a knife from me, you still wouldn't make it down to high-weight. Besides, there's Bobo."

Hugh waited a moment, as was fitting, then said, "Bobo?"

Jim grinned and replied, "We told Bobo that you were his to butcher, if he liked, if you ever stuck your head out of our compartments without us. Now he sleeps outside the door and spends a lot of his time there."

"It was only fair," put in Joe. "He was disappointed when we decided to keep you."

OFF   THE   MAIN   SEQUENCE

"Say," suggested Jim, turning his head toward his brother's, "how about some fun?" He turned back to Hugh. "Can you throw a knife?"

"Of course," Hugh answered.

"Let's see you. Here." Joe-Jim handed him their own knife. Hugh accepted it, jiggling it in his hand to try its balance. "Try my mark."

Joe-Jim had a plastic target set up at the far end of the room from his favorite chair, on which he was wont to practice his own skill. Hugh eyed it, and, with an arm motion too fast to follow, let fly. He used the economical underhand stroke, thumb on the blade, fingers together.

The blade shivered in the target, well centered in the chewed-up area which marked Joe-Jim's best efforts.

"Good boy!" Joe approved. "What do you have in mind, Jim?"

"Let's give him the knife and see how far he gets."

"No," said Joe, "I don't agree."

"Why not?"

"If Bobo wins, we're out one servant. If Hugh wins, we lose both Bobo and him. It's wasteful."

"Oh, well—if you insist."

"I do. Hugh, fetch the knife."

Hugh did so. It had not occurred to him to turn the knife against Joe-Jim. The master was the master. For servant to attack master was not simply repugnant to good morals, it was an idea so wild that it did not occur to him at all.

Hugh had expected that Joe-Jim would be impressed by his learning as a scientist. It did not work out that way. Joe-Jim, especially Jim, loved to argue. They sucked Hugh dry in short order and figuratively cast him aside. Hoyland felt humiliated. After all, was he not a scientist? Could he not read and write?

"Shut up," Jim told him. "Reading is simple. I could do it before your father was born. D'you think you're the first scientist that has served me? Scientists—bah! A pack of ignoramuses!"

In an attempt to re-establish his own intellectual conceit, Hugh expounded the theories of the younger scientists, the strictly matter-of-fact, hard-boiled realism which rejected all religious interpretation and took the Ship as it was. He confidently expected Joe-Jim to approve such a point of view; it seemed to fit their temperaments.

They laughed in his face.

"Honest," Jim insisted, when he had ceased snorting, "are you young punks so stupid as all that? Why, you're worse than your elders."

"But you just got through saying," Hugh protested in hurt tones, "that all our accepted religious notions are so much bunk. That is just what my friends think. They want to junk all that old nonsense."

Joe started to speak; Jim cut in ahead of him. "Why bother with him, Joe? He's hopeless."

"No, he's not. I'm enjoying this. He's the first one I've talked with in I don't know how long who stood any chance at all of seeing the truth. Let us be—I want to see whether that's a head he has on his shoulders, or just a place to hang his ears."

"O.K.," Jim agreed, "but keep it quiet. I'm going to take a nap." The left-hand head closed its eyes, soon it was snoring. Joe and Hugh continued their discussion in whispers.

"The trouble with you youngsters," Joe said, "is that if you can't understand a thing right off, you think it can't be true. The trouble with your elders is, anything they didn't understand they reinterpreted to mean something else and then thought they understood it. None of you has tried believing clear words the way they were written and then tried to understand them on that basis. Oh, no, you're all too bloody smart for that—if you can't see it right off, it ain't so—it must mean something different."

"What do you mean?" Hugh asked suspiciously.

"Well, take the Trip, for instance. What does it mean to you?"

"Well—to my mind, it doesn't mean anything. It's just a piece of nonsense to impress the peasants."

"And what is the accepted meaning?"

"Well—it's where you go when you die—or rather what you do. You make the Trip to Centaurus."

"And what is Centaurus?"

"It's—mind you, I'm just telling you the orthodox answers; I don't really believe this stuff—it's where you arrive when you've made the Trip, a place where everybody's happy and there's always good eating."

Joe snorted. Jim broke the rhythm of his snoring, opened one eye, and settled back again with a grunt. "That's just what I mean," Joe went on in a lower whisper. "You don't use your head. Did it ever occur to you that the Trip was just what the old books said it was—the Ship and all the Crew actually going somewhere, moving?"

Hoyland thought about it. "You don't mean for me to take you seriously. Physically, it's an impossibility. The Ship can't *go* anywhere. It already *is* everywhere. We can make a trip through it, but *the* Trip—that has to have a spiritual meaning, if it has any."

Joe called on Jordan to support him. "Now, listen," he said, "get this through that thick head of yours. Imagine a place a lot bigger than the Ship, a lot bigger, with the Ship inside it—*moving*. D'you get it?"

Hugh tried. He tried very hard. He shook his head. "It doesn't make sense," he said. "There can't be anything bigger than the Ship. There wouldn't be any place for it to *be*."

"Oh, for Huff's sake! Listen—*outside* the Ship, get that? Straight down beyond the level in every direction. Emptiness out there. Understand me?"

"But there isn't anything below the lowest level. That's why it's the lowest level."

"Look. If you took a knife and started digging a hole in the floor of the lowest level, where would it get you?"

"But you *can't*. It's too hard."

"But suppose you did and it made a hole. Where would that hole go? Imagine it."

Hugh shut his eyes and tried to imagine digging a hole in the lowest level. Digging—as if it were soft—soft as cheese.

He began to get some glimmering of a possibility, a possibility that was unsettling, soul-shaking. He was falling, falling into a hole that he had dug which had no levels under it. He opened his eyes very quickly. "That's awful!" he ejaculated. "I won't believe it."

Joe-Jim got up. "I'll *make* you believe it," he said grimly, "if I have to break your neck to do it." He strode over to the outer door and opened it. "Bobo!" he shouted. "Bobo!"

Jim's head snapped erect. "Wassa matter? Wha's going on?"

"We're going to take Hugh to no-weight."

"What for?"

"To pound some sense into his silly head."

"Some other time."

"No, I want to do it now."

"All right, all right. No need to shake. I'm awake now, anyhow."

Joe-Jim Gregory was almost as nearly unique in his, or their, mental ability as he was in his bodily construction. Under any circumstances he would have been a dominant personality; among the muties it was inevitable that he should bully them, order them about, and live on their services. Had he had the will-to-power, it is conceivable that he could have organized the muties to fight and overcome the Crew proper.

But he lacked that drive. He was by native temperament an intellectual, a bystander, an observer. He was interested in the "how" and the "why," but this will to action was satisfied with comfort and convenience alone.

Had he been born two normal twins and among the Crew, it is

likely that he would have drifted into scientisthood as the easiest and most satisfactory answer to the problem of living and as such would have entertained himself mildly with conversation and administration. As it was, he lacked mental companionship and had whiled away three generations reading and rereading books stolen for him by his stooges.

The two halves of his dual person had argued and discussed what they had read, and had almost inevitably arrived at a reasonably coherent theory of history and the physical world—except in one respect, the concept of fiction was entirely foreign to them; they treated the novels that had been provided for the Jordan expedition in exactly the same fashion that they did text and reference books.

This led to their one major difference of opinion. Jim regarded Allan Quartermain as the greatest man who had ever lived; Joe held out for John Henry.

They were both inordinately fond of poetry; they could recite page after page of Kipling, and were nearly as fond of Rhysling, "the blind singer of the spaceways."

Bobo backed in. Joe-Jim hooked a thumb toward Hugh. "Look," said Joe, "he's going out."

"Now?" said Bobo happily, and grinned, slavering.

"You and your stomach!" Joe answered, rapping Bobo's pate with his knuckles. "No, you don't eat him. You and him—blood brothers. Get it?"

"Not eat 'im?"

"No. Fight for him. He fights for you."

"O.K." The pinhead shrugged his shoulders at the inevitable. "Blood brothers. Bobo know."

"All right. Now we go up to the place-where-everybody-flies. You go ahead and make lookout."

They climbed in single file, the dwarf running ahead to spot the lie of the land, Hoyland behind him, Joe-Jim bringing up the rear, Joe with eyes to the front, Jim watching their rear, head turned over his shoulder.

Higher and higher they went, weight slipping imperceptibly from them with each successive deck. They emerged finally into a level beyond which there was no further progress, no opening above them. The deck curved gently, suggesting that the true shape of the space was a giant cylinder, but overhead a metallic expanse which exhibited a similar curvature obstructed the view and prevented one from seeing whether or not the deck in truth curved back on itself.

There were no proper bulkheads; great stanchions, so huge and squat as to give an impression of excessive, unnecessary strength, grew thickly about them, spacing deck and overhead evenly apart.

Weight was imperceptible. If one remained quietly in one place, the undetectable residuum of weight would bring the body in a gentle drift down to the "floor," but "up" and "down" were terms largely lacking in meaning. Hugh did not like it; it made him gulp, but Bobo seemed delighted by it and not unused to it. He moved through the air like an uncouth fish, banking off stanchion, floor plate, and overhead as suited his convenience.

Joe-Jim set a course parallel to the common axis of the inner and outer cylinders, following a passageway formed by the orderly spacing of the stanchions. There were handrails set along the passage, one of which he followed like a spider on its thread. He made remarkable speed, which Hugh floundered to maintain. In time, he caught the trick of the easy, effortless, overhand pull, the long coast against nothing but air resistance, and the occasional flick of the toes or the hand against the floor. But he was much too busy to tell how far they went before they stopped. Miles, he guessed it to be, but he did not know.

When they did stop, it was because the passage had terminated. A solid bulkhead, stretching away to right and left, barred their way. Joe-Jim moved along it to the right, searching.

He found what he sought, a man-sized door, closed, its presence distinguishable only by a faint crack which marked its outline and a cursive geometrical design on its surface. Joe-Jim studied this and scratched his right-hand head. The two heads whispered to each other. Joe-Jim raised his hand in an awkward gesture.

"No, no!" said Jim. Joe-Jim checked himself. "How's that?" Joe answered. They whispered together again, Joe nodded, and Joe-Jim again raised his hand.

He traced the design on the door without touching it, moving his forefinger through the air perhaps four inches from the surface of the door. The order of succession in which his finger moved over the lines of the design appeared simple but certainly not obvious.

Finished, he shoved a palm against the adjacent bulkhead, drifted back from the door, and waited.

A moment later there was a soft, almost inaudible insufflation; the door stirred and moved outward perhaps six inches, then stopped. Joe-Jim appeared puzzled. He ran his hands cautiously into the open crack and pulled. Nothing happened. He called to Bobo, "Open it."

Bobo looked the situation over, with a scowl on his forehead which wrinkled almost to his crown. He then placed his feet against the bulkhead, steadying himself by grasping the door with one hand. He took hold of the edge of the door with both hands, settled his feet firmly, bowed his body, and strained.

He held his breath, chest rigid, back bent, sweat breaking out from the effort. The great cords in his neck stood out, making of his head a misshapen pyramid. Hugh could hear the dwarf's joints crack. It was easy to believe that he would kill himself with the attempt, too stupid to give up.

But the door gave suddenly, with a plaint of binding metal. As the door, in swinging out, slipped from Bobo's fingers, the unexpectedly released tension in his legs shoved him heavily away from the bulkhead; he plunged down the passageway, floundering for a handhold. But he was back in a moment, drifting awkwardly through the air as he massaged a cramped calf.

Joe-Jim led the way inside, Hugh close behind him. "What is this place?" demanded Hugh, his curiosity overcoming his servant manners.

"The Main Control Room," said Joe.

Main Control Room! The most sacred and taboo place in the Ship, its very location a forgotten mystery. In the credo of the young men it was nonexistent. The older scientists varied in their attitude between fundamentalist acceptance and mystical belief. As enlightened as Hugh believed himself to be, the very words frightened him. The Control Room! Why, the very spirit of Jordan was said to reside there.

He stopped.

Joe-Jim stopped and Joe looked around. "Come on," he said. "What's the matter?"

"Why—uh—uh—"

"Speak up."

"But—but this place is haunted—this is Jordan's—"

"Oh, for Jordan's sake!" protested Joe, with slow exasperation. "I thought you told me you young punks didn't take any stock in Jordan."

"Yes, but—but this is—"

"Stow it. Come along, or I'll have Bobo drag you." He turned away. Hugh followed, reluctantly, as a man climbs a scaffold.

They threaded through a passageway just wide enough for two to use the handrails abreast. The passage curved in a wide sweeping arc of full ninety degrees, then opened into the control room proper. Hugh peered past Joe-Jim's broad shoulders, fearful but curious.

He stared into a well-lighted room, huge, quite two hundred feet across. It was spherical, the interior of a great globe. The surface of the globe was featureless, frosted silver. In the geometrical center of the sphere Hugh saw a group of apparatus about fifteen feet across. To his inexperienced eye, it was completely unintelligible; he could not have described it, but he saw that it floated steadily, with no apparent support.

Running from the end of the passage to the mass at the center of the globe was a tube of metal latticework, wide as the passage itself. It offered the only exit from the passage. Joe-Jim turned to Bobo, and ordered him to remain in the passageway, then entered the tube.

He pulled himself along it, hand over hand, the bars of the latticework making a ladder. Hugh followed him; they emerged into the mass of apparatus occupying the center of the sphere. Seen close up, the gear of the control station resolved itself into its individual details, but it still made no sense to him. He glanced away from it to the inner surface of the globe which surrounded them.

That was a mistake. The surface of the globe, being featureless silvery white, had nothing to lend it perspective. It might have been a hundred feet away, or a thousand, or many miles. He had never experienced an unbroken height greater than that between two decks, nor an open space larger than the village common. He was panic-stricken, scared out of his wits, the more so in that he did not know what it was he feared. But the ghost of long-forgotten jungle ancestors possessed him and chilled his stomach with the basic primitive fear of falling.

He clutched at the control gear, clutched at Joe-Jim.

Joe-Jim let him have one, hard across the mouth with the flat of his hand. "What's the matter with you?" growled Jim.

"I don't know," Hugh presently managed to get out. "I don't know, but I don't *like* this place. Let's get out of here!"

Jim lifted his eyebrows to Joe, looked disgusted, and said, "We might as well. That weak-bellied baby will never understand anything you tell him."

"Oh, he'll be all right," Joe replied, dismissing the matter. "Hugh, climb into one of the chairs—there, that one."

In the meantime, Hugh's eyes had fallen on the tube whereby they had reached the control center and had followed it back by eye to the passage door. The sphere suddenly shrank to its proper focus and the worst of his panic was over. He complied with the order, still trembling, but able to obey.

The control center consisted of a rigid framework, made up of chairs, or frames, to receive the bodies of the operators, and consolidated instrument and report panels, mounted in such a fashion as to be almost in the laps of the operators, where they were readily visible but did not obstruct the view. The chairs had high supporting sides, or arms, and mounted in these arms were the controls appropriate to each officer on watch—but Hugh was not yet aware of that.

He slid under the instrument panel into his seat and settled back, glad of its enfolding stability. It fitted him in a semi-reclining position, footrest to head support.

But something was happening on the panel in front of Joe-Jim; he caught it out of the corner of his eye and turned to look. Bright red letters glowed near the top of the board: 2ND ASTROGATOR POSTED. What was a second astrogator? He didn't know—then he noticed that the extreme top of his own board was labeled 2ND ASTROGATOR and concluded it must be himself, or rather, the man who should be sitting there. He felt momentarily uncomfortable that the proper second astrogator might come in and find him usurping his post, but he put it out of his mind—it seemed unlikely.

But what was a second astrogator, anyhow?

The letters faded from Joe-Jim's board, a red dot appeared on the left-hand edge and remained. Joe-Jim did something with his right hand; his board reported: ACCELERATION—ZERO, then MAIN DRIVE. The last two words blinked several times, then were replaced with NO REPORT. These words faded out, and a bright green dot appeared near the right-hand edge.

"Get ready," said Joe, looking toward Hugh; "the light is going out."

"You're not going to turn out the light?" protested Hugh.

"No—you are. Take a look by your left hand. See those little white lights?"

Hugh did so, and found, shining up through the surface of the chair arm, eight bright little beads of light arranged in two squares, one above the other.

"Each one controls the light of one quadrant," explained Joe. "Cover them with your hand to turn out the light. Go ahead—do it."

Reluctantly, but fascinated, Hugh did as he was directed. He placed a palm over the tiny lights, and waited. The silvery sphere turned to dull lead, faded still more, leaving them in darkness complete save for the silent glow from the instrument panels. Hugh felt nervous but exhilarated. He withdrew his palm; the sphere remained dark, the eight little lights had turned blue.

"Now," said Joe, "I'm going to show you the stars!"

In the darkness, Joe-Jim's right hand slid over another pattern of eight lights.

Creation.

Faithfully reproduced, shining as steady and serene from the walls of the stellarium as did their originals from the black deeps of space, the mirrored stars looked down on him. Light after jeweled light, scattered in careless bountiful splendor across the simulacrum sky, the countless suns lay before him—before him, over him, under him, behind him, in every direction from him. He hung alone in the center of the stellar universe.

"Oooooh!" It was an involuntary sound, caused by his indrawn breath. He clutched the chair arms hard enough to break fingernails, but he was not aware of it. Nor was he afraid at the moment; there was room in his being for but one emotion. Life within the Ship, alternately harsh and workaday, had placed no strain on his innate capacity to experience beauty; for the first time in his life he knew the intolerable ecstasy of beauty unalloyed. It shook him and hurt him, like the first trembling intensity of sex.

It was some time before Hugh sufficiently recovered from the shock and the ensuing intense preoccupation to be able to notice Jim's sardonic laugh, Joe's dry chuckle. "Had enough?" inquired Joe. Without waiting for a reply, Joe-Jim turned the lights back on, using the duplicate controls mounted in the left arm of his chair.

Hugh sighed. His chest ached and his heart pounded. He realized suddenly that he had been holding his breath the entire time that the lights had been turned out. "Well, smart boy," asked Jim, "are you convinced?"

Hugh sighed again, not knowing why. With the lights back on, he felt safe and snug again, but was possessed of a deep sense of personal loss. He knew, subconsciously, that, having seen the stars, he would never be happy again. The dull ache in his breast, the vague inchoate yearning for his lost heritage of open sky and stars, was never to be silenced, even though he was yet too ignorant to be aware of it at the top of his mind. "What was it?" he asked in a hushed voice.

"That's *it*," answered Joe. "That's the world. That's the universe. That's what I've been trying to tell you about."

Hugh tried furiously to force his inexperienced mind to comprehend. "That's what you mean by Outside?" he asked. "All those beautiful little lights?"

"Sure," said Joe, "only they aren't little. They're a long way off, you see—maybe thousands of miles."

"What?"

"Sure, sure," Joe persisted. "There's lots of room out there. Space. It's big. Why, some of those stars may be as big as the Ship—maybe bigger."

Hugh's face was a pitiful study in overstrained imagination. "Bigger than the Ship?" he repeated. "But—but—"

Jim tossed his head impatiently and said to Joe, "Wha'd' I tell you? You're wasting our time on this lunk. He hasn't got the capacity—"

"Easy, Jim," Joe answered mildly; "don't expect him to run before he can crawl. It took us a long time. I seem to remember that you were a little slow to believe your own eyes."

"That's a lie," said Jim nastily. "*You* were the one that had to be convinced."

"O.K., O.K.," Joe conceded, "let it ride. But it was a long time before we both had it all straight."

Hoyland paid little attention to the exchange between the two brothers. It was a usual thing; his attention was centered on matters decidedly not usual. "Joe," he asked, "what became of the Ship while we were looking at the stars? Did we stare right through it?"

"Not exactly," Joe told him. "You weren't looking directly at the stars at all, but at a kind of picture of them. It's like— Well, they do it with mirrors, sort of. I've got a book that tells about it."

"But you *can* see 'em directly," volunteered Jim, his momentary pique forgotten. "There's a compartment forward of here—"

"Oh, yes," put in Joe, "it slipped my mind. The Captain's veranda. 'S got one all of glass; you can look right out."

"The Captain's veranda? But—"

"Not *this* Captain. He's never been near the place. That's the name over the door of the compartment."

"What's a 'veranda'?"

"Blessed if I know. It's just the name of the place."

"Will you take me up there?"

Joe appeared to be about to agree, but Jim cut in. "Some other time. I want to get back—I'm hungry."

They passed back through the tube, woke up Bobo, and made the long trip back down.

It was long before Hugh could persuade Joe-Jim to take him exploring again, but the time intervening was well spent. Joe-Jim turned him loose on the largest collection of books that Hugh had ever seen. Some of them were copies of books Hugh had seen before, but even these he read with new meanings. He read incessantly, his mind soaking up new ideas, stumbling over them, struggling, striving to grasp them. He begrudged sleep, he forgot to eat until his breath grew sour and compelling pain in his midriff forced him to pay attention to his body. Hunger satisfied, he would be back at it until his head ached and his eyes refused to focus.

Joe-Jim's demands for service were few. Although Hugh was never off duty, Joe-Jim did not mind his reading as long as he was within earshot and ready to jump when called. Playing checkers with one of the pair when the other did not care to play was the service which used up the most time, and even this was not a total loss, for, if the player were Joe, he could almost always be diverted into a discussion of the Ship, its history, its machinery and equipment, the sort of people who had built it and first manned it— and *their* history, back on Earth, Earth the incredible, that strange place where people had lived on the *outside* instead of the *inside*.

Hugh wondered why they did not fall off.

He took the matter up with Joe and at last gained some notion of gravitation. He never really understood it emotionally—it was too wildly improbable—but as an intellectual concept he was able to accept it and use it, much later, in his first vague glimmerings of the science of ballistics and the art of astrogation and ship maneuvering. And it led in time to his wondering about weight in the Ship, a matter that had never bothered him before. The lower the level the greater the weight had been to his mind simply the order of nature, and nothing to wonder at. He was familiar with centrifugal force as it applied to slingshots. To apply it also to the whole Ship, to think of the Ship as spinning like a slingshot and thereby causing weight, was too much of a hurdle—he never really believed it.

Joe-Jim took him back once more to the Control Room and showed him what little Joe-Jim knew about the manipulation of the controls and the reading of the astrogation instruments.

The long-forgotten engineer-designers employed by the Jordan Foundation had been instructed to design a ship that would not—*could not*—wear out, even though the Trip were protracted beyond the expected sixty years. They builded better than they knew. In planning the main drive engines and the auxiliary machinery, largely automatic, which would make the Ship habitable, and in designing the controls necessary to handle all machinery not entirely automatic, the very idea of moving parts had been rejected. The engines and auxiliary equipment worked on a level below mechanical motion, on a level of pure force, as electrical transformers do. Instead of push buttons, levers, cams, and shafts, the controls and the machinery they served were planned in terms of balance between static fields, bias of electronic flow, circuits broken or closed by a hand placed over a light.

On this level of action, friction lost its meaning, wear and erosion took no toll. Had all hands been killed in the mutiny, the Ship would still have plunged on through space, still lighted, its air still fresh and moist, its engines ready and waiting. As it was, though elevators and conveyor belts fell into disrepair, disuse, and finally into the oblivion of forgotten function, the essential machinery of the Ship continued its automatic service to its ignorant human freight, or waited, quiet and ready, for someone bright enough to puzzle out its key.

Genius had gone into the building of the Ship. Far too huge to be assembled on Earth, it had been put together piece by piece in its own orbit out beyond the Moon. There it had swung for fifteen silent years while the problems presented by the decision to make its machinery foolproof and enduring had been formulated and solved. A whole new field of submolar action had been conceived in the process, struggled with, and conquered.

So— When Hugh placed an untutored, questing hand over the first of a row of lights marked ACCELERATION, POSITIVE, he got an immediate response, though not in terms of acceleration. A red light at the top of the chief pilot's board blinked rapidly and the annunciator panel glowed with a message: MAIN ENGINES—NOT MANNED.

"What does that mean?" he asked Joe-Jim.

"There's no telling," said Jim. "We've done the same thing in the main engine room," added Joe. "There, when you try it, it says 'Control Room Not Manned.'"

Hugh thought a moment. "What would happen," he persisted, "if all the control stations had somebody at 'em at once, and then I did that?"

"Can't say," said Joe. "Never been able to try it."

Hugh said nothing. A resolve which had been growing, formless, in his mind was now crystallizing into decision. He was busy with it.

He waited until he found Joe-Jim in a mellow mood, both of him, before broaching his idea. They were in the Captain's veranda at the time Hugh decided the moment was ripe. Joe-Jim rested gently in the Captain's easy chair, his belly full of food, and gazed out through the heavy glass of the view port at the serene stars. Hugh floated beside him. The spinning of the Ship caused the stars to appear to move in stately circles.

Presently he said, "Joe-Jim—"

"Eh? What's that, youngster?" It was Joe who had replied.

"It's pretty swell, isn't it?"

"What is?"

"All that. The stars." Hugh indicated the view through the port with a sweep of his arm, then caught at the chair to stop his own backspin.

"Yeah, it sure is. Makes you feel good." Surprisingly, it was Jim who offered this.

Hugh knew the time was right. He waited a moment, then said, "Why don't we finish the job?"

Two heads turned simultaneously, Joe leaning out a little to see past Jim. "What job?"

"The Trip. Why don't we start up the main drive and go on with it? Somewhere out there," he said hurriedly to finish before he was interrupted, "there are planets like Earth—or so the First Crew thought. Let's go find them."

Jim looked at him, then laughed. Joe shook his head.

"Kid," he said, "you don't know what you are talking about. You're as balmy as Bobo. No," he went on, "that's all over and done with. Forget it."

"Why is it over and done with, Joe?"

"Well, because— It's too big a job. It takes a crew that understands what it's all about, trained to operate the Ship."

"Does it take so many? You have shown me only about a dozen places, all told, for men actually to be at the controls. Couldn't a dozen men run the Ship—if they knew what you know," he added slyly.

Jim chuckled. "He's got you, Joe. He's right."

Joe brushed it aside. "You overrate our knowledge. Maybe we *could* operate the Ship, but we wouldn't get anywhere. We don't know where we are. The Ship has been drifting for I don't know how many generations. We don't know where we're headed, or how fast we're going."

"But look," Hugh pleaded, "there are instruments. You showed them to me. Couldn't we learn how to use them? Couldn't *you* figure them out, Joe, if you really wanted to?"

"Oh, I suppose so," Jim agreed.

"Don't boast, Jim," said Joe.

"I'm not boasting," snapped Jim. "If a thing'll work, I can figure it out."

"Humph!" said Joe.

The matter rested in delicate balance. Hugh had got them disagreeing among themselves—which was what he wanted—with the less tractable of the pair on his side. Now, to consolidate his gain—

"I had an idea," he said quickly, "to get you men to work with, Jim, if you were able to train them."

"What's your idea?" demanded Jim suspiciously.

"Well, you remember what I told you about a bunch of the younger scientists—"

"Those fools!"

"Yes, yes, sure—but they don't know what you know. In their way they were trying to be reasonable. Now, if I could go back down and tell them what you've taught me, I could get you enough men to work with."

Joe cut in. "Take a good look at us, Hugh. What do you see?"

"Why—why—I see *you*—Joe-Jim."

"You see a mutie," corrected Joe, his voice edged with sarcasm. "We're a *mutie*. Get that? Your scientists won't work with us."

"No, no," protested Hugh, "that's not true. I'm not talking about peasants. Peasants wouldn't understand, but these are *scientists,* and the smartest of the lot. They'll understand. All you need to do is to arrange safe conduct for them through mutie country. You can do that, can't you?" he added, instinctively shifting the point of the argument to firmer ground.

"Why, sure," said Jim.

"Forget it," said Joe.

"Well, O.K.," Hugh agreed, sensing that Joe really was annoyed at his persistence, "but it would be fun—" He withdrew some distance from the brothers.

He could hear Joe-Jim continuing the discussion with himself in low tones. He pretended to ignore it. Joe-Jim had this essential defect in his joint nature: being a committee, rather than a single individual, he was hardly fitted to be a man of action, since all decisions were necessarily the result of discussion and compromise.

Several moments later Hugh heard Joe's voice raised. "All right, all *right*—have it your own way!" He then called out, "Hugh! Come here!"

Hugh kicked himself away from an adjacent bulkhead and shot over to the immediate vicinity of Joe-Jim, arresting his flight with both hands against the framework of the Captain's chair.

"We've decided," said Joe without preliminaries, "to let you go back down to the high-weight and try to peddle your goods. But you're a fool," he added sourly.

Bobo escorted Hugh down through the dangers of the levels frequented by muties and left him in the uninhabited zone above high-weight. "Thanks, Bobo," Hugh said in parting. "Good eating." The dwarf grinned, ducked his head, and sped away, swarming up the ladder they had just descended.

Hugh turned and started down, touching his knife as he did so. It was good to feel it against him again. Not that it was his original knife. That had been Bobo's prize when he was captured, and Bobo had been unable to return it, having inadvertently left it sticking in a big one that got away. But the replacement Joe-Jim had given him was well balanced and quite satisfactory.

Bobo had conducted him, at Hugh's request and by Joe-Jim's order, down to the area directly over the auxiliary Converter used by the scientists. He wanted to find Bill Ertz, Assistant Chief Engineer and leader of the bloc of younger scientists, and he did not want to have to answer too many questions before he found him.

Hugh dropped quickly down the remaining levels and found himself in a main passageway which he recognized. Good! A turn to the left, a couple of hundred yards' walk and he found himself at the door of the compartment which housed the Converter. A guard lounged in front of it. Hugh started to push on past, was stopped. "Where do you think you're going?"

"I want to find Bill Ertz."

"You mean the Chief Engineer? Well, he's not here."

"Chief? What's happened to the old one?" Hoyland regretted the remark at once—but it was already out.

"Huh? The old Chief? Why, he's made the Trip long since." The guard looked at him suspiciously. "What's wrong with you?"

"Nothing," denied Hugh. "Just a slip."

"Funny sort of a slip. Well, you'll find Chief Ertz around his office probably."

"Thanks. Good eating."

"Good eating."

Hugh was admitted to see Ertz after a short wait. Ertz looked up from his desk as Hugh came in. "Well," he said, "so you're back, and not dead after all. This *is* a surprise. We had written you off, you know, as making the Trip."

"Yes, I suppose so."

"Well, sit down and tell me about it—I've a little time to spare at the moment. Do you know, though, I wouldn't have recognized you. You've changed a lot—all that gray hair. I imagine you had some pretty tough times."

Gray hair? Was his hair gray? And Ertz had changed a lot, too, Hugh now noticed. He was paunchy and the lines in his face had set. Good Jordan! How long had he been gone?

Ertz drummed on his desk top, and pursed his lips. "It makes a problem—your coming back like this. I'm afraid I can't just assign you to your old job; Mort Tyler has that. But we'll find a place for you, suitable to your rank."

Hugh recalled Mort Tyler and not too favorably. A precious sort of a chap, always concerned with what was proper and according to regulations. So Tyler had actually made scientisthood, and was on Hugh's old job at the Converter. Well, it didn't matter. "That's all right," he began. "I wanted to talk to you about—"

"Of course, there's the matter of seniority," Ertz went on. "Perhaps the Council had better consider the matter. I don't know of a precedent. We've lost a number of scientists to the muties in the past, but you are the first to escape with his life in my memory."

"That doesn't matter," Hugh broke in. "I've something much more pressing to talk about. While I was away I found out some amazing things, Bill, things that it is of paramount importance for you to know about. That's why I came straight to you. Listen, I—"

Ertz was suddenly alert. "Of course you have! I must be slowing down. You must have had a marvelous opportunity to study the muties and scout out their territory. Come on, man, spill it! Give me your report."

Hugh wet his lips. "It's not what you think," he said. "It's much more important than just a report on the muties, though it concerns them, too. In fact, we may have to change our whole policy with respect to the mu—"

"Well, go ahead, go ahead! I'm listening."

"All right." Hugh told him of his tremendous discovery as to the actual nature of the Ship, choosing his words carefully and trying very hard to be convincing. He dwelt lightly on the difficulties presented by an attempt to reorganize the Ship in accordance with the new concept and bore down heavily on the prestige and honor that would accrue to the man who led the effort.

He watched Ertz's face as he talked. After the first start of complete surprise when Hugh launched his key idea, the fact that the Ship was actually a moving body in a great outside space, his face became impassive and Hugh could read nothing in it, except that he seemed to detect a keener interest when Hugh spoke of how Ertz was just the man for the job because of his leadership of the younger, more progressive scientists.

When Hugh concluded, he waited for Ertz's response. Ertz said nothing at first, simply continued with his annoying habit of drumming on the top of his desk. Finally he said, "These are important matters, Hoyland, much too important to be dealt with casually. I must have time to chew it over."

"Yes, certainly," Hugh agreed. "I wanted to add that I've made arrangements for safe passage up to no-weight. I can take you up and let you see for yourself."

"No doubt that is best," Ertz replied. "Well—are you hungry?"

"No."

"Then we'll both sleep on it. You can use the compartment at the back of my office. I don't want you discussing this with anyone else until I've had time to think about it; it might cause unrest if it got out without proper preparation."

"Yes, you're right."

"Very well, then"—Ertz ushered him into a compartment behind his office which he very evidently used for a lounge—"have a good rest," he said, "and we'll talk later."

"Thanks," Hugh acknowledged. "Good eating."

"Good eating."

Once he was alone, Hugh's excitement gradually dropped away from him, and he realized that he was fagged out and very sleepy. He stretched out on a built-in couch and fell asleep.

When he awoke he discovered that the only door to the compartment was barred from the other side. Worse than that, his knife was gone.

He had waited an indefinitely long time when he heard activity at the door. It opened; two husky, unsmiling men entered. "Come along," said one of them. He sized them up, noting that neither of them carried a knife. No chance to snatch one from their belts, then. On the other hand he might be able to break away from them.

But beyond them, a wary distance away in the outer room, were two other equally formidable men, each armed with a knife. One balanced his for throwing; the other held his by the grip, ready to stab at close quarters.

He was boxed in and he knew it. They had anticipated his possible moves.

He had long since learned to relax before the inevitable. He composed his face and marched quietly out. Once through the door he saw Ertz, waiting and quite evidently in charge of the party of men. He spoke to him, being careful to keep his voice calm. "Hello, Bill. Pretty extensive preparations you've made. Some trouble, maybe?"

Ertz seemed momentarily uncertain of his answer, then said, "You're going before the Captain."

"Good!" Hugh answered. "Thanks, Bill. But do you think it's wise to try to sell the idea to him without laying a little preliminary foundation with the others?"

Ertz was annoyed at his apparent thickheadedness and showed it. "You don't get the idea," he growled. "You're going before the Captain to stand trial—for heresy!"

Hugh considered this as if the idea had not before occurred to him. He answered mildly, "You're off down the wrong passage, Bill. Perhaps a charge and trial is the best way to get at the matter, but I'm not a peasant, simply to be hustled before the Captain. I must be tried by the Council. I am a scientist."

"Are you now?" Ertz said softly. "I've had advice about that. You were written off the lists. Just what you are is a matter for the Captain to determine."

Hugh held his peace. It was against him, he could see, and there was no point in antagonizing Ertz. Ertz made a signal; the two unarmed men each grasped one of Hugh's arms. He went with them quietly.

❖

Hugh looked at the Captain with new interest. The old man had not changed much—a little fatter, perhaps.

The Captain settled himself slowly down in his chair, and picked up the memorandum before him.

"What's this all about?" he began irritably. "I don't understand it."

Mort Tyler was there to present the case against Hugh, a circumstance which Hugh had had no way of anticipating and which added to his misgivings. He searched his boyhood recollections for some handle by which to reach the man's sympathy, found none. Tyler cleared his throat and commenced:

"This is the case of one Hugh Hoyland, Captain, formerly one of your junior scientists—"

"Scientist, eh? Why doesn't the Council deal with him?"

"Because he is no longer a scientist, Captain. He went over to the muties. He now returns among us, preaching heresy and seeking to undermine your authority."

The Captain looked at Hugh with the ready belligerency of a man jealous of his prerogatives.

"Is that so?" he bellowed. "What have you to say for yourself?"

"It is not true, Captain," Hugh answered. "All that I have said to anyone has been an affirmation of the absolute truth of our ancient knowledge. I have not disputed the truths under which we live; I have simply affirmed them more forcibly than is the ordinary custom I—"

"I still don't understand this," the Captain interrupted, shaking his head. "You're charged with heresy, yet you say you believe the Teachings. If you aren't guilty, why are you here?"

"Perhaps I can clear the matter up," put in Ertz. "Hoyland—"

"Well, I hope you can," the Captain went on. "Come—let's hear it."

Ertz proceeded to give a reasonably correct, but slanted, version of Hoyland's return and his strange story. The Captain listened, with an expression that varied between puzzlement and annoyance.

When Ertz had concluded, the Captain turned to Hugh. "Humph!" he said.

Hugh spoke immediately. "The gist of my contention, Captain, is that there is a place up at no-weight where you can actually *see* the truth of our faith that the Ship is moving, where you can actually see Jordan's Plan in operation. That is not a denial of faith; that affirms it. There is no need to take my word for it. Jordan Himself will prove it."

Seeing that the Captain appeared to be in a state of indecision, Tyler broke in: "Captain, there is a possible explanation of this incredible situation which I feel duty bound that you should hear. Offhand, there are two obvious interpretations of Hoyland's ridiculous story: He may simply be guilty of extreme heresy, or he may be a mutie at heart and engaged in a scheme to lure you into their hands. But there is a third, more charitable explanation and one which I feel within me is probably the true one.

"There is record that Hoyland was seriously considered for the Converter at his birth inspection, but that his deviation from normal was slight, being simply an overlarge head, and he was passed. It seems to me that the terrible experiences he has undergone at the hands of the muties have finally unhinged an unstable mind. The poor chap is simply not responsible for his own actions."

Hugh looked at Tyler with new respect. To absolve him of guilt and at the same time to make absolutely certain that Hugh would wind up making the Trip—how neat!

The Captain shook a palm at them. "This has gone on long enough." Then, turning to Ertz: "Is there recommendation?"

"Yes, Captain. The Converter."

"Very well, then. I really don't see, Ertz," he continued testily, "why I should be bothered with these details. It seems to me that you should be able to handle discipline in your department without my help."

"Yes, Captain."

The Captain shoved back from his desk, started to get up. "Recommendation confirmed. Dismissed."

Anger flooded through Hugh at the unreasonable injustice of it. They had not even considered looking at the only real evidence he had in his defense. He heard a shout: "Wait!"—then discovered it was his own voice.

The Captain paused, looking at him.

"Wait a moment," Hugh went on, his words spilling out of their own accord. "This won't make any difference, for you're all so damn sure you know all the answers that you won't consider a fair offer to come see with your own eyes. Nevertheless— Nevertheless—it *still* moves!"

Hugh had plenty of time to think, lying in the compartment where they confined him to await the power needs of the Converter, time to think, and to second-guess his mistakes. Telling his tale to Ertz immediately—that had been mistake number one. He should have waited, become reacquainted with the man and felt him out, instead of depending on a friendship which had never been very close.

Second mistake, Mort Tyler. When he heard his name he should have investigated and found out just how much influence the man had with Ertz. He had known him of old, he should have known better.

Well, here he was, condemned as a mutant—or maybe as a heretic. It came to the same thing. He considered whether or not he should have tried to explain why mutants happened. He had learned about it himself in some of the old records in Joe-Jim's possession. No, it wouldn't wash. How could you explain about radiations from the Outside causing the birth of mutants when the listeners did not believe there was such a place as Outside? No, he had messed it up before he was ever taken before the Captain.

His self-recriminations were disturbed at last by the sound of his door being unfastened. It was too soon for another of the infrequent meals; he thought that they had come at last to take him away, and renewed his resolve to take someone with him.

But he was mistaken. He heard a voice of gentle dignity: "Son, son, how does this happen?" It was Lieutenant Nelson, his first teacher, looking older than ever and frail.

The interview was distressing for both of them. The old man, childless himself, had cherished great hopes for his protégé, even the ambition that he might eventually aspire to the captaincy, though he had kept his vicarious ambition to himself, believing it not good for the young to praise them too highly. It had hurt his heart when the youth was lost.

Now he had returned, a man, but under disgraceful conditions and under sentence of death.

The meeting was no less unhappy for Hugh. He had loved the old man, in his way, wanted to please him and needed his approval. But he could see, as he told his story, that Nelson was not capable of treating the story as anything but an aberration of Hugh's mind, and he suspected that Nelson would rather see him meet a quick death in the Converter, his atoms smashed to hydrogen and giving up clean useful power, than have him live to make a mock of the ancient teachings.

In that he did the old man an injustice; he underrated Nelson's mercy, but not his devotion to "science." But let it be said for Hugh that, had there been no more at issue than his own personal welfare, he might have preferred death to breaking the heart of his benefactor—being a romantic and more than a bit foolish.

Presently the old man got up to leave, the visit having grown unendurable to each of them. "Is there anything I can do for you, son? Do they feed you well enough?"

"Quite well, thanks," Hugh lied.

"Is there anything else?"

"No—yes, you might send me some tobacco. I haven't had a chew in a long time."

"I'll take care of it. Is there anyone you would like to see?"

"Why, I was under the impression that I was not permitted visitors—ordinary visitors."

"You are right, but I think perhaps I may be able to get the rule relaxed. But you will have to give me your promise not to speak of your heresy," he added anxiously.

Hugh thought quickly. This was a new aspect, a new possibility. His uncle? No, while they had always got along well, their minds did not meet—they would greet each other as strangers. He had never made friends easily; Ertz had been his obvious next friend and now look at the damned thing! Then he recalled his village chum, Alan Mahoney, with whom he had played as a boy. True, he had seen practically nothing of him since the time he was apprenticed to Nelson. Still—

"Does Alan Mahoney still live in our village?"

"Why, yes."

"I'd like to see him, if he'll come."

Alan arrived, nervous, ill at ease, but plainly glad to see Hugh and very much upset to find him under sentence to make the Trip. Hugh pounded him on the back. "Good boy," he said. "I knew you would come."

"Of course, I would," protested Alan, "once I knew. But nobody in the village knew it. I don't think even the Witnesses knew it."

"Well, you're here, that's what matters. Tell me about yourself. Have you married?"

"Huh, uh, no. Let's not waste time talking about me. Nothing ever happens to me anyhow. How in Jordan's name did you get in this jam, Hugh?"

"I can't talk about that, Alan. I promised Lieutenant Nelson that I wouldn't."

"Well, what's a promise—*that* kind of a promise? You're in a *jam,* fellow."

"Don't I know it!"

"Somebody have it in for you?"

"Well—our old pal Mort Tyler didn't help any; I think I can say that much."

Alan whistled and nodded his head slowly. "That explains a lot."

"How come? You know something?"

"Maybe, maybe not. After you went away he married Edris Baxter."

"So? Hm-m-m—yes, that clears up a lot." He remained silent for a time.

Presently Alan spoke up: "Look, Hugh. You're not going to sit here and take it, are you? Particularly with Tyler mixed in it. We gotta get you outa here."

"How?"

"I don't know. Pull a raid, maybe. I guess I could get a few knives to rally round and help us—all good boys, spoiling for a fight."

"Then, when it's over, we'd all be for the Converter. You, me, and your pals. No, it won't wash."

"But we've *got* to do something. We can't just sit here and wait for them to burn you."

"I know that." Hugh studied Alan's face. Was it a fair thing to ask? He went on, reassured by what he had seen. "Listen. You would do anything you could to get me out of this, wouldn't you?"

"You know that." Alan's tone showed hurt.

"Very well, then. There is a dwarf named Bobo. I'll tell you how to find him—"

Alan climbed, up and up, higher than he had ever been since Hugh had led him, as a boy, into foolhardy peril. He was older now, more conservative; he had no stomach for it. To the very real danger of leaving the well-traveled lower levels was added his superstitious ignorance. But still he climbed.

This should be about the place—unless he had lost count. But he saw nothing of the dwarf.

Bobo saw him first. A slingshot load caught Alan in the pit of the stomach, even as he was shouting, "Bobo!"

Bobo backed into Joe-Jim's compartment and dumped his load at the feet of the twins. "Fresh meat," he said proudly.

"So it is," agreed Jim indifferently. "Well, it's yours; take it away."

The dwarf dug a thumb into a twisted ear, "Funny," he said, "he knows Bobo's name."

Joe looked up from the book he was reading—Browning's *Collected Poems,* L-Press, New York, London, Luna City, cr. 35. "That's interesting. Hold on a moment."

Hugh had prepared Alan for the shock of Joe-Jim's appearance. In reasonably short order he collected his wits sufficiently to be able to tell his tale. Joe-Jim listened to it without much comment, Bobo with interest but little comprehension.

When Alan concluded, Jim remarked, "Well, you win, Joe. He didn't make it." Then, turning to Alan, he added, "You can take Hoyland's place. Can you play checkers?"

Alan looked from one head to the other. "But you don't understand," he said. "Aren't you going to do anything about it?"

Joe looked puzzled. "Us? Why should we?"

"But you've *got* to. Don't you see? He's depending on you. There's nobody else he can look to. That's why I came. Don't you see?"

"Wait a moment," drawled Jim, "wait a moment. Keep your belt on. Supposing we did want to help him—which we don't—how in Jordan's Ship could we? Answer me that."

"Why—why—" Alan stumbled in the face of such stupidity. "Why, get up a rescue party, of course, and go down and get him out!"

"Why should we get ourselves killed in a fight to rescue your friend?"

Bobo pricked his ears. "Fight?" he inquired eagerly.

"No, Bobo," Joe denied. "No fight. Just talk."

"Oh," said Bobo and returned to passivity.

Alan looked at the dwarf. "If you'd even let Bobo and me—"

"No," Joe said shortly. "It's out of the question. Shut up about it."

Alan sat in a corner, hugging his knees in despair. If only he could get out of there. He could still try to stir up some help down below. The dwarf seemed to be asleep, though it was difficult to be sure with him. If only Joe-Jim would sleep, too.

Joe-Jim showed no indication of sleepiness. Joe tried to continue reading, but Jim interrupted him from time to time. Alan could not hear what they were saying.

Presently Joe raised his voice. "Is that your idea of fun?" he demanded.

"Well," said Jim, "it beats checkers."

"It does, does it? Suppose you get a knife in your eye—where would I be then?"

"You're getting old, Joe. No juice in you any more."

"You're as old as I am."

"Yeah, but I got young ideas."

"Oh, you make me sick. Have it your own way—but don't blame me. Bobo!"

The dwarf sprang up at once, alert. "Yeah, Boss."

"Go out and dig up Squatty and Long Arm and Pig." Joe-Jim got up, went to a locker, and started pulling knives out of their racks.

Hugh heard the commotion in the passageway outside his prison. It could be the guards coming to take him to the Converter, though they probably wouldn't be so noisy. Or it could be just some excitement unrelated to him. On the other hand it might be—

It was. The door burst open, and Alan was inside, shouting at him and thrusting a brace of knives into his hands. He was hurried out of the door, while stuffing the knives in his belt and accepting two more.

Outside he saw Joe-Jim, who did not see him at once, as he was methodically letting fly, as calmly as if he had been engaging in target practice in his own study. And Bobo, who ducked his head and grinned with a mouth widened by a bleeding cut, but continued the easy flow of the motion whereby he loaded and let fly. There were three others, two of whom Hugh recognized as belonging to Joe-Jim's privately owned gang of bullies—muties by definition and birthplace; they were not deformed.

The count does not include still forms on the floor plates.

"Come on!" yelled Alan. "There'll be more in no time." He hurried down the passage to the right.

Joe-Jim desisted and followed him. Hugh let one blade go for luck at a figure running away to the left. The target was poor, and he had no time to see if he had drawn blood. They scrambled along the passage, Bobo bringing up the rear, as if reluctant to leave the fun, and came to a point where a side passage crossed the main one.

Alan led them to the right again. "Stairs ahead," he shouted.

They did not reach them. An airtight door, rarely used, clanged in their faces ten yards short of the stairs. Joe-Jim's bravoes checked their flight and they looked doubtfully at their master. Bobo broke his thickened nails trying to get a purchase on the door.

The sounds of pursuit were clear behind them.

"Boxed in," said Joe softly. "I hope you like it, Jim."

Hugh saw a head appear around the corner of the passage they had quitted. He threw overhand but the distance was too great; the knife clanged harmlessly against steel. The head disappeared. Long Arm kept his eye on the spot, his sling loaded and ready.

Hugh grabbed Bobo's shoulder. "Listen! Do you see that light?"

The dwarf blinked stupidly. Hugh pointed to the intersection of the glowtubes where they crossed in the overhead directly above the junction of the passages. "That light. Can you hit them where they cross?"

Bobo measured the distance with his eye. It would be a hard shot under any conditions at that range. Here, constricted as he was by the low passageway, it called for a fast, flat trajectory, and allowance for higher weight then he was used to.

He did not answer. Hugh felt the wind of his swing but did not see the shot. There was a tinkling crash; the passage became dark.

"Now!" yelled Hugh, and led them away at a run. As they neared the intersection he shouted, "Hold your breaths! Mind the gas!" The radioactive vapor poured lazily out from the broken tube above and filled the crossing with a greenish mist.

Hugh ran to the right, thankful for his knowledge as an engineer of the lighting circuits. He had picked the right direction; the passage ahead was black, being serviced from beyond the break. He could hear footsteps around him; whether they were friend or enemy he did not know.

They burst into light. No one was in sight but a scared and harmless peasant who scurried away at an unlikely pace. They took a quick muster. All were present, but Bobo was making heavy going of it.

Joe looked at him. "He sniffed the gas, I think. Pound his back."

Pig did so with a will. Bobo belched deeply, was suddenly sick, then grinned.

"He'll do," decided Joe.

The slight delay had enabled one at least to catch up with them. He came plunging out of the dark, unaware of, or careless of, the strength against him. Alan knocked Pig's arm down, as he raised it to throw.

"Let me at 'im!" he demanded. "He's mine!"

It was Tyler.

"Man-fight?" Alan challenged, thumb on his blade.

Tyler's eyes darted from adversary to adversary and accepted the invitation to individual duel by lunging at Alan. The quarters were too cramped for throwing; they closed, each achieving his grab in parry, fist to wrist.

Alan was stockier, probably stronger; Tyler was slippery. He attempted to give Alan a knee to the crotch. Alan evaded it, stamped on Tyler's planted foot. They went down. There was a crunching crack.

A moment later, Alan was wiping his knife against his thigh. "Let's get goin'," he complained. "I'm scared."

They reached a stairway, and raced up it, Long Arm and Pig ahead to fan out on each level and cover their flanks, and the third of the three choppers—Hugh heard him called Squatty—covering the rear. The others bunched in between.

Hugh thought they had won free, when he heard shouts and the clatter of a thrown knife just above him. He reached the level above in time to be cut not deeply but jaggedly by a ricocheted blade.

Three men were down. Long Arm had a blade sticking in the fleshy part of his upper arm, but it did not seem to bother him. His slingshot was still spinning. Pig was scrambling after a thrown knife, his own armament exhausted. But there were signs of his work; one man was down on one knee some twenty feet away. He was bleeding from a knife wound in the thigh.

As the figure steadied himself with one hand against the bulkhead and reached toward an empty belt with the other, Hugh recognized him.

Bill Ertz.

He had led a party up another way and flanked them, to his own ruin. Bobo crowded behind Hugh and got his mighty arm free for the cast. Hugh caught at it. "Easy, Bobo," he directed. "In the stomach, and easy."

The dwarf looked puzzled, but did as he was told. Ertz folded over at the middle and slid to the deck.

"Well placed," said Jim.

"Bring him along, Bobo," directed Hugh, "and stay in the middle." He ran his eye over their party, now huddled at the top of that flight of stairs. "All right, gang—up we go again! Watch it."

Long Arm and Pig swarmed up the next flight, the others disposing themselves as usual. Joe looked annoyed. In some fashion—a fashion by no means clear at the moment—he had been eased out as leader of this gang—*his* gang—and Hugh was giving orders. He reflected that there was no time now to make a fuss. It might get them all killed.

Jim did not appear to mind. In fact, he seemed to be enjoying himself.

They put ten more levels behind them with no organized opposition. Hugh directed them not to kill peasants unnecessarily. The three bravoes obeyed; Bobo was too loaded down with Ertz to constitute a problem in discipline. Hugh saw to it that they put thirty-odd more decks below them and were well into no man's land before he let vigilance relax at all. Then he called a halt and they examined wounds.

The only deep ones were to Long Arm's arm and Bobo's face. Joe-Jim examined them and applied presses with which he had outfitted himself before starting. Hugh refused treatment for his flesh wound. "It's stopped bleeding," he insisted, "and I've got a lot to do."

"You've got nothing to do but to get up home," said Joe, "and that will be an end to this foolishness."

"Not quite," denied Hugh. "You may be going home, but Alan and I and Bobo are going up to no-weight—to the Captain's veranda."

"Nonsense," said Joe. "What for?"

"Come along if you like, and see. All right, gang. Let's go."

Joe started to speak, stopped when Jim kept still. Joe-Jim followed along.

They floated gently through the door of the veranda, Hugh, Alan, Bobo with his still-passive burden—and Joe-Jim. "That's it," said Hugh to Alan, waving his hand at the splendid stars, "that's what I've been telling you about."

Alan looked and clutched at Hugh's arm. "Jordan!" he moaned. "We'll fall out!" He closed his eyes tightly.

Hugh shook him. "It's all right," he said. "It's grand. Open your eyes."

Joe-Jim touched Hugh's arm. "What's it all about?" he demanded. "Why did you bring *him* up here?" He pointed to Ertz.

"Oh—him. Well, when he wakes up I'm going to show him the stars, prove to him that the Ship moves."

"Well? What for?"

"Then I'll send him back down to convince some others."

"Hm-m-m—suppose he doesn't have any better luck than you had?"

"Why, then"—Hugh shrugged his shoulders—"why, then we shall just have to do it all over, I suppose, till we do convince them."

"We've got to do it, you know."

ELSEWHEN

Astounding Science Fiction, September 1941

as by Caleb Saunders

Excerpt from the *Evening* STANDARD:

SOUGHT SAVANT EVADES POLICE

———

CITY HALL SCANDAL LOOMS

———

Professor Arthur Frost, wanted for questioning in connection with the mysterious disappearance from his home of five of his students, escaped today from under the noses of a squad of police sent to arrest him. Police Sergeant Izowski claimed that Frost disappeared from the interior of the Black Maria under conditions which leave the police puzzled. District Attorney Karnes labeled Izowski's story as preposterous and promised the fullest possible investigation.

"BUT, CHIEF, I didn't leave him alone for a second!"

"Nuts!" answered the Chief of Police. "You claim you put Frost in the Wagon, stopped with one foot on the tailboard to write in your notebook, and when you looked up he was gone. D'yuh expect the Grand Jury to believe that? D'yuh expect *me* to believe that?"

"Honest, Chief," persisted Izowski, "I just stopped to write down—"

"Write down what?"

"Something he said. I said to him, 'Look, Doc, why don't you tell us where you hid 'em? You know we're bound to dig 'em up in time.' And he just gives me a funny faraway look, and says, 'Time—ah, time . . . yes, you could dig them up, in Time.' I thought it was an important admission and stops to write it down. But I was standing in the only door he could use to get out of the Wagon. You know, I ain't little; I kinda fill up a door."

"That's all you do," commented the Chief bitterly. "Izowski, you were either drunk, or crazy—or somebody got to you. The way you tell it, it's impossible!"

Izowski was honest, nor was he drunk, nor crazy.

Four days earlier Doctor Frost's class in speculative metaphysics had met as usual for their Friday evening seminar at the professor's home. Frost was saying, "And why not? Why shouldn't time be a fifth as well as a fourth dimension?"

Howard Jenkins, hard-headed engineering student, answered, "No harm in speculating, I suppose, but the question is meaningless."

"Why?" Frost's tones were deceptively mild.

"No question is meaningless," interrupted Helen Fisher.

"Oh, yeah? How high is up?"

"Let him answer," meditated Frost.

"I will," agreed Jenkins. "Human beings are constituted to perceive three spatial dimensions and one time dimension. Whether there are more of either is meaningless to us for there is no possible way for us to know—*ever*. Such speculation is a harmless waste of time."

"So?" said Frost. "Ever run across J. W. Dunne's theory of serial universe with serial time? And he's an engineer, like yourself. And don't forget Ouspensky. He regarded time as multi-dimensional."

"Just a second, Professor," put in Robert Monroe. "I've seen their writings—but I still think Jenkins offered a legitimate objection. How can the question mean anything to us if we aren't built to perceive more dimensions? It's like in mathematics—you can invent any mathematics you like, on any set of axioms, but unless it can be used to describe some sort of phenomena, it's just so much hot air."

"Fairly put," conceded Frost. "I'll give a fair answer. Scientific belief is based on observation, either one's own or that of a competent observer. I believe in a two-dimensional time because I have actually observed it."

The clock ticked on for several seconds.

Jenkins said, "But that is impossible, Professor. You aren't built to observe two time dimensions."

"Easy, there . . ." answered Frost. "I am built to perceive them *one at a time*—and so are you. I'll tell you about it, but before I do so, I must explain the theory of time I was forced to evolve in order to account for my experience. Most people think of time as a track that they run on from birth to death as inexorably as a train follows its rails—they feel instinctively that time follows a straight line, the past lying behind, the future lying in front. Now I have reason to believe—to know—that time is analogous to a surface rather than a line, and a rolling hilly surface at that. Think of this track we follow over the surface of time as a winding road cut through hills. Every little way the road branches and the branches follow side canyons. At these branches the crucial decisions of your life take place. You can turn right or left into entirely different futures. Occasionally there is a switchback where one can scramble up or down a bank and skip over a few thousand or million years—if you don't have your eyes so fixed on the road that you miss the short cut.

"Once in a while another road crosses yours. Neither its past nor its future has any connection whatsoever with the world we know. If you happened to take that turn you might find yourself on another planet in another space-time with nothing left of you or your world but the continuity of your ego.

"Or, if you have the necessary intellectual strength and courage, you may leave the roads, or paths of high probability, and strike out over the hills of possible time, cutting through the roads as you come to them, following them for a little way, even following them backwards, with the past *ahead* of you, and the future *behind* you. Or you might roam around the hilltops doing nothing but the extremely improbable. I can not imagine what that would be like—perhaps a bit like Alice-through-the-Looking-Glass.

"Now as to my evidence—When I was eighteen I had a decision to make. My father suffered financial reverses and I decided to quit college. Eventually I went into business for myself, and, to make a long story short, in nineteen-fifty-eight I was convicted of fraud and went to prison."

Martha Ross interrupted. "Nineteen-fifty-eight, Doctor? You mean forty-eight?"

"No, Miss Ross. I am speaking of events that did not take place on this time track."

"Oh!" She looked blank, then muttered, "With the Lord all things are possible."

"While in prison I had time to regret my mistakes. I realized that I had never been cut out for a business career, and I earnestly wished that I had stayed in school many years before. Prison has a peculiar effect on a man's mind. I drifted further and further away from reality, and lived more and more in an introspective world of my own. One night, in a way not then clear to me, my ego left my cell, went back along the time track, and I awoke in my room at my college fraternity house.

"This time I was wiser—Instead of leaving school, I found part-time work, graduated, continued as a graduate fellow, and eventually arrived where you now see me." He paused and glanced around.

"Doctor," asked young Monroe, "can you give us any idea as to how the stunt was done?"

"Yes, I can," Frost assented. "I worked on that problem for many years, trying to recapture the conditions. Recently I have succeeded and have made several excursions into possibility."

Up to this time the third woman, Estelle Martin, had made no comment, although she had listened with close attention. Now she leaned forward and spoke in an intense whisper.

"Tell us how, Professor Frost!"

"The means is simple. The key lies in convincing the subconscious mind that it can be done—"

"Then the Berkeleian idealism is proved!"

"In a way, Miss Martin. To one who believes in Bishop Berkeley's philosophy the infinite possibilities of two-dimensional time offer proof that the mind creates its own world, but a Spencerian determinist, such as good friend Howard Jenkins, would never leave the road of maximum probability. To him the world would be mechanistic and real. An orthodox free-will Christian, such as Miss Ross, would have her choice of several of the side roads, but would probably remain in a physical environment similar to Howard's.

"I have perfected a technique which will enable others to travel about in the pattern of times as I have done. I have the apparatus ready and any who wish can try it. That is the real reason why these Friday evening meetings have been held in my home—so that when the time came you all might try it, if you wished." He got up and went to a cabinet at the end of the room.

"You mean we could go tonight, Doctor?"

"Yes, indeed. The process is one of hypnotism and suggestion. Neither are necessary, but that is the quickest way of teaching the subconscious to break out of its groove and go where it pleases. I use a revolving ball to tire the conscious mind into hypnosis. During that period the subject listens to a recording which suggests the time-road to be followed, whereupon he does. It is as simple as that. Do any of you care to try it?"

"Is it likely to be dangerous, Doctor?"

He shrugged his shoulders. "The process isn't—just a deep sleep and a phonograph record. But the world of the time track you visit will be as real as the world of this time track. You are all over twenty-one. I am not urging you, I am merely offering you the opportunity."

Monroe stood up. "I'm going, Doctor."

"Good! Sit here and use these earphones. Anyone else?"

"Count me in." It was Helen Fisher.

Estelle Martin joined them. Howard Jenkins went hastily to her side. "Are you going to try this business?"

"Most certainly."

He turned to Frost. "I'm in, Doc."

Martha Ross finally joined the others. Frost seated them where they could wear the ear-phones and then asked,

"You will remember the different types of things you could do; branch off into a different world, skip over into the past or the future, or cut straight through the maze of probable tracks on a path of extreme improbability. I have records for all of those."

Monroe was first again. "I'll take a right angle turn and a brand new world."

Estelle did not hesitate. "I want to—How did you put it?—climb up a bank to a higher road somewhere in the future."

"I'll try that, too." It was Jenkins.

"I'll take the remote-possibilities track," put in Helen Fisher.

"That takes care of everybody but Miss Ross," commented the professor. "I'm afraid you will have to take a branch path in probability. Does that suit you?"

She nodded. "I was going to ask for it."

"That's fine. All of these records contain the suggestion for you to return to this room two hours from now, figured along this time track. Put on your ear-phones. The records run thirty minutes. I'll start them and the ball together."

He swung a glittering many-faceted sphere from a hook in the ceiling, started it whirling, and turned a small spotlight on it. Then he turned off the other lights, and started all the records by throwing a master switch. The scintillating ball twirled round and round, slowed and reversed and twirled back again. Doctor Frost turned his eyes away to keep from being fascinated by it. Presently he slipped out into the hall for a smoke. Half an hour passed and there came the single note of a gong. He hurried back and switched on the light.

Four of the five had disappeared.

The remaining figure was Howard Jenkins, who opened his eyes and blinked at the light. "Well, Doctor, I guess it didn't work."

The Doctor raised his eyebrows. "No? Look around you."

The younger man glanced about him. "Where are the others?"

"Where? Anywhere," replied Frost, with a shrug, "and any*when*."

Jenkins jerked off his ear-phones and jumped to his feet. "Doctor, *what have you done to Estelle?*"

Frost gently disengaged a hand from his sleeve. "I haven't done anything, Howard. She's out on another time track."

"But I meant to go with her!"

"And I tried to send you with her."

"But why didn't I go?"

"I can't say—probably the suggestion wasn't strong enough to overcome your skepticism. But don't be alarmed, son—We expect her back in a couple of hours, you know."

"Don't be alarmed!—that's easy to say. I didn't want her to try this damn fool stunt in the first place, but I knew I couldn't change her mind, so I wanted to go along to look out for her—she's so impractical! But see here, Doc—where are their bodies? I thought we would just stay here in the room in a trance."

"Apparently you didn't understand me. These other time tracks are real, as real as this one we are in. Their whole beings have gone off on other tracks, as if they had turned down a side street."

"But that's impossible—it contradicts the law of the conservation of energy!"

"You must recognize a fact when you see one—they are gone. Besides, it doesn't contradict the law; it simply extends it to include the total universe."

Jenkins rubbed a hand over his face. "I suppose so. But in that case, anything can happen to her—she could even be *killed* out there. And I can't do a damn thing about it. Oh, I wish we had never seen this damned seminar!"

The professor placed an arm around his shoulders. "Since you can't help her, why not calm down? Besides, you have no reason to believe that she is in any danger. Why borrow trouble? Let's go out to the kitchen and open a bottle of beer while we wait for them." He gently urged him toward the door.

After a couple of beers and a few cigarettes, Jenkins was somewhat calmed down. The professor made conversation.

"How did you happen to sign up for this course, Howard?"

"It was the only course I could take with Estelle."

"I thought so. I let you take it for reasons of my own. I knew you weren't interested in speculative philosophy, but I thought that your hard-headed materialism would hold down some of the loose thinking that is likely to go on in such a class. You've been a help to me. Take Helen Fisher for example. She is prone to reason brilliantly from insufficient data. You help to keep her down to earth."

"To be frank, Doctor Frost, I could never see the need for all this high-falutin discussion. I like facts."

"But you engineers are as bad as metaphysicians—you ignore any fact that you can't weigh in scales. If you can't bite it, it's not real. You believe in a mechanistic, deterministic universe, and ignore the facts of human consciousness, human will, and human freedom of choice—facts that you have directly experienced."

"But those things can be explained in terms of reflexes."

The professor spread his hands. "You sound just like Martha Ross—she can explain anything in terms of Bible-belt fundamentalism. Why don't both of you admit that there a few things you don't understand?" He paused and cocked his head. "Did you hear something?"

"I think I did."

"Let's check. It's early, but perhaps one of them is back."

They hurried to the study, where they were confronted by an incredible and awe-inspiring sight.

Floating in the air near the fireplace was a figure robed in white and shining with a soft mother-of-pearl radiance. While they stood hesitant at the door, the figure turned its face to them and they saw that it had the face of Martha Ross, cleansed and purified to an unhuman majesty. Then it spoke.

"Peace be unto you, my brothers." A wave of peace and lovingkindness flowed over them like a mother's blessing. The figure approached them, and they saw, curving from its shoulders, the long, white, sweeping wings of a classical angel. Frost cursed under his breath in a dispassionate monotone.

"Do not be afraid. I have come back, as you asked me to. To explain and to help you."

The Doctor found his voice. "Are you Martha Ross?"

"I answer to that name."

"What happened after you put on the ear-phones?"

"Nothing. I slept for a while. When I woke, I went home."

"Nothing else? How do you explain your appearance?"

"My appearance is what you earthly children expect of the Lord's Redeemed. In the course of time I served as a missionary in South America. There it was required of me that I give up my mortal life in the service of the Lord. And so I entered the Eternal City."

"You went to Heaven?"

"These many eons I have sat at the foot of the Golden Throne and sung hosannas to His name."

Jenkins interrupted them. "Tell me, Martha—or Saint Martha—*Where is Estelle?* Have you seen her?"

The figure turned slowly and faced him. "Fear not."

"But tell me where she is!"

"It is not needful."

"That's no help," he answered bitterly.

"I will help you. Listen to me; Love the Lord thy God with all thy heart, and Love thy neighbor as thyself. That is all you need to know."

Howard remained silent, at a loss for an answer, but unsatisfied. Presently the figure spoke again. "I must go. God's blessing on you." It flickered and was gone.

The professor touched the young man's arm. "Let's get some fresh air." He led Jenkins, mute and unresisting, out into the garden. They walked for some minutes in silence. Finally Howard asked a question,

"Did we see an angel in there?"

"I think so, Howard."

"But that's insane!"

"There are millions of people who wouldn't think so—unusual certainly, but not insane."

"But it's contrary to all modern beliefs—Heaven—Hell—a personal God—Resurrection. Everything I've believed in must be wrong, or I've gone screwy."

"Not necessarily—not even probably. I doubt very much if you will ever see Heaven or Hell. You'll follow a time track in accordance with your nature."

"But she seemed *real.*"

"She *was* real. I suspect that the conventional hereafter is real to any one who believes in it whole-heartedly, as Martha evidently did, but I expect you to follow a pattern in accordance with the beliefs of an agnostic—except in one respect; when you die, you won't die all over, no matter how intensely you may claim to expect to. *It is an emotional impossibility for any man to believe in his own death.* That sort of self-annihilation can't be done. You'll have a hereafter, but it will be one appropriate to a materialist."

But Howard was not listening. He pulled at his under lip and frowned. "Say, doc, why wouldn't Martha tell me what happened to Estelle? That was a dirty trick."

"I doubt if she knew, my boy. Martha followed a time track only slightly different from that we are in; Estelle chose to explore one far in the past, or in the distant future. For all practical purposes, each is non-existent to the other."

They heard a call from the house, a clear contralto voice, "Doctor! Doctor Frost!"

Jenkins whirled around. "That's Estelle!" They ran back into the house, the Doctor endeavoring manfully to keep up.

But it was not Estelle. Standing in the hallway was Helen Fisher, her sweater torn and dirty, her stockings missing, and a barely-healed scar puckering one cheek. Frost stopped and surveyed her. "Are you all right, child?" he demanded.

She grinned boyishly. "I'm okay. You should see the other guy."

"Tell us about it."

"In a minute. How about a cup of coffee for the prodigal? And I wouldn't turn up my nose at scrambled eggs and some—lots—of toast. Meals are inclined to be irregular where I've been."

"Yes, indeed. Right away," answered Frost, "but where *have* you been?"

"Let a gal eat, please," she begged. "I won't hold out on you. What is Howard looking so sour about?"

The professor whispered an explanation. She gave Jenkins a compassionate glance. "Oh, she hasn't? I thought I'd be the last man in; I was away so long. What day is this?"

Frost glanced at his wrist watch. "You're right on time; it's just eleven o'clock."

"The hell you say! Oh, excuse me, Doctor. 'Curiouser and curiouser, said Alice.' All in a couple of hours. Just for the record, I was gone several weeks at least."

When her third cup of coffee had washed down the last of the toast, she began:

"When I woke up I was falling upstairs—through a nightmare, several nightmares. Don't ask me to describe *that*—nobody could. That went on for a week, maybe, then things started to come into focus. I don't know in just what order things happened, but when I first started to notice clearly I was standing in a little barren valley. It was cold, and the air was thin and acrid. It burned my throat. There were two suns in the sky, one big and reddish, the other smaller and too bright to look at."

"Two suns!" exclaimed Howard. "That's not possible—binary stars don't have planets."

She looked at him. "Have it your own way—I was *there*. Just as I was taking this all in, something whizzed overhead and I ducked. That was the last I saw of *that* place.

"I slowed down next back on earth—at least it looked like it—and in a city. It was a big and complicated city. I was in trafficway with a lot of fast-moving traffic. I stepped out and tried to flag one of the vehicles—a long crawling caterpillar thing with about fifty wheels—when I caught sight of what was driving it and dodged back in a hurry. It wasn't a man and it wasn't an animal either—not one I've ever seen or heard of. It wasn't a bird, or a fish, nor an insect. The god that thought up the inhabitants of that city doesn't deserve worship. I don't know what they were, but they crawled and they crept and they *stank*. Ugh!"

"I slunk around holes in that place," she continued, "for a couple of weeks before I recovered the trick of jumping the time track. I was desperate, for I thought that the suggestion to return to now hadn't worked. I couldn't find much to eat and I was light-headed part of the time. I drank out of what I suspect was their drainage system, but there was nobody to ask and I didn't want to know. I was thirsty."

"Did you see any human beings?"

"I'm not sure. I saw some shapes that might have been men squatting in a circle down in the tunnels under the city, but something frightened them, and they scurried away before I could get close enough to look."

"What else happened there?"

"Nothing. I found the trick again that same night and got away from there as fast as I could. I am afraid I lost the scientific spirit, Professor—I didn't care how the other half lived.

"This time I had better luck. I was on earth again, but in pleasant rolling hills, like the Blue Ridge Mountains. It was summer, and very lovely. I found a little stream and took off my clothes and bathed. It was wonderful. After I had found some ripe berries, I lay down in the sun and went to sleep.

"I woke wide awake with a start. Someone was bending over me. It was a man, but no beauty. He was a Neanderthal. I should have run, but I tried to grab my clothes first, so he grabbed me. I was led back into camp, a Sabine woman, with my new spring sports outfit tucked fetchingly under one arm.

"I wasn't so bad off. It was the Old Man who had found me, and he seemed to regard me as a strange pet, about on a par with the dogs that snarled around the bone heap, rather than as a member of his harem. I fed well enough, if you aren't fussy—I wasn't fussy after living in the bowels of that awful city.

"The Neanderthal isn't a bad fellow at heart, rather good-natured, although inclined to play rough. That's how I got this." She fingered the scar on her cheek. "I had about decided to stay a while and study them, when one day I made a mistake. It was a chilly morning, and I put on my clothes for the first time since I had arrived. One of the young bucks saw me, and I guess it aroused his romantic nature. The Old Man was away at the time and there was no one to stop him.

"He grabbed me before I knew what was happening and tried to show his affection. Have you ever been nuzzled by a cave man, Howard? They have halitosis, not to mention B.O. I was too startled to concentrate on the time trick, or else I would have slipped right out into space-time and left him clutching air."

Doctor Frost was aghast. "Dear God, child! What did you do?"

"I finally showed him a jiu jitsu trick I learned in Phys. Ed. II, then I ran like hell and skinned up a tree. I counted up to a hundred and tried to be calm. Pretty soon I was shooting upstairs in a nightmare again and very happy to be doing it."

"Then you came back here?"

"Not by a whole lot—worse luck! I landed in this present all right, and apparently along this time dimension, but there was plenty that was wrong about it. I was standing on the south side of Forty-second street in New York. I knew where I was for the first thing I noticed was the big lighted letters that chase around the TIMES building and spell out news flashes. It was running backwards. I was trying to figure out 'DETROIT BEAT TO HITS NINE GET YANKEES' when I saw two cops close to me running as hard as they could—backwards, away from me." Doctor Frost smothered an ejaculation. "What did you say?"

"Reversed entropy—you entered the track backwards—your time arrow was pointing backwards."

"I figured that out, when I had time to think about it. Just then I was too busy. I was in a clearing in the crowd, but the ring of people was closing in on me, all running backwards. The cops disappeared in the crowd, and the crowd ran right up to me, stopped, and started to scream. Just as that happened, the traffic lights changed, cars charged out from both directions, driving backwards. It was too much for little Helen. I fainted.

"Following that I seemed to slant through a lot of places—"

"Just a second," Howard interrupted, "just what happened before that? I thought I savvied entropy, but that got me licked."

"Well," explained Frost, "The easiest way to explain it is to say that she was travelling backwards in time. Her future was their past, and vice versa. I'm glad she got out in a hurry. I'm not sure that human metabolism can be maintained in such conditions."

"Hmm—Go ahead, Helen."

"This slanting through the axes would have been startling, if I hadn't been emotionally exhausted. I sat back and watched it, like a movie. I think Salvador Dali wrote the script. I saw landscapes heave and shift like a stormy sea. People melted into plants—I think my own body changed at times, but I can't be sure. Once I found myself in a place that was all *insides,* instead of outsides. Some of the things we'll skip—I don't believe them myself.

"Then I slowed down in a place that must have had an extra spatial dimension. Everything looked three dimensional to me, but they changed their shapes when I *thought* about them. I found I could look inside solid objects simply by wanting to. When I tired of prying into the intimate secrets of rocks and plants, I took a look at myself, and it worked just as well. I know more about anatomy and physiology now than an M.D. It's fun to watch your heart beat—kind o'cute.

"But my appendix was swollen and inflamed. I found I could reach in and touch it—it was tender. I've had trouble with it so I decided to perform an emergency operation. I nipped it off with my nails. It didn't hurt at all, bled a couple of drops and closed right up."

"Good Heavens, child! You might have gotten peritonitis and died."

"I don't think so. I believe that ultra-violet was pouring all through me and killing the bugs. I had a fever for a while, but I think what caused it was a bad case of internal sunburn.

"I forgot to mention that I couldn't walk around in this place, for I couldn't seem to touch anything but myself. I sliced right through anything I tried to get a purchase on. Pretty soon I quit trying and relaxed. It was comfortable and I went into a warm happy dope, like a hibernating bear.

"After a long time—a long, long time, I went sound asleep and came to in your big easy-chair. That's all."

Helen answered Howard's anxious inquiries by telling him that she had seen nothing of Estelle. "But why don't you calm down and wait? She isn't really overdue."

They were interrupted by the opening of the door from the hallway. A short wiry figure in a hooded brown tunic and tight brown breeches strode into the room.

"Where's Doctor Frost? Oh—Doctor, I need help!"

It was Monroe, but changed almost beyond recognition. He had been short and slender before, but was now barely five feet tall, and stocky, with powerful shoulder muscles. The brown costume with its peaked hood, or helmet, gave him a strong resemblance to the popular notion of gnome.

Frost hurried to him. "What is it, Robert? How can I help?"

"This first." Monroe hunched forward for inspection of his left upper arm. The fabric was tattered and charred, exposing an ugly burn. "He just grazed me, but it had better be fixed, if I am to save the arm."

Frost examined it without touching it. "We must rush you to a hospital."

"No time. I've got to get back. They need me—and the help I can bring."

The Doctor shook his head. "You've got to have treatment, Bob. Even if there is strong need for you to go back wherever you have been, you are in a different time track now. Time lost here isn't necessarily lost there."

Monroe cut him short. "I think this world and my world have connected time rates. I must hurry."

Helen Fisher placed herself between them. "Let me see that arm, Bob. Hm—pretty nasty, but I think I can fix it. Professor, put a kettle on the fire with about a cup of water in it. As soon as it boils, chuck in a handful of tea leaves."

She rummaged through the kitchen cutlery drawer, found a pair of shears, and did a neat job of cutting away the sleeve and cleaning the burned flesh for dressing. Monroe talked as she worked.

"Howard, I want you to do me a favor. Get a pencil and paper and take down a list. I want a flock of things to take back—all of them things that you can pick up at the fraternity house. You'll have to go for me—I'd be thrown out with my present appearance—What's the matter? Don't you want to?"

Helen hurriedly explained Howard's preoccupation. He listened sympathetically. "Oh! Say, that's tough lines, old man." His brow wrinkled. "But look—You can't do Estelle any good by waiting here, and I really do need your help for the next half hour. Will you do it?"

Jenkins reluctantly agreed. Monroe continued,

"Fine! I do appreciate it. Go to my room first and gather up my reference books on math—also my slide rule. You'll find an India-paper radio manual, too. I want that. And I want your twenty-inch log-log duplex slide rule, as well. You can have my Rabelais and the *Droll Stories.* I want your *Marks' Mechanical Engineers' Handbook,* and any other technical reference books that you have and I haven't. Take anything you like in exchange.

"Then go up to Stinky Beanfield's room, and get his *Military Engineer's Handbook,* his *Chemical Warfare,* and his texts on ballistics and ordnance. Yes, and *Miller's Chemistry of Explosives,* if he has one. If not, pick up one from some other of the R.O.T.C. boys; it's important." Helen was deftly applying a poultice to his arm. He winced as the tea leaves, still warm, touched his seared flesh, but went ahead.

"Stinky keeps his service automatic in his upper bureau drawer. Swipe it, or talk him out of it. Bring as much ammunition as you can find—I'll write out a bill of sale for my car for you to leave for him. Now get going. I'll tell Doc all about it, and he can tell you later. Here. Take my car." He fumbled at his thigh, then looked annoyed. "Cripes! I don't have my keys."

Helen came to the rescue. "Take mine. The keys are in my bag on the hall table."

Howard got up. "OK, I'll do my damndest. If I get flung in the can, bring me cigarettes." He went out.

Helen put the finishing touches on the bandages. "There! I think that will do. How does it feel?"

He flexed his arm cautiously. "Okay. It's a neat job, kid. It takes the sting out."

"I believe it will heal if you keep tannin solution on it. Can you get tea leaves where you are going?"

"Yes, and tannic acid, too. I'll be all right. Now you deserve an explanation. Professor, do you have a cigaret on you? I could use some of that coffee, too."

"Surely, Robert." Frost hastened to serve him.

Monroe accepted a light and began.

"It's all pretty cock-eyed. When I came out of the sleep, I found myself, dressed as I am now and looking as I now look, marching down a long, deep fosse. I was one of a column of threes in a military detachment. The odd part about it is that I felt perfectly natural. I knew where I was and why I was there—and who I was. I don't mean Robert Monroe; my name over there is Igor." Monroe pronounced the gutteral deep in his throat and trilled the "r." "I hadn't forgotten Monroe; it was more as if I had suddenly remembered him. I had *one* identity and *two* pasts. It was something like waking up from a clearly remembered dream, only the dream was perfectly real. I *knew* Monroe was real, just as I knew Igor was real.

"My world is much like earth; a bit smaller, but much the same surface gravity. Men like myself are the dominant race, and we are about as civilized as you folks, but our culture has followed a difficult course. We live underground about half the time. Our homes are there and a lot of our industry. You see it's warm underground in our world, and not entirely dark. There is a mild radioactivity; it doesn't harm us.

"Nevertheless we are a surface-evolved race, and can't be healthy nor happy if we stay underground all the time. Now there is a war on and we've been driven underground for eight or nine months. The war is going against us. As it stands now, we have lost control of the surface and my race is being reduced to the status of hunted vermin.

"You see, we aren't fighting human beings. I don't know just what it is we are fighting—maybe beings from outer space. We don't know. They attacked us several places at once from great flying rings the like of which we had never seen. They burned us down without warning. Many of us escaped underground where they haven't followed us. They don't operate at night either—seem to need sunlight to be active. So it's a stalemate—or was until they started gassing our tunnels.

"We've never captured one and consequently don't know what makes them tick. We examined a ring that crashed, but didn't learn much. There was nothing inside that even vaguely resembled animal life, nor was there anything to support animal life. I mean there were no food supplies, nor sanitary arrangements. Opinion is divided between the idea that the one we examined was remotely controlled and the idea that the enemy are some sort of non-protoplasmic intelligence, perhaps force patterns, or something equally odd.

"Our principal weapon is a beam which creates a stasis in the ether, and freezes 'em solid. Or rather it should, but it will destroy all life and prevent molar action—but the rings are simply put temporarily out of control. Unless we can keep a beam on a ring right to the moment it crashes, it recovers and gets away. Then its pals come and burn out our position.

"We've had better luck with mining their surface camps, and blowing them up at night. We're accomplished sappers, of course. But we need better weapons. That's what I sent Howard after. I've got two ideas. If the enemy are simply some sort of intelligent force patterns, or something like that, radio may be the answer. We might be able to fill up the ether with static and jam them right out of existence. If they are too tough for that, perhaps some good old-fashioned anti-aircraft fire might make them say 'Uncle.' In any case there is a lot of technology here that we don't have, and which may have the answer. I wish I had time to pass on some of our stuff in return for what I'm taking with me."

"You are determined to go back, Robert?"

"Certainly. It's where I belong. I've no family here. I don't know how to make you see it, Doc, but those are my people—that is my world. I suppose if conditions were reversed, I'd feel differently."

"I see," said Helen, "you're fighting for the wife and kids."

He turned a weary face toward her. "Not exactly. I'm a bachelor over there, but I do have a family to think about; my sister is in command of the attack unit I'm in. Oh, yes, the women are in it—they're little and tough, like you, Helen."

She touched his arm lightly. "How did you pick up this?"

"That burn? You remember we were on the march. We were retreating down that ditch from a surface raid. I thought we had made good our escape when all of a sudden a ring swooped down on us. Most of the detachment scattered, but I'm a junior technician armed with the stasis ray. I tried to get my equipment unlimbered to fight back, but I was burned down before I could finish. Luckily it barely grazed me. Several of the others were fried. I don't know yet whether or not Sis got hers. That's one of the reasons why I'm in a hurry.

"One of the other techs who wasn't hit got his gear set up and covered our retreat. I was dragged underground and taken to a dressing station. The medicos were about to work on me when I passed out and came to in the Professor's study."

The doorbell rang and the Professor got up to answer it. Helen and Robert followed him. It was Howard, bearing spoils.

"Did you get everything?" Robert asked anxiously.

"I think so. Stinky was in, but I managed to borrow his books. The gun was harder, but I telephoned a friend of mine and had him call back and ask for Stinky. While he was out of the room, I lifted it. Now I'm a criminal—government property, too."

"You're a pal, Howard. After you hear the explanation, you'll agree that it was worth doing. Won't he, Helen?"

"Absolutely!"

"Well, I hope you're right," he answered dubiously. "I brought along something else, just in case. Here it is." He handed Robert a book.

"*Aerodynamics and Principles of Aircraft Construction,*" Robert read aloud. "My God, yes! Thanks, Howard."

In a few minutes, Monroe had his belongings assembled and fastened to his person. He had announced that he was ready when the Professor checked him:

"One moment, Robert. How do you know that these books will go with you?"

"Why not? That's why I'm fastening them to me."

"Did your earthly clothing go through the first time?"

"Noo—" His brow furrowed. "Good grief, Doc, what can I do? I couldn't possibly memorize what I need to know."

"I don't know, Son. Let's think about it a bit." He broke off and stared at the ceiling. Helen touched his hand.

"Perhaps I can help, Professor."

"In what way, Helen?"

"Apparently I don't metamorphize when I change time tracks. I had the same clothes with me everywhere I went. Why couldn't I ferry this stuff over for Bob?"

"Hm, perhaps you could."

"No, I couldn't let you do that," interposed Monroe. "You might get killed or badly hurt."

"I'll chance it."

"I've got an idea," put in Jenkins. "Couldn't Doctor Frost set his instructions so that Helen would go over and come right back? How about it, Doc?"

"Mmm, yes, perhaps." But Helen held up a hand.

"No good. The boodle might come bouncing back with me. I'll go over without any return instructions. I like the sound of this world of Bob's anyway. I may stay there. Cut out the chivalry, Bob. One of the things I liked about your world was the notion of treating men and women alike. Get unstuck from that stuff and start hanging it on me. I'm going."

She looked like a Christmas tree when the dozen-odd books had been tied to various parts of her solid little figure, the automatic pistol strapped on, and the two slide rules, one long and one short, stuck in the pistol belt.

Howard fondled the large slide rule before he fastened it on. "Take good care of this slipstick, Bob," he said, "I gave up smoking for six months to pay for it."

Frost seated the two side by side on the sofa in the study. Helen slipped a hand into Bob's. When the shining ball had been made to spin, Frost motioned for Jenkins to leave, closed the door after him and switched out the light. Then he started repeating hypnotic suggestions in a monotone.

Ten minutes later he felt a slight swish of air and ceased. He snapped the light switch. The sofa was empty, even of books.

Frost and Jenkins kept an uneasy vigil while awaiting Estelle's return. Jenkins wandered nervously around the study, examining objects that didn't interest him and smoking countless cigarets. The Professor sat quietly in his easy chair, simulating a freedom from anxiety that he did not feel. They conversed in desultory fashion.

"One thing I don't see," observed Jenkins, "is why in the world Helen could go a dozen places and not change, and Bob goes just one place and comes back almost unrecognizable—shorter, heavier, decked out in outlandish clothes. What happened to his ordinary clothes anyhow? How do you explain those things, Professor?"

"Eh? I don't explain them—I merely observe them. I think perhaps he changed, while Helen didn't, because Helen was just a visitor to the places she went to, whereas Monroe belonged over there—as witness he fitted into the pattern of that world. Perhaps the Great Architect intended for him to cross over."

"Huh? Good heavens, Doctor, surely you don't believe in divine predestination!"

"Perhaps not in those terms. But, Howard, you mechanistic skeptics make me tired. Your naive ability to believe that things 'jest growed' approaches childishness. According to you a fortuitous accident of entropy produced Beethoven's Ninth Symphony."

"I think that's unfair, Doctor. You certainly don't expect a man to believe in things that run contrary to his good sense without offering him any reasonable explanation."

Frost snorted. "I certainly do—if he has observed it with his own eyes and ears, or gets it from a source known to be credible. A fact doesn't have to be understood to be true. Sure, any reasonable mind wants explanations, but it's silly to reject facts that don't fit your philosophy.

"Now these events tonight, which you are so anxious to rationalize in orthodox terms, furnish a clue to a lot of things that scientists have been rejecting because they couldn't explain them. Have you ever heard the tale of the man who walked around the horses? No? Around 1810 Benjamin Bathurst, British Ambassador to Austria, arrived in his carriage at an inn in Perleberg, Germany. He had his valet and secretary with him. They drove into the lighted courtyard of the inn. Bathurst got out, and, in the presence of bystanders and his two attaches, walked around the horses. He hasn't been seen since."

"What happened?"

"Nobody knows. I think he was preoccupied and inadvertently wandered into another time track. But there are literally hundreds of similar cases, way too many to laugh off. The two-time-dimensions theory accounts for most of them. But I suspect that there are other as-yet-undreamed-of natural principles operating in some of the rejected cases."

Howard stopped pacing and pulled at his lower lip. "Maybe so, Doctor. I'm too upset to think. Look here—it's one o'clock. Oughtn't she to be back by now?"

"I'm afraid so, Son."

"You mean she's not coming back."

"It doesn't look like it."

The younger man gave a broken cry and collapsed on the sofa. His shoulders heaved. Presently he calmed down a little. Frost saw his lips move and suspected that he was praying. Then he showed a drawn face to the Doctor.

"Isn't there *anything* we can do?"

"That's hard to answer, Howard. We don't know where she's gone; all we do know is that she left here under hypnotic suggestion to cross over into some other loop of the past or future."

"Can't we go after her the same way and trace her?"

"I don't know. I haven't had any experience with such a job."

"I've got to do something or I'll go nuts."

"Take it easy, son. Let me think about it." He smoked in silence while Howard controlled an impulse to scream, break furniture, anything!

Frost knocked the ash off his cigar and placed it carefully in a tray. "I can think of one chance. It's a remote one."

"Anything!"

"I'm going to listen to the record that Estelle heard, and cross over.

I'll do it wide awake, while concentrating on her. Perhaps I can establish some rapport, some extra-sensory connection, that will serve to guide me to her." Frost went immediately about his preparations as he spoke. "I want you to remain in the room when I go so that you will really believe that it can be done."

In silence Howard watched him don the head-phones. The Professor stood still, eyes closed. He remained so for nearly fifteen minutes, then took a short step forward. The ear-phones clattered to the floor. He was gone.

Frost felt himself drift off into the timeless limbo which precedes transition. He noticed again that it was exactly like the floating sensation that ushers in normal sleep, and wondered idly, for the hundredth time, whether or not the dreams of sleep were real experiences. He was inclined to think they were. Then he recalled his mission with a guilty start, and concentrated hard on Estelle.

He was walking along a road, white in the sunshine. Before him were the gates of a city. The gateman stared at his odd attire, but let him pass. He hurried down the broad tree-lined avenue which (he knew) led from the space port to Capitol Hill. He turned aside into the Way of the Gods and continued until he reached the Grove of the Priestesses. There he found the house which he sought, its marble walls pink in the sun, its fountains tinkling in the morning breeze. He turned in.

The ancient janitor, nodding in the sun, admitted him to the house. The slender maidservant, barely nubile, ushered him into the inner chamber, where her mistress raised herself on one elbow and regarded her visitor through languid eyes. Frost addressed her,

"It is time to return, Estelle."

Her eyesbrows showed her surprise. "You speak a strange and barbarous tongue, old man, and yet, here is a mystery, for I know it. What do you wish of me?"

Frost spoke impatiently. "Estelle, I say it is time to return!"

"Return? What idle talk is this? Return where? And my name is Star-Light, not Ess Tell. Who are you, and from where do you come?" She searched his face, then pointed a slender finger at him. "I know you now! You are out of my dreams. You were a Master and instructed me in the ancient wisdom."

"Estelle, do you remember a youth in those dreams?"

"That odd name again! Yes, there was a youth. He was sweet—sweet and straight and tall like pine on the mountain. I have dreamed of him often." She swung about with a flash of long white limbs. "What of this youth?"

"He waits for you. It is time to return."

"Return!—There is no return to the place of dreams!"

"I can lead you there."

"What blasphemy is this? Are you a priest, that you should practice magic? Why should a sacred courtesan go to the place of dreams?"

"There is no magic in it. He is heartsick at your loss. I will lead you back to him."

She hesitated, doubt in her eyes, then she replied, "Suppose you could; why should I leave my honorable sacred station for the cold nothingness of that dream?"

He answered her gently, "What does your heart tell you, Estelle?"

She stared at him, eyes wide, and seemed about to burst into tears. Then she flung herself across the couch, and showed him her back. A muffled voice answered him,

"Be off with you! There is no youth, except in my dreams. I'll seek him there!"

She made no further reply to his importunities. Presently he ceased trying and left with a heavy heart.

Howard seized him by the arm as he returned. "Well, Professor? Well? Did you find her?"

Frost dropped wearily into his chair. "Yes, I found her."

"Was she all right? Why didn't she come back with you?"

"She was perfectly well, but I couldn't persuade her to return."

Howard looked as if he had been slapped across the mouth. "Didn't you tell her I wanted her to come back?"

"I did, but she didn't believe me."

"Not believe you?"

"You see she's forgotten most of this life, Howard. She thinks you are simply a dream."

"But that's not possible!"

Frost looked more weary than ever. "Don't you think it is about time you stopped using that term, son?"

Instead of replying he answered, "Doctor, you must take me to her!" Frost looked dubious.

"Can't you do it?"

"Perhaps I could, if you have gotten over your disbelief, but still—"

"Disbelief!—I've been forced to believe. Let's get busy."

Frost did not move. "I'm not sure that I agree. Howard, conditions are quite different where Estelle has gone. It suits her, but I'm not sure that it would be a kindness to take you through to her."

"Why not? Doesn't she want to see me?"

"Yes—I think she does. I'm sure she would welcome you, but conditions are very different."

"I don't give a damn what the conditions are. Let's go."

Frost got up. "Very well. It shall be as you wish."

He seated Jenkins in the easy cair and held the young man's eyes with his gaze. He spoke slowly in calm, unmodulated tones.

Frost assisted Howard to his feet and brushed him off. Howard laughed and wiped the white dust of the road from his hands.

"Quite a tumble, Master. I feel as if some lout had pulled a stool from under me."

"I shouldn't have had you sit down."

"I guess not." He pulled a large multi-flanged pistol from his belt and examined it. "Lucky the safety catch was set on my blaster or we might have been picking ourselves out of the stratosphere. Shall we be on our way?"

Frost looked his companion over; helmet, short military kilt, short sword and accoutrements slapping at his thighs. He blinked and answered, "Yes. Yes, of course."

As they swung into the city gates, Frost inquired, "Do you know where you are headed?"

"Yes, certaintly. To Star-Light's villa in the Grove."

"And you know what to expect there?"

"Oh, you mean our discussion. I know the customs here, Master and am quite undismayed, I assure you. Star-Light and I understand each other. She's one of these 'Out of sight, out of mind' girls. Now that I'm back from Ultima Thule, she'll give up the priesthood and we'll settle down and raise a lot of fat babies."

"Ultima Thule? Do you remember my study?"

"Of course I do—and Robert and Helen and all the rest."

"Is that what you meant by Ultima Thule?"

"Not exactly. I can't explain it, Master. I'm a practical military man. I'll leave such things to you priests and teachers."

They paused in front of Estelle's house. "Coming in, Master?"

"No, I think not. I must be getting back."

"You know best." Howard clapped him on the shoulder. "You have been a true friend, Master. Our first brat shall be named for you."

"Thank you, Howard. Good-bye, and good luck to both of you."

"And to you." He entered the house with a confident stride.

Frost walked slowly back toward the gates, his mind preoccupied with myriad thoughts. There seemed to be no end to the permutations and combinations; either of matter, or of mind. Martha, Robert, Helen—now Howard and Estelle. It should be possible to derive a theory that would cover them all.

As he mused, his heel caught on a loose paving block and he stumbled across his easy chair.

The absence of the five students was going to be hard to explain, Frost knew—so he said nothing to anyone. The weekend passed before anyone took the absences seriously. On Monday a policeman came to his house, asking questions.

His answers were not illuminating, for he had reasonably refrained from trying to tell the true story. The District Attorney smelled a serious crime, kidnapping or perhaps a mass murder. Or maybe one of these love cults—you can never tell about these professors!

He caused a warrant to be issued Tuesday morning; Sergeant Izowski was sent to pick him up.

The professor came quietly and entered the black wagon without protest. "Look, Doc," said the sergeant, encouraged by his docile manner, "why don't you tell us where you hid 'em? You know we're bound to dig them up in time."

Frost turned, looked him in the eyes, and smiled, "Time," he said softly, "ah, time . . . yes, you could dig them up, in Time." He then got into the wagon and sat down quietly, closed his eyes, and placed his mind in the necessary calm receptive condition.

The sergeant placed one foot on the tailboard, braced his bulk in the only door, and drew out his notebook. When he finished writing he looked up.

Professor Frost was gone.

Frost had intended to look up Howard and Estelle. Inadvertently he let his mind dwell on Helen and Robert at the crucial moment. When he "landed" it was not in the world of the future he had visited twice before. He did not know where he was—on earth apparently, somewhere and some*when*.

It was wooded rolling country, like the hills of southern Missouri, or New Jersey. Frost had not sufficient knowledge of botany to be able to tell whether the species of trees he saw around him were familiar or not. But he was given no time to study the matter.

He heard a shout, an answering shout. Human figures came bursting out of the trees in a ragged line. He thought that they were attacking him, looked wildly around for shelter, and found none. But they kept on past him, ignoring him, except that the one who passed closest to him glanced at him hastily, and shouted something. Then he, too, was gone.

Frost was left standing, bewildered, in the small natural clearing in which he had landed.

Before he had had time to integrate these events one of the fleeing figures reappeared and yelled to him, accompanying the words with a gesture unmistakable—he was to come along.

Frost hesitated. The figure ran toward and hit him with a clean tackle. The next few seconds were very confused, but he pulled himself together sufficiently to realize that he was seeing the world upside down; the stranger was carrying him at a strong dogtrot, thrown over one shoulder.

Bushes whipped at his face, then the way led downward for several yards, and he was dumped casually to the ground. He sat up and rubbed himself.

He found himself in a tunnel which ran upwards to daylight and downward the Lord knew where. Figures milled around him but ignored him. Two of them were setting up some apparatus between the group and the mouth of the tunnel. They worked with extreme urgency, completing what they were doing in seconds, and stepped back. Frost heard a soft gentle hum.

The mouth of the tunnel became slightly cloudy. He soon saw why—the apparatus was spinning a web from wall to wall, blocking the exit. The web became less tenuous, translucent, opaque. The hum persisted for minutes thereafter and the strange machine continued to weave and thicken the web. One of the figures glanced at its belt, spoke one word in the tone of command, and the humming ceased.

Frost could feel relief spread over the group like a warm glow. He felt it himself and relaxed, knowing intuitively that some acute danger had been averted.

The member of the group who had given the order to shut off the machine turned around, happened to see Frost, and approached him, asking some questions in a sweet but peremptory soprano. Frost was suddenly aware of three things; the leader was a woman, it was the leader who had rescued him, and the costume and general appearance of these people *matched that of the transformed Robert Monroe.*

A smile spread over his face. Everything was going to be all right!

The question was repeated with marked impatience. Frost felt that an answer was required, though he did not understand the language and was sure that she could not possibly know English. Nevertheless—

"Madame," he said in English, getting to his feet and giving her a courtly bow, "I do not know your language and do not understand your question, but I suspect that you have saved my life. I am grateful."

She seemed puzzled and somewhat annoyed, and demanded something else—at least Frost though it was a different question; he could not be sure. This was getting nowhere. The language difficulty was almost insuperable, he realized. It might take days, weeks, months to overcome it. In the meantime these people were busy with a war, and would be in no frame of mind to bother with a useless incoherent stranger.

He did not want to be turned out on the surface.

How annoying, he thought, how stupidly annoying! Probably Monroe and Helen were somewhere around, but he could die of old age and never find them. They might be anywhere on the planet. How would an American, dumped down in Tibet, make himself understood if his only possible interpreter were in South America? Or whereabouts unknown? How would he make the Tibetans understand that there even was an interpreter? Botheration!

Still, he must make a try. What was it Monroe had said his name was *here*? Egan—no, Igor. That was it—Igor.

"Igor," he said.

The leader cocked her head. "Igor?" she said.

Frost nodded vigorously. "Igor."

She turned and called out, "Igor!" giving it the marked guttural, the liquid "r" that Monroe had given it. A man came forward. The professor looked eagerly at him, but he was a stranger, like the rest. The leader pointed to the man and stated, "Igor."

This is growing complicated, though Frost, apparently Igor is a common name here—too common. Then he had a sudden idea:

If Monroe and Helen got through, their badly-needed chattels might have made them prominent. "Igor," he said, "Helen Fisher."

The leader was attentive at once, her face alive. "Elen Feesher?" she repeated.

"Yes, yes—Helen Fisher."

She stood quiet, thinking. It was plain that the words meant something to her. She clapped her hands together and spoke, commandingly. Two men stepped forward. She addressed them rapidly for several moments.

The two men stepped up to Frost, each taking an arm. They started to lead him away. Frost held back for a moment and said over his shoulder, "Helen Fisher?"

"'Elen Feesher'!" the leader assured him. He had to be content with that.

❖

Two hours passed, more or less. He had not been mistreated and the room in which they had placed him was comfortable but it was a cell—at least the door was fastened. Perhaps he had said the wrong thing, perhaps those syllables meant something quite different here from a simple proper name.

The room in which he found himself was bare and lighted only by a dim glow from the walls, as had all of this underground world which he had seen so far. He was growing tired of the place and was wondering whether or not it would do any good to set up a commotion when he heard someone at the door.

The door slid back; he saw the leader, a smile on her rather grim, middle-aged features. She spoke in her own tongue, then added, "Igor . . . Ellenfeesher."

He followed her.

Glowing passageways, busy squares where he was subjected to curious stares, an elevator which startled him by dropping suddenly when he was not aware that it *was* an elevator, and finally a capsule-like vehicle in which they were sealed airtight and which went somewhere very fast indeed to judge by the sudden surge of weight when it started and again when it stopped—through them all he followed his guide, not understanding and lacking means of inquiring. He tried to relax and enjoy the passing moment, as his companion seemed to bear him no ill-will, though her manner was brusque—that of a person accustomed to giving orders and not in the habit of encouraging casual intimacy.

They arrived at a door which she opened and strode in. Frost followed and was almost knocked off his feet by a figure which charged into him and grasped him with both arms. "Doctor! Doctor Frost!"

It was Helen Fisher, dressed in the costume worn by both sexes here. Behind her stood Robert—or Igor, his gnome-like face widened with a grin.

He detached Helen's arms gently. "My dear," he said inanely, "imagine finding you here."

"Imagine finding *you* here," she retorted. "Why, professor—you're crying!"

"Oh, no, not at all," he said hastily, and turned to Monroe. "It's good to see you, too, Robert."

"That goes double for me, Doc," Monroe agreed.

The leader said something to Monroe. He answered her rapidly in their tongue and turned to Frost. "Doctor, this is my elder sister, Margri, Actoon Margri—Major Margri, you might translate it roughly."

"She has been very kind to me," said Frost, and bowed to her, acknowledging the introduction. Margri clapped her hands smartly together at the waist and ducked her head, features impassive.

"She gave the salute of equals," explained Robert-Igor. "I translated the title doctor as best I could which causes her to assume that your rank is the same as hers."

"What should I do?"

"Return it."

Frost did so, but awkwardly.

Doctor Frost brought his erstwhile students up to "date"—using a term which does not apply, since they were on a different time axis. His predicament with the civil authorities brought a cry of dismay from Helen. "Why, you poor thing! How awful of them!"

"Oh, I wouldn't say so," protested Frost. "It was reasonable so far as they knew. But I'm afraid I can't go back."

"You don't need to," Igor assured him. "You're more than welcome here."

"Perhaps I can help out in your war."

"Perhaps—but you've already done more than anyone here by what you've enabled me to do. We are working on it now." He swung his arm in a gesture which took in the whole room.

Igor had been detached from combat duty and assigned to staff work, in order to make available earth techniques. Helen was helping. "Nobody believes my story but my sister," he admitted, "But I've been able to show them enough for them to realize that what I've got is important, so they've given me a free hand and are practically hanging over my shoulder, waiting to see what we can produce. I've already got them started on a jet fighter and attack rockets to arm it."

Frost expressed surprise. How could so much be done so fast? Were the time rates different? Had Helen and Igor crossed over many weeks before, figured along this axis?

No, he was told, but Igor's countrymen, though lacking many earth techniques, were far ahead of earth in manufacturing skill. They used a single general type of machine to manufacture almost anything. They fed into it a plan which Igor called for want of a better term the blueprints—it was in fact, a careful scale model of the device to be manufactured; the machine retooled itself and produced the artifact. One of them was, at that moment, moulding the bodies of fighting planes out of plastic, all in one piece and in one operation.

"We are going to arm these jobs with both the stasis ray and rockets," said Igor. "Freeze 'em and then shoot the damn things down while they are out of control."

They talked a few minutes, but Frost could see that Igor was getting fidgety. He guessed the reason, and asked to be excused. Igor seized on the suggestion. "We will see you a little later," he said with relief. "I'll have some one dig up quarters for you. We *are* pretty rushed. War work—I know you'll understand."

Frost fell asleep that night planning how he could help his two young friends, and their friends, in their struggle.

But it did not work out that way. His education had been academic rather than practical; he discovered that the reference books which Igor and Helen had brought along were so much Greek to him—worse, for he understood Greek. He was accorded all honor and a comfortable living because of Igor's affirmation that he had been the indispensable agent whereby this planet had received the invaluable new weapons, but he soon realized that for the job at hand he was useless, not even fit to act as an interpreter.

He was a harmless nuisance, a pensioner—and he knew it.

And underground life got on his nerves. The everpresent light bothered him. He had an unreasoned fear of radioactivity, born of ignorance, and Igor's reassurances did not stifle the fear. The war depressed him. He was not temperamentally cut out to stand up under the nervous tension of war. His helplessness to aid in the war effort, his lack of companionship, and his idleness all worked to increase the malaise.

He wandered into Igor and Helen's workroom one day, hoping for a moment's chat, if they were not too busy. They were not. Igor was pacing up and down, Helen followed them with worried eyes.

He cleared his throat. "Uh—I say, something the matter?"

Igor nodded, answered, "Quite a lot," and dropped back into his preoccupation.

"It's like this," said Helen. "In spite of the new weapons, things are still going against us. Igor is trying to figure out what to try next."

"Oh, I see. Sorry." He started to leave.

"Don't go. Sit down." He did so, and started mulling the matter over in his mind. It was annoying, very annoying!

"I'm afraid I'm not much use to you," he said at last to Helen. "Too bad Howard Jenkins isn't here."

"I don't suppose it matters," she answered. "We have the cream of modern earth engineering in these books."

"I don't mean that. I mean Howard himself, as he is where he's gone. They had a little gadget there in the future called a blaster. I gathered that it was a very powerful weapon indeed."

Igor caught some of this and whirled around. "What was it? How did it work?"

"Why, really," said Frost, "I can't say. I'm not up on such things, you know. I gathered that it was sort of a disintegrating ray."

"Can you sketch it? Think, man, think!"

Frost tried. Presently he stopped and said, "I'm afraid this isn't any good. I don't remember clearly and anyhow I don't know anything about the inside of it."

Igor sighed, sat down, and ran his hand through his hair.

After some minutes of gloomy silence, Helen said, "Couldn't we go get it?"

"Eh? How's that? How would you find him?"

"Could you find him, Professor?"

Frost sat up. "I don't know," he said slowly, "—but I'll try!"

There was the city. Yes, and there was the same gate he had passed through once before. He hurried on.

Star Light was glad to see him, but not particularly surprised. Frost wondered if anything could surprise this dreamy girl. But Howard more than made up for her lack of enthusiasm. He pounded Frost's back hard enough to cause pleurisy. "Welcome home, Master! Welcome home! I didn't know whether or not you would ever come, but we are ready for you. I had a room built for you and you alone, in case you ever showed up. What do you think of that? You are to live with us, you know. No sense in ever going back to that grubby school."

Frost thanked him, but added, "I came on business. I need your help, urgently."

"You do? Well, tell me, man, tell me!"

Frost explained. "So you see, I've got to take the secret of your blaster back to them. They need it. They must have it."

"And they shall have it," agreed Howard.

Some time later the problem looked more complicated. Try as he would Frost was simply not able to soak up the technical knowledge necessary to be able to take the secret back. The pedagogical problem presented was as great as if an untutored savage were to be asked to comprehend radio engineering sufficiently to explain to engineers unfamiliar with radio how to build a major station. And Frost was by no means sure that he could take a blaster with him through the country of Time.

172

"Well," said Howard at last, "I shall simply have to go with you."

Star-Light, who had listened quietly, showed her first acute interest. "Darling! You must not—"

"Stop it," said Howard, his chin set stubbornly. "This is a matter of obligation and duty. You keep out of it."

Frost felt the acute embarrassment one always feels when forced to overhear a husband and wife having a difference of opinion.

When they were ready, Frost took Howard by the wrist. "Look me in the eyes," he said. "You remember how we did it before?"

Howard was trembling. "I remember. Master, do you think you can do it—and not lose me?"

"I hope so," said Frost, "now relax."

They got back to the chamber from which Frost had started, a circumstance which Frost greeted with relief. It would have been awkward to have to cross half a planet to find his friends. He was not sure yet just how the spatial dimensions fitted into the time dimensions. Someday he would have to study the matter, work out an hypothesis and try to check it.

Igor and Howard wasted little time on social amenities. They were deep into engineering matters before Helen had finished greeting the professor.

At long last—"There," said Howard, "I guess that covers everything. I'll leave my blaster for a model. Any more questions?"

"No," said Igor, "I understand it, and I've got every word you've said recorded. I wonder if you know what this means to us, old man? It unquestionably will win the war for us."

"I can guess," said Howard. "This little gadget is the mainstay of our systemwide pax. Ready, Doctor. I'm getting kinda anxious."

"But you're not going, Doctor?" cried Helen. It was both a question and a protest.

"I've got to guide him back," said Frost.

"Yes," Howard confirmed, "but he is staying to live with us. Aren't you, Master?"

"Oh, no!" It was Helen again.

Igor put an arm around her. "Don't coax him," he told her. "You know he has not been happy here. I gather that Howard's home would suit him better. If so, he's earned it."

Helen thought about it, then came up to Frost, placed both hands on his shoulders, and kissed him, standing on tiptoe to do so. "Goodbye, Doc," she said in a choky voice, "or anyhow, *au revoir!*"

He reached up and patted one of her hands.

Frost lay in the sun, letting the rays soak into his old bones. It was certainly pleasant here. He missed Helen and Igor a little, but he suspected that they did not really miss him. And life with Howard and Star-Light was more to his liking. Officially he was tutor to their children, if and when. Actually he was just as lazy and useless as he had always wanted to be, with time on his hands. Time . . . Time.

There was just one thing that he would liked to have known: What did Sergeant Izowski say when he looked up and saw that the police wagon was empty? Probably thought it was impossible.

It did not matter. He was too lazy and sleepy to care. Time enough for a little nap before lunch. Time enough . . .

Time.

COMMON SENSE

Astounding Science Fiction, October 1941

JOE, THE RIGHT hand head of Joe-Jim, addressed his words to Hugh Hoyland. "All right, smart boy, you've convinced the Chief Engineer—" He gestured toward Bill Ertz with the blade of his knife, then resumed picking Jim's teeth with it. "So what? Where does it get you?"

"I've explained that," Hugh Hoyland answered irritably. "We keep on, until every scientist in the Ship, from the Captain to the greenest probationer, *knows* that the Ship moves and believes that we can make it move. Then we'll finish the Trip, as Jordan willed. How many knives can you muster?" he added.

"Well, for the love o' Jordan! Listen—have you got some fool idea that we are going to *help* you with this crazy scheme?"

"Naturally. You're necessary to it."

"Then you had better think up another think. That's out. Bobo! Get out the checkerboard."

"O.K., Boss." The microcephalic dwarf hunched himself up off the floor plates and trotted across Joe-Jim's apartment.

"Hold it, Bobo." Jim, the left-hand head, had spoken. The dwarf stopped dead, his narrow forehead wrinkled. The fact that his two-headed master occasionally failed to agree as to what Bobo should do was the only note of insecurity in his tranquil bloodthirsty existence.

"Let's hear what he has to say," Jim continued. "There may be some fun in this."

"Fun! The fun of getting a knife in your ribs. Let me point out that they are my ribs, too. I don't agree to it."

"I didn't ask you to agree; I asked you to listen. Leaving fun out of it, it may be the only way to keep a knife out of our ribs."

"What do you mean?" Joe demanded suspiciously.

"You heard what Ertz had to say." Jim flicked a thumb toward the prisoner. "The Ship's officers are planning to clean out the upper levels. How would you like to go into the Converter, Joe? You can't play checkers after we're broken down into hydrogen."

"Bunk! The Crew can't exterminate the muties—they've tried before."

Jim turned to Etrz. "How about it?"

Ertz answered somewhat diffidently, being acutely aware of his own changed status from a senior Ship's officer to prisoner of war. He felt befuddled anyhow; too much had happened and too fast. He had been kidnaped, hauled up to the Captain's veranda, and had there gazed out at the stars—the *stars*.

His hard-boiled rationalism included no such concept. If an Earth astronomer had had it physically demonstrated to him that the globe spun on its axis because someone turned a crank, the upset in evaluations could have been no greater.

Besides that, he was acutely aware that his own continued existence hung in fine balance. Joe-Jim was the first upper-level mutie he had ever met other than in combat, knife to knife. A word from him to that great ugly dwarf sprawled on the deck—

He chose his words. "I think the Crew would be successful, this time. We . . . they have organized for it. Unless there are more of you than we think there are and better organized, I think it could be done. You see . . . well, uh, I organized it."

"You?"

"Yes. A good many of the Council don't like the policy of letting the muties alone. Maybe it's sound religious doctrine and maybe it isn't, but we lose a child here and a couple of pigs there. It's annoying."

"What do you expect muties to eat?" demanded Jim belligerently. "Thin air?"

"No, not exactly. Anyhow, the new policy was not entirely destructive. Any muties that surrendered and could be civilized we planned to give to masters and put them to work as part of the Crew. That is, any that weren't, uh . . . that were—" He broke off in embarrassment, and shifted his eyes from the two-headed monstrosity before him.

"You mean any that weren't physical mutations, like me," Joe filled in nastily. "Don't you?" he persisted. "For the likes of me it's the Converter, isn't it?" He slapped the blade of his knife nervously on the palm of his hand.

Ertz edged away, his own hand shifting to his belt. But no knife was slung there; he felt naked and helpless without it. "Just a minute," he said defensively, "you asked me; that's the situation. It's out of my hands. I'm just telling you."

"Let him alone, Joe. He's just handing you the straight dope. It's like I was telling you—either go along with Hugh's plan, or wait to be hunted down. And don't get any ideas about killing him—we're going to need him." As Jim spoke he attempted to return the knife to its sheath. There was a brief and silent struggle between the twins for control of the motor nerves to their right arm, a clash of will below the level of physical activity. Joe gave in.

"All right," he agreed surlily, "but if I go to the Converter, I want to take this one with me for company."

"Stow it," said Jim. "You'll have me for company."

"Why do you believe him?"

"He has nothing to gain by lying. Ask Alan."

Alan Mahoney, Hugh's friend and boyhood chum, had listened to the argument round-eyed, without joining it. He, too, had suffered the nerve-shaking experience of viewing the outer stars, but his ignorant peasant mind had not the sharply formulated opinions of Ertz, the Chief Engineer. Ertz had been able to see almost at once that the very existence of a world outside the Ship changed all his plans and everything he had believed in; Alan was capable only of wonder.

"What about this plan to fight the muties, Alan?"

"Huh? Why, I don't know anything about it. Shucks, I'm not a scientist. Say, wait a minute—there was a junior officer sent in to help our village scientist, Lieutenant Nelson—" He stopped and looked puzzled.

"What about it? Go ahead."

"Well, he has been organizing the cadets in our village, and the married men, too, but not so much. Making 'em practice with their blades and slings. Never told us what for, though."

Ertz spread his hands. "You see?"

Joe nodded. "I see," he admitted grimly.

Hugh Hoyland looked at him eagerly. "Then you're with me?"

"I suppose so," Joe admitted. "Right!" added Jim.

Hoyland looked back to Ertz. "How about you, Bill Ertz?"

"What choice have I got?"

"Plenty. I want you with me wholeheartedly. Here's the layout: The Crew doesn't count; it's the officers we have to convince. Any that aren't too addlepated and stiff-necked to understand after they've seen the stars and the Control Room, we keep. The others"—he drew a thumb across his throat while making a harsh sibilance in his cheek—"the Converter."

Bobo grinned happily and imitated the gesture and the sound.

Ertz nodded. "Then what?"

"Muties and Crew together, under a new Captain, we move the Ship to Far Centaurus! Jordan's Will be done!"

Ertz stood up and faced Hoyland. It was a heady notion, too big to be grasped at once, but, by Jordan! he liked it. He spread his hands on the table and leaned across it. "I'm with you, Hugh Hoyland!"

A knife clattered on the table before him, one from the brace at Joe-Jim's belt. Joe looked startled, seemed about to speak to his brother, then appeared to think better of it. Ertz looked his thanks and stuck the knife in his belt.

The twins whispered to each other for a moment, then Joe spoke up. "Might as well make it stick," he said. He drew his remaining knife and, grasping the blade between thumb and forefinger so that only the point was exposed, he jabbed himself in the fleshly upper part of his left arm. "Blade for blade!"

Ertz's eyebrows shot up. He whipped out his newly acquired blade and cut himself in the same location. The blood spurted and ran down to the crook of his arm. "Back to back!" He shoved the table aside and pressed his gory shoulder against the wound on Joe-Jim.

Alan Mahoney, Hugh Hoyland, Bobo—all had their blades out, all nicked their arms till the skin ran red and wet. They crowded in, bleeding shoulders pushed together so that the blood dripped united to the deck.

"Blade for blade!"

"Back to back!"

"Blood to blood!"

"Blood brothers—*to the end of the Trip!*"

An apostate scientist, a kidnapped scientist, a dull peasant, a two-headed monster, a apple-brained moron—five knives, counting Joe-Jim as one; five brains, counting Joe-Jim as two and Bobo as none—five brains and five knives to overthrow an entire culture.

"But I don't want to go back, Hugh." Alan shuffled his feet and looked dogged. "Why can't I stay here with you? I'm a good blade."

"Sure you are, old fellow. But right now you'll be more useful as a spy."

"But you've got Bill Ertz for that."

"So we have, but we need you too. Bill is a public figure; he can't duck out and climb to the upper levels without it being noticed and causing talk. That's where you come in—you're his go-between."

"I'll have a Huff of a time explaining where I've been."

"Don't explain any more than you have to. But stay away from the Witness." Hugh had a sudden picture of Alan trying to deceive the old village historian, with his searching tongue and lust for details. "Keep clear of the Witness. The old boy would trip you up."

"Him? You mean the old one—he's dead. Made the Trip long since. The new one don't amount to nothing."

"Good. If you're careful, you'll be safe." Hugh raised his voice. "Bill! Are you ready to go down?"

"I suppose so." Ertz picked himself up and reluctantly put aside the book he had been reading—*The Three Musketeers,* illustrated, one of Joe-Jim's carefully stolen library. "Say, that's a wonderful book. Hugh, is *Earth* really like that?"

"Of course. Doesn't it say so in the book?"

Ertz chewed his lip and thought about it. "What is a house?"

"A house? A house is a sort of a . . . a sort of a compartment."

"That's what I thought at first, but how can you ride on a compartment?"

"Huh? What do you mean?"

"Why, all through the book they keep climbing on their houses and riding away."

"Let me see that book," Joe ordered. Ertz handed it to him. Joe-Jim thumbed through it rapidly. "I see what you mean. Idiot! They ride horses, not houses."

"Well, what's a horse?"

"A horse is an animal, like a big hog, or maybe like a cow. You squat up on top of it and let it carry you along."

Ertz considered this. "It doesn't seem practical. Look—when you ride in a litter, you tell the chief porter where you want to go. How can you tell a cow where you want to go?"

"That's easy. You have a porter lead it."

Ertz conceded the point. "Anyhow, you might fall off. It isn't practical. I'd rather walk."

"It's quite a trick," Joe explained. "Takes practice."

"Can *you* do it?"

Jim sniggered. Joe looked annoyed. "There are no horses in the Ship."

"O.K., O.K. But look—These guys Athos, Porthos, and Aramis, they had something—"

"We can discuss that later," Hugh interrupted. "Bobo is back. Are you ready to go, Bill?"

"Don't get in a hurry, Hugh. This is important. These chaps had knives—"

"Sure. Why not?"

"But they were better than our knives. They had knives as long as your arm—maybe longer. If we are going to fight the whole Crew, think what an advantage that would be."

"Hm-m-m—" Hugh drew his knife and looked at it, cradling it in his palm. "Maybe. You couldn't throw it as well."

"We could have throwing knives, too."

"Yes, I suppose we could."

The twins had listened without comment. "He's right," put in Joe. "Hugh, you take care of placing the knives. Jim and I have some reading to do." Both of Joe-Jim's heads were busy thinking of other books they owned, books that discussed in saguinary detail the infinitely varied methods used by mankind to shorten the lives of enemies. He was about to institute a War College Department of Historical Research, although he called his project by no such fancy term.

"O.K.," Hugh agreed, "but you will have to say the word to them."

"Right away." Joe-Jim stepped out of his apartment into the passageway where Bobo had assembled a couple of dozen of Joe-Jim's henchmen among the muties. Save for Long Arm, Pig, and Squatty, who had taken part in the rescue of Hugh, they were all strangers to Hugh, Alan, and Bill—and they were all sudden death to strangers.

Joe-Jim motioned for the three from the lower decks to join him. He pointed them out to the muties, and ordered them to look closely and not to forget—these three were to have safe passage and protection wherever they went. Furthermore, in Joe-Jim's absence his men were to take orders from any of them.

They stirred and looked at each other. Orders they were used to, but from Joe-Jim only.

A big-nosed individual rose up from his squat and addressed them. He looked at Joe-Jim, but his words were intended for all. "I am Jack-of-the-Nose. My blade is sharp and my eye is keen. Joe-Jim with the two wise heads is my Boss and my knife fights for him. But Joe-Jim is my Boss, not strangers from heavy decks. What do you say, knives? Is that not the Rule?"

He paused. The others had listened to him nervously, stealing glances at Joe-Jim. Joe muttered something out of the corner of his mouth to Bobo. Jack O'Nose opened his mouth to continue. There was a smash of breaking teeth, a crack from a broken neck; his mouth was stopped with a missile.

Bobo reloaded his slingshot. The body, not yet dead, settled slowly to the deck. Joe-Jim waved a hand toward it. "Good eating!" Joe announced. "He's yours." The muties converged on the body as if they had suddenly been unleashed. They concealed it completely in a busy grunting pile-up. Knives out, they cuffed and crowded each other for a piece of the prize.

Joe-Jim waited patiently for the undoing to be finished, then, when the place where Jack O'Nose had been was no more than a stain on the deck and the several private arguments over the sharing had died down, he spoke again—Joe spoke. "Long Arm, you and Forty-one and the Ax go down with Bobo, Alan, and Bill. The rest wait here."

Bobo trotted away in the long loping strides permitted by the low pseudogravity near the axis of rotation of the Ship. Three of the muties detached themselves from the pack and followed. Ertz and Alan Mahoney hurried to catch up.

When he reached the nearest staircase trunk, Bobo skipped out into space without breaking his stride and let centrifugal force carry him down to the next deck. Alan and the muties followed, but Ertz paused at the edge and looked back. "Jordan keep you, brothers!" he sang out.

Joe-Jim waved to him. "And you," acknowledged Joe.

"Good eating!" Jim added.

"Good eating!"

Bobo led them down forty-odd decks, well into the no man's land inhabited neither by mutie nor crew, and stopped. He pointed in succession to Long Arm, Forty-one, and the Ax. "Two Wise Heads say for you to keep watch here. You first," he added, pointing again to Forty-one.

"It's like this," Ertz amplified. "Alan and I are going down to heavy-weight level. You three are to keep a guard here, one at a time, so that I will be able to send messages back up to Joe-Jim. Get it?"

"Sure. Why not?" Long Arm answered.

"Joe-Jim says it," Forty-one commented with a note of finality in his voice. The Ax grunted agreeably.

"O.K.," said Bobo. Forty-one sat down at the stairwell, letting his feet hang over, and turned his attention to food which he had been carrying tucked under his left arm.

Bobo slapped Ertz and Alan on their backs. "Good eating," he bade them, grinning. When he could get his breath, Ertz acknowledged the courteous thought, then dropped at once to the next lower deck, Alan close after him. They had still many decks to go to "civilization."

Commander Phineas Narby, Executive Assistant to Jordan's Captain, in rummaging through the desk of the Chief Engineer was amused to find that Bill Ertz had secreted therein a couple of Unnecessary books. There were the usual Sacred books, of course, including the priceless *Care and Maintenance of the Auxiliary Four-stage Converter* and the *Handbook of Power, Light, and Conditioning—Starship* Vanguard. These were Sacred books of the first order, bearing the imprint of Jordan himself, and could lawfully be held only by the Chief Engineer.

Narby considered himself a skeptic and rationalist. Belief in Jordan was a good thing—for the Crew. Nevertheless the sight of a title page with the words "Jordan Foundation" on it stirred up within him a trace of religious awe such as he had not felt since before he was admitted to scientisthood.

He knew that the feeling was irrational—probably there had been at some time in the past some person or persons called Jordan. Jordan might have been an early engineer or captain who codified the common sense and almost instinctive rules for running the Ship. Or, as seemed more likely, the Jordan myth went back much farther than this book in his hand, and its author had simply availed himself of the ignorant superstitions of the Crew to give his writings authority. Narby knew how such things were done—he planned to give the new policy with respect to the muties the same blessing of Jordan when the time was ripe for it to be put into execution. Yes, order and discipline and belief in authority were good things—for the Crew. It was equally evident that a rational, coolheaded common sense was a proper attribute for the scientists who were custodians of the Ship's welfare—common sense and a belief in nothing but facts.

He admired the exact lettering on the pages of the book he held. They certainly had excellent clerks in those ancient times—not the sloppy draftsmen he was forced to put up with, who could hardly print two letters alike.

He made a mental note to study these two indispensable handbooks of the engineering department before turning them over to Ertz's successor. It would be well, he thought, not to be too dependent on the statements of the Chief Engineer when he himself succeeded to the captaincy. Narby had no particular respect for engineers, largely because he had no particular talent for engineering. When he had first reached scientisthood and had been charged to defend the spiritual and material welfare of the Crew, had sworn to uphold the Teachings of Jordan, he soon discovered that administration and personnel management were more in his lines than tending the converter or servicing the power lines. He had served as clerk, village administrator, recorder to the Council, personnel officer, and was now chief executive for Jordan's Captain himself—ever since an unfortunate and rather mysterious accident had shortened the life of Narby's predecessor in that post.

His decision to study up on engineering before a new Chief Engineer was selected brought to mind the problem of choosing a new chief. Normally the Senior Watch Officer for the Converter would become Chief Engineer when a chief made the Trip, but in this case, Mort Tyler, the Senior Watch, had made the Trip at the same time—his body had been found, stiff and cold, after the mutie raid which had rescued the heretic, Hugh Hoyland. That left the choice wide open and Narby was a bit undecided as to whom he should suggest to the Captain.

One thing was certain—the new chief must not be a man with as much aggressive initiative as Ertz. Narby admitted that Ertz had done a good job in organizing the Crew for the proposed extermination of the muties, but his very efficiency had made him too strong a candidate for succession to the captaincy—if and when. Had he thought about it overtly Narby might have admitted to himself that the present Captain's life span had extended unduly because Narby was not absolutely certain that Ertz would not be selected.

What he did think was that this might be a good time for the old Captain to surrender his spirit to Jordan. The fat old fool had long outlived his usefulness; Narby was tired of having to wheedle him into giving the proper orders. If the Council were faced with the necessity of selecting a new Captain at this time, there was but one candidate available—

Narby put the book down, his mind made up.

The simple decision to eliminate the old Captain carried with it in Narby's mind no feeling of shame, nor sin, nor disloyalty. He felt contempt but not dislike for the Captain, and no mean spirit colored his decision to kill him. Narby's plans were made on the noble level of statesmanship. He honestly believed that his objective was the welfare of the entire Crew—common-sense administration, order and discipline, good eating for everyone. He selected himself because it was obvious to him that he was best fitted to accomplish those worthy ends. That some must make the Trip in order that these larger interests be served he did not find even mildly regrettable, but he bore them no malice.

"What in the Huff are you doing at my desk?"

Narby looked up to see the late Bill Ertz standing over him, not looking pleased. He looked again, then as an afterthought closed his mouth. He had been so certain, when Ertz failed to reappear after the raid, that he had made the Trip and was in all probability butchered and eaten—so certain that it was now a sharp wrench to his mind to see Ertz standing before him, aggressively alive. But he pulled himself together.

"Bill! Jordan bless you, man—we thought you had made the Trip! Sit down, sit down, and tell me what happened to you."

"I will if you will get out of my chair," Ertz answered bitingly.

"Oh—sorry!" Narby hastily vacated the chair at Ertz's desk and found another.

"And now," Ertz continued, taking the seat Narby had left, "you might explain why you were going through my writings."

Narby managed to look hurt. "Isn't that obvious? We assumed you were dead. Someone had to take over and attend to your department until a new chief was designated. I was acting on behalf of the Captain."

Ertz looked him in the eyes. "Don't give me that guff, Narby. You know and I know who puts words in the Captain's mouth—we've planned it often enough. Even if you did think I was dead, it seems to me you could wait longer than the time between two sleeps to pry through my desk."

"Now really, old man—when a person is missing after a mutie raid, it's a common-sense assumption that he has made the Trip."

"O.K., O.K., skip it. Why didn't Mort Tyler take over in the meantime?"

"He's in the Converter."

"Killed, eh? But who ordered him put in the Converter? That much mass will make a terrific peak in the load."

"I did, in place of Hugh Hoyland. Their masses were nearly the same, and your requisition for the mass of Hugh Hoyland was unfilled."

"Nearly the same isn't good enough in handling the Converter. I'll have to check on it." He started to rise.

"Don't get excited," said Narby. "I'm not an utter fool in engineering, you know. I ordered his mass to be trimmed according to the same schedule you had laid out for Hoyland."

"Well—all right. That will do for now. But I will have to check it. We can't afford to waste mass."

"Speaking of waste mass," Narby said sweetly, "I found a couple of Unnecessary books in your desk."

"Well?"

"They are classed as mass available for power, you know."

"So? And who is the custodian of mass allocated for power?"

"You are certainly. But what were they doing in your desk?"

"Let me point out to you, my dear Captain's Best Boy, that it lies entirely within my discretion where I choose to store mass available for power."

"Hm-m-m—I suppose you are right. By the way, if you don't need them for the power schedule at once, would you mind letting me read them?"

"Not at all, if you want to be reasonable about it. I'll check them out to you—have to do that; they've already been centrifuged. Just be discreet about it."

"Thanks. Some of those ancients had vivid imaginations. Utterly crazy, of course, but amusing for relaxation."

❖

Ertz got out the two volumes and prepared a receipt for Narby to sign. He did this absent-mindedly, being preoccupied with the problem of how and when to tackle Narby. Phineas Narby he knew to be a key man in the task he and his blood brothers had undertaken—perhaps *the* key man. If he could be won over—

"Fin," he said, when Narby had signed, "I wonder if we followed the wisest policy in Hoyland's case."

Narby looked surprised, but said nothing.

"Oh, I don't mean that I put any stock in his story," Ertz added hastily, "but I feel that we missed an opportunity. We should have kidded him along. He was a contact with the muties. The worst handicap we work under in trying to bring mutie country under the rule of the Council is the fact that we know very little about them. We don't know how many of them there are, nor how strong they are, or how well organized. Besides that, we will have to carry the fight to them and that's a big disadvantage. We don't really know our way around the upper decks. If we had played along with him and pretended to believe his story, we might have learned a lot of things."

"But we couldn't rely on what he told us," Narby pointed out.

"We didn't need to. He offered us an opportunity to go all the way to no-weight, and look around."

Narby looked astounded. "You surely aren't serious? A member of the Crew that trusted the muties' promise not to harm him wouldn't get up to no-weight; he'd make the Trip—fast!"

"I'm not so certain about that," Ertz objected. "Hoyland believed his own story—I'm sure of that. And—"

"What! All that utter nonsense about the Ship being capable of *moving*. The solid Ship." He pounded the bulkhead. "No one could believe that."

"But I tell you he did. He's a religious fanatic—granted. But he saw something up there, and that was how he interpreted it. We could have gone up to see whatever it was he was raving about and used the chance to scout out the muties."

"Utterly foolhardy!"

"I don't think so. He must have a great deal of influence among the muties; look at the trouble they went to just to rescue him. If he says he can give us safe passage up to no-weight, I think he can."

"Why this sudden change of opinion?"

"It was the raid that changed my mind. If anyone had told me that a gang of muties would come clear down to high-weight and risk their necks to save the life of one man I would not have believed him. But it happened. I'm forced to revise my opinions. Quite aside from his story, it's evident that the muties will fight for him and probably take orders from him. If that is true, it would be worth while to pander to his religious convictions if it would enable us to gain control over the muties without having to fight for it."

Narby shrugged it off. "Theoretically you may have something there. But why waste time over might-have-beens? If there was such an opportunity, we missed it."

"Maybe not. Hoyland is still alive and back with the muties. If I could figure out some way of getting a message to him, we might still be able to arrange it."

"But how could you?"

"I don't know exactly. I might take a couple of the boys and do some climbing. If we could capture a mutie without killing him, it might work out."

"A slim chance."

"I'm willing to risk it."

Narby turned the matter over in his mind. The whole plan seemed to him to be filled with long chances and foolish assumptions. Nevertheless if Ertz were willing to take the risk and it *did* work, Narby's dearest ambition would be much nearer realization. Subduing the muties by force would be a long and bloody job, perhaps an impossible job. He was clearly aware of its difficulty.

If it did not work, nothing was lost—but Ertz. Now that he thought it over, Ertz would be no loss at this point in the game. Hm-m-m.

"Go ahead," he said. "You are a brave man, but it's a worth-while venture."

"O.K.," Ertz agreed. "Good eating."

Narby took the hint. "Good eating," he answered, gathered up the books, and left. It did not occur to him until later that Ertz had not told him where he had been for so long.

And Ertz was aware that Narby had not been entirely frank with him, but, knowing Narby, he was not surprised. He was pleased enough that his extemporaneous groundwork for future action had been so well received. It never did occur to him that it might have been simpler and more effective to tell the truth.

Ertz busied himself for a short time in making a routine inspection of the Converter and appointed an acting Senior Watch Officer. Satisfied that his department could then take care of itself during a further absence, he sent for his chief porter and told the servant to fetch Alan Mahoney from his village. He had considered ordering his litter and meeting Mahoney halfway, but he decided against it as being too conspicuous.

Alan greeted him with enthusiasm. To him, still an unmarried cadet and working for more provident men when his contemporaries were all heads of families and solid men of property, the knowledge that he was blood brother to a senior scientist was quite the most important thing that had ever happened to him, even overshadowing his recent adventures, the meaning of which he was hardly qualified to understand anyway.

Ertz cut him short, and hastily closed the door to the outer engineering office. "Walls have ears," he said quietly, "and certainly clerks have ears, and tongues as well. Do you want us both to make the Trip?"

"Aw, gosh, Bill . . . I didn't mean to—"

"Never mind. I'll meet you on the same stair trunk we came down by, ten decks above this one. Can you count?"

"Sure, I can count that much. I can count twice that much. One and one makes two, and one more makes three, and one more makes four, and one makes five, and—"

"That's enough. I see you can. But I'm relying more on your loyalty and your knife than I am on your mathematical ability. Meet me there as soon as you can. Go up somewhere where you won't be noticed."

Forty-one was still on watch when they reached the rendezvous. Ertz called him by name while standing out of range of slingshot or thrown knife, a reasonable precaution in dealing with a creature who had grown to man size by being fast with his weapons. Once identification had been established, he directed the guard to find Hugh Hoyland. He and Alan sat down to wait.

Forty-one failed to find Hugh Hoyland at Joe-Jim's apartment. Nor was Joe-Jim there. He did find Bobo, but the pinhead was not very helpful. Hugh, Bobo told him, had gone up where-everybody-flies. That meant very little to Forty-one; he had been up to no-weight only once in his life. Since the level of weightlessness extended the entire length of the Ship, being in fact the last concentric cylinder around the Ship's axis—not that Forty-one could conceive it in those terms—the information that Hugh had headed for no-weight was not helpful.

Forty-one was puzzled. An order from Joe-Jim was not to be ignored and he had got it through his not overbright mind that an order from Ertz carried the same weight. He woke Bobo up again. "Where is the Two Wise Heads?"

"Gone to see knifemaker." Bobo closed his eyes again.

That was better. Forty-one knew where the knifemaker lived. Every mutie had dealings with her; she was the indispensable artisan and tradesman of mutie country. Her person was necessarily taboo; her workshop and the adjacent neighborhood were neutral territory for all. He scurried up two decks and hurried thence.

A door reading THERMODYNAMIC LABORATORY—KEEP OUT was standing open. Forty-one could not read; neither the name nor the injunction mattered to him. But he could hear voices, one of which he identified as coming from the twins, the other from the knife-maker. He walked in. "Boss—" he began.

"Shut up," said Joe. Jim did not look around but continued his argument with the Mother of Blades. "You'll make knives," he said, "and none of your lip."

She faced him, her four calloused hands set firmly on her broad hips. Her eyes were reddened from staring into the furnace in which she heated her metal; sweat ran down her wrinkled face into the sparse gray mustache which disfigured her upper lip, and dripped onto her bare chest. "Sure I make knives," she snapped. "Honest knives. Not pig-stickers like you want me to make. Knives as long as your arm— *ptui!*" She spat at the cherry-red lip of the furnace.

"Listen, you old Crew bait," Jim replied evenly, "you'll make knives the way I tell you to, or I'll toast your feet in your own furnace. Hear me?"

Forty-one was struck speechless. No one *ever* talked back to the Mother of Blades; the Boss was certainly a man of power!

The knifemaker suddenly cracked. "But that's not the *right* way to make knives," she complained shrilly. "They wouldn't balance right. I'll show you—" She snatched up two braces of knives from her work-bench and let fly at a cross-shaped target across the room—not in succession, but all four arms swinging together, all four blades in the air at once. They *spunged* into the target, a blade at the extreme end of each arm of the cross. "See? You couldn't do that with a long knife. It would fight with itself and not go straight."

"Boss—" Forty-one tried again. Joe-Jim handed him a mouthful of knuckles without looking around.

"I see your point," Jim told the knifemaker, "but we don't want these knives for throwing. We want them for cutting and stabbing up close. Get on with it—I want to see the first one before you eat again."

The old woman bit her lip. "Do I get my usuals?" she said sharply.

"Certainly you get your usuals," he assured her. "A tithe on every kill till the blades are paid for—and good eating all the time you work."

She shrugged her misshapen shoulders. "O.K." She turned, tonged up a long flat fragment of steel with her two left hands and clanged the stock into the furnace. Joe-Jim turned to Forty-one.

"What is it?" Joe asked.

"Boss, Ertz sent me to get Hugh."

"Well, why didn't you do it?"

"I don't find him. Bobo says he's gone up to no-weight."

"Well, go get him. No, that won't do—you wouldn't know where to find him. I'll have to do it myself. Go back to Ertz and tell him to wait."

Forty-one hurried off. The Boss was all right, but it was not good to tarry in his presence.

"Now you've got us running errands," Jim commented sourly. "How do you like being a blood brother, Joe?"

"You got us into this."

"So? The blood-swearing was your idea."

"Damn it, you know why I did that. *They* took it seriously. And we are going to need all the help we can get, if we are to get out of this with a skin that will hold water."

"Oh? So *you* didn't take it seriously?"

"Did you?"

Jim smiled cynically. "Just about as seriously as you do, my dear, deceitful brother. As matters stand now, it is much, much healthier for you and me to keep to the bargain right up to the hilt. 'All for one and one for all.' "

"You've been reading Dumas again."

"And why not?"

"That's O.K. But don't be a damn fool about it."

"I won't be. I know which side of the blade is edged."

Joe-Jim found Squatty and Pig sleeping outside the door which led to the Control Room. He knew then that Hugh must be inside, for he had assigned the two as personal bodyguards to Hugh. It was a foregone conclusion anyhow; if Hugh had gone up to no-weight, he would be heading either for Main Drive, or the Control Room—more probably the Control Room. The place held a tremendous fascination for Hugh. Ever since the earlier time when Joe-Jim had almost literally dragged him into the Control Room and had forced him to see with his own eyes that the Ship was not the whole world but simply a vessel adrift in a much larger world—a vessel that could be driven and *moved*—ever since that time and throughout the period that followed while he was still a captured slave of Joe-Jim's, he had been obsessed with the idea of moving the Ship, of sitting at the controls and making it *go!*

It meant more to him than it could possibly have meant to a space pilot from Earth. From the time that the first rocket made the little jump from Terra to the Moon, the spaceship pilot has been the standard romantic hero whom every boy wished to emulate. But Hugh's ambition was of no such picayune caliber—he wished to move his *world*. In Earth standards and concepts it would be less ambitious to dream of equipping the Sun with jets and go gunning it around the Galaxy.

Young Archimedes had his lever; he sought a fulcrum.

Joe-Jim paused at the door of the great silver stellarium globe which constituted the Control Room and peered in. He could not see Hugh, but he knew that he must be at the controls in the chair of the chief astrogator, for the lights were being manipulated. The images of the stars were scattered over the inner surface of the sphere producing a simulacrum of the heavens outside the Ship. The illusion was not fully convincing from the door where Joe-Jim rested; from the center of the sphere it would be complete.

Sector by sector the stars snuffed out, as Hugh manipulated the controls from the center of the sphere. A sector was left shining on the far side forward. It was marked by a large and brilliant orb, many times as bright as its companions. Joe-Jim ceased watching and pulled himself hand over hand up to the control chairs. "Hugh!" Jim called out.

"Who's there?" demanded Hugh and leaned his head out of the deep chair. "Oh, it's you. Hello."

"Ertz wants to see you. Come on out of there."

"O.K. But come here first. I want to show you something."

"Nuts to him," Joe said to his brother. But Jim answered, "Oh, come on and see what it is. Won't take long."

The twins climbed into the control station and settled down in the chair next to Hugh's. "What's up?"

"That star out there," said Hugh, pointing at the brilliant one. "It's grown bigger since the last time I was here."

"Huh? Sure it has. It's been getting brighter for a long time. Couldn't see it at all first time I was ever in here."

"Then we're closer to it."

"Of course," agreed Joe. "I knew that. It just goes to prove that the Ship is moving."

"But why didn't you tell me about this?"

"About what?"

"About that star. About the way it's been growing bigger."

"What difference does it make?"

"What difference does it make! Why, good Jordan, man—that's it. That's where we're going. That's *the End of the Trip!*"

Joe-Jim—both of him—was momentarily startled. Not being himself concerned with any objective other than his own safety and comfort, it was hard for him to realize that Hugh, and perhaps Bill Ertz as well, held as their first objective the recapturing of the lost accomplishments of their ancestors in order to complete the long-forgotten, half-mythical Trip to Far Centaurus.

Jim recovered himself. "Hm-m-m—maybe. What makes you think that star is Far Centaurus?"

"Maybe it isn't. I don't care. But it's the star we are closest to and we are moving toward it. When we don't know which star is which, one is as good as another. Joe-Jim, the ancients must have had *some* way of telling the stars apart."

"Sure they did," Joe confirmed, "but what of it? You've picked the one you want to go to. Come on. I want to get back down."

"All right," Hugh agreed reluctantly. They began the long trip down.

Ertz sketched out to Joe-Jim and Hugh his interview with Narby. "Now my idea in coming up," he continued, "is this: I'll send Alan back down to heavy-weight with a message to Narby, telling him that I've been able to get in contact with you, Hugh, and urging him to meet us somewhere above Crew country to hear what I've found out."

"Why don't you simply go back and fetch him yourself?" objected Hugh.

Ertz looked slightly sheepish. "Because *you* tried that method on *me*—and it didn't work. You returned from mutie country and told me the wonders you had seen. I didn't believe you and had you tried for heresy. If Joe-Jim hadn't rescued you, you would have gone to the Converter. If you had not hauled me up to no-weight and forced me to see with my own eyes, I never would have believed you. I assure you Narby won't be any easier a lock to force than I was. I want to get him up here, then show him the stars and make him see—peacefully if we can; by force if we must."

"I don't get it," said Jim. "Why wouldn't it be simpler to cut his throat?"

"It would be a pleasure. But it wouldn't be smart. Narby can be a tremendous amount of help to us. Jim, if you knew the Ship's organization the way I do, you would see why. Narby carries more weight in the Council than any other Ship's officer *and* he speaks for the Captain. If we win him over, we may never have to fight at all. If we don't—well, I'm not sure of the outcome, not if we have to fight."

"I don't think he'll come up. He'll suspect a trap."

"Which is another reason why Alan must go rather than myself. He would ask me a lot of embarrassing questions and be dubious about the answers. Alan he won't expect so much of." Ertz turned to Alan and continued, "Alan, you don't know anything when he asks you but just what I'm about to tell you. Savvy?"

"Sure. I don't know nothing, I ain't seen nothing, I ain't heard nothing." With frank simplicity he added, "I never did know much."

"Good. You've never laid eyes on Joe-Jim, you've never heard of the stars. You're just my messenger, a knife I took along to help me. Now here's what you are to tell him—" He gave Alan the message for Narby, couched in simple but provocative terms, then made sure that Alan had it all straight. "All right—on your way! Good eating."

Alan slapped the grip of his knife, answered, "Good eating!" and sped away.

It is not possible for a peasant to burst precipitously into the presence of the Captain's Executive—Alan found that out. He was halted by the master-at-arms on watch outside Narby's suite, cuffed around a bit for his insistence on entering, referred to a boredly unsympathetic clerk who took his name and told him to return to his village and wait to be summoned. He held his ground and insisted that he had a message of immediate importance from the Chief Engineer to Commander Narby. The clerk looked up again. "Give me the writing."

"There is no writing."

"What? That's ridiculous. There is always a writing. Regulations."

"He had no time to make a writing. He gave me a word message."

"What is it?"

Alan shook his head. "It is private, for Commander Narby only. I have orders."

The clerk looked his exasperation.

But, being only a probationer, he forewent the satisfaction of direct and immediate disciplining of the recalcitrant churl in favor of the safer course of passing the buck higher up.

The chief clerk was brief. "Give me the message."

Alan braced himself and spoke to a scientist in a fashion he had never used in his life, even to one as junior as this passed clerk. "Sir, all I ask is for you to tell Commander Narby that I have a message for him from Chief Engineer Ertz. If the message is not delivered, I won't be the one to go to the Converter! But I don't dare give the message to anyone else."

The under official pulled at his lip, and decided to take a chance on disturbing his superior.

Alan delivered his message to Narby in a low voice in order that the orderly standing just outside the door might not overhear. Narby stared at him. "Ertz wants *me* to come along with *you* up to mutie country?"

"Not all the way up to mutie country, sir. To a point in between, where Hugh Hoyland can meet you."

Narby exhaled noisily. "It's preposterous. I'll send a squad of knives up to fetch him down to me."

Alan delivered the balance of his message. This time he carefully raised his voice to ensure that the orderly, and, if possible, others might hear his words. "Ertz said to tell you that if you were *afraid* to go, just to forget the whole matter. He will take it up with the Council himself."

Alan owed his continued existence thereafter to the fact that Narby was the sort of man who lived by shrewdness rather than by direct force. Narby's knife was at his belt; Alan was painfully aware that he had been required to deposit his own with the master-at-arms.

Narby controlled his expression. He was too intelligent to attribute the insult to the oaf before him, though he promised himself to give said oaf a little special attention at a more convenient time. Pique, curiosity, and potential loss of face all entered into his decision. "I'm coming with you," he said savagely. "I want to ask him if you got his message straight."

Narby considered having a major guard called out to accompany him, but he discarded the idea. Not only would it make the affair extremely public before he had an opportunity to judge its political aspects, but also it would lose him almost as much face as simply refusing to go. But he inquired nervously of Alan as Alan retrieved his weapon from the master-at-arms, "You're a good knife?"

"None better," Alan agreed cheerfully.

Narby hoped that the man was not simply boastful. Muties—Narby wished that he himself had found more time lately for practice in the manly arts.

Narby gradually regained his composure as he followed Alan up toward low-weight. In the first place nothing happened, no alarms; in the second place Alan was obviously a cautious and competent scout, one who moved alertly and noiselessly and never entered a deck without pausing to peer cautiously around before letting his body follow his eye. Narby might have been more nervous had he heard what Alan did hear—little noises from the depths of the great dim passageways, rustlings which told him that their progress was flanked on all sides. This worried Alan subconsciously, although he had expected something of the sort—he knew that both Hugh and Joe-Jim were careful captains who would not neglect to cover an approach. He would have worried more if he had *not* been able to detect a reconnaissance which should have been present.

When he approached the rendezvous some twenty decks above the highest civilized level, he stopped and whistled. A whistle answered him. "It's Alan," he called out.

"Come up and show yourself." Alan did so, without neglecting his usual caution. When he saw no one but his friends—Ertz, Hugh, Joe-Jim, and Bobo, he motioned for Narby to follow him.

The sight of Joe-Jim and Bobo broke Narby's restored calm with a sudden feeling that he had been trapped. He snatched at his knife and backed clumsily down the stairs—turned. Bobo's knife was out even faster. For a split moment the outcome hung balanced, ready to fall either way. But Joe-Jim slapped Bobo across the face, took his knife from him and let it clatter to the deck, then relieved him of his slingshot.

Narby was in full flight, with Hugh and Ertz calling vainly after him. "Fetch him, Bobo!" Jim commanded, "and don't hurt him." Bobo lumbered away.

He was back in fairly short order. "Run fast," he commented. He dropped Narby to the deck where the officer lay almost quiet while he fought to catch his breath. Bobo took Narby's knife from his own belt and tried it by shaving coarse black hairs from his left forearm. "Good blade," he approved.

"Give it back to him," Jim ordered. Bobo looked extremely startled but complied wistfully. Joe-Jim returned Bobo's own weapons to him.

Narby matched Bobo's surprise at regaining his side-arm, but he concealed it better. He even managed to accept it with dignity.

"Look," Ertz began in worried tones, "I'm sorry you got your wind up, Fin. Bobo's not a bad sort. It was the only way to get you back."

Narby fought with himself to regain the cool self-discipline with which he habitually met the world. Damn! he told himself, this situation is preposterous. Well—"Forget it," he said shortly. "I was expecting to meet you; I didn't expect a bunch of armed muties. You have an odd taste in playmates, Ertz."

"Sorry," Bill Ertz replied, "I guess I should have warned you"—a piece of mendacious diplomacy. "But they're all right. Bobo you've met. This is Joe-Jim. He's a . . . a sort of a Ship's officer among the muties."

"Good eating," Joe acknowledged politely.

"Good eating," Narby replied mechanically.

"Hugh you know, I think." Narby agreed that he did. An embarrassed pause followed. Narby broke it.

"Well," he said, "you must have had some reason to send word for me to come up here. Or was it just to play games?"

"I did," Ertz agreed. "I—Shucks, I hardly know where to start. See here, Narby, you won't believe this, but I've *seen*. Everything Hugh told us was true. I've been in the Control Room. I've seen the stars. I *know*."

Narby stared at him. "Ertz," he said slowly, "you've gone out of your mind."

Hugh Hoyland spoke up excitedly. "That's because you haven't *seen*. It *moves*, I tell you. The Ship *moves* like a—"

"I'll handle this," Ertz cut in. "Listen to me, Narby. What it all means you will soon decide for yourself, but I can tell you what I saw. They took me up to no-weight and into the Captain's veranda. That's a compartment with a glass wall. You can stare right out through into a great black empty space—big—bigger than anything could be. Bigger than the Ship. And there were lights out there, stars, just like the ancient myths said."

Narby looked both amazed and disgusted. "Where's your logic, man? I thought you were a scientist. What do you mean, 'bigger than the Ship'? That's an absurdity, a contradiction in terms. By definition, the Ship is the Ship. All else is a part of it."

Ertz shrugged helplessly. "I know it sounds that way. I can't explain it; it defies all logic. It's—Oh, Huff! You'll know what I mean when you see it."

"Control yourself," Narby advised him. "Don't talk nonsense. A thing is logical or it isn't. For a thing to be it must occupy space. You've seen, or thought you saw, something remarkable, but whatever it was, it can be no larger than the compartment it was in. You can't show me anything that contradicts an obvious fact of nature."

"I told you I couldn't explain it."

"Of course you can't."

The twins had been whispering disgustedly, one head to the other. "Stop the chatter," Joe said in louder tones. "We're ready to go. Come on."

"Sure," Ertz agreed eagerly, "let's drop it, Narby, until you have seen it. Come on now—it's a long climb."

"What?" Narby demanded. "Say, what is this? Go where?"

"Up to the Captain's veranda, and the Control Room."

"Me? Don't be ridiculous. I'm going down at once."

"No, Narby," Ertz denied. "That's why I sent for you. You've got to see."

"Don't be silly—I don't need to see; common sense gives sufficient answer. However," he went on, "I do want to congratulate you on making a friendly contact with the muties. We should be able to work out some means of cooperation. I think—"

Joe-Jim took one step forward. "You're wasting time," he said evenly. "We're going up—you, too. I really do insist."

Narby shook his head. "It's out of the question. Some other time, perhaps, after we have worked out a method of cooperation."

Hugh stepped in closer to him from the other side. "You don't seem to understand. You're going *now*."

Narby glanced the other way at Ertz. Ertz nodded. "That's how it is, Narby."

Narby cursed himself silently. Great Jordan! What in the Ship was he thinking of to let himself get into such a position? He had a distinct feeling that the two-headed man would rather that he showed fight. Impossible, preposterous situation. He cursed again to himself, but gave way as gracefully as he could. "Oh, well! Rather than cause an argument I'll go now. Let's get on with it. Which way?"

"Just stick with me," advised Ertz. Joe-Jim whistled loudly in a set pattern. Muties seemed to grow out of the floor plates, the bulkheads, the overhead, until six or eight more had been added to the party. Narby was suddenly sick with the full realization of just how far he had strayed from the way of caution. The party moved up.

It took them a long time to get up to no-weight, as Narby was not used to climbing. The steady reduction in weight as they rose from deck to deck relieved him somewhat but the help afforded was more than offset by the stomach qualms he felt as weight dropped away from him. He did not have a true attack of space-sickness—like all born in the Ship, muties and Crew, he was more or less acclimated to lessened weight, but he had done practically no climbing since reckless adolescence. By the time they reached the innermost deck of the Ship he was acutely uncomfortable and hardly able to proceed.

Joe-Jim sent the added members of the party back below and told Bobo to carry Narby. Narby waved him away. "I can make it," he protested, and by sheer stubborn will forced his body to behave. Joe-Jim looked him over and countermanded the order. By the time a long series of gliding dives had carried them as far forward as the transverse bulkhead beyond which lay the Control Room, he was reasonably comfortable again.

They did not stop first at the Control Room, but, in accordance with a plan of Hugh's, continued on to the Captain's veranda. Narby was braced for what he saw there, not only by Ertz's confused explanation, but because Hugh had chattered buoyantly to him about it all the latter part of the trip. Hugh was feeling warmly friendly to Narby by the time they arrived—it was wonderful to have somebody to listen!

Hugh floated in through the door ahead of the others, executed a neat turn in mid-air, and steadied himself with one hand on the back of the Captain's easy chair. With the other he waved at the great view port and the starry firmament beyond it. "There it is!" he exulted. "There it is. Look at it—isn't it wonderful?"

Narby's face showed no expression, but he looked long and intently at the brilliant display. "Remarkable," he conceded at last, "remarkable. I've never seen anything like it."

"'Remarkable' ain't half," protested Hugh. "Wonderful is the word."

"O.K.—'wonderful,'" Narby assented. "Those bright little lights—you say those are the stars that the ancients talked about?"

"Why, yes," agreed Hugh, feeling slightly disconcerted without knowing why, "only they're not little. They are big, enormous things, like the Ship. They just look little because they are so far away. See that very bright one, that big one, down to the left? It looks big because it's closer. I *think* that is Far Centaurus—but I'm not sure," he admitted in a burst of frankness.

Narby glanced quickly at him, then back to the big star. "How far away is it?"

"I don't know. But I'll find out. There are instruments to measure such things in the Control Room, but I haven't got the hang of them entirely. It doesn't matter, though. We'll get there yet!"

"Huh?"

"Sure. Finish the Trip."

Narby looked blank, but said nothing. His was a careful and orderly mind, logical to a high degree. He was a capable executive and could make rapid decisions when necessary, but he was by nature inclined to reserve his opinions when possible, until he had had time to chew over the data and assess it.

He was even more taciturn in the Control Room. He listened and looked, but asked very few questions. Hugh did not care. This was his toy, his gadget, his baby. To show it off to someone who had never seen it and who would listen was all he asked.

At Ertz's suggestion the party stopped at Joe-Jim's apartment on the way back down. Narby must be committed to the same course of action as the blood brotherhood and plans must be made to carry out such action, if the stratagem which brought Narby to them was to be fruitful. Narby agreed to stop unreluctantly, having become convinced of the reality of the truce under which he made this unprecedented sortie into mutie country. He listened quietly while Ertz outlined what they had in mind. He was still quiet when Ertz had finished.

"Well?" said Ertz at last, when the silence had dragged on long enough to get on his nerves.

"You expect some comment from me?"

"Yes, of course. You figure into it." Narby knew that he did and knew that an answer was expected from him; he was stalling for time.

"Well—" Narby pursed his lips and fitted his fingertips together. "It seems to me that this problem divides itself into two parts. Hugh

Hoyland, as I understand it, your purpose of carrying out the ancient Plan of Jordan cannot be realized until the Ship as a whole is pacified and brought under one rule—you need order and discipline for your purpose from Crew country clear to the Control Room. Is that right?"

"Certainly. We have to man the Main Drive and that means—"

"Please. Frankly, I am not qualified to understand things that I have seen so recently and have had no opportunity to study. As to your chances of success in that project, I would prefer to rely on the opinion of the Chief Engineer. Your problem is the second phase; it appears that you are necessarily interested in the first phase."

"Of course."

"Then let's talk about the first phase only. It involves matters of public policy and administration—I feel more at home there; perhaps my advice will be useful. Joe-Jim, I understand that you are looking for an opportunity to effect a peace between the muties and the members of the Crew—peace and good eating? Right?"

"That's correct," Jim agreed.

"Good. It has been my purpose for a long time and that of many of the Ship's officers. Frankly it never occurred to me that it could be achieved other than by sheer force. We had steeled ourselves to the prospect of a long and difficult and bloody war. The records of the oldest Witness, handed down to him by his predecessors clear back to the time of the mythical Mutiny, make no mention of anything but war between muties and the Crew. But this is a better way—I am delighted."

"Then you're with us!" exclaimed Ertz.

"Steady—there are many other things to be considered. Ertz, you and I know, and Hoyland as well I should think, that not all of the Ship's officers will agree with us. What of that?"

"That's easy," put in Hugh Hoyland. "Bring them up to no-weight one at a time, let them see the stars and learn the truth."

Narby shook his head. "You have the litter carrying the porters. I told you this problem is in two phases. There is no point in trying to convince a man of something he won't believe when you need him to agree to something he can understand. *After* the Ship is consolidated it will be simple enough then to let the officers experience the Control Room and the stars."

"But—"

"He's right," Ertz stopped him. "No use getting cluttered up with a lot of religious issues when the immediate problem is a practical one. There are numerous officers whom we could get on our side for the purpose of pacifying the Ship who would raise all kinds of fuss if we tackled them first on the idea that the Ship *moves*."

198

"But—"

"No 'buts' about it. Narby is right. It's common sense. Now, Narby—about this matter of those officers who may not be convinced—here's how we see it: In the first place it's your business and mine to win over as many as we can. Any who hold out against us—well, the Converter is always hungry."

Narby nodded, completely undismayed by the idea of assassination as a policy. "That seems the safest plan. Mightn't it be a little bit difficult?"

"That is where Joe-Jim comes in. We'll have the best knives in the Ship to back us up."

"I see. Joe-Jim is, I take it, Boss of all the muties?"

"What gave you that idea?" growled Joe, vexed without knowing why.

"Why, I supposed . . . I was given to understand—" Narby stopped. No one had *told* him that Joe-Jim was king of the upper decks; he had assumed it from appearances. He felt suddenly very uneasy. Had he been negotiating uselessly? What was the point in a pact with this two-headed monstrosity if he did not speak for the muties?

"I should have made that clear," Ertz said hastily. "Joe-Jim helps us to establish a new administration, then we will be able to back him up with knives to pacify the rest of the muties. Joe-Jim isn't Boss of all the muties, but he has the largest, strongest gang. With our help he soon will be Boss of all of them."

Narby quickly adjusted his mind to the new data. Muties against muties, with only a little help from the cadets of the Crew, seemed to him a good way to fight. On second thoughts, it was better than an outright truce at once—for there would be fewer muties to administer when it was all over, less chance of another mutiny. "I see," he agreed. "So—Have you considered what the situation will be afterwards?"

"What do you mean?" inquired Hoyland.

"Can you picture the present Captain carrying out these plans?"

Ertz saw what he was driving at, and so did Hoyland—vaguely.

"Go on," said Ertz.

"Who is to be the new Captain?" Narby looked squarely at Ertz.

Ertz had not thought the matter through; he realized now that the question was very pertinent, if the *coup d'état* was not to be followed by a bloody scramble for power. He had permitted himself to dream of being selected as Captain—sometime. But he knew that Narby was pointed that way, too.

Ertz had been as honestly struck by the romantic notion of moving the Ship as Hoyland. He realized that his old ambition stood in the way of the new; he renounced the old with only a touch of wistfulness.

"You will have to be Captain, Fin. Are you willing to be?"

Phineas Narby accepted gracefully. "I suppose so, if that's the way you want it. You would make a fine Captain yourself, Ertz."

Ertz shook his head, understanding perfectly that Narby's full cooperation turned on this point. "I'll continue as Chief Engineer—I want to handle the Main Drive for the Trip."

"Slow down!" Joe interrupted. "I don't agree to this. Why should *he* be Captain?"

Narby faced him. "Do you want to be Captain?" He kept his voice carefully free of sarcasm. A mutie for Captain!

"Huff's name—no! But why should you be? Why not Ertz or Hugh?"

"Not me," Hugh disclaimed. "I'll have no time for administration. I'm the astrogator."

"Seriously, Joe-Jim," Ertz explained, "Narby is the only one of the group who can get the necessary cooperation out of the Ship's officers."

"Damn it—if they won't cooperate we can slit their throats."

"With Narby as Captain we won't have to slit throats."

"I don't like it," groused Joe. His brother shushed him. "Why get excited about it, Joe? Jordan knows *we* don't want the responsibility."

"I quite understand your misgivings," Narby suggested suavely, "but I don't think you need worry. I would be forced to depend on you, of course, to administer the muties. I would administer the lower decks, a job I am used to, and you would be Vice-Captain, if you are willing to serve, for the muties. It would be folly for me to attempt to administer directly a part of the Ship I'm not familiar with and people whose customs I don't know. I really can't accept the captaincy unless you are willing to help me in that fashion. Will you do it?"

"I don't want any part of it," protested Joe.

"I'm sorry. Then I must refuse to be Captain—I really can't undertake it if you won't help me that much."

"Oh, go ahead, Joe," Jim insisted. "Let's take it—for the time being at least. The job has to be done."

"All right," Joe capitulated, "but I don't like it."

Narby ignored the fact that Joe-Jim had not specifically agreed to Narby's elevation to the captaincy; no further mention was made of it.

The discussion of ways and means was tedious and need not be repeated. It was agreed that Ertz, Alan, and Narby should all return to their usual haunts and occupations while preparations were made to strike.

Hugh detailed a guard to see them safely down to high-weight.

"You'll send Alan up when you are ready?" he said to Narby as they were about to leave.

"Yes," Narby agreed, "but don't expect him soon. Ertz and I will have to have time to feel out friends—and there's the matter of the old Captain, I'll have to persuade him to call a meeting of all the Ship's officers—he's never too easy to handle."

"Well, that's your job. Good eating!"

"Good eating."

On the few occasions when the scientist priests who ruled the Ship under Jordan's Captain met in full assembly they gathered in a great hall directly above the Ship's offices on the last civilized deck. Forgotten generations past, before the time of the mutiny led by Ship's Metalsmith Roy Huff, the hall had been a gymnasium, a place for fun and healthy exercise, as planned by the designers of the great starship—but the present users knew nothing of that.

Narby watched the roster clerk check off the Ship's officers as they arrived, worried under a bland countenance. There were only a few more to arrive; he would soon have no excuse not to notify the Captain that the meeting was ready—but he had received no word from Joe-Jim and Hoyland. Had that fool Alan managed to get himself killed on the way up to deliver the word? Had he fallen and broken his worthless neck? Was he dead with a mutie's knife in his belly?

Ertz came in, and before seeking his seat among the department heads, went up to where Narby sat in front of the Captain's chair. "How about it?" he inquired softly.

"All right," Narby told him, "but no word yet."

"Hm-m-m—" Ertz turned around and assayed his support in the crowd. Narby did likewise. Not a majority, not a *certain* majority, for anything as drastic as this. Still—the issue would not depend on voting.

The roster clerk touched his arm. "All present, sir, except those excused for sickness, and one on watch at the Converter."

Narby directed that the Captain be notified, with a sick feeling that something had gone wrong. The Captain, as usual, with complete disregard for the comfort and convenience of others, took his time about appearing. Narby was glad of the delay, but miserable in enduring it. When the old man finally waddled in, flanked by his orderlies, and settled heavily into his chair, he was, again as usual, impatient to get the meeting over. He waved for the others to be seated and started in on Narby.

"Very well, Commander Narby, let's have the agenda—you have an agenda, I hope?"

"Yes, Captain, there is an agenda."

"Then have it read, man, have it read! Why are you delaying?"

"Yes, sir." Narby turned to the reading clerk and handed him a sheaf of writings. The clerk glanced at them, looked puzzled, but, receiving no encouragement from Narby, commenced to read: "Petition, to Council and Captain: Lieutenant Braune, administrator of the village of Sector 9, being of frail health and advanced age, prays that he be relieved of all duty and retired—" The clerk continued, setting forth the recommendations of the officers and departments concerned.

The Captain twisted impatiently in his chair, finally interrupted the reading. "What's is this, Narby? Can't you handle routine matters without all this fuss?"

"I understood that the Captain was displeased with the fashion in which a similar matter was lately handled. I have no wish to trespass on the Captain's prerogatives."

"Nonsense, man! Don't read Regulations to me. Let the Council act, then bring their decision to me for review."

"Yes, sir." Narby took the writing from the clerk and gave him another. The clerk read.

It was an equally fiddling matter. Sector 3 village, because of an unexplained blight which had infected their hydroponic farms, prayed for relief and a suspension of taxes. The Captain put up with still less of this item before interrupting. Narby would have been sorely pressed for any excuse to continue the meeting had not the word he awaited arrived at that moment. It was a mere scrap of parchment, brought in from outside the hall by one of his own men. It contained the single word, "Ready." Narby looked at it, nodded to Ertz, and addressed the Captain:

"Sir, since you have no wish to listen to the petitions of your Crew, I will continue at once with the main business of this meeting." The veiled insolence of the statement caused the Captain to stare at him suspiciously, but Narby went on. "For many generations, through the lives of a succession of Witnesses, the Crew has suffered from the depredations of the muties. Our livestock, our children, even our own persons, have been in constant jeopardy. Jordan's Regulations are not honored above the levels where we live. Jordan's Captain himself is not free to travel in the upper levels of the Ship.

"It has been an article of faith that Jordan so ordained it, that the children pay with blood for the sins of their ancestors. It was the will of Jordan—we were told.

"I, for one, have never been reconciled to this constant drain on the Ship's mass." He paused.

The old Captain had been having some difficulty in believing his ears. But he found his voice. Pointing, he squealed, "Do you dispute the Teachings?"

"I do not. I maintain that the Teachings do not command us to leave the muties outside the Regulations, and never did. I demand that they be brought under the Regulations!"

"You . . . you—You are relieved of duty, sir!"

"Not," answered Narby, his insolence now overt, "until I have had my say."

"Arrest that man!" But the Captain's orderlies stood fast, though they shuffled and looked unhappy—Narby himself had selected them.

Narby turned back to the amazed Council, and caught the eye of Ertz. "All right," he said. "Now!" Ertz got up and trotted toward the door. Narby continued, "Many of you think as I do, but we always supposed that we would have to fight for it. With the help of Jordan, I have been able to establish a contact with the muties and arrange a truce. Their leaders are coming here to negotiate with us. There!" He pointed dramatically at the door.

Ertz reappeared; following him came Hugh Hoyland, Joe-Jim, and Bobo. Hoyland turned to the right along the wall and circled the company. He was followed single file by a string of muties—Joe-Jim's best butcher boys. Another such column trailed after Joe-Jim and Bobo to the left.

Joe-Jim, Hugh, and half a dozen more in each wing were covered with crude armor which extended below their waists. The armor was topped off with clumsy helms, latticeworks of steel, which protected their heads without greatly interfering with vision. Each of the armored ones, a few of the others, carried unheard-of knives—long as a man's arm!

The startled officers might have stopped the invasion at the bottleneck through which it entered had they been warned and led. But they were disorganized, helpless, and their strongest leaders had invited the invaders in. They shifted in their chairs, reached for their knives, and glanced anxiously from one to another. But no one made the first move which would start a general bloodletting.

Narby turned to the Captain. "What about it? Do you receive this delegation in peace?"

It seemed likely that age and fat living would keep the Captain from answering, from ever answering anything again. But he managed to croak, "Get 'em out of here! Get 'em out! You—You'll make the Trip for this!"

Narby turned back to Joe-Jim and jerked his thumb upward. Jim spoke to Bobo—and a knife was buried to the grip in the Captain's fat belly. He squawked, rather than screamed, and a look of utter bewilderment spread over his features. He plucked awkwardly at the hilt as if to assure himself that it was really there. "Mutiny—" he stated. "Mutiny—" The word trailed off as he collapsed into his chair, and fell heavily forward to the deck on his face.

Narby shoved it with his foot and spoke to the two orderlies. "Carry it outside," he commanded. They obeyed, seeming relieved at having something to do and someone to tell them to do it. Narby turned back to the silent watching mass. "Does anyone else object to a peace with the muties?"

An elderly officer, one who had dreamed away his life as judge and spiritual adviser to a remote village, stood up and pointed a bony finger at Narby, while his white beard jutted indignantly. "Jordan will punish you for this! Mutiny and sin—the spirit of Huff!"

Narby nodded to Joe-Jim; the old man's words gurgled in his throat, the point of a blade sticking out under one ear. Bobo looked pleased with himself.

"There has been enough talk," Narby announced. "It is better to have a little blood now than much blood later. Let those who stand with me in this matter get up and come forward."

Ertz set the precedent by striding forward and urging his surest personal supporters to come with him. Reaching the front of the room, he pulled out his knife and raised the point. "I salute Phineas Narby, Jordan's Captain!"

His own supporters were left with no choice. "Phineas Narby, Jordan's Captain!"

The hard young men in Narby's clique—the backbone of the dissident rationalist bloc among the scientist priests—joined the swing forward *en masse,* points raised high and shouting for the new Captain. The undecided and the opportunists hastened to join, as they saw which side of the blade was edged. When the division was complete, there remained a handful only of Ship's officers still hanging back, almost all of whom were either elderly or hyper-religious.

Ertz watched Captain Narby look them over, then pick up Joe-Jim with his eyes. Ertz put a hand on his arm. "There are few of them and practically helpless," he pointed out. "Why not disarm them and let them retire?"

Narby gave him an unfriendly look. "Let them stay alive and breed mutiny. I am quite capable of making my own decisions, Ertz."

Ertz bit his lip. "Very well, Captain."

"That's better." He signaled to Joe-Jim.

The long knives made short work.

Hugh hung back from the slaughter. His old teacher, Lieutenant Nelson, the village scientist who had seen his ability and selected him

for scientisthood, was one of the group. It was a factor he had not anticipated.

World conquest—and consolidation. Faith, or the Sword. Joe-Jim's
bullies, amplified by hot-blooded young cadets supplied by Captain
Narby, combed the middle decks and the upper decks. The muties, individualists by the very nature of their existence and owing no alle-
giance higher than that to the leaders of their gangs, were no match for
the planned generalship of Joe-Jim, nor did their weapons match the
strange, long knives that bit before a man was ready.

The rumor spread through mutie country that it was better to surrender quietly to the gang of the Two Wise-Heads—good eating for
those who surrendered, death inescapable for those who did not.

But it was nevertheless a long slow process—there were so many,
many decks, so many miles of gloomy corridors, so many countless
compartments in which unreconstructed muties might lurk. Furthermore, the process grew slower as it advanced, as Joe-Jim attempted to
establish a police patrol, an interior guard, over each sector, deck, and
stairway trunk, as fast as his striking groups mopped them up.

To Narby's disappointment, the two-headed man was not killed in
his campaigns. Joe-Jim had learned from his own books that a general
need not necessarily expose himself to direct combat.

Hugh buried himself in the Control Room. Not only was he more interested in the subtle problems of mastering the how and why of the complex controls and the parallel complexity of starship ballistics, but also
the whole matter of the blood purge was distasteful to him—because of
Lieutenant Nelson. Violence and death he was used to; they were commonplace even on the lower levels—but the incident made him vaguely
unhappy, even though his own evaluations were not sufficiently clean-cut
for him to feel personal responsibility for the old man's death.

He just wished it had not happened.

But the controls—ah! There was something a man could put his
heart into. He was attempting a task that an Earthman would have rejected as impossible—an Earthman would have *known* that the piloting and operation of an interstellar ship was a task so difficult that
the best possible technical education combined with extensive experience in the handling of lesser spacecraft would constitute a barely adequate grounding for additional intensive highly specialized training for
the task.

Hugh Hoyland did not know that. So he went ahead and did it
anyhow.

In which attempt he was aided by the genius of the designers. The *controls* of most machinery may be considered under the head of simple pairs, stop-and-go, push-and-pull, up-and-down, in-and-out, on-and-off, right-and-left, their permutations and combinations. The real difficulties have to do with upkeep and repair, adjustment, and replacements.

But the controls and main drive machinery of the starship *Vanguard* required no upkeep and no repair; their complexities were below the molar level, they contained no moving parts, friction took no toll and they did not fall out of adjustment. Had it been necessary for him to understand and repair the machines he dealt with, it would have been impossible. A fourteen-year-old child may safely be entrusted with a family skycar and be allowed to make thousand-mile jaunts overnight unaccompanied; it is much more probable that he will injure himself on the trip by overeating than by finding some way to mismanage or damage the vehicle. But if the skycar *should* fall out of adjustment, ground itself, and signal for a repair crew, the repair crew is essential; the child cannot fix it himself.

The *Vanguard* needed no repair crew—save for nonessential auxiliary machinery such as transbelts, elevators, automassagers, dining services, and the like. Such machinery which necessarily used moving parts had worn out before the time of the first Witness; the useless mass involved had gone into the auxiliary Converter, or had been adapted to other simpler purposes. Hugh was not even aware that there ever had been such machinery; the stripped condition of most compartments was a simple fact of nature to him, no cause for wonder.

Hugh was aided in his quest for understanding by two other facts:

First, spaceship ballistics is a very simple subject, being hardly more than the application of the second law of motion to an inverse-square field. That statement runs contrary to our usual credos; it happens to be true. Baking a cake calls for much greater, though subconscious, knowledge of engineering; knitting a sweater requires a grasp of much more complex mathematical relationships. The topology of a knitted garment—but try it yourself sometime!

For a complex subject, consider neurology, or catalysts—but don't mention ballistics.

Second, the designers had clearly in mind that the *Vanguard* would reach her destination not sooner than two generations after her departure; they wished to make things easy for the then-not-yet-born pilots who would control her on arrival. Although they anticipated no such hiatus in technical culture as took place, they did their best to make the controls simple, self-explanatory, and foolproof. The sophisticated fourteen-year-old mentioned above oriented as he would be to the concept of space travel, would doubtless have figured them out in a few hours. Hugh, reared in a culture which believed that the Ship was the whole world, made no such quick job of it.

He was hampered by two foreign concepts, *deep* space and *metrical* time. He had to learn to operate the distance finder, a delayed-action, long-base, parallax type especially designed for the *Vanguard,* and had taken readings on a couple of dozen stellar bodies before it occurred to him that the results he was getting could possibly mean anything. The readings were in parsecs and meaningless emotionally. The attempt with the aid of the Sacred books to translate his readings into linear units he could understand resulted in figures which he felt sure were wrong, obviously preposterous. Check and recheck, followed by long periods of brooding, forced him unwillingly into some dim comprehension of astronomical magnitudes.

The concepts frightened him and bewildered him. For a period of several sleeps he stayed away from the Control Room, and gave way to a feeling of futility and defeat. He occupied the time in sorting over the women available; it being the first time since his capture by Joe-Jim long ago that he had had both the opportunity and the mood to consider the subject. The candidates were numerous, for, in addition to the usual crop of village maidens, Joe-Jim's military operations had produced a number of prime widows. Hugh availed himself of his leading position in the Ship's new setup to select two women. The first was a widow, a strong competent woman, adept at providing a man with domestic comforts. He set her up in his new apartment, high up in low-weight, gave her a free hand, and allowed her to retain her former name of Chloe.

The other was a maiden, untrained and wild as a mutie. Hugh could not have told himself why he picked her. Certainly she had no virtues, but—she made him feel funny. She had bitten him while he was inspecting her; he had slapped her, naturally, and that should have been an end to the matter. But he sent word back later for her father to send her along.

He had not got around to naming her.

Metrical time caused him as much mental confusion as astronomical distances, but no emotional upset. The trouble was again the lack of the concept in the Ship. The Crew had the notion of topological time; they understood "now," "before," "after," "has been," "will be," even such notions as long time and short time, but the notion of measured time had dropped out of the culture. The lowest of earthbound cultures has some idea of measured time, even if limited to days and seasons, but every earthly concept of measured time originates in astronomical phenomena—the Crew had been insulated from all astronomical phenomena for uncounted generations.

Hugh had before him, on the control consoles, the only working timepieces in the Ship—but it was a long, long time before he grasped what they were for, and what bearing they had on other instruments. But until he did, he could not control the Ship. Speed, and its derivatives, acceleration and flexure, are based on *measured* time.

But when these two new concepts were finally grasped, chewed over, and ancient books reread in the light of these concepts, he was, in a greatly restricted and theoretical sense, an astrogator.

Hugh sought out Joe-Jim to ask him a question. Joe-Jim's minds were brilliantly penetrating when he cared to exert himself; he remained a superficial dilettante because he rarely cared.

Hugh found Narby just leaving. In order to conduct the campaign of pacification of the muties it had been necessary for Narby and Joe-Jim to confer frequently; to their mutual surprise they got along well together. Narby was a capable administrator, able to delegate authority and not given to useless elbow jogging; Joe-Jim surprised and pleased Narby by being more able than any subordinate he had ever dealt with before. There was no love wasted between them, but each recognized in the other both intelligence and a hard self-interest which matched his own. There was respect and grudging contemptuous liking.

"Good eating, Captain," Hugh greeted Narby formally.

"Oh—hello, Hugh," Narby answered, then turned back to Joe-Jim. "I'll expect a report, then."

"You'll get it," Joe agreed. "There can't be more than a few dozen stragglers. We'll hunt them out, or starve them."

"Am I butting in?" Hugh asked.

"No—I'm just leaving. How goes the great work, my dear fellow?" He smiled irritatingly.

"Well enough, but slowly. Do you wish a report?"

"No hurry. Oh, by the bye, I've made the Control Room and Main Drive, in fact the entire level of no-weight, taboo for everyone, muties and Crew alike."

"So? I see your point, I guess. There is no need for any but officers to go up there."

"You don't understand me. It is a general taboo, applying to officers as well. Not to ourselves, of course."

"But . . . but—That won't work. The only effective way to convince the officers of the truth is to take them up and show them the stars!"

"That's exactly my point. I can't have my officers upset by disturbing ideas while I am consolidating my administration. It will create religious differences and impair discipline."

Hugh was too upset and astounded to answer at once. "But," he said at last, "but that's the *point*. That's why you were made Captain."

"And as Captain I will have to be the final judge of policy. The matter is closed. You are not to take anyone to the Control Room, nor any part of no-weight, until I deem it advisable. You'll have to wait."

"It's a good idea, Hugh," Jim commented. "We shouldn't stir things up while we've got a war to attend to."

"Let me get this straight," Hugh persisted. "You mean this is a temporary policy?"

"You could put it that way."

"Well—all right," Hugh conceded. "But wait—Ertz and I need to train assistants at once."

"Very well. Nominate them to me and I'll pass on them. Whom do you have in mind?"

Hugh thought. He did not actually need assistance himself; although the Control Room contained acceleration chairs for half a dozen, one man, seated in the chief astrogator's chair, could pilot the Ship. The same applied to Ertz in the Main Drive station, save in one respect. "How about Ertz? He needs porters to move mass to the Main Drive."

"Let him. I'll sign the writing. See that he uses porters from the former muties—but no one goes to the Control Room save those who have been there before." Narby turned and left with an air of dismissal.

Hugh watched him leave, then said, "I don't like this, Joe-Jim."

"Why not?" Jim asked. "It's reasonable."

"Perhaps it is. But—well, damn it! It seems to me, somehow, that truth ought to be free to anyone—any time!" He threw up his hands in a gesture of baffled exasperation.

Joe-Jim looked at him oddly. "What a curious idea," said Joe.

"Yeah, I know. It's not common sense, but it seems like it ought to be. Oh, well, forget it ! That's not what I came to see you about."

"What's on your mind, Bud?"

"How do we—Look, we finish the Trip; see? We've got the Ship touching a planet, like this—" He brought his two fists together.

"Yes. Go on."

"Well, when that's done, *how do we get out of the Ship?*"

The twins looked confused, started to argue between themselves. Finally Joe interrupted his brother. "Wait a bit, Jim. Let's be logical about this. It was intended for us to get out—that implies a door, doesn't it?"

"Yeah. Sure."

"There's no door up here. It must be down in high-weight."

"But it isn't," objected Hugh. "All that country is known. There isn't any door. It has to be up in mutie country."

"In that case," Joe continued, "it should be either all the way forward, or all the way aft—otherwise it would not go anywhere. It isn't aft. There's nothing back of Main Drive but solid bulkheads. It would need to be forward."

"That's silly," Jim commented. "There's the Control Room and the Captain's veranda. That's all."

"Oh, yeah? How about the locked compartments?"

"Those aren't doors—not to the Outside anyway. That bulkhead's abaft the Control Room."

"No, stupid, but they might lead to doors."

"Stupid, eh? Even so, how are you going to open them—answer me that, bright boy?"

"What," demanded Hugh, "*are* the 'locked compartments'?"

"Don't you know? There are seven doors, spaced around the main shaft in the same bulkhead as the door to the Main Control Room. We've never been able to open them."

"Well, maybe that's what we're looking for. Let's go see!"

"It's a waste of time," Jim insisted.

But they went.

Bobo was taken along to try his monstrous strength on the doors. But even his knotted swollen muscles could not budge the levers which appeared to be intended to actuate the doors. "Well?" Jim sneered to his brother. "You see?"

Joe shrugged. "O.K.—you win. Let's go down."

"Wait a little," Hugh pleaded. "The second door back—the handle seemed to turn a little. Let's try it again."

"I'm afraid it's useless," Jim commented. But Joe said, "Oh, all right, as long as we're here."

Bobo tried again, wedging his shoulder under the lever and pushing from his knees. The lever gave suddenly, but the door did not open. "He's broken it," Joe announced.

"Yeah," Hugh acknowledged. "I guess that's that." He placed his hand against the door.

It swung open easily.

The door did not lead to outer space, which was well for the three, for nothing in their experience warned them against the peril of the outer vacuum. Instead a very short and narrow vestibule led them to another door which was just barely ajar. The door stuck on its hinges, but the fact that it was slightly ajar prevented it from binding anywhere else. Perhaps the last man to use it left it so as a precaution against the metal surfaces freezing together—but no one would ever know.

Bobo's uncouth strength opened it easily. Another door lay six feet beyond. "I don't understand this," complained Jim, as Bobo strained at the third door. "What's the sense in an endless series of doors?"

"Wait and find out," advised his brother.

Beyond the third door lay, not another door, but a compartment, a group of compartments, odd ones, small, crowded together and of unusual shapes. Bobo shot on ahead and explored the place, knife in teeth, his ugly body almost graceful in flight. Hugh and Joe-Jim proceeded more slowly, their eyes caught by the strangeness of the place.

Bobo returned, killed his momentum skillfully against a bulkhead, took his blade from his teeth, and reported, "No door. No more door any place. Bobo look."

"There *has* to be," Hugh insisted, irritated at the dwarf for demolishing his hopes.

The moron shrugged. "Bobo look."

"We'll look." Hugh and the twins moved off in different directions, splitting the reconnaissance between them.

Hugh found no door, but what he did find interested him even more—an impossibility. He was about to shout for Joe-Jim, when he heard his own name called. "Hugh! Come here!"

Reluctantly he left his discovery, and sought out the twins. "Come see what I've found," he began.

"Never mind," Joe cut him short. "Look at that."

Hugh looked. "That" was a Converter. Quite small, but indubitably a Converter. "It doesn't make sense," Jim protested. "An apartment this size doesn't need a Converter. That thing would supply power and light for half the Ship. What do you make of it, Hugh?"

Hugh examined it. "I don't know," he admitted, "but if you think this is strange, come see what I've found."

"What have you found?"

"Come see."

The twins followed him, and saw a small compartment, one wall of which appeared to be of glass—black, as if the far side were obscured. Facing the wall were two acceleration chairs, side by side. The arms and the lap desks of the chairs were covered with patterns of little shining lights of the same sort as the control lights on the chairs in the Main Control Room.

Joe-Jim made no comment at first, save for a low whistle from Jim.

He sat down in one of the chairs and started experimenting cautiously with the controls. Hugh sat down beside him. Joe-Jim covered a group of white lights on the right-hand arm of his chair; the lights in the apartment went out. When he lifted his hand the tiny control lights were blue instead of white. Neither Joe-Jim nor Hugh was startled when the lights went out; they had expected it, for the control involved corresponded to similar controls in the Control Room.

Joe-Jim fumbled around, trying to find controls which would produce a simulacrum of the heavens on the blank glass before him. There were no such controls and he had no way of knowing that the glass was an actual view port, obscured by the hull of the Ship proper, rather than a view screen.

But he did manage to actuate the controls that occupied the corresponding position. These controls were labeled LAUNCHING; Joe-Jim had disregarded the label because he did not understand it. Actuating them produced no very remarkable results, except that a red light blinked rapidly and a transparency below the label came into life. It read: AIR-LOCK OPEN.

Which was very lucky for Joe-Jim, Hugh, and Bobo. Had they closed the doors behind them and had the little Converter contained even a few grams of mass available for power, they would have found themselves launched suddenly into space, in a Ship's boat unequipped for a trip and whose controls they understood only by analogy with those in the Control Room. Perhaps they could have maneuvered the boat back into its cradle; more likely they would have crashed attempting it.

But Hugh and Joe-Jim were not yet aware that the "apartment" they had entered was a spacecraft; the idea of a Ship's boat was still foreign to them.

"Turn on the lights," Hugh requested. Joe-Jim did so.

"Well?" Hugh went on. "What do you make of it?"

"It seems pretty obvious," answered Jim. "This is another Control Room. We didn't guess it was here because we couldn't open the door."

"That doesn't make sense," Joe objected. "Why should there be two Control Rooms for one Ship?"

"Why should a man have two heads?" his brother reasoned. "From my point of view, you are obviously a supernumerary."

"It's not the same thing; we were born that way. But this didn't just happen—the Ship was *built*."

"So what?" Jim argued. "We carry two knives, don't we? And we weren't born with 'em. It's a good idea to have a spare."

"But you can't control the Ship from here," Joe protested. "You can't *see* anything from here. If you wanted a second set of controls, the place to put them would be the Captain's veranda, where you can see the stars."

"How about that?" Jim asked, indicating the wall of glass.

"Use your head," his brother advised. "It faces the wrong direction. It looks into the Ship, not out. And it's not an arrangement like the Control Room; there isn't any way to mirror the stars on it."

"Maybe we haven't located the controls for it."

"Even *so,* you've forgotten something. How about that little Converter?"

"What about it?"

"It must have some significance. It's not here by accident. I'll bet you that these controls have something to do with that Converter."

"Why?"

"Why not? Why are they here together if there isn't some connection?"

Hugh broke his puzzled silence. Everything the twins had said seemed to make sense, even the contradictions. It was all very confusing. But the Converter, the little Conter—"Say, look," he burst out.

"Look at what?"

"Do you suppose—Do you think that maybe this part of the Ship could *move?*"

"Naturally. The whole Ship moves."

"No," said Hugh, "no, no. I don't mean that at all. Suppose it moved by *itself*. These controls and the little Converter—suppose it could *move* right away from the Ship."

"That's pretty fantastic."

"Maybe so—but if it's true, *this is the way out*."

"Huh?" said Joe. "Nonsense. No door to the Outside here either."

"But there would be if this apartment were moved away from the Ship—the way we came in!"

The two heads snapped simultaneously toward him as if jerked by the same string. Then they looked at each other and fell to arguing. Joe-Jim repeated his experiment with the controls. "See?" Joe pointed out. " 'Launching.' It means to start something, to push something away."

"Then why doesn't it?"

" 'Air-Lock Open.' The doors we came through—it has to be that. Everything else is closed."

"Let's try it."

"We would have to start the Converter first."

"O.K."

"Not so fast. Get out, and maybe you can't come back. We'd starve."

"Hm-m-m—we'll wait a while."

Hugh listened to the discussion while snooping around the control panels, trying to figure them out. There was a stowage space under the lap desk of his chair; he fished into it, encountered something, and hauled it out. "See what I've found!"

"What is it?" asked Joe. "Oh—a book. Lot of them back in the room next to the Converter." "Let's see it," said Jim.

But Hugh had opened it himself. "'Log, Starship *Vanguard*,'" he spelled out, "'2 June, 2172. Cruising as before—'"

"What!" yelled Joe. "Let me see that!"

"'3 June. Cruising as before. 4 June. Cruising as before. Captain's mast for rewards and punishments held at 1300. See Administration Log. 5 June. Cruising as before—'"

"Gimme that!"

"Wait!" said Hugh. "'6 June. Mutiny broke out at 0431. The watch became aware of it by visiplate. Huff, Metalsmith Ordinary, screened the control station and called on the watch to surrender, designating himself as "Captain." The officer of the watch ordered him to consider himself under arrest and signaled the Captain's cabin. No answer.

"'0435. Communications failed. The officer of the watch dispatched a party of three to notify the Captain, turn out the chief proctor, and assist in the arrest of Huff.

"'0441. Converter power off; free flight.

"'0502. Lacy, Crewman Ordinary, messenger-of-the-watch, one of the party of three sent below, returned to the control station alone. He reported verbally that the other two, Malcolm Young and Arthur Sears, were dead and that he had been permitted to return in order to notify the watch to surrender. The mutineers gave 0515 as a deadline.'"

The next entry was in a different hand: "'0545. I have made every attempt to get into communication with other stations and officers in the Ship, without success. I conceive it as my duty, under the circumstances, to leave the control station without being properly relieved, and attempt to restore order down below. My decision may be faulty, since we are unarmed, but I see no other course open to me.

"'Jean Baldwin, Pilot Officer Third Class, Officer of the Watch.'"

"Is that all?" demanded Joe.

"No," said Hugh. "'1 October (approximately), 2172. I, Theodor Mawson, formerly Storekeeper Ordinary, have been selected this date as Captain of the *Vanguard*. Since the last entry in this log there have been enormous changes. The mutiny has been suppressed, or more properly, has died out, but with tragic cost. Every pilot officer, every engineering officer, is dead, or believed to be dead. I would not have been chosen Captain had there been a qualified man left.

" 'Approximately ninety per cent of the personnel are dead. Not all of that number died in the original outbreak; no crops have been planted since the mutiny; our food-stocks are low. There seems to be clear evidence of cannibalism among the mutineers who have not surrendered.

" 'My immediate task must be to restore some semblance of order and discipline among the Crew. Crops must be planted. A regular watch must be instituted at the auxiliary Converter on which we are dependent for heat and light and power.' "

The next entry was undated. " 'I have been far too busy to keep this log up properly. Truthfully, I do not know the date even approximately. The Ship's clocks no longer run. That may be attributable to the erratic operation of the auxiliary Converter, or it may possibly be an effect of radiations from outer space. We no longer have an anti-radiation shield around the Ship, since the Main Converter is not in operation. My Chief Engineer assures me that the Main Converter could be started, but we have no one fitted to astrogate. I have tried to teach myself astrogation from the books at hand, but the mathematics involved are very difficult.

" 'About one newborn child out of twenty is deformed. I have instituted a Spartan code—such children are not permitted to live. It is harsh, but necessary.

" 'I am growing very old and feeble and must consider the selection of my successor. I am the last member of the crew to be born on Earth, and even I have little recollection of it—I was five when my parents embarked. I do not know my own age, but certain unmistakable signs tell me that the time is not far away when I, too, must make the Trip to the Converter.

" 'There has been a curious change in orientation in my people. Never having lived on a planet, it becomes more difficult as time passes for them to comprehend anything not connected with the Ship. I have ceased trying to talk to them about it—it is hardly a kindness anyhow, as I have no hope of leading them out of the darkness. Theirs is a hard life at best; they raise a crop only to have it raided by the outlaws who still flourish on the upper levels. Why speak to them of better things?

" 'Rather than pass this on to my successor I have decided to attempt to hide it, if possible, in the single Ship's boat left by the mutineers who escaped. It will be safe there a long time—otherwise some witless fool may decide to use it for fuel for the Converter. I caught the man on watch feeding it with the last of a set of *Encyclopaedia Terrestriana*—priceless books. The idiot had never been taught to read! Some rule must be instituted concerning books.

" 'This is my last entry. I have put off making the attempt to place this log in safekeeping, because it is very perilous to ascend above the lower decks. But my life is no longer valuable; I wish to die knowing that a true record is left.

" 'Theodor Mawson, Captain.' "

Even the twins were silent for a long time after Hugh stopped reading. At last Joe heaved a long sigh and said, "So that's how it happened."

"The poor guy," Hugh said softly.

"Who? Captain Mawson? Why so?"

"No, not Captain Mawson. That other guy, Pilot Officer Baldwin. Think of him going out through that door, with *Huff* on the other side." Hugh shivered. In spite of his enlightenment, he subconsciously envisioned Huff, "Huff the Accursed, first to sin," as about twice as high as Joe-Jim, twice as strong as Bobo, and having fangs rather than teeth.

Hugh borrowed a couple of porters from Ertz—porters whom Ertz was using to fetch the pickled bodies of the war casualties to the Main Converter for fuel—and used them to provision the Ship's boat; water, breadstuffs, preserved meats, mass for the Converter. He did not report the matter to Narby, nor did he report the discovery of the boat itself. He had no conscious reason—Narby irritated him.

The star of their destination grew and grew, swelled until it showed a visible disc and was too bright to be stared at long. Its bearing changed rapidly, for a star; it pulled across the backdrop of the stellarium dome. Left uncontrolled, the Ship would have swung part way around it in a broad hyperbola and receded again into the depths of the darkness. It took Hugh the equivalent of many weeks to calculate the elements of the trajectory; it took still longer for Ertz and Joe-Jim to check his figures and satisfy themselves that the preposterous answers were right. It took even longer to convince Ertz that the way to rendezvous in space was to apply a force that pushed one *away* from where one wished to go—that is to say, dig in the heels, put on the brakes, kill the momentum.

In fact it took a series of experiments in free flight on the level of weightlessness to sell him the idea—otherwise he would have favored finishing the Trip by the simple expedient of crashing headlong into the star at top speed. Thereafter Hugh and Joe-Jim calculated how to apply acceleration to kill the speed of the *Vanguard* and warp her into an eccentric ellipse around the star. After that they would search for planets.

Ertz had a little trouble understanding the difference between a planet and a star. Alan never did get it.

"If my numbering is correct," Hugh informed Ertz "we should start accelerating any time now."

"O.K.," Ertz told him. "Main Drive is ready—over two hundred bodies and a lot of waste mass. What are we waiting for?"

"Let's see Narby and get permission to start."

"Why ask him?"

Hugh shrugged. "He's Captain. He'll want to know."

"All right. Let's pick up Joe-Jim and get on with it." They left Hugh's apartment and went to Joe-Jim's. Joe-Jim was not there, but they found Alan looking for him, too.

"Squatty says he's gone down to the Captain's office," Alan informed him.

"So? It's just as well—we'll see him there. Alan, old boy, you know what?"

"What?"

"The time has arrived. We're going to do it! Start moving the Ship!"

Alan looked round-eyed. "Gee! Right now?"

"Just as soon as we can notify the Captain. Come along, if you like."

"You bet! Wait while I tell my woman." He darted away to his own quarters nearby.

"He pampers that wench," remarked Ertz.

"Sometimes you can't help it," said Hugh with a faraway look.

Alan returned promptly, although it was evident that he had taken time to change to a fresh breechcloth. "O.K.," he bubbled. "Let's go!"

Alan approached the Captain's office with a proud step. He was an important guy now, he exulted to himself—he'd march on through with his friends while the guards saluted—no more of this business of being pushed around.

But the doorkeeper did not stand aside, although he did salute—while placing himself so that he filled the door. "Gangway, man!" Ertz said gruffly.

"Yes, sir," acknowledged the guard, without moving. "Your weapons, please."

"What! Don't you know me, you idiot? I'm the Chief Engineer."

OFF THE MAIN SEQUENCE

"Yes, sir. Leave your weapons with me, please. Regulations."

Ertz put a hand on the man's shoulder and shoved. The guard stood firm. "I'm sorry, sir. No one approaches the Captain wearing weapons. No one."

"Well, I'll be damned!"

"He remembers what happened to the old Captain," Hugh observed *sotto voce*. "He's smart." He drew his own knife and tossed it to the guard, who caught it neatly by the hilt. Ertz looked, shrugged, and handed over his own. Alan, considerably crestfallen, passed his own pair over with a look that should have shortened the guard's life.

Narby was talking; Joe-Jim was scowling on both his faces; Bobo looked puzzled, and naked, unfinished, without his ubiquitous knives and slingshot. "The matter is closed, Joe-Jim. That is my decision. I've granted you the favor of explaining my reasons, but it does not matter whether you like them or not."

"What's the trouble?" inquired Hugh.

Narby looked up. "Oh—I'm glad you came in. Your mutie friend seems to be in doubt as to who is Captain."

"What's up?"

"He," growled Jim, hooking a thumb toward Narby, "seems to think he's going to disarm all the muties."

"Well, the war's over, isn't it?"

"It wasn't agreed on. The muties were to become part of the Crew. Take the knives away from the muties and the Crew will kill them off in no time. It's not fair. The Crew have knives."

"The time will come when they won't," Narby predicted, "but I'll do it at my own time in my own way. This is the first step. What did you want to see me about, Ertz?"

"Ask Hugh." Narby turned to Hugh.

"I've come to notify you, Captain Narby," Hugh stated formally, "that we are about to start the Main Converter and move the Ship."

Narby looked surprised but not disconcerted. "I'm afraid you will have to postpone that. I am not yet ready to permit officers to go up to no-weight."

"It won't be necessary," Hugh explained. "Ertz and I can handle the first maneuvers alone. But we can't wait. If the Ship is not moved at once, the Trip won't be finished in your lifetime nor mine."

"Then it must," Narby replied evenly, "wait."

"What?" cried Hugh. "Narby, don't you *want* to finish the Trip?"

"I'm in no hurry."

"What sort of damn foolishness is this?" Ertz demanded. "What's got into you, Fin? Of course we move the Ship."

Narby drummed on his desk top before replying. Then he said, "Since there seems to be some slight misunderstanding as to who gives orders around here, I might as well let you have it straight. Hoyland, as long as your pastimes did not interfere with the administration of the Ship, I was willing for you to amuse yourself. I granted that willingly, for you have been very useful in your own way. But when your crazy beliefs become a possible source of corruption to good morals and a danger to the peace and security of the Ship, I have to crack down."

Hugh had opened and closed his mouth several times during this speech. Finally he managed to get out: "Crazy? Did you say crazy?"

"Yes, I did. For a man to believe that the solid Ship can move means that he is either crazy, or an ignorant religious fanatic. Since both of you have the advantage of a scientist's training, I assume that you have lost your minds."

"Good Jordan!" said Hugh. "The man has seen with his own eyes, he's seen the immortal stars—yet he sits there and calls *us* crazy!"

"What's the meaning of this, Narby?" Ertz inquired coldly. "Why the razzle-dazzle? You aren't kidding anyone—you've been to the Control Room, you've been to the Captain's veranda, you *know* the Ship moves."

"You interest me, Ertz," commented Narby, looking him over. "I've wondered whether you were playing up to Hoyland's delusions, or were deluded yourself. Now I see that you are crazy too."

Ertz kept his temper. "Explain yourself. You've seen the Control Room; how can you contend that the Ship does not move?"

Narby smiled. "I thought you were a better engineer than you appear to be, Ertz. The Control Room is an enormous hoax. You know yourself that those lights are turned on and off by switches—a very clever piece of engineering. My theory is that it was used to strike awe in the minds of the superstitious and make them believe in the ancient myths. But we don't need it any more, the Crew believe without it. It's a source of distraction now—I'm going to have it destroyed and the door sealed up."

Hugh went all to pieces at this, sputtered incoherently, and would have grappled with Narby had not Ertz restrained him. "Easy, Hugh," he admonished. Joe-Jim took Hugh by the arm, his own faces stony masks.

Ertz went on quietly, "Suppose what you say is true. Suppose that the Main Converter and the Main Drive itself are nothing but dummies and that we can never start them, what about the Captain's veranda? You've *seen* the stars there, not just an engineered shadow show."

Narby laughed. "Ertz, you are stupider than I ever guessed. I admit that the display in the veranda had me mystified at first—not that I ever believed in it! But the Control Room gave the clue—it's an illusion, a piece of skillful engineering. Behind that glass is another compartment, about the same size and unlighted. Against that darkness those tiny moving lights give the effect of a bottomless hole. It's essentially the same trick as the one used in the Control Room.

"It's obvious," he went on. "I'm surprised that you did not see it. When an apparent fact runs contrary to logic and common sense, it's obvious that you have failed to interpret the fact correctly. The most obvious fact of nature is the reality of the Ship itself, solid, immutable, complete. Any so-called fact which appears to dispute that is bound to be an illusion. Knowing that, I looked for the trick behind the illusion and found it."

"Wait," said Ertz. "Do you mean that you have been on the other side of the glass in the Captain's veranda and seen these trick lights you talk about?"

"No," admitted Narby, "it wasn't necessary. No doubt it would be easy enough to do so, but it isn't necessary. I don't have to cut myself to know that knives are sharp."

"So—" Ertz paused and thought a moment. "I'll make a deal with you. If Hugh and I are crazy in our beliefs, no harm is done as long as we keep our mouths shut. We'll try to move the Ship. If we fail we're wrong and you're right."

"The Captain does not bargain," Narby pointed out. "However— I'll consider it. That's all. You may go."

Ertz turned to go, unsatisfied but checked for the moment. He caught sight of Joe-Jim's faces, and turned back. "One more thing," he said. "What's this about the muties? Why are you shoving Joe-Jim around? He and his boys made you Captain—you've got to be fair about this."

Narby's smiling superiority cracked for a moment.

"Don't interfere, Ertz! Groups of armed savages can't be tolerated. That's final."

"You can do what you like with the prisoners," Jim stated, "but my own gang keep their knives. They were promised good eating forever if they fought for you. They keep their knives. And that's final!"

Narby looked him up and down. "Joe-Jim," he remarked, "I have long believed that the only good mutie was a dead mutie. You do much to confirm my opinion. It will interest you to know that, by this time, your gang *is* disarmed—and dead in the bargain. That's why I sent for you!"

The guards piled in, whether by signal or previous arrangement it was impossible to say. Caught flatfooted, naked, weaponless, the five found themselves each with an armed man at his back before they could rally. "Take them away," ordered Narby.

Bobo whined and looked to Joe-Jim for guidance. Joe caught his eye. "Up, Bobo!"

The dwarf jumped straight for Joe-Jim's captor, careless of the knife at his back. Forced to split his attention, the man lost a vital half second. Joe-Jim kicked him in the stomach, and appropriated his blade.

Hugh was on the deck, deadlocked with his man, his fist clutched around the knife wrist. Joe-Jim thrust and the struggle ceased. The two-headed man looked around, saw a mixed pile-up of four bodies, Ertz, Alan, two others. Joe-Jim used his knife judiciously, being careful to match the faces with the bodies. Presently his friends emerged. "Get their knives," he ordered superfluously.

His words were drowned by a high, agonized scream. Bobo, still without a knife, had resorted to his primal weapons. His late captor's face was a bloody mess, half bitten away.

"Get his knife," said Joe.

"Can't reach it," Bobo admitted guiltily. The reason was evident—the hilt protruded from Bobo's ribs, just below his right shoulder blade.

Joe-Jim examined it, touched it gently. It was stuck. "Can you walk?"

"Sure," grunted Bobo, and grimaced.

"Let it stay where it is. Alan! With me. Hugh and Bill—cover rear. Bobo in the middle."

"Where's Narby?" demanded Ertz, dabbing at a wound on his cheekbone.

But Narby was gone—ducked out through the rear door behind his desk. And it was locked.

Clerks scattered before them in the outer office; Joe-Jim knifed the guard at the outer door while he was still raising his whistle. Hastily they retrieved their own weapons and added them to those they had seized. They fled upward.

Two decks above inhabited levels Bobo stumbled and fell. Joe-Jim picked him up. "Can you make it?"

The dwarf nodded dumbly, blood on his lips. They climbed. Twenty decks or so higher it became evident that Bobo could no longer climb, though they had taken turns in boosting him from the rear. But weight was lessened appreciably at that level; Alan braced himself and picked up the solid form as if it were a child. They climbed.

Joe-Jim relieved Alan. They climbed.

Ertz relieved Joe-Jim. Hugh relieved Ertz.

They reached the level on which they lived forward of their group apartments. Hugh turned in that direction. "Put him down," commanded Joe. "Where do you think you are going?"

Hugh settled the wounded man to the deck. "Home. Where else?"

"Fool! That's where they will look for us first."

"Where *do* we go?"

"Nowhere—in the Ship. We go out of the Ship!"

"Huh?"

"The Ship's boat."

"He's right," agreed Ertz. "The whole Ship's against us now."

"But . . . but—" Hugh surrendered. "It's a long chance—but we'll try it." He started again in the direction of their homes.

"Hey!" shouted Jim. "Not that way."

"We have to get our women."

"To Huff with the women! You'll get caught. There's no time." But Ertz and Alan started off without question. "Oh—all right!" Jim snorted. "But hurry! I'll stay with Bobo."

Joe-Jim sat down, took the dwarf's head in his lap, and made a careful examination. His skin was gray and damp; a long red stain ran down from his right shoulder. Bobo sighed bubblingly and rubbed his head against Joe-Jim's thigh. "Bobo tired, Boss."

Joe-Jim patted his head. "Easy," said Jim, "this is going to hurt." Lifting the wounded man slightly, he cautiously worked the blade loose and withdrew it from the wound. Blood poured out freely.

Joe-Jim examined the knife, noted the deadly length of steel, and measured it against the wound. "He'll never make it," whispered Joe.

Jim caught his eye. "Well?"

Joe nodded slowly. Joe-Jim tried the blade he had just extracted from the wound against his own thigh, and discarded it in favor of one of his own razor-edged tools. He took the dwarf's chin in his left hand and Joe commanded, "Look at me, Bobo!"

Bobo looked up, answered inaudibly. Joe held his eye. "Good Bobo! Strong Bobo!" The dwarf grinned as if he heard and understood, but made no attempt to reply. His master pulled his head a little to one side; the blade bit deep, snicking the jugular vein without touching the windpipe. "Good Bobo!" Joe repeated. Bobo grinned again.

When the eyes were glassy and breathing had unquestionably stopped, Joe-Jim stood up, letting the head and shoulders roll from him.

He shoved the body with his foot to the side of the passage, and stared down the direction in which the others had gone. They should be back by now.

He stuck the salvaged blade in his belt and made sure that all his weapons were loose and ready.

They arrived on a dead run. "A little trouble," Hugh explained breathlessly. "Squatty's dead. No more of your men around. Dead maybe—Narby probably meant it. Here—" He handed him a long knife and the body armor that had been built for Joe-Jim, with its great wide cage of steel, fit to cover two heads.

Ertz and Alan wore armor, as did Hugh. The women did not—none had been built for them. Joe-Jim noted that Hugh's younger wife bore a fresh swelling on her lip, as if someone had persuaded her with a heavy hand. Her eyes were stormy though her manner was docile. The older wife, Chloe, seemed to take the events in her stride. Ertz's was crying softly; Alan's wench reflected the bewilderment of her master.

"How's Bobo?" Hugh inquired, as he settled Joe-Jim's armor in place.

"Made the Trip," Joe informed him.

"So? Well, that's that—let's go."

They stopped short of the level of no-weight and worked forward, because the women were not adept at weightless flying. When they reached the bulkhead which separated the Control Room and boat pockets from the body of the Ship, they went up. There was neither alarm nor ambush, although Joe thought that he saw a head show as they reached one deck. He mentioned it to his brother but not to the others.

The door to the boat pocket stuck and Bobo was not there to free it. The men tried it in succession, sweating with the strain. Joe-Jim tried it a second time, Joe relaxing and letting Jim control their muscles, that they might not fight each other. The door gave. "Get 'em inside!" snapped Jim.

"And fast!" Joe confirmed. "They're on us." He had kept lookout while his brother strove. A shout from down the line reinforced his warning.

The twins faced around to meet the threat while the men shoved the women in. Alan's fuzzy-headed mate chose that moment to go to pieces, squalled, and tried to run, but weightlessness defeated her. Hugh nabbed her, headed her inside and booted her heartily with his foot.

Joe-Jim let a blade go at long throwing range to slow down the advance. It accomplished its purpose; his opponents, half a dozen of them, checked their advance. Then, apparently on signal, six knives cut the air simultaneously.

Jim felt something strike him, felt no pain, and concluded that the armor had saved him. "Missed us, Joe," he exulted.

There was no answer. Jim turned his head, tried to look at his brother. A few inches from his eye a knife stuck through the bars of the helmet; its point was buried deep in Joe's left eye.

His brother was dead.

Hugh stuck his head back out of the door. "Come on, Joe-Jim," he shouted. "We're all in."

"Get inside," ordered Jim. "Close the door."

"But—"

"Get inside!" Jim turned, and shoved him in the face, closing the door as he did so. Hugh had one startled glimpse of the knife and sagging, lifeless face it pinned. Then the door closed against him, and he heard the lever turn.

Jim turned back at the attackers. Shoving himself away from the bulkhead with legs which were curiously heavy, he plunged toward them, his great armlong knife, more a bolo than a sword, grasped with both hands. Knives sang toward him, clattered against his breastplate, bit into his legs. He swung—a wide awkward two-handed stroke which gutted an opponent—nearly cut him in two. "That's for Joe!"

The blow stopped him. He turned in the air, steadied himself, and swung again. "That's for Bobo!"

They closed on him; he swung widely, caring not where he hit as long as his blade met resistance. "And that's for me!"

A knife planted itself in his thigh. It did not even slow him up; legs were dispensable in no-weight. " 'One for all!' "

A man was on his back now—he could feel him. No matter—here was one before him, too—one who could feel steel. As he swung, he shouted, "All for o—" The words trailed off, but the stroke was finished.

Hugh tried to open the door which had been slammed in his face. He was unable to do so—if there were means provided to do so, he was unable to figure them out. He pressed an ear against the steel and listened, but the airtight door gave back no clue.

Ertz touched him on the shoulder. "Come on," he said. "Where's Joe-Jim?"

"He stayed behind."

"What! Open the door—get him."

"I can't, it won't open. He meant to stay, he closed it himself."

"But we've got to get him—we're blood-sworn."

"I think," said Hugh, with a sudden flash of insight, "that's why he stayed behind." He told Ertz what he had seen.

"Anyhow," he concluded, "it's the *End of the Trip* to him. Get on back and feed mass to that Converter. I want power." They entered the Ship's boat proper; Hugh closed the air-lock doors behind them. "Alan!" he called out. "We're going to start. Keep those damned women out of the way."

He settled himself in the pilot's chair, and cut the lights.

In the darkness he covered a pattern of green lights. A transparency flashed on the lap desk: DRIVE READY. Ertz was on the job. Here goes! he thought, and actuated the launching combination. There was a short pause, a short and sickening lurch—*a twist*. It frightened him, since he had no way of knowing that the launching tracks were pitched to offset the normal spinning of the Ship.

The glass of the view port before him was speckled with stars; they were free—moving!

But the spread of jeweled lights was not unbroken, as it invariably had been when seen from the veranda, or seen mirrored on the Control Room walls; a great, gross, ungainly shape gleamed softly under the light of the star whose system they had entered. At first he could not account for it. Then with a rush of superstitious awe he realized that he was looking at the Ship itself, the true Ship, seen from the Outside. In spite of his long intellectual awareness of the true nature of the Ship, he had never visualized looking at it. The stars, yes—the surface of a planet, he had struggled with that concept—but the outer surface of the Ship, no.

When he did see it, it shocked him.

Alan touched him. "Hugh, what is it?"

Hoyland tried to explain to him. Alan shook his head, and blinked his eyes. "I don't get it."

"Never mind. Bring Ertz up here. Fetch the women, too—we'll let them see it."

"All right. But," he added, with sound intuition, "it's a mistake to show the women. You'll scare 'em silly—they ain't even seen the stars."

Luck, sound engineering design, and a little knowledge. Good design, ten times that much luck, and a precious little knowledge. It was luck that had placed the Ship near a star with a planetary system, luck that the Ship arrived there with a speed low enough for Hugh to counteract it in a ship's auxiliary craft, luck that he learned to handle it after a fashion before they starved or lost themselves in deep space.

It was good design that provided the little craft with a great reserve of power and speed. The designers had anticipated that the pioneers might need to explore the far-flung planets of a solar system; they had provided for it in the planning of the Ship's boats, with a large factor of safety. Hugh strained that factor to the limit.

It was luck that placed them near the plane of planetary motion, luck that, when Hugh did manage to gun the tiny projectile into a closed orbit, the orbit agreed in direction with the rotation of the planets.

Luck that the eccentric ellipse he achieved should cause them to crawl up on a giant planet so that he was eventually able to identify it as such by sight.

For otherwise they might have spun around that star until they all died of old age, ignoring for the moment the readier hazards of hunger and thirst, without ever coming close enough to a planet to pick it out from the stars.

There is a misconception, geocentric and anthropomorphic, common to the large majority of the earthbound, which causes them to visualize a planetary system stereoscopically. The mind's eye sees a sun, remote from a backdrop of stars, and surrounded by spinning apples—the planets. Step out on your balcony and look. Can you tell the planets from the stars? Venus you may pick out with ease, but could you tell it from Canopus, if you had not previously been introduced? That little red speck—is it Mars, or is it Antares? How would you know, if you were as ignorant as Hugh Hoyland? Blast for Antares, believing it to be a planet, and you will never live to have grandchildren.

The great planet that they crawled up on, till it showed a visible naked-eye disc, was larger than Jupiter, a fit companion to the star, somewhat younger and larger than the Sun, around which it swung at a lordly distance. Hugh blasted back, killing his speed over many sleeps, to bring the Ship into a path around the planet. The maneuver brought him close enough to see its moons.

Luck helped him again. He had planned to ground on the great planet, knowing no better. Had he been able to do so they would have lived just long enough to open the air-lock.

But he was short of mass, after the titanic task of pulling them out of the headlong hyperbolic plunge around and past the star and warping them into a closed orbit about the star, then into a subordinate orbit around the great planet. He pored over the ancient books, substituted endlessly in the equations the ancients had set down as the laws for moving bodies, figured and refigured, and tried even the calm patience of Chloe.

The other wife, the unnamed one, kept out of his sight after losing a tooth, quite suddenly.

But he got no answer that did not require him to use some, at least, of the precious, irreplaceable ancient books for fuel. Yes, even though they stripped themselves naked and chucked in their knives, the mass of the books would still be needed.

He would have preferred to dispense with one of his wives. He decided to ground on one of the moons.

Luck again. Coincidence of such colossal proportions that one need not be expected to believe it—for the moon-planet was suitable for human terrestrial life. Never mind—skip over it rapidly; the combination of circumstances is of the same order needed to produce such a planet in the first place. Our own planet, under our feet, is of the "There ain't no such animal!" variety. It is a ridiculous improbability.

Hugh's luck was a ridiculous improbability.

Good design handled the next phase. Although he had learned to maneuver the little Ship out in space where there is elbow room, landing is another and a ticklish matter. He would have crashed any spacecraft designed before the designing of the *Vanguard*. But the designers of the *Vanguard* had known that the Ship's auxiliary craft would be piloted and grounded by at least the second generation of explorers; green pilots must make those landings unassisted. They planned for it.

Hugh got the vessel down into the stratosphere and straightened it triumphantly into a course that would with certainty kill them all.

The autopilots took over.

Hugh stormed and swore, producing some words which diverted Alan's attention and admiration from the view out of the port. But nothing he could do would cause the craft to respond. It settled in its own way and leveled off at a thousand feet, an altitude which it maintained regardless of changing contour.

"Hugh, the stars are gone!"

"I know it."

"But Jordan! Hugh—what happened to them?"

Hugh glared at Alan. "I—don't—know—and—I—don't care! You get aft with the women and stop asking silly questions."

Alan departed reluctantly with a backward look at the surface of the planet and the bright sky. It interested him, but he did not marvel much at it—his ability to marvel had been overstrained.

It was some hours before Hugh discovered that a hitherto ignored group of control lights set in motion a chain of events whereby the autopilot would ground the Ship. Since he found this out experimentally he did not exactly choose the place of landing. But the unwinking stereo-eyes of the autopilot fed its data to the "brain"; the submolar mechanism selected and rejected; the Ship grounded gently on a rolling high prairie near a clump of trees.

Ertz came forward. "What's happened, Hugh?"

Hugh waved at the view port. "We're there." He was too tired to make much of it, too tired and too emotionally exhausted. His weeks of fighting a fight he understood but poorly, hunger, and lately thirst—years of feeding on a consuming ambition, these left him with little ability to enjoy his goal when it arrived.

But they had landed, they had finished Jordan's Trip. He was not unhappy; at peace rather, and very tired.

Ertz stared out. "Jordan!" he muttered. Then, "Let's go out."

"All right."

Alan came forward, as they were opening the air-lock, and the women pressed after him. "Are we there, Captain?"

"Shut up," said Hugh.

The women crowded up to the deserted view port; Alan explained to them, importantly and incorrectly, the scene outside. Ertz got the last door open.

They sniffed at the air. "It's *cold*," said Ertz. In fact the temperature was perhaps five degrees less than the steady monotony of the Ship's temperature, but Ertz was experiencing weather for the first time.

"Nonsense," said Hugh, faintly annoyed that any fault should be found with "his" planet. "It's just your imagination."

"Maybe," Ertz conceded. He paused uneasily. "Going out?" he added.

"Of course." Mastering his own reluctance, Hugh pushed him aside and dropped five feet to the ground "Come on—it's fine."

Ertz joined him, and stood close to him. Both of them remained close to the Ship. "It's big, isn't it?" Ertz said in a hushed voice.

"Well, we knew it would be," Hugh snapped, annoyed with himself for having the same lost feeling.

"Hi!" Alan peered cautiously out of the door. "Can I come down? Is it all right?"

"Come ahead."

Alan eased himself gingerly over the edge and joined them. He looked around and whistled. "Gosh!"

Their first sortie took them all of fifty feet from the Ship.

They huddled close together for silent comfort, and watched their feet to keep from stumbling on this strange uneven deck. They made it without incident until Alan looked up from the ground and found himself for the first time in his life with nothing *close* to him. He was hit by vertigo and acute agoraphobia; he moaned, closed his eyes and fell.

"What in the Ship?" demanded Ertz, looking around. Then it hit him.

Hugh fought against it. It pulled him to his knees, but he fought it, steadying himself with one hand on the ground. However, he had the advantage of having stared out through the view port for endless time—neither Alan nor Ertz were cowards.

"Alan!" his wife shrilled from the open door. "Alan! Come back here!" Alan opened one eye, managed to get it focused on the Ship, and started inching back on his belly.

"Alan!" commanded Hugh. "Stop that! Sit up."

Alan did so, with the air of a man pushed too far. "Open your eyes!" Alan obeyed cautiously, reclosed them hastily.

"Just sit still and you'll be all right," Hugh added. "I'm all right already." To prove it he stood up. He was still dizzy, but he made it. Ertz sat up.

The sun had crossed a sizable piece of the sky, enough time had passed for a well-fed man to become hungry—and they were not well fed. Even the women were outside—that had been accomplished by the simple expedient of going back in and pushing them out. They had not ventured away from the side of the Ship, but sat huddled against it. But their menfolk had even learned to walk singly, even in open spaces. Alan thought nothing of strutting a full fifty yards away from the shadow of the Ship, and did so more than once, in full sight of the women.

It was on one such journey that a small animal native to the planet let his curiosity exceed his caution. Alan's knife knocked him over and left him kicking. Alan scurried to the spot, grabbed his fat prize by one leg, and bore it proudly back to Hugh. "Look, Hugh, look! Good eating!"

Hugh looked with approval. His first strange fright of the place had passed and had been replaced with a warm deep feeling, a feeling that he had come at last to his long home. This seemed a good omen.

"Yes," he agreed. "Good eating. From now on, Alan, always Good Eating."

BY HIS BOOTSTRAPS
Atounding Science Fiction, October 1941

as by Anson MacDonald

BOB WILSON DID not see the circle grow.

Nor, for that matter, did he see the stranger who stepped out of the circle and stood staring at the back of Wilson's neck—stared, and breathed heavily, as if laboring under strong and unusual emotion.

Wilson had no reason to suspect that anyone else was in his room; he had every reason to expect the contrary. He had locked himself in his room for the purpose of completing his thesis in one sustained drive. He *had* to—tomorrow was the last day for submission, yesterday the thesis had been no more than a title: "An Investigation into Certain Mathematical Aspects of a Rigor of Metaphysics."

Fifty-two cigarettes, four pots of coffee, and thirteen hours of continuous work had added seven thousand words to the title. As to the validity of his thesis he was far too groggy to give a damn. Get it done, was his only thought, get it done, turn it in, take three stiff drinks and sleep for a week.

He glanced up and let his eyes rest on his wardrobe door, behind which he had cached a gin bottle, nearly full. No, he admonished himself, one more drink and you'll never finish it, Bob, old son.

The stranger behind him said nothing.

Wilson resumed typing. "—nor is it valid to assume that a conceivable proposition is necessarily a possible proposition, even when it is possible to formulate mathematics which describes the proposition with exactness. A case in point is the concept 'Time Travel.' Time travel may be imagined and its necessities may be formulated under any and all theories of time, formulae which resolve the paradoxes of each theory. Nevertheless, we know certain things about the empirical nature of time which preclude the possibility of the conceivable proposition. Duration is an attribute of consciousness and not of the plenum. It has no *Ding an Sich*. Therefore—"

A key of the typewriter stuck, three more jammed up on top of it.

Wilson swore dully and reached forward to straighten out the cantankerous machinery. "Don't bother with it," he heard a voice say. "It's a lot of utter hogwash anyhow."

Wilson sat up with a jerk, then turned his head slowly around. He fervently hoped that there was someone behind him. Otherwise—

He perceived the stranger with relief. "Thank God," he said to himself. "For a moment I thought I had come unstuck." His relief turned to extreme annoyance. "What the devil are you doing in my room?" he demanded. He shoved back his chair, got up and strode over to the one door. It was still locked, and bolted on the inside.

The windows were no help; they were adjacent to his desk and three stories above a busy street. "How *did* you get in?" he added.

"Through that," answered the stranger, hooking a thumb toward the circle. Wilson noticed it for the first time, blinked his eyes and looked again. There it hung between them and the wall, a great disk of nothing, of the color one sees when the eyes are shut tight.

Wilson shook his head vigorously. The circle remained. "Gosh," he thought, "I was right the first time. I wonder when I slipped my trolley?" He advanced toward the disk, put out a hand to touch it.

"Don't!" snapped the stranger.

"Why not?" said Wilson edgily. Nevertheless he paused.

"I'll explain. But let's have a drink first." He walked directly to the wardrobe, opened it, reached in and took out the bottle of gin without looking.

"Hey!" yelled Wilson. "What are you doing there? That's *my* liquor."

"*Your* liquor—" The stranger paused for a moment. "Sorry. You don't mind if I have a drink, do you?"

"I suppose not," Bob Wilson conceded in a surly tone. "Pour me one while you're about it."

"O.K.," agreed the stranger, "then I'll explain."

"It had better be good," Wilson said ominously. Nevertheless he drank his drink and looked the stranger over.

He saw a chap about the same size as himself and much the same age—perhaps a little older, though a three-day growth of beard may have accounted for that impression. The stranger had a black eye and a freshly cut and badly swollen upper lip. Wilson decided he did not like the chap's face. Still, there was something familiar about the face; he felt that he should have recognized it, that he had seen it many times before under different circumstances.

"Who are you?" he asked suddenly.

"Me?" said his guest. "Don't you recognize me?"

"I'm not sure," admitted Wilson. "Have I ever seen you before?"

"Well—not exactly," the other temporized. "Skip it—you wouldn't know about it."

"What's your name?"

"My name? Uh . . . just call me Joe."

Wilson set down his glass. "O.K., Joe Whatever-your-name-is, trot out that explanation and make it snappy."

"I'll do that," agreed Joe. "That dingus I came through"—he pointed to the circle—"that's a Time Gate."

"A what?"

"A Time Gate. Time flows along side by side on each side of the Gate, but some thousands of years apart—just how many thousands I don't know. But for the next couple of hours that Gate is open. You can walk into the future just by stepping through that circle." The stranger paused.

Bob drummed on the desk. "Go ahead. I'm listening. It's a nice story."

"You don't believe me, do you? I'll show you." Joe got up, went again to the wardrobe and obtained Bob's hat, his prized and only hat, which he had mistreated into its present battered grandeur through six years of undergraduate and graduate life. Joe chucked it toward the impalpable disk.

It struck the surface, went on through with no apparent resistance, disappeared from sight.

Wilson got up, walked carefully around the circle and examined the bare floor. "A neat trick," he conceded. "Now I'll thank you to return to me my hat."

The stranger shook his head. "You can get it for yourself when you pass through."

"Huh?"

"That's right. Listen—" Briefly the stranger repeated his explanation about the Time Gate. Wilson, he insisted, had an opportunity that comes once in a millennium—if he would only hurry up and climb through that circle. Furthermore, though Joe could not explain in detail at the moment, it was very important that Wilson go through.

Bob Wilson helped himself to a second drink, and then a third. He was beginning to feel both good and argumentative. "Why?" he said flatly.

Joe looked exasperated. "Dammit, if you'd just step through once, explanations wouldn't be necessary. However—" According to Joe, there was an old guy on the other side who needed Wilson's help. With Wilson's help the three of them would run the country. The exact nature of the help Joe could not or would not specify. Instead he bore down on the unique possibilities for high adventure. "You don't want to slave your life away teaching numskulls in some freshwater college," he insisted. "This is your chance. Grab it!"

Bob Wilson admitted to himself that a Ph.D. and an appointment as an instructor was not his idea of existence. Still, it beat working for a living. His eye fell on the gin bottle, its level now deplorably lowered. That explained it. He got up unsteadily.

"No, my dear fellow," he stated, "I'm not going to climb on your merry-go-round. You know why?"

"Why?"

"Because I'm drunk, that's why. You're not there at all. *That* ain't there." He gestured widely at the circle. "There ain't anybody here but me, and I'm drunk. Been working too hard," he added apologetically. "I'm goin' to bed."

"You're not drunk."

"I *am* drunk. Peter Piper pepped a pick of pippered peckles." He moved toward his bed.

Joe grabbed his arm. "You can't do that," he said.

"Let him alone!"

They both swung around. Facing them, standing directly in front of the circle was a third man. Bob looked at the newcomer, looked back at Joe, blinked his eyes and tried to focus them. The two looked a good bit alike, he thought, enough alike to be brothers. Or maybe he was seeing double. Bad stuff, gin. Should 'ave switched to rum a long time ago. Good stuff, rum. You could drink it, or take a bath in it. No, that was gin—he meant Joe.

How silly! Joe was the one with the black eye. He wondered why he had ever been confused.

Then who was this other lug? Couldn't a couple of friends have a quiet drink together without people butting in?

"Who are you?" he said with quiet dignity.

The newcomer turned his head, then looked at Joe. "*He* knows me," he said meaningly.

Joe looked him over slowly. "Yes," he said, "yes, I suppose I do. But what the deuce are you here for? And why are you trying to bust up the plan?"

"No time for long-winded explanations. I know more about it than you do—you'll concede that—and my judgment is bound to be better than yours. He doesn't go through the Gate."

"I don't concede anything of the sort—"

The telephone rang.

"Answer it!" snapped the newcomer.

Bob was about to protest the peremptory tone, but decided he wouldn't. He lacked the phlegmatic temperament necessary to ignore a ringing telephone. "Hello?"

"Hello," he was answered. "Is that Bob Wilson?"

"Yes. Who is this?"

"Never mind. I just wanted to be sure you were there. I *thought* you would be. You're right in the groove, kid, right in the groove."

Wilson heard a chuckle, then the click of the disconnection. "Hello," he said. "Hello!" He jiggled the bar a couple of times, then hung up.

"What was it?" asked Joe.

"Nothing. Some nut with a misplaced sense of humor." The telephone bell rang again. Wilson added, "There he is again," and picked up the receiver. "Listen, you butterfly-brained ape! I'm a busy man, and this is *not* a public telephone."

"Why, Bob!" came a hurt feminine voice.

"Huh? Oh, it's you, Genevieve. Look—I'm sorry. I apologize—"

"Well, I should think you would!"

"You don't understand, honey. A guy has been pestering me over the phone and I thought it was him. You know I wouldn't talk that way to you, Babe."

"Well, I should think not. Particularly after all you said to me this afternoon, and all we *meant* to each other."

"Huh? This afternoon? Did you say *this* afternoon?"

"Of course. But what I called up about was this: You left your hat in my apartment. I noticed it a few minutes after you had gone and just thought I'd call and tell you where it is. Anyhow," she added coyly, "it gave me an excuse to hear your voice again."

"Sure. Fine," he said mechanically. "Look, Babe, I'm a little mixed up about this. Trouble I've had all day long, and more trouble now. I'll look you up tonight and straighten it out. But I *know* I didn't leave your hat in my apartment—"

"*Your* hat, silly!"

"Huh? Oh, sure! Anyhow, I'll see you tonight. 'By." He rang off hurriedly. Gosh, he thought, that woman is getting to be a problem. Hallucinations. He turned to his two companions.

"Very well, Joe. I'm ready to go if you are." He was not sure just when or why he had decided to go through the time gadget, but he had. Who did this other mug think he was, anyhow, trying to interfere with a man's freedom of choice?

OFF THE MAIN SEQUENCE

"Fine!" said Joe, in a relieved voice. "Just step through. That's all there is to it."

"No, you don't!" It was the ubiquitous stranger. He stepped between Wilson and the Gate.

Bob Wilson faced him. "Listen, you! You come butting in here like you think I was a bum. If you don't like it, go jump in the lake—and I'm just the kind of guy who can do it! You and who else?"

The stranger reached out and tried to collar him. Wilson let go a swing, but not a good one. It went by nothing faster than parcel post. The stranger walked under it and let him have a mouthful of knuckles—large, hard ones. Joe closed in rapidly, coming to Bob's aid. They traded punches in a free-for-all, with Bob joining in enthusiastically but inefficiently. The only punch he landed was on Joe, theoretically his ally. However, he had intended it for the third man.

It was this *faux pas* which gave the stranger an opportunity to land a clean left jab on Wilson's face. It was inches higher than the button, but in Bob's bemused condition it was sufficient to cause him to cease taking part in the activities.

Bob Wilson came slowly to awareness of his surroundings. He was seated on a floor which seemed a little unsteady. Someone was bending over him. "Are you all right?" the figure inquired.

"I guess so," he answered thickly. His mouth pained him; he put his hand to it, got it sticky with blood. "My head hurts."

"I should think it would. You came through head over heels. I think you hit your head when you landed."

Wilson's thoughts were coming back into confused focus. Came through? He looked more closely at his succorer. He saw a middle-aged man with gray-shot bushy hair and a short, neatly trimmed beard. He was dressed in what Wilson took to be purple lounging pajamas.

But the room in which he found himself bothered him even more. It was circular and the ceiling was arched so subtly that it was difficult to say how high it was. A steady glareless light filled the room from no apparent source. There was no furniture save for a high dais or pulpit-shaped object near the wall facing him. "Came through? Came through what?"

"The Gate, of course." There was something odd about the man's accent. Wilson could not place it, save for a feeling that English was not a tongue he was accustomed to speaking.

Wilson looked over his shoulder in the direction of the other's gaze, and saw the circle.

That made his head ache even more. "Oh, Lord," he thought, "now I really am nuts. Why don't I wake up?" He shook his head to clear it.

That was a mistake. The top of his head did not quite come off—not quite. And the circle stayed where it was, a simple locus hanging in the air, its flat depth filled with the amorphous colors and shapes of no-vision. "Did I come through that?"

"Yes."

"Where am I?"

"In the Hall of the Gate in the High Palace of Norkaal. But what is more important is *when* you are. You have gone forward a little more than thirty thousand years."

"Now I know I'm crazy," thought Wilson. He got up unsteadily and moved toward the Gate.

The older man put a hand on his shoulder. "Where are you going?"

"Back!"

"Not so fast. You will go back all right—I give you my word on that. But let me dress your wounds first. And you should rest. I have some explanations to make to you, and there is an errand you can do for me when you get back—to our mutual advantage. There is a great future in store for you and me, my boy—a great future!"

Wilson paused uncertainly. The elder man's insistence was vaguely disquieting. "I don't like this."

The other eyed him narrowly. "Wouldn't you like a drink before you go?"

Wilson most assuredly would. Right at the moment a stiff drink seemed the most desirable thing on earth—or in time. "O.K."

"Come with me." The older man led him back of the structure near the wall and through a door which led into a passageway. He walked briskly; Wilson hurried to keep up.

"By the way," he asked, as they continued down the long passage, "what is your name?"

"My name? You may call me Diktor—everyone else does."

"O.K., Diktor. Do you want my name?"

"Your name?" Diktor chuckled. "I know your name. It's Bob Wilson."

"Huh? Oh—I suppose Joe told you."

"Joe? I know no one by that name."

"You don't? He seemed to know you. Say—maybe you aren't that guy I was supposed to see."

"But I am. I have been expecting you—in a way. Joe . . . Joe—Oh!" Diktor chuckled. "It had slipped my mind for a moment. He told you to call him Joe, didn't he?"

"Isn't it his name?"

"It's as good a name as any other. Here we are." He ushered Wilson into a small, but cheerful, room. It contained no furniture of any sort, but the floor was soft and warm as live flesh. "Sit down. I'll be back in a moment."

Bob looked around for something to sit on, then turned to ask Diktor for a chair. But Diktor was gone, furthermore the door through which they had entered was gone. Bob sat down on the comfortable floor and tried not to worry.

Diktor returned promptly. Wilson saw the door dilate to let him in, but did not catch on to how it was done. Diktor was carrying a carafe, which gurgled pleasantly, and a cup. "Mud in your eye," he said heartily and poured a good four fingers. "Drink up."

Bob accepted the cup. "Aren't you drinking?"

"Presently. I want to attend to your wounds first."

"O.K." Wilson tossed off the first drink in almost indecent haste—it was good stuff, a little like Scotch, he decided, but smoother and not as dry—while Diktor worked deftly with salves that smarted at first, then soothed. "Mind if I have another?"

"Help yourself."

Bob drank more slowly the second cup. He did not finish it; it slipped from relaxed fingers, spilling a ruddy, brown stain across the floor. He snored.

Bob Wilson woke up feeling fine and completely rested. He was cheerful without knowing why. He lay relaxed, eyes still closed, for a few moments and let his soul snuggle back into his body. This was going to be a good day, he felt. Oh, yes—he had finished that double-damned thesis. No, he hadn't either! He sat up with a start.

The sight of the strange walls around him brought him back into continuity. But before he had time to worry—at once, in fact—the door relaxed and Diktor stepped in. "Feeling better?"

"Why, yes, I do. Say, what is this?"

"We'll get to that. How about some breakfast?"

In Wilson's scale of evaluations breakfast rated just after life itself and ahead of the chance of immortality. Diktor conducted him to another room—the first that he had seen possessing windows. As a matter of fact half the room was open, a balcony hanging high over a green countryside. A soft, warm, summer breeze wafted through the place. They broke their fast in luxury, Roman style, while Diktor explained.

Bob Wilson did not follow the explanations as closely as he might have done, because his attention was diverted by the maidservants who served the meal. The first came in bearing a great tray of fruit on her head. The fruit was gorgeous. So was the girl. Search as he would he could discern no fault in her.

Her costume lent itself to the search.

She came first to Diktor, and with a single, graceful movement dropped to one knee, removed the tray from her head, and offered it to him. He helped himself to a small, red fruit and waved her away. She then offered it to Bob in the same delightful manner.

"As I was saying," continued Diktor, "it is not certain where the High Ones came from or where they went when they left Earth. I am inclined to think they went away into Time. In any case they ruled more than twenty thousand years and completely obliterated human culture as you knew it. What is more important to you and to me is the effect they had on the human psyche. One twentieth-century style go-getter can accomplish just about anything he wants to accomplish around here—Aren't you listening?"

"Huh? Oh, yes, sure. Say, that's one mighty pretty girl." His eyes still rested on the exit through which she had disappeared.

"Who? Oh, yes, I suppose so. She's not exceptionally beautiful as women go around here."

"That's hard to believe. I could learn to get along with a girl like that."

"You like her? Very well, she is yours."

"Huh?"

"She's a slave. Don't get indignant. They are slaves by nature. If you like her, I'll make you a present of her. It will make her happy." The girl had just returned. Diktor called to her in a language strange to Bob. "Her name is Arma," he said in an aside, then spoke to her briefly.

Arma giggled. She composed her face quickly, and, moving over to where Wilson reclined, dropped on both knees to the floor and lowered her head, with both hands cupped before her. "Touch her forehead," Diktor instructed.

Bob did so. The girl arose and stood waiting placidly by his side. Diktor spoke to her. She looked puzzled, but moved out of the room. "I told her that, notwithstanding her new status, you wished her to continue serving breakfast."

Diktor resumed his explanations while the service of the meal continued. The next course was brought in by Arma and another girl. When

Bob saw the second girl he let out a low whistle. He realized he had been a little hasty in letting Diktor give him Arma. Either the standard of pulchritude had gone up incredibly, he decided, or Diktor went to a lot of trouble in selecting his servants.

"—for that reason," Diktor was saying, "it is necessary that you go back through the Time Gate at once. Your first job is to bring this other chap back. Then there is one other task for you to do, and we'll be sitting pretty. After that it is share and share alike for you and me. And there is plenty to share, I—You aren't listening!"

"Sure I was, chief. I heard every word you said." He fingered his chin. "Say, have you got a razor I could borrow? I'd like to shave."

Diktor swore softly in two languages. "Keep your eyes off those wenches and listen to me! There's work to be done."

"Sure, sure. I understand that—and I'm your man. When do we start?" Wilson had made up his mind some time ago—just shortly after Arma had entered with the tray of fruit, in fact. He felt as if he had walked into some extremely pleasant dream. If co-operation with Diktor would cause that dream to continue, so be it. To hell with an academic career!

Anyhow, all Diktor wanted was for him to go back where he started and persuade another guy to go through the Gate. The worst that could happen was for him to find himself back in the twentieth century. What could he lose?

Diktor stood up. "Let's get on with it," he said shortly, "before you get your attention diverted again. Follow me." He set off at a brisk pace with Wilson behind him.

Diktor took him to the Hall of the Gate and stopped. "All you have to do," he said, "is to step through the Gate. You will find yourself back in your own room, in your own time. Persuade the man you find there to go through the Gate. We have need of him. Then come back yourself."

Bob held up a hand and pinched thumb and forefinger together. "It's in the bag, boss. Consider it done." He started to step through the Gate.

"Wait!" commanded Diktor. "You are not used to time travel. I warn you that you are going to get one hell of a shock when you step through. This other chap—you'll recognize him."

"Who is he?"

"I won't tell you because you wouldn't understand. But you will when you see him. Just remember this—There are some very strange paradoxes connected with time travel. Don't let anything you see throw you. You do what I tell you to and you'll be all right."

"Paradoxes don't worry me," Bob said confidently. "Is that all? I'm ready."

"One minute." Diktor stepped behind the raised dais. His head appeared above the side a moment later. "I've set the controls. O.K. Go!"

Bob Wilson stepped through the locus known as the Time Gate.

There was no particular sensation connected with the transition. It was like stepping through a curtained doorway into a darker room. He paused for a moment on the other side and let his eyes adjust to the dimmer light. He was, he saw, indeed in his own room.

There was a man in it, seated at his own desk. Diktor had been right about that. This, then, was the chap he was to send back through the Gate. Diktor had said he would recognize him. Well, let's see who it is.

He felt a passing resentment at finding someone at *his* desk in *his* room, then thought better of it. After all, it was just a rented room; when he disappeared, no doubt it had been rented again. He had no way of telling how long he had been gone—shucks, it might be the middle of next week!

The chap did look vaguely familiar, although all he could see was his back. Who was it? Should he speak to him, cause him to turn around? He felt vaguely reluctant to do so until he knew who it was. He rationalized the feeling by telling himself that it was desirable to know with whom he was dealing before he attempted anything as outlandish as persuading this man to go through the Gate.

The man at the desk continued typing, paused to snuff out a cigarette by laying it in an ash tray, then stamping it with a paper weight.

Bob Wilson knew that gesture.

Chills trickled down his back. "If he lights his next one," he whispered to himself, "the way I think he is going to—"

The man at the desk took out another cigarette, tamped it on one end, turned it and tamped the other, straightened and crimped the paper on one end carefully against his left thumbnail and placed that end in his mouth.

Wilson felt the blood beating in his neck. *Sitting there with his back to him was himself, Bob Wilson!*

He felt that he was going to faint. He closed his eyes and steadied himself on a chair back. "I knew it," he thought, "the whole thing is absurd. I'm crazy. I know I'm crazy. Some sort of split personality. I shouldn't have worked so hard."

The sound of typing continued.

He pulled himself together, and reconsidered the matter. Diktor had warned him that he was due for a shock, a shock that could not be explained ahead of time, because it could not be believed. "All right—suppose I'm not crazy. If time travel can happen at all, there is no reason why I can't come back and see myself doing something I did in the past. If I'm sane, that is what I'm doing.

"And if I am crazy, it doesn't make a damn bit of difference what I do!

"And furthermore," he added to himself, "if I'm crazy, maybe I can stay crazy and go back through the Gate! No, that does not make sense. Neither does anything else—the hell with it!"

He crept forward softly and peered over the shoulder of his double. "Duration is an attribute of the consciousness," he read, "and not of the plenum."

"That tears it," he thought, "right back where I started, and watching myself write my thesis."

The typing continued. "It has no *Ding an Sich*. Therefore—" A key stuck, and others piled up on top of it. His double at the desk swore and reached out a hand to straighten the keys.

"Don't bother with it," Wilson said on sudden impulse. "It's a lot of utter hogwash anyhow."

The other Bob Wilson sat up with a jerk, then looked slowly around. An expression of surprise gave way to annoyance. "What the devil are you doing in my room?" he demanded. Without waiting for an answer he got up, went quickly to the door and examined the lock. "How did you get in?"

"This," thought Wilson, "is going to be difficult."

"Through that," Wilson answered, pointing to the Time Gate. His double looked where he had pointed, did a double take, then advanced cautiously and started to touch it.

"Don't!" yelled Wilson.

The other checked himself. "Why not?" he demanded.

Just why he must not permit his other self to touch the Gate was not clear to Wilson, but he had had an unmistakable feeling of impending disaster when he saw it about to happen. He temporized by saying, "I'll explain. But let's have a drink." A drink was a good idea in any case. There had never been a time when he needed one more than he did right now. Quite automatically he went to his usual cache of liquor in the wardrobe and took out the bottle he expected to find there.

"Hey!" protested the other. "What are you doing there? That's *my* liquor."

"*Your* liquor—" Hell's bells! It was *his* liquor. No, it wasn't; it was—*their* liquor. Oh, the devil! It was much too mixed up to try to explain. "Sorry. You don't mind if I have a drink, do you?"

"I suppose not," his double said grudgingly. "Pour me one while you're about it."

"O.K.," Wilson assented, "then I'll explain." It was going to be much, much too difficult to explain until he had had a drink, he felt. As it was, he couldn't explain it fully to himself.

"It had better be good," the other warned him, and looked Wilson over carefully while he drank his drink.

❖

Wilson watched his younger self scrutinizing him with confused and almost insupportable emotions. Couldn't the stupid fool recognize his own face when he saw it in front of him? If he could not *see* what the situation was, how in the world was he ever going to make it clear to him?

It had slipped his mind that his face was barely recognizable in any case, being decidedly battered and unshaven. Even more important, he failed to take into account the fact that a person does not look at his own face, even in mirrors, in the same frame of mind with which he regards another's face. No sane person ever expects to see his own face hanging on another.

Wilson could see that his companion was puzzled by his appearance, but it was equally clear that no recognition took place. "Who are you?" the other man asked suddenly.

"Me?" replied Wilson. "Don't you recognize me?"

"I'm not sure. Have I ever seen you before?"

"Well—not exactly," Wilson stalled. How did you go about telling another guy that the two of you were a trifle closer than twins? "Skip it—you wouldn't know about it."

"What's your name?"

"My name? Uh—" Oh, oh! This was going to be sticky! The whole situation was utterly ridiculous. He opened his mouth, tried to form the words "Bob Wilson," then gave up with a feeling of utter futility. Like many a man before him, he found himself forced into a lie because the truth simply would not be believed. "Just call me Joe," he finished lamely.

He felt suddenly startled at his own words. It was at this point that he realized that he was *in fact,* "Joe," the Joe whom he had encountered once before. That he had landed back in his own room at the very time at which he had ceased working on his thesis he already realized, but he had not had time to think the matter through. Hearing himself refer to himself as Joe slapped him in the face with the realization that this was not simply a similar scene, but the *same* scene he had lived through once before—save that he was living through it from a different viewpoint.

At least he thought it was the same scene. Did it differ in any respect? He could not be sure as he could not recall, word for word, what the conversation had been.

For a complete transcript of the scene that lay dormant in his memory he felt willing to pay twenty-five dollars cash, plus sales tax.

Wait a minute now—he was under no compulsion. He was sure of that. Everything he did and said was the result of his own free will. Even if he couldn't remember the script, there were some things he *knew* "Joe" hadn't said. "Mary had a little lamb," for example. He would recite a nursery rhyme and get off this damned repetitive treadmill. He opened his mouth—

"O.K., Joe Whatever-your-name-is," his alter ego remarked, setting down a glass which had contained, until recently, a quarter pint of gin, "trot out that explanation and make it snappy."

He opened his mouth again to answer the question, then closed it. "Steady, son, steady," he told himself. "You're a free agent. You want to recite a nursery rhyme—go ahead and do it. Don't answer him; go ahead and recite it—and break this vicious circle."

But under the unfriendly, suspicious eye of the man opposite him he found himself totally unable to recall any nursery rhyme. His mental processes stuck on dead center.

He capitulated. "I'll do that. That dingus I came through—that's a Time Gate."

"A what?"

"A Time Gate. Time flows along side by side on each side—" As he talked he felt sweat breaking out on him; he felt reasonably sure that he was explaining in exactly the same words in which explanation had first been offered to *him*. "—into the future just by stepping through that circle." He stopped and wiped his forehead.

"Go ahead," said the other implacably. "I'm listening. It's a nice story."

Bob suddenly wondered if the other man *could* be himself. The stupid arrogant dogmatism of the man's manner infuriated him. All right, all right! He'd show him. He strode suddenly over to the wardrobe, took out his hat and threw it through the Gate.

His opposite number watched the hat snuff out of existence with expressionless eyes, then stood up and went around in back of the Gate, walking with the careful steps of a man who is a little bit drunk, but determined not to show it. "A neat trick," he applauded, after satisfying himself that the hat was gone, "now I'll thank you to return to me my hat."

Wilson shook his head. "You can get it for yourself when you pass through," he answered absent-mindedly. He was pondering the problem of how many hats there were on the other side of the Gate.

"Huh?"

"That's right. Listen—" Wilson did his best to explain persuasively what it was he wanted his earlier *persona* to do. Or rather to cajole. Explanations were out of the question, in any honest sense of the word. He would have preferred attempting to explain tensor calculus to an Australian aborigine, even though he did not understand that esoteric mathematics himself.

The other man was not helpful. He seemed more interested in nursing the gin than he did in following Wilson's implausible protestations.

"Why?" he interrupted pugnaciously.

"Dammit," Wilson answered, "if you'd just step through once, explanations wouldn't be necessary. However—" He continued with a synopsis of Diktor's proposition. He realized with irritation that Diktor had been exceedingly sketchy with *his* explanations. He was forced to hit only the high spots in the logical parts of his argument, and bear down on the emotional appeal. He was on safe ground there—no one knew better than he did himself how fed up the earlier Bob Wilson had been with the petty drudgery and stuffy atmosphere of an academic career. "You don't want to slave your life away teaching numskulls in some fresh-water college," he concluded. "This is your chance. Grab it!"

Wilson watched his companion narrowly and thought he detected a favorable response. He definitely seemed interested. But the other set his glass down carefully, stared at the gin bottle, and at last replied:

"My dear fellow, I am not going to climb on your merry-go-round. You know why?"

"Why?"

"Because I'm drunk, that's why. You're not there at all. *That* ain't there." He gestured widely at the Gate, nearly fell, and recovered himself with effort. "There ain't anybody here but me, and I'm drunk. Been working too hard," he mumbled, "'m goin' to bed."

"You're not drunk," Wilson protested unhopefully. "Damnation," he thought, "a man who can't hold his liquor shouldn't drink."

"I *am* drunk. Peter Piper pepped a pick of pippered peckles." He lumbered over toward the bed.

Wilson grabbed his arm. "You can't do that."

"Let him alone!"

Wilson swung around, saw a third man standing in front of the Gate—recognized him with a sudden shock. His own recollection of the sequence of events was none too clear in his memory, since he had been somewhat intoxicated—damned near boiled, he admitted—the first time he had experienced this particular busy afternoon. He realized that he should have anticipated the arrival of a third party. But his memory had not prepared him for who the third party would turn out to be.

He recognized himself—another carbon copy.

He stood silent for a minute, trying to assimilate this new fact and force it into some reasonable integration. He closed his eyes helplessly. This was just a little too much. He felt that he wanted to have a few plain words with Diktor.

"Who the hell are you?" He opened his eyes to find that his other self, the drunk one, was addressing the latest edition. The newcomer turned away from his interrogator and looked sharply at Wilson.

"*He* knows me."

Wilson took his time about replying. This thing was getting out of hand. "Yes," he admitted, "yes, I suppose I do. But what the deuce are you here for? And why are you trying to bust up the plan?"

His facsimile cut him short. "No time for long-winded explanations. I know more about it than you do—you'll concede that—and my judgment is bound to be better than yours. He doesn't go through the Gate."

The offhand arrogance of the other antagonized Wilson. "I don't concede anything of the sort—" he began.

He was interrupted by the telephone bell. "Answer it!" snapped Number Three.

The tipsy Number One looked belligerent but picked up the handset. "Hello. . . . Yes. Who is this? . . . Hello. . . . Hello!" He tapped the bar of the instrument, then slammed the receiver back into its cradle.

"Who was that?" Wilson asked, somewhat annoyed that he had not had a chance to answer it himself.

"Nothing. Some nut with a misplaced sense of humor." At that instant the telephone rang again. "There he is again!" Wilson tried to answer it, but his alcoholic counterpart beat him to it, brushed him aside. "Listen, you butterfly-brained ape! I'm a busy man and this is *not* a public telephone. . . . Huh? Oh, it's you, Genevieve. Look—I'm sorry. I apologize— . . . You don't understand, honey. A guy has been pestering me over the phone and I thought it was him. You know I wouldn't talk to you that way, Babe. . . . Huh? This afternoon? Did you say *this* afternoon? Sure. Fine. Look, Babe, I'm a little mixed up about this. Trouble I've had all day long and more trouble now. I'll look you up tonight and straighten it out. But I *know* I didn't leave your hat in my apartment— . . . Huh? Oh, sure! Anyhow, I'll see you tonight. 'By."

It almost nauseated Wilson to hear his earlier self catering to the demands of that clinging female. Why didn't he just hang up on her? The contrast with Arma—there was a dish!—was acute; it made him more determined than ever to go ahead with the plan, despite the warning of the latest arrival.

After hanging up the phone his earlier self faced him, pointedly ignoring the presence of the third copy. "Very well, Joe," he announced. "I'm ready to go if you are."

"Fine!" Wilson agreed with relief. "Just step through. That's all there is to it."

"No, you don't!" Number Three barred the way.

Wilson started to argue, but his erratic comrade was ahead of him. "Listen, you! You come butting in here like you think I was a bum. If you don't like it, go jump in the lake—and I'm just the kind of a guy who can do it! You and who else?"

They started trading punches almost at once. Wilson stepped in warily, looking for an opening that would enable him to put the slug on Number Three with one decisive blow.

He should have watched his drunken ally as well. A wild swing from that quarter glanced off his already damaged features and caused him excruciating pain. His upper lip, cut, puffy, and tender from his other encounter, took the blow and became an area of pure agony. He flinched and jumped back.

A sound cut through his fog of pain, a dull *Smack!* He forced his eyes to track and saw the feet of a man disappear through the Gate. Number Three was still standing by the Gate. "Now you've done it!" he said bitterly to Wilson, and nursed the knuckles of his left hand.

The obviously unfair allegation reached Wilson at just the wrong moment. His face still felt like an experiment in sadism. "Me?" he said angrily. "*You* knocked him through. I never laid a finger on him."

"Yes, but it's your fault. If you hadn't interfered, I wouldn't have had to do it."

"*Me* interfere? Why, you bald-faced hypocrite—*you* butted in and tried to queer the pitch. Which reminds me—you owe me some explanations and I damn well mean to have 'em. What's the idea of—"

But his opposite number cut in on him. "Stow it," he said gloomily. "It's too late now. He's gone through."

"Too late for what?" Wilson wanted to know.

"Too late to put a stop to this chain of events."

"Why should we?"

"Because," Number Three said bitterly, "Diktor has played me—I mean has played *you* . . . *us*—for a dope, for a couple of dopes. Look, he told you that he was going to set you up as a big shot over *there*"—he indicated the Gate—"didn't he?"

"Yes," Wilson admitted.

"Well, that's a lot of malarkey. All he means to do is to get us so incredibly tangled up in this Time Gate thing that we'll never get straightened out again."

Wilson felt a sudden doubt nibbling at his mind. It *could* be true. Certainly there had not been much sense to what had happened so far.

After all, why should Diktor want his help, want it bad enough to offer to split with him, even-Steven, what was obviously a cushy spot? "How do you know?" he demanded.

"Why go into it?" the other answered wearily. "Why don't you just take my word for it?"

"Why should I?"

His companion turned a look of complete exasperation on him. "If you can't take my word, whose word can you take?"

The inescapable logic of the question simply annoyed Wilson. He resented this interloping duplicate of himself anyhow; to be asked to follow his lead blindly irked him. "I'm from Missouri," he said. "I'll see for myself." He moved toward the Gate.

"Where are you going?"

"Through! I'm going to look up Diktor and have it out with him."

"Don't!" the other said. "Maybe we can break the chain even now." Wilson felt and looked stubborn. The other sighed. "Go ahead," he surrendered. "It's your funeral. I wash my hands of you."

Wilson paused as he was about to step through the Gate. "It is, eh? H-m-m-m—how can it be *my* funeral unless it's *your* funeral, too?"

The other man looked blank, then an expression of apprehension raced over his face. That was the last Wilson saw of him as he stepped through.

The Hall of the Gate was empty of other occupants when Bob Wilson came through on the other side. He looked for his hat, but did not find it, than stepped around back of the raised platform, seeking the exit he remembered. He nearly bumped into Diktor.

"Ah, there you are!" the older man greeted him. "Fine! Fine! Now there is just one more little thing to take care of, then we will be all squared away. I must say I am pleased with you, Bob, very pleased indeed."

"Oh, you are, are you?" Bob faced him truculently. "Well, it's too bad I can't say the same about you! I'm not a damn bit pleased. What was the idea of shoving me into that . . . that daisy chain without warning me? What's the meaning of all this nonsense? Why didn't you warn me?"

"Easy, easy," said the older man, "don't get excited. Tell the truth now—if I had told you that you were going back to meet yourself face to face, would you have believed me? Come now, 'fess up."

Wilson admitted that he would not have believed it.

"Well, then," Diktor continued with a shrug, "there was no point in me telling you, was there? If I had told you, you would not have believed me, which is another way of saying that you would have believed false data. Is it not better to be in ignorance than to believe falsely?"

"I suppose so, but—"

"Wait! I did not intentionally deceive you. I did not deceive you at all. But had I told you the full truth, you would have been deceived because you would have rejected the truth. It was better for you to learn the truth with your own eyes. Otherwise—"

"Wait a minute! Wait a minute!" Wilson cut in. "You're getting me all tangled up. I'm willing to let bygones be bygones, if you'll come clean with me. Why did you send me back at all?"

" 'Let bygones be bygones,' " Diktor repeated. "Ah, if we only could! But we can't. That's why I sent you back—in order that you might come through the Gate in the first place."

"Huh? Wait a minute—I already *had* come through the Gate."

Diktor shook his head. "Had you, now? Think a moment. When you got back into your own time and your own place you found your earlier self there, didn't you?"

"Mmmm—yes."

"*He*—your earlier self—had not yet been through the Gate, had he?"

"No. I—"

"How could you have *been* through the Gate, unless you persuaded him to *go* through the Gate?"

Bob Wilson's head was beginning to whirl. He was beginning to wonder who did what to whom and who got paid. "But that's impossible! You are telling me that I did something because I was going to do something."

"Well, didn't you? You were there."

"No, I didn't—no . . . well, maybe I did, but it didn't *feel* like it."

"Why should you expect it to? It was something totally new to your experience."

"But . . . but—" Wilson took a deep breath and got control of himself. Then he reached back into his academic philosophical concepts and produced the notion he had been struggling to express. "It denies all reasonable theories of causation. You would have me believe that causation can be completely circular. I went through because I came back from going through to persuade myself to go through. That's silly."

"Well, didn't you?"

Wilson did not have an answer ready for that one. Diktor continued with, "Don't worry about it. The causation you have been accustomed to is valid enough in its own field but is simply a special case under the general case. *Causation in a plenum need not be and is not limited by a man's perception of duration.*"

Wilson thought about that for a moment. It sounded nice, but there was something slippery about it. "Just a second," he said. "How about entropy? You can't get around entropy."

"Oh, for Heaven's sake," protested Diktor, "shut up, will you? You remind me of the mathematician who proved that airplanes couldn't fly." He turned and started out the door. "Come on. There's work to be done."

Wilson hurried after him. "Dammit, you can't do this to me. What happened to the other two?"

"The other two what?"

"The other two of me? Where are they? How am I ever going to get unsnarled?"

"You aren't snarled up. You don't feel like more than one person, do you?"

"No, but—"

"Then don't worry about it."

"But I've got to worry about it. What happened to the guy that came through just ahead of me?"

"You remember, don't you? However—" Diktor hurried on ahead, led him down a passageway, and dilated a door. "Take a look inside," he directed.

Wilson did so. He found himself looking into a small windowless unfurnished room, a room that he recognized. Sprawled on the floor, snoring steadily, was another edition of himself.

"When you first came through the Gate," explained Diktor at his elbow, "I brought you in here, attended to your hurts, and gave you a drink. The drink contained a soporific which will cause you to sleep about thirty-six hours, sleep that you badly needed. When you wake up, I will give you breakfast and explain to you what needs to be done."

Wilson's head started to ache again. "Don't do that," he pleaded. "Don't refer to that guy as if he were me. *This* is *me,* standing here."

"Have it your own way," said Diktor. "That is the man you *were.* You remember the things that are about to happen to him, don't you?"

"Yes, but it makes me dizzy. Close the door, please."

"O.K.," said Diktor, and complied. "We've got to hurry, anyhow. Once a sequence like this is established there is no time to waste. Come on." He led the way back to the Hall of the Gate.

"I want you to return to the twentieth century and obtain certain things for us, things that can't be obtained on this side but which will be very useful to us in, ah, developing—yes, that is the word—developing this country."

"What sort of things?"

"Quite a number of items. I've prepared a list for you—certain reference books, certain items of commerce. Excuse me, please. I must adjust the controls of the Gate." He mounted the raised platform from the rear. Wilson followed him and found that the structure was boxlike, open at the top, and had a raised floor. The Gate could be seen by looking over the high sides.

The controls were unique.

Four colored spheres the size of marbles hung on crystal rods arranged with respect to each other as the four major axes of a tetrahedron. The three spheres which bounded the base of the tetrahedron were red, yellow, and blue; the fourth at the apex was white. "Three spatial controls, one time control," explained Diktor. "It's very simple. Using here-and-now as zero reference, displacing any control away from the center moves the other end of the Gate farther from here-and-now. Forward or back, right or left, up or down, past or future—they are all controlled by moving the proper sphere in or out on its rod."

Wilson studied the system. "Yes," he said, "but how do you tell where the other end of the Gate is? Or when? I don't see any graduations."

"You don't need them. You can see where you are. Look." He touched a point under the control framework on the side toward the Gate. A panel rolled back and Wilson saw there was a small image of the Gate itself. Diktor made another adjustment and Wilson found that he could see through the image.

He was gazing into his own room, as if through the wrong end of a telescope. He could make out two figures, but the scale was too small for him to see clearly what they were doing, nor could he tell which editions of himself were there present—if they were in truth himself! He found it quite upsetting. "Shut if off," he said.

Diktor did so and said, "I must not forget to give you your list." He fumbled in his sleeve and produced a slip of paper which he handed to Wilson. "Here—take it."

Wilson accepted it mechanically and stuffed it into his pocket. "See here," he began, "everywhere I go I keep running into myself. I don't like it at all. It's disconcerting. I feel like a whole batch of guinea pigs. I don't half understand what this is all about and now you want to rush me through the Gate again with a bunch of half-baked excuses. Come clean. Tell me what it's all about."

Diktor showed temper in his face for the first time. "You are a stupid and ignorant young fool. I've told you all that you are able to understand. This is a period in history entirely beyond your comprehension.

It would take weeks before you would even begin to understand it. I am offering you half a world in return for a few hours' co-operation and you stand there arguing about it. Stow it, I tell you. Now—where shall we set you down?" He reached for the controls.

"Get away from those controls!" Wilson rapped out. He was getting the glimmering of an idea. "Who are you, anyhow?"

"Me? I'm Diktor."

"That's not what I mean and you know it. How did you learn English?"

Diktor did not answer. His face became expressionless.

"Go on," Wilson persisted. "You didn't learn it here; that's a cinch. You're from the twentieth century, *aren't you?*"

Diktor smiled sourly. "I wondered how long it would take you to figure that out."

Wilson nodded. "Maybe I'm not bright, but I'm not as stupid as you think I am. Come on. Give me the rest of the story."

Diktor shook his head. "It's immaterial. Besides, we're wasting time."

Wilson laughed. "You've tried to hurry me with that excuse once too often. How can we waste time when we have *that?*" He pointed to the controls and to the Gate beyond it. "Unless you lied to me, we can use any slice of time we want to, any time. No, I think I know why you tried to rush me. Either you want to get me out of the picture here, or there is something devilishly dangerous about the job you want me to do. And I know how to settle it—you're going with me!"

"You don't know what you're saying," Diktor answered slowly. "That's impossible. I've got to stay here and manage the controls."

"That's just what you aren't going to do. You could send me through and lose me. I prefer to keep you in sight."

"Out of the question," answered Diktor. "You'll have to trust me." He bent over the controls again.

"Get away from there!" shouted Wilson. "Back out of there before I bop you one." Under Wilson's menacing fist Diktor withdrew from the control pulpit entirely. "There. That's better," he added when both of them were once more on the floor of the hall.

The idea which had been forming in his mind took full shape. The controls, he knew, were still set on his room in the boardinghouse where he lived—or had lived—back in the twentieth century. From what he had seen through the speculum of the controls, the time control was set to take him right back to the day in 1952 from which he had started. "Stand there," he commanded Diktor, "I want to see something."

He walked over to the Gate as if to inspect it. Instead of stopping when he reached it, he stepped on through.

He was better prepared for what he found on the other side than he had been on the two earlier occasions of time translation—"earlier" in the sense of sequence in his memory track. Nevertheless it is never too easy on the nerves to catch up with one's self.

For he had done it again. He was back in his own room, but there were two of himself there before him. They were very much preoccupied with each other; he had a few seconds in which to get them straightened out in his mind. One of them had a beautiful black eye and a badly battered mouth. Beside that he was very much in need of a shave. That tagged him. He had been through the Gate at least once. The other, though somewhat in need of shaving himself, showed no marks of a fist fight.

He had them sorted out now, and knew where and *when* he was. It was all still mostly damnably confusing, but after former—no, not *former,* he amended—*other* experiences with time translation he knew better what to expect. He was back at the beginning again; this time he would put a stop to the crazy nonsense once and for all.

The other two were arguing. One of them swayed drunkenly toward the bed. The other grabbed him by the arm. "You can't do that," he said.

"Let him alone!" snapped Wilson.

The other two swung around and looked him over. Wilson watched the more sober of the pair size him up, saw his expression of amazement change to startled recognition. The other, the earliest Wilson, seemed to have trouble in focusing on him at all. "This is going to be a job," thought Wilson. "The man is positively stinking." He wondered why anyone would be foolish enough to drink on an empty stomach. It was not only stupid, it was a waste of good liquor.

He wondered if they had left a drink for him.

"Who are you?" demanded his drunken double.

Wilson turned to "Joe." "He knows me," he said significantly.

"Joe," studied him. "Yes," he conceded, "yes, I suppose I do. But what the deuce are you here for? And why are you trying to bust up the plan?"

Wilson interrupted him. "No time for long-winded explanations. I know more about it than you do—you'll concede that—and my judgment is bound to be better than yours. He doesn't go through the Gate."

"I don't concede anything of the sort—"

The ringing of the telephone checked the argument. Wilson greeted the interruption with relief, for he realized that he had started out on the wrong tack. Was it possible that he was really as dense himself as this lug appeared to be? Did *he* look that way to other people? But the time was too short for self-doubts and soul-searching. "Answer it!" he commanded Bob (Boiled) Wilson.

The drunk looked belligerent, but acceded when he saw that Bob (Joe) Wilson was about to beat him to it. "Hello. . . . Yes. Who is this? . . . Hello. . . . Hello!"

"Who was that?" asked "Joe."

"Nothing. Some nut with a misplaced sense of humor." The telephone rang again. "There he is again." The drunk grabbed the phone before the others could reach it. "Listen, you butterfly-brained ape! I'm a busy man and this is *not* a public telephone. . . . Huh? Oh, it's you, Genevieve—" Wilson paid little attention to the telephone conversation—he had heard it too many times before, and he had too much on his mind. His earliest *persona* was much too drunk to be reasonable, he realized; he must concentrate on some argument that would appeal to "Joe"—otherwise he was outnumbered. "—Huh? Oh, sure!" the call concluded. "Anyhow, I'll see you tonight. 'By."

Now was the time, thought Wilson, before this dumb yap can open his mouth. What would he say? What would sound convincing?

But the boiled edition spoke first. "Very well, Joe," he stated, "I'm ready to go if you are."

"Fine!" said "Joe." "Just step through. That's all there is to it."

This was getting out of hand, not the way he had planned it at all. "No, you don't!" he barked and jumped in front of the Gate. He would have to make them realize, and quickly.

But he got no chance to do so. The drunk cussed him out, then swung on him; his temper snapped. He knew with sudden fierce exultation that he had been wanting to take a punch at someone for some time. Who did they think they were to be taking chances with his future?

The drunk was clumsy; Wilson stepped under his guard and hit him hard in the face. It was a solid enough punch to have convinced a sober man, but his opponent shook his head and came back for more. "Joe" closed in. Wilson decided that he would have to put his original opponent away in a hurry, and give his attention to "Joe"—by far the more dangerous of the two.

A slight mix-up between the two allies gave him his chance. He stepped back, aimed carefully, and landed a long jab with his left, one of the hardest blows he had ever struck in his life. It lifted his target right off his feet.

As the blow landed Wilson realized his orientation with respect to the Gate, knew with bitter certainty that he had again played through the scene to its inescapable climax.

He was alone with "Joe"; their companion had disappeared through the Gate.

His first impulse was the illogical but quite human and very common feeling of look-what-you-made-me-do. "Now you've done it!" he said angrily.

"Me?" "Joe" protested. "You knocked him through. I never laid a finger on him."

"Yes," Wilson was forced to admit. "But it's your fault," he added, "if you hadn't interfered, I wouldn't have had to do it."

"*Me* interfere? Why, you bald-faced hypocrite, you butted in and tried to queer the pitch. Which reminds me—you owe me some explanations and I damn well mean to have them. What's the idea of—"

"Stow it," Wilson headed him off. He hated to be wrong and he hated still more to have to admit that he was wrong. It had been hopeless from the start, he now realized. He felt bowed down by the utter futility of it. "It's too late now. He's gone through."

"Too late for what?"

"Too late to put a stop to this chain of events." He was aware now that it always had been too late, regardless of what time it was, what year it was, or how many times he came back and tried to stop it. He *remembered* having gone through the first time, he had *seen* himself asleep on the other side. Events would have to work out their weary way.

"Why should we?"

It was not worth while to explain, but he felt the need for self-justification. "Because," he said, "Diktor has played me—I mean has played *you* . . . us—for a dope, for a couple of dopes. Look, he told you that he was going to set you up as a big shot over there, didn't he?"

"Yes—"

"Well, that's a lot of malarkey. All he means to do is to get us so incredibly tangled up in this Gate thing that we'll never get straightened out again."

"Joe" looked at him sharply. "How do you know?"

Since it was largely hunch, he felt pressed for reasonable explanation. "Why go into it?" he evaded. "Why don't you just take my word for it?"

"Why should I?"

"Why should you? Why, you lunk, can't you see? I'm yourself, older and more experienced—you *have* to believe me." Aloud he answered, "If you can't take my word, whose word can you take?"

"Joe" grunted. "I'm from Missouri," he said. "I'll see for myself."

Wilson was suddenly aware that "Joe" was about to step through the Gate. "Where are you going?"

"Through! I'm going to look up Diktor and have it out with him."

"Don't!" Wilson pleaded. "Maybe we can break the chain even now." But the stubborn sulky look on the other's face made him realize how futile it was. He was still enmeshed in inevitability; it *had* to happen. "Go ahead," he shrugged. "It's your funeral. I wash my hands of you."

"Joe" paused at the Gate. "It is, eh? Hm-m-m—how can it be *my* funeral unless it's *your* funeral, too?"

Wilson stared speechlessly while "Joe" stepped through the Gate. Whose funeral? He had not thought of it in quite that way. He felt a sudden impulse to rush through the Gate, catch up with his alter ego, and watch over him. The stupid fool might do anything. Suppose he got himself killed? Where would that leave Bob Wilson? Dead, of course.

Or would it? Could the death of a man thousands of years in the future kill *him* in the year 1952? He saw the absurdity of the situation suddenly, and felt very much relieved. "Joe's" actions could not endanger him; he remembered everything that "Joe" had done—was going to do. "Joe" would get into an argument with Diktor and, in due course of events, would come back through the Time Gate. No, *had* come back through the Time Gate. He was "Joe." It was hard to remember that.

Yes, he was "Joe." As well as the first guy. They would thread their courses, in and out and roundabout, and end up here, with *him*. Had to.

Wait a minute—in that case the whole crazy business was straightened out. He had gotten away from Diktor, had all of his various personalities sorted out, and was back where he started from, no worse for the wear except for a crop of whiskers and, possibly, a scar on his lip. Well, he knew when to let well enough alone. Shave, and get back to work, kid.

As he shaved he stared at his face and wondered why he had failed to recognize it the first time. He had to admit that he had never looked at it objectively before. He had always taken it for granted.

He acquired a crick in his neck from trying to look at his own profile through the corner of one eye.

On leaving the bathroom the Gate caught his eye forcibly. For some reason he had assumed that it would be gone. It was not. He inspected it, walked around it, carefully refrained from touching it. Wasn't the damned thing ever going to go away? It had served its purpose; why didn't Diktor shut it off?

He stood in front of it, felt a sudden surge of the compulsion that leads men to jump from high places. What would happen if he went through? What would he find? He thought of Arma. And the other one—what was her name? Perhaps Diktor had not told him. The other maidservant, anyhow, the second one.

But he restrained himself and forced himself to sit back down at the desk. If he was going to stay here—and of course he was, he was re-solved on that point—he must finish the thesis. He had to eat; he needed the degree to get a decent job. Now where was he?

Twenty minutes later he had come to the conclusion that the thesis would have to be rewritten from one end to the other. His prime theme, the application of the empirical method to the problems of speculative metaphysics and its expression in rigorous formulae, was still valid, he decided, but he had acquired a mass of new and not yet digested data to incorporate in it. In re-reading his manuscript he was amazed to find how dogmatic he had been. Time after time he had fallen into the Cartesian fallacy, mistaking clear reasoning for correct reasoning.

He tried to brief a new version of the thesis, but discovered that there were two problems he was forced to deal with which were decid-edly not clear in his mind: the problem of the ego and the problem of free will. When there had been three of him in the room, which one was the ego—was *himself?* And how was it that he had been unable to change the course of events?

An absurdly obvious answer to the first question occurred to him at once. The ego was himself. Self is self, an unproved and unprovable first statement, directly experienced. What, then, of the other two? Surely they had been equally sure of ego-being—he remembered it. He thought of a way to state it: Ego is the point of consciousness, the latest term in a continuously expanding series along the line of memory du-ration. That sounded like a general statement, but he was not sure; he would have to try to formulate it mathematically before he could trust it. Verbal language had such queer booby traps in it.

The telephone rang.

He answered it absent-mindedly. "Yes?"

"Is that you, Bob?"

"Yes. Who is this?"

"Why, it's Genevieve, of course, darling. What's come over you to-day? That's the second time you've failed to recognize my voice."

Annoyance and frustration rose up in him. Here was another prob-lem he had failed to settle—well, he'd settle it now. He ignored her complaint. "Look here, Genevieve, I've told you not to telephone me while I'm working. Good-by!"

"Well, of all the— You can't talk that way to me, Bob Wilson! In the first place, you weren't working today. In the second place, what makes you think you can use honey and sweet words on me and two hours later snarl at me? I'm not any too sure I want to marry you."

"Marry you? What put that silly idea in your head?"

The phone sputtered for several seconds. When it had abated some-what he resumed with, "Now just calm down. This isn't the Gay

Nineties, you know. You can't assume that a fellow who takes you out a few times intends to marry you."

There was a short silence. "So that's the game, is it?" came an answer at last in a voice so cold and hard and completely shrewish that he almost failed to recognize it. "Well, there's a way to handle men like you. A woman isn't unprotected in this State!"

"You ought to know," he answered savagely. "You've hung around the campus enough years."

The receiver clicked in his ear.

He wiped the sweat from his forehead. That dame, he knew, was quite capable of causing him lots of trouble. He had been warned before he ever started running around with her, but he had been so sure of his own ability to take care of himself. He should have known better—but then he had not expected anything quite as raw as this.

He tried to get back to work on his thesis, but found himself unable to concentrate. The deadline of 10 A.M. the next morning seemed to be racing toward him. He looked at his watch. It had stopped. He set it by the desk clock—four fifteen in the afternoon. Even if he sat up all night he could not possibly finish it properly.

Besides there was Genevieve—

The telephone rang again. He let it ring. It continued; he took the receiver off the cradle. He would *not* talk to her again.

He thought of Arma. There was a proper girl with the right attitude. He walked over to the window and stared down into the dusty, noisy street. Half subconsciously he compared it with the green and placid countryside he had seen from the balcony where he and Diktor had breakfasted. This was a crummy world full of crummy people. He wished poignantly that Diktor had been on the up-and-up with him.

An idea broke surface in his brain and plunged around frantically. The Gate was still open. *The Gate was still open!* Why worry about Diktor? He was his own master. Go back and play it out—everything to gain, nothing to lose.

He stepped up to the Gate, then hesitated. Was he wise to do it? After all, how much did he know about the future?

He heard footsteps climbing the stairs, coming down the hall, no—yes, stopping at his door. He was suddenly convinced that it was Genevieve; that decided him. He stepped through.

The Hall of the Gate was empty on his arrival. He hurried around the control box to the door and was just in time to hear, "Come on. There's work to be done." Two figures were retreating down the corridor. He recognized both of them and stopped suddenly.

That was a near thing, he told himself; I'll just have to wait until they get clear. He looked around for a place to conceal himself, but found nothing but the control box. That was useless; they were coming back. Still—

He entered the control box with a plan vaguely forming in his mind. If he found that he could dope out the controls, the Gate might give him all the advantage he needed. First he needed to turn on the speculum gadget. He felt around where he recalled having seen Diktor reach to turn it on, then reached in his pocket for a match.

Instead he pulled out a piece of paper. It was the list that Diktor had given him, the things he was to obtain in the twentieth century. Up to the present moment there had been too much going on for him to look it over.

His eyebrows crawled up his forehead as he read. It was a funny list, he decided. He had subconsciously expected it to call for technical reference books, samples of modern gadgets, weapons. There was nothing of the sort. Still, there was a sort of mad logic to the assortment. After all, Diktor knew these people better than he did. It might be just what was needed.

He revised his plans, subject to being able to work the Gate. He decided to make one more trip back and do the shopping Diktor's list called for—but for his own benefit, not Diktor's. He fumbled in the semidarkness of the control booth, seeking the switch or control for the speculum. His hand encountered a soft mass. He grasped it, and pulled it out.

It was his hat.

He placed it on his head, guessing idly that Diktor had stowed it there, and reached again. This time he brought forth a small notebook. It looked like a find—very possibly Diktor's own notes on the operation of the controls. He opened it eagerly.

It was not what he had hoped. But it did contain page after page of handwritten notes. There were three columns to the page; the first was in English, the second in international phonetic symbols, the third in a completely strange sort of writing. It took no brilliance for him to identify it as a vocabulary. He slipped it into a pocket with a broad smile; it might have taken Diktor months or even years to work out the relationship between the two languages; he would be able to ride on Diktor's shoulders in the matter.

The third try located the control and the speculum lighted up. He felt again the curious uneasiness he had felt before, for he was gazing again into his own room and again it was inhabited by two figures. He did not want to break into that scene again, he was sure. Cautiously he touched one of the colored beads.

The scene shifted, panned out through the walls of the boarding-house and came to rest in the air, three stories above the campus. He was pleased to have gotten the Gate out of the house, but three stories was too much of a jump. He fiddled with the other two colored beads and established that one of them caused the scene in the speculum to move toward him or away from him while the other moved it up or down.

He wanted a reasonably inconspicuous place to locate the Gate, some place where it would not attract the attention of the curious. This bothered him a bit; there was no ideal place, but he compromised on a blind alley, a little court formed by the campus powerhouse and the rear wall of the library. Cautiously and clumsily he maneuvered his flying eye to the neighborhood he wanted and set it down carefully between the two buildings. He then readjusted his position so that he stared right into a blank wall. Good enough!

Leaving the controls as they were, he hurried out of the booth and stepped unceremoniously back into his own period.

He bumped his nose against the brick wall. "I cut that a little too fine," he mused as he slid cautiously out from between the confining limits of the wall and the Gate. The Gate hung in the air, about fifteen inches from the wall and roughly parallel to it. But there was room enough, he decided—no need to go back and readjust the controls. He ducked out of the areaway and cut across the campus toward the Students' Co-op, wasting no time. He entered and went to the cashier's window.

"Hi, Bob."

"H'lo, Soupy. Cash a check for me?"

"How much?"

"Twenty dollars."

"Well—I suppose so. Is it a good check?"

"Not very. It's my own."

"Well, I might invest in it as a curiosity." He counted out a ten, a five, and five ones.

"Do that," advised Wilson. "My autographs are going to be rare collectors' items." He passed over the check, took the money, and proceeded to the bookstore in the same building. Most of the books on the list were for sale there. Ten minutes later he had acquired title to:

"The Prince," by Niccolò Machiavelli.

"Behind the Ballots," by James Farley.

"Mein Kampf" (unexpurgated), by Adolf Schickelgruber.

"How to Make Friends and Influence People," by Dale Carnegie.

The other titles he wanted were not available in the bookstore; he went from there to the university library where he drew out "Real Estate Broker's Manual," "History of Musical Instruments," and a quarto titled "Evolution of Dress Styles." The latter was a handsome volume with beautiful colored plates and was classified as reference. He had to argue a little to get a twenty-four hour permission for it.

He was fairly well loaded down by then; he left the campus, went to a pawnshop and purchased two used, but sturdy, suitcases into one of which he packed the books. From there he went to the largest music store in the town and spent forty-five minutes in selecting and rejecting phonograph records, with emphasis on swing and torch—highly emotional stuff, all of it. He did not neglect classical and semi-classical, but he applied the same rule to those categories—a piece of music had to be sensuous and compelling, rather than cerebral. In consequence his collection included such strangely assorted items as the "Marseillaise," Ravel's "Bolero," four Cole Porters, and "L'Après-midi d'un Faune."

He insisted on buying the best mechanical reproducer on the market in the face of the clerk's insistence that what he needed was an electrical one. But he finally got his own way, wrote a check for the order, packed it all in his suitcases, and had the clerk get a taxi for him.

He had a bad moment over the check. It was pure rubber, as the one he had cashed at the Students' Co-op had cleaned out his balance. He had urged them to phone the bank, since that was what he wished them not to do. It had worked. He had established, he reflected, the all-time record for kiting checks—thirty thousand years.

When the taxi drew up opposite the court where he had located the Gate, he jumped out and hurried in.

The Gate was gone.

He stood there for several minutes, whistling softly, and assessing—unfavorably—his own abilities, mental processes, et cetera. The consequences of writing bad checks no longer seemed quite so hypothetical.

He felt a touch at his sleeve. "See here, Bud, do you want my hack, or don't you? The meter's still clicking."

" 'Huh? Oh, sure." He followed the driver, climbed back in.

"Where to?"

That was a problem. He glanced at his watch, then realized that the usually reliable instrument had been through a process which rendered its reading irrelevant. "What time is it?"

"Two fifteen." He reset his watch.

Two fifteen. There would be a jamboree going on in his room at that time of a particularly confusing sort. He did not want to go *there*—not yet. Not until his blood brothers got through playing happy fun games with the Gate.

The Gate!

It would be in his room until sometime after four fifteen. If he timed it right—"Drive to the corner of Fourth and McKinley," he directed, naming the intersection closest to his boardinghouse.

He paid off the taxi driver there, and lugged his bags into the filling station at that corner, where he obtained permission from the attendant to leave them and assurance that they would be safe. He had nearly two hours to kill. He was reluctant to go very far from the house for fear some hitch would upset his timing.

It occurred to him that there was one piece of unfinished business in the immediate neighborhood—and time enough to take care of it. He walked briskly to a point two streets away, whistling cheerfully, and turned in at an apartment house.

In response to his knock the door of Apartment 211 was opened a crack, then wider. "Bob darling! I thought you were working today."

"Hi, Genevieve. Not at all—I've got time to burn."

She glanced back over her shoulder. "I don't know whether I should let you come in—I wasn't expecting you. I haven't washed the dishes, or made the bed. I was just putting on my make-up."

"Don't be coy." He pushed the door open wide, and went on in.

When he came out he glanced at his watch. Three thirty—plenty of time. He went down the street wearing the expression of the canary that ate the cat.

He thanked the service station salesman and gave him a quarter for his trouble, which left him with a lone dime. He looked at this coin, grinned to himself, and inserted it in the pay phone in the office of the station. He dialed his own number.

"Hello," he heard.

"Hello," he replied. "Is that Bob Wilson?"

"Yes. Who is this?"

"Never mind," he chuckled. "I just wanted to be sure you were there. I *thought* you would be. You're right in the groove, kid, right in the groove." He replaced the receiver with a grin.

At four ten he was too nervous to wait any longer. Struggling under the load of the heavy suitcases he made his way to the boardinghouse. He let himself in and heard a telephone ringing upstairs. He glanced at his watch—four fifteen. He waited in the hall for three interminable minutes, then labored up the stairs and down the upper hallway to his own door. He unlocked the door and let himself in.

The room was empty, the Gate still there.

Without stopping for anything, filled with apprehension lest the Gate should flicker and disappear while he crossed the floor, he hurried to it, took a firm grip on his bags, and strode through it.

The Hall of the Gate was empty, to his great relief. What a break, he told himself thankfully. Just five minutes, that's all I ask. Five uninterrupted minutes. He set the suitcases down near the Gate to be ready for a quick departure. As he did so he noticed that a large chunk was missing from a corner of one case. Half a book showed through the opening, sheared as neatly as with a printer's trimmer. He identified it as "Mein Kampf."

He did not mind the loss of the book but the implications made him slightly sick at his stomach. Suppose he had not described a clear arc when he had first been knocked through the Gate, had hit the edge, half in and half out? Man Sawed in Half—and no illusion!

He wiped his face and went to the control booth. Following Diktor's simple instructions he brought all four spheres together at the center of the tetrahedron. He glanced over the side of the booth and saw that the Gate had disappeared entirely. "Check!" he thought. "Everything on zero—no Gate." He moved the white sphere slightly. The Gate reappeared. Turning on the speculum he was able to see that the miniature scene showed the inside of the Hall of the Gate itself. So far so good—but he would not be able to tell what time the Gate was set for by looking into the Hall. He displaced a space control slightly; the scene flickered past the walls of the palace and hung in the open air. Returning the white time control to zero he then displaced it very, very slightly. In the miniature scene the sun became a streak of brightness across the sky; the days flickered past like light from a low frequency source of illumination. He increased the displacement a little, saw the ground become sear and brown, then snow covered, and finally green again.

Working cautiously, steadying his right hand with his left, he made the seasons march past. He had counted ten winters when he became aware of voices somewhere in the distance. He stopped and listened, then very hastily returned the space controls to zero, leaving the time control as it was—set for ten years in the past—and rushed out of the booth.

He hardly had time to grasp his bags, lift them, and swing them through the Gate, himself with them. This time he was exceedingly careful not to touch the edge of the circle.

He found himself, as he had planned to, still in the Hall of the Gate, but, if he had interpreted the controls correctly, ten years away from the events he had recently participated in. He had intended to give Diktor a wider berth than that, but there had been no time for it. However, he reflected, since Diktor was, by his own statement and the evidence of the little notebook Wilson had lifted from him, a native of the twentieth century, it was quite possible that ten years was enough. Diktor might not be in this era. If he was, there was always the Time Gate for a getaway. But it was reasonable to scout out the situation first before making any more jumps.

It suddenly occurred to him that Diktor might be looking at him through the speculum of the Time Gate. Without stopping to consider that speed was no protection—since the speculum could be used to view *any* time sector—he hurriedly dragged his two suitcases into the cover of the control booth. Once inside the protecting walls of the booth he calmed down a bit. Spying could work both ways. He found the controls set at zero; making use of the same process he had used once before, he ran the scene in the speculum forward through ten years, then cautiously hunted with the space controls on zero. It was a very difficult task; the time scale necessary to hunt through several months in a few minutes caused any figure which might appear in the speculum to flash past at an apparent speed too fast for his eye to follow. Several times he thought he detected flitting shadows which might be human beings but he was never able to find them when he stopped moving the time control.

He wondered in great exasperation why whoever had built the double-damned gadget had failed to provide it with graduations and some sort of delicate control mechanism—a vernier, or the like. It was not until much later that it occurred to him that the creator of the Time Gate might have no need of such gross aids to his senses. He would have given up, was about to give up, when, purely by accident, one more fruitless scanning happened to terminate with a figure in the field.

It was himself, carrying two suitcases. He saw himself walking directly into the field of view, grow large, disappear. He looked over the rail, half expecting to see himself step out of the Gate.

But nothing came out of the Gate. It puzzled him, until he recalled that it was the setting at *that* end, ten years in the future, which controlled the time of egress. But he had what he wanted; he sat back and watched. Almost immediately Diktor and another edition of himself appeared in the scene. He recalled the situation when he saw it portrayed in the speculum. It was Bob Wilson number three, about to quarrel with Diktor and make his escape back to the twentieth century.

That was that—Diktor had not seen him, did not know that he had made unauthorized use of the Gate, did not know that he was hiding ten years in the "past," would not look for him there. He returned the controls to zero, and dismissed the matter.

But other matters needed his attention—food, especially. It seemed obvious, in retrospect, that he should have brought along food to last him for a day or two at least. And maybe a .45. He had to admit that he had not been very foresighted. But he easily forgave himself—it was hard to be foresighted when the future kept slipping up behind one. "All right, Bob, old boy," he told himself aloud, "let's see if the natives are friendly—as advertised."

A cautious reconnoiter of the small part of the Palace with which he was acquainted turned up no human beings nor life of any sort, not even insect life. The place was dead, sterile, as static and unlived-in as a window display. He shouted once just to hear a voice. The echoes caused him to shiver; he did not do it again.

The architecture of the place confused him. Not only was it strange to his experience—he had expected that—but the place, with minor exceptions, seemed totally unadapted to the uses of human beings. Great halls large enough to hold ten thousand people at once—had there been floors for them to stand on. For there frequently were no floors in the accepted meaning of a level or reasonably level platform. In following a passageway he came suddenly to one of the great mysterious openings in the structure and almost fell in before he realized that his path had terminated. He crawled gingerly forward and looked over the edge. The mouth of the passage debouched high up on a wall of the place; below him the wall was cut back so that there was not even a vertical surface for the eye to follow. Far below him, the wall curved back and met its mate of the opposite side—not decently, in a horizontal plane, but at an acute angle.

There were other openings scattered around the walls, openings as unserviceable to human beings as the one in which he crouched. "The High Ones," he whispered to himself. All his cockiness was gone out of him. He retraced his steps through the fine dust and reached the almost friendly familiarity of the Hall of the Gate.

On his second try he attempted only those passages and compartments which seemed obviously adapted to men. He had already decided what such parts of the Palace must be—servants' quarters, or, more probably, slaves' quarters. He regained his courage by sticking to such areas. Though deserted completely, by contrast with the rest of the great structure a room or a passage which seemed to have been built for men was friendly and cheerful. The sourceless ever-present illuminations and the unbroken silence still bothered him, but not to the degree to which he had been upset by the Gargantuan and mysteriously convoluted chambers of the "High Ones."

He had almost despaired of finding his way out of the Palace and was thinking of retracing his steps when the corridor he was following turned and he found himself in bright sunlight.

He was standing at the top of a broad steep ramp which spread fan-like down to the base of the building. Ahead of him and below him, distant at least five hundred yards, the pavement of the ramp met the green of sod and bush and tree. It was the same placid, lush, and familiar scene he had looked out over when he breakfasted with Diktor—a few hours ago and ten years in the future.

He stood quietly for a short time, drinking in the sunshine, soaking up the heart-lifting beauty of the warm, spring day. "This is going to be all right," he exulted. "It's a grand place."

He moved slowly down the ramp, his eyes searching for human beings. He was halfway down when he saw a small figure emerge from the trees into a clearing near the foot of the ramp. He called out to it in joyous excitement. The child—it was a child he saw—looked up, stared at him for a moment, then fled back into the shelter of the trees.

"Impetuous, Robert—that's what you are," he chided himself. "Don't scare 'em. Take it easy." But he was not made downhearted by the incident. Where there were children there would be parents, society, opportunities for a bright, young fellow who took a broad view of things. He moved on down at a leisurely pace.

A man showed up at the point where the child had disappeared. Wilson stood still. The man looked him over and advanced hesitantly a step or two. "Come here!" Wilson invited in a friendly voice. "I won't hurt you."

The man could hardly have understood his words, but he advanced slowly. At the edge of the pavement he stopped, eyed it and would not proceed farther.

Something about the behavior pattern clicked in Wilson's brain, fitted in with what he had seen in the Palace, and with the little that Diktor had told him. "Unless," he told himself, "the time I spent in 'Anthropology I' was totally wasted, this Palace is tabu, the ramp I'm standing on is tabu, and, by contagion, I'm tabu. Play your cards, son, play your cards!"

He advanced to the edge of the pavement, being careful not to step off it. The man dropped to his knees and cupped his hands in front of him, head bowed. Without hesitation Wilson touched him on the forehead. The man got back to his feet, his face radiant.

"This isn't even sporting," Wilson said. "I ought to shoot him on the rise."

His Man Friday cocked his head, looked puzzled, and answered in a deep, melodious voice. The words were liquid and strange and sounded like a phrase from a song. "You ought to commercialize that voice," Wilson said admiringly. "Some stars get by on less. However—Get along now, and fetch something to eat. Food." He pointed to his mouth.

The man looked hesitant, spoke again. Bob Wilson reached into his pocket and took out the stolen notebook. He looked up "eat," than looked up "food." It was the same word. "Blellan," he said carefully.

"Blellaaaan?"

"Blellaaaaaaaan," agreed Wilson. "You'll have to excuse my accent. Hurry up." He tried to find "hurry" in the vocabulary, but it was not there. Either the language did not contain the idea or Diktor had not thought it worth while to record it. But we'll soon fix that, Wilson thought—if there isn't such a word, I'll give 'em one.

The man departed.

Wilson sat himself down Turk-fashion and passed the time by studying the notebook. The speed of his rise in these parts, he decided, was limited only by the time it took him to get into full communication. But he had only time enough to look up a few common substantives when his first acquaintance returned, in company.

The procession was headed by an extremely elderly man, white-haired but beardless. All of the men were beardless. He walked under a canopy carried by four male striplings. Only he of all the crowd wore enough clothes to get by anywhere but on a beach. He was looking un-comfortable in a sort of toga effect which appeared to have started life as a Roman-striped awning. That he was the head man was evident.

Wilson hurriedly looked up the word for "chief."

The word for chief was "Diktor."

It should not have surprised him, but it did. It was, of course, a log-ical probability that the word "Diktor" was a title rather than a proper name. It simply had not occurred to him.

Diktor—*the* Diktor—had added a note under the word. "One of the few words," Wilson read, "which shows some probability of having been derived from the dead languages. This word, a few dozen others, and the grammatical structure of the language itself, appear to be the only link between the language of the 'Forsaken Ones' and the English language."

The chief stopped in front of Wilson, just short of the pavement. "O.K., Diktor," Wilson ordered, "kneel down. You're not exempt." He pointed to the ground. The chief knelt down. Wilson touched his fore-head.

The food that had been fetched along was plentiful and very palat-able. Wilson ate slowly and with dignity, keeping in mind the impor-tance of face. While he ate he was serenaded by the entire assemblage. The singing was excellent he was bound to admit. Their ideas of har-mony he found a little strange and the performance, as a whole, seemed primitive, but their voices were all clear and mellow and they sang as if they enjoyed it.

The concert gave Wilson an idea. After he had satisfied his hunger he made the chief understand, with the aid of the indispensable little notebook, that he and his flock were to wait where they were. He then returned to the Hall of the Gate and brought back from there the phono-graph and a dozen assorted records. He treated them to a recorded con-cert of "modern" music.

The reaction exceeded his hopes. "Begin the Beguine" caused tears to stream down the face of the old chief. The first movement of Tschaikowsky's "Concerto Number One in B Flat Minor" practically stampeded them. They jerked. They held their heads and moaned. They shouted their applause. Wilson refrained from giving them the second movement, tapered them off instead with the compelling monotony of the "Bolero."

"Diktor," he said—he was not thinking of the old chief—"Diktor, old chum, you certainly had these people doped out when you sent me shopping. By the time you show up—if you ever do—I'll own the place."

Wilson's rise to power was more in the nature of a triumphal progress than a struggle for supremacy; it contained little that was dramatic. Whatever it was that the High Ones had done to the human race it had left them with only physical resemblance and with temperament largely changed. The docile friendly children with whom Wilson dealt had little in common with the brawling, vulgar, lusty, dynamic swarms who had once called themselves the People of the United States.

The relationship was like that of Jersey cattle to longhorns, or cocker spaniels to wolves. The fight was gone out of them. It was not that they lacked intelligence, nor civilized arts; it was the competitive spirit that was gone, the will-to-power.

Wilson had a monopoly on that.

But even he lost interest in playing a game that he always won. Having established himself as boss man by taking up residence in the Palace and representing himself as the viceroy of the departed High Ones, he, for a time, busied himself in organizing certain projects intended to bring the culture "up-to-date"—the reinvention of musical instruments, establishment of a systematic system of mail service, redevelopment of the idea of styles in dress and a tabu against wearing the same fashion more than one season. There was cunning in the latter project. He figured that arousing a hearty interest in display in the minds of the womenfolk would force the men to hustle to satisfy their wishes. What the culture lacked was drive—it was slipping downhill. He tried to give them the drive they lacked.

His subjects co-operated with his wishes, but in a bemused fashion, like a dog performing a trick, not because he understands it, but because his master and godhead desires it.

He soon tired of it.

But the mystery of the High Ones, and especially the mystery of their Time Gate, still remained to occupy his mind. His was a mixed nature, half hustler, half philosopher. The philosopher had his inning.

It was intellectually necessary to him that he be able to construct in his mind a physio-mathematical model for the phenomena exhibited by the Time Gate. He achieved one, not a good one perhaps, but one which satisfied all of the requirements. Think of a plane surface, a sheet of paper, or, better yet, a silk handkerchief—silk, because it has no rigidity, folds easily, while maintaining all of the relational attributes of a two-dimensional continuum on the surface of the silk itself. Let the threads of the woof be the dimension—or direction—of time; let the threads of the warp represent all three of the space dimensions.

An ink spot on the handkerchief becomes the Time Gate. By folding the handkerchief that spot may be superposed on any other spot on the silk. Press the two spots together between thumb and forefinger; the controls are set, the Time Gate is open, a microscopic inhabitant of this piece of silk may crawl from one fold to the other without traversing any other part of the cloth.

The model is imperfect; the picture is static—but a physical picture is necessarily limited by the sensory experience of the person visualizing it.

He could not make up his mind whether or not the concept of folding the four-dimensional continuum—three of space, one of time—back on itself so that the Gate was "open" required the concept of higher dimensions through which to fold it. It seemed so, yet it might simply be an intellectual shortcoming of the human mind. Nothing but empty space was required for the "folding," but "empty space" was itself a term totally lacking in meaning—he was enough of a mathematician to know that.

If higher dimensions were required to "hold" a four-dimensional continuum, then the number of dimensions of space and of time were necessarily infinite; each order requires the next higher order to maintain it.

But "infinite" was another meaningless term. "Open series" was a little better, but not much.

Another consideration forced him to conclude that there was probably at least one more dimension than the four his senses could perceive—the Time Gate itself. He became quite skilled in handling its controls, but he never acquired the foggiest notion of how it worked, or how it had been built. It seemed to him that the creatures who built it must necessarily have been able to stand outside the limits that confined him in order to anchor the Gate to the structure of space time. The concept escaped him.

He suspected that the controls he saw were simply the part that stuck through into the space he knew. The very Palace itself might be no more than a three-dimensional section of a more involved structure. Such a condition would help to explain the otherwise inexplicable nature of its architecture.

He became possessed of an overpowering desire to know more about these strange creatures, the "High Ones," who had come and ruled the human race and built this Palace and this Gate, and gone away again—and in whose backwash he had been flung out of his setting some thirty millennia. To the human race they were no more than a sacred myth, a contradictory mass of tradition. No picture of them remained, no trace of their writing, nothing of their works save the High Palace of Norkaal and the Gate. And a sense of irreparable loss in the hearts of the race they had ruled, a loss expressed by their own term for themselves—the Forsaken Ones.

With controls and speculum he hunted back through time, seeking the Builders. It was slow work, as he had found before. A passing shadow, a tedious retracing—and failure.

Once he was sure that he had seen such a shadow in the speculum. He set the controls back far enough to be sure that he had repassed it, armed himself with food and drink and waited.

He waited three weeks.

The shadow might have passed during the hours he was forced to take out for sleep. But he felt sure that he was in the right period; he kept up the vigil.

He saw it.

It was moving toward the Gate.

When he pulled himself together he was halfway down the passageway leading away from the Hall. He realized that he had been screaming. He still had an attack of the shakes.

Somewhat later he forced himself to return to the Hall, and, with eyes averted, enter the control booth and return the spheres to zero. He backed out hastily and left the Hall for his apartment. He did not touch the controls nor enter the Hall for more than two years.

It had not been fear of physical menace that had shaken his reason, nor the appearance of the creature—he could recall nothing of *how* it looked. It had been a feeling of sadness infinitely compounded which had flooded through him at the instant, a sense of tragedy, of grief insupportable and unescapable, of infinite weariness. He had been flicked with emotions many times too strong for his spiritual fiber and which he was no more fitted to experience than an oyster is to play a violin.

He felt that he had learned all about the High Ones a man could learn and still endure. He was no longer curious. The shadow of that vicarious emotion ruined his sleep, brought him sweating out of dreams.

One other problem bothered him—the problem of himself and his meanders through time. It still worried him that he had met himself coming back, so to speak, had talked with himself, fought with himself.

Which one was *himself*?

He was all of them, he knew, for he remembered being each one. How about the times when there had been more than one present?

By sheer necessity he was forced to expand the principle of nonidentity—"Nothing is identical with anything else, not even with itself"—to include the ego. In a four-dimensional continuum each event is an absolute individual, it has its space co-ordinates and its date. The Bob Wilson he was right now was *not* the Bob Wilson he had been ten minutes ago. Each was a discrete section of a four-dimensional process. One resembled the other in many particulars, as one slice of bread resembles the slice next to it. But they were *not* the same Bob Wilson— they differed by a length of time.

When he had doubled back on himself, the difference had become apparent, for the separation was now in space rather than in time, and he happened to be so equipped as to be able to *see* a space length, whereas he could only remember a time difference. Thinking back he could remember a great many different Bob Wilsons, baby, small child, adolescent, young man. They were all different—he knew that. The only thing that bound them together into a feeling of identity was continuity of memory.

And that was the same thing that bound together the three—no, four, Bob Wilsons on a certain crowded afternoon, a memory track that ran through all of them. The only thing about it that remained remarkable was time travel itself.

And a few other little items—the nature of "free will," the problem of entropy, the law of the conservation of energy and mass. The last two, he now realized, needed to be extended or generalized to include the cases in which the Gate, or something like it, permitted a leak of mass, energy, or entropy from one neighborhood in the continuum to another. They were otherwise unchanged and valid. Free will was another matter. It could not be laughed off, because it could be directly experienced—yet his own free will had worked to create the same scene over and over again. Apparently human will must be considered as one of the factors which make up the processes in the continuum— "free" to the ego, mechanistic from the outside.

And yet his last act of evading Diktor had apparently changed the course of events. He was here and running the country, had been for many years, but Diktor had not showed up. Could it be that each act of "true" free will created a new and different future? Many philosophers had thought so.

This future appeared to have no such person as Diktor—*the* Diktor—in it, anywhere or anywhen.

As the end of his first ten years in the future approached, he became more and more nervous, less and less certain of his opinion.

Damnation, he thought, if Diktor is going to show up it was high time that he did so. He was anxious to come to grips with him, establish which was to be boss.

He had agents posted throughout the country of the Forsaken Ones with instructions to arrest any man with hair on his face and fetch him forthwith to the Palace. The Hall of the Gate he watched himself.

He tried fishing the future for Diktor, but had no significant luck. He thrice located a shadow and tracked it down; each time it was himself. From tedium and partly from curiosity he attempted to see the other end of the process; he tried to relocate his original home, thirty thousand years in the past.

It was a long chore. The further the time button was displaced from the center, the poorer the control became. It took patient practice to be able to stop the image within a century or so of the period he wanted. It was in the course of this experimentation that he discovered what he had once looked for, a fractional control—a vernier, in effect. It was as simple as the primary control, but twist the bead instead of moving it directly.

He steadied down on the twentieth century, approximated the year by the models of automobiles, types of architecture, and other gross evidence, and stopped in what he believed to be 1952. Careful displacement of the space controls took him to the university town where he had started—after several false tries; the image did not enable him to read road signs.

He located his boardinghouse, brought the Gate into his own room. It was vacant, no furniture in it.

He panned away from the room, and tried again, a year earlier. Success—his own room, his own furniture, but empty. He ran rapidly back, looking for shadows.

There! He checked the swing of the image. There were three figures in the room, the image was too small, the light too poor for him to be sure whether or not one of them was himself. He leaned over and studied the scene.

He heard a dull thump outside the booth. He straightened up and looked over the side.

Sprawled on the floor was a limp human figure. Near it lay a crushed and battered hat.

He stood perfectly still for an uncounted time, staring at the two redundant figures, hat and man, while the winds of unreason swept through his mind and shook it. He did not need to examine the unconscious form to identify it. He knew . . . *he knew*—it was his younger self, knocked willy-nilly through the Time Gate.

It was not that fact in itself which shook him. He had not particularly expected it to happen, having come tentatively to the conclusion that he was living in a different, an alternative, future from the one in which he had originally transitted the Time Gate. He had been aware that it might happen nevertheless, that it did happen did not surprise him.

When it did happen, *he himself had been the only spectator!*

He was Diktor. He was *the* Diktor. He was *the only* Diktor!

He would never find Diktor, nor have it out with him. He need never fear his coming. There never had been, never would be, any other person called Diktor, because Diktor never had been nor ever would be anyone but himself.

In review, it seemed obvious that he must be Diktor; there were so many bits of evidence pointing to it. And yet it had not been obvious. Each point of similarity between himself and the Diktor, he recalled, had arisen from rational causes—usually from his desire to ape the gross characteristics of the "other" and thereby consolidate his own position of power and authority before the "other" Diktor showed up. For that reason he had established himself in the very apartments that "Diktor" had used—so that they would be "his" first.

To be sure his people called him Diktor, but he had thought nothing of that—they called anyone who ruled by that title, even the little sub-chieftains who were his local administrators.

He had grown a beard, such as Diktor had worn, partly in imitation of the "other" man's precedent, but more to set him apart from the hair-less males of the Forsaken Ones. It gave him prestige, increased his tabu. He fingered his bearded chin. Still, it seemed strange that he had not recalled that his own present appearance checked with the appearance of "Diktor." "Diktor" had been an older man. He himself was only thirty-two, ten here, twenty-two *there*.

Diktor he had judged to be about forty-five. Perhaps an unprejudiced witness would believe himself to be that age. His hair and beard were shot with gray—had been, ever since the year he had succeeded too well in spying on the High Ones. His face was lined. Uneasy lies the head and so forth. Running a country, even a peaceful Arcadia, will worry a man, keep him awake nights.

Not that he was complaining—it had been a good life, a grand life, and it beat anything the ancient past had to offer.

In any case, he had been looking for a man in his middle forties, whose face he remembered dimly after ten years and whose picture he did not have. It had never occurred to him to connect that blurred face with his present one. Naturally not.

But there were other little things. Arma, for example. He had selected a likely-looking lass some three years back and made her one of his household staff, renaming her Arma in sentimental memory of the girl he had once fancied. It was logically necessary that they were the same girl, not two Armas, but one.

But, as he recalled her, the "first" Arma had been much prettier.

Hm-m-m—it must be his own point of view that had changed. He admitted that he had had much more opportunity to become bored with exquisite female beauty than his young friend over there on the floor. He recalled with a chuckle how he had found it necessary to surround himself with an elaborate system of tabus to keep the nubile daughters of his subjects out of his hair—most of the time. He had caused a particular pool in the river adjacent to the Palace to be dedicated to his use in order that he might swim without getting tangled up in mermaids.

The man on the floor groaned, but did not open his eyes.

Wilson, the Diktor, bent over him but made no effort to revive him. That the man was not seriously injured he had reason to be certain. He did not wish him to wake up until he had had time to get his own thoughts entirely in order.

For he had work to do, work which must be done meticulously, without mistake. Everyone, he thought with a wry smile, makes plans to provide for their future.

He was about to provide for his past.

There was the matter of the setting of the Time Gate when he got around to sending his early self back. When he had tuned in on the scene in his room a few minutes ago, he had picked up the action just before his early self had been knocked through. In sending him back he must make a slight readjustment in the time setting to an instant around two o'clock of that particular afternoon. That would be simple enough; he need only search a short sector until he found his early self alone and working at his desk.

But the Time Gate had appeared in that room at a later hour; he had just caused it to do so. He felt confused.

Wait a minute, now—if he changed the setting of the time control, the Gate would appear in his room at the earlier time, remain there, and simply blend into its "reappearance" an hour or so later. Yes, that was right. To a person in the room it would simply be as if the Time Gate had been there all along, from about two o'clock.

Which it had been. He would see to that.

Experienced as he was with the phenomena exhibited by the Time Gate, it nevertheless required a strong and subtle intellectual effort to think other than in durational terms, to take an *eternal* viewpoint.

And there was the hat. He picked it up and tried it on. It did not fit very well, no doubt because he was wearing his hair longer now. The hat must be placed where it would be found—Oh, yes, in the control booth. And the notebook, too.

The notebook, the notebook—Mm-m-m—Something funny, there. When the notebook he had stolen had become dog-eared and tattered almost to illegibility some four years back, he had carefully recopied its contents in a new notebook—to refresh his memory of English rather than from any need for it as a guide. The worn-out notebook he had destroyed; it was the new one he intended to obtain, and leave to be found.

In that case, *there never had been two notebooks*. The one he had now would become, after being taken through the Gate to a point ten years in the past, the notebook from which he had copied it. They were simply different segments of the same physical process, manipulated by means of the Gate to run concurrently, side by side, for a certain length of time.

As he had himself—one afternoon.

He wished that he had not thrown away the worn-out notebook. If he had it at hand, he could compare them and convince himself that they were identical save for the wear and tear of increasing entropy.

But when had he learned the language, in order that he might prepare such a vocabulary? To be sure, when he copied it he then *knew* the language—copying had not actually been necessary.

But he *had* copied it.

The physical process he had all straightened out in his mind, but the intellectual process it represented was completely circular. His older self had taught his younger self a language which the older self knew because the younger self, after being taught, grew up to be the older self and was, therefore, capable of teaching.

But where had it started?

Which comes first, the hen or the egg?

You feed the rats to the cats, skin the cats, and feed the carcasses of the cats to the rats who are in turn fed to the cats. The perpetual motion fur farm.

If God created the world, who created God?

Who wrote the notebook? Who started the chain?

He felt the intellectual desperation of any honest philosopher. He knew that he had about as much chance of understanding such problems as a collie has of understanding how dog food gets into cans. Applied psychology was more his size—which reminded him that there were certain books which his early self would find very useful in learning how to deal with the political affairs of the country he was to run. He made a mental note to make a list.

The man on the floor stirred again, sat up. Wilson knew that the time had come when he must insure his past. He was not worried; he felt the sure confidence of the gambler who is "hot," who *knows* what the next roll of the dice will show.

He bent over his alter ego. "Are you all right?" he asked.

"I guess so," the younger man mumbled. He put his hand to his bloody face. "My head hurts."

"I should think it would," Wilson agreed. "You came through head over heels. I think you hit your head when you landed."

His younger self did not appear fully to comprehend the words at first. He looked around dazedly, as if to get his bearings. Presently he said, "Came through? Came through what?"

"The Gate, of course," Wilson told him. He nodded his head toward the Gate, feeling that the sight of it would orient the still groggy younger Bob.

Young Wilson looked over his shoulder in the direction indicated, sat up with a jerk, shuddered and closed his eyes. He opened them again after what seemed to be a short period of prayer, looked again, and said, "Did I come through that?"

"Yes," Wilson assured him.

"Where am I?"

"In the Hall of the Gate in the High Palace of Norkaal. But what is more important," Wilson added, "is *when* you are. You have gone forward a little more than thirty thousand years."

The knowledge did not seem to reassure him. He got up and stumbled toward the Gate. Wilson put a restraining band on his shoulder. "Where are you going?"

"Back!"

"Not so fast." He did not dare let him go back yet, not until the Gate had been reset. Besides he was still drunk—his breath was staggering. "You will go back all right—I give you my word on that. But let me dress your wounds first. And you should rest. I have some explanations to make to you, and there is an errand you can do for me when you get back—to our mutual advantage. There is a great future in store for you and me, my boy—a great future!"

A great future!

LOST LEGACY

Super Science Stories, November 1941

as by Lyle Monroe

CHAPTER ONE

"Ye Have Eyes to See With!"

"HI-YAH, BUTCHER!" DOCTOR Philip Huxley put down the dice cup he had been fiddling with as he spoke, and shoved out a chair with his foot. "Sit down."

The man addressed ostentatiously ignored the salutation while handing a yellow slicker and soggy felt hat to the Faculty Clubroom attendant, but accepted the chair. His first words were to the negro attendant.

"Did you hear that, Pete? A witch doctor, passing himself off as a psychologist, has the effrontery to refer to me—to *me,* a licensed physician and surgeon, as a butcher." His voice was filled with gentle reproach.

"Don't let him kid you, Pete. If Doctor Coburn ever got you into an operating theatre, he'd open up your head just to see what makes you tick. He'd use your skull to make an ashtray."

The colored man grinned as he wiped the table, but said nothing.

Coburn clucked and shook his head. "That from a witch doctor. Still looking for the Little Man Who Wasn't There, Phil?"

"If you mean parapsychology, yes."

"How's the racket coming?"

"Pretty good. I've got one less lecture this semester, which is just as well—I get awfully tired of explaining to the wide-eyed innocents how little we really know about what goes on inside their think-tanks. I'd rather do research."

"Who wouldn't? Struck any pay dirt lately?"

"Some. I'm having a lot of fun with a law student just now, chap named Valdez."

Coburn lifted his brows. "So? E.S.P.?"

"Kinda. He's sort of a clairvoyant; if he can see one side of an object, he can see the other side, too."

"Nuts!"

" 'If you're so smart, why ain't you rich?' I've tried him out under carefully controlled conditions, and he can do it—see around corners."

"Hmmmm—well, as my Grandfather Stonebender used to say, 'God has more aces up his sleeve than were ever dealt in the game.' He would be a menace at stud poker."

"Matter of fact, he made his stake for law school as a professional gambler."

"Found out how he does it?"

"No, damn it." Huxley drummed on the table top, a worried look on his face. "If I just had a little money for research, I might get enough data to make this sort of thing significant. Look at what Rhine accomplished at Duke."

"Well, why don't you holler? Go before the Board and bite 'em in the ear for it. Tell 'em how you're going to make Western University famous."

Huxley looked still more morose. "Fat chance. I talked with my dean and he wouldn't even let me take it up with the President. Scared that the old fathead will clamp down on the department even more than he has. You see, officially, we are supposed to be behaviorists. Any suggestion that there might be something to consciousness that can't be explained in terms of physiology and mechanics is about as welcome as a Saint Bernard in a telephone booth."

The telephone signal glowed red back of the attendant's counter. He switched off the newscast and answered the call. "Hello . . . Yes, ma'am, he is. I'll call him. Telephone for you, Doctuh Coburn."

"Switch it over here." Coburn turned the telephone panel at the table around so that it faced him; as he did so it lighted up with the face of a young woman. He picked up the handset. "What is it? . . . What's that? How long ago did it happen? . . . Who made the diagnosis? . . . Read that over again . . . Let me see the chart." He inspected its image reflected in the panel, then added, "Very well. I'll be right over. Prepare the patient for operating." He switched off the instrument and turned to Huxley. "Got to go, Phil—emergency."

"What sort?"

"It'll interest you. Trephining. Maybe some cerebral excision. Car accident. Come along and watch it, if you have time." He was putting on his slicker as he spoke. He turned and swung out the west door with a long, loose-limbed stride. Huxley grabbed his own raincoat and hurried to catch up with him.

"How come," he asked as he came abreast, "they had to search for you?"

"Left my pocketphone in my other suit," Coburn returned briefly. "On purpose—I wanted a little peace and quiet. No luck."

They worked north and west through the arcades and passages that connected the Union with the Science group, ignoring the moving walkways as being too slow. But when they came to the conveyor subway under Third Avenue opposite the Pottenger Medical School, they found it flooded, its machinery stalled, and were forced to detour west to the Fairfax Avenue conveyor. Coburn cursed impartially the engineers and the planning commission for the fact that spring brings torrential rains to Southern California, Chamber of Commerce or no.

They got rid of their wet clothes in the Physicians' Room and moved on to the gowning room for surgery. An orderly helped Huxley into white trousers and cotton shoe covers, and they moved to the next room to scrub. Coburn invited Huxley to scrub also in order that he might watch the operation close up. For three minutes by the little sand glass they scrubbed away with strong green soap, then stepped through a door and were gowned and gloved by silent, efficient nurses. Huxley felt rather silly to be helped on with his clothes by a nurse who had to stand on tip-toe to get the sleeves high enough. They were ushered through the glass door into surgery III, rubber-covered hands held out, as if holding a skein of yarn.

The patient was already in place on the table, head raised up and skull clamped immobile. Someone snapped a switch and a merciless circle of blue-white lights beat down on the only portion of him that was exposed, the right side of his skull. Coburn glanced quickly around the room, Huxley following his glance—light green walls, two operating nurses, gowned, masked, and hooded into sexlessness, a 'dirty' nurse, busy with something in the corner, the anesthetist, the instruments that told Coburn the state of the patient's heart action and respiration.

A nurse held the chart for the surgeon to read. At a word from Coburn, the anesthetist uncovered the patient's face for a moment. Lean brown face, acquiline nose, closed sunken eyes. Huxley repressed an exclamation. Coburn raised his eyebrows at Huxley.

"What's the trouble?"

"It's Juan Valdez!"

"Who's he?"

"The one I was telling you about—the law student with the trick eyes."

"Hmm—Well, his trick eyes didn't see around enough corners this time. He's lucky to be alive. You'll see better, Phil, if you stand over there."

Coburn changed to impersonal efficiency, ignored Huxley's presence and concentrated the whole of his able intellect on the damaged flesh before him. The skull had been crushed, or punched, apparently by coming into violent contact with some hard object with moderately sharp edges. The wound lay above the right ear, and was, superficially, two inches, or more, across. It was impossible, before exploration, to tell just how much damage had been suffered by the bony structure and the grey matter behind.

Undoubtedly there was some damage to the brain itself. The wound had been cleaned up on the surface and the area around it shaved and painted. The trauma showed up as a definite hole in the cranium. It was bleeding slightly and was partly filled with a curiously nauseating conglomerate of clotted purple blood, white tissue, grey tissue, pale yellow tissue.

The surgeon's lean slender fingers, unhuman in their pale orange coverings, moved gently, deftly in the wound, as if imbued with a separate life and intelligence of their own. Destroyed tissue, too freshly dead for the component cells to realize it, was cleared away,—chipped fragments of bone, lacerated mater dura, the grey cortical tissue of the cerebrum itself.

Huxley became fascinated by the minuscule drama, lost track of time, and of the sequence of events. He remembered terse orders for assistance, "Clamp!" "Retractor!" "Sponge!" The sound of the tiny saw, a muffled whine, then the tooth-tingling grind it made in cutting through solid living bone. Gently a spatulate instrument was used to straighten out the tortured convolutions. Incredible and unreal, he watched a scalpel whittle at the door of the mind, shave the thin wall of reason.

Three times a nurse wiped sweat from the surgeon's face.

Wax performed its function. Vitallium alloy replaced bone, dressing shut out infection. Huxley had watched uncounted operations, but felt again that almost insupportable sense of relief and triumph that comes when the surgeon turns away, and begins stripping off his gloves as he heads for the gowning room.

When Huxley joined Coburn, the surgeon had doused his mask and cap, and was feeling under his gown for cigarets. He looked entirely human again. He grinned at Huxley and inquired,

"Well, how did you like it?"

"Swell. It was the first time I was able to watch that type of thing so closely. You can't see so well from behind the glass, you know. Is he going to be all right?"

Coburn's expression changed. "He is a friend of yours, isn't he? That had slipped my mind for the moment. Sorry. He'll be all right, I'm pretty sure. He's young and strong, and he came through the operation very nicely. You can come see for yourself in a couple of days."

"You excised quite a lot of the speech center, didn't you? Will he be able to talk when he gets well? Isn't he likely to have aphasia, or some other speech disorder?"

"Speech center? Why, I wasn't even close to the speech centers."

"Huh?"

"Put a rock in your right hand, Phil, so you'll know it next time. You're turned around a hundred and eighty degrees, was working in the *right* cerebral lobe, not the left lobe."

Huxley looked puzzled, spread both hands out in front of him, glanced from one to the other, then his face cleared and he laughed. "You're right. You know, I have the damndest time with that. I never can remember which way to deal in a bridge game. But wait a minute— I had it so firmly fixed in my mind that you were on the left side in the speech centers that I am confused. What do you think the result will be on his neurophysiology?"

"Nothing—if past experience is any criterion. What I took away he'll never miss. I was working in terra incognito, pal—No Man's Land. If that portion of the brain that I was in has any function, the best physiologists haven't been able to prove it."

CHAPTER TWO

Three Blind Mice

Brrrinng!

Joan Freeman reached out blindly with one hand and shut off the alarm clock, her eyes jammed shut in the vain belief that she could re- main asleep if she did. Her mind wondered. Sunday. Don't have to get up early on Sunday. Then why had she set the alarm? She remembered suddenly and rolled out of bed, warm feet on a floor cold in the morn- ing air. Her pajamas landed on that floor as she landed in the shower, yelled, turned the shower to warm, then back to cold again.

The last item from the refrigerator had gone into a basket, and a thermos jug was filled by the time she heard the sound of a car on the hill outside, the crunch of tires on granite in the driveway. She hur- riedly pulled on short boots, snapped the loops of her jodhpurs under them, and looked at herself in the mirror. Not bad, she thought. Not Miss America, but she wouldn't frighten any children.

A banging at the door was echoed by the doorbell, and a baritone voice, "Joan! Are you decent?"

"Practically. Come on in, Phil."

Huxley, in slacks and polo shirt, was followed by another figure.

He turned to him. "Joan, this is Ben Coburn, Doctor Ben Coburn. Doctor Coburn, Miss Freeman."

"Awfully nice of you to let me come, Miss Freeman."

"Not at all, Doctor. Phil had told me so much about you that I have been anxious to meet you." The conventionalities flowed with the ease of all long-established tribal taboo.

"Call him Ben, Joan. It's good for his ego."

While Joan and Phil loaded the car Coburn looked over the young woman's studio house. A single large room, panelled in knotty pine and dominated by a friendly field-stone fireplace set about with untidy bookcases, gave evidence of her personality. He had stepped through open french doors into a tiny patio, paved with mossy bricks and fitted with a barbecue pit and a little fishpond, brilliant in the morning sunlight, when he heard himself called.

"Doc! Stir your stumps! Time's awastin'!"

He glanced again around the patio, and rejoined the others at the car. "I like your house, Miss Freeman. Why should we bother to leave Beachwood Drive when Griffith Park can't be any pleasanter?"

"That's easy. If you stay at home, it's not a picnic—it's just breakfast. My name's Joan."

"May I put in a request for 'just breakfast' here some morning—Joan?"

"Lay off o' that mug, Joan," advised Phil in a stage whisper. "His intentions ain't honorable."

Joan straightened up the remains of what had recently been a proper-sized meal. She chucked into the fire three well-picked bones to which thick sirloin steaks were no longer attached, added some discarded wrapping paper and one lonely roll. She shook the thermos jug. It gurgled slightly. "Anybody want some more grapefruit juice?" she called.

"Any more coffee?" asked Coburn, then continued to Huxley, "His special talents are gone completely?"

"Plenty," Joan replied. "Serve yourselves."

The Doctor filled his own cup and Huxley's. Phil answered, "Gone entirely, I'm reasonably certain. I thought it might be hysterical shock from the operation, but I tried him under hypnosis, and the results were still negative—completely. Joan, you're some cook. Will you adopt me?"

"You're over twenty-one."

"I could easily have him certified as incompetent," volunteered Coburn.

"Single women aren't favored for adoption."

"Marry me, and it will be all right—we can both adopt him and you can cook for all of us."

"Well, I won't say that I won't and I won't say that I will, but I will say that it's the best offer I've had today. What were you guys talking about?"

"Make him put it in writing, Joan. We were talking about Valdez."

"Oh! You were going to run those last tests yesterday, weren't you? How did you come out?"

"Absolutely negative insofar as his special clairvoyance was concerned. It's gone."

"Hmm—How about the control tests?"

"The Humm-Wadsworth Temperament Test showed exactly the same profile as before the accident, within the inherent limits of accuracy of the technique. His intelligence quotient came within the technique limit, too. Association tests didn't show anything either. By all the accepted standards of neuropsychology he is the same individual, except in two respects; he's minus a chunk of his cortex, and he is no longer able to see around corners. Oh, yes, and he's annoyed at losing that ability."

After a pause she answered, "That's pretty conclusive, isn't it?"

Huxley turned to Coburn. "What do you think, Ben?"

"Well, I don't know. You are trying to get me to admit that that piece of grey matter I cut out of his head gave him the ability to see in a fashion not possible to normal sense organs and not accounted for by orthodox medical theory, aren't you?"

"I'm not trying to make you admit anything. I'm trying to find out something."

"Well, since you put it that way, I would say if we stipulate that all your primary data were obtained with care under properly controlled conditions—"

"They were."

"—and that you have exercised even greater care in obtaining your negative secondary data—"

"I have. Damn it, I tried for three weeks under all conceivable conditions."

"Then we have the inescapable conclusions, first—" He ticked them off on his fingers. "—that this subject could see without the intervention of physical sense organs; and second, that this unusual, to put it mildly, ability was in some way related to a portion of his cerebrum in the dexter lobe."

"Bravo!" This was Joan's contribution.

"Thanks, Ben," acknowledged Phil. "I had reached the same conclusions, of course, but it's very encouraging to have someone else agree with me."

"Well, now that you are there, where are you?"

"I don't know exactly. Let me put it this way; I got into psychology for the same reason a person joins a church—because he feels an overpowering need to understand himself and the world around him. When I was a young student, I thought modern psychology could tell me the answers, but I soon found out that the best psychologists didn't know a damn thing about the real core of the matter. Oh, I am not disparaging the work that has been done; it was badly needed and has been very useful in its way. None of 'em know what life is, what thought is, whether free will is a reality or an illusion, or whether that last question means anything. The best of 'em admit their ignorance; the worst of them make dogmatic assertions that are obvious absurdities—for example some of the mechanistic behaviorists that think just because Pavlov could condition a dog to drool at the sound of a bell that, therefore, they knew all about how Paderewski made music!"

Joan, who had been lying quietly in the shade of the big liveoaks and listening, spoke up. "Ben, you are a brain surgeon, aren't you?"

"One of the best," certified Phil.

"You've seen a lot of brains, furthermore you've seen 'em while they were *alive,* which is more than most psychologists have. What do you believe thought is? What do you think makes us tick?"

He grinned at her. "You've got me, kid. I don't pretend to know. It's not my business; I'm just a tinker."

She sat up. "Give me a cigaret, Phil. I've arrived just where Phil is, but by a different road. My father wanted me to study law. I soon found out that I was more interested in the principles behind law and I changed over to the School of Philosophy. But philosophy wasn't the answer. There really isn't anything to philosophy. Did you ever eat that cotton candy they sell at fairs? Well, philosophy is like that—it looks as if it were really something, and it's awfully pretty, and it tastes sweet, but when you go to bite it you can't get your teeth into it, and when you try to swallow, there isn't anything there. Philosophy is word-chasing, as significant as a puppy chasing its tail.

"I was about to get my Ph.D. in the School of Philosophy, when I chucked it and came to the science division and started taking courses in psychology. I thought that if I was a good little girl and patient, all would be revealed to me. Well, Phil has told us what that leads to. I began to think about studying medicine, or biology. You just gave the show away on that. Maybe it was a mistake to teach women to read and write."

Ben laughed. "This seems to be experience meeting at the village church; I might as well make my confession. I guess most medical men start out with a desire to know all about man and what makes him tick, but it's a big field, the final answers are elusive and there is always so much work that needs to be done right now, that we quit worrying about the final problems. I'm as interested as I ever was in knowing what life, and thought, and so forth, really are, but I have to have an attack of insomnia to find time to worry about them. Phil, are you seriously proposing to tackle such things?"

"In a way, yes. I've been gathering data on all sorts of phenomena that run contrary to orthodox psychological theory—all the junk that goes under the general name of metapsychics—telepathy, clairvoyance, so-called psychic manifestations, clairaudience, levitation, yoga stuff, stigmata, anything of that sort I can find."

"Don't you find that most of that stuff can be explained in an ordinary fashion?"

"Quite a lot of it, sure. Then you can strain orthodox theory all out of shape and ignore the statistical laws of probability to account for most of the rest. Then by attributing anything that is left over to charlatanism, credulity, and self-hypnosis, and refuse to investigate it, you can go peacefully back to sleep."

"Occam's razor," murmured Joan.

"Huh?"

"William of Occam's Razor. It's a name for a principle in logic; whenever two hypotheses both cover the facts, use the simpler of the two. When a conventional scientist has to strain his orthodox theories all out of shape, 'til they resemble something thought up by Rube Goldberg, to account for unorthodox phenomena, he's ignoring the principle of Occam's Razor. It's simpler to draw up a new hypothesis to cover all the facts than to strain an old one that was never intended to cover the non-conforming data. But scientists are more attached to their theories than they are to their wives and families."

"My," said Phil admiringly, "to think that that came out from under a permanent wave."

"If you'll hold him, Ben, I'll beat him with this here thermos jug."

"I apologize. You're absolutely right, darling. I decided to forget about theories, to treat these outcast phenomena like any ordinary data, and to see where it landed me."

"What sort of stuff," put in Ben, "have you dug up, Phil?"

"Quite a variety, some verified, some mere rumor, a little of it carefully checked under laboratory conditions, like Valdez. Of course, you've heard of all the stunts attributed to Yoga. Very little of it has been duplicated in the Western Hemisphere, which counts against it; nevertheless a lot of odd stuff in India has been reported by competent, cool-minded observers—telepathy, accurate soothsaying, clairvoyance, fire walking, and so forth."

"Why do you include fire walking in metapsychics?"

"On the chance that the mind can control the body and other material objects in some esoteric fashion."

"Hmm."

"Is the idea any more marvelous than the fact that you can cause your hand to scratch your head? We haven't any more idea of the actual workings of volition on matter in one case than in the other. Take the Tierra del Fuegans. They slept on the ground, naked, even in zero weather. Now the body can't make any such adjustment in its economy. It hasn't the machinery; any physiologist will tell you so. A naked human being caught outdoors in zero weather must exercise, or die. But the Tierra del Fuegans didn't know about metabolic rates and such. They just slept—nice, and warm, and cozy."

"So far you haven't mentioned anything close to home. If you are going to allow that much latitude, my Grandfather Stonebender had much more wonderful experiences."

"I'm coming to them. Don't forget Valdez."

"What's this about Ben's grandfather?" asked Joan.

"Joan, don't ever boast about anything in Ben's presence. You'll find that his Grandfather Stonebender did it faster, easier, and better."

A look of more-in-sorrow-than-in-anger shone out of Coburn's pale blue eyes. "Why, Phil, I'm surprised at you. If I weren't a Stonebender myself, and tolerant, I'd be inclined to resent that remark. But your apology is accepted."

"Well, to bring matters closer home, besides Valdez, there was a man in my home town, Springfield, Missouri, who had a clock in his head."

"What do you mean?"

"I mean he knew the exact time without looking at a clock. If your watch disagreed with him, your watch was wrong. Besides that, he was a lightning calculator—knew the answer instantly to the most complicated problems in arithmetic you cared to put to him. In other ways he was feeble-minded."

Ben nodded. "It's a common phenomenon—*idiots savants*."

"But giving it a name doesn't explain it. Besides which, while a number of the people with erratic talents are feeble-minded, not all of them are. I believe that by far the greater per cent of them are not, but that we rarely hear of them because the intelligent ones are smart enough to know that they would be annoyed by the crowd, possibly persecuted, if they let the rest of us suspect that they were different."

Ben nodded again. "You got something there, Phil. Go ahead."

"There have been a lot of these people with impossible talents who were not subnormal in other ways and who were right close to home. Boris Sidis, for example—"

"He was that child prodigy, wasn't he? I thought he played out?"

"Maybe. Personally, I think he grew cagy and decided not to let the other monkeys know that he was different. In any case he had a lot of remarkable talents, in intensity, if not in kind. He must have been able to read a page of print just by glancing at it, and he undoubtedly had complete memory. Speaking of complete memory, how about Blind Tom, the negro pianist who could play any piece of music he had ever heard once? Nearer home, there was this boy right here in Los Angeles County not so very many years ago who could play ping-pong blindfolded, or anything else, for which normal people require eyes. I checked him myself, and he could do it. And there was the 'Instantaneous Echo.'"

"You never told me about him, Phil," commented Joan. "What could he do?"

"He could talk along with you, using your words and intonations, in any language whether he knew the language or not. And he would keep pace with you so accurately that anyone listening wouldn't be able to tell the two of you apart. He could imitate your speech and words as immediately, as accurately, and as effortlessly as your shadow follows the movements of your body."

"Pretty fancy, what? And rather difficult to explain by behaviorist theory. Ever run across any cases of levitation, Phil?"

"Not of human beings. However I have seen a local medium—a nice kid, non-professional, used to live next door to me—make articles of furniture in my own house rise up off the floor and float. I was cold sober. It either happened or I was hypnotized; have it your own way. Speaking of levitating, you know the story they tell about Nijinsky?"

"Which one?"

"About him floating. There are thousands of people here and in Europe (unless they died in the Collapse) who testify that in *Le Spectre de la Rose* he used to leap up into the air, pause for a while, then come down when he got ready. Call it mass hallucination—I didn't see it."

"Occam's Razor again," said Joan.

"So?"

"Mass hallucination is harder to explain than one man floating in the air for a few seconds. Mass hallucination not proved—mustn't infer it to get rid of a troublesome fact. It's comparable to the "There aint no sech animal' of the yokel who saw the rhinoceros for the first time."

"Maybe so. Any other sort of trick stuff you want to hear about, Ben? I got a million of 'em."

"How about forerunners, and telepathy?"

"Well, telepathy is positively proved, though still unexplained, by Dr. Rhine's experiments. Of course a lot of people had observed it before then, with such frequency as to make questioning it unreasonable. Mark Twain, for example. He wrote about it fifty years before Rhine, with documentation and circumstantial detail. He wasn't a scientist, but he had hard common sense and shouldn't have been ignored. Upton Sinclair, too. Forerunners are a little harder. Every one has heard dozens of stories of hunches that came true, but they are hard to follow up in most cases. You might try J. W. Dunne's *Experiment with Time* for a scientific record under controlled conditions of forerunners in dreams."

"Where does all this get you, Phil? You aren't just collecting Believe-it-or-nots?"

"No, but I had to assemble a pile of data—you ought to look over my notebooks—before I could formulate a working hypothesis. I have one now."

"Well?"

"You gave it to me—by operating on Valdez. I had begun to suspect sometime ago that these people with odd and apparently impossible mental and physical abilities were no different from the rest of us in any sense of abnormality, but that they had stumbled on potentialities inherent in all of us. Tell me, when you had Valdez' cranium open did you notice anything abnormal in its appearance?"

"No. Aside from the wound, it presented no special features."

"Very well. Yet when you excised that damaged portion, he no longer possessed his strange clairvoyant power. You took that chunk of his brain out of an uncharted area—no known function. Now it is a primary datum of psychology and physiology that large areas of the brain have no *known* function. It doesn't seem reasonable that the most highly developed and highly specialized part of the body should have large areas with *no* function; it is more reasonable to assume that the functions are unknown. And yet men have had large pieces of their cortices cut out without any *apparent* loss in their mental powers—as long as the areas controlling the normal functions of the body were left untouched.

"Now in this one case, Valdez, we have established a direct connection between an uncharted area of the brain and an odd talent, to wit, clairvoyance. My working hypothesis comes directly from that: All normal people are potentially able to exercise all (or possibly most) of the odd talents we have referred to—telepathy, clairvoyance, special mathematical ability, special control over the body and its functions, and so forth. The potential ability to do these things is lodged in the unassigned areas of the brain."

Coburn pursed his lips. "Mmm—I don't know. If we all have these wonderful abilities, which isn't proved, how is it that we don't seem able to use them?"

"I haven't proved anything—yet. This is a working hypothesis. But let me give you an analogy. These abilities aren't like sight, hearing, and touch which we can't avoid using from birth; they are more like the ability to talk, which has its own special centers in the brain from birth, *but which has to be trained into being.* Do you think a child raised exclusively by deaf-mutes would ever learn to talk? Of course not. To outward appearance he would be a deaf-mute."

"I give up," conceded Coburn. "You set up an hypothesis and made it plausible. But how are you going to check it? I don't see any place to get hold of it. It's a very pretty speculation, but without a working procedure, it's just fantasy."

Huxley rolled over and stared unhappily up through the branches. "That's the rub. I've lost my best wild talent case. I don't know where to begin."

"But, Phil," protested Joan. "You want normal subjects, and then try to develop special abilities in them. I think it's wonderful. When do we start?"

"When do we start what?"

"On *me,* of course. Take that ability to do lightning calculations, for example. If you could develop that in me, you'd be a magician. I got bogged down in first year algebra. I don't know the multiplication tables even now!"

CHAPTER THREE

"Every Man His Own Genius"

"Shall we get busy?" asked Phil.

"Oh, let's not," Joan objected. "Let's drink our coffee in peace and let dinner settle. We haven't seen Ben for two weeks. I want to hear what he's been doing up in San Francisco."

"Thanks, darling," the doctor answered, "but I'd much rather hear about the Mad Scientist and his Trilby."

"Trilby, hell," Huxley protested, "She's as independent as a hog on ice. However, we've got something to show you this time, Doc."

"Really? That's good. What?"

"Well, as you know, we didn't make much progress for the first couple of months. It was all up hill. Joan developed a fair telepathic ability, but it was erratic and unreliable. As for mathematical ability, she had learned her multiplication tables, but as for being a lightning calculator, she was a washout."

Joan jumped up, crossed between the men and the fireplace, and entered her tiny Pullman kitchen. "I've got to scrape these dishes and put them to soak before the ants get at 'em. Talk loud, so I can hear you."

"What can Joan do now, Phil?"

"I'm not going to tell you. You wait and see. Joan! Where's the card table?"

"Back of the couch. No need to shout. I can hear plainly since I got my Foxy Grandma Stream-lined Ear Trumpet."

"Okay, wench, I found it. Cards in the usual place?"

"Yes, I'll be with you in a moment." She reappeared, whisking off a giddy kitchen apron, and sat down on the couch, hugging her knees. "The Great Gaga, the Ghoul of Hollywood is ready. Sees all, knows all, and tells a darnsight more. Fortunetelling, teethpulling, and refined entertainment for the entire family."

"Cut out the clowning. We'll start out with a little straight telepathy. Throw every thing else out of gear. Shuffle the cards, Ben."

Coburn did so. "Now what?"

"Deal 'em off, one at a time, letting you and me see 'em, but not Joan. Call 'em off, kid."

Ben dealt them out slowly. Joan commenced to recite in a singsong voice, "Seven of diamonds; jack of hearts; ace of hearts; three of spades; ten of diamonds; six of clubs; nine of spades; eight of clubs—"

"Ben, that's the first time I've ever seen you look amazed."

"Right through the deck without a mistake. Grandfather Stonebender couldn't have done better."

"That's high praise, chum. Let's try a variation. I'll sit out this one. Don't let me see them. I don't know how it will work, as we never worked with anyone else. Try it."

A few minutes later Coburn put down the last card. "Perfect! Not a mistake."

Joan got up and came over to the table. "How come this deck has two tens of hearts in it?" She riffled through the deck, and pulled out one card. "Oh! You thought the seventh card was the ten of hearts; it was the ten of diamonds. See?"

"I guess I did," Ben admitted. "I'm sorry I threw you a curve. The light isn't any too good."

"Joan prefers artistic lighting effects to saving her eyes," explained Phil. "I'm glad it happened; it shows she was using telepathy, not clairvoyance. Now for a spot of mathematics. We'll skip the usual stunts

like cube roots, instantaneous addition, logarithms of hyperbolic functions, and stuff. Take my word for it; she can do 'em. You can try her
later on those simple tricks. Here's a little honey I shot in my own
kitchen. It involves fast reading, complete memory, handling of unbelievable number of permutations and combinations, and mathematical
investigation of alternatives. You play solitaire, Ben?"

"Sure."

"I want you to shuffle the cards thoroughly, then lay out a Canfield
solitaire, dealing from left to right, then play it out, three cards at a
time, going through the deck again and again, until you are stuck and
can't go any farther."

"Okay. What's the gag?"

"After you have shuffled and cut, I want you to riffle the cards
through once, holding them up so that Joan gets a quick glimpse of the
index on each card. Then wait a moment."

Silently he did what he had been asked to do. Joan checked him.
"You'll have to do it again, Ben. I saw only fifty-one cards."

"Two of them must have stuck together. I'll do it more carefully."
He repeated it.

"Fifty-two that time. That's fine."

"Are you ready, Joan?"

"Yes, Phil. Take it down; hearts to the six, diamonds to the four,
spades to the deuce, no clubs."

Coburn looked incredulous. "Do you mean that is the way this
game is going to come out?"

"Try it and see."

He dealt the cards out from left to right, then played the game out
slowly. Joan stopped him at one point. "No, play the king of hearts'
stack into that space, rather than the king of spades. The king of spades
play would have gotten the ace of clubs out, but three less hearts would
play out if you did so." Coburn made no comment, but did as she told
him to do. Twice more she stopped him and indicated a different choice
of alternatives.

The game played out exactly as she had predicted.

Coburn ran his hand through his hair and stared at the cards.
"Joan," he said meekly, "does your head ever ache?"

"Not from doing that stuff. It doesn't seem to be an effort at all."

"You know," put in Phil, seriously, "there isn't any real reason why
it should be a strain. So far as we know, thinking requires no expendi-
ture of energy at all. A person ought to be able to think straight and accurately with no effort. I've a notion that it is faulty thinking that makes
headaches."

"But how in the devil does she do it, Phil? It makes my head ache just to try to imagine the size of that problem, if it were worked out long hand by conventional mathematics."

"I don't know how she does it. Neither does she."

"Then how did she *learn* to do it?"

"We'll take that up later. First, I want to show you our *piece de resistance*."

"I can't take much more. I'm groggy now."

"You'll like this."

"Wait a minute, Phil. I want to try one of my own. How fast can Joan read?"

"As fast as she can see."

"Hmm—". The doctor hauled a sheaf of typewritten pages out of his inside coat pocket. "I've got the second draft of a paper I've been working on. Let's try Joan on a page of it. Okay, Joan?"

He separated an inner page from the rest and handed it to her. She glanced at it and handed it back at once. He looked puzzled and said:

"What's the matter?"

"Nothing. Check me as I read back." She started in a rapid singsong, " 'page four —now according to Cunningham, fifth edition, page 547,: "Another strand of fibres, videlicet, the fasciculus spinocerebellaris (posterior), prolonged upwards in the lateral furniculus of the medulla spinallis, gradually leaves this portion of the medulla oblongata. This tract lies on the surface, and is—"

"That's enough, Joan, hold it. God knows how you did it, but you read and memorized that page of technical junk in a split second." He grinned slyly. "But your pronunciation was a bit spotty. Grandfather Stonebender's would have been perfect."

"What can you expect? I don't know what half of the words mean."

"Joan, how did you learn to do all this stuff?"

"Truthfully, Doctor, I don't know. It's something like learning to ride a bicycle—you take one spill after another, then one day you get on and just ride away, easy as you please. And in a week you are riding without handle-bars and trying stunts. It's been like that—I knew what I wanted to do, and one day I could. Come on, Phil's getting impatient."

Ben maintained a puzzled silence and permitted Phil to lead him to a little desk in the corner. "Joan, can we use any drawer? OK. Ben, pick out a drawer in this desk, remove any articles you wish, add anything you wish. Then, without looking into the drawer, stir up the contents and remove a few articles and drop them into another drawer. I want to eliminate the possibility of telepathy."

"Phil, don't worry about my housekeeping. My large staff of secretaries will be only too happy to straighten out that desk after you get through playing with it."

"Don't stand in the way of science, little one. Besides," he added, glancing into a drawer, "this desk obviously hasn't been straightened for at least six months. A little more stirring up won't hurt it."

"Humph! What can you expect when I spend all my time learning parlor tricks for you? Besides, I know where everything is."

"That's just what I am afraid of, and why I want Ben to introduce a little more of the random element—if possible. Go ahead, Ben."

When the doctor had complied and closed the drawer, Phil continued, "Better use pencil and paper on this one, Joan. First list everything you see in the drawer, then draw a little sketch to show approximate locations and arrangement."

"OK." She sat down at the desk and commenced to write rapidly:

One large black leather handbag

Six-inch ruler

Ben stopped her. "Wait a minute. This is all wrong. I would have noticed anything as big as a handbag."

She wrinkled her brow. "Which drawer did you say?"

"The second on the right."

"I thought you said the top drawer."

"Well, perhaps I did."

She started again:

Brass paper knife

Six assorted pencils and a red pencil

Thirteen rubber bands

Pearl-handled penknife

"That must be your knife, Ben. It's very pretty; why haven't I seen it before?"

"I bought it in San Francisco. Good God, girl. You haven't seen it *yet*."

One paper of matches, advertising the Sir Francis Drake Hotel

Eight letters and two bills

Two ticket stubs, the Follies Burlesque Theatre—"Doctor, I'm *surprised* at you."

"Get on with your knitting."

"Provided you promise to take me the next time you go."

One fever thermometer with a pocket clip

Art gum and a typewriter eraser

Three keys, assorted

One lipstick, Max Factor #3

A scratch pad and some file cards, used on one side

One small brown paper sack containing one pair stockings, size nine, shade Creole.—"I'd forgotten that I had bought them; I searched all through the house for a decent pair this morning."

"Why didn't you just use your X-ray eyes, Mrs. Houdini?"

She looked startled. "Do you know, it just didn't occur to me. I haven't gotten around to trying to *use* this stuff yet."

"Anything else in the drawer?"

"Nothing but a box of notepaper. Just a sec: I'll make the sketch." She sketched busily for a couple of minutes, her tongue between her teeth, her eyes darting from the paper toward the closed drawer and back again. Ben inquired,

"Do you have to look in the direction of the drawer to see inside it?"

"No, but it helps. It makes me dizzy to *see* a thing when I am looking away from it."

The contents and arrangement of the drawer were checked and found to be exactly as Joan had stated they were. Doctor Coburn sat quietly, making no comment, when they had finished. Phil, slightly irked at his lack of demonstrativeness, spoke to him.

"Well, Ben, what did you think of it? How did you like it?"

"You know what I thought of it. You've proved your theory up to the hilt—but I'm thinking about the implications, some at the possibilities. I *think* we've just been handed the greatest boon a surgeon ever had to work with. Joan, can you see inside a human body?"

"I don't know. I've never—"

"Look at me."

She stared at him for a silent moment. "Why—why, I can see your heart beat! I can see—"

"Phil, can you teach me to see the way she does?"

Huxley rubbed his nose. "I don't know. Maybe—"

Joan bent over the big chair in which the doctor was seated. "Won't he go under, Phil?"

"Hell, no. I've tried everything but tapping his skull with a bungstarter. I don't believe there's any brain there to hypnotize."

"Don't be pettish. Let's try again. How do you feel, Ben?"

"All right, but wide awake."

"I'm going out of the room this time. Maybe I'm a distracting factor. Now be a good boy and go sleepy-bye." She left them.

Five minutes later Huxley called out to her, "Come on back in, kid. He's under."

She came in and looked at Coburn where he lay sprawled in her big easy chair, quiet, eyes half closed. "Ready for me?" she asked, turning to Huxley.

"Yes. Get ready." She lay down on the couch. "You know what I want; get in rapport with Ben as soon as you go under. Need any persuasion to get to sleep?"

"No."

"Very well, then—Sleep!"

She became quiet, lax.

"Are you under, Joan?"

"Yes, Phil."

"Can you reach Ben's mind?"

A short pause: "Yes."

"What do you find?"

"Nothing. It's like an empty room, but friendly. Wait a moment—he greeted me."

"What did he say?"

"Just a greeting. It wasn't in words."

"Can you hear me, Ben?"

"Sure, Phil."

"You two are together?"

"Yes. Yes, indeed."

"Listen to me, both of you. I want you to wake up slowly, remaining in rapport. Then Joan is to teach Ben how to perceive that which is not seen. Can you do it?"

"Yes, Phil, we can." It was as if one voice had spoken.

CHAPTER FOUR

Holiday

"Frankly, Mr. Huxley, I can't understand your noncooperative attitude." The President of Western University let the stare from his slightly bulging eyes rest on the second button of Phil's vest. "You have been given every facility for sound useful research along lines of proven worth. Your program of instructing has been kept light in order that you might make use of your undoubted ability. You have been acting chairman of your sub-department this past semester. Yet instead of profiting by your unusual opportunities, you have, by your own admission, been, shall we say, frittering away your time in the childish pursuit of old wives' tales and silly superstitions. Bless me, man, I don't understand it!"

Phil answered, with controlled exasperation, "But Doctor Brinckley, if you would permit me to show you—"

The president interposed a palm. "Please, Mr. Huxley. It is not necessary to go over that ground again. One more thing, it has come to my attention that you have been interfering in the affairs of the medical school."

"The medical school! I haven't set foot inside it in weeks."

"It has come to me from unquestioned authority that you have influenced Doctor Coburn to disregard the advice of the staff diagnosticians in performing surgical operations—the best diagnosticians, let me add, on the West Coast."

Huxley maintained his voice at toneless politeness. "Let us suppose for the moment that I have influenced Doctor Coburn—I do not concede the point—has there been any case in which Coburn's refusal to follow diagnosis has failed to be justified by the subsequent history of the case?"

"That is beside the point. The point is—I can't have my staff from one school interfering in the affairs of another school. You see the justice of that, I am sure."

"I do not admit that I have interfered. In fact, I deny it."

"I am afraid I shall have to be the judge of that." Brinckley rose from his desk and came around to where Huxley stood. "Now Mr. Huxley—may I call you Philip? I like to have my juniors in our institution think of me as a friend. I want to give you the same advice that I would give to my son. The semester will be over in a day or two. I think you need a vacation. The Board has made some little difficulty over renewing your contract inasmuch as you have not yet completed your doctorate. I took the liberty of assuring them that you would submit a suitable thesis this coming academic year—and I feel sure that you can if you will only devote your efforts to sound, constructive work. You take your vacation, and when you come back you can outline your proposed thesis to me. I am quite sure the Board will make no difficulty about your contract then."

"I had intended to write up the results of my current research for my thesis."

Brinckley's brows raised in polite surprise. "Really? But that is out of the question, my boy, as you know. You do need a vacation. Goodbye then; if I do not see you again before commencement, let me wish you a pleasant holiday now."

When a stout door separated him from the president, Huxley dropped his pretense of good manners and hurried across the campus, ignoring students and professors alike. He found Ben and Joan waiting for him at their favorite bench, looking across the La Brea Tar Pits toward Wilshire Boulevard.

He flopped down on the seat beside them. Neither of the men spoke, but Joan was unable to control her impatience. "Well, Phil? What did the old fossil have to say?"

"Gimme a cigaret." Ben handed him a pack and waited. "He didn't say much—just threatened me with the loss of my job and the ruination of my academic reputation if I didn't knuckle under and be his tame dog—all in the politest of terms of course."

"But Phil, didn't you offer to bring me in and show him the progress you had already made?"

"I didn't bring your name into it; it was useless. He knew who you were well enough—he made a sidelong reference to the inadvisability of young instructors seeing female students socially except under formal, fully chaperoned conditions—talked about the high moral tone of the university, and our obligation to the public!"

"Why, the dirty minded old so-and-so! I'll tear him apart for that!"

"Take it easy, Joan." Ben Coburn's voice was mild and thoughtful. "Just how did he threaten you, Phil?"

"He refused to renew my contract at this time. He intends to keep me on tenterhooks all summer, then if I come back in the fall and make a noise like a rabbit, he might renew—if he feels like it. Damn him! The thing that got me the sorest was a suggestion that I was slipping and needed a rest."

"What are you going to do?"

"Look for a job, I guess. I've got to eat."

"Teaching job?"

"I suppose so, Ben."

"Your chances aren't very good, are they, without a formal release from Western? They can blacklist you pretty effectively. You've actually got about as much freedom in the matter as a professional ballplayer."

Phil looked glum and said nothing. Joan sighed and looked out across the marshy depression surrounding the tar pits. Then she smiled and said, "We could lure old Picklepuss down here and push him in."

Both men smiled but did not answer. Joan muttered to herself something about sissies. Ben addressed Phil. "You know, Phil, the old boy's idea about a vacation wasn't too stupid; I could do with one myself."

"Anything in particular in mind?"

"Why, yes, more or less. I've been out here seven years and never really seen the state. I'd like to start out and drive, with no particular destination in mind. Then we could go on up past Sacramento and into northern California. They says it's magnificent country up there. We could take in the High Sierras and the Big Trees on the way back."

"That certainly sounds inviting."

"You could take along your research notes and we could talk about your ideas as we drove. If you decided you wanted to write up some phase, we could just lay over while you did it."

Phil stuck out his hand. "It's a deal, Ben. When do we start?"

"As soon as the term closes."

"Let's see—we ought to be able to get underway late Friday afternoon then. Which car will we use, yours or mine?"

"My coupe ought to be about right. It has lots of baggage space."

Joan, who had followed the conversation with interest, broke in on them. "Why use your car, Ben? Three people can't be comfortable in a coupe."

"Three people? Wha' d'yu mean, three people? You aren't going, bright eyes."

"So? That's what you think. You can't get rid of me at this point; I'm the laboratory case. Oh no, you can't leave me behind."

"But Joan, this is a stag affair."

"Oh, so you want to get rid of me?"

"Now Joan, we didn't say that. It just would look like the devil for you to be barging about the country with a couple of men—"

"Sissies! Tissyprissles! Pantywaists! Worried about your reputations."

"No, we're not. We're worried about yours."

"It won't wash. No girl who lives alone has any reputation. She can be as pure as Ivory soap and the cats on the campus, both sexes, will take her to pieces anyway. What are you so scared of? We aren't going to cross any state lines."

Coburn and Huxley exchanged the secret look that men employ when confronted by the persistence of an unreasonable woman.

"Look out, Joan!" A big red Santa Fe bus took the shoulder on the opposite side of the highway and slithered past. Joan switched the tail of the grey sedan around an oil tanker truck and trailer on their own side of the road before replying. When she did, she turned her head to speak directly to Phil who was riding in the back seat.

"What's the matter, Phil?"

"You darn near brought us into a head on collision with about twenty tons of the Santa Fe's best rolling stock!"

"Don't be nervous; I've been driving since I was sixteen and I've never had an accident."

"I'm not surprised; you'll never have but one. Anyhow," Phil went on, "can't you keep your eyes on the road? That's not too much to ask, is it?"

"I don't need to watch the road. Look." She turned her head far around and showed him that her eyes were jammed shut. The needle of the speedometer hovered around ninety.

"Joan! Please!"

She opened her eyes and faced front once more. "But I don't have to look in order to see. You taught me that yourself, Smarty. Don't you remember?"

"Yes, yes, but I never thought you'd apply it to driving a car!"

"Why not? I'm the safest driver you ever saw; I can see everything that's on the road, even around a blind curve. If I need to, I read the other driver's minds to see what they are going to do next."

"She's right, Phil. The few times I've paid attention to her driving she's been doing just exactly what I would have done in the same circumstances. That's why I haven't been nervous."

"All right. All right," Phil answered, "but would you two supermen keep in mind that there is a slightly nervous ordinary mortal in the back seat who can't see around corners?"

"I'll be good," said Joan soberly. "I didn't mean to scare you, Phil."

"I'm interested," resumed Ben, "in what you said about not looking toward anything you wanted to see. I can't do it too satisfactorily. I remember once you said it made you dizzy to look away and still use direct perception."

"It used to, Ben, but I got over it, and so will you. It's just a matter of breaking old habits. To me, every direction is in 'front'—all around and up and down. I can focus my attention in any direction, or two or three directions at once. I can even pick a point of away from where I am physically, and look at the other side of things—but that is harder."

"You two make me feel like the mother of the Ugly Duckling," said Phil bitterly. "Will you still think of me kindly when you have passed beyond human communication?"

"Poor Phil!" exclaimed Joan, with sincere sympathy in her voice. "You taught us, but no one has bothered to teach you. Tell you what, Ben, let's stop tonight at an auto camp—pick a nice quiet one on the outskirts of Sacramento—and spend a couple of days doing for Phil what he has done for us."

"Okay by me. It's a good idea."

"That's mighty white of you, pardner," Phil conceded, but it was obvious that he was pleased and mollified. "After you get through with me will I be able to drive a car on two wheels, too?"

"Why not learn to levitate?" Ben suggested "It's simpler—less expensive and nothing to get out of order."

"Maybe we will some day," returned Phil, quite seriously, "there no telling where this line of investigation may lead."

"Yeah, you're right," Ben answered him with equal sobriety. "I'm getting so that I can believe seven impossible things before breakfast. What were you saying just before we passed that oil tanker?"

"I was just trying to lay before you an idea I've been mulling over in my mind the past several weeks. It's a big idea, so big that I can hardly believe it myself."

"Well, spill it."

Phil commenced checking points off on his fingers. "We've proved, or tended to prove, that the normal human mind has powers previously unsuspected, haven't we?"

"Tentatively—yes. It looks that way."

"Powers way beyond any that the race as a whole makes regular use of."

"Yes, surely. Go on."

"And we have reason to believe that these powers exist, have their being, by virtue of certain areas of the brain to which functions were not previously assigned by physiologists? That is to say, they have organic basis, just as the eye and the sight centers in the brain are the organic basis for normal sight?"

"Yes, of course."

"You can trace the evolution of any organ from a simple beginning to a complex, highly developed form. The organ develops through use. In an evolutionary sense function begets organ."

"Yes. That's elementary."

"Don't you see what that implies?"

Coburn looked puzzled, then a look of comprehension spread over his face. Phil continued, with delight in his voice, "You see it, too?" The conclusion is inescapable: there must have been a time when the entire race used these strange powers as easily as they heard, or saw, or smelled. And there must have been a long, long period—hundreds of thousands, probably millions of years—during which these powers were developed as a race. Individuals couldn't do it, any more than I could grow wings. It had to be done racially, over a long period of time. Mutation theory is no use either—mutation goes by little jumps, with use confirming the change. No indeed—these strange powers are vestigial—hangovers from a time when the whole race had 'em and used 'em."

Phil stopped talking, and Ben did not answer him, but sat in a brown study while some ten miles spun past. Joan started to speak once, then thought better of it. Finally Ben commenced to speak slowly.

"I can't see any fault in your reasoning. It's not reasonable to assume that whole areas of the brain with complex functions 'jest growed'. But, brother, you've sure raised hell with modern anthropology."

"That worried me when I first got the notion, and that's why I kept my mouth shut. Do you know anything about anthropology?"

"Nothing except the casual glance that any medical student gets."

"Neither did I, but I had quite a lot of respect for it. Professor Whoosistwitchell would reconstruct one of our great grand-daddies from his collar bone and his store teeth and deliver a long dissertation on his most intimate habits, and I would swallow it, hook, line, and sinker, and be much impressed. But I began to read up on the subject. Do you know what I found?"

"Go ahead."

"In the first place there isn't a distinguished anthropologist in the world but what you'll find one equally distinguished who will call him a diamond-studded liar. They can't agree on the simplest elements of their alleged science. In the second place, there isn't a corporal's guard of really decent exhibit to back up their assertions about the ancestry of mankind never saw so much stew from one oyster. They write book after book and what have they got to go on?—The Dawson Man, the Pekin Man, the Heidelberg Man and a couple of others. And those aren't complete skeletons, a damaged skull, a couple of teeth, maybe another bone or two."

"Oh now, Phil, there were lots of specimens found on Cro-Magnon men."

"Yes, but they were true men. I'm talking about submen our evolutionary predecessors. You see, I was trying to prove myself wrong. If man's ascent had been a long steady climb submen into savages, savages to barbarians, barbarians perfecting their cultures into civilization . . . all this with only minor setbacks of a few centuries, or a few thousands years at the most . . . and with our present culture the highest the race had ever reached . . . If all that was true, then my idea was wrong.

"You follow me, don't you? The internal evidence of the brain proves that mankind, sometime in its lost history climbed to heights undreamed of today. In some fashion the race slipped back. And this happened so long ago that we have found no record of it anywhere. These brutish submen, that the anthropologists set such store by, *can't* be our ancestors; they are too new, too primitive, too young. They are too recent; they allow for no time for the race to develop these abilities whose existence we have proved. Either anthropology is all wet, or Joan can't do the things we have seen her do."

The center of the controversy said nothing. She sat at the wheel, as the big car sped along, her eyes closed against the slanting rays of the setting sun, seeing the road with an inner impossible sight.

Five days were spent in coaching Huxley and a sixth on the open road. Sacramento lay far behind them. For the past hour Mount Shasta had been visible from time to time through openings in the trees. Phil brought the car to a stop on a view point built out from the pavement of U.S. Highway 99. He turned to his passengers. "All out, troops," he said. "Catch a slice of scenery."

The three stood and stared over the canyon of the Sacramento River at Mount Shasta, thirty miles away. It was sweater weather and the air was as clear as a child's gaze. The peak was framed by two of the great fir trees which marched down the side of the canyon. Snow still lay on the slopes of the cone and straggled down as far as the timberline.

Joan muttered something. Ben turned his head. "What did you say, Joan?"

"Me? Nothing—I was saying over a bit of poetry to myself."

"What was it?"

"Tietjens' *Most Sacred Mountain:*

" *'Space and the twelve clean winds are here;*

And with them broods eternity—a swift white peace, a presence manifest.

The rhythm ceases here. Time has no place. This is the end that has no end'."

Phil cleared his throat and self-consciously broke the silence. "I think I see what you mean."

Joan faced them. "Boys," she stated, "I am going to climb Mount Shasta."

Ben studied her dispassionately. "Joan," he pronounced, "You are full of hop."

"I mean it. I didn't say you were going to—I said I was."

"But we are responsible for your safety and welfare—and I for one don't relish the thought of a fourteen-thousand foot climb."

"You are *not* responsible for my safety; I'm a free citizen. Anyhow a climb wouldn't hurt you any; it would help to get rid of some of that fat you've been storing up against winter."

"Why," inquired Phil, "are you so determined so suddenly to make this climb?"

"It's really not a sudden decision, Phil. Ever since we left Los Angeles I've had a recurring dream that I was climbing, climbing, up to some high place . . . and that I was very happy because of it. Today I know that it was Shasta I was climbing."

"How do you know it?"

"I know it."

"Ben, what do you think?"

The doctor picked up a granite pebble and shied it out in the general direction of the river. He waited for it to come to rest several hundred feet down the slope. "I guess," he said, "we'd better buy some hobnailed boots."

Phil paused and the two behind him on the narrow path were forced to stop, too. "Joan," he asked, with a worried tone, "is this the way we came?"

They huddled together, icy wind cutting at their faces like rusty razor blades and gusts of snow eddying about them and stinging their eyes, while Joan considered her answer. "I think so," she ventured at last, "but even with my eyes closed this snow makes everything look different."

"That's my trouble, too. I guess we pulled a boner when we decided against a guide . . . but who would have thought that a beautiful summer day could end up in a snow storm?"

Ben stamped his feet and clapped his hands together. "Let's get going," he urged. "Even if this is the right road, we've got the worst of it ahead of us before we reach the rest cabin. Don't forget that stretch of glacier we crossed."

"I wish I could forget it," Phil answered him soberly. "I don't fancy the prospect of crossing it in this nasty weather."

"Neither do I, but if we stay here we freeze."

With Ben now in the lead they resumed their cautious progress, heads averted to the wind, eyes half closed. Ben checked them again after a couple of hundred yards. "Careful, gang," he warned, "the path is almost gone here, and it's slippery." He went forward a few steps. "It's rather—" They heard him make a violent effort to recover his balance, then fall heavily.

"Ben! Ben!" Phil called out, "are you all right?"

"I guess so," he gasped. "I gave my left leg an awful bang. Be careful."

They saw that he was on the ground, hanging part way over the edge of the path. Cautiously they approached until they were alongside him. "Lend me a hand, Phil. Easy, now."

Phil helped him wiggle back onto the path. "Can you stand up?"

"I'm afraid not. My left leg gave me the devil when I had to move just now. Take a look at it, Phil. No, don't bother to take the boot off; look right through it."

"Of course. I forgot." Phil studied the limb for a moment. "It's pretty bad, fella—a fracture of the shin bone about four inches below the knee."

Coburn whistled a couple of bars of *Suwannee River,* then said, "Isn't that just too, too lovely? Simple or compound fracture, Phil?"

"Seems like a clean break, Ben."

"Not that it matters much one way or the other just now. What do we do next?"

Joan answered him. "We must build a litter and get you down the mountain!"

"Spoken like a true girl scout, kid. Have you figured how you and Phil can maneuver a litter, with me in it, over that stretch of ice?"

"We'll *have* to—somehow." But her voice lacked confidence.

"It won't work, kid. You two will have to straighten me out and bed me down, then go on down the mountain and stir out a rescue party with proper equipment. I'll get some sleep while you're gone. I'd appreciate it if you'd leave me some cigarets."

"No!" Joan protested. "We won't leave you here alone."

Phil added his objections. "Your plan is as bad as Joan's, Ben. It's all very well to talk about sleeping until we get back, but you know as well as I do that you would die of exposure if you spent a night like this on the ground with no protection."

"I'll just have to chance it. What better plan can you suggest?"

"Wait a minute. Let me think." He sat down on the ledge beside his friend and pulled at his left ear. "This is the best I can figure out: "We'll have to get you to some place that is a little more sheltered, and build a fire to keep you warm. Joan can stay with you and keep the fire going while I go down after help."

"That's all right," put in Joan, "except that I will be the one to go after help. You couldn't find your way in the dark and the snow, Phil. You know yourself that your direct perception isn't reliable as yet—you'd get lost."

Both men protested. "Joan, you're not going to start off alone."— "We can't permit that, Joan."

"That's a lot of gallant nonsense. Of course I'm going."

"No." It was a duet.

"Then we all stay here tonight, and huddle around a fire. I'll go down in the morning."

"That might do," Ben conceded, "if—"

"Good evening, friends." A tall, elderly man stood on the ledge behind them. Steady blue eyes regarded them from under shaggy white eyebrows. He was smooth shaven but a mane of white hair matched the eyebrows. Joan thought he looked like Mark Twain.

Coburn recovered first. "Good evening," he answered, "if it is a good evening—which I doubt."

The stranger smiled with his eyes. "My name is Ambrose, ma'am. But your friend is in need of some assistance. If you will permit me, sir—" He knelt down and examined Ben's leg, without removing the boot. Presently he raised his head. "This will be somewhat painful. I suggest, son, that you go to sleep." Ben smiled at him, closed his eyes, and gave evidence by his slow, regular breathing that he was asleep.

The man who called himself Ambrose slipped away into the shadows. Joan tried to follow him with perception, but this she found curiously hard to do. He returned in a few minutes with several straight sticks which he broke to a uniform length of about twenty inches. These he proceeded to bind firmly to Ben's left shin with a roll of cloth which he had removed from his trouser pocket.

When he was satisfied that the primitive splint was firm, he picked Coburn up in his arms, handling the not inconsiderable mass as if it were a child. "Come," he said.

They followed him without a word, back the way they had come, single file through the hurrying snowflakes. Five hundred yards, six hundred yards, then he took a turn that had not been on the path followed by Joan and the two men, and strode confidently away in the gloom. Joan noticed that he was wearing a light cotton shirt with neither coat nor sweater, and wondered that he had come so far with so little protection against the weather. He spoke to her over his shoulder, "I like cold weather, ma'am."

He walked between two large boulders, apparently disappeared into the side of the mountain. They followed him and found themselves in a passageway which led diagonally into the living rock. They turned a corner and were in an octagonal living room, high ceilinged and panelled in some mellow, light-colored wood. It was softly illuminated by indirect lighting, but possessed no windows. One side of the octagon was a fireplace with a generous hearth in which a wood fire burned hospitably. There was no covering on the flagged floor, but it was warm to the feet.

The old man paused with his burden and indicated the comfortable fittings of the room—three couches, old-fashioned heavy chairs, a chaise longue—with a nod. "Be seated, friends, and make yourselves comfortable. I must see that your companion is taken care of, then we will find refreshment for you." He went out through a door opposite the one by which they had entered, still carrying Coburn in his arms.

Phil looked at Joan and Joan looked at Phil. "Well," he said, "what do you make of it?"

"I think we've found a 'home from home.' This is pretty swell."

"What do we do next?"

"I'm going to pull that chaise longue up to the fire, take off my boots, and get my feet warm and my clothes dry."

When Ambrose returned ten minutes later he found them blissfully toasting their tired feet before the fire. He was bearing a tray from which he served them big steaming bowls of onion soup, hard rolls, apple pie, and strong black tea. While doing so he stated, "Your friend is resting. There is no need to see him until tomorrow. When you have eaten, you will find sleeping rooms in the passageway, with what you need for your immediate comfort." He indicated the door from which he had just come. "No chance to mistake them; they are the lighted rooms immediately at hand. I bid you goodnight now." He picked up the tray and turned to leave.

"Oh, I say," began Phil hesitantly, "This is awfully good of you, Mister, uh—"

"You are very welcome, sir. Bierce is my name. Ambrose Bierce. Goodnight." And he was gone.

CHAPTER FIVE

"—Through a Glass, Darkly"

When Phil entered the living room the next morning he found a small table set with a very sound breakfast for three. While he was lifting plate covers and wondering whether good manners required him to wait until joined by others, Joan entered the room. He looked up.

"Oh! It's you. Good morning, and stuff. They set a proper table here. Look." He lifted a plate cover. "Did you sleep well?"

"Like a corpse." She joined his investigations. "They do understand food, don't they? When do we start?"

"When number three gets here, I guess. Those aren't the clothes you had on last night."

"Like it?" She turned around slowly with a swaying mannequin walk. She had on a pearl grey gown that dropped to her toes. It was high waisted; two silver cords crossed between her breasts and encircled her waist, making a girdle. She was shod in silver sandals. There was an air of ancient days about the whole costume.

"It's swell. Why is it a girl always looks prettier in simple clothes?"

"Simple—hmmf! If you can buy this for three hundred dollars on Wilshire Boulevard, I'd like to have the address of the shop."

"Hello, troops." Ben stood in the doorway. They both stared at him. "What's the trouble?"

Phil ran his eye down Ben's frame. "How's your leg, Ben?"

"I wanted to ask you about that. How long have I been out? The leg's all well. Wasn't it broken after all?"

"How about it, Phil?" Joan seconded. "You examined it—I didn't."

Phil pulled his ear. "It was broken—or I've gone completely screwy. Let's have a look at it."

Ben was dressed in pajamas and bathrobe. He slid up the pajama leg, and exposed a shin that was pink and healthy. He pounded it with his fist. "See that? Not even a bruise."

"Hmm—You haven't been out long, Ben. Just since last night. Maybe ten or eleven hours."

"Huh?"

"That's right."

"Impossible."

"Maybe so. Let's eat breakfast."

They ate in thoughtful silence, each under pressing necessity of taking stock and reaching some reasonable reorientation. Toward the end of the meal they all happened to look up at once. Phil broke the silence,

"Well . . . How about it?"

"I've just doped it out," volunteered Joan. "We all died in the snow storm and went to Heaven. Pass the marmalade, will you, please?"

"That can't be right," objected Phil, as he complied, "else Ben wouldn't be here. He led a sinful life. But seriously, things have happened which require explanation. Let's tick 'em off: One; Ben breaks a leg last night, it's all healed this morning."

"Wait a minute—are we sure he broke his leg?"

"I'm sure. Furthermore, our host acted as if he thought so too—else why did he bother to carry him? Two; our host has direct perception, or an uncanny knowledge of the mountainside."

"Speaking of direct perception," said Joan, "have either of you tried to look around you and size up the place?"

"No, why?"—"Neither have I."

"Don't bother to. I tried, and it can't be done. I can't perceive past the walls of the room."

"Hmm—we'll put that down as point three. Four; our host says that his name is Ambrose Bierce. Does he mean that he is *the* Ambrose Bierce? You know who Ambrose Bierce was, Joan?"

"Of course I do—I got eddication. He disappeared sometime before I was born."

"That's right—at the time of the outbreak of the first World War. If this is the same man, he must be over a hundred years old."

"He didn't look that old by forty years."

"Well, we'll put it down for what it's worth. Point five;—We'll make this one an omnibus point—why does our host live up here? How come this strange mixture of luxury hotel and cliff dwellers cave anyhow? How can one old man run such a joint? Say, have either of you seen anyone else around the place?"

"I haven't," said Ben. "Someone woke me, but I think it was Ambrose."

"I have," offered Joan. "It was a woman who woke me. She offered me this dress."

"Mrs. Bierce, maybe?"

"I don't think so—she wasn't more than thirty-five. I didn't really get acquainted—she was gone before I was wide awake."

Phil looked from Joan to Ben. "Well, what have we got? Add it up and give us an answer."

"Good morning, young friends!" It was Bierce, standing in the doorway, his rich, virile voice resounding around the many-sided room. The three started as if caught doing something improper.

Coburn recovered first. He stood up and bowed. "Good morning, sir. I believe that you saved my life. I hope to be able to show my gratitude."

Bierce bowed formally. "What service I did I enjoyed doing, sir. I hope that you are all rested?"

"Yes, thank you, and pleasantly filled from your table."

"That is good. Now, if I may join you, we can discuss what you wish to do next. Is it your pleasure to leave, or may we hope to have your company for a while longer?"

"I suppose," said Joan, rather nervously, "that we should get started down as soon as possible. How is the weather?"

"The weather is fair, but you are welcome to remain here as long as you like. Perhaps you would like to see the rest of our home and meet the other members of our household?"

"Oh, I think that would be lovely!"

"It will be my pleasure, ma'am."

"As a matter of fact, Mr. Bierce—" Phil leaned forward a little, his face and manner serious. "—we are quite anxious to see more of your place here and to know more about you. We were speaking of it when you came in."

"Curiosity is natural and healthy. Please ask any question you wish."

"Well—" Phil plunged in. "Ben had a broken leg last night. Or didn't he? It's well this morning."

"He did indeed have a broken leg. It was healed in the night."

Coburn cleared his throat. "Mr. Bierce, my name is Coburn. I am a physician and surgeon, but my knowledge does not extend to such healing as that. Will you tell me more about it?"

"Certainly. You are familiar with regeneration as practiced by the lower life forms. The principle used is the same, but it is consciously controlled by the will and the rate of healing is accelerated. I placed you in hypnosis last night, then surrendered control to one of our surgeons who directed your mind in exerting its own powers to heal its body."

Coburn looked baffled. Bierce continued, "There is really nothing startling about it. The mind and will have always the possibility of complete domination over the body. Our operator simply directs your will to master its body. The technique is simple; you may learn it, if you wish. I assure you that to learn it is easier than to explain it in our cumbersome and imperfect language. I spoke of mind and will as if they were separate. Language forced me to that ridiculous misstatement. There is neither mind, nor will, as entities; there is only—" His voice stopped. Ben felt a blow within his mind like the shock of a sixteen inch rifle, yet it was painless and gentle. What ever it was, it was as alive as a hummingbird, or a struggling kitten, yet it was calm and untroubled.

He saw Joan nodding her head in agreement, her eyes on Bierce.

Bierce went on in his gentle, resonant voice. "Was there any other matter troubling any one of you?"

"Why, yes, Mr. Bierce," replied Joan, "several things. What is this place where we are?"

"It is my home, and the home of several of my friends. You will understand more about us as you become better acquainted with us."

"Thank you. It is difficult for me to understand how such a community could exist on this mountaintop without a being a matter of common knowledge."

"We have taken certain precautions, ma'am, to avoid notoriety. Our reasons, and the precautions they inspired will become evident to you."

"One more question; this is rather personal; you may ignore it if you like. Are you the Ambrose Bierce who disappeared a good many years ago?"

"I am. I first came up here in 1880 in search of a cure for asthma. I retired here in 1914 because I wished to avoid direct contact with the tragic world events which I saw coming and was powerless to stop." He spoke with some reluctance, as if the subject were distasteful, and turned the conversation. "Perhaps you would like to meet some of my friends now?"

❖

The apartments extended for a hundred yards along the face of the mountain and for unmeasured distances into the mountain. The thirty-odd persons in residence were far from crowded; there were many rooms not in use. In the course of the morning Bierce introduced them to most of the inhabitants.

They seemed to be of all sorts and ages and of several nationalities. Most of them were occupied in one way, or another, usually with some form of research, or with creative art. At least Bierce assured them in several cases that research was in progress—cases in which no apparatus, no recording device, nothing was evident to indicate scientific research.

Once they were introduced to a group of three, two women and a man, who were surrounded by the physical evidence of their work—biological research. But the circumstances were still confusing; two of the trio sat quietly by, doing nothing, while the third labored at a bench. Bierce explained that they were doing some delicate experiments in the possibility of activating artificial colloids. Ben inquired,

"Are the other two observing the work?"

Bierce shook his head. "Oh, no. They are all three engaged actively in the work, but at this particular stage they find it expedient to let three brains in rapport direct one set of hands."

Rapport, it developed, was the usual method of collaboration. Bierce had led them into a room occupied by six persons. One or two of them looked up and nodded, but did not speak. Bierce motioned for the three to come away. "They were engaged in a particularly difficult piece of reconstruction; it would not be polite to disturb them."

"But Mr. Bierce," Phil commented, "two of them were playing chess."

"Yes. They did not need that part of their brains, so they left it out of rapport. Nevertheless they were very busy."

It was easier to see what the creative artists were doing. In two instances, however, their methods were startling. Bierce had taken them to the studio of a little gnome of a man, a painter in oil, who was introduced simply as Charles. He seemed glad to see them and chatted vivaciously, without ceasing his work. He was doing, with meticulous realism but with a highly romantic effect, a study of a young girl dancing, a wood nymph, against a pine forest background.

The young people each made appropriate appreciative comments, Coburn commented that it was remarkable that he should be able to be so accurate in his anatomical detail without the aid of a model.

"But I have a model," he answered. "She was here last week. See?" He glanced toward the empty model's throne. Coburn and his companions followed the glance, and saw, poised on the throne, a young girl, obviously the model for the picture, frozen in the action of the painting. She was as real as bread and butter.

Charles glanced away. The model's throne was again vacant.

The second instance was not so dramatic, but still less comprehensible. They had met, and chatted with, a Mrs. Draper, a comfortable, matronly soul, who knitted and rocked as they talked. After they had left her Phil inquired about her.

"She is possibly our most able and talented artist," Bierce told him.

"In what field?"

Bierce's shaggy eyebrows came together as he chose his words. "I don't believe I can tell you adequately at this time. She composes moods—arranges emotional patterns in harmonic sequences. It's our most advanced and our most completely human form of art, and yet, until you have experienced it, it is very difficult for me to tell you about it."

"How is it possible to *arrange* emotions?"

"Your great grandfather no doubt thought it impossible to record music. We have a technique for it. You will understand later."

"Is Mrs. Draper the only one who does this?"

"Oh, no. Most of us try our hand at it. It's our favorite art form. I work at it myself but my efforts aren't popular—too gloomy."

The three talked it over that night in the living room they had first entered. This suite had been set aside for their use, and Bierce had left them with the simple statement that he would call on them on the morrow.

They felt a pressing necessity to exchange views, and yet each was reluctant to express opinion. Phil broke the silence.

"What kind of people are these? They make me feel as if I were a child who had wandered in where adults were working, but that they were too polite to put me out."

"Speaking of working—there's something odd about the way they work. I don't mean what it is they do—that's odd, too, but it's something else, something about their attitude, or the tempo at which they work."

"I know what you mean, Ben," Joan agreed, "they are busy all the time, and yet they act as if they had all eternity to finish it. Bierce was like that when he was strapping up your leg. They never hurry." She turned to Phil. "What are you frowning about?"

"I don't know. There is something else we haven't mentioned yet. They have a lot of special talents, sure, but we three know something about special talents—that ought not to confuse us. But there is something else about them that is *different*."

The other two agreed with him but could offer no help. Sometime later Joan said that she was going to bed and left the room. The two men stayed for a last cigaret.

Joan stuck her head back in the room. "I know what it is that is so different about these people," she announced,—"They are so *alive*."

CHAPTER SIX

Ichabod!

Philip Huxley went to bed and to sleep as usual. From there on nothing was usual.

He became aware that he was inhabiting another's body, thinking with another's mind. The Other was aware of Huxley, but did not share Huxley's thoughts.

The Other was at home, a home never experienced by Huxley, yet familiar. It was on Earth, incredibly beautiful, each tree and shrub fitting into the landscape as if placed there in the harmonic scheme of an artist. The house grew out of the ground.

The Other left the house with his wife and prepared to leave for the capital of the planet. Huxley thought of the destination as a "capital" yet he knew that the idea of government imposed by force was foreign to the nature of these people. The "capital" was merely the accustomed meeting place of the group whose advice was followed in matters affecting the entire race.

The Other and his wife, accompanied by Huxley's awareness, stepped into the garden, shot straight up into the air, and sped over the countryside, flying hand in hand. The country was green, fertile, park-like, dotted with occasional buildings, but nowhere did Huxley see the jammed masses of a city.

They passed rapidly over a large body of water, perhaps as large as the modern Mediterranean, and landed in a clearing in a grove of olive trees.

The Young Men—so Huxley thought of them—demanded a sweeping change in custom, first, that the ancient knowledge should henceforth be the reward of ability rather than common birthright, and second, that the greater should rule the lesser. Loki urged their case, his arrogant face upthrust and crowned with bright red hair. He spoke in words, a method which disturbed Huxley's host, telepathic rapport being the natural method of mature discussion. But Loki had closed his mind to it.

Jove answered him, speaking for all:

"My son, your words seem vain and without serious meaning. We cannot tell your true meaning, for you and your brothers have decided to shut your minds to us. You ask that the ancient knowledge be made the reward of ability. Has it not always been so? Does our cousin, the ape, fly through the air? Is not the infant soul bound by hunger, and sleep, and the ills of the flesh? Can the oriole level the mountain with his glance? The powers of our kind that set us apart from the younger spirits on this planet are now exercised by those who possess the ability, and none other. How can we make that so which is already so?

"You demand that the greater shall rule the lesser. Is it not so now? Has it not always been so? Are you ordered about by the babe at the breast? Does the waving of the grass cause the wind? What dominion do you desire other than over yourself? Do you wish to tell your brother when to sleep and when to eat? If so, to what purpose?"

Vulcan broke in while the old man was still speaking. Huxley felt a stir of shocked repugnance go through the council at this open disregard of good manners.

"Enough of this playing with words. We know what we want; you know what we want. We are determined to take it, council or no. We are sick of this sheeplike existence. We are tired of this sham equality. We intend to put on end to it. We are the strong and the able, the natural leaders of mankind. The rest shall follow us and serve us, as is the natural order of things."

Jove's eyes rested thoughtfully on Vulcan's crooked leg. "You should let me heal that twisted limb, my son."

"No one can heal my limb!"

"No. No one but yourself. And until you heal the twist in your mind, you can not heal the twist in your limb."

"There is no twist in my mind!"

"Then heal your limb."

The young man stirred uneasily. They could see that Vulcan was making a fool of himself. Mercury separated himself from the group and came forward.

"Hear me, Father. We do not purpose warring with you. Rather it is our intention to add to your glory. Declare yourself king under the sun. Let us be your legates to extend your rule to every creature that walks, or crawls, or swims. Let us create for you the pageantry of dominion, the glory of conquest. Let us conserve the ancient knowledge for those who understand it, and provide instead for lesser beings the drama they need. There is no reason why every way should be open to everyone. Rather, if the many serve the few, then will our combined efforts speed us faster on our way, to the profit of master and servant alike. Lead us, Father! Be our King!"

Slowly the elder man shook his head. "Not so. There is no knowledge, other than knowledge of oneself, and that should be free to every man who has the wit to learn. There is no power, other than the power to rule oneself, and that can be neither given, nor taken away. As for the poetry of empire, that has all been done before. There is no need to do it again. If such romance amuses you, enjoy it in the records—there is no need to bloody the planet again."

"That is the final word of the council, Father?"

"That is our final word." He stood up and gathered his robe about him, signifying that the session had ended. Mercury shrugged his shoulders and joined his fellows.

There was one more session of the council—the last—called to decide what to do about the ultimatum of the Young Men. Not every member of the council thought alike; they were as diverse as many group of human beings. They *were* human beings—not supermen. Some held out for opposing the Young Men with all the forces at their command—translate them to another dimension, wipe their minds clean, even crush them by major force.

But to use force on the Young Men was contrary to their whole philosophy. "Free will is the primary good of the Cosmos. Shall we degrade, destroy, all that we have worked for by subverting the will of even one man?"

Huxley became aware that these Elders had no need to remain on Earth. They were anxious to move on to another place, the nature of which escaped Huxley, save that it was not of the time and space he knew.

The issue was this: Had they done what they could to help the incompletely developed balance of the race? Were they justified in abdicating?

The decision was yes, but a female member of the council, whose name, it seemed to Huxley, was Demeter, argued that records should be left to help those who survived the inevitable collapse. "It is true that each member of the race must make himself strong, must make himself wise. We cannot make them wise. Yet, after famine and war and hatred have stalked the earth, should there not be a message, telling them of their heritage?"

The council agreed, and Huxley's host, recorder for the council, was ordered to prepare records and to leave them for those who would come after. Jove added an injunction:

"Bind the force patterns so that they shall not dissipate while this planet endures. Place them where they will outlast any local convulsions of the crust, so that some at least will carry down through time."

So ended that dream. But Huxley did not wake—he started at once to dream another dream, not through the eyes of another, but rather as if he watched a stereo-movie, every scene of which was familiar to him.

The first dream, for all its tragic content, had not affected him tragically; but throughout the second dream he was oppressed by a feeling of heartbreak and overpowering weariness.

After the abdication of the Elders, the Young Men carried out their purpose, they established their rule. By fire and sword, searing rays and esoteric forces, chicanery and deception. Convinced of their destiny to rule, they convinced themselves that the end justified the means.

The end was empire—Mu, mightiest of empires and mother of empires.

Huxley saw her in her prime and felt almost that the Young Men had been right—for she was glorious! The heart-choking magnificence filled his eyes with tears; he mourned for the glory, the beautiful breathtaking glory that was hers, and is no more.

Gargantuan silent liners in her skies, broadbeamed vessels at her wharves, loaded with grain and hides and spices, procession of priest and acolyte and humble believer, pomp and pageantry of power—he saw her intricate patterns of beauty and mourned her passing.

But in her swelling power there was decay. Inevitably Atlantis, her richest colony, grew to political maturity and was irked by subordinate status. Schism and apostasy, disaffection and treason, brought harsh retaliation—and new rebellion.

Rebellions rose, were crushed. At last one rose that was not crushed. In less than a month two-thirds of the people of the globe were dead; the remainder were racked by disease and hunger, and left with germ plasm damaged by the forces they had loosed.

But priests still held the ancient knowledge.

Not priests secure in mind and proud of their trust, but priests hunted and fearful, who had seen their hierarchy totter. There were such priests on both sides—and they unchained forces compared with which the previous fighting had been gentle.

The forces disturbed the isostatic balance of the earth's crust.

Mu shuddered and sank some two thousand feet. Tidal waves met at her middle, broke back, surged twice around the globe, climbed the Chinese plains, lapped the feet of Alta Himalaya.

Atlantis shook and rumbled and split for three days before the water covered it. A few escaped by air, to land on ground still wet with the ooze of exposed seabottom, or on peaks high enough to fend off the tidal waves. There they had still to wring a living from the bare soil, with minds unused to primitive art—but some survived.

Of Mu there was not a trace. As for Atlantis, a few islands, mountaintops short days before, marked the spot. Water rolled over the twin Towers of the Sun and fish swam through the gardens of the viceroy.

The woebegone feeling which had pursued Huxley now overwhelmed him. He seemed to hear a voice in his head:

"Woe! Cursed be Loki! Cursed be Venus! Cursed be Vulcan! Thrice cursed am I, their apostate servant, Orab, Archpriest of the Isles of the Blessed. Woe is me! Even as I curse I long for Mu, mighty and sinful. Twenty-one years ago, seeking a place to die, on this mountaintop I stumbled on this record of the mighty ones who were before us. Twenty-one years I have labored to make the record complete, searching the dim recesses of my mind for knowledge long unused, roaming the other planes for knowledge I never had. Now in the eight hundred and ninety-second year of my life, and of the destruction of Mu the three hundred and fifth, I, Orab, return to my fathers."

Huxley was very happy to wake up.

CHAPTER SEVEN

"The Fathers Have Eaten Sour Grapes, and the Children's Teeth Are Set on Edge."

Ben was in the living room when Phil came in to breakfast. Joan arrived almost on Phil's heels. There were shadows under her eyes and she looked unhappy. Ben spoke in a tone that was almost surly,

"What's troubling you, Joan? You look like the wrath to come."

"Please, Ben," she answered, in a tired voice, "don't heckle me. I've had bad dreams all night."

"That so? Sorry—but if you think you had bad dreams all night, you should have seen the cute little nightmares I've been riding."

Phil looked at the two of them. "Listen—have you both had odd dreams all night?"

"Wasn't that what we were just saying?" Ben sounded exasperated.

"What did you dream about?"

Neither one answered him.

"Wait a minute. I had some very strange dreams myself." He pulled his notebook out of a pocket and tore out three sheets. "I want to find out something. Will you each write down what your dreams were about, before anyone says anything more? Here's a pencil, Joan."

They balked a little, but complied.

"Read them aloud, Joan."

She picked up Ben's slip and read, " 'I dreamed that your theory about the degeneracy of the human race was perfectly correct.' "

She put it down and picked up Phil's slip. " 'dreamt that I was present at the Twilight of the Gods, and that I saw the destruction of Mu and Atlantis.' "

There was dead silence as she took the last slip, her own.

"My dream was about how the people destroyed themselves by rebelling against Odin."

Ben was first to commit himself. "Anyone of those slips could have applied to my dreams." Joan nodded. Phil got up again, went out, and returned at once with his diary. He opened it and handed it to Joan.

"Kid, will you read that aloud—starting with 'June sixteenth'?"

She read it through slowly, without looking up from the pages. Phil waited until she had finished and closed the book before speaking. "Well," he said, "well?"

Ben crushed out a cigaret which had burned down to his fingers. "It's a remarkably accurate description of my dream, except that the elder you call Jove, I thought of as Ahuramazda."

"And I thought Loki was Lucifer."

"You're both right," agreed Phil. "I don't remember any spoken names for any of them. It just seemed that I knew what their names were."

"Me, too."

"Say," interjected Ben, "we are talking as if these dreams were real—as if we had all been to the same movie."

Phil turned on him. "Well, what do *you* think?"

"Oh, the same as you do, I guess. I'm stumped. Does anybody mind if I eat breakfast—or drink some coffee, at least?"

Bierce came in before they had a chance to talk it over after breakfast—by tacit consent they had held their tongues during a sketchy meal.

"Good morning, ma'am. Good morning, gentlemen."

"Good morning, Mr. Bierce."

"I see," he said, searching their faces, "that none of you look very happy this morning. That is not surprising; no one does immediately after experiencing the records."

Ben pushed back his chair and leaned across the table at Bierce. "Those dreams were deliberately arranged for us?"

"Yes, indeed—but we were sure that you were ready to profit by them. But I have come to ask you to interview the Senior. If you can hold your questions for him, it will be simpler."

"The Senior?"

"You haven't met him as yet. It is the way we refer to the one we judge best fitted to co-ordinate our activities."

Ephraim Howe had the hills of New England in his face, lean gnarled cabinet-maker's hands. He was not young. There was courtly grace in his lanky figure. Everything about him—the twinkle in his pale blue eyes, the clasp of his hand, his drawl—bespoke integrity.

"Sit yourselves down," he said, "I'll come straight to the point"—
he called it 'pint.' "You've been exposed to a lot of curious things and
you've a right to know why. You've seen the Ancient Records now—
part of 'em. I'll tell you how this institution came about, what it's for,
and why you are going to be asked to join us.

"Wait a minute, Waaaait a minute," he added, holding up a hand.
"Don't say anything just yet . . ."

When Fra Junipero Serra first laid eyes on Mount Shasta in 1781,
the Indians told him it was a holy place, only for medicine men. He assured them that he was a medicine man, serving a greater Master, and
to keep face, dragged his sick, frail old body up to the snow line, where
he slept before returning.

The dream he had there—of the Garden of Eden, the Sin, the Fall,
and the Deluge—convinced him that it was indeed a holy place. He returned to San Francisco, planning to found a mission at Shasta. But
there was too much for one old man to do—so many souls to save, so
many mouths to feed. He surrendered his soul to rest two years later,
but laid an injunction on a fellow monk to carry out his intention.

It is recorded that this friar left the northernmost mission in 1785
and did not return.

The Indians fed the holy man who lived on the mountain until
1843, by which time he had gathered about him a group of neophytes,
three Indians, a Russian, a Yankee mountainman. The Russian carried
on after the death of the friar until joined by a Chinese, fled from his in-
denture. The Chinese made more progress in a few weeks than the
Russian had in half of a lifetime; the Russian gladly surrendered first
place to him.

The Chinese was still there over a hundred years later, though long
since retired from administration. He tutored in esthetics and humor.

"And this establishment has just one purpose," continued Ephraim
Howe. "We aim to see to it that Mu and Atlantis don't happen again.
Everything that the Young Men stood for, we are against.

"We see the history of the world as a series of crises in a conflict
between two opposing philosophies. Ours is based on the notion that
life, consciousness, intelligence, ego is the important thing in the
world." For an instant only he touched them telepathically; they felt
again the vibrantly alive thing that Ambrose Bierce had showed them
and been unable to define in words. "That puts us in conflict with every
force that tends to destroy, deaden, degrade the human spirit, or to
make it act contrary to its nature. We see another crisis approaching; we
need recruits. You've been selected.

"This crisis has been growing on us since Napoleon. Europe has gone, and Asia—surrendered to authoritarianism, nonsense like the 'leader principle,' totalitarianism, all the bonds placed on liberty which treat men as so many economic and political units with no importance as individuals. No dignity—do what you're told, believe what you are told, and shut your mouth! Workers, soldiers, breeding units . . .

"If *that* were the object of life, there would have been no point in including consciousness in the scheme at all!

"This continent," Howe went on, "has been a refuge of freedom, a place where the soul could grow. But the forces that killed enlightenment in the rest of the world are spreading here. Little by little they have whittled away at human liberty and human dignity. A repressive law, a bullying school board, a blind dogma to be accepted under pain of persecution—doctrines that will shackle men and put blinders on their eyes so that they will never regain their lost heritage.

"We need help to fight it."

Huxley stood up. "You can count on us."

Before Joan and Coburn could speak the Senior interposed. "Don't answer yet. Go back to your chambers and think about it. Sleep on it. We'll talk again."

CHAPTER EIGHT

"Precept Upon Precept . . ."

Had the place on Mount Shasta been a university and possessed a catalog (which it did not), the courses offered therein might have included the following:

TELEPATHY. Basic course required of all students not qualified by examination. Practical instruction up to and including rapport. Prerequisite in all departments. Laboratory.

RATIOCINATION, I, II, III, IV. R.I. Memory. R.II. Perception; clairvoyance, clairaudience, discretion of mass, -time, -and -space, nonmathematical relation, order, and structure, harmonic form and interval.

R.III. Dual and parallel thought processes. Detachment.

R.IV. Meditation (seminar)

AUTOKINETICS. Discrete kinesthesia. Endocrine control with esp. application to the affective senses and to suppression of fatigue, regeneration, transformation (clinical aspects of lycanthropy), sex determination, inversion, autoanaesthesia, rejuvenation.

TELEKINETICS. Life-mass-space-time continua. Prerequisite; autokinetics. Teleportation and general action at a distance. Projection. Dynamics. Statics. Orientation.

HISTORY. Courses by arrangement. Special discussions of psychometry with reference to telepathic records, and of metempsychosis. Evaluation is a prerequisite for all courses in this department.

HUMAN ESTHETICS. Seminar. Autokinetics and technique of telepathic recording (psychometry) a prerequisite.

HUMAN ETHICS. Seminar. Given concurrently with all other courses. Consult with instructor.

Perhaps some of the value of the instruction would have been lost had it been broken up into disjointed courses as outlined above. In any case the adepts on Mount Shasta could and did instruct in all these subjects. Huxley, Coburn, and Joan Freeman learned from tutors who led them to teach themselves, and they took it as an eel seeks the sea, with a sense of returning home after a long absence.

All three made rapid progress; being possessed of rudimentary perception and some knowledge of telepathy, their instructors could teach them directly. First they learned to control their bodies. They regained the control over each function, each muscle, each tissue, each gland, that a man should possess, but has largely forgotten—save a few obscure students in the far east. There was a deep, welling delight in willing the body to obey and having it comply. They became intimately aware of their bodies, but their bodies no longer tyrannized them. Fatigue, hunger, cold, pain—these things no longer drove them, but rather were simply useful signals that a good engine needed attention.

Nor did the engine need as much attention as before; the body was driven by a mind that knew precisely both the capacity and its limitations. Furthermore, through understanding their bodies, they were enabled to increase those capacities to their full potential. A week of sustained activity, without rest, or food, or water, was as easy as a morning's work had been. As for mental labor, it did not cease at all, save when they willed it—despite sleep, digestive languor, ennui, external stimuli, or muscular activity.

The greatest delight was levitation.

To fly through the air, to hang suspended in the quiet heart of a cloud, to sleep, like Mohamet, floating between ceiling and floor—these were sensuous delights unexpected, and never before experienced, except in dreams, dimly. Joan in particular drank this new joy with lusty abandon. Once she remained away two days, never setting foot to ground, sharing the sky and wind and swallow, the icy air of the heights smoothing her bright body. She dove and soared, looped and spiralled, and dropped, a dead weight, knees drawn up to forehead, from stratosphere to treetop.

During the night she paced a transcontinental plane, flying unseen above it for a thousand miles. When she grew bored with this, she pressed her face for a moment against the one lighted port of the plane, and looked inside. The startled wholesale merchant who stared back into her eyes thought that he had been vouchsafed a glimpse of an angel. He went promptly from the airport of his destination to the office of his lawyer, who drew up for him a will establishing scholarships for divinity students.

Huxley found it difficult to learn to levitate. His inquiring mind demanded a reason why the will should apparently be able to set at naught the inexorable "law" of gravitation, and his doubt dissipated his volition. His tutor reasoned with him patiently.

"You know that intangible will can affect the course of mass in the continuum; you experience it whenever you move your hand. Are you powerless to move your hand because you can not give a full rational explanation of the mystery? Life has power to affect matter; you know that—you have experienced it directly. It is a fact. Now there is no 'why' about any fact in the unlimited sense in which you ask the question. There it stands, serene, demonstrating itself. One may observe relations between facts, the relations being other facts, but to pursue those relations back to final meanings is not possible to a mind which is itself relative. First you tell me *why* you *are* . . . then I will tell you why levitation is possible.

"Now come," he continued, "place yourself in rapport with me, and try to feel how I do, as I levitate."

Phil tried again. "I don't get it," he concluded miserably.

"Look down."

Phil did so, gasped, and fell three feet to the floor. That night he joined Ben and Joan in a flight over the High Sierras.

Their tutor enjoyed with quiet amusement the zest with which they entered into the sport made possible by the newly acquired mastery of their bodies. He knew that their pleasure was natural and healthy, suited to their stage of development, and he knew that they would soon learn, of themselves, its relative worth, and then be ready to turn their minds to more serious work.

"Oh, no, Brother Junipero wasn't the only man to stumble on the records," Charles assured them, talking as he painted. "You must have noticed how high places have significance in the religions of every race. Some of them must be repositories of the ancient records."

"Don't you know for certain?" asked Phil.

"Indeed yes, in many cases—Alta Himalaya, for example. I was speaking of what an intelligent man might infer from matters of common knowledge. Consider how many mountains are of prime importance in as many different religions. Mount Olympus, Popocatepetl, Mauna Loa, Everest, Sinai, Tai Shan, Ararat, Fujiyama, several places in the Andes. And in every religion there are accounts of a teacher bringing back inspired messages from high places—Gautama, Jesus, Joseph Smith, Confucius, Moses. They all come down from high places and tell stories of creation, and downfall, and redemption.

"Of all the old accounts the best is found in Genesis. Making allowance for the fact that it was first written in the language of uncivilized nomads, it is an exact, careful account."

Huxley poked Coburn in the ribs. "How do you like that, my skeptical friend?" Then to Charles, "Ben has been a devout atheist since he first found out that Santa Claus wore false whiskers; it hurts him to have his fondest doubts overturned."

Coburn grinned, unperturbed. "Take it easy, son. I can express my own doubts, unassisted. You've brought to mind another matter, Charles. Some of these mountains don't seem old enough to have been used for the ancient records—Shasta, for example. It's volcanic and seems a little new for the purpose."

Charles went rapidly ahead with his painting as he replied. "You are right. It seems likely that Orab made copies of the original record which he found, and placed the copies with his supplement on several high places around the globe. And it is possible that others after Orab, but long before our time, read the records and moved them for safe-keeping. The copy that Junipero Serra found may have been here a mere twenty thousand years, or so."

CHAPTER NINE

Fledglings Fly

"We could hang around here for fifty years, learning new things, but in the mean time we wouldn't be getting anywhere. I, for one, am ready to go back." Phil crushed out a cigaret and looked around at his two friends.

Coburn pursed his lips and slowly nodded his head. "I feel the same way, Phil. There is no limit to what we could learn here, of course, but there comes a time when you just have to use some of the things you learn, or it just boils up inside. I think we had better tell the Senior, and get about doing it."

Joan nodded vigorously. "Uh huh. I think so, too. There's work to be done, and the place to do it is Western U.—not up here in Never-Never land. Boy, I can hardly wait to see old Brinckley's face when we get through with him!"

Huxley sought out the mind of Ephraim Howe. The other two waited for him to confer, courteously refraining from attempting to enter the telepathic conversation. "He says he had been expecting to hear from us, and that he intends to make it a full conference. He'll meet us here."

"Full conference? Everybody on the mountain?"

"Everybody—on the mountain, or not. I gather it's customary when new members decide what their work will be."

"Whew!" exclaimed Joan, "that gives me stage fright just to think about it. Who's going to speak for us? It won't be little Joan."

"How about you, Ben?"

"Well . . . if you wish."

"Take over."

They meshed into rapport. As long as they remained so, Ben's voice would express the combined thought of the trio. Ephraim Howe entered alone, but they were aware that he was in rapport with, and spokesman for, not only the adepts on the mountainside, but also the two-hundred-odd full-geniuses scattered about the country.

The conference commenced with direct mind-to-mind exchange:

—*"We feel that it is time we were at work. We have not learned all that there is to learn, it is true; nevertheless, we need to use our present knowledge."*

—*"That is well and entirely as it should be, Benjamin. You have learned all that we can teach you at this time. Now you must take what you have learned out into the world, and use it, in order that knowledge may mature into wisdom."*

—*"Not only for that reason do we wish to leave, but for another more urgent. As you yourself have taught us, the crisis approaches. We want to fight it."*

—*"How do you propose to fight the forces bringing on the crisis?"*

—*"Well . . ."* Ben did not use the word, but the delay in his thought produced the impression. *"As we see it, in order to make men free, free so that they may develop as men and not as animals; it is necessary that we undo what the Young Men did. The Young Men refused to permit any but their own select few to share in the racial heritage of ancient knowledge. For men again to become free and strong and independent it is necessary to return to each man his ancient knowledge and his ancient powers."*

—*"That is true; what do you intend to do about it?"*

—*"We will go out and tell about it. We all three are in the educational system; we can make ourselves heard—I, in the medical school at Western; Phil and Joan in the department of psychology. With the training you have given us we can overturn the traditional ideas in short order. We can start a renaissance in education that will prepare the way for everyone to receive the wisdom that you, our elders, can offer them."*

—*"Do you think that it will be as simple as that?"*

—*"Why not? Oh, we don't expect it to be simple. We know that we will run head on into some of the most cherished misconceptions of everyone, but we can use that very fact to help. It will be spectacular; we can get publicity through it that will call attention to our work. You have taught us enough that we can prove that we are right. For example—suppose we put on a public demonstration of levitation, and proved before thousands of people that human mind could do the things we know it can? Suppose we said that anyone could learn such things who first learned the techniques of telepathy? Why, in a year, or two, the whole nation could be taught telepathy, and be ready for the reading of the records, and all that that implies!"*

Howe's mind was silent for several long minutes—no message reached them. The three stirred uneasily under his thoughtful, sober gaze. Finally,

—*"If it were as simple as that, would we not have done it before?"*

It was the turn of the three to be silent. Howe continued kindly,— *"Speak up, my children. Do not be afraid. Tell us your thoughts freely. You will not offend us."*

The thought that Coburn sent in answer was hesitant—*"It is difficult . . . Many of you are very old, and we know that all of you are wise. Nevertheless, it seems to us, in our youth, that you have waited overly long in acting. We feel—we feel that you have allowed the pursuit of understanding to sap your will to action. From our standpoint, you have waited from year to year, perfecting an organization that will never be perfected, while the storm that overturns the world is gathering its force."*

The elders pondered before Ephraim Howe answered.— *"It may be that you are right, dearly beloved children, yet it does not seem so to us. We have not attempted to place the ancient knowledge in the hands of all men because few are ready for it. It is no more safe in childish minds than matches in childish hands.*

—*"And yet . . . you may be right. Mark Twain thought so, and was given permission to tell all that he had learned. He did so, writing so that anyone ready for the knowledge could understand. No one did. In desperation he set forth specifically how to become telepathic. Still no one took him seriously. The more seriously he spoke, the more his readers laughed. He died embittered.*

—*"We would not have you believe that we have done nothing. This republic, with its uncommon emphasis on personal freedom and human dignity, would not have endured as long as it has had we not helped. We chose Lincoln. Oliver Wendell Holmes was one of us. Walt Whitman was our beloved brother. In a thousand ways we have supplied help, when needed, to avert a setback toward slavery and darkness."*

The thought paused, then continued.—*"Yet each must act as he sees it. It is still your decision to do this?"*

Ben spoke aloud, in a steady voice, "It is!"

—*"So let it be! Do you remember the history of Salem?"*

—*"Salem? Where the witchcraft trials were held? . . . Do you mean to warn us that we may be persecuted as witches?"*

—*"No. There are no laws against witchcraft today, of course. It would be better if there were. We hold no monopoly on the power of knowledge; do not expect an easy victory. Beware of those who hold some portion of the ancient knowledge and use it to a base purpose— witches . . . black magicians!"*

The conference concluded and rapport loosed, Ephraim Howe shook hands solemnly all around and bade them goodby.

"I envy you kids," he said, "going off like Jack the Giant Killer to tackle the whole educational system. You've got your work cut out for you. Do you remember what Mark Twain said? 'God made an idiot for practice, then he made a school board.' Still, I'd like to come along."

"Why don't you, sir?"

"Eh? No, 'twouldn't do. I don't really believe in your plan. F'r instance—it was frequently a temptation during the years I spent ped- dlin' hardware in the State of Maine to show people better ways of do- ing things. But I didn't do it; people are used to paring knives and ice cream freezers, and they won't thank you to show them how to get along without them, just by the power of the mind. Not all at once, anyhow. They'd read you out of meetin'—and lynch you, too, most probably.

"Still, I'll be keeping an eye on you."

Joan reached up and kissed him good-bye. They left.

C H A P T E R   T E N

Lion's Mouth

Phil picked his largest class to make the demonstration which was to get the newspapers interested in them.

They had played safe to the extent of getting back to Los Angeles and started with the fall semester before giving anyone cause to suspect that they possessed powers out of ordinary. Joan had been bound over not to levitate, not to idulge in practical jokes involving control over inanimate objects, not to startle strangers with weird abilities of any sort. She had accepted the injunctions meekly, so meekly that Coburn claimed to be worried.

"It's not normal," he objected. "She can't grow up as fast as all that. Let me see your tongue, my dear."

"Pooh," she answered, displaying that member in a most undiagnostic manner, "Master Ling said I was further advanced along the Way than either one of you."

" 'The heathen Chinee is peculiar.' He was probably just encouraging you to grow up. Seriously, Phil, hadn't we better put her into a deep hypnosis and scoot her back up the mountain for diagnosis and readjustment?"

"Ben Coburn, you cast an eye in my direction and I'll bung it out!"

Phil built up to his key demonstration with care. His lectures were sufficiently innocuous that he could afford to have his head of department drop in without fear of reprimand or interference. But the combined effect was to prepare the students emotionally for what was to come. Carefully selected assignments for collateral reading heightened his chances.

"Hypnosis is a subject but vaguely understood," he began his lecture on the selected day, "and formerly classed with witchcraft, magic, and so forth, as a silly superstition. But it is a commonplace thing today and easily demonstrated. Consequently the most conservative psychologists must recognize its existence and try to observe its characteristics." He went on cheerfully uttering bromides and commonplaces, while he sized up the emotional attitude of the class.

When he felt that they were ready to accept the ordinary phenomena of hypnosis without surprise, he called Joan, who had attended for the purpose, up to the front of the room. She went easily into a state of light hypnosis. They ran quickly through the small change of hypnotic phenomena—catalepsy, compulsion, post-hypnotic suggestion—while he kept up a running chatter about the relation between the minds of the operator and the subject, the possibility of direct telepathic control, the Rhine experiments, and similar matters, orthodox in themselves, but close to the borderline of heterodox thought.

Then he offered to attempt to reach the mind of the subject telepathically.

Each student was invited to write something on a slip of paper. A volunteer floor committee collected the slips, and handed them to

Huxley one at a time. He solemnly went through the hocus-pocus of glancing at each one, while Joan read them off as his eyes rested on them. She stumbled convincingly once or twice.—*"Nice work, kid."—"Thanks, pal. "Can't I pep it up a little?"—"None of your bright ideas. Just keep on as you are. They're eating out of our hands now."*

By such easy stages he led them around to the idea that mind and will could exercise control over the body much more complete than that ordinarily encountered. He passed lightly over the tales of Hindu holy men who could lift themselves up into the air and even travel from place to place.

"We have an exceptional opportunity to put such tales to practical test," he told them. "The subject believes fully any statement made by the operator. I shall tell Miss Freeman that she is to exert her will power, and rise up off the floor. It is certain that she will believe that she can do it. Her will will be in an optimum condition to carry out the order, if it can be done. Miss Freeman!"

"Yes, Mr. Huxley."

"Exert your will. Rise up in the air!"

Joan rose straight up into the air, some six feet—until her head nearly touched the high ceiling.—*"How'm doin,' pal?"—Swell, kid, you're wowin' 'em. Look at 'em stare!"*

At that moment Brinckley burst into the room, rage in his eyes.

"Mr. Huxley, you have broken your word to me, and disgraced this university!" It was some ten minutes after the fiasco ending the demonstration. Huxley faced the president in Brinckley's private office.

"I made you no promise. I have not disgraced the school," Phil answered with equal pugnacity.

"You have indulged in cheap tricks of fake magic to bring your department into disrepute."

"So I'm a faker, am I? You stiff-necked old fossil—explain this one!" Huxley levitated himself until he floated three feet above the rug.

"Explain what?" To Huxley's amazement Brinckley seemed unaware that anything unusual was going on. He continued to stare at the point where Phil's head had been. His manner showed nothing but a slight puzzlement and annoyance at Huxley's apparently irrelevant remark.

Was it possible that the doddering old fool was so completely self-deluded that he could not observe anything that ran counter to his own preconceptions even when it happened directly under his eyes? Phil reached out with his mind and attempted to see what went on inside

Brinckley's head. He got one of the major surprises of his life. He expected to find the floundering mental processes of near senility; he found . . . cold calculation, keen ability, set in a matrix of pure evil that sickened him.

It was just a glimpse, then he was cast out with a wrench that numbed his brain. Brinckley had discovered his spying and thrown up his defences—the hard defences of a disciplined mind.

Phil dropped back to the floor, and left the room, without a word, nor a backward glance.

From THE WESTERN STUDENT, October 3rd:

PSYCH PROF FIRED FOR FRAUD

. . . students' accounts varied, but all agreed that it had been a fine show. Fullback 'Buzz' Arnold told your reporter, "I hated to see it happen; Prof Huxley is a nice guy and he certainly put on a clever skit with some good deadpan acting. I could see how it was done, of course—it was the same the Great Arturo used in his turn at the Orpheum last spring. But I can see Doctor Brinckley's viewpoint; you can't permit monkey shines at a serious center of learning."

President Brinckley gave the STUDENT the following official statement: "It is with real regret that I announce the termination of Mr. Huxley's association with the institution—for the good of the University. Mr. Huxley had been repeatedly warned as to where his steps were leading him. He is a young man of considerable ability. Let us devoutly hope that this experience will serve as a lesson to him in whatever line of endeavor . . ."

Coburn handed the paper back to Huxley. "You know what happened to me?" he inquired.

"Something new?"

"Invited to resign . . . No publicity—just a gentle hint. My patients got well too fast; I'd quit using surgery, you know."

"How perfectly stinking!" This from Joan.

"Well," Ben considered, "I don't blame the medical director; Brinckley forced his hand. I guess we underrated the old cuss."

"Rather! Ben, he's every bit as capable as any one of us, and as for his motives—I gag when I think about it."

"And I thought he was just a were-mouse," grieved Joan. "We should have pushed him into the tar pits last spring. I told you to. What do we do now?"

"Go right ahead." Phil's reply was grim. "We'll turn the situation to our own advantage; we've gotten some publicity—we'll use it."

"What's the gag?"

"Levitation again. It's the most spectacular thing we've got for a crowd. Call in the papers, and tell 'em that we will publicly demonstrate levitation at noon tomorrow in Pershing Square."

"Won't the papers fight shy of sticking their necks out on anything that sounds as fishy as that?"

"Probably they would, but here's how we'll handle that: Make the whole thing just a touch screwball and give 'em plenty of funny angles to write up. Then they can treat it as a feature rather than as straight news. The lid's off, Joan—you can do anything you like; the screwier the better. Let's get going, troops—I'll call the News Service. Ben, you and Joan split up the dailies between you."

The reporters were interested, certainly. They were interested in Joan's obvious good looks, cynically amused by Phil's flowing tie and bombastic claims, and seriously impressed by his taste in whiskey. They began to take notice when Coburn courteously poured drinks for them without bothering to touch the bottle.

But when Joan floated around the room while Phil rode a nonexistent bicycle across the ceiling, they balked. "Honest, doc," as one of them put it, "we've got to eat—you don't expect us to go back and tell a city editor anything like this. Come clean; is it the whiskey, or just plain hypnotism?"

"Put it any way you like, gentlemen. Just be sure that you say that we will do it all over again in Pershing Square at noon tomorrow."

Phil's diatribe against Brinckley came as an anticlimax to the demonstration, but the reporters obligingly noted it.

Joan got ready for bed that night with a feeling of vague depression. The exhilaration of entertaining the newspaper boys had worn off. Ben had proposed supper and dancing to mark their last night of private life, but it had not been a success. To start with, they had blown a tire while coming down a steep curve on Beachwood Drive, and Phil's gray sedan had rolled over and over. They would have all been seriously injured had it not been for the automatic body control which they possessed.

When Phil examined the wreck, he expressed puzzlement as to its cause. "Those tires were perfectly all right," he maintained. "I had examined them all the way through this morning." But he insisted on continuing with their evening of relaxation.

The floor show seemed dull, the jokes crude and callous, after the light, sensitive humor they had learned to enjoy through association with Master Ling. The ponies in the chorus were young and beautiful—Joan had enjoyed watching them, but she made the mistake of reaching out to touch their minds. The incongruity of the vapid, insensitive spirits she found—in almost every instance—added to her malaise.

She was relieved when the floor show ended and Ben asked her to dance. Both of the men were good dancers, especially Coburn, and she fitted herself into his arms contentedly. Her pleasure didn't last; a drunken couple bumped into them repeatedly. The man was quarrelsome, the woman shrilly vitriolic. Joan asked her escorts to take her home.

These things bothered her as she prepared for bed. Joan, who had never known acute physical fear in her life, feared just one thing—the corrosive, dirty emotions of the poor in spirit. Malice, envy, spite, the snide insults of twisted, petty minds; these things could hurt her, just by being in her presence, even if she were not the direct object of the attack. She was not yet sufficiently mature to have acquired a smooth armor of indifference to the opinions of the unworthy.

After a summer in the company of men of good will, the incident with the drunken couple dismayed her. She felt dirtied by the contact. Worse still, she felt an outlander, a stranger in a strange land.

She awakened sometime in the night with the sense of loneliness increased to overwhelming proportions. She was acutely aware of the three-million-odd living beings around her, but the whole city seemed alive only with malignant entities, jealous of her, anxious to drag her down to their own ignoble status. This attack on her spirit, this attempt to despoil the sanctity of her inner being, assumed an almost corporate nature. It seemed to her that it was nibbling at the edges of her mind, snuffling at her defences.

Terrified, she called out to Ben and Phil. There was no answer; her mind could not find them.

The filthy thing that threatened her was aware of her failure; she could feel it leer. In open panic she called to the Senior.

No answer. This time the thing spoke—"That way, too, is closed."

As hysteria claimed her, as her last defences crumbled, she was caught in the arms of a stronger spirit, whose calm, untroubled goodness encysted her against the evil thing that stalked her.

"Ling!" she cried, "Master Ling!" before racking sobs claimed her.

She felt the quiet, reassuring humor of his smile while the fingers of his mind reached out and smoothed away the tensions of her fear. Presently she slept.

His mind stayed with her all through the night, and talked with her, until she awakened.

Ben and Phil listened to her account of the previous night with worried faces. "That settles it," Phil decided. "We've been too careless. From now on until this thing is finished, we stay in rapport day and night, awake and asleep. As a matter of fact, I had a bad time of it myself last night, though nothing equal to what happened to Joan."

"So did I, Phil. What happened to you?"

"Nothing very much—just a long series of nightmares in which I kept losing confidence in my ability to do any of the things we learned on Shasta. What about you?"

"Same sort of thing, with variations. I operated all night long, and all of my patients died on the table. Not very pleasant—but something else happened that wasn't a dream. You know I still use an old-fashioned straight-razor; I was shaving away, paying no attention to it, when it jumped in my hand and cut a big gash in my throat. See? It's not entirely healed yet." He indicated a thin red line which ran diagonally down the right side of his neck.

"Why, Ben!" squealed Joan, "you might have been killed."

"That's what I thought," he agreed dryly.

"You know, kids," Phil said slowly, "these things aren't accidental—"

"Open up in there!" The order was bawled from the other side of the door. As one mind, their senses of direct perception jumped through solid oak and examined the speaker. Plainclothes did not conceal the profession of the over-size individual waiting there, even had they not been able to see the gold shield on his vest. A somewhat smaller, but equally officious, man waited with him.

Ben opened the door and inquired gently, "What do you want?"

The larger man attempted to come in. Coburn did not move.

"I asked you your business."

"Smart guy, eh? I'm from police headquarters. You Huxley?"

"No."

"Coburn?" Ben nodded.

"You'll do. That Huxley behind you? Don't either of you ever stay home? Been here all night?"

"No," said Coburn frostily, "not that it is any of your business."

"I'll decide about that. I want to talk to you two. I'm from the bunco squad. What's this game you were giving the boys yesterday?"

"No game, as you call it. Come down to Pershing Square at noon today, and see for yourself."

"You won't be doing anything in Pershing Square today, Bud."

"Why not?"

"Park Commission's orders."

"What authority?"

"Huh?"

"By what act, or ordinance, do they deny the right of private citizens to make peaceful use of a public place? Who is that with you?"

The smaller man identified himself. "Name's Ferguson, D.A.'s office. I want your pal Huxley on a criminal libel complaint. I want you two's witnesses."

Ben's stare became colder, if possible. "Do either of you," he inquired, in gently snubbing tones, "have a warrant?"

They looked at each other and failed to reply. Ben continued, "Then it is hardly profitable to continue this conversation, is it?" and closed the door in their faces.

He turned around to his companions and grinned. "Well, they are closing in. Let's see what the papers gave us."

They found just one story. It said nothing about their proposed demonstration, but related that Doctor Brinckley had sworn a complaint charging Phil with criminal libel. "That's the first time I ever heard of four metropolitan papers refusing a juicy news story," was Ben's comment, "what are you going to do about Brinckley's charge?"

"Nothing," Phil told him, "except possibly libel him again. If he goes through with it, it will be a beautiful opportunity to prove our claims in court. Which reminds me—we don't want our plans interfered with today; those bird dogs may be back with warrants most any time. Where'll we hide out?"

On Ben's suggestion they spent the morning buried in the downtown public library. At five minutes to twelve, they flagged a taxi, and rode to Pershing Square.

They stepped out of the cab into the arms of six sturdy policemen.

—"Ben, Phil, how much longer do I have to put up with this?"

—"Steady, kid. Don't get upset."

—"I'm not, but why should we stay pinched when we can duck out anytime?"

—"That's the point; we can escape anytime. We've never been arrested before; let's see what it's like."

❖

They were gathered that night late around the fireplace in Joan's house. Escape had presented no difficulties, but they had waited until an hour when the jail was quiet to prove that stone walls do not a prison make for a person adept in the powers of the mind.

Ben was speaking, "I'd say we had enough data to draw a curve now."

"Which is?"

"You state it."

"All right. We came down from Shasta thinking that all we had to overcome was stupidity, ignorance, and a normal amount of human contrariness and cussedness. Now we know better. Any attempt to place the essentials of the ancient knowledge in the hands of the common people is met by a determined, organized effort to prevent it, and to destroy, or disable the one who tries it."

"It's worse than that," amended Ben, "I spent our rest in the clink looking over the city. I wondered why the district attorney should take such an interest in us, so I took a look into his mind. I found out who his boss was, and took a look at *his* mind. What I found there interested me so much that I had to run up to the state capital and see what made things tick there. That took me back to Spring Street and the financial district. Believe it or not, from there I had to look up some of the most sacred cows in the community—clergymen, clubwomen, business leaders, and stuff." He paused.

"Well, what about it? Don't tell me everybody is out of step but Willie—I'll break down and cry."

"No—that was the odd part about it. Nearly all of these heavyweights were good Joes, people you'd like to know. But usually—not always, but usually—the good Joes were dominated by someone they trusted, someone who had helped them to get where they were, and these dominants were not good Joes, to state it gently. I couldn't get into all of their minds, but where I was able to get in, I found the same sort of thing that Phil found in Brinckley—cold calculated awareness that their power lay in keeping the people in ignorance."

Joan shivered. "That's a sweet picture you paint, Ben—just the right thing for a bed-time story. What's our next move?"

"What do you suggest?"

"Me? I haven't reached any conclusion. Maybe we should take on these tough babies one at a time, and smear 'em."

"How about you, Phil?"

"I haven't anything better to offer. We'll have to plan a shrewd campaign, however."

"Well, I do have something to suggest myself."

"Let's have it."

"Admit that we blindly took on more than we could handle. Go back to Shasta and ask for help."

"Why, Ben!" Joan's dismay was matched by Phil's unhappy face. Ben went on stubbornly, "Sure, I know it's gravelling, but pride is too expensive and the job is too—"

He broke off when he noticed Joan's expression. "What is it kid?"

"We'll have to make some decision quickly—that is a police car that just stopped out in front."

Ben turned back to Phil. "What'll it be; stay and fight, or go back for re-inforcements?"

"Oh, you're right. I've known it ever since I got a look at Brinckley's mind—but I hated to admit it."

The three stepped out into the patio, joined hands, and shot straight up into the air.

CHAPTER ELEVEN

"A Little Child Shall Lead Them."

"Welcome home!" Ephraim Howe met them when they landed. "Glad to have you back." He led them into his own private apartment. "Rest yourselves while I stir up the fire a mite." He chucked a wedge of pinewood into the wide grate, pulled his homely old rocking chair around so that it faced both the fire and his guests, and settled down. "Now suppose you tell me all about it. No, I'm not hooked in with the others—you can make a full report to the council when you're ready."

"As a matter of fact, don't you already know everything that happened to us, Mr. Howe?" Phil looked directly at the Senior as he spoke.

"No, I truly don't. We let you go at it your own way, with Ling keeping an eye out to see that you didn't get hurt. He has made no report to me."

"Very well, sir." They took turns telling him all that had happened to them, occasionally letting him see directly through their minds the events they had taken part in.

When they were through Howe gave them his quizzical smile and inquired, "So you've come around to the viewpoint of the council?"

"No, sir!" It was Phil who answered him. "We are more convinced of the need for positive, immediate action than we were when we left— but we are convinced, too, that we aren't strong enough nor wise enough to handle it alone. We've come back to ask for help, and to urge the council to abandon its policy of teaching only those who show that they are ready, and, instead, to reach out and teach as many minds as can accept your teachings.

"You see, sir, our antagonists don't wait. They are active all the time. They've won in Asia, they are in the ascendancy in Europe, they may win here in America, while we wait for an opportunity."

"Have you any method to suggest for tackling the problem?"

"No, that's why we came back. When we tried to teach others what we knew, we were stopped."

"That's the rub," Howe agreed. "I've been pretty much of your opinion for a good many years, but it is hard to do. What we have to give can't be printed in a book, nor broadcast over the air. It must be passed directly from mind to mind, wherever we find a mind ready to receive it."

They finished the discussion without finding a solution. Howe told them not to worry. "Go along," he said, "and spend a few weeks in meditation and rapport. When you get an idea that looks as if it might work, bring it in and we'll call the council together to consider it."

"But, Senior," Joan protested for the trio, "you see—Well, we had hoped to have the advice of the council in working out a plan. We don't know where to start, else we wouldn't have come back."

He shook his head. "You are the newest of the brethren, the youngest, the least experienced. Those are your virtues, not your disabilities. The very fact that you have not spent years of this life in thinking in terms of eons and races gives you an advantage. Too broad a viewpoint, too philosophical an outlook paralyzes the will. I want you three to consider it alone."

They did as he asked. For weeks they discussed it in rapport as a single mind, hammered at it in spoken conversation, meditated its ramifications. They roamed the nation with their minds, examining the human spirits that lay behind political and social action. With the aid of the archives they learned the techniques by which the brotherhood of adepts had interceded in the past when freedom of thought and action in America had been threatened. They proposed and rejected dozens of schemes.

"We should go into politics," Phil told the other two, "as our brothers did in the past. If we had a Secretary of Education, appointed from among the elders, he could found a national academy in which freedom of thought would really prevail, and it could be the source from which the ancient knowledge could spread."

Joan put in an objection.

"Suppose you lose the election?"

"Huh?"

"Even with all the special powers that the adepts have, it 'ud be quite a chore to line up delegates for a national convention to get our candidate nominated, then get him elected in the face of all the political machines, pressure groups, newspapers, favorite sons, et cetera, et cetera, et cetera.

"And remember this, the opposition can fight as dirty as it pleases, but we have to fight fair, or we defeat our own aims."

Ben nodded. "I am afraid she is right, Phil. But you are absolutely right in one thing; this is a problem of education." He stopped to meditate, his mind turned inward.

Presently he resumed. "I wonder if we have been tackling this job from the right end? We've been thinking of reeducating adults, already set in their ways. How about the children? They haven't crystallized; wouldn't they be easier to teach?"

Joan sat up, her eyes bright. "Ben, you've got it!"

Phil shook his head doggedly. "No. I hate to throw cold water, but there is no way to go about it. Children are constantly in the care of adults; we couldn't get to them. Don't think for a moment that you could get past local school boards; they are the tightest little oligarchies in the whole political system."

They were sitting in a group of pine trees on the lower slopes of Mount Shasta. A little group of human figures came into view below them and climbed steadily toward the spot where the three rested. The discussion was suspended until the group moved beyond earshot. The trio watched them with casual, friendly interest.

They were all boys, ten to fifteen years old, except the leader, who bore his sixteen years with the serious dignity befitting one who is responsible for the safety and wellbeing of younger charges. They were dressed in khaki shorts and shirts, campaign hats, neckerchiefs embroidered with a conifer and the insignia ALPINE PATROL, TROOP I, Each carried a staff and a knapsack.

As the procession came abreast of the adults, the patrol leader gave them a wave in greeting, the merit badges on his sleeve flashing in the sun. The three waved back and watched them trudge out of sight up the slope.

Phil watched them with a faraway look. "Those were the good old days," he said; "I almost envy them."

"Were you one?" Ben said, his eyes still on the boys. "I remember how proud I was the day I got my merit badge in first aid."

"Born to be a doctor, eh, Ben?" commented Joan, her eyes maternal, approving. "I didn't—say!"

"What's up?"

"Phil! That's your answer! That's how to reach the children in spite of parents and school boards."

She snapped into telepathic contact, her ideas spilling excitedly into their minds. They went into rapport and ironed out the details. After a time Ben nodded and spoke aloud.

"It might work," he said, "let's go back and talk it over with Ephraim."

"Senator Moulton, these are the young people I was telling you about." Almost in awe, Joan looked at the face of the little white-haired, old man whose name had become a synonym for integrity. She felt the same impulse to fold her hands across her middle and bow which Master Ling inspired. She noted that Ben and Phil were having trouble not to seem gawky and coltish.

Ephraim Howe continued, "I have gone into their scheme and I think it is practical. If you do too, the council will go ahead with it. But it largely depends on you."

The Senator took them to himself with a smile, the smile that had softened the hearts of two generations of hard politicians. "Tell me about it," he invited.

They did so—how they had tried and failed at Western University, how they had cudgeled their brains for a way, how a party of boys on a hike up the mountain had given them an inspiration. "You see, Senator, if we could just get enough boys up here all at once, boys too young to have been corrupted by their environment, and already trained, as these boys are, in the ideals of the ancients,—human dignity, helpfulness, self-reliance, kindness, all those things set forth in their code—if we could get even five thousand such boys up here all at once, we could train them in telepathy, and how to impart telepathy to others.

"Once they were taught, and sent back to their homes, each one would be a center for spreading the knowledge. The antagonists could never stop it; it would be too wide spread, epidemic. In a few years every child in the country would be telepathic, and they would even teach their elders—those that haven't grown too calloused to learn.

"And once a human being is telepathic, we can lead him along the path of the ancient wisdom!"

Moulton was nodding, and talking to himself. "Yes. Yes indeed. It could be done. Fortunately Shasta is a national park. Let me see, who is on that committee? It would take a joint resolution and a small appropriation. Ephraim, old friend, I am afraid I shall have to practice a little logrolling to accomplish this, will you forgive me?"

Howe grinned broadly.

"Oh, I mean it," Moulton continued, "people are so cynical, so harsh, about political expediency—even some of our brothers. Let me see, this will take about two years, I think, before the first camp can be held—"

"As long as that?" Joan was disappointed.

"Oh, yes, my dear. There are two bills to get before Congress, and much arranging to do to get them passed in the face of a full legislative calendar. There are arrangements to be made with the railroads and bus companies to give the boys special rates so that they can afford to come. We must start a publicity campaign to make the idea popular. Then there must be time for as many of our brothers as possible to get into the administration of the movement in order that the camp executives may be liberally interspersed with adepts. Fortunately I am a national trustee of the organization. Yes, I can manage it in two years' time, I believe."

"Good heavens!" protested Phil; "why wouldn't it be more to the point to teleport them here, teach them, and teleport them back?"

"You do not know what you are saying, my son. Can we abolish force by using it? Every step must be voluntary, accomplished by reason and persuasion. Each human being must free himself; freedom cannot be thrust on him. Besides, is two years long to wait to accomplish a job that has been waiting since the Deluge?"

"I'm sorry, sir."

"Do not be. Your youthful impatience has made it possible to do the job at all."

CHAPTER TWELVE

"Ye Shall Know the Truth—"

On the lower slopes of Mount Shasta, down near McCloud, the camp grew up. When the last of the spring snow was still hiding in the deeper gullies and on the north sides of ridges, U.S. Army Quartermaster trucks came lumbering over a road built the previous fall by the army engineers. Pyramid tents were broken out and were staked down in rows on the bosom of a gently rolling alp. Cook shacks, an infirmary, a headquarters building took shape. Camp Mark Twain was changing from blueprint to actuality.

Senator Moulton, his toga laid aside for breeches, leggings, khaki shirt, and a hat marked CAMP DIRECTOR, puttered around the field, encouraging, making decisions for the straw bosses, and searching, ever searching the minds of all who came into or near the camp for any purpose. Did anyone suspect? Had anyone slipped in who might be associated with partial adepts who opposed the real purpose of the camp? Too late to let anything slip now—too late, and too much at stake.

In the middle west, in the deep south, in New York City and New England, in the mountains and on the coast, boys were packing suitcases, buying special Shasta Camp round-trip tickets, talking about it with their envious contemporaries.

And all over the country the antagonists of human liberty, of human dignity—the racketeers, the crooked political figures, the shysters, the dealers in phony religions, the sweat-shoppers, the petty authoritarians, all of the key figures among the traffickers in human misery and human oppression, themselves somewhat adept in the arts of the mind and acutely aware of the danger of free knowledge—all of this unholy breed stirred uneasily and wondered what was taking place. Moulton had never been associated with anything but ill for them; Mount Shasta was one place they had never been able to touch—they hated the very name of the place. They recalled old stories, and shivered.

They shivered, but they acted.

Special transcontinental buses loaded with the chosen boys—could the driver be corrupted? Could his mind be taken over? Could tires, or engine, be tampered with? Trains were taken over by the youngsters. Could a switch be thrown? Could the drinking water be polluted?

Other eyes watched. A trainload of boys moved westward; in it, or flying over it, his direct perception blanketing the surrounding territory, and checking the motives of every mind within miles of his charges, was stationed at least one adept whose single duty it was to see that those boys reached Shasta safely.

Probably some of the boys would never have reached there had not the opponents of human freedom been caught off balance, doubtful, unorganized. For vice has this defect; it cannot be truly intelligent. Its very motives are its weakness. The attempts made to prevent the boys reaching Shasta were scattered and abortive. The adepts had taken the offensive for once, and their moves were faster and more rationally conceived than their antagonists'.

Once in camp a tight screen surrounded the whole of Mount Shasta National Park. The Senior detailed adepts to point patrol night and day to watch with every sense at their command for mean or malignant spirits. The camp itself was purged. Two of the councilors, and some twenty of the boys, were sent home when examination showed them to be damaged souls. The boys were not informed of their deformity, but plausible excuses were found for the necessary action.

The camp resembled superficially a thousand other such camps.

The courses in woodcraft were the same. The courts of honor met as usual to examine candidates. There were the usual sings around the campfire in the evening, the same setting-up exercises before breakfast. The slightly greater emphasis on the oath and the law of the organization was not noticeable.

Each one of the boys made at least one overnight hike in the course of the camp. In groups of fifteen or twenty they would set out in the morning in company of a councilor. That each councilor supervising such hikes was an adept was not evident, but it so happened. Each boy carried his blanket roll, and knapsack of rations, his canteen, knife, compass, and hand axe.

They camped that night on the bank of a mountain stream, fed by the glaciers, whose rush sounded in their ears as they ate supper.

Phil started out with such a group one morning during the first week of the camp. He worked around the mountain to the east in order to keep well away from the usual tourist haunts.

After supper they sat around the campfire. Phil told them stories of the holy men of the east and their reputed powers, and of Saint Francis and the birds. He was in the middle of one of his yarns when a figure appeared within the circle of firelight.

Or rather figures. They saw an old man, in clothes that Davy Crockett might have worn, flanked by two beasts, on his left side a mountain lion, who purred when he saw the fire, on his right a buck of three points, whose soft brown eyes stared calmly into theirs.

Some of the boys were alarmed at first, but Phil told them quietly to widen their circle and make room for the strangers. They sat in decent silence for a while, the boys getting used to the presence of the animals. In time one of the boys timidly stroked the big cat, who responded by rolling over and presenting his soft belly. The boy looked up at the old man and asked,

"What is his name, Mister—"

"Ephraim. His name is Freedom."

"My, but he's tame? How do you get him to be so tame?"

"He reads my thoughts and trusts me. Most things are friendly when they know you—and most people."

The boy puzzled for a moment. "How can he read your thoughts?"

"It's simple. You can read his, too. Would you like to learn how?"

"Jiminy!"

"Just look into my eyes for a moment. There! Now look into his."

"Why—Why—I really believe I can!"

—*"Of course you can. And mine, too. I'm not talking out loud. Had you noticed?"*

—*"Why, so you're not. I'm reading your thoughts!"*

—*"And I'm reading yours. Easy, isn't it?"*

With Phil's help Howe had them all conversing by thought transference inside an hour. Then to calm them down he told them stories for another hour, stories that constituted an important part of their curriculum. He helped Phil get them to sleep, then left, the animals following after him.

The next morning Phil was confronted at once by a young sceptic. "Say, did I dream all that about an old man and a puma and a deer?"

—*"Did you?"*

—*"You're doing it now!"*

—*"Certainly I am. And so are you. Now go tell the other boys the same thing."*

Before they got back to camp, he advised them not to speak about it to any other of the boys who had not as yet had their overnight hike, but that they test their new powers by trying it on any boy who had had his first all-night hike.

All was well until one of the boys had to return home in answer to a message that his father was ill. The elders would not wipe his mind clean of his new knowledge; instead they kept careful track of him. In time he talked, and the word reached the antagonists almost at once. Howe ordered the precautions of the telepathic patrol redoubled.

The patrol was able to keep out malicious persons, but it was not numerous enough to keep everything out. Forest fire broke out on the windward side of the camp late one night. No human being had been close to the spot; telekinetics was the evident method.

But what control over matter from a distance can do, it can also undo. Moulton squeezed the flame out with his will, refused it permisson to burn, bade its vibrations to stop.

For the time being the enemy appeared to cease attempts to do the boys physical harm. But the enemy had not given tap. Phil received a frantic call from one of the younger boys to come at once to the tent the boy lived in; his patrol leader was very sick. Phil found the lad in a state of hysteria, and being restrained from doing himself an injury by the other boys in the tent. He had tried to cut his throat with his jack knife and had gone berserk when one of the other boys had grabbed his hand.

Phil took in the situation quickly and put in a call to Ben.

—*"Ben! Come at once. I need you."*

Ben did so, zipping through the air and flying in through the door of the tent almost before Phil had time to lay the boy on his cot and start forcing him into a trance. The lad's startled tent mates did not have time to decide that Dr. Ben had been flying before he was standing in a normal fashion alongside their councilor.

Ben greeted him with tight communication, shutting the boys out of the circuit.—*"What's up?"*

—*"They've gotten to him . . . and damn near wrecked him."*

—*"How?"*

—*"Preyed on his mind. Tried to make him suicide. But I tranced back the hookup. Who do you think tried to do him in?—Brinckley!"*

—*"No!"*

—*"Definitely. You take over here, I'm going after Brinckley. Tell the Senior to have a watch put on all the boys who have been trained to be sensitive to telepathy. I'm afraid that any of them may be gotten at before we can teach them how to defend themselves."* With that he was gone, leaving the boys half convinced of levitation.

He had not gone very far, was still gathering speed, when he heard a welcome voice in his head,

—*"Phil! Phil! Wait for me."*

He slowed down for a few seconds. A smaller figure flashed alongside his and grasped his hand. "It's a good thing I stay hooked in with you two. You'd have gone off to tackle that dirty old so-and-so without me."

He tried to maintain his dignity. "If I had thought that you should be along on this job, I'd have called you, Joan."

"Nonsense! And also fiddlesticks! You might get hurt, tackling him all alone. Besides, I'm going to push him into the tar pits."

He sighed and gave up. "Joan, my dear, you are a bloodthirsty wench with ten thousand incarnations to go before you reach beatitude."

"I don't want to reach beatitude; I want to do old Brinckley in."

"Come along, then. Let's make some speed."

They were south of the Tehachapi by now and rapidly approaching Los Angeles. They flitted over the Sierra Madre range, shot across San Fernando Valley, clipped the top of Mount Hollywood, and landed on the lawn of the President's Residence at Western University. Brinckley saw, or felt, them coming and tried to run for it, but Phil grappled with him.

He shot one thought to Joan.—*"You stay out of this, kid, unless I yell for help."*

342

Brinckley did not give up easily. His mind reached out and tried to engulf Phil's. Huxley felt himself slipping, giving way before the evil onslaught. It seemed as though he were being dragged down, drowned, in filthy quicksand.

But he steadied himself and fought back.

When Phil had finished that which was immediately necessary with Brinckley, he stood up and wiped his hands, as if to cleanse himself of the spiritual slime he had embraced. "Let's get going," he said to Joan, "we're pushed for time."

"What did you do to him, Phil?" She stared with fascinated disgust at the thing on the ground.

"Little enough. I placed him in stasis. I've got to save him for use—for a time. Up you go, girl. Out of here—before we're noticed."

Up they shot, with Brinckley's body swept along behind by tight telekinetic bond. They stopped above the clouds. Brinckley floated beside them, starfished, eyes popping, mouth loose, his smooth pink face expressionless.—*"Ben!"* Huxley was sending, *"Ephraim Howe! Ambrose! To me! To me! Hurry!"*

—*"Coming, Phil!"* came Coburn's answer.

—*"I hear."* The strong calm thought held the quality of the Senior. *"What is it, son? Tell me."*

—*"Not time!"* snapped Phil. *"Yourself, Senior, and all others that can. Rendezvous! Hurry!"*

—*"We come."* The thought was still calm, unhurried. But there were two ragged holes in the roof of Moulton's tent. Moulton and Howe were already out of sight of Camp Mark Twain.

Slashing, slicing through the air they came, the handful of adepts who guarded the fire. From five hundred miles to the north they came, racing pigeons hurrying home. Camp councilors, two-thirds of the small group of camp matrons, some few from scattered points on the continent, they came in response to Huxley's call for help and the Senior's unprecedented tocsin. A housewife turned out the fire in the oven and disappeared into the sky. A taxi driver stopped his car and left his fares without a word. Research groups on Shasta broke their tight rapport, abandoned their beloved work, and came—fast!

"And now, Philip?" Howe spoke orally as he arrested his trajectory and hung beside Huxley.

Huxley flung a hand toward Brinckley. "He has what we need to know to strike now! Where's Master Ling?"

"He and Mrs. Draper guard the Camp."

"I need him. Can she do it alone?"

Clear and mellow, her voice rang in his head from half a state away. —*"I can!"*

—*"The tortoise flies."* The second thought held the quality of deathless merriment which was the unmistakable characteristic of the ancient Chinese.

Joan felt a soft touch at her mind, then Master Ling was among them, seated carefully tailor-fashion on nothingness. "I attend; my body follows," he announced. "Can we not proceed?"

Whereupon Joan realized that he had borrowed the faculties of her mind to project himself into their presence more quickly than he could levitate the distance. She felt unreasonably flattered by the attention.

Huxley commenced at once. "Through *his* mind—" He indicated Brinckley, "I have learned of many others with whom there can be no truce. We must search them out, deal with them at once, before they can rally from what has happened to him. But I need help. Master, will you extend the present and examine him?"

Ling had tutored them in discrimination of time and perception of the present, taught them to stand off and perceive duration from eternity. But he was incredibly more able than his pupils. He could split the beat of a fly's wing into a thousand discrete instants, or grasp a millenium as a single flash of experience. His discrimination of time and space was bound neither by his metabolic rate nor by his molar dimensions.

Now he poked gingerly at Brinckley's brain like one who seeks a lost jewel in garbage. He felt out the man's memory patterns and viewed his life as one picture. Joan, with amazement, saw his everpresent smile give way to a frown of distaste. His mind had been left open to any who cared to watch. She peered through his mind, then cut off. If there were that many truly vicious spirits in the world, she preferred to encounter them one at a time, as necessary, not experience them all at once.

Master Ling's body joined the group, melted into his projection.

Huxley, Howe, Moulton, and Bierce followed the Chinese's delicate work with close attention. Howe's face was bleakly impassive; Moulton's face, aged to androgynous sensitivity, moved from side to side while he clucked disapproval of such wickedness. Bierce looked more like Mark Twain than ever, Twain in an implacable, lowering rage.

Master Ling looked up. "Yes, yes," said Moulton, "I suppose we must act, Ephraim."

"We have no choice," Huxley stated, with a completely unconscious disregard of precedent. "Will you assign the tasks, Senior?"

Howe glanced sharply at him. "No, Philip. No. Go ahead. Carry on."

Huxley checked himself in surprise for the briefest instant, then took his cue. "You'll help me, Master Ling. Ben!"

"Waiting!"

He meshed mind to mind, had Ling show him his opponent and the data he needed.—*"Got it? Need any help?"*

—*"Grandfather Stonebender is enough."*

—*"Okay. Nip off and attend to it."*

—*"Chalk it up."* He was gone, a rush of air in his wake.

—*"This one is yours, Senator Moulton."*

—*"I know."* And Moulton was gone.

By ones and twos he gave them their assignments, and off they went to do that which must be done. There was no argument. Many of them had been aware long before Huxley was that a day of action must inevitably come to pass, but they had waited with quiet serenity, busy with the work at hand, till time should incubate the seed.

In a windowless study of a mansion on Long Island, soundproofed, cleverly locked and guarded, ornately furnished, a group of five was met—three men, one woman, and a thing in a wheel chair. It glared at the other four in black fury, glared without eyes, for its forehead dropped unbroken to its cheekbones, a smooth sallow expanse.

A lap robe, tucked loosely across the chair masked, but did not hide, the fact that the creature had no legs.

It gripped the arms of the chair. "Must I do *all* the thinking for you fools?" it asked in a sweet gentle voice. "You, Arthurson—you let Moulton slip that Shasta Bill past the Senate. Moron." The epithet was uttered caressingly.

Arthurson shifted in his chair. "I examined his mind. The bill was harmless. It was a swap on the Missouri Valley deal. I told you."

"You examined his mind, eh? Hmm—he led you on a personally conducted tour, you fool. A *Shasta* bill! When will you mindless idiots learn that no good ever came out of Shasta?" It smiled approvingly.

"Well, how was I to know? I thought a camp near the mountain might confuse . . . *them.*"

"Mindless idiot. The time will come when I will find you dispensable." The thing did not wait for the threat to sink in, but continued, "Enough of that now. We must move to repair the damage. *They* are on the offensive now. Agnes—"

"Yes." The woman answered.

"Your preaching has got to pick up—"

"I've done my best."

"Not good enough. I've got to have a wave of religious hysteria that will wash out the Bill of Rights—*before* the Shasta camp breaks up for the summer. We will have to act fast before that time and we can't be hampered by a lot of legalisms."

"It can't be done."

"Shut up. It can be done. Your temple will receive endowments this week which you are to use for countrywide television hookups. At the proper time you will discover a new messiah."

"Who?"

"Brother Artemis."

"*That* cornbelt pipsqueak? Where do I come in on this?"

"You'll get yours. But you can't head this movement; the country won't take a woman in the top spot. The two of you will lead a march on Washington and take over. The Sons of '76 will fill out your ranks and do the street fighting. Weems, that's your job."

The man addressed demurred. "It will take three, maybe four months to indoctrinate them."

"You have three weeks. It would be well not to fail."

The last of the three men broke his silence. "What's the hurry, Chief? Seems to me that you are getting yourself in a panic over a few kids."

"I'll be the judge. Now you are to time an epidemic of strikes to tie the country up tight at the time of the march on Washington."

"I'll need some incidents."

"You'll get them. You worry about the unions; I'll take care of the Merchants' and Commerce League myself. You give me one small strike tomorrow. Get your pickets out and I will have four or five of them shot. The publicity will be ready. Agnes, you preach a sermon about it."

"Slanted which way?"

It rolled its non-existent eyes up to the ceiling. "Must I think of everything? It's elementary. Use your minds."

The last man to speak laid down his cigar carefuly and said, "What's the real rush, Chief?"

"I've told you."

"No, you haven't. You've kept your mind closed and haven't let us read your thoughts once. You've known about the Shasta camp for months. Why this sudden excitement? You aren't slipping, are you? Come on, spill it. You can't expect us to follow if you are slipping."

The eyeless one looked him over carefully. "Hanson," he said, in still sweeter tones, "you have been feeling your size for months. Would you care to match your strength with mine?"

The other looked at his cigar. "I don't mind if I do."

"You will. But not tonight. I haven't time to select and train new lieutenants. Therefore I will tell you what the urgency is. I can't raise Brinckley. He's fallen out of communication. There is not *time*—"

"You are correct," said a new voice. "There is not time."

The five jerked puppetlike to face its source. Standing side by side in the study were Ephraim Howe and Joan Freeman.

Howe looked at the thing. "I've waited for this meeting," he said cheerfully, "and I've saved you for myself."

The creature got out of its wheelchair and moved through the air at Howe. Its height and position gave an unpleasant sensation that it walked on invisible legs. Howe signalled to Joan—*"It starts. Can you hold the others, my dear?"*

—*"I think so."*

—*"Now!"* Howe brought to bear everything he had learned in one hundred and thirty busy years, concentrated on the single problem of telekinetic control. He avoided, refused contact with the mind of the evil thing before him and turned his attention to destroying its physical envelope.

The thing stopped.

Slowly, slowly, like a deepsea diver caught in an implosion, like an orange in a squeezer, the spatial limits in which it existed were reduced. A spherical locus in space enclosed it, diminished.

The thing was drawn in and in. The ungrown stumps of its legs folded against its thick torso. The head ducked down against the chest to escape the unrelenting pressure. For a single instant it gathered its enormous perverted power and fought back. Joan was disconcerted, momentarily nauseated, by the backwash of evil.

But Howe withstood it without change of expression; the sphere shrank again.

The eyeless skull split. At once, the sphere shrank to the least possible dimension. A twenty-inch ball hung in the air, a ball whose repulsive superficial details did not invite examination.

Howe held the harmless, disgusting mess in place with a fraction of his mind, and inquired—*"Are you all right, my dear?"*

—*"Yes, Senior. Master Ling helped me once when I needed it."*

—*"That I anticipated. Now for the others."* Speaking aloud he said, "Which do you prefer: To join your leader, or to forget what you know?" He grasped air with his fingers and made a squeezing gesture.

The man with the cigar screamed.

"I take that to be an answer," said Howe. "Very well, Joan, pass them to me, one at a time."

He operated subtly on their minds, smoothing out the patterns of colloidal gradients established by their corporal experience.

A few minutes later the room contained four sane but infant adults—and a gory mess on the rug.

❖

Coburn stepped into a room to which he had not been invited. "School's out, boys," he announced cheerfully. He pointed a finger at one occupant. "That goes for you." Flame crackled from his finger tip, lapped over his adversary. "Yes, and for you." The flames spouted forth a second time. "And for you." A third received his final cleansing.

Brother Artemis, "God's Angry Man," faced the television pick-up. "And if these things be not true," he thundered, "then may the Lord strike me down dead!"

The coroner's verdict of heart failure did not fully account for the charred condition of his remains.

A political rally adjourned early because the principal speaker failed to show up. An anonymous beggar was found collapsed over his pencils and chewing gum. A director of nineteen major corporations caused his secretary to have hysterics by breaking off in the midst of dictating to converse with the empty air before lapsing into cheerful idiocy. A celebrated stereo and television star disappeared. Obituary stories were hastily dug out and completed for seven members of Congress, several judges, and two governors.

The usual evening sing at Camp Mark Twain took place that night without the presence of Camp Director Moulton. He was attending a full conference of the adepts, assembled all in the flesh for the first time in many years.

Joan looked around as she entered the hall. "Where is Master Ling?" she inquired of Howe.

He studied her face for a moment. For the first time since she had first met him nearly two years before she thought he seemed momentarily at a loss. "My dear," he said gently, "you must have realized that Master Ling remained with us, not for his own benefit, but for ours. The crisis for which he waited has been met; the rest of the work we must do alone."

A hand went to her throat. "You . . . you mean . . . ?"

"He was very old and very weary. He had kept his heart beating, his body functioning, by continuous control for these past forty-odd years."

"But why did he not renew and regenerate?"

"He did not wish it. We could not expect him to remain here indefinitely after he had grown up."

"No." She bit her trembling lip. "No. That it true. We are children and he has other things to do . . . but—Oh, Ling! Ling! Master Ling!" She buried her head on Howe's shoulder.

—*"Why are you weeping, Little Flower?"*

Her head jerked up.—*"Master Ling!"*

—*"Can that not be which has been? Is there past or future? Have you learned my lessons so poorly? Am I not now with you, as always?"*
She felt in the thought the vibrant timeless merriment, the gusto for living which was the hallmark of the gentle Chinese.

With a part of her mind she squeezed Howe's hand. "Sorry," she said. "I was wrong." She relaxed as Ling had taught her, let her consciousness flow in the revery which encompasses time in a single deathless now.

Howe, seeing that she was at peace, turned his attention to the meeting.

He reached out with his mind and gathered them together into the telepathic network of full conference.—*"I think that you all know why we meet,"* he thought.—*"I have served my time; we enter another and more active period when other qualities than mine are needed. I have called you to consider and pass on my selection of a successor."*

Huxley was finding the thought messages curiously difficult to follow. I must be exhausted from the effort, he thought to himself.

But Howe was thinking aloud again.—*"So be it; we are agreed."* He looked at Huxley. *"Philip, will you accept the trust?"*

"What?!!"

"You are Senior now—by common consent."

"But . . . but . . . I am not ready."

"We think so," answered Howe evenly. "Your talents are needed now. You will grow under responsibility."

—*"Chin up, pal!"* It was Coburn, in private message.

—*"It's all right, Phil."* Joan, that time.

For an instant he seemed to hear Ling's dry chuckle, his calm acceptance.

"I will try!" he answered.

On the last day of camp Joan sat with Mrs. Draper on a terrace of the Home on Shasta, overlooking the valley. She sighed. Mrs. Draper looked up from her knitting and smiled. "Are you sad that the camp is over?"

"Oh, no! I'm glad it is."

"What is it, then?"

"I was just thinking . . . we go to all this effort and trouble to put on this camp. Then we have to fight to keep it safe. Tomorrow those boys go home—then they must be watched, each one of them, while they grow strong enough to protect themselves against all the evil things there are still in the world. Next year there will be another crop of boys, and then another, and then another. Isn't there any end to it?"

"Certainly there is an end to it. Don't you remember, in the ancient records, what became of the elders? When we have done what there is for us to do here, we move on to where there is more to do. The human race was not meant to stay here forever."

"It still seems endless."

"It does, when you think of it that way, my dear. The way to make it seem short and interesting is to think about what you are going to do next. For example, what are you going to do next?"

"Me?" Joan looked perplexed. Her face cleared. "Why . . . why I'm going to get married!"

"I thought so." Mrs. Draper's needles clicked away.

CHAPTER THIRTEEN

"—and the Truth Shall Make You Free!"

The globe still swung around the sun. The seasons came and the seasons went. The sun still shone on the mountainsides, the hills were green, and the valleys lush. The river sought the bosom of the sea, then rode the cloud, and found the hills as rain. The cattle cropped in the brown plains, the fox stalked the hare through the brush. The tides answered the sway of the moon, and the gulls picked at the wet sand in the wake of the tide. The earth was fair and the earth was full; it teemed with life, swarmed with life, overflowed with life—a stream in spate.

Nowhere was man.

Seek the high hills; search him in the plains. Hunt for his spoor in the green jungles; call for him; shout for him. Follow where he has been in the bowels of earth; plumb the dim deeps of the sea.

Man is gone; his house stands empty; the door open.

A great ape, with a brain too big for his need and a spirit that troubled him, left his tribe and sought the quiet of the high place that lay above the jungle. He climbed it, hour after hour, urged on by a need that he half understood. He reached a resting place, high above the green trees of his home, higher than any of his tribe had ever climbed. There he found a broad flat stone, warm in the sun. He lay down upon it and slept.

But his sleep was troubled. He dreamed strange dreams, unlike anything he knew. They woke him and left him with an aching head.

It would be many generations before one of his line could understand what was left there by those who had departed.

"MY OBJECT ALL SUBLIME"

Future, February 1942

as by Lyle Monroe

THE CITY EDITOR tells me to go to Seventh and Spring.

"There's a story there," he says. "Go down and check it."

"What kind"

"They say it smells."

"Why shouldn't it?" I told him. "Columbia Bank on one corner, Fidelity-First National on the other, and the City Hall and the Daily Tide building just down the street."

"Wise guy," he answers. "I mean a real smell—like yourself."

Dobbs is all right—with him it's stomach ulcers and matrimony. "What's the sketch?" I asked, ignoring the crack.

"Seems like it ain't safe to drive a car through that intersection," he answered seriously. "You come out smelling like a telephone booth. Find out why."

I eased down there and looked the situation over. Nothing I could put my finger on, but a general air of nervousness and uncertainty. Now and then I'd catch a whiff of something, some ancient rottenness. It put me in mind of the morgue, again it was more like a Chinese river boat. When something happened that gave me a lead—

A truck came charging through as the lights were changing. He had time to stop, but didn't—and just missed a feeble old gal in the crosswalk. There was a sharp *"fsss"*; the truck driver got a look of agonized surprise, and wipes at his eyes. As he passed me I smelled it.

No mistake this time—it stunk like a convention of pole kitties, with prizes for range and distance.

The truck wobbled along for a few yards, then double-parked on the car tracks. I came alongside. "What happened, Buddy?" I asked the driver, but he is too far gone with choking and gasping. I left, not wanting the perfume to soak into my clothes.

I went back to the corner, having an idea and wanting to check it. In the next thirty minutes seventeen drivers did things I didn't like, bulling their way through left turns, jumping signals, ignoring pedestrians, and the like. And every one of them gets dosed with *eau de cologne*. Usually with the sound of a hiss just before it happened.

I was beginning to plot a curve, as it were, when I leaned up against a postal storage box on the corner. "Oh, excuse me!" comes this polite voice in my ear.

"No harm done, chum," I answered, and looked around. Nobody near me, nobody at all.

The stuff a leg-man drinks has to be cheap, but I was sure I hadn't gotten any quite that green. I considered it, then moved my hand toward the box. I encountered something solid in the air about a foot over the box, and grabbed. There was a smothered gasp, then silence.

I waited, then said very soft, "Well, Cagliostro, it seems to be your move." No answer. I clamped down on the chunk of breeze and twisted it. "Well?"

"Oh, dear!" comes this same mild little voice. "You seem to have captured me. What shall I do?"

I thought. "We can't stand here playing statues. People would talk. There's a beer joint just around the corner. If I let you go, will you meet me there?"

"Oh, yes, indeed," I'm answered, "anything to get out of this predicament."

"No tricks now," I warned. "Fail to show up and I'll have them search for you with a paint spray gun. That'll put a stop to your fun games."

"Oh, no!" empty air assures me, and I let go.

I had killed a bottle of suds in the joint in question when this mousy little bird shows up. He glanced nervously around, came up to my booth and gulped at me.

"Are you," I asked incredulously, "Cagliostro?"

He gulped again and nodded.

"Well, I'll be a—skip it. Draw up a chair. Beer?"

He fidgeted. "Uh, might I have a little Bourbon whiskey?"

"You know best, Pop." I fingered the waiter. "Joe, bring this gentleman some eight-year-old Kentucky." When Joe got back Caspar Milquetoast took a tumbler, poured four fingers in it, and drank it, swallowing steadily. Then he sighed.

"I feel better," he announced. "My heart, you know."

"Yes, I know," I agreed. "I hated to upset you, but it's in the interest of science."

His face lit up. "You are a student of science, too? In what field, pray tell?"

"Mob psychology," I told him. "I'm a reporter for the *Graphic*."

He seemed upset at once, so I calmed him. "Take it easy. We'll make it off the record for the moment and talk about a story later." He relaxed a little and I continued, "Right now I'm curious on my own account. I figure you had something to do with that gymkhana around the corner on Spring—not to mention finding you holed up in a slice of air. Come clean, professor."

"But I am not a professor," he protests in that same diffident voice, after tucking away another four fingers of corn. "I am a private research student in spectroscopy. My name is Cuthbert Higgins."

"Okay, Cuthbert. Mine's Carter. Call me Cleve. Let's get to it. What is it? Mirrors?"

"Not precisely. It may be hard to explain to a layman. Are you versed in advanced mathematics? The use of tensors, for example?"

"I was doing all right," I said, "up to improper fractions. Do they come after that?"

"I am, uh, afraid so."

"Okay," I told him, "I'll hang on where I can."

"Very well," he agreed, "you are familiar with the gross phenomena associated with seeing. Light strikes an object, is reflected or refracted by it to the eye, where it is interpreted as sight. The only ordinary substance which reflects or refracts so little as to be invisible is air."

"Sure."

"For a number of reasons it is difficult to change the optical characteristics of the human body to the point where it would match air and be invisible. But there remains two possibilities: To bend the light rays around the body is one way. The other is psychological invisibility."

"Huh?" I demanded. "Come again. Do you mean hypnosis?"

"Not at all," he told me. "Invisibility by suggestion is a common phenomenon . . . a stock in trade of stage magicians. They suggest that an object in plain sight is not in plain sight, and surely enough, it is not."

I nodded. "I catch. Thurston used to do that in his levitation stunt. The frame that supports the gal is in plain sight, but the audience never sees it. I never saw it until it was pointed out to me, then I couldn't see why in the hell I hadn't seen it."

Higgins nodded happily. "Exactly. The eye ignores what is actually there and the brain fills in the background. Lots of people have that quality. Good detectives. Pickpockets. I have it myself—that is what got me interested in the problem of invisibility."

"Slow up!" I said. "Don't sit there and tell me that I didn't see you a while ago simply because you are inconspicuous. Dammit, I looked *through* you."

"Not quite," he corrected. "You looked *around* me."

"How?"

"By application of the laws of optics."

"Listen," I said, slightly irked, "I'm not quite as ignorant as I made out. I never heard of any optical laws that would fit."

"It *does*," he conceded, "involve certain advances of my own. The principle is similar to total reflection. I throw a prolate ellipsoid field around my body. Light strikes the screen at any point, runs on the surface of the field for a hundred and eighty degrees, and departs at the antipodal point with its direction and intensity unchanged. In effect, it makes a detour around me."

"It sounds simple," I commented, "but I don't think I could build one."

"It is hard to make it clearer without recourse to higher mathematics," he apologized, "but perhaps I can give a somewhat analogous example with prisms and mirrors. When a ray of light strikes a surface, it may be reflected through twice the angle of incidence or refracted through the angle of refraction, thusly—" and he started to sketch on the menu. "When an optical system is arranged in *this* fashion—" He sketched a sort of daisy chain of mirrors and prisms. "—a beam of light striking the system at any point 'A' and at any angle 'theta,' will be reflected and refracted around the system to point 'A prime,' and exit at angle theta. So you see—"

"Skip it," I cut in. "I can see that it gallops half way around and heads out in the same direction; the rest is over my head. All right, that clears up half the mystery, but how about that reign of terror in the traffic?"

"Oh, *that*." He gives me a silly grin and hauls out a gat as long as my foot.

I don't like that look in his eyes. "Put that thing down!" I yelled.

He does so reluctantly. "I don't see why you should make such a fuss," he protests. "It's not dangerous—not very. It's just a squirt gun."

"Huh?" I looked at it more closely. "Pardon My I.Q., Cuthbert. I begin to see the sketch. What's it got in it?"

His face lit up. "Synthetic essence *mephitis*—skunk juice!"

"Mmm . . ."

"Hmmm!"

"It was a by-product of an attempt to find a synthetic base for perfume," he explained. "No real use, but I had made up quite a supply for experimental purposes—"

"And squirting it on traffic is your idea of a joke."

"Oh, no! For years I have been incensed—as who hasn't?—at the reckless drivers that infest our city. It would never have occurred to me that I might do anything about it myself, had I not heard a less inhibited victim refer to one of these loutish persons as 'stinking'—along with less repeatable things. It brought a whimsical thought to mind—would it not be a capital jest to make dangerous drivers smell physically the way they already smelled spiritually. At first the project seemed impractical; then I recalled the invisibility apparatus which had been gathering dust in my laboratory for ten years."

"What!" I demanded. "You mean to say you've had this gadget for years and have not used it?"

He gave me a big-eyed stare. "Why, certainly. Obviously there was no use for it. In the hands of an irresponsible person it could be the source of much wrong doing."

"But—Hell, you could turn it over to the government."

He shook his head.

"All right, then," I persisted. "You could use it yourself. Think of the things you could do. You could start out by cleaning up that mess down at the City Hall. Sit in on the crooked deals and expose them."

He shook his head again. "I am forced to regard your viewpoint as naive. Good government grows out of the people; it cannot be handed to them."

"Oh, well," I shrugged. "You're probably right. Still, think of the fun you could have—" I was thinking about backstage at the Follies.

But he shook his head again. "Uses for amusement only would almost certainly involve some violation of the right of privacy."

I gave up. "Go on with your story, Cuthbert."

"Having determined to try the jest, I made my preparations. They were simple. A water gun suggested itself as an applicator and a hot water bottle served as a source of supply. Earlier today I sought an outlying intersection and experimented. The results exceeded my fondest hopes—there are at least a dozen drivers who regret having jumped the light.

"Then I came down here where the hunting is better. I was just warming up when you apprehended me."

I stood up. "Cuthbert Higgins," I said, "you are a public benefactor. Long may you squirt!"

He was pleased as a kid. "Would you like to try it?"

"Would I! Half a sec while I phone in my story."

His face fell. "Oh dear!" he moaned. "I had forgotten you were connected with the press."

" 'Chained' is the word, Cuthbert. But don't give it a thought. I'll cover you like a grave."

Dobbs was difficult as usual, but I convinced him, gave my story to a rewrite man, along with the license numbers of the cars I had seen sprayed, and rang off.

Cuthbert's car was a couple of streets away. I wanted to drive, but he managed to convince me that he was sober, in spite of the $6.40 worth of liquor in him, by balancing a pencil by its point. Besides, I really wanted to try the invisibility gadget.

It fit like a knapsack between the shoulders, with a switch on the straps in front. I threw the switch.

It was as dark as the inside of a dog. "Get me out of here, Cuthbert!" I demanded.

He flipped the switch, and came the dawn. "Naturally you were in darkness," he said. "Try these."

"These" were a pair of trick spectacles. "Rectifiers," he explained. "The shield bypasses visible light but not ultra-violet. With these you can see by ultra-violet."

"I get it," I announced, feeling smug. " 'Black light.' I've read about it."

"Not exactly," he said, "but that will do. Try them."

I did. They worked. No color, black-and-white like a movie peep show, but I could see with the shield up.

From then on it was "Tallyho!" and "Yoicks! Yoicks!" More fun than a Legion Convention. We penalized everything from cutting in and out to jaywalking. But a guy had to be doing something actually stupid and dangerous before we court-martialed him.

All but one. We got a horn-tooter behind us at a signal change. One of those lugs who wants the driver ahead to jump the lights so he can hurry on about his all-important business. You've met 'em.

Well, when this item pulled in behind us and started his serenade, I glanced at Cuthbert. "It's a moot point," he said, "but I think there is justification."

I slipped out of the car and sprayed him just as he was leaning out to cuss Cuthbert. So I sprayed the upholstery too, just to teach him not to use naughty words.

But the high point of the day was a motorcycle cop. He had a meek little citizen backed up to the curb and was bawling the bejasus out of him for a little technicality not actually dangerous—failing to signal a right-hand turn on a clear street.

I gave the overgrown ape a liberal dose, not neglecting his pretty uniform and his shiny motorcycle.

The *Graphic* played it big: "STENCH STALKS STREETS; POLICE PUZZLED" and "WAR WAGED ON DANGEROUS DRIVERS." The other papers copied in the later editions—all except the *Tide*. The *Tide* waited to the final, then let forth a blast that would curl your teeth, demanding immediate apprehension of "the lawless terror prowling the city streets." Poor old Cuthbert was made out to be something between Jack the Ripper and Dracula, with a dash of Nero.

When I looked over the list of victims in the *Graphic*, I understood. On it was Felix Harris, owner-publisher of the *Tide*.

Felix Harris arrived in this town riding the rods. He got a job on the *Tide*, married the boss's daughter, and has looked down on the common peepul ever since. He owns a pew in the right church, chairmans all the stuffed-shirt committees, and takes his cut on every racket in town. And he and his fat-headed son are notoriously bad drivers.

But Heaven help the cop silly enough to give one of them a ticket!

I could smell trouble, but saw no way for Cuthbert to be nabbed, if we were cautious. Dobbs kept me on the story; Cuthbert and I spent four colossal days, taking turns driving and squirting the stinkum.

Then I get a call from the jailhouse; Cuthbert is on ice.

They had gotten onto him through me—seems I had been tailed for three days. They had nothing against him but suspicion, but a dick had snooped around his house and had smelled him cooking up a fresh batch of the skunk juice. They nabbed him.

I ducked out to see a lawyer pal of mine. He thought it was a cinch for habeas corpus, but he was mistaken. There wasn't a judge in town who would issue a writ—we knew the squeeze was on. And Cuthbert was booked for everything from malicious mischief to criminal syndicalism. Maximum bail on each offense, total *seventy thousand dollars*!

The paper would go bail for a story, I knew—but not that much.

Cuthbert was unperturbed, though I did my best to explain what a jam he was in. "I know I have a loyal friend in you," he said, talking soft so the turnkey would not hear. "Can you go to my home and get the invisibility apparatus?"

"What?" I almost shouted. Then I lowered my voice in a hurry. "Didn't they grab it?"

"I think not, else they would have questioned me about it."

It was there when I looked for it, right where we always hid it. I locked it into the trunk of my car and started back downtown, thinking that I would have Cuthbert out of clink with its held in less time than it takes to buy a hat. When it suddenly occurs to me that I have no way to use it.

Here was the hitch: If I carried it down to the jail, they would never let me hand it to him. If I wore it in, invisible myself, how would I get to his cell with it? Supposing I managed to take advantage of doors as they were opened to get into the cell blocks, and managed to find his cell—another unlikely point—how would I get out after slipping him the gear? I'd be left in the cell myself. I was already connected with the case; I had a dirty suspicion that they would throw away the key and pipe me fresh air and sunlight on alternate Wednesdays.

I pulled up to the curb.

A half hour later I had a headache and a plan, but it called for an accomplice. The plan, I mean. The headache I could manage alone.

There is a little actress, name o' Dorothy Bardou, with whom I've had many a swell time. There isn't a mean streak in her—however, she would blow up the County Courthouse if it appealed to her imagination. I phoned her, found she was in, told her to stay that way, and drove over.

I brought her up to date and then broke my plan, "You see, Dotty," I told her, trying to make it both reasonable and intriguing, "all you do is wear the shield and follow me. I do all the explaining. When we get to his cell, you slip him the shield, and out he walks, a free man."

"Leaving Dorothy in the Bastille," she adds coldly. "Had you thought of that, Cleve—or didn't it seem to matter?"

"Yes, darling," I said, "but that is the whole point in you doing it instead of me. You aren't connected with the case, they've got no excuse to hold you, they don't dare sweat you, and the whole thing is a mystery. Think of the publicity."

She did not answer right away; I could see the idea had taken hold. I relaxed.

Presently she said, "I'd better dress my smartest for this. The nearer I come to looking Junior League, the better I can put over the part."

❧

We got her fur coat out of hock, which I charged to expense account, and I showed her how to use the gear. It all worked per plan, except that Dorothy sneezed in the elevator going up to the cell blocks and I had to cover with some fast pantomime.

Cuthbert was stuffy about it, but I convinced him that no other caper would work, and he gave in. I left them to work it out.

I had to get the details from Cuthbert later. "She is an intelligent and charming young lady," he opined, "as well as courageous."

"You're cookin' with gas, Cuthbert."

"Assuredly. We had a most interesting conversation during the two hours we allowed for you to establish an alibi. At the end of that time, she took off the pack, permitted me to assume it, and gave vent to the most startling outcry it has ever been my privilege to hear. The turnkey came most immediately. When he found my cubicle occupied by a beautiful young lady, his face was a study in conflicting emotions. He felt unequal to the situation and hurriedly fetched the jailer.

"Miss Bardou gave that worthy no time to think. She demanded to be released at once, and met his request for an explanation by demanding one of him. When the jailer, sweating copiously, opened the door for her, I slipped out in the confusion.

"She was not content to let well enough alone, but demanded to be taken to the Chief of Police at once. Having no choice in the matter of doors, I, perforce, followed along. There were gentlemen of the press there—"

"My work," I stuck in.

"Excellent. She distressed the chief very much by propounding the theory that she had been drugged and kidnaped by his own men."

"Good girl! Did the boys get pictures?"

"In quantity."

We hid Cuthbert, for the time being, with an aunt of mine, since he obviously could not stay at his place nor mine. The *Tide* was still howling for his blood. I wrote an opus for the *Graphic* which suggested, in a nice way of course, that he had been done away with in jail, and that the Dotty incident had been framed up to cover it.

I told Cuthbert to keep indoors, and in particular not to play with his squirt gun as it would queer my "foul play" story. This irked him. He wanted especially to draw a bead on the judge of the traffic court, as I had inadvertently let him in on how the old fraud fixed tickets for the "right" people. Cuthbert's indignation you wouldn't believe. How a man could reach his age and still be that naive I don't see.

He sputtered about "equality before the law" and such matters. I had to calm him down and exact promises.

He didn't keep the promises very well. I have to piece this part of the yarn together as I did not see all of it. It seems he was taking a walk, in the shield of course, which wasn't so bad, but carrying his squirt gun, which was strictly against contract.

He has just crossed the intersection of two boulevards, when a big sedan, doing about sixty, goes through against the signals. It just misses two cars going with the lights, and one of them climbs the curb and crashes into a store window.

This is too much for Cuthbert. He steps off the curb, takes careful aim, and gets the driver of the sedan right in the eye. Then he jumps back, for they almost run him down. He is tripped by the curbstone, and falls over a fireplug, which dislodges the invisibility gear and it falls into the gutter, but he is much too busy to notice.

When he got to his feet he saw that the sedan had climbed the curb and skidded into a terrace a little further down. Filled with remorse, he went down to see if he could help. As he does, four men pile out of the car. One of them is wiping his eyes, two of them are carrying guns, and one is lugging a small child.

"I felt instinctively," Cuthbert tells me later, "that they were malefactors of some sort. So I shouted for them to put up their hands, meanwhile brandishing my water pistol."

I arrived on the scene right after this, in a police squad car. I had been at the station when the call came in and went along to cover it. For it's a kidnaping and a big one—old Felix Harris's grandson and probably the only person in the world he really cares about.

We find a curious scene. One of the kidnappers is down, shot in the leg by Cuthbert with one of their own gats, two of them are wiping their eyes and moaning, and one is very quiet. The kid is sitting on the grass, crying.

When Cuthbert sees us, he crumples up at the knees.

Cuthbert is not only a hero; the charges against him are quietly dropped. The secret of the shield is still safe, as the police car ran over it there in the gutter, and crushed it beyond recognition. The boys are puzzled as to how he can have spread so much skunk juice with the entire town looking for him, and question him not a little before they let him go but he has an answer ready. "I'm naturally inconspicuous," he told them. "Nobody ever notices me. You just didn't see me."

Which was true, as far as it went.

I groaned so much over the destruction of the shield that Cuthbert promised to build me a new one for my birthday. I'm looking forward to it. I've got some plans of my own.

GOLDFISH BOWL

Astounding Science Fiction, March 1942

as by Anson MacDonald

ON THE HORIZON lay the immobile cloud which capped the incredible
waterspouts known as the Pillars of Hawaii.

Captain Blake lowered his binoculars. "There they stand, gentlemen."

In addition to the naval personnel of the watch, the bridge of the
hydrographic survey ship U. S. S. *Mahan* held two civilians; the captain's words were addressed to them. The elder and smaller of the pair
peered intently through a spy-glass he had borrowed from the quartermaster. "I can't make them out," he complained.

"Here—try my glasses, doctor," Blake suggested, passing over his
binoculars. He turned to the officer of the deck and added, "Have the
forward range finder manned, if you please, Mr. Mott." Lieutenant Mott
caught the eye of the bos'n's mate of the watch, listening from a discreet distance, and jerked a thumb upward. The petty officer stepped to
the microphone, piped a shrill stand-by, and the metallic voice of the
loud-speaker filled the ship, drowning out the next words of the captain:

"Raaaaange one! Maaaaaaaan and cast loose!"

"I asked," the captain repeated, "if that was any better."

"I think I see them," Jacobson Graves acknowledged. "Two dark
vertical stripes, from the cloud to the horizon."

"That's it."

The other civilian, Bill Eisenberg, had taken the telescope when
Graves had surrendered it for the binoculars. "I got 'em, too," he announced. "There's nothing wrong with this 'scope, Doc. But they don't
look as big as I had expected," he admitted.

"They are still beyond the horizon," Blake explained. "You see
only the upper segments. But they stand just under eleven thousand feet
from water line to cloud—if they are still running true to form."

Graves looked up quickly. "Why the mental reservation? Haven't
they been?"

Captain Blake shrugged. "Sure. Right on the nose. But they ought not to be there at all—four months ago they did not exist. How do I know what they will be doing today—or tomorrow?"

Graves nodded. "I see your point—and agree with it. Can we estimate their height from the distance?"

"I'll see." Blake stuck his head into the charthouse. "Any reading, Archie?"

"Just a second, captain." The navigator stuck his face against a voice tube and called out, "Range!"

A muffled voice replied, "Range one—no reading."

"Something greater than twenty miles," Blake told Graves cheerfully. "You'll have to wait, doctor."

Lieutenant Mott directed the quartermaster to make three bells; the captain left the bridge, leaving word that he was to be informed when the ship approached the critical limit of three miles from the Pillars. Somewhat reluctantly, Graves and Eisenberg followed him down; they had barely time enough to dress before dining with the captain.

Captain Blake's manners were old-fashioned; he did not permit the conversation to turn to shop talk until the dinner had reached the coffee and cigars stage. "Well, gentlemen," he began, as he lit up, "just what is it you propose to do?"

"Didn't the Navy Department tell you?" Graves asked with a quick look.

"Not much. I have had one letter, directing me to place my ship and command at your disposal for research concerning the Pillars, and a dispatch two days ago telling me to take you aboard this morning. No details."

Graves looked nervously at Eisenberg, then back to the captain. He cleared his throat. "Uh—we propose, captain, to go up the Kanaka column and down the Wahini."

Blake gave him a sharp look, started to speak, reconsidered, and started again. "Doctor—you'll forgive me, I hope; I don't mean to be rude—but that sounds utterly crazy. A fancy way to commit suicide."

"It may be a little dangerous—"

"Hummph!"

"—but we have the means to accomplish it, if, as we believe to be true, the Kanaka column supplies the water which becomes the Wahini column on the return trip." He outlined the method. He and Eisenberg totaled between them nearly twenty-five years of bathysphere experience, eight for Eisenberg, seventeen for himself. They had brought aboard the *Mahan,* at present in an uncouth crate on the fantail, a modified bathysphere. Externally it was a bathysphere with its anchor weights removed; internally it much more nearly resembled some of the complicated barrels in which foolhardy exhibitionists have essayed the spectacular, useless trip over Niagara Falls. It would supply air, stuffy but breathable, for forty-eight hours; it held water and concentrated food for at least that period; there were even rude but adequate sanitary arrangements.

But its principal feature was an anti-shock harness, a glorified corset, a strait jacket, in which a man could hang suspended clear of the walls by means of a network of Gideon cord and steel springs. In it, a man might reasonably hope to survive most violent pummeling. He could perhaps be shot from a cannon, bounced down a hillside, subjected to the sadistic mercy of a baggage smasher, and still survive with bones intact and viscera unruptured.

Blake poked a finger at a line sketch with which Graves had illustrated his description. "You actually intend to try to ascend the Pillars in that?"

Eisenberg replied. "Not him, captain. Me."

Graves reddened. "My damned doctor—"

"*And* your colleagues," Eisenberg added. "It's this way, captain: There's nothing wrong with Doc's nerve, but he has a leaky heart, a pair of submarine ears, and a set of not-so-good arteries. So the Institute has delegated me to kinda watch over him."

"Now look here," Graves protested, "Bill, you're not going to be stuffy about this. I'm an old man; I'll never have another such chance."

"No go," Eisenberg denied. "Captain, I wish to inform you that the Institute vested title of record to that gear we brought aboard in me, just to keep the old war horse from doing anything foolish."

"That's your pidgin," Blake answered testily. "My instructions are to facilitate Dr. Graves' research. Assuming that one or the other of you wish to commit suicide in that steel coffin, how do you propose to enter the Kanaka Pillar?"

"Why, that's your job, captain. You put the sphere into the up column and pick it up again when it comes down the down column."

Blake pursed his lips, then slowly shook his head. "I can't do that."

"Huh? Why not?"

"I will not take my ship closer than three miles to the Pillars. The *Mahan* is a sound ship, but she is not built for speed. She can't make more than twelve knots. Some place inside that circle the surface current which feeds the Kanaka column will exceed twelve knots. I don't care to find out where, by losing my ship.

"There have been an unprecedented number of unreported fishing vessels out of the islands lately. I don't care to have the *Mahan* listed."

"You think they went up the column?"

"I do."

"But, look, captain," suggested Bill Eisenberg, "you wouldn't have to risk the ship. You could launch the sphere from a power boat."

Blake shook his head. "Out of the question," he said grimly. "Even if the ship's boats were built for the job, which they aren't, I will not risk naval personnel. This isn't war."

"I wonder," said Graves softly.

"What's that?"

Eisenberg chuckled. "Doc has a romantic notion that all the odd phenomena turned up in the past few years can be hooked together into one smooth theory with a single, sinister cause—everything from the Pillars to LaGrange's fireballs."

"LaGrange's fireballs? How could there be any connection there? They are simply static electricity, allee samee heat lightning. I know; I've seen 'em."

The scientists were at once attentive, Graves' pique and Eisenberg's amusement alike buried in truth-tropism. "You did? When? Where?"

"Golf course at Hilo. Last March. I was—"

"*That* case! That was one of the disappearance cases!"

"Yes, of course. I'm trying to tell you. I was standing in a sand trap near the thirteenth green, when I happened to look up—" A clear, balmy island day. No clouds, barometer normal, light breeze. Nothing to suggest atmospheric disturbance, no maxima of sunspots, no static on the radio. Without warning a half dozen, or more, giant fireballs— ball "lightning" on a unprecedented scale—floated across the golf course in a sort of skirmish line, a line described by some observers as mathematically even—an assertion denied by others.

A woman player, a tourist from the mainland, screamed and began to run. The flanking ball nearest her left its place in line and danced after her. No one seemed sure that the ball touched her—Blake could not say although he had watched it happen—but when the ball had passed on, there she lay on the grass, dead.

A local medico of somewhat flamboyant reputation insisted that he found evidence in the cadaver of both co-agulation and electrolysis, but the jury that sat on the case followed the coroner's advice in calling it heart failure, a verdict heartily approved by the local chamber of commerce and tourist bureau.

The man who disappeared did not try to run; his fate came to meet him. He was a caddy, a Japanese-Portygee-Kanaka mixed breed, with no known relatives, a fact which should have made it easy to leave his name out of the news reports had not a reporter smelled it out. "He was standing on the green, not more than twenty-five yards away from me," Blake recounted, "when the fireballs approached. One passed on each side of me. My skin itched, and my hair stood up. I could smell ozone. I stood still—"

"That saved you," observed Graves.

"Nuts," said Eisenberg. "Standing in the dry sand of the trap was what saved him."

"Bill, you're a fool," Graves said wearily. "These fireball things perform with intelligent awareness."

Blake checked his account. "Why do you assume that, doctor?"

"Never mind, for the moment, please. Go on with your story."

"Hm-m-m. Well, they passed on by me. The caddy fellow was directly in the course of one of them. I don't believe he saw it—back toward it, you see. It reached him, enveloped him, passed on—but the boy was gone."

Graves nodded. "That checks with the accounts I have seen. Odd that I did not recall your name from the reports."

"I stayed in the background," Blake said shortly. "Don't like reporters."

"Hm-m-m. Anything to add to the reports that did come out? Any errors in them?"

"None that I can recall. Did the reports mention the bag of golf clubs he was carrying?"

"I think not."

"They were found on the beach, six miles away."

Eisenberg sat up. "That's news," he said. "Tell me: Was there anything to suggest how far they had fallen? Were they smashed or broken?"

Blake shook his head. "They weren't even scratched, nor was the beach sand disturbed. But they were—ice-cold."

Graves waited for him to go on; when the captain did not do so he inquired, "What do you make of it?"

"Me? I make nothing of it."

"How do you explain it?"

"I don't. Unclassified electrical phenomena. However, if you want a rough guess, I'll give you one. This fireball is a static field of high potential. It englobes the caddy and charges him, whereupon he bounces away like a pith ball—electrocuted, incidentally. When the charge dissipates, he falls into the sea."

"So? There was a case like it in Kansas, rather too far from the sea."

"The body might simply never have been found."

"They never are. But even so—how do you account for the clubs being deposited so gently? And why were they cold?"

"Dammit, man, *I* don't know! I'm no theoretician; I'm a maritime engineer by profession, an empiricist by disposition. Suppose you tell me."

"All right—but bear in mind that my hypothesis is merely tentative, a basis for investigation. I see in these several phenomena, the Pillars, the giant fireballs, a number of other assorted phenomena which should never have happened, but did—including the curious case of a small mountain peak south of Boulder, Colorado, which had its tip leveled off 'spontaneously'—I see in these things evidence of intelligent direction, a single conscious cause." He shrugged. "Call it the 'X' factor. I'm looking for X."

Eisenberg assumed a look of mock sympathy. "Poor old Doc," he sighed. "Sprung a leak at last."

The other two ignored the crack. Blake inquired, "You are primarily an ichthyologist, aren't you?"

"Yes."

"How did you get started along this line?"

"I don't know. Curiosity, I suppose. My boisterous young friend here would tell you that ichthyology is derived from 'icky.' "

Blake turned to Eisenberg. "But aren't *you* an ichthyologist?"

"Hell, no! I'm an oceanographer specializing in ecology."

"He's quibbling," observed Graves. "Tell Captain Blake about Cleo and Pat."

Eisenberg looked embarrassed. "They're damned nice pets," he said defensively.

Blake looked puzzled; Graves explained. "He kids me, but *his* secret shame is a pair of goldfish. Goldfish! You'll find 'em in the washbasin in his stateroom this minute."

"Scientific interest?" Blake inquired with a dead pan.

"Oh, no! He thinks they are devoted to him."

"They're damned nice pets," Eisenberg insisted. "They don't bark, they don't scratch, they don't make messes. And Cleo does so have expression!"

In spite of his initial resistance to their plans Blake cooperated actively in trying to find a dodge whereby the proposed experiment could be performed without endangering naval personnel or matériel. He liked these two; he understood their curious mixture of selfless recklessness and extreme caution; it matched his own—it was professionalism, as distinguished from economic motivation.

He offered the services of his master diver, an elderly commissioned warrant officer, and his technical crew in checking their gear. "You know," he added, "there is some reason to believe that your bathysphere could make the round trip, aside from the proposition that what goes up must come down. You know of the *VJ-14?*"

"Was that the naval plane lost in the early investigation?"

"Yes." He buzzed for his orderly. "Have my writer bring up the jacket on the *VJ-14,*" he directed.

Attempts to reconnoiter the strange "permanent" cloud and its incredible waterspouts had been made by air soon after its discovery. Little was learned. A plane would penetrate the cloud. Its ignition would fail; out it would glide, unharmed, whereupon the engines would fire again. Back into the cloud—engine failure. The vertical reach of the cloud was greater than the ceiling of any plane.

"The *VJ-14,*" Blake stated, referring occasionally to the file jacket which had been fetched, "made an air reconnaissance of the Pillars themselves on 12 May, attended by the U. S. S. *Pelican.* Besides the pilot and radioman she carried a cinematographer and a chief aerographer. Mm-m-m—only the last two entries seem to be pertinent: 'Changing course. Will fly between the Pillars—*14,*' and '0913—Ship does not respond to controls—*14.*' Telescopic observation from the *Pelican* shows that she made a tight upward spiral around the Kanaka Pillar, about one and a half turns, and was sucked into the column itself. Nothing was seen to fall.

"Incidentally the pilot, Lieutenant—m-m-m-m, yes—Mattson—Lieutenant Mattson was exonerated posthumously by the court of inquiry. Oh, yes, here's the point pertinent to our question: From the log of the *Pelican:* '1709—Picked up wreckage identified as part of *VJ-14.* See additional sheet for itemized description.' We needn't bother with that. Point is, they picked it up four miles from the base of the Wahini Pillar on the side away from the Kanaka. The inference is obvious and your scheme might work. Not that you'd live through it."

"I'll chance it," Eisenberg stated.

"Mm-m-m—yes. But I was going to suggest we send up a dead load, say a crate of eggs packed into a hogshead." The buzzer from the bridge sounded; Captain Blake raised his voice toward the brass funnel of a voice tube in the overhead. "Yes?"

"Eight o'clock, Captain. Eight o'clock lights and galley fires out; prisoners secured."

"Thank you, sir." Blake stood up. "We can get together on the details in the morning."

A fifty-foot motor launch bobbed listlessly astern the *Mahan.* A nine-inch coir line joined it to its mother ship; bound to it at fathom intervals was a telephone line ending in a pair of headphones worn by a signalman seated in the stern sheets of the launch. A pair of flags and a spyglass lay on the thwart beside him; his blouse had crawled up, exposing part of the lurid cover of a copy of *Dynamic Tales,* smuggled along as a precaution against boredom.

Already in the boat were the coxswain, the engineman, the boat officer, Graves, and Eisenberg. With them, forward in the boat, was a breaker of water rations, two fifty-gallon drums of gasoline—and a hogshead. It contained not only a carefully packed crate of eggs but also a jury-rigged smoke-signal device, armed three ways—delayed action set for eight, nine and ten hours; radio relay triggered from the ship; and simple salt-water penetration to complete an electrical circuit. The torpedo gunner in charge of diving hoped that one of them might work and thereby aid in locating the hogshead. He was busy trying to devise more nearly foolproof gear for the bathysphere.

The boat officer signaled ready to the bridge. A megaphoned bellow responded, "Pay her out handsomely!" The boat drifted slowly away from the ship and directly toward the Kanaka Pillar, three miles away.

The Kanaka Pillar loomed above them, still nearly a mile away but loweringly impressive nevertheless. The place where it disappeared in cloud seemed almost overhead, falling toward them. Its five-hundred-foot-thick trunk gleamed purplish-black, more like polished steel than water.

"Try your engine again, coxswain."

"Aye, aye, sir!" The engine coughed, took hold; the engineman eased in the clutch, the screw bit in, and the boat surged forward, taking the strain off the towline. "Slack line, sir."

"Stop your engine." The boat officer turned to his passengers. "What's the trouble, Mr. Eisenberg? Cold feet?"

"No, dammit—seasick. I *hate* a small boat."

"Oh, that's too bad. I'll see if we haven't got a pickle in that chow up forward."

"Thanks, but pickles don't help me. Never mind, I can stand it."

The boat officer shrugged, turned and let his eye travel up the dizzy length of the column. He whistled, something which he had done every time he had looked at it. Eisenberg, made nervous by his nausea, was beginning to find it cause for homicide. "*Whew!* You really intend to try to go up that thing, Mr. Eisenberg?"

"I do!"

The boat officer looked startled at the tone, laughed uneasily, and added, "Well, you'll be worse than seasick, if you ask me."

Nobody had. Graves knew his friend's temperament; he made conversation for the next few minutes.

"Try your engine, coxswain." The petty officer acknowledged, and reported back quickly:

"Starter doesn't work, sir."

"Help the engineman get a line on the flywheel. I'll take the tiller."

The two men cranked the engine over easily, but got no answering cough. "Prime it!" Still no results.

The boat officer abandoned the useless tiller and jumped down into the engine space to lend his muscle to heaving on the cranking line. Over his shoulder he ordered the signalman to notify the ship.

"Launch Three, calling bridge. Launch Three, calling bridge. Bridge—reply! Testing—testing." The signalman slipped a phone off one ear. "Phone's dead, sir."

"Get busy with your flags. Tell 'em to haul us in!" The officer wiped sweat from his face and straightened up. He glanced nervously at the current *slap-slapping* against the boat's side.

Graves touched his arm. "How about the barrel?"

"Put it over the side if you like. I'm busy. Can't you raise them, Sears?"

"I'm trying, sir."

"Come on, Bill," Graves said to Eisenberg. The two of them slipped forward in the boat, threading their way past the engine on the side away from the three men sweating over the flywheel. Graves cut the hogshead loose from its lashings, then the two attempted to get a purchase on the awkward, unhandy object. It and its light load weighed less than two hundred pounds, but it was hard to manage, especially on the uncertain footing of heaving floorboards.

They wrestled it outboard somehow, with one smashed finger for Eisenberg, a badly banged shin for Graves. It splashed heavily, drenching them with sticky salt water, and bobbed astern, carried rapidly toward the Kanaka Pillar by the current which fed it.

"Ship answers, sir!"

"Good! Tell them to haul us in—*carefully*." The boat officer jumped out of the engine space and ran forward, where he checked again the secureness with which the towline was fastened.

Graves tapped him on the shoulder. "Can't we stay here until we see the barrel enter the column?"

"No! Right now you had better pray that that line holds, instead of worrying about the barrel—or we go up the column, too. Sears, has the ship acknowledged?"

"Just now, sir."

"Why a coir line, Mr. Parker?" Eisenberg inquired, his nausea forgotten in the excitement. "I'd rather depend on steel, or even good stout Manila."

"Because coir floats, and the others don't," the officer answered snappishly. "Two miles of line would drag us to the bottom. *Sears!* Tell them to ease the strain. We're shipping water."

"Aye, aye, sir!"

The hogshead took less than four minutes to reach the column, enter it, a fact which Graves ascertained by borrowing the signalman's glass to follow it on the last leg of its trip—which action won him a dirty look from the nervous boat officer. Some minutes later, when the boat was about five hundred yards farther from the Pillar than it had been at nearest approach, the telephone came suddenly to life. The starter of the engine was tested immediately; the engine roared into action.

The trip back was made with engine running to take the strain off the towline—at half speed and with some maneuvering, in order to avoid fouling the screw with the slack bight of the line.

The smoke signal worked—one circuit or another. The plume of smoke was sighted two miles south of the Wahini Pillar, elapsed time from the moment the vessel had entered the Kanaka column just over eight hours.

Bill Eisenberg climbed into the saddle of the exerciser in which he was to receive antibends treatment—thirty minutes of hard work to stir up his circulation while breathing an atmosphere of helium and oxygen, at the end of which time the nitrogen normally dissolved in his blood stream would be largely replaced by helium. The exerciser itself was simply an old bicycle mounted on a stationary platform. Blake looked it over. "You needn't have bothered to bring this," he remarked. "We've a better one aboard. Standard practice for diving operations these days."

"We didn't know that," Graves answered. "Anyhow, this one will do. All set, Bill?"

"I guess so." He glanced over his shoulder to where the steel bulk of the bathysphere lay, uncrated, checked and equipped, ready to be swung outboard by the boat crane. "Got the gasket-sealing compound?"

"Sure. The Iron Maiden is all right. The gunner and I will seal you in. Here's your mask."

Eisenberg accepted the inhaling mask, started to strap it on, checked himself. Graves noticed the look on his face. "What's the trouble, son?"

"Doc . . . uh—"

"Yes?"

"I say—you'll look out for Cleo and Pat, won't you?"

"Why, sure. But they won't need anything in the length of time you'll be gone."

"Um-m-m, no, I suppose not. But you'll look out for 'em?"

"Sure."

"O.K." Eisenberg slipped the inhaler over his face, waved his hand to the gunner waiting by the gas bottles. The gunner eased open the cutoff valves, the gas lines hissed, and Eisenberg began to pedal like a six-day racer.

With thirty minutes to kill, Blake invited Graves to go forward with him for a smoke and a stroll on the fo'c's'le. They had completed about twenty turns when Blake paused by the wildcat, took his cigar from his mouth and remarked, "Do you know, I believe he has a good chance of completing the trip."

"So? I'm glad to hear that."

"Yes, I do, really. The success of the trial with the dead load convinced me. And whether the smoke gear works or not, if that globe comes back down the Wahini Pillar, *I'll find it*."

"I know you will. It was a good idea of yours, to paint it yellow."

"Help us to spot it, all right. I don't think he'll learn anything, however. He won't see a thing through those ports but blue water, from the time he enters the column to the time we pick him up."

"Perhaps so."

"What else *could* he see?"

"I don't know. Whatever it is that *made* those Pillars, perhaps."

Blake dumped the ashes from his cigar carefully over the rail before replying. "Doctor, I don't understand you. To my mind, those Pillars are a natural, even though strange, phenomenon."

"And to me it's equally obvious that they are not 'natural.' They exhibit intelligent interference with the ordinary processes of nature as clearly as if they had a sign saying so hung on them."

"I don't see how you can say that. Obviously, they are not man-made."

"No."

"Then who did make them—if they were made?"

"I don't know."

Blake started to speak, shrugged, and held his tongue. They resumed their stroll. Graves turned aside to chuck his cigarette overboard, glancing outboard as he did so.

He stopped, stared, then called out: "Captain Blake!"

"Eh?" The captain turned and looked where Graves pointed. "Great God! Fireballs!"

"That's what I thought."

"They're some distance away," Blake observed, more to himself than to Graves. He turned decisively. "Bridge!" he shouted. "Bridge! Bridge ahoy!"

"Bridge, aye aye!"

"Mr. Weems—pass the word: 'All hands, below decks.' Dog down all ports. Close all hatches. And close up the bridge itself! Sound the general alarm."

"Aye aye, sir!"

"Move!" Turning to Graves, he added, "Come inside." Graves followed him; the captain stopped to dog down the door by which they entered, himself. Blake pounded up the inner ladders to the bridge, Graves in his train. The ship was filled with whine of the bos'n pipe, the raucous voice of the loud-speaker, the clomp of hurrying feet, and the monotonous, menacing *cling-cling-cling!* of the general alarm.

The watch on the bridge were still struggling with the last of the heavy glass shutters of the bridge when the captain burst into their midst. "I'll take it, Mr. Weems," he snapped. In one continuous motion he moved from one side of the bridge to the other, letting his eye sweep the port side aft, the fo'c's'le, the starboard side aft, and finally rest on the fireballs—distinctly nearer and heading straight for the ship. He cursed. "Your friend did not get the news," he said to Graves. He grasped the crank which could open or close the after starboard shutter of the bridge.

Graves looked past his shoulder, saw what he meant—the after-deck was empty, save for one lonely figure pedaling away on the stationary bicycle. The LaGrange fireballs were closing in.

The shutter stuck, jammed tight, would not open. Blake stopped trying, swung quickly to the loud-speaker control panel, and cut in the whole board without bothering to select the proper circuit. "Eisenberg! *Get below!*"

Eisenberg must have heard his name called, for he turned his head and looked over his shoulder—Graves saw distinctly—just as the fireball reached him. It passed on, and the saddle of the exerciser was empty.

The exerciser was undamaged, they found, when they were able to examine it. The rubber hose to the inhaler mask had been cut smoothly. There was no blood, no marks. Bill Eisenberg was simply gone.

"I'm going up."

"You are in no physical shape to do so, doctor."

"You are in no way responsible, Captain Blake."

"I know that. You may go if you like—after we have searched for your friend's body."

"Search be damned! I'm going up to *look* for him."

"Huh? Eh? How's that?"

"If you are right, he's dead, and there is no point in searching for his body. If I'm right, there is just an outside chance of finding him— up there!" He pointed toward the cloud cap of the Pillars.

Blake looked him over slowly, then turned to the master diver. "Mr. Hargreave, find an inhaler mask for Dr. Graves."

They gave him thirty minutes of conditioning against the caisson disease while Blake looked on with expressionless silence. The ship's company, bluejackets and officers alike, stood back and kept quiet; they walked on eggs when the Old Man had that look.

Exercise completed, the diver crew dressed Graves rapidly and strapped him into the bathysphere with dispatch, in order not to expose him too long to the nitrogen in the air. Just before the escape port was dogged down Graves spoke up. "Captain Blake."

"Yes, doctor?"

"Bill's goldfish—will you look out for them?"

"Certainly, doctor."

"Thanks."

"Not at all. Are you ready?"

"Ready."

Blake stepped forward, stuck an arm through the port of the sphere and shook hands with Graves. "Good luck." He withdrew his arm. "Seal it up."

They lowered it over the side; two motor launches nosed it half a mile in the direction of the Kanaka Pillar where the current was strong enough to carry it along. There they left it and bucked the current back to the ship, were hoisted in.

Blake followed it with his glasses from the bridge. It drifted slowly at first, then with increased speed as it approached the base of the column. It whipped into rapid motion the last few hundred yards; Blake saw a flash of yellow just above the water line, then nothing more.

Eight hours—no plume of smoke. Nine hours, ten hours, nothing. After twenty-four hours of steady patrol in the vicinity of the Wahini Pillar, Blake radioed the Bureau.

Four days of vigilance—Blake knew that the bathysphere's passenger must be dead; whether by suffocation, drowning, implosion, or other means was not important. He so reported and received orders to proceed on duty assigned. The ship's company was called to quarters; Captain Blake read the service for the dead aloud in a harsh voice, dropped over the side some rather wilted hibiscus blooms—all that his steward could produce at the time—and went to the bridge to set his course for Pearl Harbor.

On the way to the bridge he stopped for a moment at his cabin and called to his steward: "You'll find some goldfish in the stateroom occupied by Mr. Eisenberg. Find an appropriate container and place them in my cabin."

"Yes, suh, Cap'n."

When Bill Eisenberg came to his senses he was in a Place.

Sorry, but no other description is suitable; it lacked features. Oh, not entirely, of course—it was not dark where he was, nor was it in a state of vacuum, nor was it cold, nor was it too small for comfort. But it did lack features to such a remarkable extent that he had difficulty in estimating the size of the place. Consider—stereo vision, by which we estimate the size of things *directly,* does not work beyond twenty feet or so. At greater distances we depend on previous knowledge of the true size of familiar objects, usually making our estimates subconsciously— a man *so high* is about *that far* away, and vice versa.

But the Place contained no familiar objects. The ceiling was a considerable distance over his head, too far to touch by jumping. The floor curved up to join the ceiling and thus prevented further lateral progress of more than a dozen paces or so. He would become aware of the obstacle by losing his balance. (He had no reference lines by which to judge the vertical; furthermore, his sense of innate balance was affected by the mistreatment his inner ears had undergone through years of diving. It was easier to sit than to walk, nor was there any reason to walk, after the first futile attempt at exploration.)

When he first woke up he stretched and opened his eyes, looked around. The lack of detail confused him. It was as if he were on the inside of a giant eggshell, illuminated from without by a soft, mellow, slightly amber light. The formless vagueness bothered him; he closed his eyes, shook his head, and opened them again—no better.

He was beginning to remember his last experience before losing consciousness—the fireball swooping down, his frenzied, useless attempt to duck, the "Hold your hats, boys!" thought that flashed through his mind in the long-drawn-out split second before contact. His orderly mind began to look for explanations. Knocked cold, he thought, and my optic nerve paralyzed. Wonder if I'm blind for good.

Anyhow, they ought not to leave him alone like this in his present helpless condition. "Doc!" he shouted. "Doc Graves!"

No answer, no echo—he became aware that there was *no* sound, save for his own voice, none of the random little pounds that fill completely the normal "dead" silence. This place was as silent as the inside of a sack of flour. Were his ears shot, too?

No, he had heard his own voice. At that moment he realized that he was looking at his own hands. Why, there was nothing wrong with his eyes—he could see them plainly!

And the rest of himself, too. He was naked.

It might have been several hours later, it might have been moments, when he reached the conclusion that he was dead. It was the only hypothesis which seemed to cover the facts. A dogmatic agnostic by faith, he had expected no survival after death; he had expected to go out like a light, with a sudden termination of consciousness. However, he had been subjected to a charge of static electricity more than sufficient to kill a man; when he regained awareness, he found himself without all the usual experience which makes up living. Therefore—he was dead. Q.E.D.

To be sure, he seemed to have a body, but he was acquainted with the subjective-objective paradox. He still had memory, the strongest pattern in one's memory is body awareness. This was not his body, but his detailed sensation memory of it. So he reasoned. Probably, he thought, my dream-body will slough away as my memory of the object-body fades.

There was nothing to do, nothing to experience, nothing to distract his mind. He fell asleep at last, thinking that, if this were death, it was damned dull!

He awoke refreshed, but quite hungry and extremely thirsty. The matter of dead, or not-dead, no longer concerned him; he was interested in neither theology nor metaphysics. He was hungry.

Furthermore, he experienced on awakening a phenomenon which destroyed most of the basis for his intellectual belief in his own death—it had never reached the stage of emotional conviction. Present there with him in the Place he found material objects other than himself, objects which could be seen and touched.

And eaten.

Which last was not immediately evident, for they did not look like food. There were two sorts. The first was an amorphous lump of nothing in particular, resembling a grayish cheese in appearance, slightly greasy to the touch, and not appetizing. The second sort was a group of objects of uniform and delightful appearance. They were spheres, a couple of dozen; each one seemed to Bill Eisenberg to be a duplicate of a crystal ball he had once purchased—true Brazilian rock crystal the perfect beauty of which he had not been able to resist; he had bought it and smuggled it home to gloat over in private.

The little spheres were like that in appearance. He touched one. It was smooth as crystal and had the same chaste coolness, but it was soft as jelly. It quivered like jelly, causing the lights within it to dance delightfully, before resuming its perfect roundness.

Pleasant as they were, they did not look like food, whereas the cheesy, soapy lump might be. He broke off a small piece, sniffed it, and tasted it tentatively. It was sour, nauseating, unpleasant. He spat it out, made a wry face, and wished heartily that he could brush his teeth. If that was food, he would have to be much hungrier—

He turned his attention back to the delightful little spheres of crystallike jelly. He balanced them in his palms, savoring their soft, smooth touch. In the heart of each he saw his own reflection, imagined in miniature, made elfin and graceful. He became aware almost for the first time of the serene beauty of the human figure, almost any human figure, when viewed as a composition and not as a mass of colloidal detail.

But thirst became more pressing than narcissist admiration. It occurred to him that the smooth, cool spheres, if held in the mouth, might promote salivation, as pebbles will. He tried it; the sphere he selected struck against his lower teeth as he placed it in his mouth, and his lips and chin were suddenly wet, while drops trickled down his chest. The spheres were water, nothing but water, no cellophane skin, no container of any sort. Water had been delivered to him, neatly packaged, by some esoteric trick of surface tension.

He tried another, handling it more carefully to insure that it was not pricked by his teeth until he had it in his mouth. It worked; his mouth was filled with cool, pure water—too quickly; he choked. But he had caught on to the trick; he drank four of the spheres.

His thirst satisfied, he became interested in the strange trick whereby water became its own container. The spheres were tough; he could not squeeze them into breaking down, nor did smashing them hard against the floor disturb their precarious balance. They bounced like golf balls and came up for more. He managed to pinch the surface of one between thumb and fingernail. It broke down at once, and the water trickled between his fingers—water alone, no skin nor foreign substance. It seemed that a cut alone could disturb the balance of tensions; even wetting had no effect, for he could hold one carefully in his mouth, remove it, and dry it off on his own skin.

He decided that, since his supply was limited, and no more water was in prospect, it would be wise to conserve what he had and experiment no further.

The relief of thirst increased the demands of hunger. He turned his attention again to the other substance and found that he could force himself to chew and swallow. It might not be food, it might even be poison, but it filled his stomach and stayed the pangs. He even felt well fed, once he had cleared but the taste with another sphere of water.

After eating he rearranged his thoughts. He was not dead, or, if he were, the difference between living and being dead was imperceptible, verbal. OK, he was alive. But he was shut up alone. Somebody knew where he was and was aware of him, for he had been supplied with food and drink—mysteriously but cleverly. *Ergo*—he was a prisoner, a word which implies a warden.

Whose prisoner? He had been struck by a LaGrange fireball and had awakened in his cell. It looked, he was forced to admit, as if Doc Graves had been right; the fireballs were intelligently controlled. Furthermore, the person or persons behind them had novel ideas as to how to care for prisoners as well as strange ways of capturing them.

Eisenberg was a brave man, as brave as the ordinary run of the race from which he sprang—a race as foolhardy as Pekingese dogs. He had the high degree of courage so common in the human race, a race capable of conceiving death, yet able to face its probability daily, on the highway, on the obstetrics table, on the battlefield, in the air, in the subway—and to face lightheartedly the certainty of death in the end.

Eisenberg was apprehensive, but not panic-stricken. His situation was decidedly interesting; he was no longer bored. If he were a prisoner, it seemed likely that his captor would come to investigate him presently, perhaps to question him, perhaps to attempt to use him in some fashion. The fact that he had been saved and not killed implied some sort of plans for his future. Very well, he would concentrate on meeting whatever exigency might come with a calm and resourceful mind. In the meantime, there was nothing he could do toward freeing himself; he had satisfied himself of that. This was a prison which would baffle Houdini—smooth continuous walls, no way to get a purchase.

He had thought once that he had a clue to escape; the cell had sanitary arrangements of some sort, for that which his body rejected went elsewhere. But he got no further with that lead; the cage was self-cleaning—and that was that. He could not tell how it was done. It baffled him.

Presently he slept again.

❖

When he awoke, one element only was changed—the food and water had been replenished. The "day" passed without incident, save for his own busy fruitless thoughts.

And the next "day." And the next.

He determined to stay awake long enough to find out how food and water were placed in his cell. He made a colossal effort to do so, using drastic measures to stimulate his body into consciousness. He bit his lips, he bit his tongue. He nipped the lobes of his ears viciously with his nails. He concentrated on difficult mental feats.

Presently he dozed off; when he awoke, the food and water had been replenished.

The waking periods were followed by sleep, renewed hunger and thirst, the satisfying of same, and more sleep. It was after the sixth or seventh sleep that he decided that some sort of a calendar was necessary to his mental health. He had no means of measuring time except by his sleeps; he arbitrarily designated them as days. He had no means of keeping records, save his own body. He made that do. A thumbnail shred, torn off, made a rough tattooing needle. Continued scratching of the same area on his thigh produced a red welt which persisted for a day or two, and could be renewed. Seven welts made a week. The progression of such welts along ten fingers and ten toes gave him the means to measure twenty weeks—which was a much longer period than he anticipated any need to measure.

He had tallied the second set of seven thigh welts on the ring finger of his left hand when the next event occurred to disturb his solitude. When he awoke from the sleep following said tally, he became suddenly and overwhelmingly aware that he was not alone!

There was a human figure sleeping beside him. When he had convinced himself that he was truly wide awake—his dreams were thoroughly populated—he grasped the figure by the shoulder and shook it. "Doc!" he yelled. "Doc! Wake up!"

Graves opened his eyes, focused them, sat up, and put out his hand. "Hi, Bill," he remarked. "I'm damned glad to see you."

"Doc!" He pounded the older man on the back. "Doc! For Criminy sake! You don't know how glad *I* am to see *you*."

"I can guess."

"Look, Doc—where have you been? How did you get here? Did the fireballs snag you, too?"

"One thing at a time, son. Let's have breakfast." There was a double ration of food and water on the "floor" near them. Graves picked up a sphere, nicked it expertly, and drank it without losing a drop. Eisenberg watched him knowingly.

"You've been here for some time."

"That's right."

"Did the fireballs get you the same time they got me?"

"No." He reached for the food. "I came up the Kanaka Pillar."

"What!"

"That's right. Matter of fact, I was looking for you."

"The hell you say!"

"But I do say. It looks as if my wild hypothesis was right; the Pillars and the fireballs are different manifestations of the same cause—X!"

It seemed almost possible to hear the wheels whir in Eisenberg's head. "But, Doc . . . look here, Doc, that means your whole hypothesis was correct. Somebody *did* the whole thing. Somebody has us locked up here now."

"That's right." He munched slowly. He seemed tired, older and thinner than the way Eisenberg remembered him. "Evidence of intelligent control. Always was. No other explanation."

"But *who?*"

"Ah!"

"Some foreign power? Are we up against something utterly new in the way of an attack?"

"Hummph! Do you think the Russians, for instance, would bother to serve us water like *this?*" He held up one of the dainty little spheres.

"Who, then?"

"I wouldn't know. Call 'em Martians—that's a convenient way to think of them."

"Why Martians?"

"No reason. I said that was a convenient way to think of them."

"Convenient how?"

"Convenient because it keeps you from thinking of them as human beings—which they obviously aren't. Nor animals. Something very intelligent, but not animals, because they are smarter than we are. Martians."

"But . . . but—Wait a minute. Why do you assume that your X people aren't human? Why not humans who have a lot of stuff on the ball that we don't have? New scientific advances?"

"That's a fair question," Graves answered, picking his teeth with a forefinger. "I'll give you a fair answer. Because in the present state of the world we know pretty near where all the best minds are and what they are doing. Advances like these couldn't be hidden and would be a long time in developing. X indicates evidence of a half a dozen different lines of development that are clear beyond our ken and which would require years of work by hundreds of researchers, to say the very least. *Ipso facto,* nonhuman science.

"Of course," he continued, "if you want to postulate a mad scientist and a secret laboratory, I can't argue with you. But I'm not writing Sunday supplements."

Bill Eisenberg kept very quiet for some time, while he considered what Graves said in the light of his own experience. "You're right, Doc," he finally admitted. "Shucks—you're usually right when we have an argument. It has to be Martians. Oh, I don't mean inhabitants of Mars; I mean some form of intelligent life from outside this planet."

"Maybe."

"But you just said so!"

"No, I said it was a convenient way to look at it."

"But it has to be, by elimination."

"Elimination is a tricky line of reasoning."

"What else could it be?"

"Mm-m-m. I'm not prepared to say just what I do think—yet. But there are stronger reasons than we have mentioned for concluding that we are up against nonhumans. Psychological reasons."

"What sort?"

"X doesn't treat prisoners in any fashion that arises out of human behavior patterns. Think it over."

They had a lot to talk about; much more than X, even though X was a subject they were bound to return to. Graves gave Bill a simple bald account of how he happened to go up the Pillar—an account which Bill found very moving for what was left out, rather than told. He felt suddenly very humble and unworthy as he looked at his elderly, frail friend.

"Doc, you don't look well."

"I'll do."

"That trip up the Pillar was hard on you. You shouldn't have tried it."

Graves shrugged. "I made out all right." But he had not, and Bill could see that he had not. The old man was "poorly."

They slept and they ate and they talked and they slept again. The routine that Eisenberg had grown used to alone continued, save with company. But Graves grew no stronger.

"Doc, it's up to us to do something about it."

"About what?"

"The whole situation. This thing that has happened to us is an intolerable menace to the whole human race. We don't know what may have happened down below—"

"Why do you say 'down below'?"

"Why, you came up the Pillar."

"Yes, true—but I don't know when or how I was taken out of the bathysphere, nor where they may have taken me. But go ahead. Let's have your idea."

"Well, but—OK—we don't know what may have happened to the rest of the human race. The fireballs may be picking them off one at a time, with no chance to fight back and no way of guessing what has been going on. We have some idea of the answer. It's up to us to escape and warn them. There may be some way of fighting back. It's our duty, the whole future of the human race may depend on it."

Graves was silent so long after Bill had finished his tocsin that Bill began to feel embarrassed, a bit foolish. But when he finally spoke it was to agree. "I think you are right, Bill. I think it quite possible that you are right. Not necessarily, but distinctly possible. And that possibility does place an obligation on us to all mankind. I've known it. I knew it before we got into this mess, but I did not have enough data to justify shouting. 'Wolf!'

"The question is," he went on, "how can we give such a warning—now?"

"We've got to escape!"

"Ah!"

"There *must* be some way."

"Can you suggest one?"

"Maybe. We haven't been able to find any way in or out of this place, but there must be a way—has to be; we were brought in. Furthermore, our rations are put inside every day—somehow. I tried once to stay awake long enough to see how it was done, but I fell asleep—"

"So did I."

"Uh-huh. I'm not surprised. But there are two of us now; we could take turns, watch on and watch off, until something happened."

Graves nodded. "It's worth trying."

Since they had no way of measuring the watches, each kept the vigil until sleepiness became intolerable, then awakened the other. But nothing happened. Their food ran out, was not replaced. They conserved their water balls with care, were finally reduced to one, which was not drunk because each insisted on being noble about it—the other must drink it! But still no manifestation of any sort from their unseen captors.

After an unmeasured and unestimated length of time—but certainly long, almost intolerably long—at a time when Eisenberg was in a light, troubled sleep, he was suddenly awakened by a touch and the sound of his name. He sat up, blinking, disoriented. "Who? What? Wha'sa matter?"

"I must have dozed off," Graves said miserably. "I'm sorry, Bill." Eisenberg looked where Graves pointed. Their food and water had been renewed.

Eisenberg did not suggest a renewal of the experiment. In the first place, it seemed evident that their keepers did not intend for them to learn the combination to their cell and were quite intelligent enough to outmaneuver their necessarily feeble attempts. In the second place, Graves was an obviously sick man; Eisenberg did not have the heart to suggest another long, grueling, half-starved vigil.

But, lacking knowledge of the combination, it appeared impossible to break jail. A naked man is a particularly helpless creature; lacking materials wherewith to fashion tools, he can do little. Eisenberg would have swapped his chances for eternal bliss for a diamond drill, an acetylene torch, or even a rusty, secondhand chisel. Without tools of some sort it was impressed on him that he stood about as much chance of breaking out of his cage as his goldfish, Cleo and Patra, had of chewing their way out of a glass bowl.

"Doc."

"Yes, son."

"We've tackled this the wrong way. We know that X is intelligent; instead of trying to escape, we should be trying to establish communication."

"How?"

"I don't know. But there must be *some* way."

But if there was, he could never conjure it up. Even if he assumed that his captors could see and hear him, how was he to convey intelligence to them by word or gesture? Was it theoretically possible for any nonhuman being, no matter how intelligent, to find a pattern of meaning in human speech symbols, if he encountered them without context, without background, without pictures, without *pointing?* It is certainly true that the human race, working under much more favorable circumstances, has failed almost utterly to learn the languages of the other races of animals.

What should he do to attract their attention, stimulate their interest? Recite the "Gettysburg Address"? Or the multiplication table? Or, if he used gestures, would deaf-and-dumb language mean any more, or any less, to his captors than the sailor's hornpipe?

"Doc."

"What is it, Bill?" Graves was sinking; he rarely initiated a conversation these "days."

"Why are we here? I've had it in the back of my mind that *eventually* they would take us out and do something with us. Try to question us, maybe. But it doesn't look like they meant to."

"No, it doesn't."

"Then why are we here? Why do they take care of us?"

Graves paused quite a long time before answering: "I think that they are expecting us to reproduce."

"What!"

Graves shrugged.

"But that's ridiculous."

"Surely. But would they know it?"

"But they are intelligent."

Graves chuckled, the first time he had done so in many sleeps. "Do you know Roland Young's little verse about the flea:

> " 'A funny creature is the Flea
> You cannot tell the She from He.
> But He can tell—and so can She.'

"After all, the visible differences between men and women are quite superficial and almost negligible—except to men and women!"

Eisenberg found the suggestion repugnant, almost revolting; he struggled against it. "But look, Doc—even a little study would show them that the human race is divided up into sexes. After all, we aren't the first specimens they've studied."

"Maybe they don't study us."

"Huh?"

"Maybe we are just—pets."

Pets! Bill Eisenberg's morale had stood up well in the face of danger and uncertainty. This attack on it was more subtle. Pets! He had thought of Graves and himself as prisoners of war, or, possibly, objects of scientific research. But pets!

"I know how you feel," Graves went on, watching his face. "It's . . . it's *humiliating* from an anthropocentric viewpoint. But I think it may be true. I may as well tell you my own private theory as to the possible nature of X, and the relation of X to the human race. I haven't up to now, as it is almost sheer conjecture, based on very little data. But it does cover the known facts.

"I conceive of the X creatures as being just barely aware of the existence of men, unconcerned by them, and almost completely uninterested in them."

"But they hunt us!"

"Maybe. Or maybe they just pick us up occasionally by accident. A lot of men have dreamed about an impingement of nonhuman intelligences on the human race. Almost without exception the dream has taken one of two forms, invasion and war, or exploration and mutual social intercourse. Both concepts postulate that nonhumans are enough like us either to fight with us or talk to us—treat us as equals, one way or the other.

"I don't believe that X is sufficiently interested in human beings to want to enslave them, or even exterminate them. They may not even study us, even when we come under their notice. They may lack the scientific spirit in the sense of having a monkeylike curiosity about everything that moves. For that matter, how thoroughly do *we* study other life forms? Did you ever ask your goldfish for their views on goldfish poetry or politics? Does a termite think that a woman's place is in the home? Do beavers prefer blondes or brunettes?"

"You are joking."

"No, I'm not. Maybe the life forms I mentioned don't have such involved ideas. My point is: if they did, or do, we'd never guess it. I don't think X conceives of the human race as intelligent."

Bill chewed this for a while, then added: "Where do you think they came from, Doc? Mars, maybe? Or clear out of the Solar System?"

"Not necessarily. Not even probably. It's my guess that they came from the same place we did—*from up out of the slime of this planet.*"

"Really, Doc—"

"I mean it. And don't give me that funny look. I may be sick, but I'm not balmy. *Creation took eight days!*"

"Huh?"

"I'm using biblical language. 'And God blessed them, and God said unto them, Be fruitful and multiply, and replenish the earth, and subdue it: and have dominion over the fish of the sea, and over the fowl of the air, and over every living thing that moveth upon the earth.' And so it came to pass. But nobody mentioned the stratosphere."

"Doc—are you sure you feel all right?"

"Dammit—quit trying to psychoanalyze me! I'll drop the allegory.

What I mean is: We aren't the latest nor the highest stage in evolution. First the oceans were populated. Then lungfish to amphibian, and so on up, until the continents were populated, and, in time, man ruled the surface of the earth—or thought he did. But did evolution stop there? I think not. Consider—from a fish's point of view air is a hard vacuum. From our point of view the upper reaches of the atmosphere, sixty, seventy, maybe a hundred thousand feet up seem like a vacuum and unfit to sustain life. But it's not vacuum. It's thin, yes, but there is matter there and radiant energy. Why not life, intelligent life, highly evolved as it would have to be—but evolved from the same ancestry as ourselves and fish? We wouldn't see it happen; man hasn't been aware, in a scientific sense, that long. When our grand-daddies were swinging in the trees, it had already happened."

Eisenberg took a deep breath. "Just wait a minute, Doc. I'm not disputing the theoretical possibility of your thesis, but it seems to me it is out on direct evidence alone. We've never seen them, had no direct evidence of them. At least, not until lately. And we *should* have seen them."

"Not necessarily. Do ants see men? I doubt it."

"Yes—but, consarn it, a man has better eyes than an ant."

"Better eyes for what? For his own needs. Suppose the X creatures are too high up, or too tenuous, or too fast-moving for us to notice them. Even a thing as big and as solid and as slow as an airplane can go up high enough to pass out of sight, even on a clear day. If X is tenuous and even semitransparent, we never *would* see them—not even as occultations of stars, or shadows against the moon—though as a matter of fact there have been some very strange stories of just that sort of thing."

Eisenberg got up and stomped up and down. "Do you mean to suggest," he demanded, "that creatures so insubstantial they can float in a soft vacuum built the Pillars?"

"Why not? Try explaining how a half-finished, naked embryo like *homo sapiens* built the Empire State Building."

Bill shook his head. "I don't get it."

"You don't try. Where do you think *this* came from?" Graves held up one of the miraculous little water spheres. "My guess is that life on this planet is split three ways, with almost no intercourse between the three. Ocean culture, land culture, and another—call it stratoculture. Maybe a fourth, down under the crust—but we don't know. We know a little about life under the sea, because we are curious. But how much do they know of us? Do a few dozen bathysphere descents constitute an invasion? A fish that sees our bathysphere might go home and take to his bed with a sick headache, but he wouldn't talk about it, and he wouldn't be believed if he did. If a lot of fish see us and swear out affidavits, along comes a fish-psychologist and explains it as mass hallucination.

"No, it takes something at least as large and solid and permanent as the Pillars to have any effect on orthodox conceptions. Casual visitations have no real effect."

Eisenberg let his thoughts simmer for some time before commenting further. When he did, it was half to himself. "I don't believe it. I won't believe it!"

"Believe what?"

"Your theory. Look, Doc—if you are right, don't you see what it means? We're helpless, we're outclassed."

"I don't think they will bother much with human beings. They haven't, up till now."

"But that isn't it. Don't you see? We've had some dignity as a race. We've striven and accomplished things. Even when we failed, we had the tragic satisfaction of knowing that we were, nevertheless, superior and more able than the other animals. We've had faith in the race—we would accomplish great things yet. But if we are just one of the lower animals ourselves, what does our great work amount to? Me, I couldn't go on pretending to be a 'scientist' if I thought I was just a fish, mucking around in the bottom of a pool. My work wouldn't *signify* anything."

"Maybe it doesn't."

"No, maybe it doesn't." Eisenberg got up and paced the constricted area of their prison. "Maybe not. But I won't surrender to it. I *won't!* Maybe you're right. Maybe you're wrong. It doesn't seem to matter very much *where* the X people came from. One way or the other, they are a threat to our own kind. Doc, we've got to get out of here and warn them!"

"How?"

Graves was comatose a large part of the time before he died. Bill maintained an almost continuous watch over him, catching only occasional cat naps. There was little he could do for his friend, even though he did watch over him, but the spirit behind it was comfort to them both.

But he was dozing when Graves called his name. He woke at once, though the sound was a bare whisper. "Yes, Doc?"

"I can't talk much more, son. Thanks for taking care of me."

"Shucks, Doc."

"Don't forget what you're here for. Some day you'll get a break. Be ready for it and don't muff it. People have to be warned."

"I'll do it, Doc. I swear it."

"Good boy." And then, almost inaudibly, "G'night, son."

❖

Eisenberg watched over the body until it was quite cold and had begun to stiffen. Then, exhausted by his long vigil and emotionally drained, he collapsed into a deep sleep. When he woke up the body was gone.

It was hard to maintain his morale, after Graves was gone. It was all very well to resolve to warn the rest of mankind at the first possible chance, but there was the endless monotony to contend with. He had not even the relief from boredom afforded the condemned prisoner— the checking off of limited days. Even his "calendar" was nothing but a counting of his sleeps.

He was not quite sane much of the time, and it was the twice-tragic insanity of intelligence, aware of its own instability. He cycled between periods of elation and periods of extreme depression, in which he would have destroyed himself, had he the means.

During the periods of elation he made great plans for fighting against the X creatures—after he escaped. He was not sure how or when, but, momentarily, he was sure. He would lead the crusade himself; rockets could withstand the dead zone of the Pillars and the cloud; atomic bombs could destroy the dynamic balance of the Pillars. They would harry them and hunt them down; the globe would once again be the kingdom of man, to whom it belonged.

During the bitter periods of relapse he would realize clearly that the puny engineering of mankind would be of no force against the powers and knowledge of the creatures who built the Pillars, who kidnaped himself and Graves in such a casual and mysterious a fashion. They were outclassed. Could codfish plan a sortie against the city of Boston? Would it matter if the chattering monkeys in Guatemala passed a resolution to destroy the navy?

They were outclassed. The human race had reached its highest point—the point at which it began to be aware that it was not the highest race, and the knowledge was death to it, one way or the other—the mere knowledge alone, even as the knowledge was now destroying him, Bill Eisenberg, himself. Eisenberg—*homo piscis*. Poor fish!

His overstrained mind conceived a means by which he might possibly warn his fellow beings. He could not escape as long as his surroundings remained unchanged. That was established and he accepted it; he no longer paced his cage. But certain things *did* leave his cage: left-over food, refuse—and Graves' body. If he died, his own body would be removed, he felt sure. Some, at least, of the things which had gone up the Pillars had come down again—he knew that. Was it not likely that the X creatures disposed of any heavy mass for which they had no further use by dumping it down the Wahini Pillar? He convinced himself that it was so.

Very well, his body would be returned to the surface, eventually. How could he use it to give a message to his fellow men, if it were found? He had no writing materials, nothing but his own body.

But the same make-do means which served him as a calendar gave him a way to write a message. He could make welts on his skin with a shred of thumbnail. If the same spot were irritated over and over again, not permitted to heal, scar tissue would form. By such means he was able to create permanent tattooing.

The letters had to be large; he was limited in space to the fore part of his body; involved argument was impossible. He was limited to a fairly simple warning. If he had been quite right in his mind, perhaps he would have been able to devise a more cleverly worded warning—but then he was not.

In time, he had covered his chest and belly with cicatrix tattooing worthy of a bushman chief. He was thin by then and of an unhealthy color; the welts stood out plainly.

His body was found floating in the Pacific, by Portuguese fishermen who could not read the message, but who turned it into the harbor police of Honolulu. They, in turn, photographed the body, fingerprinted it, and disposed of it. The fingerprints were checked in Washington, and William Eisenberg, scientist, fellow of many distinguished societies, and high type of *homo sapiens,* was officially dead for the second time, with a new mystery attached to his name.

The cumbersome course of official correspondence unwound itself and the record of his reappearance reached the desk of Captain Blake, at a port in the South Atlantic. Photographs of the body were attached to the record, along with a short official letter telling the captain that, in view of his connection with the case, it was being provided for his information and recommendation.

Captain Blake looked at the photographs for the dozenth time. The message told in scar tissue was plain enough: "BEWARE—CREATION TOOK EIGHT DAYS." But what did it mean?

Of one thing he was sure—Eisenberg had not had those scars on his body when he disappeared from the *Mahan*.

The man had lived for a considerable period after he was grabbed up by the fireball—that was certain. And he had learned something. What? The reference to the first chapter of Genesis did not escape him; it was not such as to be useful.

He turned to his desk and resumed making a draft in painful longhand of his report to the bureau. "—the message in scar tissue adds to the mystery, rather than clarifying it. I am now forced to the opinion that the Pillars and the LaGrange fireballs are connected in some way. The patrol around the Pillars should not be relaxed. If new opportunities or methods for investigating the nature of the Pillars should develop, they should be pursued thoroughly. I regret to say that I have nothing of the sort to suggest—"

He got up from his desk and walked to a small aquarium supported by gimbals from the inboard bulkhead, and stirred up the two goldfish therein with a forefinger. Noticing the level of the water, he turned to the pantry door. "Johnson, you've filled this bowl too full again. Pat's trying to jump out again!"

"I'll fix it, captain." The steward came out of the pantry with a small pan. ("Don't know why the Old Man keeps these tarnation fish. He ain't interested in 'em—*that's certain*.") Aloud he added: "That Pat fish don't want to stay in there, captain. Always trying to jump out. And he don't *like* me, captain."

"What's that?" Captain Blake's thoughts had already left the fish; he was worrying over the mystery again.

"I say that fish don't *like* me, captain. Tries to bite my finger every time I clean out the bowl."

"Don't be silly, Johnson."

PIED PIPER

Astonishing Stories, March 1942

as by Lyle Monroe

"THE PRIME MINISTER—and Field Marshal Yler!" Doctor Groot's secretary was obviously excited.

Doctor Groot did not lift his eyes from the laboratory bench. With a gentle, steady grip he held a tiny furry animal while he shaved an area on its thigh.

"So? Have them wait."

"But Doctor, it's the—"

"Are they more important than this?" He reached for a hypodermic needle, loaded and waiting. His little specimen, a fieldmouse, did not resist the needle.

The secretary started to speak, bit her lip, and withdrew.

The statesman endured the wait somewhat better than the soldier. "I don't like this, Excellency," the field marshal grumbled. "Why should we be kept waiting while our host fiddles around among his stinks and bottles? Mind you, I'm not complaining on my own account; I learned to wait when I was a cadèt; but you represent the state."

The Prime Minister twisted around in his chair to face Yler. "Patience, John. What does it matter if we are treated like job-seekers? We must have him to win the war, but does he need us? I doubt it—from his viewpoint. Would you and I be here at all if we were not already beaten?"

The general turned a darker red. "With due respect to you, sir, our armies are not yet beaten."

"True. True," the statesman conceded testily, "but they will be in the end. You told me so."

The soldier muttered to himself.

"What," asked his companion, "did you say?"

"I said I would rather go down in honorable defeat."

"Oh, that! Of course you would. All your training is to fight. My anxiety is to win. That is the difference between politicians and soldiers—we know when to give way in order to win. Resign yourself to it; we must have the services of Doctor Groot in order to win this war!"

The soldier's answer was cut short by the secretary appearing to announce that Doctor Groot could now see them. She led the way; the politician followed; the soldier brought up the rear, still fuming. As they entered Groot's study, the doctor was entering it also, from the laboratory door on the far side.

His visitors saw a vigorous elderly man, a little below middle height, stocky and a bit full about the equator. Live, merry eyes peered out of a face appropriate to an old bull ape. This was surmounted by a pink, hairless dome of startling size. He was dressed in dirty linen pajamas and a rubber apron.

"Sit down," he said, waving them to big leather armchairs and seating himself in one, after pushing several books and assorted oddments to the floor to clear the chair. "I'm sorry to have kept you waiting, but I was up to my eyes in some research that couldn't wait. But I found the answer to the problem."

The field marshal leaned forward eagerly. "You've found the weapon, Doctor?"

"The weapon? What weapon? I've found why field mice have herpies [*sic*]. Odd business—hysteric, just as in humans. I induced a neurosis; they responded by developing herpies. Quite interesting."

The soldier did not conceal his annoyance. "Field mice! Wasting time with such trifles! Man, don't you know there's a war?"

Groot lifted his shoulders a fraction of an inch. "Field mice, or field marshals, who shall say what is important? To me, all life is important, and interesting."

The Prime Minister interrupted suavely, "No doubt you are right, Doctor, but Field Marshal Yler and I are faced with another problem of paramount importance to us. The sound of battle hardly reaches the quiet of your laboratory, but for us who are charged with the public responsibility of prosecuting the war, there is no escaping it. We have come to you because we are at our wit's end and need the help of your genius. Will you give us that help?"

Groot pushed out his lips. "How can I help? You have hundreds of able research men in your laboratories. Why do you think that one old man can help you win a war?"

"I am no expert in these things," replied the politician, "but I know your reputation. Everywhere among our experts and technical men I hear the same thing: 'If only Groot were here, he could do it.' . . . 'Why isn't Doctor Groot called in on this?' They all seemed convinced that you can solve any problem you put your mind to."

"And what do you wish me to do?"

The Prime Minister turned to the soldier. "Tell him, John."

Rapidly Yler sketched out the progress of the war; the statistics of men and materials involved, the factors of supply and distribution, the techniques employed in fighting, the types of weapons; the strategical principles.

"So you see that even though we started practically equal in man-power and technical equipment, because of the enemy's greater reserves of capital goods, the tide has swung against us. Under the law of decrements, each battle leaves us worse off than before; the ratio against us has increased."

Groot considered this, then answered.

"The second differential is even worse, is it not so? The rate of increase of your losses climbs even more rapidly than the losses themselves. And it would seem from your figures that the third differential, the speed with which the rate is increasing spells disaster—you cannot even hold out until winter."

The Field Marshal admitted that such was true. "However," he added, "we have dug in and are holding the strategic situation practically static while we try to decide what to do about it. That is where you come in, Doctor; we need some radically new weapon or technique to change the ratio of losses to our favor, or the end is in sight. I can hold this situation together with very little change for six weeks or so. If you can go into your laboratory and produce some new and powerful weapon of offense in that length of time, you can save the country."

Groot looked at him quizzically, "So? What would you like? An incendiary ray from a portable projector, perhaps? Or how about a bomb that would not cease to explode, but would continue to destroy for days of weeks? Or perhaps you would like a means of disabling their aircraft in midair?"

The soldier nodded eagerly, "That's the idea, Doctor, any of those things. If you can do even one of them, you will be the greatest hero in the history of our country. But can you really give us such weapons?"

Groot nodded casually. "But certainly, any of those things are obvious possibilities. You provide me with the money and help and I can deliver such weapons, or better ones, in fairly short order."

The politician intervened. "Anything you like, Doctor, anything at all. I shall direct the Secretary of the Exchequer to provide you with an unlimited drawing account. Any personnel you require will be ordered to report to you forthwith. Now suppose I leave you two to confer as to the most immediately important work to be done."

He arose and reached for his gloves and hat. "I may say, Doctor, that the reward will be commensurate with your service. Your country will not forget."

Groot motioned him back to his chair. "Don't be hasty, my friend. I did not say I *would* do these things. I said I *could*."

"Do you mean you might not—"

"In fact, I will not."

The field marshal was on his feet at once.

"This is treason," he raged. "Excellency, permit me to arrest him at once. I'll make him produce—or kill him in the process!"

Groot's tones were soft, mild. "Do you really think a man my age fears death? And let me tell you, my friend, a man with your blood pressure should not get into rages—it is quite likely to bring on a thrombosis, and result in your demise."

The politician's years of practice in controlling his temper and concealing his feelings stood him in good stead. He placed a hand on the marshal's shoulder. "Sit down, John, and be quiet. You know as well as I that we can't make Doctor Groot work, if he refuses. To talk of revenge on him is silly." He turned to Groot. "Doctor, when your fellow countrymen are dying to accomplish a particular end, don't you think you owe them some explanation if you refuse to help them in any way you can?"

Groot had watched the little by-play with amusement. He replied courteously, "Certainly, Your Excellency. I will not assist in this mass killing because I see no reason why either side should win. The cultures are similar; the racial stocks are the same in about the same proportions. What difference will it make which side wins?"

"Don't you feel any obligation of patriotism, or loyalty?"

"Only," Groot shrugged, "to the race itself. Not to a particular gang."

"I don't suppose it would do any good to discuss with you the question of which side is morally justified?"

Groot shook his head. "None at all, I'm afraid."

"I thought not. We are realists, you and I." He gathered up his gloves again. "I shall do what I can, Doctor, to protect you from the results of your decision, but political necessities may force my hand. You will understand."

"Stay." Groot stopped him again. "I refused to help you win this war. Suppose I undertook to keep you from losing?"

"But that is the same thing," exploded the field marshal.

The Prime Minister simply raised his brows.

Groot proceeded. "I will *not* help you to win. But if you wish it, I will show you how to stop this war with no victory on either side, provided—" He paused—"provided you agree now to my kind of a peace."

He stopped and waited for the effect of his words. The Prime Minister nodded. "Go ahead. We will at least listen."

"If the war is finished with no victor and no vanquished, if the terms of the peace set up a new government which welds the two countries into one nation, indistinguishable, free, and equal, I shall be satisfied. If you can assure me of that, I will help you—otherwise not."

The politician withdrew to the far end of the room, and stood staring out the window. He traced a triangle with his forefinger on his right cheek, and repeated it, endlessly, his brows furrowed in thought.

The old soldier got up and joined him and expostulated in whispers, "—utopian! . . . impractical! . . . Different languages, different traditions . . ."

The politician left the soldier abruptly and faced the scientist. "I agree to your terms, Doctor. What do you plan to do?"

"First you answer a question for me: why are men willing to fight and die in a war?"

"Why? For their country, for patriotic reasons. Oh, I suppose a few regard it as an adventure."

"No reason is necessary for the men themselves," put in the field marshal, "under compulsory service. They *have* to."

"But even under compulsory service," said Groot, "there must be good morale, a willingness to die fighting, else you would be faced with chronic mutiny. Not so?"

"Mmmm—well, yes. You're right."

"Doctor, why do you think men are willing to die in war?" inquired the Prime Minister.

Groot answered solemnly, "To be willing to die in war has nothing to do with personal self-preservation. To go to war is suicide—for the individual. Men are willing to be killed in war for one reason only—that their tribe may live after them. That is to say, they fight for their children. To a nation without children, war is meaningless, not worth fighting. That is a primary datum of mass psychology!"

"Go on."

"I propose that we kidnap their children!"

"It's an infamous scheme. I will not agree to it."

"It is humane."

"It is contrary to international law."

"Naturally. International law defines the legal ways to kill men. This proposes an illegal way to avoid killing them."

"It violates every rule of civilized warfare!"

"Quiet, John! You'll do as you are told."

Deep behind the enemy's lines in a moderate-sized city, life flowed quietly along. True, there were few men on the streets, and those few usually showed the marks of battle. The motor busses were driven by women; the clerks were women; even the street sweepers and rubbish collectors were women. On a hill at the outskirts of town, there stood a large boarding school, an orphanage for the children of the war dead. Here matriarchy was the natural thing.

It was recess time. The pleasant, gardened grounds swarmed and boiled with young life. Their high young voices were raised in shouts and calls that attend the age-old games of childhood; tag, ball games, and the like.

In her private office, Madame Curan, superintendent, pored over her reports. The voices of the children outside reached her as a wordless, tuneless obligato, which she heard subconsciously and responded to by relaxing the tired wrinkles between her eyes.

She pushed a stack of papers to one side, and pressed a button. The outer office door opened almost at once, and she glanced up to find, not the stenographer she had rung for, but her second-in-command. The woman was plainly excited.

"Madame! Air raid!"

Madame Curan's finger was at once on another button. A siren mourned, and the shouts of the children were snuffed out.

"Are you sure?" she asked her assistant as they hurried out. "I don't understand it. They've never raided schoolhouses before."

Out on the grounds the children had formed into four queues and were being hurried down four covered ramps which led underground. The playground supervisors, young widows, most of them with a too bitter knowledge of war, were urging them on.

Madame Curan glanced up. Settling out of the sky was a huge helicopter of bombing type. It was attended by a dancing swooping swarm of little fighting planes. Three little white clouds appeared suddenly among the planes; then a few seconds later the breeze brought three short dry coughs. The anti-aircraft batteries had opened up.

Her assistant clutched at her arm. "Where are our planes?"

"There they come."

Three tiny specks, higher than the enemy, burst out of the glare of the sun from the southwest. They dropped their *V* formation, shifted into open column, and dived at full throttle, disregarding the convoying fighting planes in their eagerness to reach the big bomber. The bomber jerked away to the east, like a hummingbird shifting to another blossom. But the column followed. It was plain that the leading pilot intended suicide by diving into the bomber.

One of the fast little fighters of the convoy beat him to it. The two planes, defender and convoy, collided a short distance over the helicopter. They seemed to disintegrate noiselessly into disorganized rubbish. The other two planes in the column ducked, one under, one over the floating rubbish, and passed harmlessly beyond the bomber. A few seconds later came the sound of the collision—the noise of a giant tearing a thousand yards of muslin.

The helicopter landed on the playground.

From the control cabin on the port side forward, a small door opened, a light metal ladder swung down, and two men debarked. They approached the women. The younger of the two men addressed them.

"Madame Curan, is it not? I am Lieutenant Bunes. Allow me to present Flight Commander Dansic. I will translate for him."

"It is not necessary. I know your language. What is the meaning of this cowardly attack?"

The commander saluted smartly, and made a slight bow from the waist. "Please, Madame. I am so happy that you speak our language. It will make everything so much simpler. I regret to inform you that you are my prisoner."

"Obviously."

He smiled as if she had been exceptionally witty. "Yes, of course. You, and your assistants. I am forced to require a certain service of you."

"I shall not help you!"

"Please, Madame. It will not be anything you do not wish to do. You will simply continue with your present duties of caring for the children. You see, I must take the children back to my country. You will be needed to care for them."

"I will not! I shall tell them to resist. You cannot possibly control three thousand children."

He shrugged his shoulders. "As you like, Madame. Did I not promise that you would not be required to do anything that [you] do not wish to do?"

While they were talking, a great door opened from the fat body of the aircraft, swung down like a drawbridge, and a dozen men trotted out at double time. They broke into two single file columns and deployed rapidly around the buildings until they completely surrounded the school at fifty-yard intervals. Each carried a large tripod and had a pack slung on his back.

Once at their posts, they set up the tripods, unslung the packs, clamped them hastily on the tripods, and stripped the covers from the packs. Then each one grasped the end of a reel of wire which was slung on his tripod, trotted away in a counter-clockwise direction toward the next adjacent tripod, paying out the wire as he ran. Each man clamped the end of his wire to the tripod of his left-hand neighbor, and ran quickly back to his post.

A non-commissioned officer standing at the helicopter door bellowed, "Report!"

"One!" "Two!" "Three!" "Four!" "Five!" "Six!" "Seven!" "Eight!" "Nine!" "Ten!" "Eleven!" "Twelve!"

The non-commissioned officer brought his right hand down smartly.

Nothing much happened. The trees and buildings beyond the line of tripods shimmered slightly as if seen through a soap bubble film. But a motorcycle squad of civic guards came charging up the boulevard from the city a moment later, and crashed into this iridescent phantom. They piled up in a tangled, sickening heap.

Inside the helicopter a young technician sat before a complex control board, his bony, nervous hands busy with knurled levers, a triple bank of numbered keys, and numerous switches. His eyes followed the responses on the instrument panel back of the control board, noting the readings shown by quivering needles, watched the wandering of the little lighted "bugs" in the zero readers, saw the ready lights flash on.

A green light flashed near the top of the panel. He pulled a screen down in front of his face and threw a switch. A picture rapidly built up on the screen of another pale-faced nervous man. The picture spoke.

"Hi, Jan. Ready on your side?"

"Yeah. I'll give you a stand-by warning."

"I don't like this, Jan."

"Neither do I. I'll run any machine that they put in front of me, but I prefer to take 'em apart first and see what makes 'em tick."

"Right. How the hell do I know what goes on back of that board? I'm just punching keys in the dark. Besides, how do we know those kids won't be hurt? Nobody has ever seen this gadget in operation."

A shadow fell across the board. The technician looked up and saw the non-commissioned officer gesturing to him. He spoke again to the panel.

"Stand by! We're starting the music." He pressed three buttons in rapid succession.

The music reached the four standing on the grounds; Madame Curan, nervous and defiant; her assistant, frightened and looking for guidance; the commander and his aide, urbane and alert. It tinkled in their ears like a child's song. It sang to them of a child's cosmos, a child's heaven, wonderful, free from care.

Dansic smiled at Madame Curan. "Is it not silly to be at war when there is music like that in the world?"

In spite of herself she smiled back.

The music swelled and developed a throbbing almost below the audible range. Then a thin reedy piping was distinguishable. It wove in and out of the melody, embroidered it, and took it over. *Come away,* it said. *Come away with me.* It was piercing, but not painful—it seemed to vibrate in the very brain itself.

The children boiled up out of the underground ramps like so many puppies. They laughed and shouted and ran in circles. They rushed out of the ground and danced towards the helicopter. Up the incline they jostled, pushing and giggling.

The technician took a quick look over his shoulder, and barked, "Here they come!"

He threw a switch, and an empty frame beside the control board, six feet high, suddenly filled with opaque, velvet blackness.

The first of the children skipped up to the frame, jumped into it and disappeared.

Commander Dansic led Madame Curan into the helicopter as the last of the children were entering. She suppressed a scream when she saw what was happening to her charges, and turned furiously at the commander. But he silenced her with a wave of his hand.

"Regard, please."

Following the direction of his pointing finger, she saw, framed in the television panel, a screen similar to the one in which she stood, except that in the picture the children were popping out of a frame of blackness.

"Where are they? What have you done with them?"

"They are in my country—safe."

The last of the staff of the school was persuaded or coerced into passing through the blackness; the helicopter crew followed, two at a time. Finally the commander was left alone, save for the technician, with Madame Curan. He turned to her and bowed.

"And now, Madame, will you come with me and resume your duties to your wards?" He offered her the crook of his right elbow.

She bit her lip, then grasped the profferred [*sic*] arm. They marched steadily into the black.

The technician pulled off his earphones, made some last adjustments, and faced the framed darkness. He entered it with the air of a man about to take a cold shower.

Fifteen seconds later the packs on the circle of tripods blew up in a series of overlapping little pops. Ten seconds after that the helicopter blossomed into a giant mushroom, with a dull *whooo-hooom!* that shook the ground.

The two technicians need not have worried about the safety of the children. Back deep in the territory of their home country, Doctor Groot sprawled in a chair and watched the arrival of one consignment of the children. A small, warm smile lightened his ugly face, induced by the sound of the unearthly music perhaps, or possibly by the sight of so many happy children. The Prime Minister stood near him, too nervous to sit down.

Groot crooked a finger at an elderly gray-haired female in the white uniform of a chief nurse.

"Come here, Elda."

"Yes, Doctor."

"You must see to the music yourself. Reduce the volume now to the least that will keep them quiet, free from tears. Put them to sleep with it tonight. But no music—*this* sort of music—tomorrow, unless absolutely necessary. It is not good for them to be happy as angels too long. They have still to be men and women."

"I understand, Doctor."

"See that they all understand." He turned to the Prime Minister, who pulled at his lip and looked distrait. "What is worrying you, my friend?"

"Well—Are you sure no harm can come to these children?"

"Do you not see?" Groot waved a hand at the frolicsome children, being herded in little groups to the quarters prepared for them.

"Yes—but suppose two of your receiving stations were tuned in the same fashion. What would happen to the children?"

Groot smiled. "You are confusing this with radio. My fault, perhaps. I called it mass-radio when speaking of it. But it is nothing of the sort. It is—how are you in mathematics?"

The Prime Minister made a grimace.

"Very well, then," continued Groot, "I cannot answer you properly. But I can tell you this: Those children were not broadcast like radio waves. They simply stepped through a door. It is as if I took that door"—he pointed to one in the end of the hall—"and twisted this building so that it fitted up against the door." He pointed to another on the other end of the hall. "I have tampered a little, oh, such a very little, with world lines, and pinned a piece of space to another piece of space with which it was not normally in contact." He pointed to the mass-radio receiver present with them in the room. "That is one end of my pin. You understand?"

"Well—not entirely."

Groot nodded. "I did not expect you to. I did not truly explain it. Without the language of tensor calculus it cannot be explained; I can only tell you an allegory."

An orderly trotted up and handed Groot a sheef [*sic*] of reports. Groot glanced at them. "Two more stations and we shall be ready for the shield. Have you wondered how that worked, too?"

The statesman admitted that he had.

"It is the same thing and yet different," said Groot. "This time we lock the door, very softly. The world lines are given a gentle twist and mass will not pass along them. But pshaw! Those are monkey tricks, mere gadgets, complex as they seem to the layman. But the music now—that is another matter. There we tamper with the powers of heaven itself, which is why I am so careful with it."

The Prime Minister was surprised and said so. He had been impressed by the engineering miracles. The use of music he regarded as a harmless crotchet of Groot's.

"Oh, no," said Groot. "No. No indeed. Have you ever thought about music? Why is music? What is it? Can you define it?"

"Why—uh—music is certain rhythmical arrangements of sounds which produce emotional responses—"

Groot held up a hand. "Yes, but what arrangements? And what emotions? And why? Never mind. I have analyzed the matter. And now I hold the secret of Orpheus' lute, the magic of the Pied Piper."

He lowered his voice. "It is a serious matter, friend—a dangerous matter. These other toys will go to the state, but this one secret I keep always to myself—and try to forget."

The orderly hurried up again, and handed him another report. Groot looked at it and passed it over to the Prime Minister.

"Time," he said. "They are all back. We will set the shield."

A few minutes later the lead wires of some thousands of tripods, spaced equally along four hundred and seventy miles of battle front, were joined. Telephonic reports were relayed to GHQ, two switches were thrown, and a shimmering intangible screen separated the opposing armies.

The war was over—*de facto*.

❖

OFFICIAL PRIORITY MESSAGE

FROM: PRIME MINISTER

TO: CHANCELLOR

VIA: NEUTRAL LIAISON

EXCELLENCY, YOU ARE AWARE THAT HOSTILITIES HAVE CEASED BE-
CAUSE OF OUR DEFENSIVE SCREEN. WE HOLD THREE HUNDRED FIFTY-
SEVEN THOUSAND AND TWELVE OF YOUR CHILDREN AS HOSTAGES.
PLEASE SEND OBSERVERS UNDER FLAG OF TRUCE TO ASSURE YOU OF
THEIR WELL-BEING. WE ARE PREPARED TO MAINTAIN STATUS QUO IN-
DEFINITELY. WE ARE READY TO TREAT WITH YOU FOR AN EQUITABLE
PEACE WITHOUT VICTORY TO REPLACE PRESENT DE FACTO ARMISTICE.

SIGNED AND SEALED BY THE

PRIME MINISTER

On the eleventh day of the peace conference, the chancellor asked
for a recapitulation of the points agreed on. The chief clerk complied.

"First consideration: it is agreed that henceforth the two subscrib-
ing nations are one nation. Dependent considerations:—" The clerk
droned on. The two parliaments were to meet together, pending a cen-
sus and a constitutional convention. The currencies were to be joined,
and so forth, and so forth. It was provided that the war orphans in each
territory were to be reared in the land of the former enemy, and that
subsidies were to be provided to encourage marriages which would
mingle the blood of the former two countries.

The armies were to be demobilized and a corps of technical experts were to be trained in the use of the new defensive weapons developed by Doctor Groot.

Doctor Groot himself lolled in a chair near the middle of the horseshoe of desks. When the clerk had concluded, the Prime Minister and
the chancellor looked at Groot.

"Well," he said testily, when the pause had grown, "let's sign it and
go home. The rest is routine."

"Had you considered," observed the chancellor, "that this new nation we have created must have a head, a chief executive?"

"What of it?"

"I cannot be it, nor can it be"—he bowed to the Prime Minister—
"my honorable friend."

"Well! Pick one!"

"We have. There is only one man universally trusted here. He and
no other will do, if this agreement is to be more than a scrap of paper.
And that one is yourself, Doctor."

At this, the field marshal arose at his place at the head of his nation's table of military officials.

"Stop!" he shouted. "There is no need to go further with this fool's play. I shall not stand by while my country is dishonored and prostituted." He clapped his hands together. As if prearranged, two officers left the table, ran to the horseshoe and grasped Groot on each side.

"You are relieved of office, Mr. Prime Minister. I shall conduct the affairs of our country until the war is over. Safe conduct will be provided for the representatives of the enemy. Hostilities will be resumed at once. And that"—he pointed at Dr. Groot and bristled in rage—"that meddler must be removed—completely."

Groot sat quietly, making no attempt to resist his captors. But under the table, his shoe pressed down on a button concealed in the rug. In another room some relays clicked.

And the music started.

Not children's music this time. No, rather the *Ride of the Valkyrie*, the *Marseillaise*. Not these exactly, but rather that quality of each, and of every martial song, that promises men Valhalla after battle.

The field marshal heard it and stopped in his tracks; his fine old head reared up, listening. The two officers grasping Groot heard it, and dropped his arms. One by one almost every one of the uniformed men stood up and quested for the sound. Here and there an occasional frock-coated dignitary joined them. Almost immediately they formed a column of fours and swung away down the great hall, their heels pounding to two-four time.

At the end of the hall a tapestry swung aside and revealed . . . nothingness . . . nothingness, in a large frame.

The column marched into the blackness. When the last man had disappeared, Groot released the pressure from the button. The blackness vanished, leaving an empty frame, with the wall just beyond it. A murmur of expelled breath filled the room.

The Prime Minister turned to Groot and dabbed at his brow with a fine linen handkerchief. "Good God, man, where have you sent them?"

Groot shook his head. "I am sorry. I do not know."

"You don't know?"

"No. You see, I anticipated some trouble, but did not have time to fasten the other end of my 'pin.' "

The Prime Minister was horror-stricken.

"Poor old John," he muttered.

Groot nodded soberly. "Yes. I am sorry I had to do it. Poor old John. He was such a *good* man—I liked him so very much."

FREE MEN

Written 1947; first appeared in
The Worlds of Robert A. Heinlein, 1966

"THAT MAKES THREE provisional presidents so far," the Leader said. "I wonder how many more there are?" He handed the flimsy sheet back to the runner, who placed it in his mouth and chewed it up like gum.

The third man shrugged. "No telling. What worries me—" A mockingbird interrupted. "Doity, doity, doity," he sang. "Terloo, terloo, terloo, purty-purty-purty-purty."

The clearing was suddenly empty.

"As I was saying," came the voice of the third man in a whisper in the Leader's ear, "it ain't how many worries me, but how you tell a de Gaulle from a Laval. See anything?"

"Convoy. Stopped below us." The Leader peered through bushes and down the side of a bluff. The high ground pushed out toward the river here, squeezing the river road between it and the water. The road stretched away to the left, where the valley widened out into farmland, and ran into the outskirts of Barclay ten miles away.

The convoy was directly below them, eight trucks preceded and followed by halftracks. The following halftrack was backing, vortex gun cast loose and ready for trouble. Its commander apparently wanted elbow room against a possible trap.

At the second truck helmeted figures gathered around its rear end, which was jacked up. As the Leader watched he saw one wheel removed.

"Trouble?"

"I think not. Just a breakdown. They'll be gone soon." He wondered what was in the trucks. Food, probably. His mouth watered. A few weeks ago an opportunity like this would have meant generous rations for all, but the conquerors had smartened up.

He put useless thoughts away. "It's not that that worries me, Dad," he added, returning to the subject. "We'll be able to tell quislings from loyal Americans. But how do you tell men from boys?"

"Thinking of Joe Benz?"

"Maybe. I'd give a lot to know how far we can trust Joe. But I could have been thinking of young Morrie."

"You can trust him."

"Certainly. At thirteen he doesn't drink—and he wouldn't crack if they burned his feet off. Same with Cathleen. It's not age or sex— but how can you tell? And you've *got* to be able to tell."

There was a flurry below. Guards had slipped down from the trucks and withdrawn from the road when the convoy had stopped, in accordance with an orderly plan for such emergencies. Now two of them returned to the convoy, hustling between them a figure not in uniform.

The mockingbird set up a frenetic whistling.

"It's the messenger," said the Leader. "The dumb fool! Why didn't he lie quiet? Tell Ted we've seen it."

Dad pursed his lips and whistled: "Keewah, keewah, keewah, terloo."

The other "mockingbird" answered, "Terloo," and shut up.

"We'll need a new post office now," said the Leader. "Take care of it, Dad."

"Okay."

"There's no real answer to the problem," the Leader said. "You can limit size of units, so that one person can't give away too many—but take a colony like ours. It needs to be a dozen or more to work. That means they all have to be dependable, or they all go down together. So each one has a loaded gun at the head of each other one."

Dad grinned, wryly. "Sounds like the United Nations before the Blow Off. Cheer up, Ed. Don't burn your bridges before you cross them."

"I won't. The convoy is ready to roll."

When the convoy had disappeared in the distance, Ed Morgan, the Leader, and his deputy Dad Carter stood up and stretched. The "mockingbird" had announced safety loudly and cheerfully. "Tell Ted to cover us into camp," Morgan ordered.

Dad wheepled and chirruped and received acknowledgment. They started back into the hills. Their route was roundabout and included check points from which they could study their back track and receive reports from Ted. Morgan was not worried about Ted being followed—he was confident that Ted could steal baby 'possums from mama's pouch. But the convoy breakdown might have been a trap—there was no way to tell that all of the soldiers had got back into the trucks. The messenger might have been followed; certainly he had been trapped too easily.

Morgan wondered how much the messenger would spill. He could not spill much about Morgan's own people, for the "post office" rendezvous was all that he knew about them.

❖

The base of Morgan's group was neither better nor worse than average of the several thousand other camps of recalcitrant guerrillas throughout the area that once called itself the United States. The Twenty Minute War had not surprised everyone. The mushrooms which had blossomed over Washington, Detroit, and a score of other places had been shocking but expected—by some.

Morgan had made no grand preparations. He had simply conceived it as a good period in which to stay footloose and not too close to a target area. He had taken squatter's rights in an abandoned mine and had stocked it with tools, food, and other useful items. He had had the simple intention to survive; it was during the weeks after Final Sunday that he discovered that there was no way for a man with foresight to avoid becoming a leader.

Morgan and Dad Carter entered the mine by a new shaft and tunnel which appeared on no map, by a dry rock route which was intended to puzzle even a bloodhound. They crawled through the tunnel, were able to raise their heads when they reached the armory, and stepped out into the common room of the colony, the largest chamber, ten by thirty feet and as high as it was wide.

Their advent surprised no one, else they might not have lived to enter. A microphone concealed in the tunnel had conveyed their shibboleths before them. The room was unoccupied save for a young woman stirring something over a tiny, hooded fire and a girl who sat at a typewriter table mounted in front of a radio. She was wearing earphones and shoved one back and turned to face them as they came in.

"Howdy, Boss!"

"Hi, Margie. What's the good word?" Then to the other, "What's for lunch?"

"Bark soup and a notch in your belt."

"Cathleen, you depress me."

"Well . . . mushrooms fried in rabbit fat, but darn few of them."

"That's better."

"You better tell your boys to be more careful what they bring in. One more rabbit with tularemia and we won't have to worry about what to eat."

"Hard to avoid, Cathy. You must be sure you handle them the way Doc taught you." He turned to the girl. "Jerry in the upper tunnel?"

"Yes."

"Get him down here, will you?"

"Yes, sir." She pulled a sheet out of her typewriter and handed it to him, along with others, then left the room.

Morgan glanced over them. The enemy had abolished soap opera and singing commercials but he could not say that radio had been improved. There was an unnewsy sameness to the propaganda which now came over the air. He checked through while wishing for just one old-fashioned, uncensored newscast.

"Here's an item!" he said suddenly. "Get this, Dad—"

"Read it to me, Ed." Dad's spectacles had been broken on Final Sunday. He could bring down a deer, or a man, at a thousand yards—but he might never read again.

" 'New Center, 28 April—It is with deep regret that Continental Coordinating Authority for World Unification, North American District, announces that the former city of St. Joseph, Missouri, has been subjected to sanitary measures. It is ordered that a memorial plaque setting forth the circumstances be erected on the former site of St. Joseph as soon as radioactivity permits. Despite repeated warnings the former inhabitants of this lamented city encouraged and succored marauding bands of outlaws skulking around the outskirts of their community. It is hoped that the sad fate of St. Joseph will encourage the native authorities of all North American communities to take all necessary steps to suppress treasonable intercourse with the few remaining lawless elements in our continental society.' "

Dad cocked a brow at Morgan. "How many does that make since they took over?"

"Let's see . . . Salinas . . . Colorado Springs . . . uh, six, including St. Joe."

"Son, there weren't more than sixty million Americans left after Final Sunday. If they keep up, we'll be kind of thinned out in a few years."

"I know." Morgan looked troubled. "We've got to work out ways to operate without calling attention to the towns. Too many hostages."

A short, dark man dressed in dirty dungarees entered from a side tunnel, followed by Margie. "You wanted me, boss?"

"Yes, Jerry. I want to get word to McCracken to come in for a meeting. Two hours from now, if he can get here."

"Boss, you're using radio too much. You'll get him shot and us, too."

"I thought that business of bouncing it off the cliff face was foolproof?"

"Well . . . a dodge I can work up, somebody else can figure out. Besides, I've got the chassis unshipped. I was working on it."

"How long to rig it?"

"Oh, half an hour—twenty minutes."

"Do it. This may be the last time we'll use radio, except as utter last resort."

"Okay, boss."

The meeting was in the common room. Morgan called it to order once all were present or accounted for. McCracken arrived just as he had decided to proceed without him. McCracken had a pass for the countryside, being a veterinarian, and held proxy for the colony's underground associates in Barclay.

"The Barclay Free Company, a provisional unit of the United States of America, is now in session," Morgan announced formally. "Does any member have any item to lay before the Company?"

He looked around; there was no response. "How about you?" he challenged Joe Benz. "I heard that you had some things you thought the Company ought to hear."

Benz started to speak, shook his head. "I'll wait."

"Don't wait too long," Morgan said mildly. "Well, I have two points to bring up for discussion—"

"Three," corrected Dr. McCracken. "I'm glad you sent for me." He stepped up to Morgan and handed him a large, much folded piece of paper. Morgan looked it over, refolded it, and put it in his pocket.

"It fits in," he said to McCracken. "What do the folks in town say?"

"They are waiting to hear from you. They'll back you up—so far, anyway."

"All right." Morgan turned back to the group. "First item—we got a message today, passed by hand and about three weeks old, setting up another provisional government. The courier was grabbed right under our noses. Maybe he was a stooge; maybe he was careless—that's neither here nor there at the moment. The message was that the Honorable Albert M. Brockman proclaimed himself provisional President of these United States, under derived authority, and appointed Brigadier General Dewey Fenton commander of armed forces including irregular militia—meaning us—and called on all citizens to unite to throw the Invader out. All formal and proper. So what do we do about it?"

"And who the devil is the Honorable Albert M. Brockman?" asked someone in the rear.

"I've been trying to remember. The message listed government jobs he's held, including some assistant secretary job—I suppose that's the 'derived authority' angle. But I can't place him."

"I recall him," Dr. McCracken said suddenly. "I met him when I was in the Bureau of Animal Husbandry. A career civil servant . . . and a stuffed shirt."

There was a gloomy silence. Ted spoke up. "Then why bother with him?"

The Leader shook his head. "It's not that simple, Ted. We can't assume that he's no good. Napoleon might have been a minor clerk under different circumstances. And the Honorable Mr. Brockman may be a revolutionary genius disguised as a bureaucrat. But that's not the point. We need nationwide unification more than anything. It doesn't matter right now who the titular leader is. The theory of derived authority may be shaky but it may be the only way to get everybody to accept one leadership. Little bands like ours can never win back the country. We've got to have unity—and that's why we can't ignore Brockman."

"The thing that burns me," McCracken said savagely, "is that it need never have happened at all! It could have been prevented."

"No use getting in a sweat about it," Morgan told him. "It's easy to see the government's mistakes now, but just the same I think there was an honest effort to prevent war right up to the last. It takes all nations to keep the peace, but it only takes one to start a war."

"No, no, no—I don't mean that, Captain," McCracken answered. "I don't mean the War could have been prevented. I suppose it could have been—once. But everybody knew that another war could happen, and everybody—*everybody,* I say, knew that if it came, it would start with the blasting of American cities. Every congressman, every senator knew that a war would destroy Washington and leave the country with no government, flopping around like a chicken with its head off. They *knew*—why didn't they *do* something!"

"What could they do? Washington couldn't be protected."

"Do? Why, they could have made plans for their own deaths! They could have slapped through a constitutional amendment calling for an alternate president and alternate congressmen and made it illegal for the alternates to be in target areas—or any scheme to provide for orderly succession in case of disaster. They could have set up secret and protected centers of government to use for storm cellars. They could have planned the same way a father takes out life insurance for his kids. Instead they went stumbling along, fat, dumb, and happy, and let themselves get killed, with no provision to carry out their sworn duties after they were dead. Theory of 'derived authority,' pfui! It's not just disastrous; it's ridiculous! We used to be the greatest country in the world—now look at us!"

"Take it easy, Doc," Morgan suggested. "Hindsight is easier than foresight."

"Hummm! *I* saw it coming. I quit my Washington job and took a country practice, five years ahead of time. Why couldn't a congressman be as bright as I am?"

"Hmmm . . . well—you're right. But we might just as well worry over the Dred Scott Decision. Let's get on with the problem. How about Brockman? Ideas?"

"What do you propose, boss?"

"I'd rather have it come from the floor."

"Oh, quit scraping your foot, boss," urged Ted. "We elected you to lead."

"Okay. I propose to send somebody to backtrack on the message and locate Brockman—smell him out and see what he's got. I'll consult with as many groups as we can reach in this state and across the river, and we'll try to manage unanimous action. I was thinking of sending Dad and Morrie."

Cathleen shook her head. "Even with faked registration cards and travel permits they'd be grabbed for the Reconstruction Battalions. I'll go."

"In a pig's eye," Morgan answered. "You'd be grabbed for something a danged sight worse. It's got to be a man."

"I am afraid Cathleen is right," McCracken commented. "They shipped twelve-year-old boys and old men who could hardly walk for the Detroit project. They don't care how soon the radiation gets them— it's a plan to thin us out."

"Are the cities still that bad?"

"From what I hear, yes. Detroit is still 'hot' and she was one of the first to get it."

"I'm going to go." The voice was high and thin, and rarely heard in conference.

"Now, Mother—" said Dad Carter.

"You keep out of this, Dad. The men and young women would be grabbed, but they won't bother with *me*. All I need is a paper saying I have a permit to rejoin my grandson, or something."

McCracken nodded. "I can supply that."

Morgan paused, then said suddenly, "Mrs. Carter will contact Brockman. It is so ordered. Next order of business," he went on briskly. "You've all seen the news about St. Joe—this is what they posted in Barclay last night." He hauled out and held up the paper McCracken had given him. It was a printed notice, placing the City of Barclay on probation, subject to the ability of "local authorities" to suppress "bands of roving criminals."

There was a stir, but no comment. Most of them had lived in Barclay; all had ties there.

"I guess you're waiting for me," McCracken began. "We held a meeting as soon as this was posted. We weren't all there—it's getting harder to cover up even the smallest gathering—but there was no disagreement. We're behind you but we want you to go a little easy. We suggest that you cut out pulling raids within, oh, say twenty miles of Barclay, and that you stop all killing unless absolutely necessary to avoid capture. It's the killings they get excited about—it was killing of the district director that touched off St. Joe."

Benz sniffed. "So we don't do anything. We just give up—and stay here in the hills and starve."

"Let me finish, Benz. We don't propose to let them scare us out and keep us enslaved forever. But casual raids don't do them any real harm. They're mostly for food for the Underground and for minor retaliations. We've got to conserve our strength and increase it and organize, until we can hit hard enough to make it stick. We won't let you starve. I can do more organizing among the farmers and some animals can be hidden out, unregistered. We can get you meat—some, anyhow. And we'll split our rations with you. They've got us on 1800 calories now, but we can share it. Something can be done through the black market, too. There are ways."

Benz made a contemptuous sound. Morgan looked at him.

"Speak up, Joe. What's on your mind?"

"I will. It's not a plan; it's a disorderly retreat. A year from now we'll be twice as hungry and no further along—and they'll be better dug in and stronger. Where does it get us?"

Morgan shook his head. "You've got it wrong. Even if we hadn't had it forced on us, we would have been moving into this stage anyhow. The Free Companies have got to quit drawing attention to themselves. Once the food problem is solved we've got to build up our strength and weapons. We've got to have organization and weapons—nationwide organization and guns, knives, and hand grenades. We've got to turn this mine into a factory. There are people down in Barclay who can use the stuff we can make here—but we can't risk letting Barclay be blasted in the meantime. Easy does it."

"Ed Morgan, you're kidding yourself and you know it."

"How?"

"'How?' Look, you sold me the idea of staying on the dodge and joining up—"

"You volunteered."

"Okay, I volunteered. It was all because you were so filled with fire and vinegar about how we would throw the enemy back into the ocean. You talked about France and Poland and how the Filipinos kept on fighting after they were occupied. You sold me a bill of goods. But there was something you didn't tell me—"

"Go on."

"There never was an Underground that freed its own country. All of them had to be pulled out of the soup by an invasion from outside. Nobody is going to pull *us* out."

There was silence after this remark. The statement had too much truth in it, but it was truth that no member of the Company could afford to think about. Young Morrie broke it. "Captain?"

"Yes, Morrie." Being a fighting man, Morrie was therefore a citizen and a voter.

"How can Joe be so sure he knows what he's talking about? History doesn't repeat. Anyhow, maybe we will get some help. England, maybe—or even the Russians."

Benz snorted. "Listen to the punk! Look, kid, England was smashed like we were, only worse—and Russia, too. Grow up; quit daydreaming."

The boy looked at him doggedly. "You don't know that. We only know what they chose to tell us. And there aren't enough of them to hold down the whole world, everybody, everywhere. We never managed to lick the Yaquis, or the Moros. And they can't lick us *unless we let them*. I've read some history too."

Benz shrugged. "Okay, okay. Now we can all sing 'My Country 'Tis of Thee' and recite the Scout oath. That ought to make Morrie happy—"

"Take it easy, Joe!"

"We have free speech here, don't we? What I want to know is: How long does this go on? I'm getting tired of competing with coyotes for the privilege of eating jackrabbits. You know I've fought with the best of them. I've gone on the raids. Well, haven't I? Haven't I? You can't call *me* yellow."

"You've been on some raids," Morgan conceded.

"All right. I'd go along indefinitely if I could see some sensible plan. That's why I ask, 'How long does this go on?' When do we move? Next spring? Next year?"

Morgan gestured impatiently. "How do I know? It may be next spring; it may be ten years. The Poles waited three hundred years."

"That tears it," Benz said slowly. "I was hoping you could offer some reasonable plan. Wait and arm ourselves—that's a pretty picture! Homemade hand grenades against atom bombs! Why don't you quit kidding yourselves? We're *licked!*" He hitched at his belt. "The rest of you can do as you please—I'm through."

Morgan shrugged. "If a man won't fight, I can't make him. You're assigned noncombatant duties. Turn in your gun. Report to Cathleen."

"You don't get me, Ed. I'm *through*."

"You don't get *me,* Joe. You don't resign from an Underground."

"There's no risk, I'll leave quietly, and let myself be registered as a straggler. It doesn't mean anything to the rest of you. I'll keep my mouth shut—that goes without saying."

Morgan took a long breath, then answered, "Joe, I've learned by bitter experience not to trust statements set off by 'naturally,' 'of course,' or 'that goes without saying.' "

"Oh, so you don't trust me?"

"As Captain of this Company I can't afford to. Unless you can get the Company to recall me from office, my rulings stand. You're under arrest. Hand over your gun."

Benz glanced around, at blank, unfriendly faces. He reached for his waist. "With your left hand, Joe!"

Instead of complying, Benz drew suddenly, backed away. "Keep clear!" he said shrilly. "I don't want to hurt anybody—but keep clear!"

Morgan was unarmed. There might have been a knife or two in the assembly, but most of them had come directly from the dinner table. It was not their custom to be armed inside the mine.

Young Morrie was armed with a rifle, having come from lookout duty. He did not have room to bring it into play, but Morgan could see that he intended to try. So could Benz.

"Stop it, Morrie!" Morgan assumed obedience and turned instantly to the others. "Let him go. Nobody move. Get going, Joe."

"That's better." Benz backed down the main tunnel, toward the main entrance, weed and drift choked for years. Its unused condition was their principal camouflage, but it could be negotiated.

He backed away into the gloom, still covering them. The tunnel curved; shortly he was concealed by the bend.

Dad Carter went scurrying in the other direction as soon as Benz no longer covered them. He reappeared at once, carrying something. "Heads down!" he shouted, as he passed through them and took out after Benz.

"Dad!" shouted Morgan. But Carter was gone.

Seconds later a concussion tore at their ears and noses.

Morgan picked himself up and brushed at his clothes, saying in annoyed tones, "I never did like explosives in cramped quarters. Cleve—Art. Go check on it. Move!"

"Right, boss!" They were gone.

"The rest of you get ready to carry out withdrawal plan—full plan, with provisions and supplies. Jerry, don't disconnect either the receiver or the line-of-sight till I give the word. Margie will help you. Cathleen, get ready to serve anything that can't be carried. We'll have one big meal. 'The condemned ate hearty.' "

"Just a moment, Captain." McCracken touched his sleeve. "I had better get a message into Barclay."

"Soon as the boys report. You better get back into town."

"I wonder. Benz knows me. I think I'm here to stay."

"Hm . . . well, you know best. How about your family?"

McCracken shrugged. "They can't be worse off than they would be if I'm picked up. I'd like to have them warned and then arrangements made for them to rejoin me if possible."

"We'll do it. You'll have to give me a new contact."

"Planned for. This message will go through and my number two man will step into my shoes. The name is Hobart—runs a feed store on Pelham Street."

Morgan nodded. "Should have known you had it worked out. Well, what we don't know—" He was interrupted by Cleve, reporting.

"He got away, Boss."

"Why didn't you go after him?"

"Half the roof came down when Dad chucked the grenade. Tunnel's choked with rock. Found a place where I could see but couldn't crawl through. He's not in the tunnel."

"How about Dad?"

"He's all right. Got clipped on the head with a splinter but not really hurt."

Morgan stopped two of the women hurrying past, intent on preparations for withdrawal. "Here—Jean, and you, Mrs. Bowen. Go take care of Dad Carter and tell Art to get back here fast. Shake a leg!"

When Art reported Morgan said, "You and Cleve go out and find Benz. Assume that he is heading for Barclay. Stop him and bring him in if you can. Otherwise kill him. Art is in charge. Get going." He turned to McCracken. "Now for a message." He fumbled in his pocket for paper, found the poster notice that McCracken had given him, tore off a piece, and started to write. He showed it to McCracken. "How's that?" he asked.

The message warned Hobart of Benz and asked him to try to head him off. It did not tell him that the Barclay Free Company was moving but did designate the "post office" through which next contact would be expected—the men's rest room of the bus station.

"Better cut out the post office," McCracken advised. "Hobart knows it and we may contact him half a dozen other ways. But I'd like to ask him to get my family out of sight. Just tell him that we are sorry to hear that Aunt Dinah is dead."

"Is that enough?"

"Yes."

"Okay." Morgan made the changes, then called, "Margie! Put this in code and tell Jerry to get it out fast. Tell him it's the strike-out edition. He can knock down his sets as soon as it's out."

"Okay, boss." Margie had no knowledge of cryptography. Instead she had command of jive talk, adolescent slang, and high school double-talk which would be meaningless to any but another American bobby-soxer. At the other end a fifteen-year-old interpreted her butchered English by methods which impressed her foster parents as being telepathy—but it worked.

The fifteen-year-old could be trusted. Her entire family, save herself, had been in Los Angeles on Final Sunday.

Art and Cleve had no trouble picking up Benz's trail. His tracks were on the tailings spilling down from the main entrance to the mine. The earth and rock had been undisturbed since the last heavy rain; Benz's flight left clear traces.

But the trail was cold by more than twenty minutes; they had left the mine by the secret entrance a quarter of a mile from where Benz had made his exit.

Art picked it up where Benz had left the tailings and followed it through brush with the woodsmanship of the Eagle Scout he had been. From the careless signs he left behind Benz was evidently in a hurry and heading by the shortest route for the highway. The two followed him as fast as they could cover ground, discarding caution for speed.

They checked just before entering the highway. "See anything?" asked Cleve.

"No."

"Which way would he go?"

"The Old Man said to head him off from Barclay."

"Yeah, but suppose he headed south instead? He used to work in Wickamton. He might head that way."

"The Boss said to cover Barclay. Let's go."

They had to cache their guns; from here on it would be their wits and their knives. An armed American on a highway would be as conspicuous as a nudist at a garden party.

Their object now was speed; they must catch up with him, or get ahead of him and waylay him.

Nine miles and two and a half hours later—one hundred and fifty minutes of dog trot, with time lost lying in the roadside brush when convoys thundered past—they were in the outskirts of Barclay. Around a bend, out of sight, was the roadblock of the Invaders' check station. The point was a bottleneck; Benz must come this way if he were heading for Barclay.

"Is he ahead or behind us?" asked Cleve, peering out through bushes.

"Behind, unless he was picked up by a convoy—or sprouted wings. We'll give him an hour."

A horse-drawn hayrack lumbered up the road. Cleve studied it. Americans were permitted no power vehicles except under supervision, but this farmer and his load could go into town with only routine check at the road block. "Maybe we ought to hide in that and look for him in town."

"And get a bayonet in your ribs? Don't be silly."

"Okay. Don't blow your top." Cleve continued to watch the rig. "Hey," he said presently. "Get a load of that!"

"That" was a figure which dropped from the tail of the wagon as it started around the bend, rolled to the ditch on the far side, and slithered out of sight.

"That was Joe!"

"Are you sure?"

"Sure! Here we go."

"How?" Art objected. "Take it easy. Follow me." They faded back two hundred yards, to where they could cross the road on hands and knees through a drainage pipe. Then they worked up the other side to where Benz had disappeared in weeds.

They found the place where he had been; grass and weeds were still straightening up. The route he must have taken was evident—down toward the river bank, then upstream to the city. There were drops of blood. "Dad must have missed stopping him by a gnat's whisker," Cleve commented.

"Bad job he didn't."

"Another thing—he said he was going to give himself up. I don't think he is, or he would have stayed with the wagon and turned himself in at the check station. He's heading for some hideout. Who does he know in Barclay?"

"I don't know. We'd better get going."

"Wait a minute. If he touches off an alarm, they'll shoot him for us. If he gets by the 'eyes,' we've lost him and we'll have to pick him up inside. Either way, we don't gain anything by blundering ahead. We've got to go in by the chute."

Like all cities the Invader had consolidated, Barclay was girdled by electric-eye circuits. The enemy had trimmed the town to fit, dynamiting and burning where necessary to achieve unbroken sequence of automatic sentries. But the "chute"—an abandoned and forgotten aqueduct—passed under the alarms. Art knew how to use it; he had been in town twice since Final Sunday.

They worked back up the highway, crossed over, and took to the hills. Thirty minutes later they were on the streets of Barclay, reasonably safe as long as they were quick to step off the sidewalk for the occasional Invader.

The first "post office," a clothesline near their exit, told them nothing—the line was bare. They went to the bus station. Cleve studied the notices posted for inhabitants while Art went into the men's rest room. On the wall, defaced by scrawlings of every sort, mostly vulgar, he found what he sought: "Killroy was here." The misspelling of Kilroy was the clue—exactly eighteen inches below it and six to the right was an address: "1745 Spruce—ask for Mabel."

He read it as 2856 Pine—one block beyond Spruce. Art passed the address to Cleve, then they set out separately, hurrying to beat the curfew but proceeding with caution—at least one of them must get through. They met in the backyard of the translated address. Art knocked on the kitchen door. It was opened a crack by a middle-aged man who did not seem glad to see them. "Well?"

"We're looking for Mabel."

"Nobody here by that name."

"Sorry," said Art. "We must have made a mistake." He shivered. "Chilly out," he remarked. "The nights are getting longer."

"They'll get shorter by and by," the man answered.

"We've got to think so, anyhow," Art countered.

"Come in," the man said. "The patrol may see you." He opened the door and stepped aside. "My name's Hobart. What's your business?"

"We're looking for a man named Benz. He may have sneaked into town this afternoon and found someplace to—"

"Yes, yes," Hobart said impatiently. "He got in about an hour ago and he's holed up with a character named Moyland." As he spoke he removed a half loaf of bread from a cupboard, cut four slices, and added cold sausage, producing two sandwiches. He did not ask if they were hungry; he simply handed them to Art and Cleve.

"Thanks, pal. So he's holed up. Haven't you done anything about it? He has got to be shut up at once or he'll spill his guts."

"We've got a tap in on the telephone line. We had to wait for dark. You can't expect me to sacrifice good boys just to shut his mouth unless it's absolutely necessary."

"Well, it's dark now, and we'll be the boys you mentioned. You can call yours off."

"Okay." Hobart started pulling on shoes.

"No need for you to stick your neck out," Art told him. "Just tell us where this Moyland lives."

"And get your throat cut, too. I'll take you."

"What sort of a guy is this Moyland? Is he safe?"

"You can't prove it by me. He's a black market broker, but that doesn't prove anything. He's not part of the organization but we haven't anything against him."

Hobart took them over his back fence, across a dark side street, through a playground, where they lay for several minutes under bushes because of a false alarm, then through many more backyards, back alleys, and dark byways. The man seemed to have a nose for the enemy; there were no more alarms. At last he brought them through a cellar door into a private home. They went upstairs and through a room where a woman was nursing a baby. She looked up, but otherwise ignored them. They ended up in a dark attic. "Hi, Jim," Hobart called out softly. "What's new?"

The man addressed lay propped on his elbows, peering out into the night through opera glasses held to slots of a ventilating louvre. He rolled over and lowered the glasses, pushing one of a pair of earphones from his head as he did so. "Hello, Chief. Nothing much. Benz is getting drunk, it looks like."

"I'd like to know where Moyland gets it," Hobart said. "Has he telephoned?"

"Would I be doing nothing if he had? A couple of calls came in, but they didn't amount to anything, so I let him talk."

"How do you know they didn't amount to anything?"

Jim shrugged, turned back to the louvre. "Moyland just pulled down the shade," he announced.

Art turned to Hobart. "We can't wait. We're going in.

Benz arrived at Moyland's house in bad condition. The wound in his shoulder, caused by Carter's grenade, was bleeding. He had pushed a handkerchief up against it as a compress, but his activity started the blood again; he was shaking for fear his condition would attract attention before he could get under cover.

Moyland answered the door. "Is that you, Zack?" Benz demanded, shrinking back as he spoke.

"Yes. Who is it?"

"It's me—Joe Benz. Let me in, Zack—quick!"

Moyland seemed about to close the door, then suddenly opened it. "Get inside." When the door was bolted, he demanded, "Now—what's your trouble? Why come to me?"

"I had to go someplace, Zack. I had to get off the street. They'd pick me up."

Moyland studied him. "You're not registered. Why not?"

Benz did not answer. Moyland waited, then went on, "You know what I can get for harboring a fugitive. You're in the Underground—aren't you?"

"Oh, no, Zack! I wouldn't do that to you. I'm just a—a straggler. I gotta get registered, Zack."

"That's blood on your coat. How?"

"Uh . . . just an accident. Maybe you could let me have clean rags and some iodine."

Moyland stared at him, his bland face expressionless, then smiled. "You've got no troubles we can't fix. Sit down." He stepped to a cabinet and took out a bottle of bourbon, poured three fingers in a water glass, and handed it to Benz. "Work on that and I'll fix you up."

He returned with some torn toweling and a bottle. "Sit here with your back to the window, and open your shirt. Have another drink. You'll need it before I'm through."

Benz glanced nervously at the window. "Why don't you draw the shade?"

"It would attract attention. Honest people leave their shades up these days. Hold still. This is going to hurt."

Three drinks later Benz was feeling better. Moyland seemed willing to sit and drink with him and to soothe his nerves. "You did well to come in," Moyland told him. "There's no sense hiding like a scared rabbit. It's just butting your head against a stone wall. Stupid."

Benz nodded. "That's what I told them."

"Told who?"

"Hunh? Oh, nobody. Just some guys I was talking to. Tramps."

Moyland poured him another drink. "As a matter of fact you *were* in the Underground."

"Me? Don't be silly, Zack."

"Look, Joe, you don't have to kid me. I'm your friend. Even if you did tell me it wouldn't matter. In the first place, I wouldn't have any proof. In the second place, I'm sympathetic to the Underground—any American is. I just think they're wrong-headed and foolish. Otherwise I'd join 'em myself."

"They're foolish all right! You can say that again."

"So you *were* in it?"

"Huh? You're trying to trap me. I gave my word of honor—"

"Oh, relax!" Moyland said hastily. "Forget it. I didn't hear anything; I can't tell anything. Hear no evil, see no evil—that's me." He changed the subject.

The level of the bottle dropped while Moyland explained current events as he saw them. "It's a shame we had to take such a shellacking to learn our lesson but the fact of the matter is, we were standing in the way of the natural logic of progress. There was a time back in '45 when we could have pulled the same stunt ourselves, only we weren't bright enough to do it. World organization, world government. We stood in the way, so we got smeared. It had to come. A smart man can see that."

Benz was bleary but he did not find this comment easy to take. "Look, Zack—you don't mean you *like* what happened to us?"

"Like it? Of course not. But it was necessary. You don't have to like having a tooth pulled—but it has to be done. Anyhow," he went on, "it's not all bad. The big cities were economically unsound anyway. We should have blown them up ourselves. Slum clearance, you might call it."

Benz banged his empty glass down. "Maybe so—but they made slaves out of us!"

"Take it easy, Joe," Moyland said, filling his glass, "you're talking abstractions. The cop on the corner could push you around whenever he wanted to. Is that freedom? Does it matter whether the cop talks with an Irish accent or some other accent? No, chum, there's a lot of guff talked about freedom. No man is free. There is no such thing as freedom. There are only various privileges. Free speech—we're talking freely now, aren't we? After all, you don't want to get up on a platform and shoot off your face. Free press? When did *you* ever own a newspaper? Don't be a chump. Now that you've shown sense and come in, you are going to find that things aren't so very different. A little more orderly and no more fear of war, that's all. Girls make love just like they used to, the smart guys get along, and the suckers still get the short end of the deal."

Benz nodded. "You're right, Zack. I've been a fool."

"I'm glad you see it. Now take those wild men you were with. What freedom have they got? Freedom to starve, freedom to sleep on the cold ground, freedom to be hunted."

"That was it," Benz agreed. "Did you ever sleep in a mine, Zack? Cold. That ain't half of it. Damp, too."

"I can imagine," Moyland agreed. "The Capehart Lode always was wet."

"It wasn't the Capehart; it was the Harkn—" He caught himself and looked puzzled.

"The Harkness, eh? That's the headquarters?"

"I didn't say that! You're putting words in my mouth! You—"

"Calm yourself, Joe. Forget it." Moyland got up and drew down the shade. "You didn't say anything."

"Of course I didn't." Benz stared at his glass. "Say, Zack, where do I sleep? I don't feel good."

"You'll have a nice place to sleep any minute now."

"Huh? Well, show me. I gotta fold up."

"Any minute. You've got to check in first."

"Huh? Oh, I can't do that tonight, Zack. I'm in no shape."

"I'm afraid you'll have to. See me pull that shade down? They'll be along any moment."

Benz stood up, swaying a little. "You framed me!" he yelled, and lunged at his host.

Moyland sidestepped, put a hand on his shoulder and pushed him down into the chair. "Sit down, sucker," he said pleasantly. "You don't expect me to get A-bombed just for you and your pals, do you?" Benz shook his head, then began to sob.

Hobart escorted them out of the house, saying to Art as they left, "If you get back, tell McCracken that Aunt Dinah is resting peacefully."

"Okay."

"Give us two minutes, then go in. Good luck."

Cleve took the outside; Art went in. The back door was locked, but the upper panel was glass. He broke it with the hilt of his knife, reached in and unbolted the door. He was inside when Moyland showed up to investigate the noise.

Art kicked him in the belly, then let him have the point in the neck as he went down. Art stopped just long enough to insure that Moyland would stay dead, then went looking for the room where Benz had been when the shade was drawn.

He found Benz in it. The man blinked his eyes and tried to focus them, as if he found it impossible to believe what he saw. "Art!" he got out at last. "Jeez, boy! Am I glad to see you! Let's get out of here—this place is 'hot.' "

Art advanced, knife out.

Benz looked amazed. "Hey, Art! Art! You're making a mistake. Art. You can't do this—" Art let him have the first one in the soft tissues under the breast bone, then cut his throat to be sure. After that he got out quickly.

Thirty-five minutes later he was emerging from the country end of the chute. His throat was burning from exertion and his left arm was useless—he could not tell whether it was broken or simply wounded.

Cleve lay dead in the alley behind Moyland's house, having done a good job of covering Art's rear.

❖

It took Art all night and part of the next morning to get back near the mine. He had to go through the hills the entire way; the highway was, he judged, too warm at the moment.

He did not expect that the Company would still be there. He was reasonably sure that Morgan would have carried out the evacuation pending certain evidence that Benz's mouth had been shut. He hurried.

But he did not expect what he did find—a helicopter hovering over the neighborhood of the mine.

He stopped to consider the matter. If Morgan had got them out safely, he knew where to rejoin. If they were still inside, he had to figure out some way to help them. The futility of his position depressed him—one man, with a knife and a bad arm, against a helicopter.

Somewhere a bluejay screamed and cursed. Without much hope he chirped his own identification. The bluejay shut up and a mockingbird answered him—Ted.

Art signaled that he would wait where he was. He considered himself well hidden; he expected to have to signal again when Ted got closer, but he underestimated Ted's ability. A hand was laid on his shoulder.

He rolled over, knife out, and hurt his shoulder as he did so. "Ted! Man, do you look good to me!"

"Same here. Did you get him?"

"Benz? Yes, but maybe not in time. Where's the gang?"

"A quarter mile north of back door. We're pinned down. Where's Cleve?"

"Cleve's not coming back. What do you mean 'pinned down'?"

"That damned 'copter can see right down the draw we're in. Dad's got 'em under an overhang and they're safe enough for the moment, but we can't move."

"What do you mean 'Dad's got 'em'?" demanded Art. "Where's the Boss?"

"He ain't in such good shape, Art. Got a machine gun slug in the ribs. We had a dust-up. Cathleen's dead."

"The hell you say!"

"That's right. Margie and Maw Carter have got her baby. But that's one reason why we're pinned down—the Boss and the kid, I mean."

A mockingbird's call sounded far away. "There's Dad," Ted announced. "We got to get back."

"Can we?"

"Sure. Just keep behind me. I'll watch out that I don't get too far ahead."

Art followed Ted in, by a circuitous and, at one point, almost perpendicular route. He found the Company huddled under a shelf of rock which had been undercut by a stream, now dry. Against the wall Morgan was on his back, with Dad Carter and Dr. McCracken squatting beside him. Art went up and made his report.

Morgan nodded, his face gray with pain. His shirt had been cut away; bandaging was wrapped around his ribs, covering a thick pad. "You did well, Art. Too bad about Cleve. Ted, we're getting out of here and you're going first, because you're taking the kid."

"The baby? How—"

"Doc'll dope it so that it won't let out a peep. Then you strap it to your back, papoose fashion."

Ted thought about it. "No, to my front. There's some knee-and-shoulder work on the best way out."

"Okay. It's your job."

"How do *you* get out, boss?"

"Don't be silly."

"Look here, boss, if you think we're going to walk off and leave you, you've got another—"

"Shut up and scram!" The exertion hurt Morgan; he coughed and wiped his mouth.

"Yes, sir." Ted and Art backed away.

"Now, Ed—" said Carter.

"You shut up, too. You still sure you don't want to be Captain?"

"You know better than that, Ed. They took things from me while I was your deppity, but they wouldn't have me for Captain."

"That puts it up to you, Doc."

McCracken looked troubled. "They don't know me that well, Captain."

"They'll take you. People have an instinct for such things."

"Anyhow, if I am Captain, I won't agree to your plan of staying here by yourself. We'll stay till dark and carry you out."

"And get picked up by an infrared spotter, like sitting ducks? That's supposing they let you alone until sundown—that other 'copter will be back with more troops before long."

"I don't think they'd let me walk off on you."

"It's up to you to *make* them. Oh, I appreciate your kindly thoughts, Doc, but you'll think differently as soon as you're Captain. You'll know you have to cut your losses."

McCracken did not answer. Morgan turned his head to Carter. "Gather them around, Dad."

They crowded in, shoulder to shoulder. Morgan looked from one troubled face to another and smiled. "The Barclay Free Company, a provisional unit of the United States of America, is now in session," he announced, his voice suddenly firm. "I'm resigning the captaincy for reasons of physical disability. Any nominations?"

The silence was disturbed only by calls of birds, the sounds of insects.

Morgan caught Carter's eyes. Dad cleared his throat. "I nominate Doc McCracken."

"Any other nominations?" He waited, then continued, "All right, all in favor of Doc make it known by raising your right hand. Okay—opposed the same sign. Dr. McCracken is unanimously elected. It's all yours, Captain. Good luck to you."

McCracken stood up, stooping to avoid the rock overhead. "We're evacuating at once. Mrs. Carter, give the baby about another tablespoon of the syrup, then help Ted. He knows what to do. You'll follow Ted. Then Jerry. Margie, you are next. I'll assign the others presently. Once out of the canyon, spread out and go it alone. Rendezvous at dusk, same place as under Captain Morgan's withdrawal plan—the cave." He paused. Morgan caught his eye and motioned him over, "That's all until Ted and the baby are ready to leave. Now back away and give Captain Morgan a little air."

When they had withdrawn McCracken leaned over Morgan the better to hear his weak words. "Don't be too sure you've seen the last of me, Captain. I might join up in a few days."

"You might at that. I'm going to leave you bundled up warm and plenty of water within reach. I'll leave you some pills, too—that'll give you some comfort and ease. Only half a pill for you—they're intended for cows." He grinned at his patient.

"Half a pill it is. Why not let Dad handle the evacuation? He'll make you a good deputy—and I'd like to talk with you until you leave."

"Right." He called Carter over, instructed him, and turned back to Morgan.

"After you join up with Powell's outfit," whispered Morgan, "your first job is to get into touch with Brockman. Better get Mrs. Carter started right away, once you've talked it over with Powell."

"I will."

"That's the most important thing we've got to worry about, Doc. We've got to have unity, and one plan, from coast to coast. I look forward to a day when there will be an American assigned, by name, to each and every one of them. Then at a set time—zzzt!" He drew a thumb across his throat.

McCracken nodded. "Could be. It *will* be. How long do you think it will take us?"

"I don't know. I don't think about 'how long.' Two years, five years, ten years—maybe a century. That's not the point. The only question is whether or not there are any guts left in America." He glanced out where the fifth person to leave was awaiting a signal from Carter, who in turn was awaiting a signal from Art, hidden out where he could watch for the helicopter. "Those people will stick."

"I'm sure of that."

Presently Morgan added, "There's one thing this has taught me: You can't enslave a free man. Only person can do that to a man is himself. No, sir—you can't enslave a free man. The most you can do is kill him."

"That's a fact, Ed."

"It is. Got a cigarette, Doc?"

"It won't do you any good, Ed."

"It won't do me any harm, either—now, will it?"

"Well, not much." McCracken unregretfully gave him his last and watched him smoke it.

Later, Morgan said, "Dad's ready for you, Captain. So long."

"So long. Don't forget. Half a pill at a time. Drink all the water you want, but don't take your blankets off, no matter how hot you get."

"Half a pill it is. Good luck."

"I'll have Ted check on you tomorrow."

Morgan shook his head. "That's too soon. Not for a couple of days at least."

McCracken smiled. "I'll decide that, Ed. You just keep yourself wrapped up. Good luck." He withdrew to where Carter waited for him. "You go ahead, Dad. I'll bring up the rear. Signal Art to start."

Carter hesitated. "Tell me straight, Doc. What kind of shape is he in?"

McCracken studied Carter's face, then said in a low voice, "I give him about two hours."

"I'll stay behind with him."

"No, Dad, you'll carry out your orders." Seeing the distress in the old man's eyes, he added, "Don't you worry about Morgan. A free man can take care of himself. Now get moving."

"Yes, sir."

ON THE SLOPES OF VESUVIUS

Written 1947; first appeared in *Expanded Universe*, 1980

"PADDY, SHAKE HANDS with the guy who built the atom bomb," Professor Warner said to the bartender. "He and Einstein rigged it up in their own kitchen one evening."

"With the help of about four hundred other guys," amended the stranger, raising his voice slightly to cut through the rumble of the subway.

"Don't quibble over details. Paddy, this is Doctor Mansfield. Jerry, meet Paddy—Say, Paddy, what *is* your last name?"

"Francis X. Hughes," answered the barkeep as he wiped his hand and stuck it out. "I'm pleased to meet any friend of Professor Warner."

"I'm pleased to meet you, Mr. Hughes."

"Call me Paddy, they all do. You really are one of the scientists who built the atom bomb?"

"I'm afraid so."

"May the Lord forgive you. Are you at N.Y.U., too?"

"No, I'm out at the new Brookhaven Laboratory."

"Oh, yes."

"You've been there?"

Hughes shook his head. "About the only place I go is home to Brooklyn. But I read the papers."

"Paddy's in a well-padded rut," explained Warner. "Paddy, what are you going to do when they blow up New York? It'll break up your routine."

He set their drinks before them and poured himself a short beer. "If that's all I've got to worry about I guess I'll die of old age and still in my rut, Professor."

Warner's face lost its cheerful expression for a moment; he stared at his drink as if it had suddenly become bitter. "I wish I had your optimism, Paddy, but I haven't. Sooner or later, we're in for it."

"You shouldn't joke about such things, Professor."

"I'm not joking."

"You can't be serious."

"I wish I weren't. Ask him. After all, he built the damned thing."

Hughes raised his brows at Mansfield who replied, "I'm forced to agree with Professor Warner. They will be able to do it—atom-bomb New York I mean. I *know* that; it's not a guess—it's a certainty. Being able to do it, I'm strongly of the opinion that they *will* do it."

"Who do you mean by 'they'?" demanded the bartender. "The Russians?"

"Not necessarily. It might be anybody who first worked up the power to smash us."

"Sure," said Warner. "Everybody wants to kick the fat boy. We're envied and hated. The only reason we haven't been smeared is that no one has had what it takes to do it—up to now, that is!"

"Just a minute, gentlemen—" put in Hughes. "I don't get it. You're talking about somebody—anybody—atom-bombing New York. How can they do it? Didn't we decide to hang on to the secret? Do you think some dirty spy has gotten away with it while we weren't watching?"

Mansfield looked at Warner, then back at Hughes and said gently, "I hate to disturb your peace of mind, Mr. Hughes—Paddy—but there is no secret. Any nation that is willing to go to the trouble and expense can build an atom bomb."

"And that's official," added Warner, "and it's a lead-pipe cinch that, power politics being what it is, a dozen different nations are working on the problem right now."

Hughes had been looking perturbed; his face cleared. "Oh, I see what you mean. In time, they can dig it out for themselves. In that case, gentlemen, let's have a round on the house and drink to their frustration. I can't be worrying about what might happen twenty years from now. We might none of us be spared that long what with taxicabs and the like."

Mansfield's brows shot up. "Why do you say twenty years, Paddy?"

"Eh? Oh, I seem to remember reading it in the papers. That general, wasn't it? The one who was in charge of the atom-bomb business."

Mansfield brushed the general aside. "Poppycock! That estimate is based on entirely unwarranted national conceit. The time will be much shorter."

"How much shorter?" demanded Hughes. Mansfield shrugged.

"What would you do, Paddy," Warner asked curiously, "if you thought some nation—let's say some nation that didn't like us—had already managed to manufacture atom bombs?"

The saloon cat came strolling along the top of the bar. Hughes stopped to feed it a slice of cheese before replying. "I do not have your learning, gentlemen, but Paddy Hughes is no fool. If someone is loose in the world with those devil's contraptions, New York is a doomed city. America is the champion and must be beaten before any new bully boy can hope to win—and New York is one of the spots he would shoot at first. Even Sad Sack—" He jerked a thumb at the cat. "—is bright enough to flee from a burning building."

"Well, what do you think you would do?"

"I don't 'think' what I'd do, I *know* what I'd do; I've done it before. When I was a young man and the Black-and-Tans were breathing down the back o' my neck, I climbed on a ship with never a thought of looking back—and any man who wanted them could have my pigs and welcome to them."

Warner chuckled. "You must have been quite the lad, Paddy. But I don't believe you would do it—not now. You're firmly rooted in your rut and you like it—like me and six million others in this town. That's why decentralization is a fantasy."

Hughes nodded. "It would be hard." That it would be hard he understood. Like leaving home it would be to quit Schreiber's Bar-Grill after all these years—Schreiber couldn't run it without him; he'd chase all the customers away. It would be hard to leave his friends in the parish, hard to leave his home—what with Molly's grave being just around the corner and all. And if the cities were to be blown up a man would have to go back to farming. He'd promised himself when he hit the new country that he'd never, never, never tackle the heartbreaking load of tilling the soil again. Well, perhaps there would be no landlords when the cities were gone. If a man must farm, at least he might be spared that. Still, it would be hard—and Molly's grave off somewhere in the rubble. "But I'd do it."

"You think you would."

"I wouldn't even go back to Brooklyn to pick up my other shirt. I've my week's pay envelope right here." He patted his vest. "I'd grab my hat and start walking." The bartender turned to Mansfield. "Tell me the truth, Doctor—if it's not twenty years, how long will it be?"

Mansfield took out an envelope and started figuring on the back of it. Warner started to speak, but Hughes cut him off. "Quiet while he's working it out!" he said sharply.

"Don't let him kid you, Paddy," Warner said wryly. "He's been lying awake nights working out this problem ever since Hiroshima."

Mansfield looked up. "That's true. But I keep hoping I'll come out with a different answer. I never do."

"Well, what *is* the answer?" Hughes insisted.

Mansfield hesitated. "Paddy, you understand that there are a lot of factors involved, not all of them too clear. Right? In the first place, it took us about four years. But we were lavish with money and lavish with men, more so maybe than any other nation could be, except possibly Russia. Figured on that alone it might take several times four years for another country to make a bomb. But that's not the whole picture; it's not even the important part. There was a report the War Department put out, the Smyth Report—you've heard of it?—which gives anyone who can read everything but the final answers. With that report, with competent people, uranium ore, and a good deal less money than it cost us, a nation ought to be able to develop a bomb in a good deal less time than it took us."

Hughes shook his head. "I don't expect you to explain, Doctor; I just want to know your answer. How long?"

"I was just explaining that the answer had to be indefinite. I make it not less than two and not more than four years."

The bartender whistled softly. "Two years. Two years to get away and start a new life."

"No, no, no! Mr. Hughes," Mansfield objected. "Not two years from now—two years from the time the first bomb was dropped."

Hughes' face showed a struggle to comprehend. "But, gentlemen," he protested, "it's been *more* than two years since the first bomb was dropped."

"That's right."

"Don't blow your top, Paddy," Warner cautioned him. "The bomb isn't everything. It might be ten years before anybody develops the sort of robot carrier that can go over the north pole or the ocean and seek out a particular city with an atom bomb. In the meantime we don't have too much to fear from an ordinary airplane attack."

Mansfield looked annoyed. "You started this, Dick. Why try to hand out soothing syrup now? With a country as wide open as this one you don't need anything as fancy as guided missiles to pull a Pearl Harbor on it. The bombs would be assembled secretly and set off by remote control. Why, there might be a tramp steamer lying out there in the East River right now—"

Warner let his shoulders slump. "You're right, of course."

Hughes threw down his bar towel. "You're telling me that New York is as likely to be blown up right now as at any other time."

Mansfield nodded. "That's the size of it," he said soberly.

Hughes looked from one to the other. The cat jumped down and commenced rubbing up against his ankle, purring. He pushed it away with his foot. "It's not true! I know it's not true!"

"Why not?"

"Because! If it was true would you be sitting here, drinking quietly? You've been having a bit of fun with me, pulling my leg. Oh, I can't pick the flaw in your argument, but you don't believe it yourselves."

"I wish I didn't believe it," said Mansfield.

"Oh, we believe it, Paddy," Warner told him. "To tell you the truth, I'm planning to get out. I've got letters out to half a dozen cow colleges; I'm just waiting until my contract expires. As for Doc Mansfield, he can't leave. This is where his lab is located."

Hughes considered this, then shook his head. "No, it won't wash. No man in his right mind will hang on to a job when it means sitting on the hot squat, waiting for the Warden to throw the switch. You're pulling my leg."

Mansfield acted as if Hughes had not spoken. "Anyhow," he said to Warner, "the political factors might delay the blow-off indefinitely."

Warner shook his head angrily. "Now who's handing out soothing syrup? The political factors speed up the event, not delay it. If a country intends to defeat us someday, it's imperative that she do it as quickly as possible, before we catch wind of her plans and strike first. Or before we work out a real counter weapon—if that's possible."

Mansfield looked tired, as if he had been tired for a long time. "Oh, you're right. I was just whistling to keep my courage up. But we won't develop a counter weapon, not a real one. The only possible defense against atomic explosion is not to be there when it goes off." He turned to the barman. "Let's have another round, Paddy."

"Make mine a Manhattan," added Warner.

"Just a minute. Professor Warner. Doctor Mansfield. You were not fooling with me? Every word you had to say is God's own truth?"

"As you're standing there, Paddy."

"And Doctor Mansfield—Professor Warner, do you trust Doctor Mansfield's figuring?"

"There's no man in the United States better qualified to make such an estimate. That's the truth, Paddy."

"Well, then—" Hughes turned toward where his employer sat nodding over the cash register on the restaurant side of the room and whistled loudly between his teeth. "Schreiber! Come take the bar." He started stripping off his apron.

"Hey!" said Warner, "where you going? I ordered a Manhattan."

"Mix it yourself," said Hughes. "I've quit." He reached for his hat with one hand, his coat with the other, and then he was out the door.

Forty seconds later he was on an uptown express; he got off at 34th Street and three minutes thereafter he was buying a ticket, west. It was ten minutes later that he felt the train start to roll under him, headed out of the city.

But it was less than an hour later when his misgivings set in. Had he been too hasty? Professor Warner was a fine man, to be sure, but given to his little jokes, now and again. Had he been taken in by a carefully contrived hoax? Had Warner said to his friend, we'll have some fun and scare the living daylights out of the old Irishman?

Nor had he made any arrangements for someone to feed Sad Sack. The cat had a weak stomach, he was certain, and no one else gave the matter any attention at all. And Molly's grave—Wednesday was his day to do his gardening there. Of course Father Nelson would see that it was watered, just for kindness' sake, but still—

When the train paused at Princeton Junction he slipped off and sought out a telephone. He had in mind what he meant to say if he was able to reach Professor Warner—a good chance, he thought, for considering the hour the gentlemen probably stayed on for a steak. Professor Warner, he would say, you've had your fun and a fine joke it was as I would be the first to say and to buy a drink on it, but tell me—man to man—was there anything to what you and your friend was telling me? That would settle it, he thought.

The call went through promptly and he heard Schreiber's irritated voice. "Hello," he said.

The line went dead. He jiggled the hook. The operator answered, "One moment, please—" then, "This is the Princeton operator. Is this the party with the call to New York?"

"Yes. I—"

"There has been a temporary interruption in service. Will you hang up and try again in a few minutes, please?"

"But I was just talking—"

"Will you hang up and try again in a few minutes, puh*lease*?"

He heard the shouting as he left the booth. As he got outdoors he could see the great, gloriously beautiful, gold and purple mushroom still mounting over where had been the City of New York.

COLUMBUS WAS A DOPE

Startling Stories, May 1947

"I DO LIKE to wet down a sale," the fat man said happily, raising his voice above the sighing of the air-conditioner. "Drink up, Professor, I'm two ahead of you."

He glanced up from their table as the elevator door opposite them opened. A man stepped out into the cool dark of the bar and stood blinking, as if he had just come from the desert glare outside.

"Hey, Fred—Fred Nolan," the fat man called out. "Come over!" He turned to his guest. "Man I met on the hop from New York. Siddown, Fred. Shake hands with Professor Appleby, Chief Engineer of the Starship *Pegasus*—or will be when she's built. I just sold the Professor an order of bum steel for his crate. Have a drink on it."

"Glad to, Mr. Barnes," Nolan agreed. "I've met Dr. Appleby. On business—Climax Instrument Company."

"Huh?"

"Climax is supplying us with precision equipment," offered Appleby.

Barnes looked surprised, then grinned. "That's one on me. I took Fred for a government man, or one of your scientific johnnies. What'll it be, Fred? Old-fashioned? The same, Professor?"

"Right. But please don't call me 'Professor.' I'm not one and it ages me. I'm still young."

"I'll say you are, uh—Doc, Pete! Two old-fashioneds and another double Manhattan! I guess I expected a comic book scientist, with a long white beard. But now that I've met you, I can't figure out one thing."

"Which is?"

"Well, at your age you bury yourself in this god-forsaken place—"

"We couldn't build the *Pegasus* on Long Island," Appleby pointed out, "and this is the ideal spot for the take-off."

"Yeah, sure, but that's not it. It's—well, mind you, I sell steel. You want special alloys for a starship; I sell it to you. But just the same, now that business is out of the way, why do you want to do it? Why try to go to Proxima Centauri, or any other star?"

Appleby looked amused. "It can't be explained. Why do men try to climb Mount Everest? What took Perry to the North Pole? Why did Columbus get the Queen to hock her jewels? Nobody has ever been to Proxima Centauri—so we're going."

Barnes turned to Nolan. "Do you get it, Fred?"

Nolan shrugged. "I sell precision instruments. Some people raise chrysanthemums; some build starships. I sell instruments."

Barnes' friendly face looked puzzled. "Well—" The bartender put down their drinks. "Say, Pete, tell me something. Would you go along on the *Pegasus* expedition if you could?"

"Nope."

"Why not?"

"I like it here."

Dr. Appleby nodded. "There's your answer, Barnes, in reverse. Some have the Columbus spirit and some haven't."

"It's all very well to talk about Columbus," Barnes persisted, "but he expected to come back. You guys don't expect to. Sixty years—you told me it would take sixty years. Why, you may not even live to get there."

"No, but our children will. And our grandchildren will come back."

"But— Say, you're not *married?*"

"Certainly I am. Family men only on the expedition. It's a two-to-three generation job. You know that." He hauled out a wallet. "There's Mrs. Appleby with Diane. Diane is three and a half."

"She's a pretty baby," Barnes said soberly and passed it on to Nolan, who smiled at it and handed it back to Appleby. Barnes went on. "What happens to her?"

"She goes with us, naturally. You wouldn't want her put in an orphanage, would you?"

"No, but—" Barnes tossed off the rest of his drink, "I don't get it," he admitted. "Who'll have another drink?"

"Not for me, thanks," Appleby declined, finishing his more slowly and standing up. "I'm due home. Family man, you know." He smiled.

Barnes did not try to stop him. He said goodnight and watched Appleby leave.

"My round," said Nolan. "The same?"

"Huh? Yeah, sure." Barnes stood up. "Let's get up to the bar, Fred, where we can drink properly. I need about six."

"Okay," Nolan agreed, standing up. "What's the trouble?"

"Trouble? Did you see that picture?"

"Well?"

"Well, how do *you* feel about it? I'm a salesman too, Fred. I sell steel. It don't matter what the customer wants to use it for; I sell it to him.

I'd sell a man a rope to hang himself. But I do love kids. I can't stand to think of that cute little kid going along on that—that crazy expedition!"

"Why not? She's better off with her parents. She'll get as used to steel decks as most kids are to sidewalks."

"But look, Fred. You don't have any silly idea they'll make it, do you?"

"They might."

"Well, they won't. They don't stand a chance. I know. I talked it over with our technical staff before I left the home office. Nine chances out of ten they'll burn up on the take-off. That's the best that can happen to them. If they get out of the solar system, which ain't likely, they'll still never make it. They'll never reach the stars."

Pete put another drink down in front of Barnes. He drained it and said:

"Set up another one, Pete. They can't. It's a theoretical impossibility. They'll freeze—or they'll roast—or they'll starve. But they'll never get there."

"Maybe so."

"No maybe about it. They're *crazy*. Hurry up with that drink, Pete. Have one yourself."

"Coming up. Don't mind if I do, thanks." Pete mixed the cocktail, drew a glass of beer, and joined them.

"Pete, here, is a wise man," Barnes said confidentially. "You don't catch him monkeying around with any trips to the stars. Columbus— Pfui! Columbus was a dope. He shoulda stood in bed."

The bartender shook his head. "You got me wrong, Mr. Barnes. If it wasn't for men like Columbus, we wouldn't be here today—now, would we? I'm just not the explorer type. But I'm a believer. I got nothing against the *Pegasus* expedition."

"You don't approve of them taking kids on it, do you?"

"Well . . . there were kids on the *Mayflower,* so they tell me."

"It's not the same thing." Barnes looked at Nolan, then back to the bartender. "If the Lord had intended us to go to the stars, he would have equipped us with jet propulsion. Fix me another drink, Pete."

"You've had about enough for a while, Mr. Barnes."

The troubled fat man seemed about to argue, thought better of it.

"I'm going up to the Sky Room and find somebody that'll dance with me," he announced. "G'night." He swayed softly toward the elevator.

Nolan watched him leave. "Poor old Barnes." He shrugged. "I guess you and I are hard-hearted, Pete."

"No. I believe in progress, that's all. I remember my old man wanted a law passed about flying machines, keep 'em from breaking their fool necks. Claimed nobody ever could fly, and the government should put a stop to it. He was wrong. I'm not the adventurous type myself but I've seen enough people to know they'll try anything once, and that's how progress is made."

"You don't look old enough to remember when men couldn't fly."

"I've been around a long time. Ten years in this one spot."

"Ten years, eh? Don't you ever get a hankering for a job that'll let you breathe a little fresh air?"

"Nope. I didn't get any fresh air when I served drinks on Forty-second Street and I don't miss it now. I like it here. Always something new going on here, first the atom laboratories and then the big observatory and now the Starship. But that's not the real reason. I like it here. It's my home. Watch this."

He picked up a brandy inhaler, a great fragile crystal globe, spun it and threw it, straight up, toward the ceiling. It rose slowly and gracefully, paused for a long reluctant wait at the top of its rise, then settled slowly, slowly, like a diver in a slow-motion movie. Pete watched it float past his nose, then reached out with thumb and forefinger, nipped it easily by the stem, and returned it to the rack.

"See that," he said. "One-sixth gravity. When I was tending bar on earth my bunions gave me the dickens all the time. Here I weigh only thirty-five pounds. I like it on the Moon."

JERRY WAS A MAN

Thrilling Wonder Stories, October 1947

DON'T BLAME THE Martians. The human race would have developed plasto-biology in any case.

Look at the older registered Kennel Club breeds—glandular giants like the St. Bernard and the Great Dane, silly little atrocities like the Chihuahua and the Pekingese. Consider fancy goldfish.

The damage was done when Dr. Morgan produced new breeds of fruit flies by kicking around their chromosomes with X-ray. After that, the third generation of the Hiroshima survivors did not teach us anything new; those luckless monstrosities merely publicized standard genetic knowledge.

Mr. and Mrs. Bronson van Vogel did not have social reform in mind when they went to the Phoenix Breeding Ranch; Mr. van Vogel simply wanted to buy a Pegasus. He had mentioned it at breakfast. "Are you tied up this morning, my dear?"

"Not especially. Why?"

"I'd like to run out to Arizona and order a Pegasus designed."

"A Pegasus? A flying horse? Why, my sweet?"

He grinned. "Just for fun. Pudgy Dodge was around the Club yesterday with a six-legged dachshund—must have been over a yard long. It was clever, but he swanked so much I want to give him something to stare at. Imagine, Martha—me landing on the Club 'copter platform on a winged horse. That'll snap his eyes back!"

She turned her eyes from the Jersey shore to look indulgently at her husband. She was not fooled; this would be expensive. But Brownie was such a dear! "When do we start?"

They landed two hours earlier than they started. The airsign read, in letters fifty feet high:

PHOENIX BREEDING RANCH
Controlled Genetics—licensed Labor Contractors

" 'Labor Contractors'?" she read. "I thought this place was used just to burbank new animals?"

"They both design and produce," he explained importantly. "They distribute through the mother corporation 'Workers'. You ought to know; you own a big chunk of Workers common."

"You mean I own a bunch of apes? Really?"

"Perhaps I didn't tell you. Haskell and I—" He leaned forward and informed the field that he would land manually; he was a bit proud of his piloting.

He switched off the robot and added, briefly as his attention was taken up by heading the ship down, "Haskell and I have been plowing your General Atomics dividends back into Workers, Inc. Good diversification—still plenty of dirty work for the anthropoids to do." He slapped the keys; the scream of the nose jets stopped conversation.

Bronson had called the manager in flight; they were met—not with red carpet, canopy, and footmen, though the manager strove to give that impression. "Mr. van Vogel? And *Mrs.* van Vogel! We are honored indeed!" He ushered them into a tiny, luxurious unicar; they jeeped off the field, up a ramp, and into the lobby of the administration building. The manager, Mr. Blakesly, did not relax until he had seated them around a fountain in the lounge of his offices, struck cigarettes for them, and provided tall, cool drinks.

Bronson van Vogel was bored by the attention, as it was obviously inspired by his wife's Dun & Bradstreet rating (ten stars, a sunburst, and heavenly music). He preferred people who could convince him that he had invented the Briggs fortune, instead of marrying it.

"This is business Blakesly. I've an order for you."

"So? Well, our facilities are at your disposal. What would you like, sir?"

"I want you to make me a Pegasus."

"A Pegasus? A flying horse?"

"Exactly."

Blakesly pursed his lips. "You seriously want a horse that will fly? An animal like the mythical Pegasus?"

"Yes, yes—that's what I said."

"You embarrass me, Mr. van Vogel. I assume you want a unique gift for your lady. How about a midget elephant, twenty inches high, perfectly housebroken, and able to read and write? He holds the stylus in his trunk—very cunning."

"Does he talk?" demanded Mrs. van Vogel.

"Well, now, my dear lady, his voice box, you know—and his tongue—he was not designed for speech. If you insist on it, I will see what our plasticians can do."

"Now, Martha—"

"You can have your Pegasus, Brownie, but I think I may want this toy elephant. May I see him?"

"Most surely. Hartstone!"

The air answered Blakesly. "Yes, boss?"

"Bring Napoleon to my lounge."

"Right away, sir."

"Now about your Pegasus, Mr. van Vogel . . . I see difficulties but I need expert advice. Dr. Cargrew is the real heart of this organization, the most eminent bio-designer—of terrestrial origin, of course—on the world today." He raised his voice to actuate relays. "Dr. Cargrew!"

"What is it, Mr. Blakesly?"

"Doctor, will you favor me by coming to my office?"

"I'm busy. Later."

Mr. Blakesly excused himself, went into his inner office, then returned to say that Dr. Cargrew would be in shortly. In the mean time Napoleon showed up. The proportions of his noble ancestors had been preserved in miniature; he looked like a statuette of an elephant, come amazingly to life.

He took three measured steps into the lounge, then saluted them each with his trunk. In saluting Mrs. van Vogel he dropped on his knees as well.

"Oh, how cute!" she gurgled. "Come here, Napoleon."

The elephant looked at Blakesly, who nodded. Napoleon ambled over and laid his trunk across her lap. She scratched his ears; he moaned contentedly.

"Show the lady how you can write," ordered Blakesly. "Fetch your things from my room."

Napoleon waited while she finished treating a particularly satisfying itch, then oozed away to return shortly with several sheets of heavy white paper and an oversize pencil. He spread a sheet in front of Mrs. van Vogel, held it down daintily with a fore foot, grasped the pencil with his trunk finger, and printed in large, shaky letters, "I LIKE YOU."

"The darling!" She dropped to her knees and put her arms around his neck. "I simply must have him. How much is he?"

"Napoleon is part of a limited edition of six," Blakesly said carefully. "Do you want an exclusive model, or may the others be sold?"

"Oh, I don't care. I just want Nappie. Can I write him a note?"

"Certainly, Mrs. van Vogel. Print large letters and use Basic English. Napoleon knows most of it. His price, nonexclusive is $350,000. That includes five years salary for his attending veterinary."

"Give the gentleman a check, Brownie," she said over her shoulder.

"But Martha—"

"Don't be tiresome, Brownie." She turned back to her pet and began printing. She hardly looked up when Dr. Cargrew came in.

Cargrew was a chilly figure in white overalls and skull cap. He shook hands brusquely, struck a cigarette and sat down. Blakesly explained.

Cargrew shook his head. "It's a physical impossibility."

Van Vogel stood up. "I can see," he said distantly, "That I should have taken my custom to NuLife Laboratories. I came here because we have a financial interest in this firm and because I was naive enough to believe the claims of your advertisements."

"Siddown, young man!" Cargrew ordered. "Take your trade to those thumb-fingered idiots if you wish—but I warn you they couldn't grow wings on a grasshopper. First you listen to me.

"We can grow anything and make it live. I can make you a living thing—I won't call it an animal—the size and shape of that table over there. It wouldn't be good for anything, but it would be alive. It would ingest food, use chemical energy, give off excretions, and display irritability. But it would be a silly piece of manipulation. Mechanically a table and an animal are two different things. Their functions are different, so their shapes are different. Now I can make you a winged horse—"

"You just said you couldn't."

"Don't interrupt. I can make a winged horse that will look just like the pictures in the fairy stories. If you want to pay for it; we'll make it— we're in business. But it won't be able to fly."

"Why not?"

"Because it's not built for flying. The ancient who dreamed up that myth knew nothing about aerodynamics and still less about biology. He stuck wings on a horse, just stuck them on, thumb tacks and glue. But that doesn't make a flying machine. Remember, son, that an animal is a machine, primarily a heat engine with a control system to operate levers and hydraulic systems, according to definite engineering laws. You savvy aerodynamics?"

"Well, I'm a pilot."

"Hummph! Well, try to understand this. A horse hasn't got the heat engine for flight. He's a hayburner and that's not efficient. We might mess around with a horse's insides so that he could live on a diet of nothing but sugar and then he might have enough energy to fly short distances. But he still would not look like the mythical Pegasus. To anchor his flying muscles he would need a breast bone maybe ten feet long. He might have to have as much as eighty feet wing spread.

Folded, his wings would cover him like a tent. You're up against the cube-square disadvantage."

"Huh?"

Cargrew gestured impatiently. "Lift goes by the square of a given dimension; dead load by the cube of the same dimension, other things being equal. I might be able to make you a Pegasus the size of a cat without distorting the proportions too much."

"No, I want one I can ride. I don't mind the wing spread and I'll put up with the big breast bone. When can I have him?"

Cargrew looked disgusted, shrugged, and replied, "I'll have to consult with B'na Kreeth." He whistled and chirped; a portion of the wall facing them dissolved and they found themselves looking into a laboratory. A Martian, life-size, showed in the forepart of the three-dimensional picture.

When the creature chirlupped back at Cargrew, Mrs. van Vogel looked up, then quickly looked away. She knew it was silly but she simply could not stand the sight of Martians—and the ones who had modified themselves to a semi-manlike form disgusted her the most.

After they had twittered and gestured at each other for a minute or two Cargrew turned back to van Vogel. "B'na says that you should forget it; it would take too long. He wants to know how you'd like a fine unicorn, or a pair, guaranteed to breed true?"

"Unicorns are old hat. How long would the Pegasus take?"

After another squeaky-door conversation Cargrew answered, "Ten years probably, sixteen years on the guarantee."

"Ten years? That's ridiculous!"

Cargrew looked shirty. "*I* thought it would take fifty, but if B'na says that he can do it three to five generations, then he can do it. B'na is the finest bio-micrurgist in two planets. His chromosome surgery in un-equalled. After all, young man, natural processes would take upwards of a million years to achieve the same result, if it were achieved at all. Do you expect to be able to buy miracles?"

Van Vogel had the grace to look sheepish. "Excuse me, Doctor. Let's forget it. Ten years really is too long. How about the other possibility? You said you could make a picture-book Pegasus, as long as I did not insist on flight. Could I ride him? On the ground?"

"Oh, certainly. No good for polo, but you could ride him."

"I'll settle for that. Ask Benny creeth, or what ever his name is, how long it would take."

The Martian had faded out of the screens. "I don't need to ask him," Cargrew asserted. "This is my job—purely manipulation. B'na's collaboration is required only for rearrangement and transplanting of genes—true genetic work. I can let you have the beast in eighteen months."

"Can't you do better than that?"

"What do you expect, man? It takes eleven months to grow a new-born colt. I want one month of design and planning. The embryo will be removed on the fourth day and will be developed in an extra-uterine capsule. I'll operate ten or twelve times during gestation, grafting and budding and other things you've heard of. One year from now we'll have a baby colt, with wings. Thereafter I'll deliver to you a six-months-old Pegasus."

"I'll take it."

Cargrew made some notes, then read, "One alate horse, not capable of flight and not to breed true. Basic breed your choice—I suggest a Palomino, or an Arabian. Wings designed after a condor, in white. Simulated pin feathers with a grafted fringe of quill feathers, or reasonable facsimile." He passed the sheet over. "Initial that and we'll start in advance of formal contract."

"It's a deal," agreed van Vogel. "What is the fee?" He placed his monogram under Cargrew's.

Cargrew made further notes and handed them to Blakesly—estimates of professional man-hours, technician man-hours, purchases, and overhead. He had padded the figures to subsidize his collateral research but even he raised his eyebrows at the dollars-and-cents interpretation Blakesly put on the data. "That will be an even two million dollars."

Van Vogel hesitated; his wife had looked up at the mention of money. But she turned her attention back to the scholarly elephant.

Blakesly added hastily, "That is for an exclusive creation, of course."

"Naturally," van Vogel agreed briskly, and added the figure to the memorandum.

Van Vogel was ready to return, but his wife insisted on seeing the "apes", as she termed the anthropoid workers. The discovery that she owned a considerable share in these subhuman creatures had intrigued her. Blakesly eagerly suggested a trip through the laboratories in which the workers were developed from true apes.

They were arranged in seven buildings, the seven "Days of Creation". "First Day" was a large building occupied by Cargrew, his staff, his operating rooms, incubators, and laboratories. Martha van Vogel stared in horrified fascination at living organs and even complete embryos, living artificial lives sustained by clever glass and metal recirculating systems and exquisite automatic machinery.

She could not appreciate the techniques; it seemed depressing.

She had about decided against plasto-biology when Napoleon, by tugging at her skirts, reminded her that it produced good things as well as horrors.

The building "Second Day" they did not enter; it was occupied by B'na Kreeth and his racial colleagues. "We could not stay alive in it, you understand," Blakesly explained. Van Vogel nodded; his wife hurried on—she wanted no Martians, even behind plastiglass.

From there on the buildings were for development and production of commercial workers. "Third Day" was used for the development of variations in the anthropoids to meet constantly changing labor requirements. "Fourth Day" was a very large building devoted entirely to production-line incubators for commercial types of anthropoids. Blakesly explained that they had dispensed with normal birth. "The policy permits exact control of forced variations, such as for size, and saves hundreds of thousands of worker-hours on the part of the female anthropoids."

Martha van Vogel was delighted with "Fifth Day", the anthropoid kindergarden where the little tykes learned to talk and were conditioned to the social patterns necessary to their station in life. They worked at simple tasks such as sorting buttons and digging holes in sand piles, with pieces of candy given as incentives for fast and accurate work.

"Six Day" completed the anthropoids' educations. Each learned the particular sub-trade it would practice, cleaning, digging, and especially agricultural semi-skills such as weeding, thinning, and picking. "One Nisei farmer working three neo-chimpanzees can grow as many vegetables as a dozen old-style farm hands," Blakesly asserted. "They really *like* to work—when we get through with them."

They admired the almost incredibly heavy tasks done by modified gorillas and stopped to gaze at the little neo-Capuchins doing high picking on prop trees, then moved on toward "Seventh Day."

This building was used for the radioactive mutation of genes and therefore located some distance away from the others. They had to walk, as the sidewalk was being repaired; the detour took them past workers' pens and barracks. Some of the anthropoids crowded up to the wire and began calling to them: "Sigret! Sigret! Preese, Missy! Preese, Boss! Sigret!"

"What are they saying?" Martha van Vogel inquired.

"They are asking for cigarettes," Blakesly answered in annoyed tones. "They know better, but they are like children. Here—I'll put a stop to it." He stepped up to the wire and shouted to an elderly male, "Hey! Strawboss!"

The worker addressed wore, in addition to the usual short canvas kilt, a bedraggled arm band. He turned and shuffled toward the fence. "Strawboss," ordered Blakesly, "get those Joes away from here."

"Okay, Boss," the old fellow acknowledged and started cuffing those nearest him. "Scram, you Joes! Scram!"

"But I have some cigarettes," protested Mrs. van Vogel, "and I would gladly have given them some."

"It doesn't do to pamper them," the Manager told her. "They have been taught that luxuries come only from work. I must apologize for my poor children; those in these pens are getting old and forgetting their manners."

She did not answer but moved further along the fence to where one old neo-chimp was pressed up against the wire, staring at them with soft, tragic eyes, like a child at a bakery window. He had taken no part in the jostling demand for tobacco and had been let alone by the straw-boss. "Would you like a cigarette?" she asked him.

"Preese, Missy."

She struck one which he accepted with fumbling grace, took a long, lung-filling drag, let the smoke trickle out his nostrils, and said shyly, "Sankoo, Missy. Me Jerry."

"How do you do, Jerry?"

"Howdy, Missy." He bobbed down, bending his knees, ducking his head, and clasping his hands to his chest, all in one movement.

"Come along, Martha." Her husband and Blakesly had moved in behind her.

"In a moment," she answered. "Brownie, meet my friend Jerry. Doesn't he look just like Uncle Albert? Except that he looks so sad. Why are you unhappy, Jerry?"

"They don't understand abstract ideas," put in Blakesly.

But Jerry surprised him. "Jerry sad," he announced in tones so doleful that Martha van Vogel did not know whether to laugh or to cry.

"Why, Jerry?" she asked gently. "Why are you so sad?"

"No work," he stated. "No sigret. No candy. No work."

"These are all old workers who have passed their usefulness," Blakesly repeated. "Idleness upsets them, but we have nothing for them to do."

"Well!" she said. "Then why don't you have them sort buttons, or something like that, such as the baby ones do?"

"They wouldn't even do that properly," Blakesly answered her. "These workers are senile."

"Jerry isn't senile! You heard him talk."

"Well, perhaps not. Just a moment." He turned to the apeman, who was squatting down in order to scratch Napoleon's head with a long forefinger thrust through the fence. "You, Joe! Come here."

Blakesly felt around the worker's hairy neck and located a thin steel chain to which was attached a small metal tag. He studied it. "You're right," he admitted. "He's not really over age, but his eyes are bad. I remember the lot—cataracts as a result of an unfortunate linked mutation." He shrugged.

"But that's no reason to let him grieve his heart out in idleness."

"Really, Mrs. van Vogel, you should not upset yourself about it. They don't stay in these pens long—only a few days at the most."

"Oh," she answered, somewhat mollified, "you have some other place to retire them to, then. Do you give them something to do there? You should—Jerry wants to work. Don't you, Jerry?"

The neo-chimp had been struggling to follow the conversation. He caught the last idea and grinned. "Jerry work! Sure mike! Good worker." He flexed his fingers, then made fists, displaying fully opposed thumbs.

Mr. Blakesly seemed somewhat nonplused. "Really, Mrs. van Vogel, there is no need. You see—" He stopped.

Van Vogel had been listening irritably. His wife's enthusiasms annoyed him, unless they were also his own. Furthermore he was beginning to blame Blakesly for his own recent extravagance and had a premonition that his wife would find some way to make him pay, very sweetly, for his indulgence.

Being annoyed with both of them, he chucked in the perfect wrong remark. "Don't be silly, Martha. They don't retire them; they liquidate them."

It took a little time for the idea to soak in, but when it did she was furious. "Why . . . why—I never heard of such a thing! You ought to be ashamed. You . . . you would shoot your own grandmother."

"Mrs. van Vogel—please!"

"Don't 'Mrs. van Vogel' me! It's got to stop—you hear me?" She looked around at the death pens, at the milling hundreds of old workers therein. "It's horrible. You work them until they can't work anymore, then you take away their little comforts, and you *dispose* of them. I wonder you don't eat them!"

"They do," her husband said brutally. "Dog food."

"What! Well, we'll put a stop to that!"

"Mrs. van Vogel," Blakesly pleaded. "Let me explain."

"Hummph! Go ahead. It had better be good."

"Well, it's like this—" His eye fell on Jerry, standing with worried expression at the fence. "Scram, Joe!" Jerry shuffled away.

"Wait, Jerry!" Mrs. van Vogel called out. Jerry paused uncertainly. "Tell him to come back," she ordered Blakesly.

The Manager bit his lip, then called out, "Come back here."

449

He was beginning definitely to dislike Mrs. van Vogel, despite his automatic tendency to genuflect in the presence of a high credit rating. To be told how to run his own business—well, now, indeed! "Mrs. van Vogel, I admire your humanitarian spirit but you don't understand the situation. We understand our workers and do what is best for them. They die painlessly before their disabilities can trouble them. They live happy lives, happier than yours or mine. We trim off the bad part of their lives, nothing more. And don't forget, these poor beasts would never have been born had we not arranged it."

She shook her head. "Fiddlesticks! You'll be quoting the Bible at me next. There will be no more of it, Mr. Blakesly. I shall hold you personally responsible."

Blakesly looked bleak. "My responsibilities are to the directors."

"You think so?" She opened her purse and snatched out her telephone. So great was her agitation that she did not bother to call through, but signalled the local relay operator instead. "Phoenix? Get me Great New York Murray Hill 9Q-4004, Mr. Haskell. Priority—star subscriber 777. Make it quick." She stood there, tapping her foot and glaring, until her business manager answered. "Haskell? This is Martha van Vogel. How much Workers, Incorporated, common do I own? No, no, never mind that—what percent? . . . so? Well, it's not enough. I want 51% by tomorrow morning . . . all right, get proxies for the rest but get it . . . I didn't ask you what it would cost; I said to get it. Get busy." She disconnected abruptly and turned to her husband. "We're leaving, Brownie, and we are taking Jerry with us. Mr. Blakesly, will you kindly have him taken out of that pen? Give him a check for the amount, Brownie."

"Now, Martha—"

"My mind is made up, Brownie."

Mr. Blakesly cleared his throat. It was going to be pleasant to thwart this woman. "The workers are never sold. I'm sorry. It's a matter of policy."

"Very well then, I'll take a permanent lease."

"This worker has been removed from the labor market. He is not for lease."

"Am I going to have more trouble with you?"

"If you please, Madame! This worker is not available under any terms—but, as a courtesy to you, I am willing to transfer to you indentures for him, gratis. I want you to know that the policies of this firm are formed from a very real concern for the welfare of our charges as well as from the standpoint of good business practice. We therefore reserve the right to inspect at any time to assure ourselves that you are taking proper care of this worker." There, he told himself savagely, that will stop her clock!

"Of course. Thank you, Mr. Blakesly. You are most gracious."

The trip back to Great New York was not jolly. Napoleon hated it and let it be known. Jerry was patient but airsick. By the time they grounded the van Vogels were not on speaking terms.

"I'm sorry, Mrs. van Vogel. The shares were simply not available. We should have had proxy on the O'Toole block but someone tied them up an hour before I reached them."

"Blakesly."

"Undoubtedly. You should not have tipped him off; you gave him time to warn his employers."

"Don't waste time telling me what mistakes I made yesterday. What are you going to do today?"

"Mr. dear Mrs. van Vogel, what can I do? I'll carry out any instructions you care to give."

"Don't talk nonsense. You are supposed to be smarter than I am; that's why I pay you to do my thinking for me."

Mr. Haskell looked helpless.

His principal struck a cigarette so hard she broke it. "Why isn't Weinberg here?"

"Really, Mrs. van Vogel, there are no special legal aspects. You want the stock; we can't buy it nor bind it. Therefore—"

"I pay Weinberg to know the legal angles. Get him."

Weinberg was leaving his office; Haskell caught him on a chaseme circuit. "Sidney," Haskell called out. "Come to my office, will you? Oscar Haskell."

"Sorry. How about four o'clock?"

"Sidney, I want you—now!" cut in the client's voice. "This is Martha van Vogel."

The little man shrugged helplessly. "Right away," he agreed. That woman—why hadn't he retired on his one hundred and twenty-fifth birthday, as his wife had urged him to?

Ten minutes later he was listening to Haskell's explanations and his client's interruptions. When they had finished he spread his hands. "What do you expect, Mrs. van Vogel? These workers are chattels. You have not been able to buy the property rights involved; you are stopped. But I don't see what you are worked up about. They gave you the worker whose life you wanted preserved.

She spoke forcefully under her breath, then answered him. "That's not important. What is one worker among millions? I want to stop this killing, all of it."

Weinberg shook his head. "If you were able to prove that their methods of disposing of these beasts were inhumane, or that they were negligent of their physical welfare before destroying them, or that the destruction was wanton—"

"Wanton? It certain is!"

"Probably not in a legal sense, my dear lady. There was a case, Julius Hartman et al. vs. Hartman Estate, 1972, I believe, in which a permanent injunction was granted against carrying out a term of the will which called for the destruction of a valuable collection of Persian cats. But in order to use that theory you would have to show that these creatures, when superannuated, are notwithstanding more valuable alive than dead. You cannot compel a person to maintain chattels at a loss."

"See here, Sidney, I didn't get you over here to tell me how this can't be done. If what I want isn't legal, then get a law passed."

Weinberg looked at Haskell, who looked embarrassed and answered, "Well, the fact of the matter is, Mrs. van Vogel, that we have agreed with the other members of the Commonwealth Association not to subsidize any legislation during the incumbency of the present administration."

"How ridiculous! Why?"

"The Legislative Guild has brought out a new fair-practices code which we consider quite unfair, a sliding scale which penalizes the well-to-do—all very nice sounding, with special provisions for nominal fees for veterans' private bills and such things—but in fact the code is confiscatory. Even the Briggs Foundation can hardly afford to take a proper interest in public affairs under this so-called code."

"Hmmph! A fine day when legislators join unions—they are professional men. Bribes should be competitive. Get an injunction."

"Mrs. van Vogel," protested Weinberg, "how can you expect me to get an injunction against an organization which has no legal existence? In a legal sense, there is no Legislative Guild, just as the practice of assisting legislation by subsidy has itself no legal existence."

"And babies come under cabbage leaves. Quit stalling me, gentlemen. What are you going to do?"

Weinberg spoke when he saw that Haskell did not intend to. "Mrs. van Vogel, I think we should retain a special shyster."

"I don't employ shysters, even—I don't understand the way they think. I am a simple housewife, Sidney."

Mr. Weinberg flinched at her self-designation while noting that he must not let her find out that the salary of his own staff shyster was charged to her payroll. As convention required, he maintained the front of a simple, barefoot solicitor, but he had found out long ago that Martha van Vogel's problems required an occasional dose of the more exotic branch of the law. "The man I have in mind is a creative artist," he insisted. "It is no more necessary to understand him than it is to understand the composer in order to appreciate a symphony. I do recommand that you talk with him, at least."

"Oh, very well! Get him up here."

"Here? My dear lady!" Haskell was shocked at the suggestion; Weinberg looked amazed. "It would not only cause any action you bring to be thrown out of court if it were known that you had consulted this man, but it would prejudice any Briggs enterprise for years."

Mrs. van Vogel shrugged. "You men. I never will understand the way you think. Why shouldn't one consult a shyster as openly as one consults an astrologer?"

James Roderick McCoy was not a large man, but he seemed large. He managed to dominate even so large a room as Mrs. van Vogel's salon. His business card read:

J. R. McCOY
"THE REAL McCOY"

Licensed Shyster—Fixing, Special Contacts,
Angles. All Work Guaranteed.

TELEPHONE SKYLINE 9-8M4554
Ask for Mac

The number given was the pool room of the notorious Three Planets Club. He wasted no time on offices and kept his files in his head—the only safe place for them.

He was sitting on the floor, attempting to teach Jerry to shoot craps, while Mrs. van Vogel explained her problem. "What do you think, Mr. McCoy? Could we approach it through the SPCA? My public relations staff could give it a build up."

McCoy got to his feet. "Jerry's eyes aren't so bad; he caught me trying to palm box cars off on him as a natural. No," he continued, "the SPCA angle is no good. It's what 'workers' will expect. They'll be ready to prove that the anthropoids actually enjoy being killed off."

Jerry rattled the dice hopefully. "That's all, Jerry. Scram."

"Okay, Boss." The ape man got to his feet and went to the big stereo which filled a corner of the room. Napoleon ambled after him and switched it on. Jerry punched a selector button and got a blues singer. Napoleon immediately punched another, then another and another until he got a loud but popular band. He stood there, beating out the rhythm with his trunk.

Jerry looked pained and switched it back to his blues singer. Napoleon stubbornly reached out with his prehensile nose and switched it off.

Jerry used a swear word.

"Boys!" called out Mrs. van Vogel. "Quit squabbling. Jerry, let Nappie play what he wants to. You can play the stereo when Nappie has to take his nap."

"Okay, Missy Boss."

McCoy was interested. "Jerry likes music?"

"Like it? He loves it. He's been learning to sing."

"Huh? This I gotta hear."

"Certainly. Nappie—turn off the stereo." The elephant complied but managed to look put upon. "Now Jerry—'Jingle Bells.'" She led him in it:

"Jingle bells, jingle bells, jingle all the day—", and he followed,
"Jinger bez, jinger bez, jingle awrah day;
Oh, wot fun tiz to ride in one-hoss open sray."

He was flat, he was terrible. He looked ridiculous, patting out the time with one splay foot. But it was singing.

"Say, that's fast!" McCoy commented. "Too bad Nappie can't talk—we'd have a duet."

Jerry looked puzzled. "Nappie talk good," he stated. He bent over the elephant and spoke to him. Napoleon grunted and moaned back at him. "See, Boss?" Jerry said triumphantly.

"What did he say?"

"He say, 'Can Nappie pray stereo now?'"

"Very well, Jerry," Mrs. van Vogel interceded. The ape man spoke to his chum in whispers. Napoleon squealed and did not turn on the stereo.

"Jerry!" said his mistress. "I said nothing of the sort; he does *not* have to play your blues singer. Come away, Jerry. Nappie—play what you want to."

"You mean he tried to cheat?" McCoy inquired with interest.

"He certainly did."

"Hmm—Jerry's got the makings of a real citizen. Shave him and put shoes on him and he'd get by all right in the precinct I grew up in." He stared at the anthropoid. Jerry stared back, puzzled but patient. Mrs. van Vogel had thrown away the dirty canvas kilt which was both his badge of servitude and a concession to propriety and had replaced it with a kilt in the bright Cameron war plaid, complete to sporan, and topped off with a Glengarry.

"Do you suppose he could learn to play the bagpipes?" McCoy asked. "I'm beginning to get an angle."

"Why, I don't know. What's your idea?"

McCoy squatted down cross-legged and began practicing rolls with his dice. "Never mind," he answered when it suited him, "that angle's no good. But we're getting there." He rolled four naturals, one after the other. "You say Jerry still belongs to the Corporation?"

"In a titular sense, yes. I doubt if they will ever try to repossess him."

"I wish they would try." He scooped up the dice and stood up. "It's in the bag, Sis. Forget it. I'll want to talk to your publicity man but you can quit worrying about it."

Of course Mrs. van Vogel should have knocked before entering her husband's room—but then she would not have overheard what he was saying, nor to whom.

"That's right," she heard him say, "we haven't any further need for him. Take him away, the sooner the better. Just be sure the men you send have a signed order directing us to turn him over."

She was not apprehensive, as she did not understand the conversation, but merely curious. She looked over her husband's shoulder at the video screen.

There she saw Blakesly's face. His voice was saying, "Very well, Mr. van Vogel, the anthropoid will be picked up tomorrow."

She strode up to the screen. "Just a minute, Mr. Blakesly—" then, to her husband, "Brownie, what in the world do you think you are doing?"

The expression she surprised on his face was not one he had ever let her see before. "Why don't you knock?"

"Maybe it's a good thing I didn't. Brownie, did I hear you right. Were you telling Mr. Blakesly to pick up Jerry?" She turned to the screen. "Was that it, Mr. Blakesly?"

"That is correct, Mrs. van Vogel. And I must say I find this confusion most—"

"Stow it." She turned back. "Brownie, what have you to say for yourself?"

"Martha, you are being preposterous. Between that elephant and that ape this place is a zoo. I actually caught your precious Jerry smoking my special, personal cigars today . . . not to mention the fact that both of them play the stereo all day long until a man can't get a moment's peace. I certainly don't have to stand for such things in my own house."

"Whose house, Brownie?"

"That's beside the point. I will not stand for—"

"Never mind." She turned to the screen. "My husband seems to have lost his taste for exotic animals, Mr. Blakesly. Cancel the order for a Pegasus."

"Martha!"

"Sauce for the goose, Brownie. I'll pay for your whims; I'm damned if I'll pay for your tantrums. The contract is cancelled, Mr. Blakesly. Mr. Haskell will arrange the details."

Blakesly shrugged. "Your capricious behavior will cost you, of course. The penalties—"

"I said Mr. Haskell would arrange the details. One more thing, Mister Manager Blakesly—have you done as I told you to?"

"What do you mean?"

"You know what I mean—are those poor creatures still alive and well?"

"That is not your business." He had, in fact, suspended the killings; the directors had not wanted to take any chances until they saw what the Briggs trust could manage, but Blakesly would not give her the satisfaction of knowing.

She looked at him as if he were a skipped dividend. "It's not, eh? Well, bear this in mind, you cold-blooded little pipsqueak: I'm holding you personally responsible. If just one of them dies from *anything,* I'll have your skin for a rug." She flipped off the connection and turned to her husband. "Brownie—"

"It's useless to say anything," he cut in, in the cold voice he normally used to bring her to heel. "I shall be at the Club. Good-bye!"

"That's just what I was going to suggest."

"What?"

"I'll have your clothes sent over. Do you have anything else in this house?"

He stared at her. "Don't talk like a fool, Martha."

"I'm not talking like a fool." She looked him up and down. "My, but you are handsome, Brownie. I guess I was a fool to think I could buy a big hunk of man with a checkbook. I guess a girl gets them free, or she doesn't get them at all. Thanks for the lesson." She turned and slammed out of the room and into her own suite.

Five minutes later, makeup repaired and nerves steadied by a few whiffs of Fly-Right, she called the pool room of the Three Planets Club. McCoy came to the screen carrying a cue. "Oh, it's you, sugar puss. Well, snap it up—I've got four bits on this game."

"This is business."

"Okay, okay—spill it."

She told him the essentials. "I'm sorry about cancelling the flying horse contract, Mr. McCoy. I hope it won't make your job any harder. I'm afraid I lost my temper."

"Fine. Go lose it again."

"Huh?"

"You're barrelling down the groove, kid. Call Blakesly up again. Bawl him out. Tell him to keep his bailiffs away from you, or you'll stuff 'em and use them for hat racks. Dare him to take Jerry away from you."

"I don't understand you."

"You don't have to, girlie. Remember this: You can't have a bull fight until you get the bull mad enough to fight. Have Weinberg get a temporary injunction restraining Workers, Incorporated, from reclaiming Jerry. Have your boss press agent give me a buzz. Then you call in the newsboys and tell them what you think of Blakesly. Make it nasty. Tell them you intend to put a stop to this wholesale murder if it takes every cent you've got."

"Well . . . all right. Will you come to see me before I talk to them?"

"Nope—gotta get back to my game. Tomorrow, maybe. Don't fret about having cancelled that silly winged-horse deal. I always did think your old man was weak in the head, and it's saved you a nice piece of change. You'll need it when I send in my bill. Boy, am I going to clip you! Bye now."

The bright letters trailed around the sides of the Times Building: "WORLD'S RICHEST WOMAN PUTS UP FIGHT FOR APE MAN." On the giant video screen above showed a transcribe of Jerry, in his ridiculous Highland chief outfit. A small army of police surrounded the Briggs town house, while Mrs. van Vogel informed anyone who would listen, including several news services, that she would defend Jerry personally and to the death.

The public relations office of Workers, Incorporated, denied any intention of seizing Jerry; the denial got nowhere.

In the meantime technicians installed extra audio and video circuits in the largest court room in town, for one Jerry (no surname), described as a legal, permanent resident of these United States, had asked for a permanent injunction against the corporate person "Workers," its officers, employees, successors, or assignees, forbidding it to do him any physical harm and in particular forbidding it to kill him.

Through his attorney, the honorable and distinguished and stuffily respectable Augustus Pomfrey, Jerry brought the action *in his own name.*

❖

Martha van Vogel sat in the court room as a spectator only, but she was surrounded by secretaries, guards, maid, publicity men, and yes men, and had one television camera trained on her alone. She was nervous. McCoy had insisted on briefing Pomfrey through Weinberg, to keep Pomfrey from knowing that he was being helped by a shyster. She had her own opinion of Pomfrey—

The McCoy had insisted that Jerry not wear his beautiful new kilt but had dressed him in faded dungaree trousers and jacket. It seemed poor theater to her.

Jerry himself worried her. He seemed confused by the lights and the noise and the crowd, about to go to pieces.

And McCoy had refused to go to the trial with her. He had told her that it was quite impossible, that his mere presence would alienate the court, and Weinberg had backed him up. Men! Their minds were devious—they seemed to *like* twisted ways of doing things. It confirmed her opinion that men should not be allowed to vote.

But she felt lost without the immediate presence of McCoy's easy self-confidence. Away from him, she wondered why she had ever trusted such an important matter to an irresponsible, jumping jack, bird-brained clown as McCoy. She chewed her nails and wished he were present.

The panel of attorneys appearing for Worker's Incorporated, began by moving that the action be dismissed without trial, on the theory that Jerry was a chattel of the corporation, an integral part of it, and no more able to sue than the thumb can sue the brain.

The honorable Augustus Pomfrey looked every inch the statesman as he bowed to the court and to his opponents. "It is indeed strange," he began, "to hear the second-hand voice of a legal fiction, a soulless, imaginary quantity called a corporate 'person,' argue that a flesh-and-blood creature, a being of hopes and longings and passions, has not legal existence. I see here beside me my poor cousin Jerry." He patted Jerry on the shoulder; the ape man, needing reassurance, slid a hand into his. It went over well.

"But when I look for this abstract fancy 'Workers,' what do I find? Nothing—some words on paper, some signed bits of foolscap—"

"If the Court please, a question," put in the opposition chief attorney, "does the learned counsel contend that a limited liability stock company cannot own property?"

"Will the counsel reply?" directed the judge.

"Thank you. My esteemed colleague has set up a straw man; I contended only that the question as to whether Jerry is a chattel of Workers, Incorporated, is immaterial, nonessential, irrelevant. I am part of the corporate city of Great New York. Does that deny me my civil rights as a person of flesh and blood? In fact it does not even rob me of my right to sue that civic corporation of which I am a part, if, in my opinion, I am wronged by it. We are met today in the mellow light of equity, rather than in the cold and narrow confines of law. It seemed a fit time to dwell on the strange absurdities we live by, whereunder a nonentity of paper and legal fiction could deny the existence of this our poor cousin. I ask that the learned attorneys for the corporation stipulate that Jerry does, in fact, exist, and let us get on with the action."

They huddled; the answer was "No."

"Very well. My client asked to be examined in order that the court may determine his status and being."

"Objection! This anthropoid cannot be examined; he is a mere part and chattel of the respondent."

"That is what we are about to determine," the judge answered dryly. "Objection overruled."

"Go sit in that chair, Jerry."

"Objection! This beast cannot take an oath—it is beyond his comprehension."

"What have you to say to that, Counsel?"

"If it pleases the Court," answered Pomfrey, "the simplest thing to do is to put him in the chair and find out."

"Let him take the stand. The clerk will administer the oath." Martha van Vogel gripped the arms of her chair; McCoy had spent a full week training him for this. Would the poor thing blow up without McCoy to guide him?

The clerk droned through the oath; Jerry looked puzzled but patient.

"Your honor," said Pomfrey, "when young children must give testimony, it is customary to permit a little leeway in the wording, to fit their mental attainments. May I be permitted?" He walked up to Jerry.

"Jerry, my boy, are you a good worker?"

"Sure mike! Jerry good worker!"

"Maybe bad worker, huh? Lazy. Hide from strawboss."

"No, no, no! Jerry good worker. Dig. Weed. Not dig up vegetaber. Dig up weed. Work hard."

"You will see," Pomfrey addressed the court, "that my client has very definite ideas of what is true and what is false. Now let us attempt to find out whether or not he has moral values which require him to tell the truth. Jerry—"

"Yes, Boss."

Pomfrey spread his hand in front of the anthropoid's face. "How many fingers do you see?"

Jerry reached out and ticked them off. "One—two—sree—four, uh—five."

"Six fingers, Jerry."

"Five, Boss."

"Six fingers, Jerry. I give you cigarette. Six."

"Five, Boss. Jerry not cheat."

Pomfrey spread his hands. "Will the court accept him?"

The court did. Martha van Vogel sighed. Jerry could not count very well and she had been afraid that he would forget his lines and accept the bribe. But he had been promised all the cigarettes he wanted and chocolate as well if he would remember to insist that five was five.

"I suggest," Pomfrey went on, "that the matter has been established. Jerry is an entity; if he can be accepted as a witness, then surely he may have his day in court. Even a dog may have his day in court. Will my esteemed colleagues stipulate?"

Workers, Incorporated, through its battery of lawyers, agreed—just in time, for the judge was beginning to cloud up. He had been much impressed by the little performance.

The tide was with him; Pomfrey used it. "If it please the court and if the counsels for the respondent will permit, we can shorten these proceedings. I will state the theory under which relief is sought and then, by a few questions, it may be settled one way or another. I ask that it be stipulated that it was the intention of Workers, Incorporated, through its servants, to take the life of my client."

Stipulation was refused.

"So? Then I ask that the court take judicial notice of the well-known fact that these anthropoid workers are destroyed when they no longer show a profit; thereafter I will call witnesses, starting with Horace Blakesly, to show that Jerry was and presumably is under such sentence of death."

Another hurried huddle resulted in the stipulation that Jerry had, indeed, been scheduled for euthanasia.

"Then," said Pomfrey, "I will state my theory. Jerry is not an animal, but a man. It is not legal to kill him—it is murder."

First there was silence, then the crowd gasped. People had grown used to animals that talked and worked, but they were no more prepared to think of them as persons, humans, *men,* than were the haughty Roman citizens prepared to concede human feelings to their barbarian slaves.

Pomfrey let them have it while they were still groggy. "What is a man? A collection of living cells and tissues? A legal fiction, like this corporate 'person' that would take poor Jerry's life? No, a man is none of these things. A man is a collection of hopes and fears, of human longings, of aspirations greater than himself—more than the clay from which he came; less than the Creator which lifted him up from the clay. Jerry has been taken from his jungle and made something more than the poor creatures who were his ancestors, even as you and I. We ask that this Court recognize his manhood."

The opposing attorneys saw that the Court was moved; they drove in fast. An anthropoid, they contended, could not be a man because he lacked human shape and human intelligence. Pomfrey called his first witness—Master B'na Kreeth.

The Martian's normal bad temper had not been improved by being forced to wait around for three days in a travel tank, to say nothing of the indignity of having to interrupt his researches to take part in the childish pow-wows of terrestrials.

There was further delay to irritate him while Pomfrey forced the corporation attorneys to accept B'na as an expert witness. They wanted to refuse but could not—he was their own Director of Research. He also held voting control of all Martian-held Workers' stock, a fact unmentioned but hampering.

More delay while an interpreter was brought in to help administer the oath—B'na Kreeth, self-centered as all Martians, had never bothered to learn English.

He twittered and chirped in answer to the demand that he tell the truth, the whole truth, and so forth; the interpreter looked pained. "He says he can't do it," he informed the judge.

Pomfrey asked for exact translation.

The interpreter looked uneasily at the judge. "He says that if he told the whole truth you fools—not 'fools' exactly; it's a Martian word meaning a sort of headless worm—would not understand it."

The court discussed the idea of contempt briefly. When the Martian understood that he was about to be forced to remain in a travel tank for thirty days he came down off his high horse and agreed to tell the truth as adequately as was possible; he was accepted as a witness.

"Are you a man?" demanded Pomfrey.

"Under your laws and by your standards I am a man."

"By what theory? Your body is unlike ours; you cannot even live in our air. You do not speak our language; your ideas are alien to us. How can you be a man?"

The Martian answered carefully: *"I quote from the Terra-Martian Treaty, which you must accept as supreme law. 'All members of the Great Race, while sojourning on the Third Planet, shall have all the rights and prerogatives of the native dominant race of the Third*

Planet.' This clause has been interpreted by the Bi-Planet Tribunal to mean that members of the Great Race are 'men' whatever that may be."

"Why do you refer to your sort as the 'Great Race'?"

"Because of our superior intelligence."

"Superior to men?"

"We are men."

"Superior to the intelligence of earth men?"

"That is self-evident."

"Just as we are superior in intelligence to this poor creature Jerry?"

"That is not self-evident."

"Finished with the witness," announced Pomfrey. The opposition counsels should have left bad enough alone; instead they tried to get B'na Kreeth to define the difference in intelligence between humans and worker-anthropoids. Master B'na explained meticulously that cultural differences masked the intrinsic differences, if any, and that, in any case, both anthropoids and men made so little use of their respective potential intelligences that it was really too early to tell which race would turn out to be the superior race in the Third Planet.

He had just begun to discuss how a truly superior race could be bred by combining the best features of anthropoids and men when he was hastily asked to "stand down."

"May it please the Court," said Pomfrey, "we have not advanced the theory; we have merely disposed of respondent's contention that a particular shape and a particular degree of intelligence are necessary to manhood. I now ask that the petitioner be recalled to the stand that the court may determine whether he is, in truth, human."

"If the learned court please—" The battery of lawyers had been in a huddle ever since B'na Kreeth's travel tank had been removed from the room; the chief counsel now spoke.

"The object of the petition appears to be to protect the life of this chattel. There is no need to draw out these proceedings; respondent stipulates that this chattel will be allowed to die a natural death in the hands of its present custodian and moves that the action be dismissed."

"What do you say to that?" the Court asked Pomfrey.

Pomfrey visibly gathered his toga about him. "We ask not for cold charity from this corporation, but for the justice of the court. We ask that Jerry's humanity be established as a matter of law. Not for him to vote, nor to hold property, nor to be relieved of special police regulations appropriate to his group—but we do ask that he be adjudged at least as human as that aquarium monstrosity just removed from this court room!"

The judge turned to Jerry. "Is that what you want, Jerry?"

Jerry looked uneasily at Pomfrey, then said, "Okay, Boss."

"Come up to the chair."

"One moment—" The opposition chief counsel seemed flurried. "I ask the Court to consider that a ruling in this matter may affect a long-established commercial practice necessary to the economic life of—"

"Objection!" Pomfrey was on his feet, bristling. "Never have I heard a more outrageous attempt to prejudice a decision. My esteemed colleague might as well ask the Court to decide a murder case from political considerations. I protest—"

"Never mind," said the court. "The suggestion will be ignored. Proceed with your witness."

Pomfrey bowed. "We are exploring the meaning of this strange thing called 'manhood.' We have seen that it is not a matter of shape, nor race, nor planet of birth, nor of acuteness of mind. Truly, it cannot be defined, yet it may be experienced. It can reach from heart to heart, from spirit to spirit." He turned to Jerry. "Jerry—will you sing your new song for the judge?"

"Sure mike." Jerry looked uneasily up at the whirring cameras, the mikes, and the ikes, then cleared his throat:

"Way down upon de Suwannee Ribber
Far, far away;
Dere's where my heart is turning ebber—"

The applause scared him out of his wits; the banging of the gavel frightened him still more—but it mattered not; the issue was no longer in doubt. Jerry was a man.

WATER IS FOR WASHING
Argosy, November 1947

HE JUDGED THAT the valley was hotter than usual—but, then, it usually was. Imperial Valley was a natural hothouse, two hundred and fifty feet below sea level, diked from the Pacific Ocean by the mountains back of San Diego, protected from the Gulf of Baja California by high ground on the south. On the east, the Chocolate Mountains walled off the rushing Colorado River.

He parked his car outside the Barbara Worth Hotel in El Centro and went into the bar. "Scotch."

The bartender filled a shot glass, then set a glass of ice water beside it. "Thanks. Have one?"

"Don't mind if I do."

The customer sipped his drink, then picked up the chaser. "That's just the right amount of water in the right place. I've got hydrophobia."

"Huh?"

"I hate water. Darn near drowned when I was a kid. Afraid of it ever since."

"Water ain't fit to drink," the bartender agreed, "but I do like to swim."

"Not for me. That's why I like the Valley. They restrict the stuff to irrigation ditches, washbowls, bathtubs, and glasses. I always hate to go back to Los Angeles."

"If you're afraid of drowning," the barkeep answered, "you're better off in L.A. than in the Valley. We're below sea level here. Water all around us, higher than our heads. Suppose somebody pulled out the cork?"

"Go frighten your grandmother. The Coast Range is no cork."

"Earthquake."

"That's crazy. Earthquakes don't move mountain ranges."

"Well, it wouldn't necessarily take a quake. You've heard about the 1905 flood, when the Colorado River spilled over and formed the Salton Sea? But don't be too sure about quakes; valleys below sea level don't just grow—*something* has to cause them. The San Andreas Fault curls around this valley like a question mark. Just imagine the shake-up it must have taken to drop thousands of square miles below the level of the Pacific."

"Quit trying to get my goat. That happened thousands of years ago. Here." He laid a bill on the bar and left. Joy-killer! A man like that shouldn't be tending bar.

The thermometer in the shaded doorway showed 118 degrees. The solid heat beat against him, smarting his eyes and drying his lungs, even while he remained on the covered sidewalk. His car, he knew, would be too hot to touch; he should have garaged it. He walked around the end of it and saw someone bending over the lefthand door. He stopped. "What the hell do you think you're doing?"

The figure turned suddenly, showing pale, shifty eyes. He was dressed in a business suit, dirty and unpressed. He was tieless. His hands and nails were dirty, but not with the dirt of work; the palms were uncalloused. A weak mouth spoiled features otherwise satisfactory. "No harm intended," he apologized. "I just wanted to read your registration slip. You're from Los Angeles. Give me a lift back to the city, pal."

The car owner ignored him and glanced around inside the automobile. "Just wanted to see where I was from, eh? Then why did you open the glove compartment? I ought to run you in." He looked past the vagrant at two uniformed deputy sheriffs sauntering down the other side of the street: "On your way, bum."

The man followed the glance, then faded swiftly away in the other direction. The car's owner climbed in, swearing at the heat, then checked the glove compartment. The flashlight was missing.

Checking it off to profit-and-loss, he headed for Brawley, fifteen miles north. The heat was oppressive, even for Imperial Valley. Earthquake weather, he said to himself, giving vent to the Californian's favorite superstition, then sternly denied it—that dumb fool gin peddler had put the idea in his mind. Just an ordinary Valley day, a little hotter, maybe.

His business took him to several outlying ranchos between Brawley and the Salton Sea. He was heading back toward the main highway on a worn gravel mat when the car began to waltz around as if he were driving over corduroy. He stopped the car, but the shaking continued, accompanied by a bass grumble.

Earthquake! He burst out of the car possessed only by the primal urge to get out in the open, to escape the swaying towers, the falling bricks. But there were no buildings here—nothing but open desert and irrigated fields.

He went back to the car, his stomach lurching to every following temblor. The right front tire was flat. Stone-punctured, he decided, when the car was bounced around by the first big shock.

Changing that tire almost broke his heart. He was faint from heat and exertion when he straightened up from it.

Another shock, not as heavy as the first, but heavy, panicked him again and he began to run, but he fell, tripped by the crazy galloping of the ground. He got up and went back to the car.

It had slumped drunkenly, the jack knocked over by the quake.

He wanted to abandon it, but the dust from the shocks had closed in around him like fog, without fog's blessed coolness. He knew he was several miles from town and doubted his ability to make it on foot.

He got to work, sweating and gasping. One hour and thirteen minutes after the initial shock the spare tire was in place. The ground still grumbled and shook from time to time. He resolved to drive slowly and thereby keep the car in control if another bad shock came along. The dust forced him to drive slowly, anyhow.

Moseying back toward the main highway, he was regaining his calm, when he became aware of a train in the distance. The roar increased, over the noise of the car—an express train, he decided, plunging down the valley. The thought niggled at the back of his mind for a moment, until he realized why the sound seemed wrong: Trains should not race after a quake; they should creep along, the crew alert for spread rails.

The sound was recast in his mind. *Water!*

Out of the nightmare depths of his subconscious, out of the fright of his childhood, he placed it. This was the sound after the dam broke, when, as a kid, he had been so nearly drowned. Water! A great wall of water, somewhere in the dust, hunting for him, hunting for *him!*

His foot jammed the accelerator down to the floorboards; the car bucked and promptly stalled. He started it again and strove to keep himself calm. With no spare tire and a bumpy road he could not afford the risk of too much speed. He held himself down to a crawling thirty-five miles an hour, tried to estimate the distance and direction of the water, and prayed.

The main highway jumped at him in the dust and he was almost run down by a big car roaring past to the north. A second followed it, then a vegetable truck, then the tractor unit of a semi-trailer freighter.

It was all he needed to know. He turned north.

He passed the vegetable truck and a jalopy-load of Okie-style workers, a family. They shouted at him, but he kept going. Several cars more powerful than his passed him and he passed in turn several of the heaps used by the itinerant farm workers. After that he had the road to himself. Nothing came from the north.

The trainlike rumble behind him increased.

He peered into the rear-view mirror but could see nothing through the dusty haze.

There was a child sitting beside the road and crying—a little girl about eight. He drove on past, hardly aware of her, then braked to a stop. He told himself that she must have folks around somewhere, that it was no business of his. Cursing himself, he backed and turned, almost drove past her in the dust, then managed to turn around without backing and pulled up beside her. "Get in!"

She turned a dirty, wet, tragic face, but remained seated. "I can't. My foot hurts."

He jumped out, scooped her up and dumped her in the righthand seat, noting as he did so that her right foot was swollen. "How did you do it?" he demanded, as he threw in the clutch.

"When the *thing* happened. Is it broke?" She was not crying now. "Are you going to take me home?"

"I—I'll take care of you. Don't ask questions."

"All right," she said doubtfully. The roar behind them was increasing. He wanted to speed up but the haze and the need to nurse his unreliable spare tire held him back. He had to swerve suddenly when a figure loomed up in the dust—a Nisei boy, hurrying toward them.

The child beside him leaned out. "That's Tommy!"

"Huh? Never mind. Just a goddam Jap."

"That's Tommy Hayakawa. He's in my class." She added. "Maybe he's looking for me."

He cursed again, under his breath, and threw the car into a turn that almost toppled it. Then he was heading back, into that awful sound.

"There he is," the child shrieked. "Tommy! Oh, Tommy!"

"Get in," he commanded, when he had stopped the car by the boy.

"Get in, Tommy," his passenger added.

The boy hesitated; the driver reached past the little girl, grabbed the boy by his shirt and dragged him in. "Want to be drowned, you fool?"

He had just shifted into second, and was still accelerating, when another figure sprang up almost in front of the car—a man, waving his arms. He caught a glimpse of the face as the car gained speed. It was the sneak thief.

His conscience was easy about that one, he thought as he drove on. Good riddance! Let the water get him.

Then the horror out of his own childhood welled up in him and he saw the face of the tramp again, in a horrible fantasy. He was struggling in the water, his bloodshot eyes bulging with terror, his gasping mouth crying wordlessly for help.

The driver was stopping the car. He did not dare turn; he backed the car, at the highest speed he could manage. It was no great distance, or else the vagrant had run after them.

The door was jerked open and the tramp lurched in. "Thanks, pal," he gasped. "Let's get out of here!"

"Right!" He glanced into the mirror, then stuck his head out and looked behind. Through the haze he saw it, a lead-black wall, thirty—or was it a hundred?—feet high, rushing down on them, overwhelming them. The noise of it pounded his skull.

He gunned the car in second, then slid into high and gave it all he had, careless of the tires. "How we doing?" he yelled.

The tramp looked out the rear window. "We're gaining. Keep it up."

He skidded around a wreck on the highway, then slowed a trifle, aware that the breakneck flight would surely lose them the questionable safety of the car if he kept it up. The little girl started to cry.

"Shut up!" he snapped.

The Nisei boy twisted around and looked behind. "What is it?" he asked in an awed voice.

The tramp answered him. "The Pacific Ocean has broken through."

"It can't be!" cried the driver. "It must be the Colorado River."

"That's no river, Mac. That's the Gulf. I was in a cantina in Centro when it came over the radio from Calexico. Warned us that the ground had dropped away to the south. Tidal wave coming. Then the station went dead." He moistened his lips. "That's why I'm here."

The driver did not answer. The vagrant went on nervously, "Guy I hitched with went on without me, when he stopped for gas in Brawley." He looked back again. "I can't see it any more."

"We've gotten away from it?"

"Hell, no. It's just as loud. I just can't see it through the murk."

They drove on. The road curved a little to the right and dropped away almost imperceptibly.

The bum looked ahead. Suddenly he yelled. "Hey! Where you going?"

"Huh?"

"You got to get off the highway, man! We're dropping back toward the Salton Sea—the lowest place in the Valley."

"There's no other place to go. We *can't* turn around."

"You can't go ahead. It's suicide!"

"We'll outrun it. North of the Salton, it's high ground again."

"Not a chance. Look at your gas gauge."

The gauge was fluttering around the left side of the dial. Two gallons, maybe less. Enough to strand them by the sunken shores of the Salton Sea. He stared at it in an agony of indecision.

"Gotta cut off to the left," his passenger was saying. "Side road. Follow it up toward the hills."

"Where?"

"Coming up. I know this road. I'll watch for it."

When he turned into the side road, he realized sickly that his course was now nearly parallel to the hungry flood south of them. But the road climbed.

He looked to the left and tried to see the black wall of water, the noise of which beat loud in his ears, but the road demanded his attention. "Can you see it?" he yelled to the tramp.

"Yes! Keep trying, pal!"

He nodded and concentrated on the hills ahead. The hills must surely be above sea level, he told himself. On and on he drove, through a timeless waste of dust and heat and roar. The grade increased, then suddenly the car broke over a rise and headed down into a wash—a shallow arroyo that should have been dry, but was not.

He was into water before he knew it, hub high and higher. He braked and tried to back. The engine coughed and stalled.

The tramp jerked open the door, dragged the two children out, and, with one under each arm, splashed his way back to higher ground. The driver tried to start the car, then saw frantically that the rising water was up above the floorboards. He jumped out, stumbled to his knees in water waist-deep, got to his feet, and struggled after them.

The tramp had set the children down on a little rise and was looking around. "We got to get out of here," the car owner gasped.

The tramp shook his head. "No good. Look around you."

To the south, the wall of water had broken around the rise on which they stood. A branch had sluiced between them and the hills, filling the wash in which the car lay stalled. The main body of the rushing waters had passed east of them, covering the highway they had left, and sweeping on toward the Salton Sea.

Even as he watched, the secondary flood down the wash returned to the parent body. They were cut off, surrounded by the waters.

He wanted to scream, to throw himself into the opaque turbulence and get it over. Perhaps he did scream. He realized that the tramp was shaking him by the shoulder.

"Take it easy, pal. We've got a couple of throws left."

"Huh?" He wiped his eyes. "What do we do?"

"I want my mother," the little girl said decisively.

The tramp reached down and patted her absent-mindedly.

Tommy Hayakawa put his arm around her. "I'll take care of you, Laura," he said gravely.

The water was already over the top of the car and rising. The boiling head of the flood was well past them; its thunder was lessening; the waters rose quietly—but they rose.

"We can't stay here," he persisted.

"We'll have to," the tramp answered. . . .

Their living space grew smaller, hardly thirty feet by fifty. They were not alone now. A coyote, jack rabbits, creepers, crawlers, and gnawers, all the poor relations of the desert, were forced equally back into the narrowing circle of dry land. The coyote ignored the rabbits; they ignored the coyote. The highest point of their island was surmounted by a rough concrete post about four feet high, an obelisk with a brass plate set in its side. He read it twice before the meaning of the words came to him.

It was a bench mark, stating, as well as latitude and longitude, that this spot, this line engraved in brass, was "sea level." When it soaked into his confused brain he pointed it out to his companion. "Hey! Hey, look! We're going to make it! The water won't come any higher!"

The tramp looked. "Yes, I know. I read it. But it doesn't mean anything. That's the level it used to be before the earthquake."

"But—"

"It may be higher—or lower. We'll find out."

The waters still came up. They were ankle-deep at sundown. The rabbits and the other small things were gradually giving up. They were in an unbroken waste of water, stretching from the Chocolate Mountains beyond where the Salton Sea had been, to the nearer hills on the west. The coyote slunk up against their knees, dog fashion, then appeared to make up its mind, for it slipped into the water and struck out toward the hills. They could see its out-thrust head for a long time, until it was just a dot on the water in the gathering darkness.

When the water was knee-deep, each man took one of the children in his arms. They braced themselves against the stability of the concrete post, and waited, too tired for panic. They did not talk. Even the children had not talked much since abandoning the car.

It was getting dark. The tramp spoke up suddenly. "Can you pray?"

"Uh—not very well."

"Okay. I'll try, then." He took a deep breath. "Merciful Father,

Whose all-seeing eye notes even the sparrow in its flight, have mercy on these Thy unworthy servants. Deliver them from this peril, if it be Thy will." He paused, and then added, "And make it as fast as You can, please. Amen."

The darkness closed in, complete and starless. They could not see the water, but they could feel it and hear it. It was warm—it felt no worse when it soaked their armpits than it had around their ankles. They had the kids on their shoulders now, with their backs braced against the submerged post. There was little current.

Once something bumped against them in the darkness—a dead steer, driftwood, a corpse—they had no way of knowing. It nudged them and was gone. Once he thought he saw a light, and said suddenly to the tramp, "Have you still got that flashlight you swiped from me?"

There was a long silence and a strained voice answered, "You recognized me."

"Of course. Where's the flashlight?"

"I traded it for a drink in Centro."

"But, look, Mac," the voice went on reasonably, "if I hadn't borrowed it, it would be in your car. It wouldn't be here. And if I *did* have it in my pocket, it'd be soaked and wouldn't work."

"Oh, forget it!"

"Okay." There was silence for a while, then the voice went on, "Pal, could you hold both the kids a while?"

"I guess so. Why?"

"This water is still coming up. It'll be over our heads, maybe. You hang onto the kids; I'll boost myself up on the post. I'll sit on it and wrap my legs around it. Then you hand me the kids. That way we gain maybe eighteen inches or two feet."

"And what happens to me?"

"You hang onto my shoulders and float with your head out of the water."

"Well—we'll try it."

It worked. The kids clung to the tramp's sides, supported by water and by his arms. The driver hung onto the tramp where he could, first to his belt, then, as the waters rose and his toes no longer touched bottom, to the collar of his coat. They were still alive.

"I wish it would get light. It's worse in the darkness."

"Yeah," said the tramp. "If it was light, maybe somebody 'ud see us."

"How?"

"Airplane, maybe. They always send out airplanes, in floods."

He suddenly began to shake violently, as the horror came over him, and the memory of another flood when there had been no rescuing airplanes.

The tramp said sharply, "What's the matter, Mac? Are you cracking up?"

"No, I'm all right. I just hate water."

"Want to swap around? You hold the kids for a while and I'll hang on and float."

"Uh. . . . No, we might drop one. Stay where you are."

"We can make it. The change'll do you good." The tramp shook the children. "Hey, wake up! wake up, honey—and hold tight."

The kids were transferred to his shoulders while he gripped the post with his knees and the tramp steadied him with an arm. Then he eased himself cautiously onto the top of the post, as the tramp got off and floated free, save for one anchoring hand. "You all right?" he said to the tramp.

The hand squeezed his shoulder in the darkness. "Sure. Got a snootful of water."

"Hang on."

"Don't worry—I will!"

He was shorter than the tramp; he had to sit erect to keep his head out of water. The children clung tightly. He kept them boosted high.

Presently the tramp spoke. "You wearing a belt?"

"Yes. Why?"

"Hold still." He felt a second hand fumbling at his waist, then his trousers loosened as the belt came away. "I'm going to strap your legs to the post. That's the bad part about it; your legs cramp. Hold tight now. I'm going under."

He felt hands under water, fumbling at his legs. Then there was the tension of the belt being tightened around his knees. He relaxed to the pressure. It *was* a help; he found he could hold his position without muscular effort.

The tramp broke water near him. "Where are you?" the voice was panicky.

"Here! Over here!" he tried to peer into the inky darkness; it was hopeless. "Over this way!" The splashing seemed to come closer. He shouted again, but no hand reached out of the darkness. He continued to shout, then shouted and listened intermittently. It seemed to him that he heard splashing long after the sound had actually ceased.

He stopped shouting only when his voice gave out. Little Laura was sobbing on his shoulder. Tommy was trying to get her to stop. He could tell from their words that they had not understood what had happened and he did not try to explain.

When the water dropped down to his waist, he moved the kids so that they sat on his lap. This let him rest his arms, which had grown almost unbearably tired as the receding water ceased to support the weight of the children. The water dropped still more, and the half dawn showed him that the ground beneath him was, if not dry, at least free from flood.

He shook Tommy awake. "I can't get down, kid. Can you unstrap me?"

The boy blinked and rubbed his eyes. He looked around and seemed to recall his circumstances without dismay. "Sure. Put me down."

The boy loosened the buckle after some difficulty and the man cautiously unwound himself from his perch. His legs refused him when he tried to stand; they let him and the girl sprawl in the mud.

"Are you hurt?" he asked her as he sat up.

"No," she answered soberly.

He looked around. It was getting steadily lighter and he could see the hills to the west; it now appeared that the water no longer extended between the hills and themselves. To the east was another story; the Salton Sea no longer existed as such. An unbroken sheet of water stretched from miles to the north clear to the southern horizon.

His car was in sight; the wash was free of water except for casual pools. He walked down toward the automobile, partly to take the knots out of his legs, partly to see if the car could ever be salvaged. It was there that he found the tramp.

The body lay wedged against the right rear wheel, as if carried down there by undertow.

He walked back toward the kids. "Stay away from the car," he ordered. "Wait here. I've got something to do." He went back to the car and found the keys still in the ignition lock. He opened the trunk with some difficulty and got out a short spade he kept for desert mishaps.

It was not much of a grave, just a shallow trench in the wet sand, deep enough to receive and cover a man, but he promised himself that he would come back and do better. He had no time now. The waters, he thought, would be back with high tide. He must get himself and the children to the hills.

Once the body was out of sight, he called out to the boy and the girl, "You can come here now." He had one more chore. There was drift about, yucca stalks, bits of wood. He selected two pieces of unequal length, then dug around in his tool chest for bits of wire. He wired the short piece across the longer, in a rough cross, then planted the cross in the sand near the head of the grave.

He stepped back and looked at it, the kids at his side.

His lips moved silently for a moment, then he said, "Come on, kids. We got to get out of here." He picked up the little girl, took the boy by the hand, and they walked away to the west, the sun shining on their backs.

NOTHING EVER HAPPENS ON THE MOON

Boys' Life, April–May 1949

"I NEVER KNEW a boy from Earth who wasn't cocky."

Mr. Andrews frowned at his Senior Patrol Leader. "That's childish, Sam. And no answer. I arrive expecting to find the troop ready to hike. Instead I find you and our visitor about to fight. And both of you Eagle Scouts! What started it?"

Sam reluctantly produced a clipping. "This, I guess."

It was from the Colorado Scouting News and read: "Troop 48, Denver—LOCAL SCOUT SEEKS SKY-HIGH HONOR. Bruce Holli-field, Eagle Scout, is moving with his family to South Pole, Venus. Those who know Bruce—and who doesn't—expect him to qualify as Eagle (Venus) in jig time. Bruce will spend three weeks at Luna City, waiting for the Moon-Venus transport. Bruce has been boning up lately on lunar Scouting, and he has already qualified in space suit operation in the vacuum chamber at the Pike's Peak space port. Cornered, Bruce admitted that he hopes to pass the tests for Eagle Scout (Luna) while on the Moon.

"If he does—and we're betting on Bruce!—he's a dead cinch to be-come the first Triple Eagle in history.

"Go to it, Bruce! Denver is proud of you. Show those Moon Scouts what real Scouting is like."

Mr. Andrews looked up. "Where did this come from?"

"Uh, somebody sent it to Peewee."

"Yes?"

"Well, we all read it and when Bruce came in, the fellows ribbed him. He got sore."

"Why didn't you stop it?"

"Uh . . . well, I was doing it myself."

"Humph! Sam, this item is no sillier than the stuff our own Scribe turns in for publication. Bruce didn't write it, and you yahoos had no business making his life miserable. Send him in. Meantime call the roll."

"Yes, sir. Uh, Mr. Andrews—"

"Yes?"

"What's *your* opinion? Can this kid possibly qualify for lunar Eagle in three weeks?"

"No—and I've told him so. But he's durn well going to have his chance. Which reminds me: you're his instructor."

"Me?" Sam looked stricken.

"You. You've let me down, Sam; this is your chance to correct it. Understand me?"

Sam swallowed. "I guess I do."

"Send Hollifield in."

Sam found the boy from Earth standing alone, pretending to study the bulletin board. Sam touched his arm. "The Skipper wants you."

Bruce whirled around, then stalked away. Sam shrugged and shouted, "Rocket Patrol—fall in!"

Speedy Owens echoed, "Crescent Patrol—fall in!" As muster ended Mr. Andrews came out of his office, followed by Bruce. The Earth Scout seemed considerably chastened. .

"Mr. Andrews says I'm to report to you."

"That's right." They eyed each other cautiously. Sam said, "Look, Bruce—let's start from scratch."

"Suits me."

"Fine. Just tag along with me." At a sign from the Scoutmaster Sam shouted, "By twos! Follow me." Troop One jostled out the door, mounted a crosstown slidewalk and rode to East Air Lock.

Chubby Schneider, troop quartermaster, waited there with two assistants, near a rack of space suits. Duffel was spread around in enormous piles—packaged grub, tanks of water, huge air bottles, frames of heavy wire, a great steel drum, everything needed for pioneers on the airless crust of the Moon.

Sam introduced Bruce to the Quartermaster. "We've got to outfit him, Chubby."

"That new G.E. job might fit him."

Sam got the suit and spread it out. The suit was impregnated glass fabric, aluminum-sprayed to silvery whiteness. It closed from crotch to collar with a zippered gasket. It looked expensive; Bruce noticed a plate on the collar: DONATED BY THE LUNA CITY KIWANIS KLUB.

The helmet was a plastic bowl, silvered except where swept by the eyes of the wearer. There it was transparent, though heavily filtered.

Bruce's uniform was stowed in a locker; Chubby handed him a loose-knit coverall. Sam and Chubby stuffed him into the suit and Chubby produced the instrument belt.

Both edges of the belt zipped to the suit; there were several rows of grippers for the top edge; thus a pleat could be taken. They fastened it with maximum pleat. "How's that?" asked Sam.

"The collar cuts my shoulders."

"It won't under pressure. If we leave slack, your head will pull out of the helmet like a cork." Sam strapped the air, water, radio, and duffel-rack backpack to Bruce's shoulders. "Pressure check, Chubby."

"We'll dress first." While Chubby and Sam dressed, Bruce located his intake and exhaust valves, the spill valve inside his collar, and the water nipple beside it. He took a drink and inspected his belt.

Sam and Bruce donned helmets. Sam switched on Bruce's walkie-talkie, clipped a blood-oxygen indicator to Bruce's ear, and locked his helmet on. "Stand by for pressure," he said, his words echoing in Bruce's helmet. Chubby hooked hose from a wall gauge to Bruce's air intake.

Bruce felt the collar lift. The air in the suit grew stuffy, the helmet fogged. At thirty pounds Chubby cut the intake, and watched the gauge. Mr. Andrews joined them, a Gargantuan helmeted figure, toting a pack six feet high. "Pressure steady, sir," Chubby reported.

Sam hooked up Bruce's air supply. "Open your intake and kick your chin valve before you smother," he ordered. Bruce complied. The stale air rushed out and the helmet cleared. Sam adjusted Bruce's valves. "Watch that needle," he ordered, pointing to the blood-oxygen dial on Bruce's belt. "Keep your mix so that reads steady in the white without using your chin valve."

"I know."

"So I'll say it again. Keep that needle out of the red, or you'll explain it to Saint Peter."

The Scoutmaster asked, "What load are you giving him?"

"Oh," replied Sam, "just enough to steady him—say three hundred pounds, total."

Bruce figured—at one-sixth gravity that meant fifty pounds weight including himself, his suit, and his pack. "I'll carry my full share," he objected.

"We'll decide what's best for you," the Scoutmaster snapped. "Hurry up; the troop is ready." He left.

Sam switched off his radio and touched helmets. "Forget it," he said quietly. "The Old Man is edgy at the start of a hike." They loaded Bruce rapidly—reserve air and water bottles, a carton of grub, short, wide skis and ski poles—then hung him with field gear, first-aid kit, prospector's hammer, two climbing ropes, a pouch of pitons and snap rings, flashlight, knife. The Moon Scouts loaded up; Sam called, "Come on!"

Mr. Andrews handed the lockmaster a list and stepped inside; the three Scouts followed. Bruce felt his suit expand as the air sucked back into the underground city. A light blinked green; Mr. Andrews opened the outer door and Bruce stared across the airless lunar plain.

It dazzled him. The plain was bright under a blazing Sun. The distant needle-sharp hills seemed painted in colors too flat and harsh. He looked at the sky to rest his eyes.

It made him dizzy. He had never seen a whole skyful of stars undimmed by air. The sky was blacker than black, crowded with hard, diamond lights.

"Route march!" the Scoutmaster's voice rang in his helmet. "Heel and toe. Jack Wills out as pathfinder." A boy left the group in long, floating strides, fifteen feet at a bound. He stopped a hundred yards ahead; the troop formed single column fifty yards behind him. The Pathfinder raised his arm, swung it down, and the troop moved out.

Mr. Andrews and a Scout joined Sam and Bruce. "Speedy will help you," he told Sam, "until Bruce gets his legs. Move him along. We can't heel-and-toe and still make our mileage."

"We'll move him."

"Even if we have to carry him," added Speedy.

The Scoutmaster overtook the troop in long leaps. Bruce wanted to follow. It looked easy—like flying. He had not liked the crack about carrying him. But Sam grasped him by his left belt grip while Speedy seized the one on his right. "Here we go," Sam warned. "Feet on the ground and try to swing in with us."

Bruce started off confidently. He felt that three days of low gravity in the corridors of Luna City had given him his "legs"; being taught to walk, like a baby, was just hazing.

Nothing to it—he was light as a bird! True, it was hard to keep heel-and-toe; he wanted to float. He gained speed on a downgrade; suddenly the ground was not there when he reached for it. He threw up his hands.

He hung head down on his belt and could hear his guides laughing. "Wha' happened?" he demanded, as they righted him.

"Keep your feet on the ground."

"I know what you're up against," added Speedy, "I've been to Earth. Your mass and weight don't match and your muscles aren't used to it. You weigh what a baby weighs, Earth-side, but you've got the momentum of a fat man."

Bruce tried again. Some stops and turns showed him what Speedy meant. His pack felt like feathers, but unless he banked his turns, it would throw him, even at a walk. It *did* throw him, several times, before his legs learned.

Presently, Sam asked, "Think you're ready for a slow lope?"

"I guess so."

"Okay—but remember, if you want to turn, you've *got* to slow down first—or you'll roll like a hoop. Okay, Speedy. An eight-miler."

Bruce tried to match their swing. Long, floating strides, like flying. It *was* flying! Up! . . . float . . . brush the ground with your foot and up again. It was better than skating or skiing.

"Wups!" Sam steadied him. "Get your feet out in front."

As they swung past, Mr. Andrews gave orders for a matching lope.

The unreal hills had moved closer; Bruce felt as if he had been flying all his life. "Sam," he said, "do you suppose I can get along by myself?"

"Shouldn't wonder. We let go a couple o' miles back."

"Huh?" It was true; Bruce began to feel like a Moon hand.

Somewhat later a boy's voice called "Heel and toe!" The troop dropped into a walk. The pathfinder stood on a rise ahead, holding his skis up. The troop halted and unlashed skis. Ahead was a wide basin filled with soft, powdery stuff.

Bruce turned to Sam, and for the first time looked back to the west. "*Jee . . .* miny *Crickets!*" he breathed.

Earth hung over the distant roof of Luna City, in half phase. It was round and green and beautiful, larger than the harvest Moon and unmeasurably more lovely in forest greens, desert browns and glare white of cloud.

Sam glanced at it. "Fifteen o'clock."

Bruce tried to read the time but was stumped by the fact that the sunrise line ran mostly across ocean. He questioned Sam. "Huh? See that bright dot on the dark side? That's Honolulu—figure from there."

Bruce mulled this over while binding his skis, then stood up and turned around, without tripping. "Hmmm—" said Sam, "you're used to skis."

"Got my badge."

"Well, this is different. Just shuffle along and try to keep your feet."

Bruce resolved to stay on his feet if it killed him. He let a handful of the soft stuff trickle through his glove. It was light and flaky, hardly packed at all. He wondered what had caused it.

Mr. Andrews sent Speedy out to blaze trail; Sam and Bruce joined the column. Bruce was hard put to keep up. The loose soil flew to left and right, settling so slowly in the weak gravity that it seemed to float in air—yet a ski pole, swung through such a cloud, cut a knife-sharp hole without swirling it.

The column swung wide to the left, then back again. Off to the right was a circular depression perhaps fifty yards across; Bruce could not see the bottom. He paused, intending to question Sam; the Scoutmaster's voice prodded him. "Bruce! Keep moving!"

Much later Speedy's voice called out, "Hard ground!" Shortly the column reached it and stopped to remove skis. Bruce switched off his radio and touched his helmet to Sam's.

"What was that back where the Skipper yelled at me?"

"That? That was a morning glory. They're poison!"

"A 'morning glory'?"

"Sort of a sink hole. If you get on the slope, you never get out. Crumbles out from under you and you wind up buried in the bottom. There you stay—until your air gives out. Lot of prospectors die that way. They go out alone and are likely to come back in the dark."

"How do you know what happens if they go out alone?"

"Suppose you saw tracks leading up to one and no tracks going away?"

"Oh!" Bruce felt silly.

The troop swung into a lope; slowly the hills drew closer and loomed high into the sky. Mr. Andrews called a halt. "Camp," he said. "Sam, spot the shelter west of that outcropping. Bruce, watch what Sam does."

The shelter was an airtight tent, framed by a half cylinder of woven heavy wire. The frame came in sections. The Scoutmaster's huge pack was the air bag.

The skeleton was erected over a ground frame, anchored at corners and over which was spread an asbestos pad. The curved roof and wall sections followed. Sam tested joints with a wrench, then ordered the air bag unrolled. The air lock, a steel drum, was locked into the frame and gasketed to the bag. Meanwhile, two Scouts were rigging a Sun shade.

Five boys crawled inside and stood up, arms stretched high. The others passed in all the duffel except skis and poles. Mr. Andrews was last in and closed the air lock. The metal frame blocked radio communication; Sam plugged a phone connection from the lock to his helmet. "Testing," he said.

Bruce could hear the answer, relayed through Sam's radio. "Ready to inflate."

"Okay." The bag surged up, filling the frame. Sam said, "You go on, Bruce. There's nothing left but to adjust the shade."

"I'd better watch."

"Okay." The shade was a flimsy Venetian blind, stretched over the shelter. Sam half-opened the slats. "It's cold inside," he commented, "from expanding gas. But it warms up fast." Presently, coached by phone, he closed them a bit. "Go inside," he urged Bruce. "It may be half an hour before I get the temperature steady."

"Maybe I should," admitted Bruce. "I feel dizzy."

Sam studied him. "Too hot?"

"Yeah, I guess so."

"You've held still in the Sun too long. Doesn't give the air a chance to circulate. Here." Sam opened Bruce's supply valve wider; "Go inside."

Gratefully, Bruce complied.

As he backed in, and straightened up, two boys grabbed him. They closed his valves, unlocked his helmet, and peeled off his suit. The suit traveled from hand to hand and was racked. Bruce looked around.

Daylamps were strung from air lock to a curtain at the far end that shut off the sanitary unit. Near this curtain suits and helmets were racked. Scouts were lounging on both sides of the long room. Near the entrance a Scout was on watch at the air conditioner, a blood-oxygen indicator clipped to his ear. Nearby, Mr. Andrews phoned temperature changes to Sam. In the middle of the room Chubby had set up his commissary. He waved. "Hi, Bruce! Siddown—chow in two shakes."

Two Scouts made room for Bruce and he sat. One of them said, "Y'ever been at Yale?" Bruce had not. "That's where I'm going," the Scout confided. "My brother's there now." Bruce began to feel at home.

When Sam came in Chubby served chow, beef stew, steaming and fragrant, packaged rolls, and bricks of peach ice cream. Bruce decided that Moon Scouts had it soft. After supper, the Bugler got out his harmonica and played. Bruce leaned back, feeling pleasantly drowsy.

"Hollifield!" Bruce snapped awake. "Let's try you on first aid."

For thirty minutes Bruce demonstrated air tourniquets and emergency suit patches, artificial respiration for a man in a space suit, what to do for Sun stroke, for anoxia, for fractures. "That'll do," the Scoutmaster concluded. "One thing: What do you do if a man cracks his helmet?"

Bruce was puzzled. "Why," he blurted, "you bury him."

"Check," the Scoutmaster agreed. "So be careful. Okay, sports—six hours of sleep. Sam, set the watch."

Sam assigned six boys, including himself. Bruce asked, "Shouldn't I take a watch?"

Mr. Andrews intervened. "No. And take yourself off, Sam. You'll take Bruce on his two-man hike tomorrow; you'll need your sleep."

"Okay, Skipper." He added to Bruce, "There's nothing to it. I'll show you." The Scout on duty watched several instruments, but, as with suits, the important one was the blood-oxygen reading. Stale air was passed through a calcium oxide bath, which precipitated carbon dioxide as calcium carbonate. The purified air continued through dry sodium hydroxide, removing water vapor.

"The kid on watch makes sure the oxygen replacement is okay," Sam went on. "If anything went wrong, he'd wake us and we'd scramble into suits."

Mr. Andrews shooed them to bed. By the time Bruce had taken his turn at the sanitary unit and found a place to lie down, the harmonica was sobbing: *"Day is done. . . . . Gone the Sun . . ."*

It seemed odd to hear *Taps* when the Sun was still overhead. They couldn't wait a week for sundown, of course. These colonials kept funny hours . . . bed at what amounted to early evening, up at one in the morning. He'd ask Sam. Sam wasn't a bad guy—a little bit know-it-all. Odd to sleep on a bare floor, too—not that it mattered with low gravity. He was still pondering it when his ears were assaulted by *Reveille,* played on the harmonica.

Breakfast was scrambled eggs, cooked on the spot. Camp was struck, and the troop was moving in less than an hour. They headed for Base Camp at a lope.

The way wound through passes, skirted craters. They had covered thirty miles and Bruce was getting hungry when the pathfinder called, "Heel and toe!" They converged on an air lock, set in a hillside.

Base Camp had not the slick finish of Luna City, being rough caverns sealed to airtightness, but each troop had its own well-equipped troop room. Air was renewed by hydroponic garden, like Luna City; there was a Sun power plant and accumulators to last through the long, cold nights.

Bruce hurried through lunch; he was eager to start his two-man hike. They outfitted as before, except that reserve air and water replaced packaged grub. Sam fitted a spring-fed clip of hiking rations into the collar of Bruce's suit.

The Scoutmaster inspected them at the lock. "Where to, Sam?"

"We'll head southeast. I'll blaze it."

"Hmm—rough country. Well, back by midnight, and stay out of caves."

"Yes, sir."

Outside Sam sighed, "Whew! I thought he was going to say not to climb."

"We're going to?"

"Sure. You can, can't you?"

"Got my Alpine badge."

"I'll do the hard part, anyhow. Let's go."

Sam led out of the hills and across a baked plain. He hit an eight-mile gait, increased it to a twelve-miler. Bruce swung along, enjoying it. "Swell of you to do this, Sam."

"Nuts. If I weren't here, I'd be helping to seal the gymnasium."

"Just the same, I need this hike for my Mooncraft badge."

Sam let several strides pass. "Look, Bruce—you don't really expect to make Lunar Eagle?"

"Why not? I've got my optional badges. There are only four required ones that are terribly different: camping, Mooncraft, pathfinding, and pioneering. I've studied like the dickens and now I'm getting experience."

"I don't doubt you've studied. But the Review Board are tough eggs. You've got to be a real Moon hand to get by."

"They won't pass a Scout from Earth?"

"Put it this way. The badges you need add up to one thing, Mooncraft. The examiners are old Moon hands; you won't get by with book answers. They'll know how long you've been here and they'll *know* you don't know enough."

Bruce thought about it. "It's not fair!"

Sam snorted. "Mooncraft isn't a game; it's the real thing. 'Did you stay alive?' If you make a mistake, you flunk—and they bury you."

Bruce had no answer.

Presently they came to hills; Sam stopped and called Base Camp. "Parsons and Hollifield, Troop One—please take a bearing."

Shortly Base replied, "One one eight. What's your mark?"

"Cairn with a note."

"Roger."

Sam piled up stones, then wrote date, time, and their names on paper torn from a pad in his pouch, and laid it on top. "Now we start up."

The way was rough and unpredictable; this canyon had never been a watercourse. Several times Sam stretched a line before he would let Bruce follow. At intervals he blazed the rock with his hammer. They came to an impasse, five hundred feet of rock, the first hundred of which was vertical and smooth.

Bruce stared. "We're going up that?"

"Sure. Watch your Uncle Samuel." A pillar thrust up above the vertical pitch. Sam clipped two lines together and began casting the bight up toward it. Twice he missed and the line floated down. At last it went over.

Sam drove a piton into the wall, off to one side, clipped a snap ring to it, and snapped on the line. He had Bruce join him in a straight pull on the free end to test the piton. Bruce then anchored to the snap ring with a rope strap; Sam started to climb.

Thirty feet up, he made fast to the line with his legs and drove another piton; to this he fastened a safety line. Twice more he did this. He reached the pillar and called, "Off belay!"

Bruce unlinked the line; it snaked up the cliff. Presently Sam shouted, "On belay!"

Bruce answered, "Testing," and tried unsuccessfully to jerk down the line Sam had lowered.

"Climb," ordered Sam.

"Climbing." One-sixth gravity, Bruce decided, was a mountaineer's heaven. He paused on the way up only to unsnap the safety line.

Bruce wanted to "leapfrog" up the remaining pitches, but Sam insisted on leading. Bruce was soon glad of it; he found three mighty differences between climbing on Earth and climbing here; the first was low gravity, but the others were disadvantages: balance climbing was awkward in a suit, and chimney climbing, or any involving knees and shoulders, was clumsy and carried danger of tearing the suit.

They came out on raw, wild upland surrounded by pinnacles, bright against black sky. "Where to?" asked Bruce.

Sam studied the stars, then pointed southeast. "The photomaps show open country that way."

"Suits me." They trudged away; the country was too rugged to lope. They had been traveling a long time, it seemed to Bruce, when they came out on a higher place from which Earth could be seen. "What time is it?" he asked.

"Almost seventeen," Sam answered, glancing up.

"We're supposed to be back by midnight."

"Well," admitted Sam, "I expected to reach open country before now."

"We're lost?"

"Certainly not! I've blazed it. But I've never been here before. I doubt if anyone has."

"Suppose we keep on for half an hour, then turn back?"

"Fair enough." They continued for at least that; Sam conceded that it was time to turn.

"Let's try that next rise," urged Bruce.

"Okay." Sam reached the top first. "Hey, Bruce—we made it!"

Bruce joined him. "Golly!" Two thousand feet below stretched a dead lunar plain. Mountains rimmed it except to the south. Five miles away two small craters formed a figure eight.

"I know where we are," Sam announced. "That pair shows up on the photos. We slide down here, circle south about twenty miles, and back to Base. A cinch—how's your air?"

Bruce's bottle showed fair pressure; Sam's was down, he having done more work. They changed both bottles and got ready. Sam drove a piton, snapped on a ring, fastened a line to his belt and passed it through the ring. The end of the line he passed between his legs, around a thigh and across his chest, over his shoulder and to his other hand, forming a rappel seat. He began to "walk" down the cliff, feeding slack as needed.

He reached a shoulder below Bruce. "Off rappel!" he called, and recovered his line by pulling it through the ring.

Bruce rigged a rappel seat and joined him. The pitches became steeper; thereafter Sam sent Bruce down first, while anchoring him above. They came to a last high sheer drop. Bruce peered over. "Looks like here we roost."

"Maybe." Sam bent all four lines together and measured it. Ten feet of line reached the rubble at the base.

Bruce said, "It'll reach, but we have to leave the lines behind us."

Sam scowled. "Glass lines cost money; they're from Earth."

"Beats staying here."

Sam searched the cliff face, then drove a piton. "I'll lower you. When you're halfway, drive two pitons and hang the strap from one. That'll give me a changeover."

"I'm against it," protested Bruce.

"If we lost our lines," Sam argued, "we'll never hear the last of it. Go ahead."

"I still don't like it."

"Who's in charge?"

Bruce shrugged, snapped on the line and started down.

Sam stopped him presently. "Halfway. Pick me a nest."

Bruce walked the face to the right, but found only smooth wall. He worked back and located a crack. "Here's a crack," he reported, "but just one. I shouldn't drive two pitons in one crack."

"Spread 'em apart," Sam directed. "It's good rock."

Reluctantly, Bruce complied. The spikes went in easily but he wished he could hear the firm ring that meant a piton was biting properly. Finished, he hung the strap. "Lower away!"

In a couple of minutes he was down and unsnapped the line. "Off belay!" He hurried down the loose rock at the base. When he reached the edge of it he called, "Sam! This plain is soft stuff."

"Okay," Sam acknowledged. "Stand clear." Bruce moved along the cliff about fifty feet and stopped to bind on skis. Then he shuffled out onto the plain, kick-turned, and looked back. Sam had reached the pitons. He hung, one foot in the strap, the bight in his elbow, and recovered his line. He passed his line through the second piton ring, settled in rappel, and hooked the strap from piton to piton as an anchor. He started down.

Halfway down the remaining two hundred feet he stopped. "What's the matter?" called Bruce.

"It's reached a shackle," said Sam, "and the pesky thing won't feed through the ring. I'll free it." He raised himself a foot, then suddenly let what he had gained slip through the ring above.

To Bruce's amazement Sam leaned out at an impossible angle. He heard Sam cry "Rock!" before he understood what had happened—the piton had failed.

Sam fell about four feet, then the other piton, connected by the strap, stopped him. He caught himself, feet spread. But the warning cry had not been pointless; Bruce saw a rock settling straight for Sam's helmet. Bruce repeated the shout.

Sam looked up, then jumped straight out from the cliff. The rock passed between him and the wall; Bruce could not tell if it had struck him. Sam swung in, his feet caught the cliff—and again he leaned out crazily. The second piton had let go.

Sam again shouted, "*Rock!*" even as he kicked himself away from the cliff.

Bruce watched him, turning slowly over and over and gathering momentum. It seemed to take Sam forever to fall.

Then he struck.

Bruce fouled his skis and had to pick himself up. He forced himself to be careful and glided toward the spot.

Sam's frantic shove had saved him from crashing his helmet into rock. He lay buried in the loose debris, one leg sticking up ridiculously. Bruce felt an hysterical desire to laugh.

Sam did not stir when Bruce tugged at him. Bruce's skis got in his way; finally he stood astraddle, hauled Sam out. The boy's eyes were closed, his features slack, but the suit still had pressure. "Sam," shouted Bruce, "can you hear me?"

Sam's blood-oxygen reading was dangerously in the red; Bruce opened his intake valve wider—but the reading failed to improve. He wanted to turn Sam face down, but he had no way of straightening Sam's helmeted head, nor would he then be able to watch the blood-oxygen indicator unless he took time to remove the belt. He decided to try artificial respiration with the patient face up. He kicked off skis and belt.

The pressure in the suit got in his way, nor could he fit his hands satisfactorily to Sam's ribs. But he kept at it—swing! and one, and two and up! and one, and two and swing!

The needle began to move. When it was well into the white Bruce paused.

It stayed in the white.

Sam's lips moved but no sound came. Bruce touched helmets. "What is it, Sam?"

Faintly he heard, "Look out! Rock!"

Bruce considered what to do next.

There was little he could do until he got Sam into a pressurized room. The idea, he decided, was to get help—fast!

Send up a smoke signal? Fire a gun three times? Snap out of it, Bruce! You're on the Moon now. He wished that someone would happen along in a desert car.

He would have to try radio. He wasn't hopeful, as they had heard nothing even from the cliff. Still, he must try—

He glanced at Sam's blood-oxygen reading, then climbed the rubble, extended his antenna and tried. "*M'aidez!*" he called. "Help! Does anybody hear me?" He tried again.

And again.

When he saw Sam move he hurried back. Sam was sitting up and feeling his left knee. Bruce touched helmets. "Sam, are you all right?"

"Huh? This leg won't work right."

"Is it broken?"

"How do I know? Turn on your radio."

"It *is* on. Yours is busted."

"Huh? How'd that happen?"

"When you fell."

"Fell?"

Bruce pointed. "Don't you remember?"

Sam stared at the cliff. "Uh, I don't know. Say, this thing hurts like mischief. Where's the rest of the troop?"

Bruce said slowly, "We're out by ourselves, Sam. Remember?"

Sam frowned. "I guess so. Bruce, we've got to get out of here! Help me get my skis on."

"Do you think you can ski with that knee?"

"I've got to." Bruce lifted him to his feet, then bound a ski to the injured leg while Sam balanced on the other. But when Sam tried shifting his weight he collapsed—and fainted.

Bruce gave him air and noted that the blood-oxygen reading was still okay. He untangled the ski, straightened out Sam's legs, and waited. When Sam's eyes fluttered he touched helmets. "Sam, can you understand me?"

"Yeah. Sure."

"You can't stay on your feet. I'll carry you."

"No."

"What do you mean, 'No'?"

"No good. Rig a toboggan." He closed his eyes.

Bruce laid Sam's skis side by side. Two steel rods were clipped to the tail of each ski; he saw how they were meant to be used. Slide a rod through four ring studs, two on each ski; snap a catch—*so*! Fit the other rods. Remove bindings—the skis made a passable narrow toboggan.

He removed Sam's pack, switched his bottles around in front and told him to hold them. "I'm going to move you. Easy, now!" The space-suited form hung over the edges, but there was no help for it. He found he could thread a rope under the rods and lash his patient down. Sam's pack he tied on top.

He made a hitch by tying a line to the holes in the tips of the skis; there was a long piece left over. He said to Sam, "I'll tie this to my arm. If you want anything, just jerk."

"Okay."

"Here we go." Bruce put on his skis, brought the hitch up to his armpits and ducked his head through, forming a harness. He grasped his ski poles and set out to the south, parallel to the cliff.

The toboggan drag steadied him; he settled down to covering miles. Earth was shut off by the cliff; the Sun gave him no estimate of hour. There was nothing but blackness, stars, the blazing Sun, a burning desert underfoot, and the towering cliff—nothing but silence and the urgency to get back to base.

Something jerked his arm. It scared him before he accounted for it. He went back to the toboggan. "What is it, Sam?"

"I can't stand it. It's too hot." The boy's face was white and sweat-covered.

Bruce gave him a shot of air, then thought about it. There was an emergency shelter in Sam's pack, just a rolled-up awning with a collapsible frame. Fifteen minutes later he was ready to move. One awning support was tied upright to the sole of one of Sam's boots; the other Bruce had bent and wedged under Sam's shoulders. The contraption looked ready to fall apart but it held. "There! Are you okay?"

"I'm fine. Look, Bruce, I think my knee is all right now. Let me try it."

Bruce felt out the knee through the suit. It was twice the size of its mate; he could feel Sam wince. He touched helmets. "You're full of hop, chum. Relax." Bruce got back into harness.

Hours later, Bruce came across tracks. They swung in from northeast, turned and paralleled the hills. He stopped and told Sam.

"Say, Sam, how can I tell how old they are?"

"You can't. A track fifty years old looks as fresh as a new one."

"No point in following these?"

"No harm in it, provided they go in our direction."

"Roger." Bruce went back to towing. He called hopefully over the radio every few minutes and then listened. The tracks cheered him even though he knew how slim the chance was that they meant anything. The tracks swung out from the hills presently or, rather, the hills swung in, forming a bay. He took the shorter route as his predecessor had.

He should have seen what was coming. He knew that he should keep his eyes ahead, but the need to watch his instruments, the fact that he was leaning into harness, and the circumstance that he was following tracks combined to keep his head down. He had just glanced back at Sam when he felt his skis slipping out from under him.

Automatically he bent his knees and threw his skis into a "snowplow." He might have been able to stop had not the toboggan been scooting along behind. It plowed into him; boy, skis, and toboggan went down, tangled like jackstraws.

He struggled for footing, felt the sand slip under him. He had time to see that he had been caught—in daylight!—by that lunar equivalent of quicksand, a morning glory. Then the sifting dust closed over his helmet.

He felt himself slip, slide, fall, slide again, and come softly to rest.

Bruce tried to get his bearings. Part of his mind was busy with horror, shock, and bitter self blame for having failed Sam; another part seemed able to drive ahead with the business at hand. He did not seem hurt—and he was still breathing. He supposed that he was buried in a morning glory; he suspected that any movement would bury him deeper.

Nevertheless he had to locate Sam. He felt his way up to his neck, pushing the soft flakes aside. The toboggan hitch was still on him. He got both hands on it and heaved. It was frustrating work, like swimming in mud. Gradually he dragged the sled to him—or himself to the sled. Presently he felt his way down the load and located Sam's helmet. "*Sam!* Can you hear me?"

The reply was muffled. "Yeah, Bruce!"

"Are you okay?"

"Okay? Don't be silly! We're in a *morning glory!*"

"Yes, I know. Sam, I'm terribly sorry!"

"Well, don't cry about it. It can't be helped."

"I didn't mean to—"

"Stow it, can't you!" Sam's voice concealed panic with anger. "It doesn't matter. We're goners—don't you realize that?"

"Huh? No, we're not! Sam, I'll get you out—I swear I will."

Sam waited before replying. "Don't kid yourself, Bruce. Nobody ever gets out of a morning glory."

"Don't talk like that. We aren't dead yet."

"No, but we're going to be. I'm trying to get used to the idea." He paused. "Do me a favor, Bruce—get me loose from these confounded skis. I don't want to die tied down."

"Right away!" In total darkness, his hands in gloves, with only memory to guide him, and with the soft, flaky dust everywhere, unlashing the load was nearly impossible. He shifted position, then suddenly noticed something—his left arm was free of the dust.

He shifted and got his helmet free as well. The darkness persisted; he fumbled at his belt, managed to locate his flashlight.

He was lying partly out and mostly in a sloping mass of soft stuff. Close overhead was a rocky roof; many feet below the pile spilled over a floor of rock. Sideways the darkness swallowed up the beam.

He still clutched the toboggan; he hauled at it, trying to drag Sam out. Failing, he burrowed back in. "Hey, Sam! We're in a cave!"

"Huh?"

"Hang on. I'll get you out." Bruce cautiously thrashed around in an attempt to get his entire body outside the dust. It kept caving down on him. Worse, his skis anchored his feet. He kicked one loose, snaked his arm in, and dragged it out. It slid to the base of the pile. He repeated the process, then rolled and scrambled to the floor, still clinging to the hitch.

He set the light on the rock floor, and put the skis aside, then heaved mightily. Sam, toboggan, and load came sliding down, starting a small avalanche. Bruce touched helmets. "Look! We're getting somewhere!"

Sam did not answer. Bruce persisted, "Sam, did you hear me?"

"I heard you. Thanks for pulling me out. Now untie me, will you?"

"Hold the light." Bruce got busy. Shortly he was saying, "There you are. Now I'll stir around and find the way out."

"What makes you think there is a way out?"

"Huh? Don't talk like that. Who ever heard of a cave with no exit?"

Sam answered slowly, "*He* didn't find one."

" 'He'?"

"Look." Sam shined the light past Bruce. On the rock a few feet away was a figure in an old-fashioned space suit.

Bruce took the light and cautiously approached the figure. The man was surely dead; his suit was limp. He lay at ease, hands folded across his middle, as if taking a nap. Bruce pointed the torch at the glass face plate. The face inside was lean and dark, skin clung to the bones; Bruce turned the light away.

He came back shortly to Sam. "He didn't make out so well," Bruce said soberly. "I found these papers in his pouch. We'll take them with us so we can let his folks know."

"You *are* an incurable optimist, aren't you? Well, all right." Sam took them. There were two letters, an old-style flat photograph of a little girl and a dog, and some other papers. One was a driver's license for the Commonwealth of Massachusetts, dated June 1995 and signed *Abner Green.*

Bruce stared. "1995! Gee whiz!"

"I wouldn't count on notifying his folks."

Bruce changed the subject. "He had one thing we can use. This." It was a coil of manila rope. "I'll hitch all the lines together, one end to your belt and one to mine. That'll give me five or six hundred feet. If you want me, just pull."

"Okay. Watch your step."

"I'll be careful. You'll be all right?"

"Sure. I've got *him* for company."

"Well . . . here goes."

One direction seemed as good as another. Bruce kept the line taut to keep from walking in a circle. The rock curved up presently and his flash showed that it curved back on itself, a dead end. He followed the wall to the left, picking his way, as the going was very rough. He found himself in a passage. It seemed to climb, but it narrowed. Three hundred feet and more out by the ropes, it narrowed so much that he was stopped.

Bruce switched off his light and waited for his eyes to adjust. He became aware of a curious sensation. It was panic.

He forced himself not to turn on the light until he was certain that no gleam lay ahead. Then thankfully he stumbled back into the main cavern.

Another series of chambers led steadily downward. He turned back at a black and bottomless hole.

The details varied but the answers did not: At the furthest reach of the lines, or at some impassable obstacle, he would wait in the dark— but no gleam of light ever showed. He went back to Sam after having covered, he estimated, about 180 degrees.

Sam had crawled up to the heap of fallen dust. Bruce hurried to him. "Sam, are you all right?"

"Sure. I just moved to a feather bed. That rock is terribly cold. What did you find?"

"Well, nothing yet," he admitted. He sat down in the flaky pile and leaned toward Sam. "I'll start again in a moment."

"How's your air supply?" asked Sam.

"Uh, I'll have to crack my reserve bottle soon. How's yours?"

"Mine is throttled to the limit. You're doing all the work; I can save my reserve bottle for you—I think."

Bruce frowned. He wanted to protest, but the gesture wouldn't make sense. They would have to finish up all even; naturally he was using much more air than was Sam.

One thing was sure—time was running out. Finally he said, "Look, Sam—there's no end of those caves and passages. I couldn't search them all with all the air in Luna City."

"I was afraid so."

"But we *know* there's a way out right above us."

"You mean *in*."

"I mean *out*. See here—this morning glory thing is built like an hour glass; there's an open cone on top, and this pile of sand down below. The stuff trickled down through a hole in the roof and piled up until it choked the hole."

"Where does that get you?"

"Well, if we dug the stuff away we could clear the hole."

"It would keep sifting down."

"No, it wouldn't, it would reach a point where there wasn't enough dust close by to sift down any further—there would still be a hole."

Sam considered it. "Maybe. But when you tried to climb up it would collapse back on you. That's the bad part about a morning glory, Bruce; you can't get a foothold."

"The dickens I can't! If I can't climb a slope on skis without collapsing it, when I've got my wits about me and am really trying, why, you can have my reserve air bottle."

Sam chuckled. "Don't be hasty. I might hold you to it. Anyhow," he added, "I can't climb it."

"Once I get my feet on the level, I'll pull you out like a cork, even if you're buried. Time's a-wastin'." Bruce got busy.

Using a ski as a shovel he nibbled at the giant pile. Every so often it would collapse down on him. It did not discourage him; Bruce knew that many yards of the stuff would have to fall and be moved back before the hole would show.

Presently he moved Sam over to the freshly moved waste. From there Sam held the light; the work went faster. Bruce began to sweat.

After a while he had to switch air bottles; he sucked on his water tube and ate a march ration before getting back to work.

He began to see the hole opening above him. A great pile collapsed on him; he backed out, looked up, then went to Sam. "Turn out the light!"

There was no doubt; a glimmer of light filtered down. Bruce found himself pounding Sam and shouting. He stopped and said, "Sam, old boy, did I ever say what patrol I'm from?"

"No. Why?"

"Badger Patrol. Watch me dig!" He tore into it. Shortly sunlight poured into the hole and reflected dimly around the cavern. Bruce shoveled until he could see a straight rise from the base of the pile clear to the edge of the morning glory high above them. He decided that the opening was wide enough to tackle.

He hitched himself to Sam with the full length of all the glass ropes and then made a bundle of Sam's pack save air and water bottles, tied a bowline on Sam's uninjured foot, using the manila line, and secured the bundle to the end of that line. He planned to drag Sam out first, then the equipment. Finished, he bound on skis.

Bruce touched helmets. "This is it, pal. Keep the line clear of the sand."

Sam grabbed his arm. "Wait a minute."

"What's the matter?"

"Bruce—if we don't make it, I just want to say that you're all right."

"Uh . . . oh, forget it. We'll make it." He started up.

A herringbone step suited the convex approach to the hole. As Bruce neared the opening he shifted to side-step to fit the narrow passage and the concave shape of the morning glory above. He inched up, transferring his weight smoothly and gradually, and not remaining in one spot too long. At last his head, then his whole body, were in sunshine; he was starting up the morning glory itself.

He stopped, uncertain what to do. There was a ridge above him, where the flakes had broken loose when he had shoveled away their support. The break was much too steep to climb, obviously unstable. He paused only a moment as he could feel his skis sinking in; he went forward in half side-step, intending to traverse past the unstable formation.

The tow line defeated him. When Bruce moved sideways, the line had to turn a corner at the neck of the hole. It brushed and then cut into the soft stuff. Bruce felt his skis slipping backwards; with cautious haste he started to climb, tried to ride the slipping mass and keep above it. He struggled as the flakes poured over his skis. Then he was fouled, he went down, it engulfed him.

Again he came to rest in soft, feathery, darkness. He lay quiet, nursing his defeat, before trying to get out. He hardly knew which way was up, much less which way was out. He was struggling experimentally when he felt a tug on his belt. Sam was trying to help him.

A few minutes later, with Sam's pull to guide him, Bruce was again on the floor of the cave. The only light came from the torch in Sam's hand; it was enough to show that the pile choking the hole was bigger than ever.

Sam motioned him over. "Too bad, Bruce," was all he said.

Bruce controlled his choking voice to say, "I'll get busy as soon as I catch my breath."

"Where's your left ski?"

"Huh? Oh! Must have pulled off. It'll show up when I start digging."

"Hmmm . . . how much air have you?"

"Uh?" Bruce looked at his belt. "About a third of a bottle."

"I'm breathing my socks. I've got to change."

"Right away!" Bruce started to make the switch; Sam pulled him down again.

"You take the fresh bottle, and give me your bottle."

"But—"

"No 'buts' about it," Sam cut him off. "You have to do all the work; you've *got* to take the full tank."

Silently Bruce obeyed. His mind was busy with arithmetic. The answer always came out the same; he knew with certainty that there was not enough air left to permit him again to perform the Herculean task of moving that mountain of dust.

He began to believe that they would never get out. The knowledge wearied him; he wanted to lie down beside the still form of Abner Green and, like him, not struggle at the end.

However he could not. He knew that, for Sam's sake, he would have to shovel away at that endless sea of sand, until he dropped from lack of oxygen. Listlessly he took off his remaining ski and walked toward his task.

Sam jerked on the rope.

Bruce went back. "What's got into you, kid?" Sam demanded.

"Nothing. Why?"

"It's got you whipped."

"I didn't say so."

"But you think so. I could see it. Now you listen! You convinced me that you could get us out—and, by Jiminy! you're going to! You're just cocky enough to be the first guy to whip a morning glory and you can do it. Get your chin up!"

Bruce hesitated. "Look, Sam, I won't quit on you, but you might as well know the truth: there isn't air enough to do it again."

"Figured that out when I saw the stuff start to crumble."

"You knew? Then if you know any prayers, better say them."

Sam shook his arm. "It's not time to pray; it's time to get busy."

"Okay." Bruce started to straighten up.

"That's not what I meant."

"Huh?"

"There's no point in digging. Once was worth trying; twice is wasting oxygen."

"Well, what do you want me to do?"

"You didn't try *all* the ways out, did you?"

"No." Bruce thought about it. "I'll try again, Sam. But there isn't air enough to try them all."

"You can search longer than you can shovel. But don't search haphazardly; search back toward the hills. Anywhere else will be just another morning glory; we need to come out *at the hills;* away from the sand."

"Uh . . . look, Sam, where *are* the hills? Down here you can't tell north from next week."

"Over that way," Sam pointed.

"Huh? How do you know?"

"You showed me. When you broke through I could tell where the Sun was from the angle of the light."

"But the Sun is overhead."

"Was when we started. Now it's fifteen, twenty degrees to the west. Now listen: these caves must have been big blow holes once, gas pockets. You search off in that direction and find us a blow hole that's not choked with sand."

"I'll do my darndest!"

"How far away were the hills when we got caught?"

Bruce tried to remember. "Half a mile, maybe."

"Check. You won't find what we want tied to me with five or six hundred feet of line. Take that pad of paper in my pouch. Blaze your way—and be darn sure you blaze enough!"

"I will!"

"Attaboy! Good luck."

Bruce stood up.

It was the same tedious, depressing business as before. Bruce stretched the line, then set out at the end of it, dropping bits of paper and counting his steps. Several times he was sure that he was under the hills, only to come to an impasse. Twice he skirted the heaps that marked other morning glorys. Each time he retraced his steps he gathered up his blazes, both to save paper and to keep from confusing himself.

Once, he saw a glimmer of light and his heart pounded—but it filtered down from a hole too difficult even for himself and utterly impossible for Sam.

His air got low; he paid no attention, other than to adjust his mix to keep it barely in the white. He went on searching.

A passage led to the left, then down; he began to doubt the wisdom of going further and stopped to check the darkness. At first his eyes saw nothing, then it seemed as if there might be a suggestion of light ahead. Eye fatigue? Possibly. He went another hundred feet and tried again. It was light!

Minutes later he shoved his shoulders up through a twisted hole and gazed out over the burning plain.

"Hi!" Sam greeted him. "I thought you had fallen down a hole."

"Darn near did. Sam, I found it!"

"Knew you would. Let's get going."

"Right. I'll dig out my other ski."

"Nope."

"Why not?"

"Look at your air gauge. We aren't going anywhere on skis."

"Huh? Yeah, I guess not." They abandoned their loads, except for air and water bottles. The dark trek was made piggy-back, where the ceiling permitted. Some places Bruce half dragged his partner. Other places they threaded on hands and knees with Sam pulling his bad leg painfully behind him.

Bruce climbed out first, having slung Sam in a bowline before he did so. Sam gave little help in getting out; once they were above ground Bruce picked him up and set him against a rock. He then touched helmets. "There, fellow! We made it!"

Sam did not answer.

Bruce peered in; Sam's features were slack, eyes half closed. A check of his belt told why; the blood-oxygen indicator showed red.

Sam's intake valve was already wide open; Bruce moved fast, giving himself a quick shot of air, then transferring his bottle to Sam. He opened it wide.

He could see Sam's pointer crawl up even as his own dropped toward the red. Bruce had air in his suit for three or four minutes if he held still.

He did not hold still. He hooked his intake hose to the manifold of the single bottle now attached to Sam's suit and opened his valve. His own indicator stopped dropping toward the red. They were Siamese twins now, linked by one partly-exhausted bottle of utterly necessary gas. Bruce put an arm around Sam, settled Sam's head on his shoulder, helmet to helmet, and throttled down both valves until each was barely in the white. He gave Sam more margin than himself, then settled down to wait. The rock under them was in shadow, though the Sun still baked the plain. Bruce looked out, searching for anyone or anything, then extended his aerial. "*M'aidez!*" he called. "Help us! We're lost."

He could hear Sam muttering. "May day!" Sam echoed into his dead radio. "May day! We're lost."

Bruce cradled the delirious boy in his arm and repeated again, "*M'aidez! Get a bearing on us." He paused, then echoed, "May day! May day!"

After a while he readjusted the valves, then went back to repeating endlessly, "May day! Get a bearing on us."

He did not feel it when a hand clasped his shoulder. He was still muttering "May day!" when they dumped him into the air lock of the desert car.

Mr. Andrews visited him in the infirmary at Base Camp. "How are you, Bruce?"

"Me? I'm all right, sir. I wish they'd let me get up."

"My instructions. So I'll know where you are." The Scoutmaster smiled; Bruce blushed.

"How's Sam?" he asked.

"He'll get by. Cold burns and a knee that will bother him a while. That's all."

"Gee, I'm glad."

"The troop is leaving. I'm turning you over to Troop Three, Mr. Harkness. Sam will go back with the grub car."

"Uh, I think I could travel with the Troop, sir."

"Perhaps so, but I want you to stay with Troop Three. You need field experience."

"Uh—" Bruce hesitated, wondering how to say it. "Mr. Andrews?"
"Yes?"

"I might as well go back. I've learned something. You were right. A fellow can't get to be an old Moon hand in three weeks. Uh . . . I guess I was just conceited."

"Is that all?"

"Well—yes, sir."

"Very well, listen to me. I've talked with Sam and with Mr. Harkness. Mr. Harkness will put you through a course of sprouts; Sam and I will take over when you get back. You plan on being ready for the Court of Honor two weeks from Wednesday." The Scoutmaster added, "Well?"

Bruce gulped and found his voice. "Yes, sir!"

GULF

Astounding Science Fiction, November–December 1949

THE FIRST-QUARTER rocket from Moonbase put him down at Pied-a-Terre. The name he was traveling under began—by foresight—with the letter "A"; he was through port inspection and into the shuttle tube to the city ahead of the throng. Once in the tube car he went to the men's washroom and locked himself in.

Quickly he buckled on the safety belt he found there, snapped its hooks to the wall fixtures, and leaned over awkwardly to remove a razor from his bag. The surge caught him in that position; despite the safety belt he bumped his head—and swore. He straightened up and plugged in the razor. His moustache vanished; he shortened his sideburns, trimmed the corners of his eyebrows, and brushed them up.

He towelled his hair vigorously to remove the oil that had sleeked it down, combed it loosely into a wavy mane. The car was now riding in a smooth, unaccelerated 300 mph; he let himself out of the safety belt without unhooking it from the walls and, working very rapidly, peeled off his moonsuit, took from his bag and put on a tweedy casual outfit suited to outdoors on Earth and quite unsuited to Moon Colony's air-conditioned corridors.

His slippers he replaced with walking shoes from the bag; he stood up. Joel Abner, commercial traveler, had disappeared; in his place was Captain Joseph Gilead, explorer, lecturer, and writer. Of both names he was the sole user; neither was his birth name.

He slashed the moonsuit to ribbons and flushed it down the water closet, added "Joel Abner's" identification card; then peeled a plastic skin off his travel bag and let the bits follow the rest. The bag was now pearl grey and rough, instead of dark brown and smooth. The slippers bothered him; he was afraid they might stop up the car's plumbing. He contented himself with burying them in the waste receptacle.

The acceleration warning sounded as he was doing this; he barely had time to get back into the belt. But, as the car plunged into the solenoid field and surged to a stop, nothing remained of Joel Abner but some unmarked underclothing, very ordinary toilet articles, and nearly two dozen spools of microfilm equally appropriate—until examined—

to a commercial traveler or a lecturer-writer. He planned not to let them be examined as long as he was alive.

He waited in the washroom until he was sure of being last man out of the car, then went forward into the next car, left by its exit, and headed for the lift to the ground level.

"New Age Hotel, sir," a voice pleaded near his ear. He felt a hand fumbling at the grip of his travel bag.

He repressed a reflex to defend the bag and looked the speaker over. At first glance he seemed an under-sized adolescent in a smart uniform and a pillbox cap. Further inspection showed premature wrinkles and the features of a man at least forty. The eyes were glazed. A pituitary case, he thought to himself, and on the hop as well. "New Age Hotel," the runner repeated. "Best mechanos in town, chief. There's a discount if you're just down from the moon."

Captain Gilead, when in town as Captain Gilead, always stayed at the old Savoy. But the notion of going to the New Age appealed to him; in that incredibly huge, busy, and ultramodern hostelry he might remain unnoticed until he had had time to do what had to be done.

He disliked mightily the idea of letting go his bag. Nevertheless it would be out of character not to let the runner carry the bag; it would call attention to himself—and the bag. He decided that this unhealthy runt could not outrun him even if he himself were on crutches; it would suffice to keep an eye on the bag.

"Lead on, comrade," he answered heartily, surrendering the bag. There had been no hesitation at all; he had let go the bag even as the hotel runner reached for it.

"Okay, chief." The runner was first man into an empty lift; he went to the back of the car and set the bag down beside him. Gilead placed himself so that his foot rested firmly against his bag and faced forward as other travelers crowded in. The car started.

The lift was jammed; Gilead was subjected to body pressures on every side—but he noticed an additional, unusual, and uncalled-for pressure behind him.

His right hand moved suddenly and clamped down on a skinny wrist and a hand clutching something. Gilead made no further movement, nor did the owner of the hand attempt to draw away or make any objection. They remained so until the car reached the surface. When the passengers had spilled out he reached behind him with his left hand, recovered his bag and dragged the wrist and its owner out of the car.

It was, of course, the runner; the object in his fist was Gilead's wallet. "You durn near lost that, chief," the runner announced with no show of embarrassment. "It was falling out of your pocket."

Gilead liberated the wallet and stuffed it into an inner pocket.

"Fell right through the zipper," he answered cheerfully. "Well, let's find a cop."

The runt tried to pull away. "You got nothing on me!"

Gilead considered the defense. In truth, he had nothing. His wallet was already out of sight. As to witnesses, the other lift passengers were already gone—nor had they seen anything. The lift itself was automatic. He was simply a man in the odd position of detaining another citizen by the wrist. And Gilead himself did not want to talk to the police.

He let go that wrist. "On your way, comrade. We'll call it quits."

The runner did not move. "How about my tip?"

Gilead was beginning to like this rascal. Locating a loose half credit in his change pocket he flipped it at the runner, who grabbed it out of the air but still didn't leave. "I'll take your bag now. Gimme."

"No, thanks, chum. I can find your delightful inn without further help. One side, please."

"Oh, yeah? How about my commission? I gotta carry your bag, else how they gonna know I brung you in? Gimme."

Gilead was delighted with the creature's unabashed insistence. He found a two-credit piece and passed it over. "There's your cumshaw. Now beat it, before I kick your tail up around your shoulders."

"You and who else?"

Gilead chuckled and moved away down the concourse toward the station entrance to the New Age Hotel. His subconscious sentries informed him immediately that the runner had not gone back toward the lift as expected, but was keeping abreast him in the crowd. He considered this. The runner might very well be what he appeared to be, common city riff-raff who combined casual thievery with his overt occupation. On the other hand—

He decided to unload. He stepped suddenly off the sidewalk into the entrance of a drugstore and stopped just inside the door to buy a newspaper. While his copy was being printed, he scooped up, apparently as an afterthought, three standard pneumo mailing tubes. As he paid for them he palmed a pad of gummed address labels.

A glance at the mirrored wall showed him that his shadow had hesitated outside but was still watching him. Gilead went on back to the shop's soda fountain and slipped into an unoccupied booth. Although the floor show was going on—a remarkably shapely ecdysiast was working down toward her last string of beads—he drew the booth's curtain.

Shortly the call light over the booth flashed discreetly; he called, "Come in!" A pretty and very young waitress came inside the curtain. Her plastic costume covered without concealing.

She glanced around. "Lonely?"

"No, thanks, I'm tired."

"How about a redhead, then? Real cute—"

"I really am tired. Bring me two bottles of beer, unopened, and some pretzels."

"Suit yourself, sport." She left.

With speed he opened the travel bag, selected nine spools of microfilm, and loaded them into the three mailing tubes, the tubes being of the common three-spool size. Gilead then took the filched pad of address labels, addressed the top one to "Raymond Calhoun, P. O. Box 1060, Chicago" and commenced to draw with great care in the rectangle reserved for electric-eye sorter. The address he shaped in arbitrary symbols intended not to be read, but to be scanned automatically. The hand-written address was merely a precaution, in case a robot sorter should reject his hand-drawn symbols as being imperfect and thereby turn the tube over to a human postal clerk for readdressing.

He worked fast, but with the care of an engraver. The waitress returned before he had finished. The call light warned him; he covered the label with his elbow and kept it covered.

She glanced at the mailing tubes as she put down the beer and a bowl of pretzels. "Want me to mail those?"

He had another instant of split-second indecision. When he had stepped out of the tube car he had been reasonably sure, first, that the *persona* of Joel Abner, commercial traveler, had not been penetrated, and, second, that the transition from Abner to Gilead had been accomplished without arousing suspicion. The pocket-picking episode had not alarmed him, but had caused him to reclassify those two propositions from calculated certainties to unproved variables. He had proceeded to test them at once; they were now calculated certainties again—of the opposite sort. Ever since he had spotted his erstwhile porter, the New Age runner, as standing outside this same drugstore his subconscious had been clanging like a burglar alarm.

It was clear not only that he had been spotted but that they were organized with a completeness and shrewdness he had not believed possible.

But it was mathematically probable to the point of certainty that they were not operating through this girl. They had no way of knowing that he would choose to turn aside into this particular drugstore. That she could be used by them he was sure—and she had been out of sight since his first contact with her. But she was clearly not bright enough, despite her alley-cat sophistication, to be approached, subverted, instructed and indoctrinated to the point where she could seize an unexpected opportunity, all in a space of time merely adequate to fetch two bottles of beer. No, this girl was simply after a tip. Therefore she was safe.

But her costume offered no possibility of concealing three mailing tubes, nor would she be safe crossing the concourse to the post office. He had no wish that she be found tomorrow morning dead in a ditch.

"No," he answered immediately. "I have to pass the post office anyway. But it was a kind thought. Here." He gave her a half credit.

"Thanks." She waited and stared meaningfully at the beer. He fumbled again in his change pocket, found only a few bits, reached for his wallet and took out a five-pluton note.

"Take it out of this."

She handed him back three singles and some change. He pushed the change toward her, then waited, frozen, while she picked it up and left. Only then did he hold the wallet closer to his eyes.

It was not his wallet.

He should have noticed it before, he told himself. Even though there had been only a second from the time he had taken it from the runner's clutched fingers until he had concealed it in a front pocket, he should have known it—known it and forced the runner to disgorge, even if he had had to skin him alive.

But why was he sure that it was not his wallet? It was the proper size and shape, the proper weight and feel—real ostrich skin in these days of synthetics. There was the weathered ink stain which had resulted from carrying a leaky stylus in the same pocket. There was a V-shaped scratch on the front which had happened so long ago he did not recall the circumstances.

Yet it was not his wallet.

He opened it again. There was the proper amount of money, there were what seemed to be his Explorers' Club card and his other identity cards, there was a dog-eared flat-photo of a mare he had once owned. Yet the more the evidence showed that it was his, the more certain he became that it was not his. These things were forgeries; they did not *feel* right.

There was one way to find out. He flipped a switch provided by a thoughtful management; the booth became dark. He took out his penknife and carefully slit a seam back of the billfold pocket. He dipped a finger into a secret pocket thus disclosed and felt around, the space was empty—nor in this case had the duplication of his own wallet been quite perfect; the space should have been lined, but his fingers encountered rough leather.

He switched the light back on, put the wallet away, and resumed his interrupted drawing. The loss of the card which should have been in the concealed pocket was annoying, certainly awkward, and conceivably disastrous, but he did not judge that the information on it was jeopardized by the loss of the wallet. The card was quite featureless unless examined by black light; if exposed to visible light—by some one taking the real wallet apart, for example—it had the disconcerting quality of bursting explosively into flame.

He continued to work, his mind busy with the wider problem of why they had taken so much trouble to try to keep him from knowing that his wallet was being stolen—and the still wider and more disconcerting question of why they had bothered with *his* wallet. Finished, he stuffed the remainder of the pad of address labels into a crack between cushions in the booth, palmed the label he had prepared, picked up the bag and the three mailing tubes. One tube he kept separate from the others by a finger.

No attack would take place, he judged, in the drug store. The crowded concourse between himself and the post office he would ordinarily have considered equally safe—but not today. A large crowd of people, he knew, are equal to so many trees as witnesses if the dice were loaded with any sort of a diversion.

He slanted across the bordering slidewalk and headed directly across the middle toward the post office, keeping as far from other people as he could manage. He had become aware of two men converging on him when the expected diversion took place.

It was a blinding light and a loud explosion, followed by screams and startled shouts. The source of the explosion he could imagine; the screams and shouts were doubtless furnished free by the public. Being braced, not for this, but for anything, he refrained even from turning his head.

The two men closed rapidly, as on cue.

Most creatures and almost all humans fight only when pushed. This can lose them decisive advantage. The two men made no aggressive move of any sort, other than to come close to Gilead—nor did they ever attack.

Gilead kicked the first of them in the knee cap, using the side of his foot, a much more certain stroke than with the toe. He swung with his travel bag against the other at the same time, not hurting him but bothering him, spoiling his timing. Gilead followed it with a heavy kick to the man's stomach.

The man whose knee cap he had ruined was on the pavement, but still active—reaching for something, a gun or a knife. Gilead kicked him in the head and stepped over him, continued toward the post office.

Slow march—slow march all the way! He must not give the appearance of running away; he must be the perfect respectable citizen, going about his lawful occasions.

The post office came close, and still no tap on the shoulder, no denouncing shout, no hurrying footsteps. He reached the post office, was inside. The opposition's diversion had worked, perfectly—but for Gilead, not for them.

There was a short queue at the addressing machine. Gilead joined it, took out his stylus and wrote addresses on the tubes while standing. A man joined the queue almost at once; Gilead made no effort to keep him from seeing what address he was writing; it was "Captain Joseph Gilead, the Explorers' Club, New York." When it came his turn to use the symbol printing machine he still made no effort to conceal what keys he was punching—and the symbol address matched the address he had written on each tube.

He worked somewhat awkwardly as the previously prepared gummed label was still concealed in his left palm.

He went from the addressing machine to the mailing receivers; the man who had been behind him in line followed him without pretending to address anything.

Thwonk! and the first tube was away with a muted implosion of compressed air. *Thwonk!* again and the second was gone—and at the same time Gilead grasped the last one in his left hand, sticking the gummed label down firmly over the address he had just printed on it. Without looking at it he made sure by touch that it was in place, all corners sealed, then *thwonk!* it joined its mates.

Gilead turned suddenly and trod heavily on the feet of the man crowded close behind him. "Wups! pardon *me*." he said happily and turned away. He was feeling very cheerful; not only had he turned his dangerous charge over into the care of a mindless, utterly reliable, automatic machine which could not be coerced, bribed, drugged, nor subverted by any other means and in whose complexities the tube would be perfectly hidden until it reached a destination known only to Gilead, but also he had just stepped on the corns of one of the opposition.

On the steps of the post office he paused beside a policeman who was picking his teeth and staring out at a cluster of people and an ambulance in the middle of the concourse. "What's up?" Gilead demanded.

The cop shifted his toothpick. "First some damn fool sets off fireworks," he answered, "then two guys get in a fight and blame near ruin each other."

"My goodness!" Gilead commented and set off diagonally toward the New Age Hotel.

He looked around for his pick-pocket friend in the lobby, did not see him. Gilead strongly doubted if the runt were on the hotel's staff. He signed in as Captain Gilead, ordered a suite appropriate to the *persona* he was wearing, and let himself be conducted to the lift.

Gilead encountered the runner coming down just as he and his bellman were about to go up. "Hi, Shorty!" he called out while deciding not to eat anything in this hotel. "How's business?"

The runt looked startled, then passed him without answering, his eyes blank. It was not likely, Gilead considered, that the runt would be used after being detected; therefore some sort of drop box, call station, or headquarters of the opposition was actually inside the hotel. Very well, that would save everybody a lot of useless commuting—and there would be fun for all!

In the meantime he wanted a bath.

In his suite he tipped the bellman who continued to linger.

"Want some company?"

"No, thanks, I'm a hermit."

"Try this then." The bellman inserted Gilead's room key in the stereo panel, fiddled with the controls, the entire wall lighted up and faded away. A svelte blonde creature, backed by a chorus line, seemed about to leap into Gilead's lap. "That's not a tape," the bellman went on, "that's a live transmission direct from the Tivoli. We got the best equipment in town."

"So you have," Gilead agreed, and pulled out his key. The picture blanked; the music stopped. "But I want a bath, so get out—now that you've spent four credits of my money."

The bellman shrugged and left. Gilead threw off his clothes and stepped into the "fresher." Twenty minutes later, shaved from ear to toe, scrubbed, soaked, sprayed, pummeled, rubbed, scented, powdered, and feeling ten years younger, he stepped out. His clothes were gone.

His bag was still there; he looked it over. It seemed okay, itself and contents. There were the proper number of microfilm spools—not that it mattered. Only three of the spools mattered and they were already in the mail. The rest were just shrubbery, copies of his own public lectures. Nevertheless he examined one of them, unspooling a few frames.

It was one of his own lectures all right—but not one he had had with him. It was one of his published transcriptions, available in any large book store. "Pixies everywhere," he remarked and put it back. Such attention to detail was admirable.

"Room service!"

The service panel lighted up. "Yes, sir?"

"My clothes are missing. Chase 'em up for me."

"The valet has them, sir."

"I didn't order valet service. Get 'em back."

The girl's voice and face were replaced, after a slight delay, by those of a man. "It is not necessary to order valet service here, sir. 'A New Age guest receives the best.' "

"Okay, get 'em back—chop, chop! I've got a date with the Queen of Sheba."

"Very good, sir." The image faded.

With wry humor he reviewed his situation. He had already made the possibly fatal error of underestimating his opponent through—he now knew—visualizing that opponent in the unimpressive person of "the runt." Thus he had allowed himself to be diverted; he should have gone anywhere rather than to the New Age, even to the old Savoy, although that hotel, being a known stamping ground of Captain Gilead, was probably as thoroughly booby-trapped by now as this palatial dive.

He must not assume that he had more than a few more minutes to live. Therefore he must use those few minutes to tell his boss the destination of the three important spools of microfilm. Thereafter, if he still were alive, he must replenish his cash to give him facilities for action—the amount of money in "his" wallet, even if it were returned, was useless for any major action. Thirdly, he must report in, close the present assignment, and be assigned to his present antagonists as a case in themselves, quite aside from the matter of the microfilm.

Not that he intended to drop Runt & Company even if not assigned to them. True artists were scarce—nailing him down by such a simple device as stealing his pants! He loved them for it and wanted to see more of them, as violently as possible.

Even as the image on the room service panel faded he was punching the scrambled keys on the room's communicator desk. It was possible—certain—that the scramble code he used would be repeated elsewhere in the hotel and the supposed privacy attained by scrambling thereby breached at once. This did not matter; he would have his boss disconnect and call back with a different scramble from the other end. To be sure, the call code of the station to which he was reporting would thereby be breached, but it was more than worthwhile to expend and discard one relay station to get this message through.

Scramble pattern set up, he coded—not New Washington, but the relay station he had selected. A girl's face showed on the screen. "New Age service, sir. Were you scrambling?"

"Yes."

"I am veree sorree, sir. The scrambling circuits are being repaired. I can scramble for you from the main board."

"No, thanks, I'll call in clear."

"I yam ve-ree sor-ree, sir."

There was one clear-code he could use—to be used only for crash priority. This was crash priority. Very well—

He punched the keys again without scrambling and waited. The same girl's face appeared presently. "I am verree sorree, sir; that code does not reply. May I help you?"

"You might send up a carrier pigeon." He cleared the board.

The cold breath on the back of his neck was stronger now; he decided to do what he could to make it awkward to kill him just yet. He reached back into his mind and coded in clear the *Star-Times*.

No answer.

He tried the *Clarion*—again no answer.

No point in beating his head against it; they did not intend to let him talk outside to anyone. He rang for a bellman, sat down in an easy chair, switched it to "shallow massage", and luxuriated happily in the chair's tender embrace. No doubt about it; the New Age *did* have the best mechanos in town—his bath had been wonderful; this chair was superb. Both the recent austerities of Moon Colony and the probability that this would be his last massage added to his pleasure.

The door dilated and a bellman came in—about his own size, Gilead noted. The man's eyebrows went up a fraction of an inch on seeing Gilead's oyster-naked condition. "You want company?"

Gilead stood up and moved toward him. "No, dearie," he said grinning, "I want *you*"—at which he sank three stiffened fingers in the man's solar plexus.

As the man grunted and went down Gilead chopped him in the side of the neck with the edge of his hand.

The shoulders of the jacket were too narrow and the shoes too large; nevertheless two minutes later "Captain Gilead" had followed "Joel Abner" to oblivion and Joe, temporary and free-lance bellman, let himself out of the room. He regretted not being able to leave a tip with his predecessor.

He sauntered past the passengers lifts, firmly misdirected a guest who had stopped him, and found the service elevator. By it was a door to the "quick drop." He opened it, reached out and grasped a waiting pulley belt, and, without stopping to belt himself into it, contenting himself with hanging on, he stepped off the edge. In less time than it would have taken him to parachute the drop he was picking himself up off the cushions in the hotel basement and reflecting that lunar gravitation surely played hob with a man's leg muscles.

He left the drop room and started out in an arbitrary direction, but walking as if he were on business and belonged where he was—any exit would do and he would find one eventually.

He wandered in and out of the enormous pantry, then found the freight door through which the pantry was supplied.

When he was thirty feet from it, it closed and an alarm sounded. He turned back.

He encountered two policemen in one of the many corridors under the giant hotel and attempted to brush on past them. One of them stared at him, then caught his arm. "Captain Gilead—"

Gilead tried to squirm away, but without showing any skill in the attempt. "What's the idea?"

"You are Captain Gilead."

"And you're my Aunt Sadie. Let go of my arm, copper."

The policeman fumbled in his pocket with his other hand, pulled out a notebook. Gilead noted that the other officer had moved a safe ten feet away and had a Markheim gun trained on him.

"You, Captain Gilead," the first officer droned, "are charged on a sworn complaint with uttering a counterfeit five-pluton note at or about thirteen hours this date at the Grand Concourse drugstore in this city. You are cautioned to come peacefully and are advised that you need not speak at this time. Come along."

The charge might or might not have something to it, thought Gilead; he had not examined closely the money in the substituted wallet. He did not mind being booked, now that the microfilm was out of his possession; to be in an ordinary police station with nothing more sinister to cope with than crooked cops and dumb desk sergeants would be easy street compared with Runt & Company searching for him.

On the other hand the situation was too pat, unless the police had arrived close on his heels and found the stripped bellman, gotten his story and started searching.

The second policeman kept his distance and did not lower the Markheim gun. That made other consideration academic. "Okay, I'll go," he protested. "You don't have to twist my arm that way."

They went up to the weather level and out to the street—and not once did the second cop drop his guard. Gilead relaxed and waited. A police car was balanced at the curb. Gilead stopped. "I'll walk," he said. "The nearest station is just around the corner. I want to be booked in my own precinct."

He felt a teeth-chattering chill as the blast from the Markheim hit him; he pitched forward on his face.

He was coming to, but still could not co-ordinate, as they lifted him out of the car. By the time he found himself being half-carried, half-marched down a long corridor he was almost himself again, but with a gap in his memory. He was shoved through a door which clanged behind him. He steadied himself and looked around.

"Greetings, friend," a resonant voice called out. "Drag up a chair by the fire."

Gilead blinked, deliberately slowed himself down, and breathed deeply. His healthy body was fighting off the effects of the Markheim bolt; he was almost himself.

The room was a cell, old-fashioned, almost primitive. The front of the cell and the door were steel bars; the walls were concrete. Its only furniture, a long wooden bench, was occupied by the man who had spoken. He was fiftyish, of ponderous frame, heavy features set in a shrewd, good-natured expression. He was lying back on the bench, head pillowed on his hands, in animal ease. Gilead had seen him before.

"Hello, Dr. Baldwin."

The man sat up with a flowing economy of motion that moved his bulk as little as possible. "I'm not Dr. Baldwin—I'm not Doctor anything, though my name is Baldwin." He stared at Gilead. "But I know you—seen some of your lectures."

Gilead cocked an eyebrow. "A man would seem naked around the Association of Theoretical Physicists without a doctor's degree—and you were at their last meeting."

Baldwin chuckled boomingly. "That accounts for it—that has to be my cousin on my father's side, Hartley M.—Stuffy citizen Hartley. I'll have to try to take the curse off the family name, now that I've met you, Captain." He stuck out a huge hand. "Gregory Baldwin, 'Kettle Belly' to my friends. New and used helicopters is as close as I come to theoretical physics. *'Kettle Belly Baldwin, King of the Kopters'*—you must have seen my advertising."

"Now that you mention it, I have."

Baldwin pulled out a card. "Here. If you ever need one, I'll give you a ten percent off for knowing old Hartley. Matter of fact, I can do right well by you in a year-old Curtiss, a family car without a mark on it."

Gilead accepted the card and sat down. "Not at the moment, thanks. You seem to have an odd sort of office, Mr. Baldwin."

Baldwin chuckled again. "In the course of a long life these things happen, Captain. I won't ask you why you are here or what you are doing in that monkey suit. Call me Kettle Belly."

"Okay." Gilead got up and went to the door. Opposite the cell was a blank wall; there was no one in sight. He whistled and shouted—no answer.

"What's itching you, Captain?" Baldwin asked gently.

Gilead turned. His cellmate had dealt a solitaire hand on the bench and was calmly playing.

"I've got to raise the turnkey and send for a lawyer."

"Don't fret about it. Let's play some cards." He reached in a pocket. "I've got a second deck; how about some Russian bank?"

"No, thanks. I've got to get out of here." He shouted again—still no answer.

"Don't waste your lung power, Captain," Baldwin advised him. "They'll come when it suits them and not a second before. I *know*. Come play with me; it passes the time." Baldwin appeared to be shuffling the two decks; Gilead could see that he was actually stacking the cards. The deception amused him; he decided to play—since the truth of Baldwin's advice was so evident.

"If you don't like Russian bank," Kettle Belly went on, "here is a game I learned as a kid." He paused and stared into Gilead's eyes. "It's instructive as well as entertaining, yet it's simple, once you catch on to it." He started dealing out the cards. "It makes a better game with two decks, because the black cards don't mean anything. Just the twenty-six red cards in each deck count—with the heart suit coming first. Each card scores according to its position in that sequence. The ace of hearts is one and the king of hearts counts thirteen; the ace of diamonds is next at fourteen and so on. Savvy?"

"Yes."

"And the blacks don't count. They're blanks . . . spaces. Ready to play?"

"What are the rules?"

"We'll deal out one hand for free; you'll learn faster as you see it. Then, when you've caught on, I'll play you for a half interest in the atomics trust—or ten bits in cash." He resumed dealing, laying the cards out rapidly in columns, five to a row. He paused, finished. "It's my deal, so it's your count. See what you get."

It was evident that Baldwin's stacking had brought the red cards into groups, yet there was no evident advantage to it, nor was the count especially high—nor low. Gilead stared at it, trying to figure out the man's game. The cheating, as cheating seemed too bold to be probable.

Suddenly the cards jumped at him, arranged themselves in a meaningful array. He read:

XTHXY
CANXX
XXXSE
HEARX
XUSXX

The fact that there were only two fives-of-hearts available had affected the spelling but the meaning was clear. Gilead reached for the cards. "I'll try one. I can beat that score." He dipped into the tips belonging to the suit's owner. "Ten bits it is."

Baldwin covered it. Gilead shuffled, making even less attempt to cover up than had Baldwin. He dealt:

> WHATS
> XXXXX
> XYOUR
> GAMEX
> XXXXX

Baldwin shoved the money toward him and anted again. "Okay, my turn for revenge." He laid out:

> XXIMX
> XONXX
> YOURX
> XXXXX
> XSIDE

"I win again," Gilead announced gleefully. "Ante up." He grabbed the cards and manipulated them:

> YEAHX
> XXXXX
> PROVE
> XXITX
> XXXXX

Baldwin counted and said, "You're too smart for me. Gimme the cards." He produced another ten-bit piece and dealt again:

> XXILX
> HELPX
> XXYOU
> XGETX
> OUTXX

"I should have cut the cards," Gilead complained, pushing the money over. "Let's double the bets." Baldwin grunted and Gilead dealt again:

```
XNUTS
IMXXX
SAFER
XXINX
XGAOL
```

"I broke your luck," Baldwin gloated. "We'll double it again?"

```
XUXRX
XNUTS
THISX
NOXXX
XJAIL
```

The deal shifted:

```
KEEPX
XTALK
INGXX
XXXXX
XBUDX
```

Baldwin answered:

```
THISX
XXXXX
XXNEW
AGEXX
XHOTL
```

As he stacked the cards again Gilead considered these new factors. He was prepared to believe that he was hidden somewhere in the New Age Hotel; in fact the counterproposition that his opponents had permitted two ordinary cops to take him away to a normal city jail was most unlikely—unless they had the jail as fully under control as they quite evidently had the hotel. Nevertheless the point was not proven. As for Baldwin, he might be on Gilead's side; more probably he was planted as an *agent provacateur*—or he might be working for himself.

The permutations added up to six situations, only one of which made it desirable to accept Baldwin's offer for help in a jail break—said situation being the least likely of the six.

Nevertheless, though he considered Baldwin a liar, net, he tentatively decided to accept. A static situation brought him no advantage; a dynamic situation—*any* dynamic situation—he might turn to his advantage. But more data were needed. "These cards are sticky as candy," he complained. "You letting your money ride?"

"Suits." Gilead dealt again:

XXXXX
WHYXX
AMXXX
XXXXI
XHERE

"You have the damnedest luck," Baldwin commented:

FILMS
ESCAP
BFORE
XUXXX
KRACK

Gilead swept up the cards, was about to "shuffle," when Baldwin said, "Oh oh, school's out." Footsteps could be heard in the passage. "Good luck, boy," Baldwin added.

Baldwin knew about the films, but had not used any of the dozen ways to identify himself as part of Gilead's own organization. Therefore he was planted by the opposition, or he was a third factor.

More important, the fact that Baldwin knew about the films proved his assertion that this was not a jail. It followed with bitter certainty that he, Gilead, stood no computable chance of getting out alive. The footsteps approaching the cell could be ticking off the last seconds of his life.

He knew now that he should have found means to report the destination of the films before going to the New Age. But Humpty Dumpty was off the wall, entropy always increases—but the films *must* be delivered.

The footsteps were quite close.

Baldwin might get out alive.

But who was Baldwin?

All the while he was "shuffling" the cards. The action was not final; he had only to give them one true shuffle to destroy the message being set up in them. A spider settled from the ceiling, landed on the other man's hand. Baldwin, instead of knocking it off and crushing it, most carefully reached his arm out toward the wall and encouraged it to lower itself to the floor. "Better stay out of the way, shorty," he said gently, "or one of the big boys is likely to step on you."

The incident, small as it was, determined Gilead's decision—and with it, the fate of a planet. He stood up and handed the stacked deck to Baldwin. "I owe you exactly ten-sixty," he said carefully. "Be sure to remember it—I'll see who our visitors are."

The footsteps had stopped outside the cell door.

There were two of them, dressed neither as police nor as guards; the masquerade was over. One stood well back, covering the maneuver with a Markheim, the other unlocked the door. "Back against the wall, Fatso," he ordered. "Gilead, out you come. And take it easy, or, after we freeze you, I'll knock out your teeth just for fun."

Baldwin shuffled back against the wall; Gilead came out slowly. He watched for any opening but the leader backed away from him without once getting between him and the man with the Markheim. "Ahead of us and take it slow," he was ordered. He complied, helpless under the precautions, unable to run, unable to fight.

Baldwin went back to the bench when they had gone. He dealt out the cards as if playing solitaire, swept them up again, and continued to deal himself solitaire hands. Presently he "shuffled" the cards back to the exact order Gilead had left them in and pocketed them.

The message had read: XTELLXFBSXPOBOXDEBT XXXCHI.

His two guards marched Gilead into a room and locked the door behind him, leaving themselves outside. He found himself in a large window overlooking the city and a reach of the river; balancing it on the left hung a solid portraying a lunar landscape in convincing color and depth. In front of him was a rich but not ostentatious executive desk.

The lower part of his mind took in these details; his attention could be centered only on the person who sat at that desk. She was old but not senile, frail but not helpless. Her eyes were very much alive, her expression serene. Her translucent, well-groomed hands were busy with a frame of embroidery.

On the desk in front of her were two pneumo mailing tubes, a pair of slippers, and some tattered, soiled remnants of cloth and plastic.

She looked up. "How do you do, Captain Gilead?" she said in a thin, sweet soprano suitable for singing hymns.

Gilead bowed. "Well, thank you—and you, Mrs. Keithley?"

"You know me, I see."

"Madame would be famous if only for her charities."

"You are kind. Captain, I will not waste your time. I had hoped that we could release you without fuss, but—" She indicated the two tubes in front of her. "—you can see for yourself that we must deal with you further."

"So?"

"Come, now, Captain. You mailed *three* tubes. These two are only dummies, and the third did not reach its apparent destination. It is possible that it was badly addressed and has been rejected by the sorting machines. If so, we shall have it in due course. But it seems much more likely that you found some way to change its address—likely to the point of pragmatic certainty."

"Or possibly I corrupted your servant."

She shook her head slightly. "We examined him quite thoroughly before—"

"Before he died?"

"Please, Captain, let's not change the subject. I must know where you sent that other tube. You cannot be hypnotized by ordinary means; you have an acquired immunity to hypnotic drugs. Your tolerance for pain extends beyond the threshold of unconsciousness. All of these things have already been proved, else you would not be in the job you are in; I shall not put either of us to the inconvenience of proving them again. Yet I must have that tube. What is your price?"

"You assume that I have a price."

She smiled. "If the old saw has any exceptions, history does not record them. Be reasonable, Captain. Despite your admitted immunity to ordinary forms of examination, there are ways of breaking down— of *changing*—a man's character so that he becomes really quite pliant under examination . . . ways that we learned from the commissars. But those ways take time and a woman my age has no time to waste."

Gilead lied convincingly. "It's not your age, ma'am; it is the fact that you know that you must obtain that tube at once or you will never get it." He was hoping—more than that, he was *willing*—that Baldwin would have sense enough to examine the cards for one last message . . . and act on it. If Baldwin failed and he, Gilead, died, the tube would eventually come to rest in a dead-letter office and would in time be destroyed.

"You are probably right. Nevertheless, Captain, I will go ahead with the Mindszenty technique if you insist upon it. What do you say to ten million plutonium credits?"

Gilead believed her first statement. He reviewed in his mind the means by which a man bound hand and foot, or worse, could kill himself unassisted. "Ten million plutons and a knife in my back?" he answered. "Let's be practical."

"Convincing assurance would be given before you need talk."

"Even so, it is not my price. After all, you are worth at least five hundred million plutons."

She leaned forward. "I like you, Captain. You are a man of strength. I am an old woman, without heirs. Suppose you became my partner—and my successor?"

"Pie in the sky."

"No, no! I mean it. My age and sex do not permit me actively to serve myself; I must rely on others. Captain, I am very tired of inefficient tools, of men who can let things be spirited away right from under their noses. Imagine!" She made a little gesture of exasperation, clutching her hand into a claw. "You and I could go far, Captain. I need you."

"But I do not need you, madame. And I won't have you."

She made no answer, but touched a control on her desk. A door on the left dilated; two men and a girl came in. The girl Gilead recognized as the waitress from the Grand Concourse Drug Store. They had stripped her bare, which seemed to him an unnecessary indignity since her working uniform could not possibly have concealed a weapon.

The girl, once inside, promptly blew her top, protesting, screaming, using language unusual to her age and sex—an hysterical, thalmic outburst of volcanic proportions.

"Quiet, child!"

The girl stopped in midstream, looked with surprise at Mrs. Keithley, and shut up. Nor did she start again, but stood there, looking even younger than she was and somewhat aware of and put off stride by her nakedness. She was covered now with goose flesh, one tear cut a white line down her dust-smeared face, stopped at her lip. She licked at it and sniffled.

"You were out of observation once, Captain," Mrs. Keithley went on, "during which time this person saw you twice. Therefore we will examine her."

Gilead shook his head. "She knows no more than a goldfish. But go ahead—five minutes of hypno will convince you."

"Oh, no, Captain! Hypno is sometimes fallible; if she is a member of your bureau, it is certain to be fallible." She signalled to one of the men attending the girl; he went to a cupboard and opened it. "I am old-fashioned," the old woman went on. "I trust simple mechanical means much more than I do the cleverest of clinical procedures."

Gilead saw the implements that the man was removing from cupboard and started forward. "Stop that!" he commanded. "You can't do that—"

He bumped his nose quite hard.

The man paid him no attention. Mrs. Keithley said, "Forgive me, Captain. I should have told you that this room is not one room, but two. The partition is merely glass, but very special glass—I use the room for difficult interviews. There is no need to hurt yourself by trying to reach us."

"Just a moment!"

"Yes, Captain?"

"Your time is already running out. Let the girl and me go free *now*. You are aware that there are several hundred men searching this city for me even now—and that they will not stop until they have taken it apart panel by panel."

"I think not. A man answering your description to the last factor caught the South Africa rocket twenty minutes after you registered at the New Age hotel. He was carrying your very own identifications. He will not reach South Africa, but the manner of his disappearance will point to desertion rather than accident or suicide."

Gilead dropped the matter. "What do you plan to gain by abusing this child? You have all she knows; certainly you do not believe that we could afford to trust in such as she?"

Mrs. Keithley pursed her lips. "Frankly, I do not expect to learn anything from her. I may learn something from you."

"I see."

The leader of the two men looked questioningly at his mistress; she motioned him to go ahead. The girl stared blankly at him, plainly un-aware of the uses of the equipment he had gotten out. He and his part-ner got busy.

Shortly the girl screamed, continued to scream for a few moments in a high adulation. Then it stopped as she fainted.

They roused her and stood her up again. She stood, swaying and staring stupidly at her poor hands, forever damaged even for the futile purposes to which she had been capable of putting them. Blood spread down her wrists and dripped on a plastic tarpaulin, placed there earlier by the second of the two men.

Gilead did nothing and said nothing. Knowing as he did that the tube he was protecting contained matters measured in millions of lives, the problem of the girl, as a problem, did not even arise. It disturbed a deep and very ancient part of his brain, but almost automatically he cut that part off and lived for the time in his forebrain.

Consciously he memorized the faces, skulls, and figures of the two men and filed the data under "personal." Thereafter he unobtrusively gave his attention to the scene out the window. He had been noting it all through the interview but he wanted to give it explicit thought. He re-cast what he saw in terms of what it would look like had he been able to look squarely out the window and decided that he was on the ninety-first floor of the New Age hotel and approximately one hundred and thirty meters from the north end. He filed this under "professional".

When the girl died, Mrs. Keithley left the room without speaking to him. The men gathered up what was left in the tarpaulin and fol-lowed her. Presently the two guards returned and, using the same fool-proof methods, took him back to his cell.

As soon as the guards had gone and Kettle Belly was free to leave his position against the wall he came forward and pounded Gilead on the shoulders. "Hi, boy! I'm sure glad to see you—I was scared I would never lay eyes on you again. How was it? Pretty rough?"

"No, they didn't hurt me; they just asked some questions."

"You're lucky. Some of those crazy damn cops play mean when they get you alone in a back room. Did they let you call your lawyer?"

"No."

"Then they ain't through with you. You want to watch it, kid."

Gilead sat down on the bench. "The hell with them. Want to play some more cards?"

"Don't mind if I do. I feel lucky." Baldwin pulled out the double deck, riffled through it. Gilead took them and did the same. Good! they were in the order he had left them in. He ran his thumb across the edges again— yes, even the black nulls were unchanged in sequence; apparently Kettle Belly had simply stuck them in his pocket without examining them, without suspecting that a last message had been written in to them. He felt sure that Baldwin would not have left the message set up if he had read it. Since he found himself still alive, he was much relieved to think this.

He gave the cards one true shuffle, then started stacking them. His first lay-out read:

XXXXX
ESCAP
XXATX
XXXXX
XONCE

"Gotcha that time!" Baldwin crowed. "Ante up":

DIDXX
XYOUX
XXXXX
XXXXX
CRACK

"Let it ride," announced Gilead and took the deal:

XXNOX
BUTXX
XXXXX
XLETS
XXGOX

"You're too derned lucky to live," complained Baldwin. "Look—we'll leave the bets doubled and double the lay-out. I want a fair chance to get my money back."

His next lay-out read:

```
XXXXX
XTHXN
XXXXX
THXYX
NEEDX
XXXUX
ALIVX
XXXXX
PLAYX
XXXUP
```

"Didn't do you much good, did it?" Gilead commented, took the cards and started arranging them.

"There's something mighty funny about a man that wins all the time," Baldwin grumbled. He watched Gilead narrowly. Suddenly his hand shot out, grabbed Gilead's wrist. "I thought so;" he yelled. "A goddam card sharp—"

Gilead shook his hand off. "Why, you obscene fat slug!"

"Caught you! *Caught you!*" Kettle Belly reclaimed his hold, grabbed the other wrist as well. They struggled and rolled to the floor.

Gilead discovered two things: this awkward, bulky man was an artist at every form of dirty fighting and he could simulate it convincingly without damaging his partner. His nerve holds were an inch off the nerve; his kneeings were to thigh muscle rather than to the crotch.

Baldwin tried for a chancery strangle; Gilead let him take it. The big man settled the flat of his forearm against the point of Gilead's chin rather than against his Adam's apple and proceeded to "strangle" him.

There were running footsteps in the corridor.

Gilead caught a glimpse of the guards as they reached the door. They stopped momentarily; the bell of the Markheim was too big to use through the steel grating, the charge would be screened and grounded. Apparently they did not have pacifier bombs with them, for they hesitated. Then the leader quickly unlocked the door, while the man with the Markheim dropped back to the cover position.

Baldwin ignored them, while continuing his stream of profanity and abuse at Gilead. He let the first man almost reach them before he suddenly said in Gilead's ear, "Close your eyes!" At which he broke just as suddenly.

Gilead sensed an incredibly dazzling flash of light even through his eyelids. Almost on top of it he heard a muffled crack; he opened his eyes and saw that the first man was down, his head twisted at a grotesque angle.

The man with the Markheim was shaking his head; the muzzle of his weapon weaved around. Baldwin was charging him in a waddle, back and knees bent until he was hardly three feet tall. The blinded guard could hear him, let fly a charge in the direction of the noise; it passed over Baldwin.

Baldwin was on him; the two went down. There was another cracking noise of ruptured bone and another dead man. Baldwin stood up, grasping the Markheim, keeping it pointed down the corridor. "How are your eyes, kid?" he called out anxiously.

"They're all right."

"Then come take this chiller." Gilead moved up, took the Markheim. Baldwin ran to the dead end of the corridor where a window looked out over the city. The window did not open; there was no "copter step" beyond it. It was merely a straight drop. He came running back.

Gilead was shuffling possibilities in his mind. Events had moved by Baldwin's plan, not by his. As a result of his visit to Mrs. Keithley's "interview room" he was oriented in space. The corridor ahead and a turn to the left should bring him to the quick-drop shaft. Once in the basement and armed with a Markheim, he felt sure that he could fight his way out—with Baldwin in trail if the man would follow. If not— well, there was too much at stake.

Baldwin was into the cell and out again almost at once. "Come along!" Gilead snapped. A head showed at the bend in the corridor; he let fly at it and the owner of the head passed out on the floor.

"Out of my way, kid!" Baldwin answered. He was carrying the heavy bench on which they had "played" cards. He started up the corridor with it, toward the sealed window, gaining speed remarkably as he went.

His makeshift battering ram struck the window heavily. The plastic bulged, ruptured, and snapped like a soap bubble. The bench went on through, disappeared from sight, while Baldwin teetered on hands and knees, a thousand feet of nothingness under his chin.

"Kid!" he yelled. "Close in! Fall back!"

Gilead backed towards him, firing twice more as he did so. He still did not see how Baldwin planned to get out, but the big man had demonstrated that he had resourcefulness—and resources.

Baldwin was whistling through his fingers and waving. In violation of all city traffic rules a helicopter separated itself from the late afternoon throng, cut through a lane, and approached the window. It hovered

just far enough away to keep from fouling its blades. The drive opened the door, a line snaked across and Kettle Belly caught it. With great speed he made it fast to the window's polarizer knob, then grabbed the Markheim. "You first," he snapped. "Hurry!"

Gilead dropped to his knees and grasped the line; the driver immediately increased his tip speed and tilted his rotor; the line tautened. Gilead let it take his weight, then swarmed across it. The driver gave him a hand up while controlling his craft like a highschool horse with his other hand.

The 'copter bucked; Gilead turned and saw Baldwin coming across, a fat spider on a web. As he himself helped the big man in, the driver reached down and cut the line. The ship bucked again and slid away.

There were already men standing in the broken window. "Get lost, Steve!" Baldwin ordered. The driver gave his tip jets another notch and tilted the rotor still more; the 'copter swooped away. He eased it into the traffic stream and inquired, "Where to?"

"Set her for home—and tell the other boys to go home, too. No— you've got your hands full; I'll tell them!" Baldwin crowded up into the other pilot's seat, slipped on phones and settled a quiet-mike over his mouth. The driver adjusted his car to the traffic, set up a combination on his pilot, then settled back and opened a picture magazine.

Shortly Baldwin took off the phones and came back to the passenger compartment. "Takes a lot of 'copters to be sure you have one cruising by when you need it," he said conversationally. "Fortunately, I've got a lot of 'em. Oh, by the way, this is Steve Halliday. Steve, meet Joe—Joe, what is your last name?"

"Greene," answered Gilead.

"Howdy," said the driver and let his eyes go back to his magazine.

Gilead considered the situation. He was not sure that it had been improved. Kettle Belly, whatever he was, was more than a used 'copter dealer—*and* he knew about the films. This boy Steve looked like a harmless young extrovert but, then, Kettle Belly himself looked like a lunk. He considered trying to overpower both of them, remembered Kettle Belly's virtuosity in rough-and-tumble fighting, and decided against it. Perhaps Kettle Belly really was on his side, completely and utterly. He heard rumors that the Department used more than one echelon of operatives and he had no way of being sure that he himself was at the top level.

"Kettle Belly," he went on, "could you set me down at the airport first? I'm in one hell of a hurry."

Baldwin looked him over. "Sure, if you say so. But I thought you would want to swap those duds? You're as conspicuous as a preacher at a stag party. And how are you fixed for cash?"

With his fingers Gilead counted the change that had come with the suit. A man without cash had one arm in a sling. "How long would it take?"

"Ten minutes extra, maybe."

Gilead thought again about Kettle Belly's fighting ability and decided that there was no way for a fish in water to get any wetter. "Okay." He settled back and relaxed completely.

Presently he turned again to Baldwin. "By the way, how did you manage to sneak in that dazzle bomb?"

Kettle Belly chuckled. "I'm a large man, Joe; there's an awful lot of me to search." He laughed again. "You'd be amazed at where I had that hidden."

Gilead changed the subject. "How did you happen to be there in the first place?"

Baldwin sobered. "That's a long and complicated story. Come back some day when you're not in such a rush and I'll tell you all about it."

"I'll do that—soon."

"Good. Maybe I can sell you that used Curtiss at the same time."

The pilot alarm sounded; the driver put down his magazine and settled the craft on the roof of Baldwin's establishment.

Baldwin was as good as his word. He took Gilead to his office, sent for clothes—which showed up with great speed—and handed Gilead a wad of bills suitable to stuff a pillow. "You can mail it back," he said.

"I'll bring it back in person," promised Gilead.

"Good. Be careful out on the street. Some of our friends are sure to be around."

"I'll be careful." He left, as casually as if he had called there on business, but feeling less sure of himself than usual. Baldwin himself remained a mystery and, in his business, Gilead could not afford mysteries.

There was a public phone booth in the lobby of Baldwin's building. Gilead went in, scrambled, then coded a different relay station from the one he had attempted to use before. He gave his booth's code and instructed the operator to scramble back. In a matter of minutes he was talking to his chief in New Washington.

"Joe! Where the hell have you been?"

"Later, boss—get this." In departmental oral code as an added precaution, he told his chief that the films were in post office box 1060, Chicago, and insisted that they be picked up by a major force at once.

His chief turned away from the view plate, then returned, "Okay, it's done. Now what happened to you?"

"Later, boss, later. I think I've got some friends outside who are anxious to rassle with me. Keep me here and I may get a hole in my head."

"Okay—but head right back here. I want a full report; I'll wait here for you."

"Right." He switched off.

He left the booth light-heartedly, with the feeling of satisfaction that comes from a hard job successfully finished. He rather hoped that some of his "friends" would show up; he felt like kicking somebody who needed kicking.

But they disappointed him. He boarded the transcontinental rocket without alarms and slept all the way to New Washington.

He reached the Federal Bureau of Security by one of many concealed routes and went to his boss's office. After scan and voice check he was let in. Bonn looked up and scowled.

Gilead ignored the expression; Bonn usually scowled. "Agent Joseph Briggs, three-four-oh-nine-seven-two, reporting back from assignment, sir," he said evenly.

Bonn switched a desk control to "recording" and another to "covert." "You are, eh? Why, thumb-fingered idiot! how do you dare to show your face around here?"

"Easy now, boss—what's the trouble?"

Bonn fumed incoherently for a time, then said, "Briggs, twelve star men covered that pick up—and the box was empty. Post office box ten-sixty, Chicago, indeed! Where are those films? Was it a cover up? Have you got them with you?"

Gilead-Briggs restrained his surprise. "No. I mailed them at the Grand Concourse post office to the address you just named." He added, "The machine may have kicked them out; I was forced to letter by hand the machine symbols."

Bonn looked suddenly hopeful. He touched another control and said, "Carruthers! On that Briggs matter: Check the rejection stations for that routing." He thought and then added, "Then try a rejection sequence on the assumption that the first symbol was acceptable to the machine but mistaken. Also for each of the other symbols; run them simultaneously—crash priority for all agents and staff. After that try combinations of symbols taken two at a time, then three at a time, and so on." He switched off.

"The total of that series you just set up is every postal address in the continent," Briggs suggested mildly. "It can't be done."

"It's got to be done! Man, have you any idea of the *importance* of those films you were guarding?"

"Yes. The director at Moon Base told me what I was carrying."

"You don't act as if you did. You've lost the most valuable thing this or any other government can possess—the absolute weapon. Yet you stand there blinking at me as if you had mislaid a pack of cigarettes."

"Weapon?" objected Briggs. "I wouldn't call the nova effect that, unless you class suicide as a weapon. And I don't concede that I've lost it. As an agent acting alone and charged primarily with keeping it out of the hands of others, I used the best means available in an emergency to protect it. That is well within the limits of my authority. I was spotted, by some means—"

"You shouldn't have been spotted!"

"Granted. But I was. I was unsupported and my estimate of the situation did not include a probability of staying alive. Therefore I had to protect my charge by some means which did not depend on my staying alive."

"But you *did* stay alive—you're here."

"Not my doing nor yours, I assure you. I should have been covered. It was your order, you will remember, that I act alone."

Bonn looked sullen. "That was necessary."

"So? In any case, I don't see what all the shooting is about. Either the films show up, or they are lost and will be destroyed as unclaimed mail. So I go back to the Moon and get another set of prints."

Bonn chewed his lip. "You can't do that."

"Why not?"

Bonn hesitated a long time. "There were just two sets. You had the originals, which were to be placed in a vault in the Archives—and the others were to be destroyed at once when the originals were known to be secure."

"Yes? What's the hitch?"

"You don't see the importance of the procedure. Every working paper, every file, every record was destroyed when these films were made. Every technician, every assistant, received hypno. The intention was not only to protect the results of the research but to wipe out the very fact that the research had taken place. There aren't a dozen people in the system who even know of the existence of the nova effect."

Briggs had his own opinions on this point, based on recent experience, but he kept still about them. Bonn went on, "The Secretary has been after me steadily to let him know when the originals were secured. He has been quite insistent, quite critical. When you called in, I told him that the films were safe and that he would have them in a few minutes."

"Well?"

"Don't you see, you fool—he gave the order at once to destroy the other copies."

Briggs whistled. "Jumped the gun, didn't he?"

"That's not the way he'll figure it—mind you, the President was pressuring *him*. He'll say that *I* jumped the gun."

"And so you did."

"No, *you* jumped the gun. You told me the films were in that box."

"Hardly. I said I had sent them there."

"No, you didn't."

"Get out the tape and play it back."

"There is no tape—by the President's own order no records are kept on this operation."

"So? Then why are you recording now?"

"Because," Bonn answered sharply, "some one is going to pay for this and it is not going to be me."

"Meaning," Briggs said slowly, "that it is going to be me."

"I didn't say that. It might be the Secretary."

"If his head rolls, so will yours. No, both of you are figuring on using me. Before you plan on that, hadn't you better hear my report? It might affect your plans. I've got news for you, boss."

Bonn drummed the desk. "Go ahead. It had better be good."

In a passionless monotone Briggs recited all events as recorded by sharp memory from receipt of the films on the Moon to the present moment. Bonn listened impatiently.

Finished, Briggs waited. Bonn got up and strode around the room. Finally he stopped and said, "Briggs, I never heard such a fantastic pack of lies in my life. A fat man who plays cards! A wallet that wasn't your wallet—your clothes stolen! And Mrs. Keithley—Mrs. *Keithley!* Don't you know that she is one of the strongest supporters of the Administration?"

Briggs said nothing. Bonn went on, "Now I'll tell you what actually did happen. Up to the time you grounded at Pied-a-Terre your report is correct, but—"

"How do you know?"

"Because you were covered, naturally. You don't think I would trust this to one man, do you?"

"Why didn't you tell me? I could have hollered for help and saved all this."

Bonn brushed it aside. "You engaged a runner, dismissed him, went in that drugstore, came out and went to the post office. There was no fight in the concourse for the simple reason that no one was following you. At the post office you mailed three tubes, one of which may or may not have contained the films. You went from there to the New Age hotel, left it twenty minutes later and caught the transrocket for Cape Town. You—"

"Just a moment," objected Briggs. "How could I have done that and still be here now?"

"Eh?" For a moment Bonn seemed stumped. "That's just a detail; you were positively identified. For that matter, it would have been a far, far better thing for you if you had stayed on that rocket. In fact—" The bureau chief got a far-away look in his eyes. "—you'll be better off for the time being if we assume officially that you did stay on that rocket. You are in a bad spot, Briggs, a very bad spot. You did not muff this assignment—you sold out!"

Briggs looked at him levelly. "You are preferring charges?"

"Not just now. That is why it is best to assume that you stayed on that rocket—until matters settle down, clarify."

Briggs did not need a graph to show him what solution would come out when "matters clarified." He took from a pocket a memo pad, scribbled on it briefly, and handed it to Bonn.

It read: "I resign my appointment effective immediately." He had added signature, thumbprint, date, and hour.

"So long, boss," he added. He turned slightly, as if to go.

Bonn yelled, "Stop! Briggs, you are under arrest." He reached toward his desk.

Briggs cuffed him in the windpipe, added one to the pit of Bonn's stomach. He slowed down then and carefully made sure that Bonn would remain out for a satisfactory period. Examination of Bonn's desk produced a knockout kit; he added a two-hour hypodermic, placing it inconspicuously beside a mole near the man's backbone. He wiped the needle, restored everything to its proper place, removed the current record from the desk and wiped the tape of all mention of himself, including door check. He left the desk set to "covert" and "do not disturb" and left by another of the concealed routes to the Bureau.

He went to the rocket port, bought a ticket, unreserved, for the first ship to Chicago. There was twenty minutes to wait; he made a couple of minor purchases from clerks rather than from machines, letting his face be seen. When the Chicago ship was called he crowded forward with the rest.

At the inner gate, just short of the weighing-in platform, he became part of the crowd present to see passengers off, rather than a passenger himself. He waved at some one in the line leaving the weighing station beyond the gate, smiled, called out a good-by, and let the crowd carry him back from the gate as it closed. He peeled off from the crowd at the men's washroom. When he came out there were several hasty but effective changes in his appearance.

More important, his manner was different.

A short, illicit transaction in a saloon near a hiring hall provided the work card he needed; fifty-five minutes later he was headed across country as Jack Gillespie, loader and helper-driver on a diesel freighter.

Could his addressing of the pneumo tube have been bad enough to cause the automatic postal machines to reject it? He let the picture of the label, as it had been when he had completed it, build in his mind until it was as sharp as the countryside flowing past him. No, his lettering of the symbols had been perfect and correct; the machines would accept it.

Could the machine have kicked out the tube for another cause, say a turned-up edge of the gummed label? Yes, but the written label was sufficient to enable a postal clerk to get it back in the groove. One such delay did not exceed ten minutes, even during the rush hour. Even with five such delays the tube would have reached Chicago more than one hour before he reported to Bonn by phone.

Suppose the gummed label had peeled off entirely; in such case the tube would have gone to the same destination as the two cover-up tubes.

In which case Mrs. Keithley would have gotten it, since she had been able to intercept or receive the other two.

Therefore the tube had reached the Chicago post office box.

Therefore Kettle Belly *had* read the message in the stacked cards, had given instructions to some one in Chicago, had done so while at the helicopter's radio. After an event, "possible" and "true" are equivalent ideas, whereas "probable" becomes a measure of one's ignorance. To call a conclusion "improbable" *after the event* was self-confusing amphigory.

Therefore Kettle Belly Baldwin had the films—a conclusion he had reached in Bonn's office.

Two hundred miles from New Washington he worked up an argument with the top driver and got himself fired. From a local booth in the town where he dropped he scrambled through to Baldwin's business office. "Tell him I'm a man who owes him money."

Shortly the big man's face built up on the screen. "Hi, kid! How's tricks?"

"I'm fired."

"I thought you would be."

"Worse than that—I'm wanted."

"Naturally."

"I'd like to talk with you."

"Swell. Where are you?"

Gilead told him.

"You're clean?"

"For a few hours, at least."

"Go to the local air port. Steve will pick you up."

Steve did so, nodded a greeting, jumped his craft into the air, set his pilot, and went back to his reading. When the ship settled down on course, Gilead noted it and asked, "Where are we going?"

"The boss's ranch. Didn't he tell you?"

"No." Gilead knew it was possible that he was being taken for a one-way ride. True, Baldwin had enabled him to escape an otherwise pragmatically certain death—it was certain that Mrs. Keithley had not intended to let him stay alive longer that suited her uses, else she would not have had the girl killed in his presence. Until he had arrived at Bonn's office, he had assumed that Baldwin had saved him because he knew something that Baldwin most urgently wanted to know—whereas now it looked as if Baldwin had saved him for altruistic reasons.

Gilead conceded the existence in this world of altruistic reasons, but was inclined not to treat them as "least hypothesis" until all other possible hypotheses had been eliminated. Baldwin might have had his own reasons for wishing him to live long enough to report to New Washington and nevertheless be pleased to wipe him out now that he was a wanted man whose demise would cause no comment.

Baldwin might even be a partner in these dark matters of Mrs. Keithley. In some ways that was the simplest explanation though it left other factors unexplained. In any case Baldwin was a key actor—and he had the films. The risk was necessary.

Gilead did not worry about it. The factors known to him were chalked up on the blackboard of his mind, there to remain until enough variables become constants to permit a solution by logic. The ride was very pleasant.

Steve put him down on the lawn of a large rambling ranch house, introduced him to a motherly old party named Mrs. Garver, and took off. "Make yourself at home, Joe," she told him. "Your room is the last one in the east wing—shower across from it. Supper in ten minutes."

He thanked her and took the suggestion, getting back to the living room with a minue or two to spare. Several others, a dozen or more of both sexes, were there. The place seemed to be a sort of a dude ranch—not entirely dude, as he had seen Herefords on the spread as Steve and he were landing.

The other guests seemed to take his arrival as a matter of course. No one asked why he was there. One of the women introduced herself as Thalia Wagner and then took him around the group. Ma Garver came in swinging a dinner bell as this was going on and they all filed into a long, low dining room Gilead could not remember when he had had so good a meal in such amusing company.

After eleven hours of sleep, his first real rest in several days, he came fully, suddenly awake at a group of sounds his subconscious could not immediately classify and refused to discount. He opened his eyes, swept the room with them, and was at once out of bed, crouching on the side away from the door.

There were hurrying footsteps moving past his bedroom door. There were two voices, one male, one female, outside the door; the female was Thalia Wagner, the man he could not place.

Male: "tsʉmaeq?"

Female: "nø!"

Male: "zʊlntsɨ."

Female: "ɨpbit' New Jersey."

These are not precisely the sounds that Gilead heard, first because of the limitations of phonetic symbols, and second because his ears were not used to the sounds. Hearing is a function of the brain, not of the ear; his brain, sophisticated as it was, nevertheless insisted on forcing the sounds that reached his ears into familiar pockets rather than stop to create new ones.

Thalia Wagner identified, he relaxed and stood up. Thalia was part of the unknown situation he accepted in coming here; a stranger known to her he must accept also. The new unknowns, including the odd language, he filed under "pending" and put aside.

The clothes he had had were gone, but his money—Baldwin's money, rather—was where his clothes had been and with it his work card as Jack Gillespie and his few personal articles. By them some one had laid out a fresh pair of walking shorts and new sneakers, in his size.

He noted, with almost shocking surprise, that some one had been able to serve him thus without waking him.

He put on his shorts and shoes and went out. Thalia and her companion had left while he dressed. No one was about and he found the dining room empty, but three places were set, including his own of supper, and hot dishes and facilities were on the sideboard. He selected baked ham and hot rolls, fried four eggs, poured coffee. Twenty minutes later, warmly replenished and still alone, he stepped out on the veranda.

It was a beautiful day. He was drinking it in and eyeing with friendly interest a desert lark when a young woman came around the side of the house. She was dressed much as he was, allowing for difference in sex, and she was comely, though not annoyingly so. "Good morning," he said.

She stopped, put her hands on her hips, and looked him up and down. "Well!" she said. "Why doesn't somebody tell me these things?"

Then she added, "Are you married?"

"No."

"I'm shopping around. Object: matrimony. Let's get acquainted."

"I'm a hard man to marry. I've been avoiding it for years."

"They're all hard to marry," she said bitterly. "There's a new colt down at the corral. Come on."

They went. The colt's name was War Conqueror of Baldwin; hers was Gail. After proper protocol with mare and son they left. "Unless you have pressing engagements," said Gail, "now is a salubrious time to go swimming."

"If salubrious means what I think it does, yes."

The spot was shaded by cottonwoods, the bottom was sandy; for a while he felt like a boy again, with all such matters as lies and nova effects and death and violence away in some improbable, remote dimension. After a long while he pulled himself up on the bank and said, "Gail, what does 'tsɯmaeq' mean?"

"Come again?" she answered. "I had water in my ear."

He repeated all of the conversation he had heard. She looked incredulous, then laughed. "You didn't hear that, Joe, you just didn't." She added, "You got the 'New Jersey' part right."

"But I did."

"Say it again."

He did so, more carefully, and giving a fair imitation of the speakers' accents.

Gail chortled. "I got the gist of it that time. That Thalia; someday some strong man is going to wring her neck."

"But what does it mean?"

Gail gave him a long, sidewise look. "If you ever find out, I really will marry you, in spite of your protests."

Some one was whisting from the hill top. "Joe! Joe Greene—the boss wants you."

"Gotta go," he said to Gail. "G'bye."

"See you later," she corrected him.

Baldwin was waiting in a study as comfortable as himself. "Hi, Joe," he greeted him. "Grab a seatful of chair. They been treating you right?"

"Yes, indeed. Do you always set as good a table as I've enjoyed so far?"

Baldwin patted his middle. "How do you think I came by my nickname?"

"Kettle Belly, I'd like a lot of explanations."

"Joe, I'm right sorry you lost your job. If I'd had my druthers, it wouldn't have been the way it was."

"Are you working with Mrs. Keithley?"

"No. I'm against her."

"I'd like to believe that, but I've no reason to—yet. What were you doing where I found you?"

"They had grabbed me—Mrs. Keithley and her boys."

"They just happened to grab you—and just happened to stuff you in the same cell with me—and you just happened to know about the films I was supposed to be guarding—and you just happened to have a double deck of cards in your pocket? Now, really!"

"If I hadn't had the cards, we would have found some other way to talk," Kettle Belly said mildly. "Wouldn't we, now?"

"Yes. Granted."

"I didn't mean to suggest that the set up was an accident. We had you covered from Moon Base; when you were grabbed—or rather as soon as you let them suck you into the New Age, I saw to it that they grabbed me too; I figured I might have a chance to lend you a hand, once I was inside." He added, "I kinda let them think that I was an FBS man, too."

"I see. Then it was just luck that they locked us up together."

"Not luck," Kettle Belly objected. "Luck is a bonus that follows careful planning—it's never free. There was a computable probability that they would put us together in hopes of finding out what they wanted to know. We hit the jackpot because we paid for the chance. If we hadn't, I would have had to crush out of that cell and look for you— but I had to be inside to do it."

"Who is Mrs. Keithley?"

"Other than what she is publicly, I take it. She is the queen bee—or the black widow—of a gang. 'Gang' is a poor word—power group, maybe. One of several such groups, more or less tied together where their interests don't cross. Between them they divvy up the country for whatever they want like two cats splitting a gopher."

Gilead nodded; he knew what Baldwin meant, though he had not known that the enormously respected Mrs. Keithley was in such matters—not until his nose had been rubbed in the fact. "And what are you, Kettle Belly?"

"Now, Joe—I like you and I'm truly sorry you're in a jam. You led wrong a couple of times and I was obliged to trump, as the stakes were high. See here, I feel that I owe you something; what do you say to this:

we'll fix you up with a brand-new personality, vacuum tight—even new fingerprints if you want them. Pick any spot on the globe you like and any occupation; we'll supply all the money you need to start over—or money enough to retire and play with the cuties the rest of your life. What do you say?"

"No." There was no hesitation.

"You've no close relatives, no intimate friends. Think about it. I can't put you back in your job; this is the best I can do."

"I've thought about it. The devil with the job, I want to finish my case! you're the key to it."

"Reconsider, Joe. This is your chance to get out of affairs of state and lead a normal, happy life."

" 'Happy', he says!"

"Well, safe, anyhow. If you insist on going further your life expectancy becomes extremely problematical."

"I don't recall ever having tried to play safe."

"You're the doctor. Joe. In that case—" A speaker on Baldwin's desk uttered: "œnɪɛ ʀ ʰøg rylp."

Baldwin answered, "nʊ," and sauntered quickly to the fireplace. An early-morning fire still smouldered in it. He grasped the mantel piece, pulled it toward him. The entire masonry assembly, hearth, mantel, and grate, came toward him, leaving an arch in the wall. "Duck down stairs, Joe," he said. "It's a raid."

"A real priest's hole!"

"Yeah, corny, ain't it? This joint has more bolt holes than a rabbit's nest—and booby-trapped, too. Too many gadgets, if you ask me." He went back to his desk, opened a drawer, removed three film spools and dropped them in a pocket.

Gilead was about to go down the staircase; seeing the spools, he stopped. "Go ahead, Joe," Baldwin said urgently. "You're covered and outnumbered. With this raid showing up we wouldn't have time to fiddle; we'ud just have to kill you."

They stopped in a room well underground, another study much like the one above, though lacking sunlight and view. Baldwin said something in the odd language to the mike on the desk, was answered. Gilead experimented with the idea that the lingo might be reversed English, discarded the notion.

"As I was saying," Baldwin went on, "if you are dead set on knowing all the answers—"

"Just a moment. What about this raid?"

"Just the government boys. They won't be rough and not too thorough. Ma Garver can handle them. We won't have to hurt anybody as long as they don't use penetration radar."

Gilead smiled wryly at the disparagement of his own former service. "And if they do?"

"That gimmick over there squeals like a pig, if it's touched by penetration frequencies. Even then we're safe against anything short of an A-bomb. They won't do that; they want the films, not a hole in the ground. Which reminds me—here, catch."

Gilead found himself suddenly in possession of the films which were at the root of the matter. He unspooled a few frames and made certain that they were indeed the right films. He sat still and considered how he might get off this limb and back to the ground without dropping the eggs. The speaker again uttered something; Baldwin did not answer it but said, "We won't be down here long."

"Bonn seems to have decided to check my report." Some of his—former—comrades were upstairs. If he did Baldwin in, could he locate the inside control for the door?

"Bonn is a poor sort. He'll check me—but not too thoroughly; I'm rich. He won't check Mrs. Keithley at all; she's too rich. He thinks with his political ambitions instead of his head. His late predecessor was a better man—he was one of us."

Gilead's tentative plans underwent an abrupt reversal. His oath had been to a government; his personal loyalty had been given to his former boss. "Prove that last remark and I shall be much interested."

"No, you'll come to learn that it's true—if you still insist on knowing the answers. Through checking those films, Joe? Toss 'em back."

Gilead did not do so. "I suppose you have made copies in any case?"

"Wasn't necessary; I looked at them. Don't get ideas, Joe; you're washed up with the FBS, even if you brought the films and my head back on a platter. You slugged your boss—remember?"

Gilead remembered that he had not told Baldwin so. He began to believe that Baldwin did have men inside the FBS, whether his late bureau chief had been one of them or not.

"I would at least be allowed to resign with a clear record. I know Bonn—officially he would be happy to forget it." He was simply stalling for time, waiting for Baldwin to offer an opening.

"Chuck them back, Joe. I don't want to rassle. One of us might get killed—both of us, if you won the first round. You can't prove your case, because I can prove I was home teasing the cat. I sold 'copters to two very respectable citizens at the exact time you would claim I was somewhere else." He listened again to the speaker, answered it in the same gibberish.

Gilead's mind evaluated his own tactical situation to the same answer that Baldwin had expressed. Not being given to wishful thinking he at once tossed the films to Baldwin.

"Thanks, Joe." He went to a small oubliette set in the wall, switched it to full power, put the films in the hopper, waited a few seconds, and switched it off. "Good riddance to bad rubbish."

Gilead permitted his eyebrows to climb. "Kettle Belly, you've managed to surprise me."

"How?"

"I thought you wanted to keep the nova effect as a means to power."

"Nuts! Scalping a man is a hell of a poor way to cure him of dandruff. Joe, how much do you know about the nova effect?"

"Not much. I know it's a sort of atom bomb powerful enough to scare the pants off anybody who gets to thinking about it."

"It's not a bomb. It's not a weapon. It's a means of destroying a planet and everything on it completely—by turning that planet into a nova. If that's a weapon, military or political, then I'm Samson and you're Delilah.

"But I'm not Samson," he went on, "and I don't propose to pull down the Temple—nor let anybody else do so. There are moral lice around who would do just that, if anybody tried to keep them from having their own way. Mrs. Keithley is one such. Your boy friend Bonn is another such, if only he had the guts and the savvy—which he ain't. I'm bent on frustrating such people. What do you know about ballistics, Joe?"

"Grammar school stuff."

"Inexcusable ignorance." The speaker sounded again; he answered it without breaking his flow. "The problem of three bodies still lacks a neat general solution, but there are several special solutions—the asteroids that chase Jupiter in Jupiter's own orbit at the sixty degree position, for example. And there's the straight-line solution—you've heard of the asteroid 'Earth-Anti'?"

"That's the chunk of rock that is always on the other side of the Sun, where we never see it."

"That's right—only it ain't there any more. It's been novaed."

Gilead, normally immune to surprise, had been subjected to one too many. "Huh? I thought this nova effect was theory?"

"Nope. If you had had time to scan through the films you would have seen pictures of it. It's a plutonium, lithium, and heavy water deal, with some flourishes we won't discuss. It adds up to the match that can set afire a world. It did—a little world flared up and was gone.

"Nobody saw it happen. No one on Earth *could* see it, for it was behind the Sun. It couldn't have been seen from Moon Colony; the Sun still blanked it off from there—visualize the geometry. All that ever saw it were a battery of cameras in a robot ship. All who knew about it were the scientists who rigged it—and *all* of them were with us, except the director. If *he* had been, too, you would never have been in this mix up."

"Dr. Finnley?"

"Yep. A nice guy, but a mind like a pretzel. A 'political' scientist, second-rate ability. He doesn't matter; our boys will ride herd on him until he's pensioned off. But we couldn't keep him from reporting and sending the films down. So I had to grab 'em and destroy them."

"Why didn't you simply save them? All other considerations aside, they are unique in science."

"The human race doesn't need that bit of science, not this millenium. I saved all that mattered, Joe—in my head."

"You *are* your cousin Hartley, aren't you?"

"Of course. But I'm also Kettle Belly Baldwin, and several other guys."

"You can be Lady Godiva, for all of me."

"As Hartley, I was entitled to those films, Joe. It was my project. I instigated it, through my boys."

"I never credited Finnley with it. I'm not a physicist, but he obviously isn't up to it."

"Sure, sure. I was attempting to prove that an artificial nova could not be created; the political—the *racial*—importance of establishing the point is obvious. It backfired on me—so we had to go into emergency action."

"Perhaps you should have left well enough alone."

"No. It's better to know the worst; now we can be alert for it, divert research away from it." The speaker growled again; Baldwin went on, "There may be a divine destiny, Joe, unlikely as it seems, that makes really dangerous secrets too difficult to be broached until intelligence reaches the point where it can cope with them—*if* said intelligence has the will and the good intentions. Ma Garver says to come up now."

They headed for the stairs. "I'm surprised that you leave it up to an old gal like Ma to take charge during an emergency."

"She's competent, I assure you. But I *was* running things—you heard me."

"Oh."

They settled down again in the above-surface study. "I give you one more chance to back out, Joe. It doesn't matter that you know all about the films, since they are gone and you can't prove anything—but beyond that—you realize that if you come in with us, are told what is going on, you will be killed deader than a duck at the first suspicious move?"

Gilead did; he knew in fact that he was already beyond the point of no return. With the destruction of the films went his last chance of rehabilitating his former main *persona*. This gave him no worry; the matter was done. He had become aware that from the time he had admitted that he understood the first message this man had offered him concealed in a double deck of cards he had no longer been a free actor, his moves had been constrained by moves made by Baldwin. Yet there was no help for it; his future lay here or nowhere.

"I know it; go ahead."

"I know what your mental reservations are, Joe; you are simply accepting risk; not promising loyalty."

"Yes—but why are you considering taking a chance on me?"

Baldwin was more serious in manner than he usually allowed himself to be. "You're an able man, Joe. You have the savvy and the moral courage to do what is reasonable in an odd situation rather than what is conventional."

"That's why you want me?"

"Partly that. Partly because I like the way you catch on to a new card game." He grinned. "And even partly because Gail likes the way you behave with a colt."

"Gail? What's she got to do with it?"

"She reported on you to me about five minutes ago, during the raid."

"Hmm—go ahead."

"You've been warned." For a moment Baldwin looked almost sheepish. "I want you to take what I say next at its face value, Joe—don't laugh."

"Okay."

"You asked what I was. I'm sort of the executive secretary of this branch of an organization of supermen."

"I thought so."

"Eh? How long have you known?"

"Things added up. The card game, your reaction time. I knew it when you destroyed the films."

"Joe, what is a superman?"

Gilead did not answer.

"Very well, let's chuck the term," Baldwin went on. "It's been overused and misused and beat up until it has mostly comic connotations. I used it for shock value and I didn't shock you. The term 'supermen' has come to have a fairy tale meaning, conjuring up pictures of x-ray eyes, odd sense organs, double hearts, uncuttable skin, steel muscles—an adolescent's dream of the dragon-killing hero. Tripe, of course. Joe, what is a *man?* What is man that makes him more than an animal? Settle that and we'll take a crack at defining a superman—or New Man, *homo novis,* who must displace *homo sapiens—is* displacing him—because he is better able to survive than is homo sap. I'm not trying to define myself, I'll leave it up to my associates and the inexorable processes of time as to whether or not I am a superman, a member of the new species of man—same test to apply to you."

"*Me?*"

"You. You show disturbing symptoms of being *homo novis,* Joe, in a sloppy, ignorant, untrained fashion. Not likely, but you just might be one of the breed. Now—what is man? What is the one thing he can do better than animals which is so strong a survival factor that it outweighs all the things that animals of one sort or another can do much better than he can?"

"He can think."

"I fed you that answer; no prize for it. Okay, you pass yourself off a man; let's see you do something. What is the one possible conceivable factor—or factors, if you prefer—which the hypothetical superman could have, by mutation or magic or any means, and which could be added to this advantage which man already has and which has enabled him to dominate this planet against the unceasing opposition of a million other species of fauna? Some factor that would make the domination of man by his successor, as inevitable as your domination over a hound dog? Think, Joe. What is the *necessary* direction of evolution to the next dominant species?

Gilead engaged in contemplation for what was for him a long time. There were so many lovely attributes that a man might have: to be able to see both like a telescope and microscope, to see the insides of things, to see throughout the spectrum, to have hearing of the same order, to be immune to disease, to grow a new arm or leg, to fly through the air without bothering with silly gadgets like helicopters or jets, to walk unharmed the ocean bottom, to work without tiring—

Yet the eagle could fly and he was nearly extinct, even though his eyesight was better than man's. A dog has better smell and hearing; seals swim better, balance better, and furthermore can store oxygen. Rats can survive where men would starve or die of hardship; they are smart and pesky hard to kill. Rats could—

Wait! Could tougher, smarter rats displace man? No, it just wasn't in them; too small a brain.

"To be able to think better," Gilead answered almost instantly.

"Hand the man a cigar! Supermen are superthinkers; anything else is a side issue. I'll allow the possibility of super-somethings which might exterminate or dominate mankind other than by outsmarting him in his own racket—thought. But I deny that it is possible for a *man* to conceive in discrete terms what such a super-something would be or how this something would win out. New Man will beat out homo sap in homo sap's own specialty—rational thought, the ability to recognize data, store them, integrate them, evaluate correctly the result, and arrive at a correct decision. That is how man got to be champion; the creature who can do it better is the coming champion. Sure, there are other survival factors, good health, good sense organs, fast reflexes, but they aren't even comparable, as the long, rough history of mankind has proved over and over—Marat in his bath, Roosevelt in his wheelchair, Caesar with his epilepsy and his bad stomach, Nelson with one eye and one arm, blind Milton; when the chips are down it's *brain* that wins, not the body's tools."

"Stop a moment," said Gilead. "How about E.S.P.?"

Baldwin shrugged. "I'm not sneering at extra-sensory perception any more than I would at exceptional eyesight—E.S.P. is not in the same league with the ability to think correctly. E.S.P. is a grab bag name for the means other than the known sense organs by which the brain may gather data—but the trick that pays off with first prize is to make use of that data, to *reason* about it. If you would like a telepathic hook up to Shanghai, I can arrange it; we've got operators at both ends—but you can get whatever data you might happen to need from Shanghai by phone with less trouble, less chance of a bad connection, and less danger of somebody listening in. Telepaths can't pick up a radio message; it's not the same wave band."

"What wave band is it?"

"Later, later. You've got a lot to learn."

"I wasn't thinking especially of telephathy. I was thinking of all parapsychological phenomena."

"Same reasoning. Apportation would be nice, if telekinetics had gotten that far—which it ain't. But a pick-up truck moves things handily enough. Television in the hands of an intelligent man counts for more than clairvoyance in a moron. Quit wasting my time, Joe."

"Sorry."

"We defined thinking as integrating data and arriving at correct answers. Look around you. Most people do that stunt just well enough to get to the corner store and back without breaking a leg. If the average man thinks at all, he does silly things like generalizing from a single datum. He uses one-valued logics. If he is exceptionally bright, he may use two-valued, 'either-or' logic to arrive at his wrong answers. If he is hungry, hurt, or personally interested in the answer, he can't use any sort of logic and will discard an observed fact as blithely as he will stake his life on a piece of wishful thinking. He uses the technical miracles created by superior men without wonder nor surprise, as a kitten accepts a bowl of milk. Far from aspiring to higher reasoning, he is not even aware that higher reasoning exists. He classes his own mental process as being of the same sort as the genius of an Einstein. Man is not a rational animal; he is a rationalizing animal.

"For explanations of a universe that confuses him he seizes onto numerology, astrology, hysterical religions, and other fancy ways to go crazy. Having accepted such glorified nonsense, facts make no impression on him, even if at the cost of his own life. Joe, one of the hardest things to believe is the abysmal depth of human stupidity.

"That is why there is always room at the top, why a man with just a *leetle* more on the ball can so easily become governor, millionaire, or college president—and why homo sap is sure to be displaced by New Man, because there is so much room for improvement and evolution never stops.

"Here and there among ordinary men is a rare individual who really thinks, can and does use logic in at least one field—he's often as stupid as the rest outside his study or laboratory—but he can think, if he's not disturbed or sick or frightened. This rare individual is responsible for *all* the progress made by the race; the others reluctantly adopt his results. Much as the ordinary man dislikes and distrusts and persecutes the process of thinking he is forced to accept the results occasionally, because thinking is efficient compared with his own mauderings. He may still plant his corn in the dark of the Moon but he will plant better corn developed by better men than he.

"Still rarer is the man who thinks habitually, who applies reason, rather than habit pattern, to all his activity. Unless he masques himself, his is a dangerous life; he is regarded as queer, untrustworthy, subversive of public morals; he is a pink monkey among brown monkeys—a fatal mistake. Unless the pink monkey can dye himself brown before he is caught.

"The brown monkey's instinct to kill is correct; such men are dangerous to all monkey customs.

"Rarest of all is the man who can and does reason at all times, quickly, accurately, inclusively, despite hope or fear or bodily distress, without egocentric bias or thalmic disturbance, with correct memory, with clear distinction between fact, assumption, and non-fact. Such men exist, Joe; they are 'New Man'—human in all respects, indistinguishable in appearance or under the scalpel from homo sap, yet as unlike him in action as the Sun is unlike a single candle."

Gilead said, "Are you that sort?"

"You will continue to form your own opinions."

"And you think I may be, too?"

"Could be. I'll have more data in a few days."

Gilead laughed until the tears came. "Kettle Belly, if I'm the future

Gulf

hope of the race, they had better send in the second team quick. Sure I'm brighter than most of the jerks I run into, but, as you say, the competition isn't stiff. But I haven't any sublime aspirations. I've got as lecherous an eye as the next man. I enjoy wasting time over a glass of beer. I just don't *feel* like a superman."

"Speaking of beer, let's have some." Baldwin got up and obtained two cans of the brew. "Remember that Mowgli felt like a wolf. Being a New Man does not divorce you from human sympathies and pleasures. There have been New Men all through history; I doubt if most of them suspected that their difference entitled them to call themselves a different breed. Then they went ahead and bred with the daughters of men, diffusing their talents through the racial organism, preventing them from effectuating until chance brought the genetic factors together again."

"Then I take it that New Man is not a special mutation?"

"Huh? Who isn't a mutation, Joe? All of us are a collection of millions of mutations. Around the globe hundreds of mutations have taken place in our human germ plasm while we have been sitting here. No, homo novis didn't come about because great grandfather stood too close to a cyclotron; homo novis was not even a separate breed until he became aware of himself, organized, and decided to hang on to what his genes had handed him. You could mix New Man back into the race today and lose him; he's merely a variation becoming a species. A million years from now is another matter; I venture to predict that New Man, of that year and model, won't be able to interbreed with homo sap—no viable offspring."

"You don't expect present man—homo sapiens—to disappear?"

"Not necessarily. The dog adapted to man. Probably more dogs now than in umpteen B.C.—and better fed."

"And man would be New Man's dog."

"Again not necessarily. Consider the cat."

"The idea is to skim the cream of the race's germ plasm and keep it biologically separate until the two races are permanently distinct. You chaps sound like a bunch of stinkers, Kettle Belly."

"Monkey talk."

"Perhaps. The new race would necessarily run things—"

"Do you expect New Man to decide grave matters by counting common man's runny noses?"

"No, that was my point. Postulating such a new race, the result is inevitable. Kettle Belly, I confess to a monkey prejudice in favor of democracy, human dignity, and freedom. It goes beyond logic; it is the kind of a world I like. In my job I have jungled with the outcasts of society, shared their slumgullion. Stupid they may be, bad they are not— I have no wish to see them become domestic animals."

543

OFF THE MAIN SEQUENCE

For the first time the big man showed concern. His *persona* as "King of the Kopters," master merchandiser, slipped away; he sat in brooding majesty, a lonely and unhappy figure. "I know, Joe. They are of us; their little dignities, their nobilities, are not lessened by their sorry state. Yet it must be."

"Why? New Man will come—granted. But why hurry the process?"

"Ask yourself." He swept a hand toward the oubliette. "Ten minutes ago you and I saved this planet, all our race. It's the hour of the knife. Some one must be on guard if the race is to live; there is no one but us. To guard effectively we New Men must be organized, must never fumble any crisis like this—and must increase our numbers. We are few now, Joe; as the crises increase, we must increase to meet them. Eventually—and it's a dead race with time—we must take over and make certain that baby never plays with matches."

He stopped and brooded. "I confess to that same effection for democracy, Joe. But it's like yearning for the Santa Claus you believed in as a child. For a hundred and fifty years or so democracy, or something like it, could flourish safely. The issues were such as to be settled without disaster by the votes of common men, befogged and ignorant as they were. But now, if the race is simply to stay alive, political decisions depend on real knowledge of such things as nuclear physics, planetary ecology, genetic theory, even system mechanics. They aren't up to it, Joe. With goodness and more will than they possess less than one in a thousand could stay awake over one page of nuclear physics; they can't learn what they must know."

Gilead brushed it aside. "It's up to us to brief them. Their hearts are all right; tell them the score—they'll come down with the right answers."

"No, Joe. We've tried it; it does not work. As you say, most of them are good, the way a dog can be noble and good. Yet there are bad ones—Mrs. Keithley and company and more like her. Reason is poor propaganda when opposed by the yammering, unceasing lies of shrewd and evil and self-serving men. The little man has no way to judge and the shoddy lies are packaged more attractively. There is no way to offer color to a colorblind man, nor is there any way for us to give the man of imperfect brain the canny skill to distinguish a lie from a truth.

"No, Joe. The gulf between us and them is narrow, but it is very deep. We cannot close it."

"I wish," said Gilead, "that you wouldn't class me with your 'New Man'; I feel more at home on the other side."

"You will decide for yourself which side you are on, as each of us has done."

Gilead forced a change in subject. Ordinarily immune to thalamic disturbance this issue upset him; his brain followed Baldwin's argument and assured him that it was true; his inclinations fought it. He was confronted with the sharpest of all tragedy; two equally noble and valid rights, utterly opposed. "What do you people do, aside from stealing films?"

"Mmm—many things." Baldwin relaxed, looked again like a jovial sharp businessman. "Where a push here and a touch there will keep things from going to pot, we apply the pressure, by many and devious means. And we scout for suitable material and bring it into the fold when we can—we've had our eye on you for ten years."

"So?"

"Yep. That is a prime enterprise. Through public data we eliminate all but about one tenth of one per cent; that thousandth individual we watch. And then there are our horticultural societies." He grinned.

"Finish your joke."

"We weed people."

"Sorry, I'm slow today."

"Joe, didn't you ever feel a yen to wipe out some evil, obscene, rotten jerk who infected everything he touched, yet was immune to legal action? We treat them as cancers; we excise them from the body social. We keep a 'Better Dead' list; when a man is clearly morally bankrupt we close his account at the first opportunity."

Gilead smiled. "If you were sure what you were doing, it could be fun."

"We are always sure, though our methods would be no good in a monkey law court. Take Mrs. Keithley—is there doubt in your mind?"

"None."

"Why don't you have her indicted? Don't bother to answer. For example, two weeks from tonight there will be giant powwow of the new, rejuvenated, bigger-and-better-than-ever Ku Klux Klan on a mountain top down Carolina way. When the fun is at its height, when they are mouthing obscenities, working each other up to the pogrom spirit, an act of God is going to wipe out the whole kit and kaboodle. Very sad."

"Could I get in on that?"

"You aren't even a cadet as yet." Baldwin went on. "There is the project to increase our numbers, but that is a thousand-year program; you'd need a perpetual calendar to check it. More important is keeping matches away from baby. Joe, it's been eighty-five years since we beheaded the last commissar: have you wondered why so little basic progress in science has been made in that time?"

"Eh? There have been a lot of changes."

"Minor adaptations—some spectacular, almost none of them basic. Of course there was very little progress made under communism; a totalitarian political religion is incompatible with free investigation.

Let me digress: the communist interregnum was responsible for the New Men getting together and organizing. Most New Men are scientists, for obvious reasons. When the commissars started ruling on natural laws by political criteria—Lysenko-ism and similar nonsense—it did not sit well; a lot of us went underground.

"I'll skip the details. It brought us together, gave us practice in underground activity, and gave a backlog of new research, carried out underground. Some of it was obviously dangerous; we decided to hang onto it for a while. Since then such secret knowledge has grown, for we never give out an item until it has been scrutinized for social hazards. Since much of it *is* dangerous and since very few indeed outside our organization are capable of real original thinking, basic science has been almost at a—public!—standstill.

"We hadn't expected to have to do it that way. We helped to see to it that the new constitution was liberal and—we thought—workable. But the new Republic turned out to be an even poorer thing than the old. The evil ethic of communism had corrupted, even after the form was gone. We held off. Now we know that we must hold off until we can revise the whole society."

"Kettle Belly," Joe said slowly, "you speak as if you had been on the spot. How old are you?"

"I'll tell you when you are the age I am now. A man has lived long enough when he no longer longs to live. I ain't there yet. Joe, I must have your answer, or this must be continued in our next."

"You had it at the beginning—but, see here, Kettle Belly, there is one job I want promised to me."

"Which is?"

"I want to kill Mrs. Keithley."

"Keep your pants on. When you're trained, and if she's still alive then, you'll be used for that purpose—"

"Thanks!"

"—provided you are the proper tool for it." Baldwin turned toward the mike, called out, "Gail!" and added one word in the strange tongue.

Gail showed up promptly. "Joe," said Baldwin, "when this young lady gets through with you, you will be able to sing, whistle, chew gum, play chess, hold your breath, and fly a kite simultaneously—and all this while riding a bicycle under water. Take him, sis, he's all yours."

Gail rubbed her hands. "Oh, boy!"

"First we must teach you to see and to hear, then to remember, then to speak, and then to think."

Joe looked at her. "What's this I'm doing with my mouth at this moment?"

"It's not talking, it's a sort of grunting. Furthermore English is not structurally suited to thinking. Shut up and listen."

In their underground classroom Gail had available several types of apparatus to record and manipulate light and sound. She commenced throwing groups of figures on a screen, in flashes. "What was it, Joe?"

"nine-six-oh-seven-two—That was as far as I got."

"It was up there a full thousandth of a second. Why did you get only the left hand side of the group?"

"That's all the farther I had read."

"Look at *all* of it. Don't make an effort of will; just look at it." She flashed another number.

Joe's memory was naturally good; his intelligence was high—just how high he did not yet know. Unconvinced that the drill was useful, he relaxed and played along. Soon he was beginning to grasp a nine-digit array as a single *gestalt*; Gail reduced the flash time.

"What is this magic lantern gimmick?" he inquired.

"It's a Renshaw tachistoscope. Back to work."

Around World War II Dr. Samuel Renshaw at the Ohio State University was proving that most people are about one-fifth efficient in using their capacities to see, hear, taste, feel and remember. His research was swallowed in the morass of communist pseudoscience that obtained after World War III, but, after his death, his findings were preserved underground. Gail did not expose Gilead to the odd language he had heard until he had been rather thoroughly Renshawed.

However, from the time of his interview with Baldwin the other persons at the ranch used it in his presence. Sometimes someone—usually Ma Garver—would translate, sometimes not. He was flattered to feel accepted, but gravelled to know that it was at the lowest cadetship. He was a child among adults.

Gail started teaching him to hear by speaking to him single words from the odd language, requiring him to repeat them back. "No, Joe. Watch." This time when she spoke the word it appeared on the screen in sound analysis, by a means basically like one long used to show the deaf-and-dumb their speech mistakes. "Now you try it."

He did, the two arrays hung side by side. "How's that, teacher?" he said triumphantly.

"Terrible, by several decimal places. You held the final guttural too long—" She pointed. "—the middle vowel was formed with your tongue too high and you pitched it too low and you failed to let the pitch rise. And six other things. You couldn't possibly have been understood.

I heard what you said, but it was gibberish. Try again. And don't call me 'teacher'."

"Yes, ma'am," he answered solemnly.

She shifted the controls; he tried again. This time his analysis array was laid down on top of hers; where the two matched, they cancelled. Where they did not match, his errors stood out in contrasting colors. The screen looked like a sun burst.

"Try again, Joe." She repeated the word without letting it affect the display.

"Confound it, if you would tell me what the words mean instead of treating me the way Milton treated his daughters about Latin, I could remember them easier."

She shrugged. "I can't, Joe. You must learn to hear and to speak first. Speedtalk is a flexible language; the same word is not likely to recur. This practice word means: 'The far horizons draw no nearer.' That's not much help, is it?"

The definition seemed improbable, but he was learning not to doubt her. He was not used to women who were always two jumps ahead of him. He ordinarily felt sorry for the poor little helpless cuddly creatures; this one he often wanted to slug. He wondered if this response were what the romancers meant by "love"; he decided that it couldn't be.

"Try again, Joe." Speedtalk was a structurally different speech from any the race had ever used. Long before, Ogden and Richards had shown that eight hundred and fifty words were sufficient vocabulary to express anything that could be expressed by "normal" human vocabularies, with the aid of a handful of special words—a hundred odd—for each special field, such as horse racing or ballistics. About the same time phoneticians had analyzed all human tongues into about a hundred-odd sounds, represented by the letters of a general phonetic alphabet.

On these two propositions Speedtalk was based.

To be sure, the phonetic alphabet was much less in number than the words in Basic English. But the letters representing sound in the phonetic alphabet were each capable of variation several different ways—length, stress, pitch, rising, falling. The more trained an ear was the larger the number of possible variations; there was no limit to variations, but, without much refinement of accepted phonetic practice, it was possible to establish a one-to-one relationship with Basic English so that *one phonetic symbol* was equivalent to an entire word in a "normal" language, one Speedtalk word was equal to an entire sentence. The language consequently was learned by letter units rather than by word units—but each word was spoken and listened to as a single structured gestalt.

But Speedtalk was not "shorthand" Basic English. "Normal" languages, having their roots in days of superstition and ignorance, have in them inherently and unescapably wrong structures of mistaken ideas about the universe. One can think logically in English only by extreme effort, so bad it is as a mental tool. For example, the verb "to be" in English has twenty-one distinct meanings, *every single one of which is false-to-fact.*

A symbolic structure, invented instead of accepted without question, can be made similar in structure to the real-world to which it refers. The structure of Speedtalk did *not* contain the hidden errors of English; it was structured as much like the real world as the New Men could make it. For example, it did not contain the unreal distinction between nouns and verbs found in most other languages. The world—the continuum known to science and including all human activity—does not contain "noun things" and "verb things"; it contains space-time events and relationships between them. The advantage for achieving truth, or something more nearly like truth, was similar to the advantage of keeping account books in Arabic numerals rather than Roman.

All other languages made scientific, multi-valued logic almost impossible to achieve; in Speedtalk it was as difficult *not* to be logical. Compare the pellucid Boolean logic with the obscurities of the Aristotelean logic it supplanted.

Paradoxes are verbal, do not exist in the real world—and Speedtalk did not have such built into it. Who shaves the Spanish Barber? Answer: follow him around and see. In the syntax of Speedtalk the paradox of the Spanish Barber could not even be expressed, save as a self-evident error.

But Joe Greene-Gilead-Briggs could not learn it until he had learned to hear, by learning to speak. He slaved away; the screen continued to remain lighted with his errors.

Came finally a time when Joe's pronunciation of a sentence-word blanked out Gail's sample; the screen turned dark. He felt more triumph over that than anything he could remember.

His delight was short. By a circuit Gail had thoughtfully added somedays earlier the machine answered with a flourish of trumpets, loud applause, and then added in a cooing voice, "Mama's *good* boy!"

He turned to her. "Woman, you spoke of matrimony. If you ever do manage to marry me, I'll beat you."

"I haven't made up my mind about you yet," she answered evenly. "Now try this word, Joe—"

Baldwin showed up that evening, called him aside. "Joe! C'mere. Listen, lover boy, you keep your animal nature out of your work, or I'll have to find you a new teacher."

"But—"

"You heard me. Take her swimming, take her riding, after hours you are on your own. Work time—strictly business. I've got plans for you; I want you to get smarted up."

"She complained about me?"

"Don't be silly. It's my business to know what's going on."

"Hmm. Kettle Belly, what is this shopping-for-a-husband she kids about? Is she serious, or is it just intended to rattle me?"

"Ask her. Not that it matters, as you won't have any choice if she means it. She has the calm persistence of the law of gravitation."

"Ouch! I had had the impression that the 'New Men' did not bother with marriage and such like, as you put it, 'monkey customs.'"

"Some do, some don't. Me, I've been married quite a piece, but I mind a mousy little member of our lodge who had had nine kids by nine fathers—all wonderful genius-plus kids. On the other hand I can point out one with eleven kids—Thalia Wagner—who has never so much as looked at another man. Geniuses make their own rules in such matters, Joe; they always have. Here are some established statistical facts about genius, as shown by Armatoe's work—"

He ticked them off. "Geniuses are usually long lived. They are not modest, not honestly so. They have infinite capacity for taking pains. They are emotionally indifferent to accepted codes of morals—they make their own rules. You seem to have the stigmata, by the way."

"Thanks for nothing. Maybe I should have a new teacher, is there is anyone else available who can do it."

"*Any* of us can do it, just as anybody handy teaches a baby to talk. She's actually a biochemist, when she has time for it."

"When she has time?"

"Be careful of that kid, son. Her real profession is the same as yours—honorable hatchet man. She's killed upwards of three hundred people." Kettle Belly grinned. "If you want to switch teachers, just drop me a wink."

Gilead-Greene hastily changed the subject. "You were speaking of work for me: how about Mrs. Keithley? Is she still alive?"

"Yes, blast her."

"Remember, I've got dibs on her."

"You may have to go to the Moon to get her. She's reported to be building a vacation home there. Old age seems to be telling on her; you had better get on with your home work if you want a crack at her." Moon Colony even then was a center of geriatrics for the rich. The low gravity was easy on their hearts, made them feel young—and possibly extended their lives.

"Okay, I will."

Instead of asking for a new teacher Joe took a highly polished apple to their next session. Gail ate it, leaving him very little core, and put him harder to work than ever. While perfecting his hearing and pronunciation, she started him on the basic thousand-letter vocabulary by forcing him to start to talk simple three and four-letter sentences, and by answering him in different word-sentences using the same phonetic letters. Some of the vowel and consonant sequences were very difficult to pronounce.

Master them he did. He had been used to doing most things easier than could those around him; now he was in very fast company. He stretched himself and began to achieve part of his own large latent capacity. When he began to catch some of the dinner-table conversation and to reply in simple Speedtalk—being forbidden by Gail to answer in English—she started him on the ancillary vocabularies.

An economical language cannot be limited to a thousand words; although almost every idea can be expressed somehow in a short vocabulary, higher orders of abstraction are convenient. For technical words Speedtalk employed an open expansion of sixty of the thousand-odd phonetic letters. They were the letters ordinarily used as numerals; by preceding a number with a letter used for no other purpose, the symbol was designated as having a word value.

New Men numbered to the base sixty—three times four times five, a convenient, easily factored system, most economical, i. e., the symbol "100" identified the number described in English as thirty-six hundred—yet permitting quick, in-the-head translation from common notation to Speedtalk figures and vice versa.

By using these figures, each prefaced by the indicator—a voiceless Welsh or Burmese "1"—a pool of 215,999 words (one less than the cube of sixty) were available for specialized meaning without using more than four letters including the indicator. Most of them could be pronounced as one syllable. These had not the stark simplicity of basic Speedtalk; nevertheless words such as "ichthyophagous" and "constitutionality" were thus compressed to monosyllables. Such shortcuts can best be appreciated by anyone who has heard a long speech in Cantonese translated into a short speech in English. Yet English is not the most terse of "normal" languages—and expanded Speedtalk is many times more economical than the briefest of "normal" tongues.

By adding one more letter (sixty to the fourth power) just short of thirteen *million* words could be added if needed—and most of them could still be pronounced as one syllable.

When Joe discovered that Gail expected him to learn a couple of hundred thousand new words in a matter of days, he balked. "Damn it, Fancy Pants, I am not a superman. I'm in here by mistake."

"Your opinion is worthless; I think you can do it. Now listen."

"Suppose I flunk; does that put me safely off your list of possible victims?"

"If you flunk, I wouldn't have you on toast. Instead I'd tear your head off and stuff it down your throat. But you won't flunk; I *know*. However," she added, "I'm not sure you would be a satisfactory husband; you argue too much."

He made a brief and bitter remark in Speedtalk; she answered with one word which described his shortcomings in detail. They got to work.

Joe was mistaken; he learned the expanded vocabulary as fast as he heard it. He had a latent eidetic memory; the Renshawing process now enabled him to use it fully. And his mental processes, always fast, had become faster than he knew.

The ability to learn Speedtalk at all is proof of supernormal intelligence; the *use* of it by such intelligence renders that mind efficient. Even before World War II Alfred Korzybski had shown that human thought was performed, when done efficiently, only in symbols; the notion of "pure" thought, free of abstracted speech symbols, was merely fantasy. The brain was so constructed as to work without symbols only on the animal level; to speak of "reasoning" without symbols was to speak nonsense.

Speedtalk did not merely speed up communication—by its structures it made thought more logical; by its economy it made thought processes enormously faster, since it takes almost as long to *think* a word as it does to speak it.

Korzybski's monumental work went fallow during the communist interregnum; *Das Kapital* is a childish piece of work, when analyzed by semantics, so the politburo suppressed semantics—and replaced it by *ersatz* under the same name, as Lysenkoism replaced the science of genetics.

Having Speedtalk to help him learn *more* Speedtalk, Joe learned very rapidly. The Renshawing had continued; he was now able to grasp a gestalt or configuration in many senses at once, grasp it, remember it, reason about it with great speed.

Living time is not calendar time; a man's life is the thought that flows through his brain. Any man capable of learning Speedtalk had an association time at least three times as fast as an ordinary man. Speedtalk itself enabled him to manipulate symbols approximately seven times as fast as English symbols could be manipulated. Seven times three is twenty-one; a new man had an *effective* life time of at least *sixteen hundred years,* reckoned in flow of ideas.

They had time to become encyclopedic synthesists, something denied any ordinary man by the straitjacket of his sort of time.

When Joe had learned to talk, to read and write and cipher, Gail turned him over to others for his real education. But before she checked him out she played him several dirty tricks.

For three days she forbade him to eat. When it was evident that he could think and keep his temper despite low blood-sugar count, despite hunger reflex, she added sleeplessness and pain—intense, long, continued, and varied pain. She tried subtly to goad him into irrational action; he remained bedrock steady, his mind clicking away at any assigned task as dependably as an electronic computer.

"Who's not a superman?" she asked at the end of their last session.

"Yes, teacher."

"Come here, lug." She grabbed him by the ears, kissed him soundly. "So long." He did not see her again for many weeks.

His tutor in E.S.P. was an ineffectual-looking little man who had taken the protective coloration of the name Weems. Joe was not very good at producing E.S.P. phenomena. Clairvoyance he did not appear to have. He was better at precognition, but he did not improve with practice. He was best at telekinesis; he could have made a soft living with dice. But, as Kettle Belly had pointed out, from affecting the roll of dice to moving tons of freight was quite a gap—and one possibly not worth bridging.

"It may have other uses, however," Weems had said softly, lapsing into English. "Consider what might be done if one could influence the probability that a neutron would reach a particular nucleus—or change the statistical probability in a mass."

Gilead let it ride; it was an outrageous thought.

At telepathy he was erratic to exasperation. He called the Rhine cards once without a miss, then had poor scores for three weeks. More highly structured communication seemed quite beyond him, until one day without apparent cause but during an attempt to call the cards by telepathy, he found himself hooked in with Weems for all of ten seconds—time enough for a thousand words by Speedtalk standards.

—it comes out as speech!

—why not? thought is speech.

—how do we do it?

—if we knew it would not be so unreliable. as it is, some can do it by volition, some by accident, and some never seem to be able to do it.

we do know this: while thought may not be of the physical world in any fashion we can now define and manipulate, it is similar to events in continuum in its quantal nature. You are now studying the extension of the quantuum concept to all features of the continuum, you know the chronon, the mensum, and the viton, as quanta, as well as the action units of quanta such as the photon. The continuum has not only structure but texture in all its features. The least unit of thought we term the psychon.

—*define it. put salt on its tail.*

—*some day, some day. I can tell you this; the fastest possible rate of thought is one psychon per chronon; this is a basic, universal constant.*

—*how close do we come to that?*

—*less than sixty-to-the-minus-third-power of the possibility.*

—*! ! ! ! ! !*

—*better creatures than ourselves will follow us. We pick pebbles at a boundless ocean.*

—*what can we do to improve it?*

—*gather our pebbles with serene minds.*

Gilead paused for a long split second of thought.—*can psychons be destroyed?*

—*vitons may be transferred. psychons are*—

The connection was suddenly destroyed. "As I was saying," Weems went on quietly, "psychons are as yet beyond our comprehension in many respects. Theory indicates that they may not be destroyed, that thought, like action, is persistent. Whether or not such theory, if true, means that personal identity is also persistent must remain an open question. See the daily papers—a few hundred years from now—or a few hundred thousand." He stood up.

"I'm anxious to try tomorrow's session, Doc," Gilead-Greene almost bubbled. "Maybe—"

"I'm finished with you."

"But, Doctor Weems that connection was clear as a phone hook-up. Perhaps tomorrow—"

"We have established that your talent is erratic. We have no way to train it to dependability. Time is too short to waste, mine and yours." Lapsing suddenly into English, he added, "No."

Gilead left.

During his training in other fields Joe was exposed to many things best described as impressive gadgets. There was an integrating pantograph, a factory-in-a-box, which the New Men planned to turn over to ordinary men as soon as the social system was no longer dominated by economic wolves. It could and did reproduce almost any prototype placed on its stage, requiring thereto only materials and power. Its power came from a little nucleonics motor the size of Joe's thumb; its theory played hob with conventional notions of entropy. One put in "sausage"; one got out "pig."

Latent in it was the shape of an economic system as different from the current one as the assembly-line economy differed from the family-shop system—and in such a system lay possibilities of human freedom and dignity missing for centuries, if they had ever existed.

In the mean time New Men rarely bought more than one of anything—a pattern. Or they made a pattern.

Another useful but hardly wonderful gadget was a dicta-phone-typewriter-printing-press combination. The machine's analysers recognized each of the thousand-odd phonetic symbols; there was a typebar for each sound. It produced one or many copies. Much of Gilead's education came from pages printed by this gadget, saving the precious time of others.

The arrangement, classification, and accessibility of knowledge remains in all ages the most pressing problem. With the New Men, complete and organized memory licked most of the problem and rendered record keeping, most reading and writing—and most especially the time-destroying trouble of rereading—unnecessary. The autoscriber gadget, combined with a "librarian" machine that could "hear" that portion of Speedtalk built into it as a filing system, covered most of the rest of the problem. New Men were not cluttered with endless bits of paper. They *never* wrote memoranda.

The area under the ranch was crowded with technological wonders, all newer than next week. Incredibly tiny manipulators for micrurgy of all sorts, surgical, chemical, biological manipulation, oddities of cybernetics only less complex than the human brain—the list is too long to describe. Joe did not study all of them; an encyclopedic synthesist is concerned with structured shapes of knowledge; he cannot, even with Speedtalk, study details in every field.

Early in his education, when it was clear that he had had the potential to finish the course, plastic surgery was started to give him a new identity and basic appearance. His height was reduced by three inches; his skull was somewhat changed; his complexion was permanently darkened. Gail picked the facial appearance he was given; he did not object. He rather liked it; it seemed to fit his new inner personality.

With a new face, a new brain, and a new outlook, he was almost in fact a new man. Before he had been a natural genius; now he was a *trained* genius.

❖

"Joe, how about some riding?"

"Suits."

"I want to give War Conqueror some gentle exercise. He's responding to the saddle; I don't want him to forget."

"Right with you."

Kettle Belly and Gilead-Greene rode out from the ranch buildings. Baldwin let the young horse settle to a walk and began to talk. "I figure you are about ready for work son." Even in Speedtalk Kettle Belly's speech retained his own flavor.

"I suppose so, but I still have those mental reservations."

"Not sure we are on the side of the angels?"

"I'm sure you mean to be. It's evident that the organization selects for good will and humane intentions quite as carefully as for ability. I wasn't sure at one time—"

"Yes?"

"That candidate who came here about six months ago, the one who broke his neck in a riding accident."

"Oh, yes! Very sad."

"Very opportune, you mean, Kettle Belly."

"Damn it, Joe, if a bad apple gets in this far, we can't let him out." Baldwin reverted to English for swearing purposes; he maintained that it had "more juice."

"I know it. That's why I'm sure about the quality of our people."

"So it's 'our people' now?"

"Yes. But I'm not sure we are on the right track."

"What's your notion of the right track?"

"We should come out of hiding and teach the ordinary man what he can learn of what we know. He could learn a lot of it and could use it. Properly briefed and trained, he could run his affairs pretty well. He would gladly kick out the no-goods who ride on his shoulders, if only he knew how. We could show him. That would be more to the point than this business of spot assassination, now and then, here and there— mind you, I don't object to killing any man who merits killing; I simply say it's inefficient. No doubt we would have to continue to guard against such crises as the one that brought you and me together, but, in the main, people could run their own affairs if we would just stop pretending that we are so scared we can't mix with people, come out of our hole, and lend a hand."

Baldwin reined up. "Don't say that I don't mix with the common people, Joe; I sell used 'copters for a living. You can't get any commoner. And don't imply that my heart is not with them. We are not like them, but we are tied to them by the strongest bond of all, for we are all, each every one, sickening with the same certainly fatal disease—we are alive.

"As for our killings, you don't understand the principles of assassination as a political weapon. Read—" He named a Speedtalk library designation. "If I were knocked off, our organization wouldn't even hiccup, but organizations for bad purposes are different. They are personal empires; if you pick the time and the method, you can destroy such an organization by killing one man—the parts that remain will be almost harmless until assimilated by another leader—then you kill *him*. It is not inefficient; it's quite efficient, if planned with the brain and not with the emotions.

"As for keeping ourselves separate, we are about like the U-235 in U-238, not effective unless separated out. There have been potential New Men in every generation, but they were spread too thin.

"As for keeping our existence secret, it is utterly necessary if we are to survive and increase. There is nothing so danger-out as being the Chosen People—and in the minority. One group was persecuted for two thousand years merely for making the claim."

He again shifted to English to swear. "Damn it, Joe, face up to it. This world is run the way my great aunt Susie flies a 'copter. Speedtalk or no not Speedtalk, common man *can't* learn to cope with modern problems. No use to talk about the unused potential of his brain, he has not got the *will* to learn what he would have to know. We can't fit him out with new genes, so we have to lead him by the hand to keep him from killing himself—and us. We can give him personal liberty, we can give him autonomy in most things, we can give him a great measure of personal dignity—and we will, because we believe that individual freedom, at all levels, is the direction of evolution, of maximum survival value. But we can't let him fiddle with issues of racial life and death; he ain't up to it.

"No help for it. Each shape of society develops its own ethic. We are shaping this the way we are inexorably forced to, by the logic of events. We *think* we are shaping it toward survival."

"Are we?" mused Greene-Gilead.

"Remains to be seen. Survivors survive. We'll know—Wup! Meeting's adjourned."

The radio on Baldwin's pommel was shrilling his personal emergency call. He listened, then spoke one sharp word in Speedtalk. "Back to the house, Joe!" He wheeled and was away. Joe's mount came of less selected stock; he was forced to follow.

Baldwin sent for Joe soon after he got back. Joe went in; Gail was already there.

Baldwin's face was without expression. He said in English, "I've work for you, Joe, work you won't have any doubt about. Mrs. Keithley."

"Good."

"Not good." Baldwin shifted to Speedtalk. "We have been caught flat-footed. Either the second set of films was never destroyed, or there was a third set. We do not know; the man who could tell us is dead. But Mrs. Keithley obtained a set and has been using them.

"This is the situation. The 'fuse' of the nova effect has been installed in the New Age hotel. It has been sealed off and can be triggered only by radio signal from the Moon—her signal. The 'fuse' has been rigged so that any attempt to break in, as long as the firing circuit is still armed, will trigger it and set it off. Even an attempt to examine it by penetration wavelengths will set it off. Speaking as a physicist, it is my considered opinion that *no* plan for tackling the 'nova' fuse bomb itself will work unless the arming circuit is first broken on the Moon and that no attempt should be made to get at fuse before then, because of extreme danger to the entire planet.

"The arming circuit and the radio relay to the Earthside trigger is located on the Moon in a building inside her private dome. The triggering control she keeps with her. From the same control she can disarm the arming circuit temporarily; it is a combination dead-man switch and time-clock arrangement. It can be set to disarm for a maximum of twelve hours, to let her sleep, or possibly to permit her to order rearrangements. Unless it is switched off any attempt to enter the building in which the arming circuit is housed will also trigger the 'Nova' bomb circuit. While it is disarmed, the housing on the Moon may be broached by force but this will set off alarms which will warn her to rearm and then to trigger at once. The set up is such that the following sequence of events must take place:

"First, she must be killed, and the circuit disarmed.

"Second, the building housing the arming circuit and radio relay to the trigger must be broken open and the circuits destroyed *before* the time clock can rearm and trigger. This must be done with speed, not only because of guards, but because her surviving lieutenants will attempt to seize power by possessing themselves of the controls.

"Third, as soon as word is received on Earth that the arming circuit is destroyed, the New Age will be attacked in force and the 'Nova' bomb destroyed.

"Fourth, as soon as the bomb is destroyed, a general round up must be made of all persons technically capable of setting up the 'Nova' effect from plans. This alert must be maintained until it is certain that no plans remain in existence, including the third set of films, and further established by hypno that no competent person possesses sufficient knowledge to set it up without plans. This alert may compromise our secret status; the risk must be taken.

"Any questions?"

"Kettle Belly," said Joe, "Doesn't she know that if the Earth becomes a Nova, the Moon will be swallowed up in the disaster?"

"Crater walls shield her dome from line-of-sight with Earth; apparently she believes she is safe. Evil is essentially stupid, Joe; despite her brilliance, she believes what she wishes to believe. Or it may be that she is willing to risk her own death against the tempting prize of absolute power. Her plan is to proclaim power with some pious nonsense about being high priestess of peace—a euphemism for Empress of Earth. It is a typical paranoid deviation; the proof of the craziness lies in the fact that the physical arrangements make it certain—if we do not intervene—that Earth will be destroyed automatically a few hours after her death; a thing that could happen any time—and a compelling reason for all speed. No one has ever quite managed to conquer all of Earth, not even the commissars. Apparently she wishes not only to conquer it, but wants to destroy it after she is gone, lest anyone else ever manage to do so again. Any more questions?"

He went on, "The plan is this:

"You two will go to the Moon to become domestic servants to Mr. and Mrs. Alexander Copley, a rich, elderly couple living at the Elysian Rest Homes, Moon Colony. They are of us. Shortly they will decide to return to Earth; you two will decide to remain, you like it. You will advertise, offering to work for anyone who will post your return bond. About this time Mrs. Keithley will have lost through circumstances that will be arranged, two or more of her servants; she will probably hire you, since domestic service is the scarcest commodity on the Moon. If not, a variation will be arranged for you.

"When you are inside her dome, you'll maneuver yourselves into positions to carry out your assignments. When both of you are so placed, you will carry out procedures one and two with speed.

"A person named McGinty, already inside her dome, will help you in communication. He is not one of us but is our agent, a telepath. His ability does not extend past that. Your communication hook up will probably be, Gail to McGinty by telepathy, McGinty to Joe by concealed radio."

Joe glanced at Gail; it was the first that he had known that she was a telepath. Baldwin went on, "Gail will kill Mrs. Keithley; Joe will break into the housing and destroy the circuits. Are you ready to go?"

Joe was about to suggest swapping the assignments when Gail answered, "Ready"; he echoed her.

"Good. Joe, you will carry your assumed I.Q. at about 85, Gail at 95; she will appear to be the dominant member of a married couple—" Gail grinned at Joe. "—but you, Joe, will be in charge. Your personalities and histories are now being made up and will be ready with your identifications. Let me say again that the greatest of speed is necessary; government security forces here may attempt a fool-hardy attack on the New Age hotel. We shall prevent or delay such efforts, but act with speed. Good luck."

Operation Black Widow, first phase, went off as planned. Eleven days later Joe and Gail were inside Mrs. Keithley's dome on the moon and sharing a room in the servants' quarters. Gail glanced around when first they entered it and said in Speedtalk, "Now you'll have to marry me; I'm compromised."

"Shut that up, idiot! Some one might hear you."

"Pooh! They'd just think I had asthma. Don't you think it's noble of me, Joe, to sacrifice my girlish reputation for home and country?"

"What reputation?"

"Come closer so I can slug you."

Even the servants' quarter were luxurious. The dome was a sybarite's dream. The floor of it was gardened in real beauty save where Mrs. Keithley's mansion stood. Opposite it, across a little lake— certainly the only lake on the Moon—was the building housing the circuits; it was disguised as a little Doric Grecian shrine.

The dome itself was edge-lighted fifteen hours out of each twenty-four, shutting out the black sky and the harsh stars. At "night" the lighting was gradually withdrawn.

McGinty was a gardener and obviously enjoyed his work. Gail established contact with him, got out of him what little he knew. Joe left him alone save for contacts in character.

There was a staff of over two hundred, having its own social hierarchy, from engineers for dome and equipment, Mrs. Keithley's private pilot, and so on down to gardeners' helpers. Joe and Gail were midway, being inside servants. Gail made herself popular as the harmlessly flirtatious but always helpful and sympathetic wife of a meek and older husband. She had been a beauty parlor operator, so it seemed, before she "married" and had great skill in massaging aching backs and stiff necks, relieving headaches and inducing sleep. She was always ready to demonstrate.

Her duties as a maid had not yet brought her into close contact with their employer. Joe, however, had acquired the job of removing all potted plants to the "outdoors" during "night"; Mrs. Keithley, according to Mr. James, the butler, believed that plants should be outdoors at "night." Joe was thus in a position to get outside the house when the dome was dark; he had already reached the point where the night guard at the Grecian temple would sometimes get Joe to "jigger" for him while the guard snatched a forbidden cigarette.

McGinty had been able to supply one more important fact: in addition to the guard at the temple building, and the locks and armor plate of the building itself, the arming circuit was booby-trapped. Even if it were inoperative as an arming circuit for the 'Nova' bomb on Earth, it itself would blow up if tampered with. Gail and Joe discussed it in their room, Gail sitting on his lap like an affectionate wife, her lips close to his left ear. "Perhaps you could wreck it from the door, without exposing yourself."

"I've got to be sure. There is certainly some way of switching that gimmick off. She has to provide for possible repairs or replacements."

"Where would it be?"

"Just one place that matches the pattern of the rest of her planning. Right under her hand, along with the disarming switch and the trigger switch." He rubbed his other ear; it contained his short-range radio hook-up to McGinty and itched almost constantly.

"Hmm—then there's just one thing to be done; I'll have to wring it out of her before I kill her."

"We'll see."

Just before dinner the following "evening" she found him in their room. "It worked, Joe, it worked!"

"What worked?"

"She fell for the bait. She heard from her secretary about my skill as a masseuse; I was ordered up for a demonstration this afternoon. Now I am under strict instructions to come to her tonight and rub her to sleep."

"It's tonight, then."

McGinty waited in his room, behind a locked door. Joe stalled in the back hall, spinning out endlessly a dull tale to Mr. James.

A voice in his ear said, "She's in *her* room now."

"—and that's how my brother got married to two women at once," Joe concluded. "Sheer bad luck. I better get these plants outside before the missus happens to ask about 'em."

"I suppose you had. Goodnight."

"Goodnight, Mr. James." He picked up two of the pots and waddled out."

He put them down outside and heard, "She says she's started to massage. She's spotted the radio switching unit; it's on the belt that the old gal keeps at her bedside table when she's not wearing it."

"Tell her to kill her and grab it."

"She says she wants to make her tell how to unswitch the booby-trap gimmick first."

"Tell her not to delay."

Suddenly, inside his head, clear and sweet as a bell as if they were her own spoken tones, he heard her.—*Joe, I can hear you. can you hear me?*

—*yes, yes!* Aloud he added, *"Stand by the phones anyhow, Mac."*

—*it won't be long. I have her in intense pain; she'll crack soon.*

—*hurt her plenty!* He began to run toward the temple building.—*Gail, are you still shopping for a husband?*

—*I've found him.*

—*marry me and I'll beat you every Saturday night.*

—*the man who can beat me hasn't been born.*

—*I'd like to try.* He slowed down before he came near the guard's station. "Hi, Jim!"

—*it's a deal.*

"Well, if it taint Joey boy! Got a match?"

"Here." He reached out a hand—then, as the guard fell, he eased him to the ground and made sure that he would stay out. —*Gail! It's got to be now!*

The voice in his head came back in great consternation: —*Joe! She was too tough, she wouldn't crack. She's dead!*

—*good! get that belt, break the arming circuit, then see what else you find. I'm going to break in.*

He went toward the door of the temple.

—*it's disarmed, Joe. I could spot it; it has a time set on it. I can't tell about the others; they aren't marked and they all look alike.*

He took from his pocket a small item provided by Baldwin's careful planning —*twist them all from where they are to the other way. You'll probably hit it.*

—*oh, Joe, I hope so!*

He had placed the item against the lock; the metal around it turned red and now was melting away. An alarm clanged somewhere.

Gail's voice came again in his head; there was urgency in it but no fear: —*Joe! they're beating on the door. I'm trapped.*

—*McGinty! be our witness!* He went on: —*I, Joseph, take thee, Gail, to be my lawfully wedded wife—*

He was answered in tranquil rhythm: —*I, Gail, take thee, Joseph, to be my lawfully wedded husband—*

—*to have and to hold,* he went on.

to have and to hold, my beloved!

—*for better, for worse—*

—for better, for worse—Her voice in his head was singing . . . —*till death do us part. I've got it open, darling; I am going in.*

—till death do us part! They are breaking down the bedroom door, Joseph my dearest.

—hang on! I'm almost through here.

—they have broken it down, Joe. They are coming toward me. Good-bye my darling! I am very happy. Abruptly her "voice" stopped.

He was facing the box that housed the disarming circuit, alarms clanging in his ears; he took from his pocket another gadget and tried it.

The blast that shattered the box caught him full in the chest. The letters on the metal marker read:

TO THE MEMORY OF
MR. AND MRS. JOSEPH GREENE
WHO, NEAR THIS SPOT,
DIED FOR ALL THEIR FELLOW MEN

DESTINATION MOON

Short Stories Magazine, September 1950

❖

Today, with space full of ships, colonies on the inner planets, and Earth's Moon so close that pilots on the Luna run sleep home nights, it is hard to imagine when "flying to the Moon" was a figure of speech for the impossible, when men who thought it could be done were visionaries, crackpots.

It is hard to realize the opposition they faced, to understand why they persisted, what they thought—

Farquharson, *History of Transportation,* III: 414

CHAPTER ONE

THE MOJAVE DESERT was gray with first morning light, but at the construction site lights were still burning in the office of the technical director. The office was quiet, save for petulant burbling of a pot of coffee.

Three men were present—the director himself, Doctor Robert Corley, Lincoln-tall and lean, Rear Admiral "Red" Bowles, regular navy retired, and Jim Barnes, head of Barnes Aircraft, Barnes Tool Works, other enterprises.

All three needed shaves; Barnes badly needed a haircut as well. Barnes was seated at Corley's desk; Bowles sprawled on a couch, apparently asleep and looking like a fat, redheaded baby; Doctor Corley paced the room, following a well worn pattern.

He stopped, and stared out the window. A thousand yards away on the floor of the desert a great ship, pointed and sleek, thrust up into the sky, ready to punch out through Earth's thick atmosphere.

Wearily he turned away and picked up a letter from the desk; it read:

Reaction Associates, Inc.
Mojave, California.

Gentlemen:

Your request to test the engine of your atomic-powered rocket ship at the site of its construction is regretfully denied.

Although it is conceded that no real danger of atomic explosion exists, a belief in such danger does exist in the public mind. It is the policy of the Commission—Corley skipped down to the last paragraph:—*therefore, test is authorized at the Special Weapons Testing Center, South Pacific. Arrangements may be*—

He stopped and shoved the letter at Barnes. "If we've got to test at Eniwetok, we've got to find the money to do it."

Barnes' voice showed exasperation. "Doc, I've told you the syndicate won't put up another dime; there is no other money to be found."

"Confound it—we should have government money!"

Barnes grunted. "Tell that to Congress."

Without opening his eyes Bowles commented, "The United States is going to stall around and let Russia get to the Moon first—with hydrogen bombs. That's what you call 'policy.'"

Corley chewed his lip. "It's got to be *now*."

"I know it." Barnes got up and went to the window. The rising sun caught a highlight on the polished skin of the great ship. "It's got to be now," he repeated softly.

He turned and said, "Doc, when is the next favorable time to leave?"

"When we planned on it—next month."

"No, I mean this month."

Corley glanced at the wall calendar, dug into a bookcase for a well-thumbed volume, did a quick estimate. "Tomorrow morning—around four o'clock."

"That's it, then. We blast off tomorrow morning."

Admiral Bowles sat up with a jerk. "Blast off in an untested ship? Jim, you're crazy!"

"Probably. But now is the time—*now*. If we wait even a month, we will be tangled in some new snafu. That ship is ready, except for testing the power plant. So we'll skip the test!"

"But we haven't even selected a crew."

Barnes grinned. "*We're the crew!*"

Neither Corley nor Bowles answered. Barnes went on, "Why not? The takeoff is automatic. Sure, we agreed that we should have young men, fast reflexes, and all that malarkey—and every damned one of us has been trying to figure out a reason why he should be included. You, Red, you sneaked off to Moffeatt Field and took a pilot's physical.

Flunked it, too. Don't lie to me; I *know*. And you, Doc, you've been hinting that you ought to nurse the power plant yourself—you've been working on your wife, too."

"Eh?"

"She wanted me to say that the syndicate would object to your going. Don't worry; I didn't agree."

Corley looked at him levelly. "I've always intended to go. She knows that."

"That's my boy! Red?"

Bowles heaved himself to his feet. "Shucks, Jim, I didn't bust that physical much—just overweight."

"You're in. I don't want an eager young beaver as co-pilot anyhow."

" 'Co-pilot?' "

"Want to rassle me for skipper? Red, I've meant to gun this crate myself ever since the day—Lordy, four years ago!—when you brought Doc to see me with a satchelful of blueprints." He drew a breath and looked around exultantly.

Bowles said, "Let's see. You for pilot; I'm co-; Doc is chief. That leaves nobody but the radarman. You can't possibly train a man in the electronics of that ship by tomorrow morning."

Barnes shrugged. "Hobson's choice—it has to be Ward." He named the chief electronics engineer of the project.

Bowles turned to Corley. "Does Ward hanker to go?"

Corley looked thoughtful. "I'm sure he does. We haven't discussed it." He reached for the phone. "I'll call his quarters."

Barnes stuck a hand in the way. "Not so fast. Once the word got out, the Commission has twenty-four hours in which to stop us."

Bowles glanced at his watch. "Twenty-one hours."

"Long enough, anyhow."

Corley frowned. "We can't keep it secret. We've got to load that ship. I've got to reach Dr. Hastings and get our ballistic calculated."

"One thing at a time." Barnes paused, frowning.

"Here's the plan: we'll tell everybody that this is just a dress rehearsal, but complete in all details, road blocks, rations, reporters, check-off lists, the works. Doc, you get the power plant ready. Red, you're in charge of loading. Me, I'm going into Mojave and phone Hastings. Then I'll phone the University and arrange for the big computer."

"Why drive twenty miles?" Corley protested. "Call from here."

"Because these wires are probably tapped—and I don't mean the F.B.I.! Aside from us three and Ward, Hastings is the one man who *must* know the truth—when he figures that ballistic, he's got to know it matters."

Barnes reached for his hat. "Doc, you can call Ward now—here I go."

"Wait!" said Bowles. "Jim, you're going off half cocked. You can at least find out from here where Hastings is. You may have to fly down to Palomar and get him."

Barnes snapped his fingers. "I *am* half cocked, Red. I forgot the most important item—the reason why I can't use my plane myself; I need it for the Resident Inspector." He referred to the project representative of the Atomic Energy Commission.

"Holmes? Why does *he* need your plane?"

"To get lost in. I'm going to persuade Ned Holmes to go to Washington and make one last plea for us to be allowed to test our engine here. He'll do it; turning us down wasn't his idea. Our boy Andy will fly him in my plane—and Andy will be forced down in the desert, forty miles from a phone. Very sad."

Corley grudged a smile. "Sounds like kidnapping."

Barnes looked innocent.

"Of course Holmes will put the Commission's seal on the power pile before he leaves."

"And we'll break it. Any more objections? If not, let's get Andy, Holmes, and Ward, in that order."

Admiral Bowles whistled. "Doc," he said, "that engine of yours had better work, or we will spend the rest of our lives in jail. Well, let's get busy."

CHAPTER TWO

The morning was well worn by the time Jim Barnes drove back to the construction site. The company guard at the pass gate waved him through; he stopped nevertheless. "Howdy, Joe."

"Morning, Mr. Barnes."

"I see the gate is open. Any orders from the front office?"

"About the gate? No. Somebody called and said today was dress rehearsal for the Big Boy." The guard hooked a thumb toward the ship, two miles away.

"That's right. Now listen; this dress rehearsal must be letter perfect. Keep that gate locked. Clear with me, or Admiral Bowles, or Doctor Corley himself before unlocking it."

"Gotcha, Mr. Barnes."

"Just remember that there are people who would do anything to keep that ship over there from leaving the ground—and they don't necessarily have foreign accents."

"Don't worry, Mr. Barnes."

But he did worry; corking up the gate still left fourteen miles of unguarded fence.

Oh, well—it was a risk that must be accepted. He drove on past the living quarters, through the circle of shops. The area swarmed with people, on foot, in trucks, in jeeps. Trucks were lined up at the entrance to the bull pen surrounding the ship itself. Barnes pulled up at the administration building.

In Corley's office he found Bowles, Corley himself—and Corley's wife. Corley looked harassed; Mrs. Corley was quite evidently angry. "Greetings, folks," he said. "Am I butting in?"

Corley looked up. "Come in, Jim."

Barnes bowed to Mrs. Corley. "How do you do, ma'am?"

She glared at him. "You! You're responsible for this!"

"Me, Mrs. Corley? For what?"

"You know very well 'what'! Oh you . . . you . . ." She caught her breath, then gave vent to one explosive word: "Men!" She slammed out of the room.

When the door had closed behind her, Barnes let his eyebrows seek their natural level. "I see she knows. You shouldn't have told her, not yet, Doc."

"Confound it, Jim. I didn't expect her to kick up a fuss."

Bowles faced around in his chair. "Don't be a fool, Jim. Doc's wife *had* to know—wives aren't hired hands."

"Sorry. The damage is done. Doc, have you put any check on phone calls?"

"Why, no."

"Do it. Wait, I'll do it." He stepped to the door. "Countess, call our switch board. Tell Gertie to switch all outgoing calls to you. You tell 'em firmly that outside lines are all in use, find out who it is, why they want to call, and whom—then tell the Director, Admiral Bowles, or me. Same for incoming calls."

He closed the door and turned back to Bowles.

"Your wife knows?"

"Of course."

"Trouble?"

"No. Navy wives get used to such things, Jim."

"I suppose so. Well, I got Hastings squared away. He says that he will be here with the tape not later than two in the morning. I've got a plane standing by for him."

Corley frowned. "That's cutting it fine. We ought to have more time to set up the autopilot."

"He says he can't promise it sooner. How about things here?"

"Loading is coming all right," answered Bowles, "provided the trucks with the oxygen aren't late."

"You should have flown it in."

"Quit jittering. The trucks are probably in Cajon Pass this minute."

"Okay, okay. Power plant, Doc?"

"I haven't broken Ned Holmes' seal on the atomic pile yet. The water tanks are filling, but they've just started."

He was interrupted by the telephone at his elbow. "Yes?"

His secretary's voice sounded in the room. "Your wife wants to call long distance, Doctor. I'm stalling her. Are you in?"

"Put her on," he said wearily. Mrs. Corley's words could not be heard, but her angry tones came through. Corley answered, "No, dear . . . That's right, dear. I'm sorry but that's how it is . . . no, I don't know when the lines will be free; we're holding them for calls placed to the east coast . . . no, you can't have the car; I'm using it. I—" He looked surprised and replaced the instrument. "She hung up on me."

"See what I mean?" said Barnes.

"Jim, you're a fool," Bowles answered.

"No, I'm a bachelor. Why? Because I can't stand the favorite sport of all women."

"Which is?"

"Trying to geld stallions. Let's get on with the job."

"Right," agreed Corley and flipped a key on his Teletalk. "Helen, call the electronics shop and tell Mr. Ward that I want to see him."

"Haven't you broken the news to him?" demanded Barnes.

"Ward? Of course."

"How did he take it?"

"Well enough. Ward is high strung. At first he insisted there wasn't time to get all the electronic gear ready."

"But he's in?"

"He's in." Corley stood up. "I've got to get back into the ship."

"Me, too," Bowles agreed.

Barnes followed them out. As they passed the desk of Corley's secretary she was saying, "One moment, puh*lease*—I'm ringing him." She looked up and pointed to Corley.

Corley hesitated. "Uh, uh," said Barnes, "if you let 'em tie you up on the phone, we'll never take off. I'm elected. Go on, you two. Get the buggy ready to go."

"Okay." Corley added to his secretary, "Got Mr. Ward yet?"

"Not in the electronics shop. I'm chasing him."

"I want him right away."

Barnes went back inside and spent an hour handling a log jam on the telephone. Personal calls he simply stalled on the excuse that the lines were needed for priority long distance calls. If a call was concerned with getting the ship ready to go, he handled it himself or monitored it. As best he could he kept the construction site an island, cut off from the world.

He straightened out a matter with the chief metallurgist, gave the accounting office an okay on some overtime of the week before, assured Associated Press that the "dress rehearsal" was worth full coverage, and gleefully extended an invitation to the Los Angeles Associated Civic Clubs to go through the ship—next week.

That done, he took Corley's dictaphone and began a memorandum to his business manager on how to close the project in case (a) the trip was successful, (b) the ship crashed. He planned to mark it to be transcribed the following day.

A call from Dr. Corley interrupted him. "Jim? I can't find Ward."

"Tried the men's wash rooms?"

"No—but I will."

"He can't be far away. Anything wrong in his department?"

"No, but I need him."

"Well, maybe he's finished his tests and gone to his quarters to catch some sleep."

"There's no answer from his quarters."

"Phone could be off the hook. I'll send someone to dig him out."

"Do that."

While he was arranging this, Herbert Styles, public relations chief for the project, came in. The press agent slumped down in a chair and looked mournful.

"Howdy, Herb."

"Howdy. Say, Mr. Barnes, let's you and me go back to Barnes Aircraft and quit this crazy dump."

"What's biting you, Herb?"

"Well, maybe you can make some sense out of what's going on. They tell me to get everybody in here by three A.M.—A.P., U.P., INS, radio chains, television trucks, and stuff. Then you lock the joint up like a schoolhouse on Sunday. And all this for a practice drill, a dry run. Who's crazy? Me or you?"

Barnes had known Styles a long time. "It's not a drill, Herb."

"Of course not." Styles ground out a cigarette. "Now—how do we play it?"

"Herb, I'm in a squeeze. We're going to take off—at three fifty-three tomorrow morning. If word gets out before then, they'll find some way to stop us."

"Who's 'they'? And why?"

"The Atomic Energy Commission for one—for jumping off with an untested power-pile ship."

Styles whistled. "Bucking the Commission, eh? Oh, brother! But why not test it?"

Barnes explained, concluding with, "—so we can't test it. I'm busted, Herb."

"Isn't everybody?"

"That isn't all. Call it a hunch, or anything you like. If we don't take off now, we never will—even if I had the dinero to test in the South Pacific. We've had more than our share of bad luck on this project— and I don't believe in luck."

"Meaning?"

"There are people who want this enterprise to fail. Some are crackpots; some are jealous. Others—"

"Others," Styles finished for him, "don't like the United States getting space travel first any better than they liked us getting the atom bomb first."

"Check."

"So what do you want to guard against? A time bomb in the ship? Sabotage of the controls? Or the Federal marshal with a squad of soldiers to back him up?"

"I don't know!"

Styles stared at nothing.

"Boss—"

"Yeh?"

"Item: pretty soon you've got to admit publicly that it's a real take-off, for you've got to evacuate this valley. The sheriff and state police won't play games just for a drill."

"But—"

"Item: by now it is after office hours on the east coast. You're fairly safe from the Commission until morning. Item: any sabotage will be done on the spur of the moment, provided it isn't already built into the ship."

"Too late to worry about anything built into the ship."

"Just the same, if I were you, I would go over her with a toothpick. Any last minute stuff will be done with a wrench, behind a control panel or such—what they used to call 'target of opportunity.' "

"Hard to stop."

"Not too hard. There isn't anything that can be done to that ship down at its base, right? Well, if my neck depended on that heap, I wouldn't let anybody up inside it from now on, except those going along. Not *anybody*, not even if he carried a certificate of Simon-pure one-hundred-percentism from the D.A.R. I'd watch what went in and I'd stow things with my own little patty-paws."

Barnes chewed his lip. "You're right. Herb—you just bought yourself a job."

"Such as?"

"Take over here." He explained what he had been doing. "As for the press, don't tip them off until you have to make arrangements for the road blocks and evacuation—maybe you can keep things wrapped up until around midnight. I'm going up into that ship and—"

The telephone jangled; he picked it up. "Yes?"

It was Bowles.

"Jim—come to the electronics shop."

"Trouble?"

"Plenty. Ward has run out on us."

"Oh, oh! I'll be right over." He slammed the phone and said, "Take over, Herb!"

"Wilco!"

Outside, he jumped in his car and swung around the circle to the electronics shops. He found Bowles and Corley in Ward's office. With them was Emmanuel Traub, Ward's first assistant.

"What happened?"

Corley answered, "Ward is in the hospital—acute appendicitis."

Bowles snorted. "Acute funk!"

"That's not fair! Ward wouldn't run out on me."

Barnes cut in. "It doesn't matter either way. The question is: what do we do now?"

Corley looked sick. "We can't take off."

"Stow that!" Barnes turned to Bowles. "Red, can you handle the electronics?"

"Hardly! I can turn the knobs on an ordinary two-way—but that ship is *all* electronics."

"I'm in the same fix—Doc, *you* could. Or couldn't you?"

"Uh, maybe—but I can't handle radar and power plant both."

"You could teach me to handle power plant and Red could pilot."

"*Huh?* I can't make a nucleonics technician out of you in something like a matter of hours."

Barnes seemed to feel the world pressing in on him. He shook off the feeling and turned to Traub. "Mannie, you installed a lot of the electronic gear, didn't you?"

"Me? I installed all of it. Mr. Ward didn't like to go up the Gantry crane. He is a nervous type guy."

Barnes looked at Corley. "Well?"

Corley fidgeted. "I don't know."

Bowles said suddenly, "Traub, where did you go to college?"

Traub looked hurt. "I got no fancy degree but I carry a civil service classification of senior electronics engineer—a P-5. I did three years in the Raytheon labs. I had my ham license since I was fifteen, and I was a master sergeant in the Signal Corps. If it makes with electrons, I savvy it."

Barnes said mildly, "The Admiral didn't mean any harm, Mannie. What do you weigh?"

Traub shifted his eyes from one to the other. "Mr. Barnes—this is no rehearsal? This is it?"

"This is it, Mannie. We take off—" He glanced at his watch. "—in thirteen hours."

Traub was breathing hard. "You gentlemen are asking me to go to the Moon with you? Tonight?"

Before Barnes could answer, Bowles put in:

"That's it, Mannie."

Traub swallowed hard. "Yes," he said.

"Yes?" Barnes echoed.

"I'll go."

Corley said hastily, "Traub, we don't want to rush you."

"Director, take a look at my job application. I put down 'Willing to travel.'"

CHAPTER THREE

The great ship was ringed with floodlights spaced inside the bull pen. It was still framed by the skeleton arch of the Gantry crane, but the temporary anti-radiation shield which had surrounded its lower part down to the jets was gone; instead there were posted the trefoil signs used to warn of radioactivity—although the level of radiation had not yet become dangerously high.

But the power pile was unsealed and the ship was ready to go. Thirteen-fifteenths of its mass was water, ready to be flashed into incandescent steam by the atomic pile, to be thrown away at thirty thousand feet per second.

High up in the ship was the control room and adjacent air lock. Below the air lock the permanent anti-radiation shield ran across the ship, separating the pressurized crew space from the tanks, the pumps, the pile itself, and auxiliary machinery. Above the control room, the nose of the craft was unpressurized cargo space.

At its base triangular airfoils spread out like oversize fins—fins they would be as the ship blasted away; glider wings they would become when the ship returned to Earth with her tanks empty.

Jim Barnes was at the foot of the Gantry crane, giving last-minute orders. A telephone had been strung out to the crane; it rang and he turned to answer it.

"Mr. Barnes?"

"Yes, Herb."

"Sheriff's office reports road blocks in place and everybody out of the valley—it cost plenty cumshaw to clear the Idle Hour Guest Rancho, by the way."

"No matter."

"Everybody out, that is, but Pete the Hermit. He won't git."

"The old boy with the whiskers in that shack north of the gate?"

"The same. We finally told him the score, but it didn't faze him. He says he ain't never seen no ship take off for the Moon and he ain't planning to miss it, not at his age."

Barnes chuckled. "Can't blame him. Well, let him sign the release our own people sign. Tell him if he won't sign, the show won't take place."

"And if he doesn't sign?"

"Herb, I take off even if some damn fool is standing under the jets. But don't tell him."

"I got you. Now how about the press?"

"Tell them now—but keep them off my neck. And even with releases they stay in the blockhouse."

"I'll have trouble with the newsreel and television people."

"Remote control or nothing. Herd 'em in, you go in last and lock the door behind you. They can string all the wires into the blockhouse they need, but *nobody* stays inside the area unsheltered."

"Mr. Barnes—do you really think the blast will be that dangerous?"

Barnes' reply was drowned out by the bull horn from the blockhouse: "Attention! The last bus is now loading at the north entrance to the shop circle!"

Presently Styles resumed:

"Another call—you better take it, boss. Trouble."

"Who is it?"

"Commanding general at Muroc."

"Put him on." In a moment he was saying, "Jim Barnes, General. How are you?"

"Oh—hello, Mr. Barnes. I hate to buck you, but your man seems unreasonable. Is it necessary to ask us to keep radar crews up all night for your practice drill?"

"Mmm . . . General, isn't your tracking radar always manned anyhow? I thought this country had a 'radar umbrella' over it."

The general answered stiffly, "That's not a proper question, Mr. Barnes."

"I suppose not. Big difference between passing a law and getting appropriations to carry it out, isn't there?" He thought a minute. "General, suppose I guarantee blips on your tracking screens?"

"What do you mean?"

Barnes said, "General, I've known you since open cockpits. You've used a lot of my planes."

"You make good planes, Mr. Barnes."

"Tonight I want some cooperation. This is it, Whitey."

"Huh?"

"We blast off tonight. As long as you know, you can call White Sands and make sure they track us, too. And Whitey—"

"Yes, Jim?"

"What with getting your crew organized and calling White Sands it will be another hour before you can call Washington, wouldn't you think?"

Silence persisted so long that Barnes thought he had been cut off, then the general answered, "It might take that long. Anything more you had better tell me?"

"No . . . that's enough. Except one thing; I'm going, Whitey. I'm piloting it."

"Oh. Good luck, Jim."

"Thanks, Whitey."

As Barnes turned away, he saw a plane circling the area, its lights blinking. The elevator creaked behind him; he looked up to see Corley, Bowles, and Traub descending. Corley shouted, "Is that Dr. Hastings?"

"I hope so."

The plane landed and a jeep drove up to it. A few minutes later the jeep swung into the bull pen and up to the crane; Doctor Hastings got out. Corley ran to meet him.

"Doctor Hastings! You have it?"

"Greetings, gentlemen. Yes, indeed." Hastings tapped a bulging pocket.

"Give it to me!"

"Suppose we go into the ship? I'd like to discuss it with you."

"Jump aboard." The two savants mounted the elevator and started up.

Admiral Bowles touched Barnes' sleeve. "Jim—a word with you."

"Shoot."

Bowles indicated Traub with his eyes; Barnes caught the meaning and they moved inside. "Jim," Bowles asked in a whisper, "what do you know about this man Traub?"

"Nothing that you don't. Why?"

"He's foreign born, isn't he? Germany? Poland?"

"Russia, for all I know. Does it matter?"

Bowles frowned. "There's been sabotage, Jim."

"The hell you say! What sort?"

"The earth-departure radar wouldn't function. Traub opened up the front, then called me over."

"What was it?"

"A pencil mark drawn between two leads. It—"

"I get you, a carbon short. Sabotage, all right. Well?"

"My point is, he found it too easily. How would he know right where to find it if he didn't do it himself?"

Barnes thought about it. "If Traub is trying to stop us, all he has to do is to refuse to go. We can't go without him—and he knows it."

"Suppose his object was not just to stop us, but to wreck the ship?"

"And kill himself in the bargain? Be logical, Red."

"Some of those people are fanatics, Jim. Beyond logic."

Barnes considered it. "Forget it, Red."

"But—"

"I said, 'Forget it!' Get on back in that ship and prowl around. Imagine that you are a saboteur; try to think where you would hide a bomb—or what you would wreck."

"Aye, aye, sir!"

"Good. Mannie!"

"Yes, Mr. Barnes." Traub trotted up; Barnes told him to go up and continue checking. The phone at the foot of the crane rang; it was Styles again.

"Boss? Just got a call from the pass gate. The deputy there is hooked by car radio with the deputies at the road blocks—"

"Good. Nice organizing, Herb."

"Not good! The north road block reports a car with a bailiff; he has a federal court order to stop the takeoff. They let him through."

Barnes swore softly. "Call the pass gate. Tell the deputy there to stop him."

"I did. He won't. He says he can't interfere with federal business."

"That tears it!" Barnes stopped to think. "Tell him to make almighty sure that the man is what he says he is. Tell him that the court order is almost certainly phony—which it is. Tell him to hold the man while he gets in touch with the sheriff's office and has the sheriff phone the judge who is supposed to have issued the described order."

"I'll try," Styles answered, "but suppose the order is kosher, boss? Hadn't I better just put the slug on him and dump him in a closet until the fireworks are over?"

Barnes weighed this. "No—you'd spend your life breaking rocks. Gain me all the minutes you can—then hightail it for the blockhouse. Is everybody clear?"

"Everybody but the car and driver for Mrs. Corley."

"How about Admiral Bowles' wife?"

"He sent her off earlier—the Admiral doesn't like ships watched out of sight."

"Bless his superstitious heart! Send Mrs. Corley's car into the pen. I'm going to button up around here."

"Roger!"

Barnes turned around to find Corley and Hastings descending. He waited, bursting with impatience. Corley spoke as they reached bottom. "Oh, Jim, I—"

"Never mind! Is everything okay up there?"

"Yes, but—"

"No time! Say good-bye to your wife, Doctor Hastings—good-bye, and thanks! Your plane's waiting."

"Jim," protested Corley, "what's the rush? It's—"

"No time!" A car swung in through the gate of the pen, came toward them. "There's your wife. Say good-bye and get back here. Move!" Barnes turned away and went to the crane operator. "Barney!"

"Yeah?"

"We're going up now—*for the last time*. As soon as we are off the crane, back it away. The safety stops are off the tracks?"

"Sure."

"Off entirely, or just moved back?"

"Off entirely. Don't worry; I won't run her off the rails."

"Yes, you will. Run the crane right off the end."

"Huh? Mr. Barnes, if I dropped the wheels into the sand, it would take a week to get her back on."

"Check. That's exactly what I want. After you do it, don't stop to explain; just run for the blockhouse."

The operator looked baffled. "Okay—you said it."

Barnes came back to the elevator. Corley and his wife were standing near her car. She was crying.

Barnes shaded his eyes against the floodlights and tried to see the road to the pass gate. The foundry cut off his view. Suddenly headlights gleamed around that building, turned onto the shop circle and came toward the bull pen entrance. Barnes shouted, "Doc! *Now!* Hurry!"

Corley looked up, then hastily embraced his wife. Barnes shouted, "Come on! Come on!"

Corley waited to hand his wife into the car. Barnes climbed onto the elevator and, as Corley reached it, pulled him aboard. "Barney! UP!"

Cables creaked and groaned; the platform crawled upward. As Mrs. Corley's car approached the gate the other car started in. Both cars stopped, then the strange car bulled on through. It gunned in second toward the crane and slammed to a stop; a man swarmed out.

He ran to the elevator; the platform was thirty feet above his head. He waved and shouted. "Barnes! Come down here!"

Barnes shouted back, "Can't hear you! Too much racket!"

"Stop the elevator! I've got a court order!"

The driver of the car jumped out and ran toward the crane control station. Barnes watched, unable to stop whatever was to come.

Barney reached behind him and grabbed a wrench; the driver stopped short. "Good boy!" Barnes breathed.

The elevator reached the airlock door; Barnes nudged Corley. "In you go!" He followed Corley, turned and lifted the gangway off the lip of the door, shoved it clear with his foot. "Barney! Get going!"

The crane operator glanced up and shifted his controls. The crane quivered, then very slowly crawled back from the ship, cleared it, and continued.

It backed still farther, lurched out of plumb, and trembled. Its drive motor squealed and stopped. Barney slid out of his saddle and loped away toward the gate.

CHAPTER FOUR

Time checks had been completed with Muroc, with White Sands and with their blockhouse. The control room was quiet save for the sighing of air-replenishing equipment, the low hum of radio circuits, and stray sounds of auxiliary machinery. The clocks at each station read 3:29—twenty-four minutes to H-hour.

The four were at their stations; two upper bunks were occupied by pilot and co-pilot; the lowers by power engineer and electronics engineer. Across the lap of each man arched a control console; his arms were supported so that his fingers were free to handle his switches without lifting any part of his body against the terrible weight to come. His head was supported so that he might see his instruments.

Traub lifted his head and peered out one of the two large quartz ports. "It's clouding up. I can't see the Moon."

Barnes answered, "Out where we're going there won't be any clouds."

"No clouds?"

"What do you expect, out in space?"

"Uh, I don't know. I guess I got most of my ideas about space travel from Buck Rogers. Electronics is my game."

"Twenty-three minutes," announced Bowles. "Skipper, what's the name of this bucket?"

"Huh?"

"When you launch a ship you have to name her."

"Eh, I suppose so. Doc, what do you say? She's your baby."

"Me? I've never thought about it."

"How," Bowles went on, "about calling her the *Luna?*"

Corley considered. "Suits me, if it suits the rest of you."

"The space ship *Luna*," agreed Barnes. "Sounds good."

Traub chuckled nervously. "That makes us 'the Lunatics.' "

"And why not?" agreed Barnes.

"Twenty minutes," announced Bowles.

"Warm her up, Doc. Check-off lists, everybody."

"She's hot now," Corley answered. "If I increase the fission rate, I'll have to give her something to chew. Jim, I've been thinking. We could still test her."

"Huh?"

"Set her for a half-*g* lift, and clear her throat once—I've got her set for that."

"What's the point? She either works, or she blows up."

"Okay," Corley answered.

Traub gulped. "Could she blow up?"

"Don't worry," Corley reassured him. "The scale model ran an hour and twenty-three minutes before it blew up."

"Oh. Is that good?"

"Mannie," Barnes ordered. "Switch on 'Ground Pick-Up.' We might as well watch."

"Yes, sir." Above them was a large TV screen. Traub could hook it in to a scanner in the tail, another in the nose, or—as now—pick up an ordinary video channel. The screen lighted up; they saw their own ship, lonely and tall in the floodlights.

An announcer's voice came with the picture: "—this ship, the mightiest ever built, will soon plunge into outer space. Its flight was unannounced until tonight, its destination has not been revealed. Is this—"

The broadcast was interrupted by Herb Styles. "Mr. Barnes! Boss!"

Barnes leaned out and looked at Traub in the couch beneath. "Are you hooked in?"

"Just a sec—go ahead."

"What is it, Herb?"

"Somebody tearing down the road, heading this way."

"Who?"

"Don't know. We can't contact the north road block."

"Call the pass gate. Head 'em off."

"It's no longer manned. Hey—wait. North road block coming in." After a pause, Styles yelled, "Truck loaded with men—they crushed through and ran over a deputy!"

"Keep your shirt on," cautioned Barnes. "They can't reach us. If they hang around down below, it's their misfortune. I'm blasting on time."

Bowles sat up. "Don't be too sure, Jim."

"Eh? What can they do to us now?"

"What would six sticks of dynamite against one of the tail jacks do to this ship? Let's take off—now!"

"Before calculated time? Red, don't be silly."

"Blast off and correct later!"

"Doc—could we do that?"

"Eh? *No!*"

Barnes stared at the TV picture. "Mannie—tell block-house to sound sirens!"

"Jim," protested Corley, "you can't take off now!"

"Are you still set up to test? Half *g?*"

"Yes, but—"

"Stand by!" His eyes were fixed on the pictured scene outside; headlights came around the foundry, sped toward the pen. The moaning of sirens drowned out Corley's answer.

The truck was almost at the gate. Barnes' forefinger stabbed the firing button.

A whine of great pumps was blanked out by a roar they could feel in their bones. The *Luna* shivered.

In the TV screen a flower of white light burst from the tail of the ship, billowed up, blanketing the headlights, the buildings, the lower half of the ship.

Barnes jerked his finger back. The noise died out; the cloud changed from incandescent to opaque. In the silence Styles' voice came over the speaker. *"Great—Day—in the Morning!"*

"Herb—can you hear me?"

"Yes. What happened?"

"Use the bull horn to warn them off. Tell 'em to scram; if they come closer I'll fry them."

"I think you have."

"Get busy." He watched the screen, his finger raised. The cloud lifted; he made out the truck.

"Nine minutes," Bowles announced, calmly.

Through the speaker Barnes could hear a voice on the bull horn, warning the attacking party back. A man jumped down from the truck, was followed by others. Barnes' finger trembled.

They turned and ran.

Barnes sighed. "Doc, did the test suit you?"

"A mushy cutoff," Corley complained. "It should have been sharp."

"Do we blast, or don't we?"

Corley hesitated. "Well?" demanded Barnes.

"We blast."

Traub heaved a mournful sigh. Barnes snapped, "Power plant—shift to automatic! All hands—prepare for acceleration. Mannie, tell blockhouse, Muroc, and White Sands to stand by for count off at oh three five two."

" 'Oh three five two,' " Traub repeated, then went on, "Ship, calling blockhouse, Muroc, White Sands."

"Power plant, report."

"Automatic, all green."

"Co-pilot?"

"Tracking on autopilot." Bowles added, "Eight minutes."

"Doc, is she hot as she'll take?"

"I'm carrying the fission rate as high as I dare," Corley answered, strain in his voice. "She's on the ragged edge."

"Keep her so. All hands, strap down."

Corley reared up. "Jim—I forgot to pass out the drop-sick pills."

"Stay where you are! If we get seasick, we get seasick."

"One minute, coming up!" Bowles' voice was harsh.

"Take it, Mannie!"

"Blockhouse—Muroc—White Sands. Ready for count off!" Traub paused; the room was still.

"Sixty! Fifty-nine—fifty-eight—fifty-seven—"

Barnes gripped his arm rests, tried to slow down his heart. He watched the seconds click off as Traub counted them. "Thirty-nine!

Thirty-eight! Thirty-seven!" Traub's voice was shrill. "Thirty-one! *Half!*"

Barnes could hear sirens, rising and falling, out on the field. Above him in the TV screen, the *Luna* stood straight and proud, her head in darkness.

"Eleven!

"And ten!

"And nine!

"And eight!"—Barnes licked his lips and swallowed.

"Five—four——three———two—

"Fire!"

The word was lost in sound, a roar that made the test blast seem as nothing. The *Luna* shrugged—and climbed for the sky.

CHAPTER FIVE

If we are to understand those men, we must reorient. Crossing the Atlantic was high adventure—when Columbus did it. So with the early spacemen. The ships they rode in were incredibly makeshift.

They did not know what they were doing. Had they known, they would not have gone.

Farquharson, *Ibid.,* III: 415

Barnes felt himself shoved back into the cushions. He gagged and fought to keep from swallowing his tongue. He felt paralyzed by body weight of more than half a ton; he strained to lift his chest. Worse than weight was noise, a mind-killing "white" sound from unbearable ultra-sonics down to bass too low to be heard.

The sound Dopplered down the scale, rumbled off and left them. At five effective gravities they outraced their own din in six seconds, leaving an aching quiet broken only by noise of water coursing through pumps.

For a moment Barnes savored the silence. Then his eyes caught the TV screen above him; in it was a shrinking dot of fire. He realized that he was seeing himself, disappearing into the sky, and regretted that he had not watched the blast-away. "Mannie," he labored, to say, "switch on 'View After.'"

"I *can't,*" Traub groaned thickly. "I can't move a muscle."

"Do it!"

Traub managed it; the screen blurred, then formed a picture. Bowles grunted, "Great Caesar's ghost!" Barnes stared. They were high above Los Angeles; the metropolitan area was map sharp, picked out in street lights and neon. It was shrinking visibly.

Rosy light flashed through the eastern port, followed at once by dazzling sunlight. Traub yelped, *"What happened?"*

Barnes himself had been startled but he strove to control his voice and answered, "Sunrise. We're up that high." He went on, "Doc—how's the power plant?"

"Readings normal," Corley replied in tongue-clogged tones. "How long to go?"

Barnes looked at his board. "More than three minutes."

Corley did not answer; three minutes seemed too long to bear. Presently Traub said, "Look at the sky!" Corley forced his head over and looked. Despite harsh sunlight the sky was black and spangled with stars.

At three minutes and fifty seconds the jets cut off. Like the first time, the cutoff was mushy, slow. The terrible weight left them gradually. But it left them completely. Rocket and crew were all in a free orbit "falling" upward toward the Moon. Relative to each other and to ship they had no weight.

Barnes felt that retching, frightening "falling elevator" feeling characteristic of no weight, but, expecting it, he steeled himself. "Power plant," he snapped, "report!"

"Power plant okay," Corley replied weakly. "Notice the cutoff?"

"Later," decided Barnes. "Co-pilot, my track seems high."

"My display tracks on," wheezed Bowles, "—or a hair high."

"Mannie!"

No answer. Barnes repeated, "Mannie? Answer, man—are you all right?"

Traub's voice was weak. "I think I'm dying. This thing is falling—oh, God, *make it stop!*"

"Snap out of it!"

"Are we going to crash?"

"No, no! We're all right."

"'All right,' the man says," Traub muttered, then added, "I don't care if we do."

Barnes called out, "Doc, get those pills. Mannie needs one bad." He stopped to control a retch. "I could use one myself."

"Me, too," agreed Bowles. "I haven't been this seasick since I was—" He caught himself, then went on. "—since I was a midshipman."

Corley loosened his straps and pulled himself out from his couch. Weightless, he floated free and turned slowly over, like a diver in slow motion. Traub turned his face away and groaned.

"Stop it, Mannie," ordered Barnes. "Try to raise White Sands. I want a series of time-altitude readings."

"I can't—I'm sick."

"Do it!"

Corley floated near a stanchion, grabbed it, and pulled himself to a cupboard. He located the pill bottle and hastily gulped a pill. He then moved to Traub's couch, pulling himself along. "Here, Traub—take this. You'll feel better."

"What is it?"

"Some stuff called Dramamine. It's for seasickness."

Traub put a pill in his mouth. "I can't swallow."

"Better try." Traub got it down, clamped his jaw to keep it down. Corley pulled himself to Barnes. "Need one, Jim?"

Barnes started to answer, turned his head away, and threw up in his handkerchief. Tears streaming from his eyes, he accepted the pill. Bowles called out, "Doc—hurry up!" His voice cut off; presently he added, "Too late."

"Sorry." Corley moved over to Bowles. "Criminy, you're a mess!"

"Gimme that pill and no comments."

Traub was saying in a steadier voice, "Spaceship *Luna,* calling White Sands. Come in White Sands."

At last an answer came back, "White Sands to Spaceship—go ahead."

"Give us a series of radar checks, time, distance, and bearing."

A new voice cut in, "White Sands to Spaceship—we have been tracking you, but the figures are not reasonable. What is your destination?"

Traub glanced at Barnes, then answered, "*Luna,* to White Sands—destination: Moon."

"Repeat? Repeat?"

"Our destination is the Moon!"

There was a silence. The same voice replied, " 'Destination: Moon'—Good luck, Spaceship *Luna!*"

Bowles spoke up suddenly. "Hey! *Come look!*" He had unstrapped and was floating by the sunward port.

"Later," Barnes answered. "I need this tracking report first."

"Well, come look until they call back. This is once in a lifetime."

Corley joined Bowles. Barnes hesitated; he wanted very badly to see, but he was ashamed to leave Traub working. "Wait," he called out. "I'll turn ship and we can all see."

Mounted at the centerline of the ship was a flywheel. Barnes studied his orientation readings, then clutched the ship to the flywheel. Slowly the ship turned, without affecting its motion along its course. "How's that?"

"Wrong way!"

"Sorry." Barnes tried again; the stars marched past in the opposite direction; Earth swung into view. He caught sight of it and almost forgot to check the swing.

Power had cut off a trifle more than eight hundred miles up. The *Luna* had gone free at seven miles per second; in the last few minutes they had been steadily coasting upwards and were now three thousand miles above Southern California. Below—opposite them, from their viewpoint—was darkness. The seaboard cities stretched across the port like Christmas lights. East of them, sunrise cut across the Grand Canyon and shone on Lake Mead. Further east the prairies were in daylight, dun and green broken by blinding cloud. The plains dropped away into curved skyline.

So fast were they rising that the picture was moving, shrinking, and the globe drew into itself as a ball. Barnes watched from across the compartment. "Can you see all right, Mannie?" he asked.

"Yeah," answered Traub. "Yeah," he repeated softly. "Say, that's *real,* isn't it?"

Barnes said, "Hey, Red, Doc—heads down. You're not transparent."

Traub looked at Barnes. "Go ahead, skipper."

"No, I'll stick with you."

"Don't be a chump. I'll look later."

"Well—" Barnes grinned suddenly. "Thanks, Mannie." He gave a shove and moved across to the port.

Mannie continued to stare. Later the radio claimed his attention. "White Sands, calling Spaceship—ready with radar report."

The first reports, plus a further series continued as long as White Sands and Muroc were able to track them, confirmed Barnes' suspicion. They were tracking "high," ahead of their predicted positions and at speeds greater than those called for by Hastings' finicky calculations. The difference was small; on the autopilot displays it was hardly the thickness of a line between the calculated path and the true path.

But the difference would increase.

"Escape speeds" for rockets are very critical. Hastings had calculated the classical hundred-hour orbit and the *Luna* had been aimed to reach the place *where the Moon would be* four days later. But initial speed is critical. A difference of less than one percent in ship speed at cutoff can halve—or double—the transit time from Earth to Moon. The *Luna* was running very slightly ahead of schedule—but when it reached the orbit of the Moon, the Moon would not be there.

Doctor Corley tugged at his thinning hair. "Sure, the cutoff was mushy, but I was expecting it and I noted the mass readings. It's not enough to account for the boost. Here—take a look."

Corley was hunched at the log desk, a little shelf built into the space between the acceleration bunks. He was strapped to a stool fixed to the deck in front of it. Barnes floated at his shoulder; he took the calculation and scanned it. "I don't follow you," Barnes said presently; "your expended mass is considerably higher than Hastings calculated."

"You're looking at the wrong figure," Corley pointed out. "You forgot the mass of water you used up in that test. Subtract that from the total mass expended to get the effective figure for blast off—this figure here. Then you apply that—" Corley hesitated, his expression changed from annoyance to dismay. "Oh, my God!"

"Huh? What is it, Doc? Found the mistake?"

"Oh, how could I be so stupid!" Corley started frenzied figuring.

"What have you found?" Corley did not answer; Barnes grabbed his arm. "What's up?"

"Huh? Don't bother me."

"I'll bother you with a baseball bat. *What have you found?*"

"Eh? Look, Jim, what's the final speed of a rocket, ideal case?"

"What is this? A quiz show? Jet speed times the logarithm of the mass ratio. Pay me."

"And *you* changed the mass ratio! No wonder we're running high."
"Me?"

"We both did—my fault as much as yours. Listen; you spilled a mass of water in scaring off that truckload of thugs—but Hastings' figures were based on us lifting that particular mass *all the way to the Moon*. The ship should have grossed almost exactly two hundred fifty tons at takeoff; she was shy what you had used—so we're going too fast."

"Huh? I wasted reaction mass, so we're going too fast? That doesn't make sense." Barnes hooked a foot into the legs of the stool to anchor himself, and did a rough run-through of the problem with slide rule and logarithm table. "Well, boil me in a bucket!" He added humbly, "Doc, I shouldn't have asked to be skipper. I don't know enough."

Corley's worried features softened. "Don't feel that way, Jim. Nobody knows enough—yet. God knows I've put in enough time on theory, but I went ahead and urged you to make the blunder."

"Doc, how important is this ? The error is less than one percent. I'd guess that we would reach the Moon about an hour early."

"And roughly you'd be wrong. Initial speed is critical, Jim; you know that!"

"How critical? When do we reach the Moon?"

Corley looked glumly at the pitiful tools he had with him—a twenty-inch log-log slide rule, seven place tables, a Nautical Almanac, and an office-type calculator which bore the relation to a "giant brain" that a firecracker does to an A-bomb. "I don't know. I'll have to put it up to Hastings." He threw his pencil at the desk top; it bounced off and floated away. "The question is: do we get there at all?"

"Oh, it can't be that bad!"

"It *is* that bad."

From across the compartment Bowles called out, "Come and get it—or I throw it to the pigs!"

But food had to wait while Corley composed a message to Hastings. It was starkly simple: OFF TRAJECTORY. USE DATA WHITE SANDS MUROC AND COMPUTE CORRECTION VECTOR. PLEASE USE UTMOST HASTE—CORLEY.

After sending it Traub announced that he wasn't hungry and didn't guess he would eat.

Bowles left the "galley" (one lonely hot plate) and moved to Traub's couch. Traub had strapped himself into it to have stability while he handled his radio controls. "Snap out of it, man," Bowles advised. "Must eat, you know."

Traub looked gray. "Thanks, Admiral, but I couldn't."

"So you don't like my cooking? By the way, my friends call me 'Red.'"

"Thanks, uh—Red. No, I'm just not hungry."

Bowles brought his head closer and spoke in low tones. "Don't let it get you, Mannie. I've been in worse jams and come out alive. Quit worrying."

"I'm not worrying."

Bowles chuckled. "Don't be ashamed of it, son. We all get upset, first time under fire. Come eat."

"I can't eat. And I've *been* under fire."

"Really?"

"Yes, really! I've got two Purple Hearts to prove it. Admiral, leave me alone, please. My stomach is awful uneasy."

Bowles said, "I beg your pardon, Mannie." He added, "Maybe you need another seasick pill."

"Could be."

"I'll fetch one." Bowles did so, then returned again shortly with a transparent sack filled with milk—to be exact, a flexible plastic nursing cell, complete with nipple. "Sweet milk, Mannie. Maybe it'll comfort your stomach."

Traub looked at it curiously. "With this should go a diaper and a rattle," he announced. "Thanks, uh—Red."

"Not at all, Mannie. If that stays down, I'll fix you a sandwich." He turned in the air and rejoined the others.

CHAPTER SIX

The *Luna* plunged on; Earth dropped away; radio signals grew weaker— and still no word from Hastings. Corley spent the time trying endlessly and tediously to anticipate the answer he expected from Hastings, using the tools he had. Traub stood guard at the radio. Barnes and Bowles spent a lengthy time staring out the ports—back at the shrinking, cloud-striped Earth, forward at the growing gibbous Moon and brilliant steady stars— until Bowles fell asleep in mid-sentence, a softly snoring free balloon.

Barnes nudged him gently toward his couch and there strapped him loosely, to keep him from cluttering up the cramped cabin. He eyed his own couch longingly, then turned to Traub instead.

"Out of there, Mannie," he ordered. "I'll relieve you while you catch some shut-eye."

"Me? Oh, that's all right, Skipper. You get some sleep yourself and I'll take a rain check."

Barnes hesitated. "Sure you don't want to be relieved?"

"Not a bit. I feel—" He broke off and added, "Just a minute," and turned to his controls. He was on earphones now, rather than speaker. He settled them in place and said sharply, "Go ahead, Earth."

Presently Traub turned to Barnes: "Chicago *Tribune*—they want an exclusive story from you."

"No, I'm going to sleep."

Traub reported Barnes' answer, then turned back. "How about the Admiral or Doctor Corley?"

"The co-pilot is asleep and Doctor Corley is not to be disturbed."

"Mr. Barnes?" Traub's manner was diffident. "Do you mind if they get one from *me?*"

Barnes chuckled. "Not at all. But stick them plenty."

As Barnes closed his eyes he could hear Traub dickering with some faceless negotiator. He wondered if Traub would ever get to spend the fee? What was a man like Traub doing up here anyhow, in a ship headed nowhere in a hell of a hurry?

For that matter, why was Jim Barnes here?

After his interview, Traub continued guarding the radio. Signals grew fainter and presently reduced to garble. The room was quiet, save for the soft murmur of the air replenisher.

❖

After a long time the radio came suddenly to life—NAA, Washington, Traub soon learned, had rigged a reflector to beam directly at them. "Can you take code groups?" he was asked.

He assured them that he could. "Despatch for Rear Admiral Bowles," NAA rapped back at him. "Zero zero zero one: Code groups follow—love, uncle, king, easy, roger—boy, able, dog, item, peter—" The groups continued for a long time.

"Doctor Corley!"

Corley looked around vaguely, as if awakening in a strange place. "Eh? Yes, Mannie? I'm busy."

"Doctor Hastings calling."

"Oh, fine," Corley acknowledged. "Slide out of there and let me take it."

They changed places with effort, bothered by weightlessness. Traub felt a touch on his arm. "What is it, Mannie?"

He turned; Barnes and Bowles had waked up and loosed themselves. "Howdy, Skipper. It's Doctor Hastings."

"Good!"

"Uh, Admiral—got something for you." Traub hauled out the code dispatch.

Bowles stared at it. Barnes remarked, "Race results?"

Bowles did not answer. He shoved himself toward the forward bulkhead, as far away as possible. He then took a thin book from an inner pocket, and started studying the message with the aid of the book. Barnes looked surprised but said nothing.

Hastings' report was short but not sweet. They would reach the Moon's orbit where planned, but more than fifty hours too soon—and would miss the Moon by more than 90,000 miles!

Barnes whistled. "Hot pilot Barnes, they call me."

Corley said, "It's no joke."

"I wasn't laughing, Doc," Barnes answered, "but there is no use crying. It will be tragic soon enough."

Traub broke in. "Hey—what do you mean?"

"He means," Bowles said bluntly, "that we are headed out and aren't coming back."

"On out? And out—out into outer space? Where the stars are?"

"That's about it."

"Not that," Corley interrupted, "I'd estimate that we would reach our farthest point somewhere around the orbit of Mars."

Traub sighed. "So it's Mars, now? That's not so bad, is it? I mean they say people live on Mars, don't they? All those canals and things? We can get another load of water and come back."

"Don't kid yourself, Mannie," Bowles said. "Just be glad you're a bachelor."

"A bachelor? Who said I was?"

"Aren't you?"

"Me? I'm a very domestic type guy. Four kids—and married fourteen years."

Corley looked stricken. "Mannie, I didn't know."

"What's that got to do with it? Insurance I've got, with a rocket experimentation rider. I knew this was no picnic."

Barnes said, "Mannie, if I had known, I wouldn't have asked you to go. I'm sorry." He turned to Corley, "When do we run out of water—and air?"

Corley raised his voice. "Please! Everybody! I didn't say we weren't going to get back. I said—"

"But you—"

"Shut *up*, Red! I said *this* orbit is no good. We've got to vector west, toward the Moon. And we've got to do it at—" He glanced at a clock. "Good grief! Seven minutes from now."

Barnes jerked his head around. "Acceleration stations, everybody! Stand by to maneuver!"

CHAPTER SEVEN

The most treacherous maneuver known to space flight is a jet landing on an airless planet. Even today, it commands the highest pay, the most skilled pilots—

Farquharson, *Ibid.,* III: 418

For forty hours they fell toward the Moon. The maneuver had worked; one could see, even with naked eye, that they were closing with the Moon. The four took turns at the radio, ate and slept and talked and stared out at the glittering sky. Bowles and Traub discovered a common passion for chess and played off the "First Annual Interplanetary Championship"—so dubbed by the Admiral—using pencil marks on paper.

Traub won, four out of seven.

Some two hundred thousand miles out the *Luna* slid past the null point between Earth and Moon, and began to shape her final orbit. It became evident that the correction vector had somewhat overcompensated and that they were swinging toward the Moon's western limb—"western" as seen from Earth: the *Luna*'s orbit would intersect her namesake somewhere on the never-yet-seen far side—or it was possible that the ship would skim the far side at high speed, come around sharply and head back toward Earth.

Two principal styles of landing were possible—Type A, in which a ship heads in vertically, braking on her jets to a landing in one maneuver, and Type B, in which a ship is first slowed to a circular orbit, then stopped dead, then backed to a landing when she drops from the point of rest.

"Type A, Jim—it's simplest."

Barnes shook his head. "No, Doc. Simple on paper only. Too risky." If they corrected course to head straight in (Type A), their speed at instant of braking would be a mile and a half a second and an error of one second would land them 8000 feet above—or below!—the surface.

Barnes went on, "How about a modified 'A'?"

Modified Type A called for intentionally blasting too soon, then cutting the jets when the radar track showed that the ship hovered, allowing it to fall from rest, then blasting again as necessary, perhaps two or three times.

"Confound it, Jim, a modified 'A' is so damned wasteful."

"I'd like to get us down without wrecking us."

"And I would like us to get home, too. This ship was figured for a total change of twelve and a half miles per second. Our margin is paper thin."

"Just the same, I'd like to set the autopilot to kick her a couple of seconds early."

"We can't afford it and that's that."

"Land her yourself, then. I'm not Superman."

"Now, Jim—"

"Sorry." Barnes looked at the calculations. "But why Type A? Why not Type B?"

"But Jim, Type B is probably ruled out. It calls for decelerating at point of closest approach and, as things stand now, 'closest approach' may be contact."

"Crash, you mean. But don't be so damned conventional; you can vector into a circular orbit from any position."

"But that wastes reaction mass, too."

"Crashing from a sloppy Type A wastes more than reaction mass," Barnes retorted. "Get to work on a 'B'; I won't risk an 'A.' "

Corley looked stubborn. Barnes went on, "There's a bonus with Type B, Doc—two bonuses."

"Don't be silly. Done perfectly, it takes as much reaction mass as Type A; done sloppily, it takes more."

"I won't be sloppy. Here's your bonus: Type A lands us on this face, but Type B lets us swing around the Moon and *photograph the back side* before we land. How does that appeal to your scientific soul?"

Corley looked tempted. "I thought about that, but we've got too little margin. It takes a mile and a half of motion to get down to the Moon, the same to get up—three miles. For the trip back I have to save enough mass to slow from seven miles a second to five before we dip into the atmosphere. We used up seven to blast off—it all adds up to twelve. Look at the figures; what's left?"

Barnes did so and shrugged. "Looks like a slightly fat zero."

"A few seconds of margin at most. You could waste it on the transitions in a Type B landing."

"Now the second bonus, Doc," Barnes said slowly. "The Type B gives you a chance to change your mind after you get into a circular orbit; the straight-in job commits you beyond any help."

Corley looked shocked. "Jim, you mean go back to Earth *without landing?*"

Barnes lowered his voice. "Wait, Doc. I'd land on the Moon if I had enough in tanks to get down—and not worry about getting up again. I'm a bachelor. But there's Mannie Traub. No getting around it; we stampeded him. Now it turns out he has a slew of kids, waiting for poppa to come home. It makes a difference."

Corley pulled at his scalp lock. "He should have told us."

"If he had, we wouldn't have taken off."

"Confound it, things would have been all right if I hadn't suggested that you test the engine."

"Nonsense! If I hadn't scared those babies off with a blast, they probably would have wrecked the ship."

"You can't be sure."

"A man can't be sure of anything. How about Traub?"

"You're right—I suppose. Okay, we leave it up to Traub."

From the other end of the compartment Traub looked around from his chess game with Bowles.

"Somebody call me?"

"Yes," Barnes agreed. "Both of you. We've got things to decide."

Barnes outlined the situation. "Now," he said, "Doc and I agree that, after we get into a circular orbit and have had time to add up what's left, Mannie should decide whether we land, or just swing around and blast for home."

Bowles looked amazed, but said nothing.

Traub looked flustered. "Me? It ain't my business to decide. I'm the electronics department."

"Because," Barnes stated, "you're the only one with kids."

"Yes, but—Look here—is there really a chance that, if we landed, we wouldn't be able to get back?"

"Possible," Barnes answered and Corley nodded.

"But don't you *know*?"

"Look, Mannie," Barnes countered, "we've got water in the tanks to land, take off, and return to Earth—but none for mistakes."

"Yes, but you won't make any mistakes, will you?"

"I can't promise. I've already made one and it's brought us to this situation."

Traub's features worked in agonized indecision. "But it's not my business to decide!"

Bowles spoke up suddenly. "You're right; it's not!" He went on, "Gentlemen, I didn't intend to speak, because it never crossed my mind that we might not land. But now the situation demands it. As you know, I received a coded message.

"The gist was this: our trip has caused grave international repercussions. The Security Council has been in constant session, with the U.S.S.R. demanding that the Moon be declared joint property of the United Nations—"

"As it should be," Corley interrupted.

"You don't see the point, Doctor. Their only purpose is to forestall us claiming the Moon—*we,* who actually are making the trip. To forestall us, you understand, so that the United States will not be able to found a base on the Moon without permission—permission that is certain to be vetoed."

"But," pointed out Corley, "it works both ways. We would veto Russia establishing a base on the Moon. Admiral, I've worked with you because it was a way to get on with my life's ambition, but, to be frank, using the Moon as a rocket launching base—by *anybody*—sticks in my craw."

Bowles turned red. "Doctor, this is not an attempt to insure the neutrality of the Moon; this is the same double-talk they used to stop world control of atomics. The commissars simply want to tie us up in legalisms until *they* have time to get to the Moon. We'll wake up one morning to find Russia with a base on the Moon and us with none—and World War Three will be over before it starts."

"But—Admiral, you can't know that."

Bowles turned to Barnes. "Tell him, Jim."

Barnes gestured impatiently. "Come out of your ivory tower, Doc. Space travel is here now—we did it. There is bound to be a rocket base on the Moon. Sure, it ought to be a United Nations base, keeping the peace of the world. But the United Nations has been helpless from scratch. The first base is going to belong to us—or to Russia. Which one do you trust not to misuse the power? Us—or the Politburo?"

Corley covered his eyes, then looked at Bowles. "All right," he said dully. "It has to be—but I don't like it."

Traub broke the ensuing silence with "Uh, I don't see how this ties in with whether we land or not?"

Bowles turned to him. "Because of this: the rest of that message restored me to active duty and directed me to claim the Moon in the name of the United States—as quickly as possible. We would have what the diplomats call a *fait accompli*. But to claim the Moon *I have to land!*"

Traub stared. "Oh. I see."

Bowles went on in a gentle voice, "Mannie, this goes beyond you and me, or even your kids. The surest way to make sure that your kids grow up in a peaceful, free world is to risk your neck right now. So we've *got* to land."

Traub hesitated; Bowles went on, "You see that, don't you? It's for your kids—and millions of other kids."

Barnes interrupted him. "Red—quit working on him!"

"Eh?"

"He'll make a free choice—after we've leveled off and looked the situation over."

"But, Jim, I thought we saw eye to eye. You told Doc—"

"Pipe down! You've stated your case, now quit trying to work him up into being a martyr."

Bowles turned bright red. "I must inform you, sir, that besides being returned to active duty I was given authority to commandeer this ship."

Barnes locked eyes with him. "You can take your authority and—do whatever you think proper with it. I'm skipper and will stay so as long as I'm alive." He looked around. "All hands—get ready for approach. Doc, go ahead with trial calculations, Type B. Mannie, warm up the pilot radar. Bowles!"

Finally Bowles answered, "Yes, sir."

"Rig the autocamera in the starboard port. We'll take a continuous strip as we pass around the far side."

"Aye aye, sir."

Traub leaned from his couch and peered out the starboard port. "It's just like the other side."

Barnes answered, "What did you expect? Skyscrapers? Co-pilot, how do you track?"

"Speed over ground—one point three seven. Altitude, fifty-one point two, closing slowly."

"Check. I project closest approach at not less than twenty-one—no contact. What do you get?"

"Closer to twenty, but no contact."

"Check. Take over orientation. I'll blast when altitude changes from steady to opening."

"Aye aye, sir!"

The *Luna* was swinging around the unknown far face of the Moon, but her crew was too busy to see much of the craggy, devil-torn landscape. She was nearing her closest approach, travelling almost horizontally. She was pointed tail first, ready to blast back from a top speed of a mile and a half a second to a circular orbit speed of a mile a second. At Barnes' order Bowles gave his attention to placing her axis precisely horizontal.

The television screen read "View Aft"; in its center was a cross mark lying over a picture of the mountainous horizon they were approaching. He jockeyed the ship against the reaction of the flywheel, then steadied her by gyros when one cross line held steady on the horizon.

Barnes set his controls on semiautomatic, ready both to fire and cut off with one punch of the firing button. Into his autopilot he fed the speed change he wished to achieve. Altitude dropped to forty miles, to thirty, to less than twenty-five. "Power plant," Barnes called out, "stand by for blasting!"

"Ready, Jim," Corley reported quietly.

"Electronics?"

"Everything sweet, Skipper."

Barnes watched ground speed with one eye, the radar altimeter with the other . . . twenty-three, it said . . . twenty-two . . . twenty-one and a half. . . .

Twenty-one point five . . . twenty-one point four—point four again—and again. Point five! and crawling up. His finger stabbed at the firing button.

The blast was fourteen seconds only, then it cut off, but in the same mushy fashion which it had before. Barnes shook his head to clear it and looked at his board. Altitude twenty-one point five; ground speed, one plus a frog's whisker—they were in orbit as planned. He sighed happily. "That's all for now, troops. Leave everything hot but you can get out of your hammocks."

Bowles said, "Hadn't I better stay and watch the board?"

"Suit yourself—but they won't repeal the law of gravitation. Doc, let's see how much juice we have left." He glanced at a clock. "We've got an hour to make a decision. It will be almost half an hour before Earth is in sight again."

"I don't like the way she cuts off," Corley complained.

"Quit fretting. I used to have a car that sounded its horn every time I made a left turn."

Bowles got a container of coffee, then joined Traub at the starboard port. They peered around the automatic camera and watched the moonscape slide past. "Rugged terrain," Bowles remarked.

Traub agreed. "There's better stuff going to waste in California."

They continued to stare out. Presently Bowles turned in the air and slithered back to his acceleration couch.

"Traub!"

Mannie came to the desk. "Mannie," Barnes said, pointing at a lunar map, "we figure to land spang in the middle of the Earthside face—that dark spot, *Sinus Medii*. It's a plain."

"You figure to land, then?"

"It's up to you, Mannie. But you'll have to make up your mind. We'll be there in about—uh, forty minutes."

Traub looked troubled. "Look, chief, you shouldn't—"

He was interrupted by Bowles' voice. "Captain! We are closing, slowly."

"Are you sure?"

"Quite sure. Altitude nineteen point three—correction: point two . . . closing."

"Acceleration stations!"

Barnes was diving toward his couch as he shouted. Traub and Corley followed him. As he strapped down Barnes called out, "Co-pilot—get a contact prediction. All hands, stand by for maneuvers." He studied his own board. He could not doubt it; they were in something less than a perfect circle.

He was trying to make a prediction from his display when Bowles reported, "I make it contact in nine minutes, Captain, plus or minus a minute."

Barnes concentrated. The radar track was jiggling as much as five or ten percent, because of mountains below them; the prediction line was a broad band. As near as he could tell, Bowles was right.

"What now, Captain?" Bowles went on. "Shall I swing her to blast forward?" A slight nudge would speed up the ship, in effect, lift her, permit her to *fall around* the Moon rather than curve down.

It would also waste reaction mass.

Nine minutes . . . nine hundred miles, about. He tried to figure how many minutes it would be until they raised Earth over the horizon, ahead.

Seven minutes, possibly—and Earth would be in sight. A landing at *Sinus Medii* was impossible but they still might land in sight of Earth without using more precious water to correct their orbit. "Mannie," he snapped, "we land in seven minutes—or we never land. *Make up your mind!*"

Traub did not answer.

Barnes waited, while a minute coursed by. Finally he said in a weary voice, "Co-pilot—swing to blast forward. All hands, prepare for departure."

Traub suddenly spoke up. "That's what we came for, wasn't it? To land on the Moon? Well, let's land the damn thing!"

Barnes caught his breath. "Good boy! Co-pilot, cancel that last. Steady ship for deceleration. Sing out when you see Earth."

"Aye aye, sir!"

"There's Earth!"

Barnes glanced up, saw Terra pictured in the TV screen, rising behind a wall of mountains. Bowles went on, "Better land, Jim. You'll never get over those mountains."

Barnes did not argue; their altitude was barely three miles now. He shouted, "Stand by. Red, start swinging as soon as I cut off."

"Right!"

"Fire!" He stabbed the button. This maneuver was manual, intended only to stop their forward motion. He watched his ground-speed radar while the ship shivered—nine-tenths . . . seven . . . five . . . four . . . three . . . two . . . one . . . six-hundredths. He jerked his finger off just before it dropped to zero and prayed that a mushy cutoff would equal his anticipation.

He started to shout to Bowles, but the ship was already swinging.

Earth and the horizon swung up in the TV screen and out of sight.

For a crawling ten seconds, while they fell straight down, the *Luna* crept into position for a tail-first landing. They were less than three miles up now. Barnes shifted scale from miles to feet and started his prediction.

Bowles beat him to an answer. "Contact in seventy-two seconds, Skipper."

Barnes relaxed. "See the advantage of a Type 'B' landing, Doc," he remarked cheerfully. "No hurry—just like an elevator."

"Quit gabbing and get us down," Corley answered tautly.

"Right," Barnes agreed. "Co-pilot, predict the blast altitude." His own hands were busy to the same end.

Bowles answered, "Jim, you going manual or automatic?"

"Don't know yet." Automatic firing was quicker, possibly more certain—but that mushy cutoff could bounce them like a pingpong ball. He steadied cross-hairs on his autopilot display and read the answer: "Blast at five two oh feet. What do you get, Red?"

"Check." Bowles added, "That's less than three seconds blast, Jim. Better make it automatic."

"Tend to your knitting."

"My mistake."

Nearly forty seconds passed and they had fallen to eleven thousand feet before he decided. "Power plant, set for manual landing. Co-pilot, cover me at five hundred feet."

"Jim, that's too late," Bowles protested.

"You will be covering me all of a tenth of a second after I should fire."

Bowles subsided. Barnes grabbed a glance at the TV screen; the ground under them seemed level and there was no perceptible drift. He looked back at his board. "Correction—cover at five ten."

"Five ten—right."

The seconds clicked past; he had his finger poised over the button when Bowles shouted, "Jim—look at the screen!"

He looked up—the *Luna,* still carrying a trifle of drift, was now over a long crack, or rill—and they were about to land in it.

Barnes jabbed the button.

He let up at once; the *Luna* coughed to silence. The rill, canyon, or crevasse was still in sight but no longer centered. "Co-pilot—new prediction!"

"What happened?" Corley demanded.

"Quiet!"

"Prediction," Bowles chanted, "blast at—at three nine oh."

Barnes was adjusting verniers for his own prediction as Bowles reported. "Check," he answered. "Cover at three seven oh." He threw one glance at the TV screen. The crevasse was toward the edge of the screen; the ground below looked fairly smooth. Unquestionably the ship had a slight drift. All he could do was hope that the gyros would keep them from toppling. *"Brace for crash!"*

480—450—400—He jabbed the button.

The terrible pressure shoved his head back; he lost sight of the altimeter. He caught it again—190—150—125—

At "fifty" he snatched his finger away and prayed.

The jet cut off sloppily as always. A grinding jar slammed him more deeply into the cushions. The ship lurched like an unsteady top—and stayed upright.

Barnes found that he had been holding his breath a long time.

CHAPTER EIGHT

Columbus found a pleasant climate, rich land, docile natives. Nowhere in our System did explorers find conditions friendly to men—and nowhere was this more brutally true than on our nearest neighbor.

Farquharson, *Ibid.,* III: 420

Barnes felt dazed, as if wakening from a confusing dream. Bowles' voice recalled him to the present. "Jacks are down, skipper. Unclutch the gyros?"

He pulled himself together. "Check our footing first. I'll—Say! *We're on the Moon!*" Frantically he unstrapped.

"We sure are!" answered Bowles. "A fine landing, Jim. I was scared."

"It was terrible, and you know it."

"We're alive, aren't we? Never mind—*we made it.*"

Corley interrupted them. "Power plant secured."

Barnes looked startled. "Oh, sure. Traub, your department okay?"

Mannie answered weakly, "I guess so. I think I fainted."

"Nonsense!" Bowles reassured him. "Come on—let's look."

The four crowded at the portside port and stared out across an umber plain, baking under an unchecked sun, now not far from zenith. Miles away, jutting up into black, star-studded sky, were the peaks they had seen. In the middle distance was a single pock mark, a crater a mile or less across. Nothing else broke the flat desolation . . . endless, lifeless waste, vacuum sharp and kiln dry.

Traub broke the silence with an awed whisper. "Gosh, what a place! How long do we stay, Mr. Barnes?"

"Not long, Mannie." He tried to make his words carry conviction. "Doc," he went on, "let's check the mass ratio."

"Okay, Jim."

Bowles went to the starboard port; one glance through it and he sang out, "Hey—see this."

They joined him. Below was the dark chasm in which they had almost landed. It ran close to the ship; one jack almost touched the edge. Barnes looked down into its awesome depths and felt no regret about expending mass to avoid it.

Bowles stared at it. "I repeat, Jim, a fine landing."

"Too close for comfort."

Bowles pushed his face to the quartz and tried to see farther to right and left. "I'm turned around," he complained. "Which way is Earth?"

"Earth is east, of course," Corley answered.

"Which way is east?"

"Man, you certainly are confused. East is out the other port."

"But it *can't* be. We looked out there first and Earth wasn't in sight." Bowles crossed back to the other port. "See?"

Corley joined him. "That's east," he stated. "Look at the stars."

Bowles looked. "But something is screwy. I saw Earth before we landed, in the screen. You saw it, didn't you, Jim?"

"Yes, I saw it."

"You, Doc?"

"I was too busy. How high was it?"

"Just rising. But I *saw* it."

Corley looked at the sky, then at the mountains. "Sure, you did. And it's there—back of those mountains."

Barnes whistled tonelessly. "That's it. I've landed us a few miles too short."

Bowles looked whipped. "Out of line-of-sight," he said dully. "I could claim it until hell freezes—and I can't get the message back."

Traub looked startled. "We're cut off from Earth? But I saw it, too."

"Sure, you did," agreed Barnes, "you saw it while we had altitude. Now we're down too low."

"Oh." Traub looked out. "But it isn't serious, is it? Earth is back of those mountains—but it's in the east; it will rise after a bit. How fast does the Moon turn? Twenty-eight days and something?"

Barnes turned to Corley. "You tell him, Doc."

"Mannie—the Earth doesn't rise or set."

"Huh?"

"The Moon keeps the same face to the Earth all the time. From any one spot, the Earth doesn't move; it just hangs."

"Huh?" Traub raised his hands, stared at them; it could be seen that he was visualizing it, using his fists for Earth and Moon. "Oh—I get it." He looked dismayed. "Say, that's bad. That's really bad."

"Snap out of it, Mannie," Barnes said quickly. "If we can't contact Earth, we'll just have to wait until we get back." He said nothing about his own fears.

Bowles smashed a fist into a palm. "We've got to contact Earth! It doesn't matter whether we get back; four casualties is cheap. But to get a message through now—*this* message, that a United States vessel has landed and taken possession—can mean the salvation of the United States." He turned to Corley. "Doctor, we have enough power to lift us over those mountains, haven't we?"

"Eh? Why, yes."

"Then let's do it—now." He turned toward his couch.

"Hold it, Red!" Bowles stopped; Barnes went on, "If we make one lift and drop, to near those mountains, you know what that does to our chances of getting back."

"Of course! It's not important; we owe it to our country."

"Maybe so. Maybe not." Barnes paused. "If it turns out that we don't have enough juice left to break free of the Moon, I'll concede your point."

"Jim Barnes, we can't consider ourselves against the safety of our country."

"Speak for yourself, Red. Conceded that a claim to the Moon might help out the State Department this week—again it might not. It might stimulate Russia into going all out for space travel while the United States stumbles along as before, proud that we claimed it, but unwilling to spend real money to make it stick."

"Jim, that's sophistry."

"So? That's my decision. We'll try everything else first. You don't know you can't get a message through. Why don't you try?"

"When we're not in line-of-sight? Don't be silly."

"Earth is not far down behind those mountains. Find a place that *is* line-of-sight."

"Oh. Now you make sense." Bowles looked out at the mountains. "I wonder how far away they are?"

"Tell you in a moment," Traub offered. "Wait till I swing the soup bowl around." He started for his couch.

"Never mind, Mannie!" put in Barnes. "No—go ahead. It won't hurt to know. But I wasn't talking about the mountains, Red. They are too far away. But if you scout around, you may find a spot from which the mountains are low enough to let you see Earth. Or you might find some hills—we can't see all around from inside here. Mannie, is it possible to take out the radio and use it outside the ship?"

"Outside? Let me see— The transmitter is unpressurized; I guess I could jigger it. How about power?"

Bowles said, "Doc, how much cable can we dig up?"

Barnes cut in, "Find your spot, then we'll see what's needed."

"Right! Jim, I'll go out at once. Mannie, come with me and we'll find a spot."

"Outside?" Traub said blankly.

"Sure. Don't you want to be the first man to set foot on the Moon?"

"Uh, I guess so." Traub peered out at the blazing unfriendly surface.

Corley got an odd look; Barnes noted it and said, "One moment, Red. Doc is entitled to the honor of being first. After all, the Corley engine made it possible."

"Oh, sure! Doc can be first down the ladder. Let's all go."

"I'll go later," Barnes decided. "I've got work to do."

"As you wish. Come on, Doc."

Corley looked shy. "Oh, I don't have to be first. We all did it, together."

"Don't be modest. Into our suits—let's go!" Thoughts of military policy seemed to have left Bowles' mind; he was for the moment boyishly eager for adventure. He was already undogging the hatch that led down into the airlock.

Barnes helped them dress. The suits were modifications of high-altitude pressure suits used by jet pilots—cumbersome, all-enclosing skins not unlike diving suits and topped off with "goldfish bowl" helmets. The helmets were silvered except for the face plates; a walkie-talkie radio, two oxygen bottles, and an instrument belt completed the main features of a suit. When they were dressed but not helmeted, Barnes said, "Stay in sight of the ship and each other. Red, when you shift from tank one to tank two, git for home and don't dawdle."

"Aye aye."

"I'm going now." He gasketed their helmets, leaving Corley to the last. To him he said softly, "Don't stay long. I need you."

Corley nodded. Barnes fastened the doctor's helmet, then climbed up into the control room and closed the hatch. Corley waited until Barnes was clear, then said, "Check radios. Check instruments."

"Okay, Doctor," Traub's voice sounded in his earphones.

"Okay here," added Bowles.

"Ready for decompression?" They assented; Corley touched a button near the door; there came a muted whine of impellers. Gradually his suit began to lift and swell. The feeling was not new; he had practiced in their own vacuum chamber back at Mojave. He wondered how Traub felt; the first experience with trusting a Rube Goldberg skin could be frightening. "How are you doing, Mannie?"

"All right."

"The first time seems odd, I know."

"But it's not the first time," Traub answered. "I checked these walkie-talkies in the chamber at the job."

"If you gentlemen are through chatting," Bowles cut in, "you'll note that the tell-tale reads 'vacuum.'"

"Eh?" Corley turned and undogged the outer door.

He stood in the door, gazing north. The aching, sun-drenched plain stretched to a black horizon. On his right, knife sharp in the airless moonscape, was the wall of mountains they had grounded to avoid. He lifted his eyes and made out the Big Dipper, midnight clear above a dazzling, noonday desert.

Bowles touched his arm. "One side, Doc. I'll rig the ladder."

"Sorry."

Bowles linked the ends of a rope ladder to hooks outside the door. Finished, he kicked the ladder out. "Go ahead, Doc."

"Uh, thanks." Corley felt for the first rung. It was a clumsy business in the pressure suit. Finally he knelt, grasped the threshold, got a toe in and started down.

It was awkward, rather than hard work. Suit and all, he weighed less than forty pounds. He found it easier to lower himself by his hands alone. He could not see below his chin, but the shape of the ship let him know his progress. Finally he was even with the jets. He lowered himself a bit more, felt for the ground—and kicked his toe into the lunar soil.

Then he was standing on it.

He stood there a moment, his heart pounding. He was trying to realize it, take it in, and found himself unable to do so. He had lived the moment too many thousands of times in too many years of dreams. It was still a dream.

A foot brushed his shoulder; he stepped back to avoid being stepped on by Traub. Soon Bowles joined them. "So this is it," the Admiral said inanely and turned slowly around. "Look, Mannie! Hills! Not far away."

Corley saw that Bowles was looking under the jets to the south. The plain was broken there with a sharp eruption of rock. Corley touched Bowles' arm. "Let's get away from the ship. Here where the jets splashed is probably a bit radioactive."

"Okay." Bowles followed him; Traub brought up the rear.

CHAPTER NINE

Columbus had one motive; Queen Isabella had another—
Farquharson, *Ibid.*, III:421

On climbing back into the control room Barnes did not immediately get to work. Instead he sat down and thought. For the last—two days, was it? three days? four days, really—he had had no chance to collect his thoughts, drop his public mask and invite his soul.

He felt unutterably weary.

He lifted his eyes to the mountains. There they stood, tall and forbidding, witnesses that he had accomplished his driving purpose.

To what end? To let Corley explore the dark outer reaches of science? To help Bowles insure the safety of western civilization—or perhaps hasten a new crisis?

Or to make orphans of four kids whose old man was "a very domestic type guy" but could be shamed into coming along?

No, he knew it had been because Jimmy Barnes had been small for his age, clumsy with his fists, no decent clothes—so he had to make more money, boss more men, build faster planes than anyone else. He, James A. Barnes, had reached the Moon because he had never been sure of himself.

He wondered about Mannie's kids and his stomach was a rock inside him.

He threw off the mood and went to the radio controls, keyed the walkie-talkie circuit and called out, "This is Jim Barnes, kiddies, coming to you by courtesy of 'SLUMP,' the Super soap. Come in, come in, wherever you are!"

"Jim!" Bowles' voice came back. "Come on out."

"Later," Barnes answered. "Where's Doc?"

"Right here," Corley answered. "I was just coming back."

"Good," said Barnes. "Red, I'll leave this switched on. Sing out now and then."

"Sure thing," Bowles agreed.

Barnes went to the desk and began toting up mass reserves. An orbit computation is complicated; calculating what it takes to pull free of a planet is simple; he had a rough answer in a few minutes.

He ran his hand through his hair. He still needed that haircut—and no barbers on *this* block. He wondered if it were true that a man's hair continued to grow after his death.

The hatch creaked and Corley climbed into the room. "Whew!" he said. "It's good to get out of that suit. That sun is really hot."

"Wasn't the gas expansion enough to keep you cool?"

"Not cool enough. Those suits are hard to get around in, too, Jim—they need a lot of engineering."

"They'll get it," Barnes answered absently, "but reengineering this ship is more urgent. Not the Corley engine, Doc; the controls. They aren't delicate enough."

"I know," Corley admitted. "That poor cutoff—we'll have to design a prediction for it into the autopilot, and use a feedback loop."

Barnes nodded. "Yes, sure, *after* we get back—and if we get back." He tossed his fingers at the scientist. "Hum that through."

Corley glanced at it. "I know."

"Red won't find a spot in line-of-sight with home; those mountains are infernally high. But I wanted him out of the way—and Mannie. No use talking to Red; he's going to get a posthumous Congressional Medal if it kills him—and us too."

Corley nodded. "But I'm with him on trying to contact Earth; I need it worse than he does."

"Hastings?"

"Yes. Jim, if we had enough margin, we could blast off and correct after radio contact. We haven't; if we get off at all it will be close."

"I know. I spent our ticket home, when I made that extra blast."

"What good would it have done to have crashed? Forget it; I need Hastings. We need the best orbit possible."

"Fat chance!"

"Maybe not. There's libration, you know."

Barnes looked startled. "Man, am I stupid!" He went on eagerly, "What's the situation now? Is Earth swinging up, or down?"

The Moon's spin is steady, but its orbit speed is not; it moves fastest when it is closest to Earth. The amount is slight, but it causes the Moon to appear to wobble each month as if the Man-in-the-Moon were shaking his head. This moves the Earth to-and-fro in the lunar sky some seven degrees.

Corley answered, "It's rising—I think. As to whether it will rise enough—well, I'll have to compute Earth's position and then take some star sights."

"Let's get at it. Can I help?"

Before Corley could reply Bowles' voice came over the speaker: "Hey! Jim!"

Barnes keyed the walkie-talkies. "Yes, Red?"

"We're at the hills south of the ship. They might be high enough. I want to go behind them; there may be an easier place to climb."

On the airless Moon, all radio requires line-of-sight—yet Barnes hated to refuse a reasonable request. "Okay—but don't take any chances."

"Aye aye, Skipper."

Barnes turned to Corley. "We need the time anyhow."

"Yes," Corley agreed. "You know, Jim, this isn't the way I imagined it. I don't mean the Moon itself—just wait until we get some pressurized buildings here and some decent pressure suits. But what I mean is what we find ourselves doing. I expected to cram every minute with exploring and collecting specimens and gathering new data. Instead I'll beat my brains out simply trying to get us back."

"Well, maybe you'll have time later—too much time."

Corley grudged a smile. "Could be—"

He sketched out the relative positions of Earth and Moon, consulted tables. Presently he looked up. "We're in luck. Earth will rise nearly two and a half degrees before she swings back."

"Is that enough?"

"We'll see. Dig out the sextant, Jim." Barnes got it and Corley took it to the eastern port. He measured the elevations of three stars above the tops of the mountains. These he plotted on a chart and drew a line for the apparent horizon. Then he plotted Earth's position relative to those stars.

"Finicky business," he complained. "Better check me, Jim."

"I will. What do you get?"

"Well—if I haven't dropped a decimal point, Earth will be up for a few hours anyway three days from now."

Barnes grinned. "We'll get a ticker-tape parade yet, Doc."

"Maybe. Let's have another look at the ballistic situation first."

Barnes' face sobered.

Corley worked for an hour, taking Barnes' approximation and turning it into something slightly better. At last he stopped. "I don't know," he fretted. "Maybe Hastings can trim it a little."

"Doc," Barnes answered, "suppose we jettison everything we can? I hate to say it, but there's all that equipment you brought."

"What do you think I've been doing with these weight schedules? Theoretically the ship is stripped."

"Oh. And it's still bad?"

"It's still bad."

Bowles and Traub returned worn out and just short of sun stroke.

The Admiral was unhappy; he had not been able to find any way to climb the hills: "I'll go back tomorrow," he said stoutly. "I mean after we've eaten and slept."

"Forget it," advised Barnes.

"What do you mean?"

"We are going to have line-of-sight from here."

"Eh? Repeat that."

"Libration," Barnes told him. "Doc has already calculated it."

Bowles' face showed delighted comprehension. Traub looked puzzled; Barnes explained it.

"So you see," Barnes went on, "we'll have a chance to send a message in about seventy hours."

Bowles stood up, his fatigue forgotten. "That's all we need!" He pounded his palm exultantly.

"Slow down, Red," Barnes advised, "our chances of taking off look worse than ever."

"So?" Bowles shrugged. "It's not important."

"Oh, for Pete's sake! Drop the Nathan Hale act. Have the common decency to give a thought to Mannie and his four kids."

Bowles started to retort, stopped—then went on again with dignity. "Jim, I didn't mean to annoy you. But I meant what I said. It's not important to get back, as long as our message gets through. Our mistakes will make it easier for the next expedition. In a year the United States can have a dozen ships, better ships, on the Moon. Then no country would be so foolhardy as to attack us. *That* is important; we aren't."

He went on, "Every man dies; the group goes on. You spoke of Mannie's kids. You have no children, nor has Corley. Mannie has—so I know he understands what I mean better than you do." He turned to Traub. "Well, Mannie?"

Traub looked up, then dropped his eyes. "Red is right, Mr. Barnes," he answered in a low voice, "but I'd like to get home."

Barnes bit his lip. "Let's drop it," he said irritably. "Red, you might rustle up some supper."

For three days, Earth time, they labored. Bowles and Barnes stripped the ship—cameras, empty oxygen bottles, their extra clothing, the many scientific instruments Corley had hoped to use—Wilson cloud chamber, Geiger counter, a 12" Schmidt camera and clock, still cameras, the autocamera, ultra-and infra-spectrographs, other instruments. Corley stayed at his desk, computing, checking, computing again—getting the problem in the best possible shape to turn over to

Hastings. Traub overhauled his radio and lined up his directional antenna to the exact orientation at which Earth would appear.

The hour finally crept up to them. Traub was in his couch at the radio controls while the rest crowded at the eastern port. What they needed to say had been made one message:

A formal claim to the Moon, setting forth time and place of landing, a long and technical message to Hastings, and finally code groups supplied by Bowles. Traub would send it all out as one, many times if necessary.

"I see it!" It was Corley who claimed the distinction.

Barnes stared at the spot. "Your imagination, Doc; a highlight on the peaks." The sun was behind them, "afternoon" by local time; the mountains were bright in the east.

Bowles put in, "No, Jim. There's something there."

Barnes turned. "Start sending!"

Traub closed his key.

The message was repeated, with listening in between, time after time. An arc of Earth slowly, terribly slowly, crept above the horizon. No answer came back, but they did not despair, so little of Earth was as yet in sight.

Finally Barnes turned to Corley. "What does that look like, Doc? The part we can see, I mean."

Corley peered at it. "Can't say. Too much cloud."

"It looks like ocean. If so, we won't get a jingle until it's higher."

Corley's face slowly became horror struck. "What's the matter?" demanded Barnes.

"Good grief! *I forgot to figure the attitude.*"

"Huh?"

Corley did not answer. He jumped to the desk, grabbed the Nautical Almanac, started scribbling, stopped, and drew a diagram of the positions of Earth, Sun, and Moon. On the circle representing the Earth he drew a line for the Greenwich meridian.

Barnes leaned over him. "Why the panic?"

"That *is* ocean, the Pacific Ocean."

Bowles joined them. "What about it?"

"Don't you see? Earth turns to the east; America is moving away—already out of sight." Corley hurriedly consulted his earlier calculations. "Earth reaches maximum elevation in about, uh, four hours and eight minutes. Then it drops back."

Traub pushed up an earphone. "Can't you guys shut up?" he protested. "I'm trying to listen."

Corley threw down his pencil. "It doesn't matter, Mannie. You aren't ever going to be in line-of-sight with NAA."

"Huh? What did you say?"

"The Earth is faced wrong. We're seeing the Pacific Ocean now, then we'll see Asia, Europe, and finally the Atlantic. By the time we should see the United States it will have dropped back of the mountains."

"You mean I'm just wasting time?"

"Keep sending, Mannie," Barnes said quietly, "and keep listening. You may pick up another station."

Bowles shook his head. "Not likely."

"Why not? Hawaii may still be in sight. The Pearl Harbor station is powerful."

"Provided they have rigged a beam on us, same as NAA."

"Well, keep trying, Mannie."

Traub slipped his earphone back in place. Bowles went on, "It's nothing to get excited about. We'll be picked up anywhere." He chuckled. "Soviet stations will be listening to us shortly. They will be broadcasting denials at the same time stations in Australia are telling the world the truth."

Corley looked up. "But I won't get to talk to Hastings!"

Bowles said very gently:

"As I said, that isn't important in the long run."

Barnes said, "Stow it, Red. Don't get downhearted, Doc—there is a good chance that some other station will beam us. Keep trying, Mannie."

"Will you guys *please* shut up?"

He did keep trying over and over again; in the intervals he listened, not only to the beam frequency of NAA, but all over the dial.

More than eight hours later the last faint arc of Earth had vanished. No one had thought to eat and Traub had not left his post for any purpose.

They went on preparing to leave, but their hearts were not in it. Corley stayed at his desk, except for snatches of sleep, trying to make up by effort for the lack of fine tools. He set the departure ahead to give him more time. The aching, cloudless lunar day wore on and the sun sank to the west. They planned to risk it just at sundown. It was admitted by Corley—and by Barnes, who checked his figures—that the situation theoretically did not permit success. By the book, they would rise, curve around the Moon, and approach the border where the fields of Earth and Moon balance—but they would never reach it; they would fall back and crash.

It was also agreed, by everyone, that it was better to die trying than to wait for death. Bowles suggested that they wait a month until next sight of Earth, but arithmetic shut off that chance; they would not starve; they would not die of thirst—they would suffocate.

Bowles took it serenely; Traub lay in his bunk or moved like a zombie. Corley was a gray-faced automaton, buried in figures. Barnes became increasingly irritable.

As a sop to Corley, Bowles made desultory readings on the instruments Corley had not had time to use. Among the chores was developing the films taken on the flight across the back face. It had been agreed to keep them, they weighed ounces only, and it was desirable to develop them to prevent fogging by stray radioactivity. Barnes assigned Traub the task, to keep him busy.

Traub worked in the airlock, it being the only darkroom. Presently he came poking his head up through the hatch. "Mr. Barnes?"

"Yes, Mannie?" Barnes noted with satisfaction that Traub showed his first touch of animation since his ordeal.

"See what you make of this." Traub handed him a negative. Barnes spread it against a port. "See those little round things? What are they?"

"Craters, I guess."

"No, *these* are craters. See the difference?"

Barnes tried to visualize what the negative would look like in positive. "What do you think?"

"Well, they look like hemispheres. Odd formation, huh?"

Barnes looked again. "Too damned odd," he said slowly. "Mannie, let's have a print."

"There's no print paper, is there?"

"You're right; my error."

Bowles joined them. "What's the curiosity? Moon maidens?"

Barnes showed him. "What do you make of those things?"

Bowles looked, and looked again. Finally he asked, "Mannie, how can we enlarge this?"

It took an hour to jury-rig a magic lantern, using a pilfered camera lens. They all gathered in the airlock and Traub switched on his improvised projector.

Bowles said, "Focus it, for cripes' sake." Traub did so. The images of his "hemispheres" were reasonably distinct. They were six in number, arranged in a semicircle—and they were unnatural in appearance.

Barnes peered at them. "Red—you were a bit late when you claimed this planet."

Bowles said, "Hmmm—" Finally he emphatically added, "Constructions."

"Wait a minute," protested Corley. "They *look* artificial, but some very odd formations are natural."

"Look closer, Doc," Barnes advised. "There is no reasonable doubt. The question: were we a year or so late in claiming the Moon? Or millions of years?"

"Eh?"

"Those are pressure domes. Who built them? Moon people, long before history? Visiting Martians? Or Russians?"

Traub said, "Mr. Barnes—why not *live* Moon people?"

"What? Take a walk outside."

"I don't see why not. As soon as I saw them I said, 'That's where those flying saucers came from a while back.'"

"Mannie, there were no flying saucers. Don't kid yourself."

Traub said, doggedly, "I knew a man who—"

"—saw one with his own eyes," Barnes finished. "Forget it. That's our worry—there. They're real. They show on film."

"Forget Martians, too," Bowles said gruffly, "and any long-dead Moon people."

"I take it you go for Russians?" Barnes commented.

"I simply know that those films must be in the hands of military intelligence as soon as possible."

"Military intelligence? Ah, yes, on Earth—a lovely thought."

"Don't be sarcastic. I mean it."

"So do I."

From willingness to die, his mission accomplished, Bowles became frantic to live, to get back. It made him bitter that he himself had insisted on landing—with all-important new evidence even then latent in the ship.

He sweated out a possible scheme to get the films back to Washington and seized a time when Traub was out of the ship to propose it to Barnes. "Jim—could you get this ship back by yourself?"

"What do you mean?"

"You checked the figures. One man might make it—if the ship were lightened by the other three."

Barnes looked angry. "Red, that's nonsense."

"Ask the others."

"No!" Barnes added, "Four men came; four go back—or nobody does."

"Well, *I* can lighten ship, at least. That's my privilege."

"Any more such talk and it'll be your privilege to be strapped down till takeoff!"

Bowles took Barnes' arm. "Those films have *got* to reach the Pentagon."

"Quit breathing in my face. We'll make it if we can. Have you anything left to jettison?"

"Jim, this ship gets back if I have to drag it."

"Drag it, then. Answer my question."

"I've got the clothes I stand in—I'll jettison them." Bowles looked around. "Jettison, he says. Jim Barnes, you call this ship stripped. By God, I'll show you! Where's that tool kit?"

"Traub just took it outside along with other stuff."

Bowles jumped to the microphone. "Mannie? Bring back the hacksaw; I need it!" He turned to Barnes. "I'll show you how to strip ship. What's that radio doing there? Useless as a third leg. Why do I need an autopilot display? Yours is enough. Doc—get up off that stool!"

Corley looked up from his closed world of figures. He had not even heard the row. "Eh? You called me?"

"Up off that stool—I'm going to unbolt it from the deck."

Corley looked puzzled. "Certainly, if you need it." He turned to Barnes. "Jim, these are the final figures."

Barnes was watching Bowles. "Hold the figures, Doc. We may make a few revisions."

Under the drive of Bowles' will they stripped ship again, fighting against their deadline. Rations—*all* rations—men do not starve quickly. Radios. Duplicate instruments. Engineering instruments not utterly essential to blasting. The hot plate. Cupboards and doors, light fixtures and insulation; everything that could be hacksawed away or ripped out bodily. The ladder from control room to airlock—that was kicked out last, with three space suits and the rope ladder.

Bowles found no way to get rid of the fourth pressure suit; he had to wear it to stay alive while he pushed out the last items—but he found a way to minimize even that. He removed the instrument belt, the back pack, the air bottles, the insulating shoes, and stood there, gasping the air left in the suit, while the lock cycled from "vacuum" to "pressure" for the last time.

Three hands reached down and pulled him through the hatch. "Stations!" Barnes snapped. "Stand by to blast!"

They were waiting for the count off, when Traub reached up and touched Barnes' arm. "Skipper?"

"Yes, Mannie?"

Traub looked to see if the other two were noticing; they were not. "Are we really going to make it?"

Barnes decided to be truthful. "Probably not." He glanced at Bowles; the Admiral's features were sunken; his false teeth had gone with the rest. Barnes grinned warmly. "But we're sure going to give it a try!"

The monument where the proud Luna *once stood is pictured in every schoolroom. Many trips followed, some tragic, some not, before space transportation reached its present safe operation. The spaceways are paved with the bodies and glorious hopes of pioneers. With accomplishment of their dream some of the romance has gone out of space.*

Farquharson, Ibid., III: 423.

THE YEAR OF THE JACKPOT

Galaxy Science Fiction, March 1952

CHAPTER ONE

AT FIRST POTIPHAR Breen did not notice the girl who was undressing.

She was standing at a bus stop only ten feet away. He was indoors but that would not have kept him from noticing; he was seated in a drug-store booth adjacent to the bus stop; there was nothing between Potiphar and the young lady but plate glass and an occasional pedestrian.

Nevertheless he did not look up when she began to peel. Propped up in front of him was a Los Angeles *Times;* beside it, still unopened, were the *Herald-Express* and the *Daily News.* He was scanning the newspaper carefully but the headline stories got only a passing glance. He noted the maximum and minimum temperatures in Brownsville, Texas, and entered them in a neat black notebook; he did the same with the closing prices of three blue chips and two dogs on the New York Exchange, as well as the total number of shares. He then began a rapid sifting of minor news stories, from time to time entering briefs of them in his little book; the items he recorded seemed randomly unrelated— among them a publicity release in which Miss National Cottage Cheese Week announced that she intended to marry and have twelve children by a man who could prove that he had been a life-long vegetarian, a cir-cumstantial but wildly unlikely flying saucer report, and a call for prayers for rain throughout Southern California.

Potiphar had just written down the names and addresses of three residents of Watts, California, who had been miraculously healed at a tent meeting of the God-is-All First Truth Brethren by the Reverend Dickie Bottomley, the eight-year-old evangelist, and was preparing to tackle the *Herald-Express,* when he glanced over his reading glasses and saw the amateur ecdysiast on the street corner outside. He stood up, placed his glasses in their case, folded the newspapers and put them carefully in his right coat pocket, counted out the exact amount of his check and added twenty-five cents. He then took his raincoat from a hook, placed it over his arm, and went outside.

By now the girl was practically down to the buff. It seemed to Potiphar Breen that she had quite a lot of buff. Nevertheless she had not pulled much of a house. The corner newsboy had stopped hawking his disasters and was grinning at her, and a mixed pair of transvestites who were apparently waiting for the bus had their eyes on her. None of the passers-by stopped. They glanced at her, then with the self-conscious indifference to the unusual of the true Southern Californian, they went on their various ways. The transvestites were frankly staring. The male member of the team wore a frilly feminine blouse but his skirt was a conservative Scottish kilt—his female companion wore a business suit and Homburg hat; she stared with lively interest.

As Breen approached the girl hung a scrap of nylon on the bus stop bench, then reached for her shoes. A police officer, looking hot and un-happy, crossed with the lights and came up to them. "Okay," he said in a tired voice, "that'll be all, lady. Get them duds back on and clear out of here."

The female transvestite took a cigar out of her mouth. "Just," she said, "what business is it of yours, officer?"

The cop turned to her. "Keep out of this!" He ran his eyes over her get up, that of her companion. "I ought to run both of you in, too."

The transvestite raised her eyebrows. "Arrest us for being clothed, arrest her for not being. I think I'm going to like this." She turned to the girl, who was standing still and saying nothing, as if she were puzzled by what was going on. "I'm a lawyer, dear." She pulled a card from her vest pocket. "If this uniformed Neanderthal persists in annoying you, I'll be delighted to handle him."

The man in the kilt said, "Grace! Please!"

She shook him off. "Quiet, Norman—this *is* our business." She went on to the policeman, "Well? Call the wagon. In the meantime my client will answer no questions."

The official looked unhappy enough to cry and his face was get-ting dangerously red. Breen quietly stepped forward and slipped his raincoat around the shoulders of the girl. She looked startled and spoke for the first time. "Uh—thanks." She pulled the coat about her, cape fashion.

The female attorney glanced at Breen then back to the cop. "Well, officer? Ready to arrest us?"

He shoved his face close to hers. "I ain't going to give you the sat-isfaction!" He sighed and added, "Thanks, Mr. Breen—you know this lady?"

"I'll take care of her. You can forget it, Kawonski."

"I sure hope so. If she's with you, I'll do just that. But get her out of here, Mr. Breen—please!"

The lawyer interrupted. "Just a moment—you're interfering with my client."

Kawonski said, "Shut up, you! You heard Mr. Breen—she's with him. Right, Mr. Breen?"

"Well—yes. I'm a friend. I'll take care of her."

The transvestite said suspiciously, "I didn't hear *her* say that."

Her companion said, "Grace—please! There's our bus."

"And I didn't hear her say she was your client," the cop retorted. "You look like a—" His words were drowned out by the bus's brakes. "—and besides that, if you don't climb on that bus and get off my territory, I'll . . . I'll . . ."

"You'll what?"

"Grace! We'll miss our bus."

"Just a moment, Norman. Dear, is this man really a friend of yours? Are you with him?"

The girl looked uncertainly at Breen, then said in a low voice, "Uh, yes. That's right."

"Well . . ." The lawyer's companion pulled at her arm. She shoved her card into Breen's hand and got on the bus; it pulled away.

Breen pocketed the card. Kawonski wiped his forehead. "Why did you do it, lady?" he said peevishly.

The girl looked puzzled. "I . . . I don't know."

"You hear that, Mr. Breen? That's what they all say. And if you pull 'em in, there's six more the next day. The Chief said—" He sighed. "The Chief said—well, if I had arrested her like that female shyster wanted me to, I'd be out at a hundred and ninety-sixth and Ploughed Ground tomorrow morning, thinking about retirement. So get her out of here, will you?"

The girl said, "But—"

"No 'buts,' lady. Just be glad a real gentleman like Mr. Breen is willing to help you." He gathered up her clothes, handed them to her. When she reached for them she again exposed an uncustomary amount of skin; Kawonski hastily gave them to Breen instead, who crowded them into his coat pockets.

She let Breen lead her to where his car was parked, got in and tucked the raincoat around her so that she was rather more dressed than a girl usually is. She looked at him.

She saw a medium-sized and undistinguished man who was slipping down the wrong side of thirty-five and looked older. His eyes had that mild and slightly naked look of the habitual spectacles wearer who is not at the moment with glasses; his hair was gray at the temples and thin on top. His herringbone suit, black shoes, white shirt, and neat tie smacked more of the East than of California.

He saw a face which he classified as "pretty" and "wholesome" rather than "beautiful" and "glamorous." It was topped by a healthy mop of light brown hair. He set her age at twenty-five, give or take eighteen months. He smiled gently, climbed in without speaking and started his car.

He turned up Doheny Drive and east on Sunset. Near La Cienega he slowed down. "Feeling better?"

"Uh, I guess so Mr.—'Breen'?"

"Call me Potiphar. What's your name? Don't tell me if you don't want to."

"Me? I'm . . . I'm Meade Barstow."

"Thank you, Meade. Where do you want to go? Home?"

"I suppose so. I—Oh my no! I can't go home like *this*." She clutched the coat tightly to her.

"Parents?"

"No. My landlady. She'd be shocked to death."

"Where, then?"

She thought. "Maybe we could stop at a filling station and I could sneak into the ladies' room."

"Mmm. . . . maybe. See here, Meade—my house is six blocks from here and has a garage entrance. You could get inside without being seen." He looked at her.

She stared back. "Potiphar—you don't *look* like a wolf?"

"Oh, but I am! The worst sort." He whistled and gnashed his teeth. "See? But Wednesday is my day off from it."

She looked at him and dimpled. "Oh, well! I'd rather wrestle with you than with Mrs. Megeath. Let's go."

He turned up into the hills. His bachelor diggings were one of the many little frame houses clinging like fungus to the brown slopes of the Santa Monica Mountains. The garage was notched into this hill; the house sat on it. He drove in, cut the ignition, and led her up a teetery inside stairway into the living room. "In there," he said, pointing. "Help yourself." He pulled her clothes out of his coat pockets and handed them to her.

She blushed and took them, disappeared into his bedroom. He heard her turn the key in the lock. He settled down in his easy chair, took out his notebook, and opened the *Herald-Express*.

He was finishing the *Daily News* and had added several notes to his collection when she came out. Her hair was neatly rolled; her face was restored; she had brushed most of the wrinkles out of her skirt. Her sweater was neither too tight nor deep cut, but it was pleasantly filled. She reminded him of well water and farm breakfasts.

He took his raincoat from her, hung it up, and said, "Sit down, Meade."

She said uncertainly, "I had better go."

"Go if you must—but I had hoped to talk with you."

"Well—" She sat down on the edge of his couch and looked around. The room was small but as neat as his necktie, clean as his collar. The fireplace was swept; the floor was bare and polished. Books crowded bookshelves in every possible space. One corner was filled by an elderly flat-top desk; the papers on it were neatly in order. Near it, on its own stand, was a small electric calculator. To her right, French windows gave out on a tiny porch over the garage. Beyond it she could see the sprawling city; a few neon signs were already blinking.

She sat back a little. "This is a nice room—Potiphar. It looks like you."

"I take that as a compliment. Thank you." She did not answer; he went on, "Would you like a drink?"

"Oh, would I!" She shivered. "I guess I've got the jitters."

He got up. "Not surprising. What'll it be?"

She took Scotch and water, no ice; he was a Bourbon-and-ginger-ale man. She had soaked up half her highball in silence, then put it down, squared her shoulders and said, "Potiphar?"

"Yes, Meade?"

"Look—if you brought me here to make a pass, I wish you'd go ahead and make it. It won't do you a bit of good, but it makes me nervous to wait for it."

He said nothing and did not change his expression. She went on uneasily, "Not that I'd blame you for trying—under the circumstances. And I *am* grateful. But . . . well—it's just that I don't—"

He came over and took both her hands. "My dear, I haven't the slightest thought of making a pass at you. Nor need you feel grateful. I butted in because I was interested in your case."

"My case? Are you a doctor? A psychiatrist?"

He shook his head. "I'm a mathematician. A statistician, to be precise."

"Huh? I don't get it."

"Don't worry about it. But I would like to ask some questions. May I?"

"Uh, sure, sure! I owe you that much—and then some."

"You owe me nothing. Want your drink sweetened?"

She gulped it and handed him her glass, then followed him out into the kitchen. He did an exact job of measuring and gave it back. "Now tell me why you took your clothes off?"

She frowned. "I don't know. I *don't* know. I don't *know*. I guess I just went crazy." She added round-eyed, "But I don't feel crazy. Could I go off my rocker and not know it?"

"You're not crazy . . . not more so than the rest of us," he amended. "Tell me—where did you see someone else do this?"

"Huh? But I never have."

"Where did you read about it?"

"But I haven't. Wait a minute—those people up in Canada. Dooka-somethings."

"Doukhobors. That's all? No bareskin swimming parties? No strip poker?"

She shook her head. "No. You may not believe it but I was the kind of a little girl who undressed under her nightie." She colored and added, "I still do—unless I remember to tell myself it's silly."

"I believe it. No news stories?"

"No. Yes, there was too! About two weeks ago, I think it was. Some girl in a theater, in the audience, I mean. But I thought it was just publicity. You know the stunts they pull here."

He shook his head. "It wasn't. February 3rd, the Grand Theater, Mrs. Alvin Copley. Charges dismissed."

"Huh? How did *you* know?"

"Excuse me." He went to his desk, dialed the City News Bureau. "Alf? This is Pot Breen. They still sitting on that story? . . . yes, yes, the Gypsy Rose file. Any new ones today?" He waited; Meade thought that she could make out swearing. "Take it easy, Alf—this hot weather can't last forever. Nine, eh? Well, add another—Santa Monica Boulevard, late this afternoon. No arrest." He added. "Nope, nobody got her name—a middle-aged woman with a cast in one eye. I happened to see it . . . who, me? Why would I want to get mixed up? But it's rounding up into a very, very interesting picture." He put the phone down.

Meade said, "Cast in one eye, indeed!"

"Shall I call him back and give him your name?"

"Oh, no!"

"Very well. Now, Meade, we seemed to have located the point of contagion in your case—Mrs. Copley. What I'd like to know next is how you felt, what you were thinking about, when you did it?"

She was frowning intently. "Wait a minute, Potiphar—do I understand that *nine other* girls have pulled the stunt I pulled?"

"Oh, no—nine others *today*. You are—" He paused briefly. "—the three hundred and nineteenth case in Los Angeles county since the first of the year. I don't have figures on the rest of the country, but the suggestion to clamp down on the stories came from the eastern news services when the papers here put our first cases on the wire. That proves that it's a problem elsewhere, too."

"You mean that women all over the country are peeling off their clothes in public? Why, how shocking!"

He said nothing. She blushed again and insisted, "Well, it is shocking, even if it was me, this time."

"No, Meade. One case is shocking; over three hundred makes it scientifically interesting. That's why I want to know how it felt. Tell me about it."

"But—All right, I'll try. I told you I don't know why I did it; I still don't. I—"

"You remember it?"

"Oh, yes! I remember getting up off the bench and pulling up my sweater. I remember unzipping my skirt. I remember thinking I would have to hurry as I could see my bus stopped two blocks down the street. I remember how *good* it felt when I finally, uh—" She paused and looked puzzled. "But I still don't know why."

"What were you thinking about just before you stood up?"

"I don't remember."

"Visualize the street. What was passing by? Where were your hands? Were your legs crossed or uncrossed? Was there anybody near you? What were you thinking about?"

"Uh . . . nobody was on the bench with me. I had my hands in my lap. Those characters in the mixed-up clothes were standing near by, but I wasn't paying attention. I wasn't thinking much except that my feet hurt and I wanted to get home—and how unbearably hot and sultry it was. Then—" Her eyes became distant. "—suddenly I knew what I had to do and it was very urgent that I do it. So I stood up and I . . . and I—" Her voice became shrill.

"Take it easy!" he said. "Don't do it again."

"Huh? Why, Mr. Breen! I wouldn't do anything like that."

"Of course not. Then what?"

"Why, you put your raincoat around me and you know the rest." She faced him. "Say, Potiphar, what were you doing with a raincoat? It hasn't rained in weeks—this is the driest, hottest rainy season in years."

"In sixty-eight years, to be exact."

"Huh?"

"I carry a raincoat anyhow. Uh, just a notion of mine, but I feel that when it does rain, it's going to rain awfully hard." He added, "Forty days and forty nights, maybe."

She decided that he was being humorous and laughed. He went on, "Can you remember how you got the idea?"

She swirled her glass and thought. "I simply don't know."

He nodded. "That's what I expected."

"I don't understand you—unless you think I'm crazy. Do you?"

"No. I think you had to do it and could not help it and don't know why and can't know why."

"But *you* know." She said it accusingly.

"Maybe. At least I have some figures. Ever take any interest in statistics, Meade?"

She shook her head. "Figures confuse me. Never mind statistics—*I want to know why I did what I did!*"

He looked at her very soberly. "I think we're lemmings, Meade."

She looked puzzled, then horrified. "You mean those little furry mouselike creatures? The ones that—"

"Yes. The ones that periodically make a death migration, until millions, hundreds of millions of them drown themselves in the sea. Ask a lemming why he does it. If you could get him to slow up his rush toward death, even money says he would rationalize his answer as well as any college graduate. But he does it because he has to—and so do we."

"That's a horrid idea, Potiphar."

"Maybe. Come here, Meade. I'll show you figures that confuse me, too." He went to his desk and opened a drawer, took out a packet of cards. "Here's one. Two weeks ago—a man sues an entire state legislature for alienation of his wife's affection—and the judge lets the suit be tried. Or this one—a patent application for a device to lay the globe over on its side and warm up the arctic regions. Patent denied, but the inventor took in over three hundred thousand dollars in down payments on South Pole real estate before the postal authorities stepped in. Now he's fighting the case and it looks as if he might win. And here— prominent bishop proposes applied courses in the so-called facts of life in high schools." He put the card away hastily. "Here's a dilly: a bill introduced in the Alabama lower house to repeal the laws of atomic energy—not the present statutes, but the natural laws concerning nuclear physics; the wording makes that plain." He shrugged. "How silly can you get?"

"They're crazy."

"No, Meade. One such is crazy; a lot of them is a lemming death march. No, don't object—I've plotted them on a curve. The last time we had anything like this was the so-called Era of Wonderful Nonsense. But this one is much worse." He delved into a lower drawer, hauled out a graph. "The amplitude is more than twice as great and we haven't reached peak. What the peak will be I don't dare guess—three separate rhythms, reinforcing."

She peered at the curves. "You mean that the laddy with the arctic real estate deal is somewhere on this line?"

"He adds to it. And back here on the last crest are the flag-pole sitters and the goldfish swallowers and the Ponzi hoax and the marathon dancers and the man who pushed a peanut up Pikes Peak with his nose. You're on the new crest—or you will be when I add you in."

She made a face. "I don't like it."

"Neither do I. But it's as clear as a bank statement. This year the human race is letting down its hair, flipping its lip with a finger, and saying, '*Wubba, wubba, wubba.*'"

She shivered. "Do you suppose I could have another drink? Then I'll go."

"I have a better idea. I owe you a dinner for answering questions. Pick a place and we'll have a cocktail before."

She chewed her lip. "You don't owe me anything. And I don't feel up to facing a restaurant crowd. I might . . . I might—"

"No, you wouldn't," he said sharply. "It doesn't hit twice."

"You're sure? Anyhow, I don't want to face a crowd." She glanced at his kitchen door. "Have you anything to eat in there? I can cook."

"Um, breakfast things. And there's a pound of ground round in the freezer compartment and some rolls. I sometimes make hamburgers when I don't want to go out."

She headed for the kitchen. "Drunk or sober, fully dressed or—or naked, I can cook. You'll see."

He did see. Open-faced sandwiches with the meat married to toasted buns and the flavor garnished rather than suppressed by scraped Bermuda onion and thin-sliced dill, a salad made from things she had scrounged out of his refrigerator, potatoes crisp but not vulcanized. They ate it on the tiny balcony, sopping it down with cold beer.

He sighed and wiped his mouth. "Yes, Meade, you can cook."

"Some day I'll arrive with proper materials and pay you back. Then I'll prove it."

"You've already proved it. Nevertheless I accept. But I tell you three times, you owe me nothing."

"No? If you hadn't been a Boy Scout, I'd be in jail."

Breen shook his head. "The police have orders to keep it quiet at all costs—to keep it from growing. You saw that. And, my dear, you weren't a person to me at the time. I didn't even see your face; I—"

"You saw plenty else!"

"Truthfully, I didn't look. You were just a—a statistic."

She toyed with her knife and said slowly, "I'm not sure, but I think I've just been insulted. In all the twenty-five years that I've fought men off, more or less successfully, I've been called a lot of names—but a 'statistic'—why I ought to take your slide rule and beat you to death with it."

"My dear young lady—"

"I'm not a lady, that's for sure. But I'm *not* a statistic."

"My dear Meade, then. I wanted to tell you, before you did anything hasty, that in college I wrestled varsity middle-weight."

She grinned and dimpled. "That's more the talk a girl likes to hear. I was beginning to be afraid you had been assembled in an adding machine factory. Potty, you're rather a dear."

"If that is a diminutive of my given name, I like it. But if it refers to my waist line, I resent it."

She reached across and patted his stomach. "I like your waist line; lean and hungry men are difficult. If I were cooking for you regularly, I'd really pad it."

"Is that a proposal?"

"Let it lie, let it lie—Potty, do you really think the whole country is losing its buttons?"

He sobered at once. "It's worse than that."

"Huh?"

"Come inside. I'll show you." They gathered up dishes and dumped them in the sink, Breen talking all the while. "As a kid I was fascinated by numbers. Numbers are pretty things and they combine in such interesting configurations. I took my degree in math, of course, and got a job as a junior actuary with Midwestern Mutual—the insurance outfit. That was fun—no way on earth to tell when a particular man is going to die, but an absolute certainty that so many men of a certain age group would die before a certain date. The curves were so lovely—and they always worked out. Always. You didn't have to know *why;* you could predict with dead certainty and never know why. The equations worked; the curves were right.

"I was interested in astronomy too; it was the one science where individual figures worked out neatly, completely, and accurately, down to the last decimal point the instruments were good for. Compared with astronomy the other sciences were mere carpentry and kitchen chemistry.

"I found there were nooks and crannies in astronomy where individual numbers won't do, where you have to go over to statistics, and I became even more interested. I joined the Variable Star Association and I might have gone into astronomy professionally, instead of what I'm in now—business consultation—if I hadn't gotten interested in something else."

" 'Business consultation'?" repeated Meade. "Income tax work?"

"Oh, no—that's too elementary. I'm the numbers boy for a firm of industrial engineers. I can tell a rancher exactly how many of his Hereford bull calves will be sterile. Or I tell a motion picture producer how much rain insurance to carry on location. Or maybe how big a company in a particular line must be to carry its own risk in industrial accidents. And I'm right. I'm always right."

"Wait a minute. Seems to me a big company would *have* to have insurance."

"Contrariwise. A really big corporation begins to resemble a statistical universe."

"Huh?"

"Never mind. I got interested in something else—cycles. Cycles are everything, Meade. And everywhere. The tides. The seasons. Wars. Love. Everybody knows that in the spring the young man's fancy lightly turns to what the girls never stopped thinking about, but did you know that it runs in an eighteen-year-plus cycle as well? And that a girl born at the wrong swing of the curve doesn't stand nearly as good a chance as her older or younger sister?"

"What? Is *that* why I'm a doddering old maid?"

"You're twenty-five?" He pondered. "Maybe—but your chances are picking up again; the curve is swinging up. Anyhow, remember you are just one statistic; the curve applies to the group. Some girls get married every year anyhow."

"Don't call me a statistic."

"Sorry. And marriages match up with acreage planted to wheat, with wheat cresting ahead. You could almost say that planting wheat makes people get married."

"Sounds silly."

"It *is* silly. The whole notion of cause-and-effect is probably superstition. But the same cycle shows a peak in house building right after a peak in marriages, every time."

"Now that makes sense."

"Does it? How many newlyweds do you know who can afford to build a house? You might as well blame it on wheat acreage. We don't know *why;* it just *is*."

"Sun spots, maybe?"

"You can correlate sun spots with stock prices, or Columbia River salmon, or women's skirts. And you are just as much justified in blaming short skirts for sun spots as you are in blaming sun spots for salmon. We don't know. But the curves go on just the same."

"But there has to be some *reason* behind it."

"Does there? That's mere assumption. A fact has no 'why.' There it stands, self demonstrating. Why did you take your clothes off today?"

She frowned. "That's not fair."

"Maybe not. But I want to show you why I'm worried." He went into the bedroom, came out with a large roll of tracing paper. "We'll spread it on the floor. Here they are, all of them. The 54-year cycle—see the Civil War there? See how it matches in? The 18 & ⅓ year cycle, the 9-plus cycle, the 41-month shorty, the three rhythms of sun spots—everything, all combined in one grand chart. Mississippi River floods, fur catches in Canada, stock market prices, marriages, epidemics, freight-car loadings, bank clearings, locust plagues, divorces, tree growth, wars, rainfall, earth magnetism, building construction patents applied for, murders—you name it; I've got it there."

She stared at the bewildering array of wavy lines. "But, Potty, what does it mean?"

"It means that these things all happen, in regular rhythm, whether we like it or not. It means that when skirts are due to go up, all the sylists in Paris can't make 'em go down. It means that when prices are going down, all the controls and supports and government planning can't make 'em go up." He pointed to a curve. "Take a look at the grocery ads. Then turn to the financial page and read how the Big Brains try to double-talk their way out of it. It means that when an epidemic is due, it happens, despite all the public health efforts. It means we're lemmings."

She pulled her lip. "I don't like it. 'I am the master of my fate,' and so forth. I've got free will, Potty. I know I have—I can feel it."

"I imagine every little neutron in an atom bomb feels the same way. He can go *spung!* or he can sit still, just as he pleases. But statistical mechanics work out anyhow. And the bomb goes off—which is what I'm leading up to. See anything odd there, Meade?"

She studied the chart, trying not to let the curving lines confuse her. "They sort of bunch up over at the right end."

"You're dern tootin' they do! See that dotted vertical line? That's right, now—and things are bad enough. But take a look at that solid vertical; that's about six months from now—and that's when we get it. Look at the cycles—the long ones, the short ones, all of them. Every single last one of them reaches either a trough or a crest exactly on—or almost on—that line."

"That's bad?"

"What do you think? Three of the big ones troughed in 1929 and the depression almost ruined us . . . even with the big 54-year cycle supporting things. Now we've got the big one troughing—and the few crests are not things that help. I mean to say, tent caterpillars and influenza don't do us any good. Meade, if statistics mean anything, this tired old planet hasn't seen a jackpot like this since Eve went into the apple business. I'm scared."

She searched his face. "Potty—you're not simply having fun with me? You know I can't check up on you."

"I wish to heaven I were. No, Meade, I can't fool about numbers; I wouldn't know how. This is it. The Year of the Jackpot."

She was very silent as he drove her home. As they approached West Los Angeles, she said, "Potty?"

"Yes, Meade?"

"What do we *do* about it?"

"What do you do about a hurricane? You pull in your ears. What can you do about an atom bomb? You try to out-guess it, not be there when it goes off. What else can you do?"

"Oh." She was silent for a few moments, then added, "Potty? Will you tell me which way to jump?"

"Huh? Oh, sure! If I can figure it out."

He took her to her door, turned to go. She said, "Potty!"

He faced her. "Yes, Meade?"

She grabbed his head, shook it—then kissed him fiercely on the mouth. "There—is that just a statistic?"

"Uh, no."

"It had better not be," she said dangerously. "Potty, I think I'm going to have to change your curve."

CHAPTER TWO

"RUSSIANS REJECT UN NOTE"

"MISSOURI FLOOD DAMAGE EXCEEDS 1951 RECORD"

"MISSISSIPPI MESSIAH DEFIES COURT"

"NUDIST CONVENTION STORMS BAILEY'S BEACH"

"BRITISH-IRAN TALKS STILL DEAD-LOCKED"

"FASTER-THAN-LIGHT WEAPON PROMISED"

"TYPHOON DOUBLING BACK ON MANILA"

"MARRIAGE SOLEMNIZED ON FLOOR OF HUDSON—New York, 13 July, *In a specially-constructed diving suit built for two, Merydith Smithe, café society headline girl, and Prince Augie Schleswieg of New York and the Riviera were united today by Bishop Dalton in a service televised with the aid of the Navy's ultra-new—*"

As the Year of the Jackpot progressed Breen took melancholy pleasure in adding to the data which proved that the curve was sagging as predicted. The undeclared World War continued its bloody, blundering way at half a dozen spots around a tortured globe. Breen did not chart it; the headlines were there for anyone to read. He concentrated on the odd facts in the other pages of the papers, facts which, taken singly, meant nothing, but taken together showed a disastrous trend.

He listed stock market prices, rainfall, wheat futures, but it was the "silly season" items which fascinated him. To be sure, some humans were always doing silly things—but at what point had prime damfoolishness become commonplace? When, for example, had the zombie-like professional models become accepted ideals of American womanhood? What were the gradations between National Cancer Week and National Athlete's Foot Week? On what day had the American people finally taken leave of horse sense?

Take transvestism—male-and-female dress customs were arbitrary, but they had seemed to be deeply rooted in the culture. When did the breakdown start? With Marlene Dietrich's tailored suits? By the late forties there was no "male" article of clothing that a woman could not wear in public—but when had men started to slip over the line? Should he count the psychological cripples who had made the word "drag" a byword in Greenwich Village and Hollywood long before this outbreak? Or were they "wild shots" not belonging on the curve? Did it start with some unknown normal man attending a masquerade and there discovering that skirts actually were more comfortable and practical than trousers? Or had it started with the resurgence of Scottish nationalism reflected in the wearing of kilts by many Scottish-Americans?

Ask a lemming to state his motives! The outcome was in front of him, a news story. Transvestism by draft-dodgers had at last resulted in a mass arrest in Chicago which was to have ended in a giant joint trial—only to have the deputy prosecutor show up in a pinafore and defy the judge to submit to an examination to determine the judge's true sex. The judge suffered a stroke and died and the trial was postponed—postponed forever in Breen's opinion; he doubted that this particular blue law would ever again be enforced.

Or the laws about indecent exposure, for that matter. The attempt to limit the Gypsy-Rose syndrome by ignoring it had taken the starch out of enforcement; now here was a report about the All Souls Community Church of Springfield: the pastor had reinstituted ceremonial nudity. Probably the first time this thousand years, Breen thought, aside from some screwball cults in Los Angeles. The reverend gentleman claimed that the ceremony was identical with the "dance of the high priestess" in the ancient temple of Karnak.

Could be—but Breen had private information that the "priestess" had been working the burlesque & nightclub circuit before her present engagement. In any case the holy leader was packing them in and had not been arrested.

Two weeks later a hundred and nine churches in thirty-three states offered equivalent attractions. Breen entered them on his curves.

This queasy oddity seemed to him to have no relation to the startling rise in the dissident evangelical cults throughout the country. These churches were sincere, earnest and poor—but growing, ever since the War. Now they were multiplying like yeast. It seemed a statistical cinch that the United States was about to become godstruck again. He correlated it with Transcendentalism and the trek of the Latter Day Saints—hmm . . . yes, it fitted. And the curve was pushing toward a crest.

Billions in war bonds were now falling due; wartime marriages were reflected in the swollen peak of the Los Angeles school population. The Colorado River was at a record low and the towers in Lake Mead stood high out of the water. But the Angelenos committed slow suicide by watering lawns as usual. The Metropolitan Water District commissioners tried to stop it—it fell between the stools of the police powers of fifty "sovereign" cities. The taps remained open, trickling away the life blood of the desert paradise.

The four regular party conventions—Dixiecrats, Regular Republicans, the other Regular Republicans, and the Democrats—attracted scant attention, as the Know-Nothings had not yet met. The fact that the "American Rally," as the Know-Nothings preferred to be called, claimed not to be a party but an educational society did not detract from their strength. But what was their strength? Their beginnings had been so obscure that Breen had had to go back and dig into the December 1951 files—but he had been approached twice this very week to join them, right inside his own office—once by his boss, once by the janitor.

He hadn't been able to chart the Know-Nothings. They gave him chills in his spine. He kept column-inches on them, found that their publicity was shrinking while their numbers were obviously zooming.

Krakatau blew up on July 18th. It provided the first important transPacific TV-cast; its effect on sunsets, on solar constant, on mean temperature, and on rainfall would not be felt until later in the year. The San Andreas fault, its stresses unrelieved since the Long Beach disaster of 1933, continued to build up imbalance—an unhealed wound running the full length of the West Coast. Pelée and Etna erupted; Mauna Loa was still quiet.

Flying saucers seemed to be landing daily in every state. No one had exhibited one on the ground—or had the Department of Defense sat on them? Breen was unsatisfied with the off-the-record reports he had been able to get; the alcoholic content of some of them had been high. But the sea serpent on Ventura Beach was real; he had seen it. The troglodyte in Tennessee he was not in a position to verify.

Thirty-one domestic air crashes the last week in July . . . was it sabotage? Or was it a sagging curve on a chart? And that neo-polio epidemic that skipped from Seattle to New York? Time for a big epidemic? Breen's chart said it was. But how about B.W.? Could a chart *know* that a Slav biochemist would perfect an efficient virus-and-vector at the right time? Nonsense!

But the curves, if they meant anything at all, included "free will"; they averaged in all the individual "wills" of a statistical universe—and came out as a smooth function. Every morning three million "free wills" flowed toward the center of the New York megapolis; every evening they flowed out again—all by "free will," and on a smooth and predictable curve.

Ask a lemming! Ask *all* the lemmings, dead and alive—let them take a vote on it! Breen tossed his notebook aside and called Meade. "Is this my favorite statistic?"

"Potty! I was thinking about you."

"Naturally. This is your night off."

"Yes, but another reason, too. Potiphar, have you ever taken a look at the Great Pyramid?"

"I haven't even been to Niagara Falls. I'm looking for a rich woman, so I can travel."

"Yes, yes, I'll let you know when I get my first million, but—"

"That's the first time you've proposed to me this week."

"Shut up. Have you ever looked into the prophecies they found inside the pyramid?"

"Huh? Look, Meade, that's in the same class with astrology—strictly for squirrels. Grow up."

"Yes, of course. But Potty, I thought you were interested in anything odd. This is odd."

"Oh. Sorry. If it's 'silly season' stuff, let's see it."

"All right. Am I cooking for you tonight?"

"It's Wednesday, isn't it?"

"How soon?"

He glanced at his watch. "Pick you up in eleven minutes." He felt his whiskers. "No, twelve and a half."

"I'll be ready. Mrs. Megeath says that these regular dates mean that you are going to marry me."

"Pay no attention to her. She's just a statistic. And I'm a wild datum."

"Oh, well, I've got two hundred and forty-seven dollars toward that million. 'Bye!'"

Meade's prize was the usual Rosicrucian come-on, elaborately printed, and including a photograph (retouched, he was sure) of the much disputed line on the corridor wall which was alleged to prophesy, by its various discontinuities, the entire future. This one had an unusual time scale but the major events were all marked on it—the fall of Rome, the Norman Invasion, the Discovery of America, Napoleon, the World Wars.

What made it interesting was that it suddenly stopped—now.

"What about it, Potty?"

"I guess the stonecutter got tired. Or got fired. Or they got a new head priest with new ideas." He tucked it into his desk. "Thanks. I'll think about how to list it." But he got it out again, applied dividers and a magnifying glass. "It says here," he announced, "that the end comes late in August—unless that's a fly speck."

"Morning or afternoon? I have to know how to dress."

"Shoes will be worn. All God's chilluns got shoes." He put it away.

She was quiet for a moment, then said, "Potty, isn't it about time to jump?"

"Huh? Girl, don't let *that* thing affect you! That's 'silly season' stuff."

"Yes. But take a look at *your* chart."

Nevertheless he took the next afternoon off, spent it in the reference room of the main library, confirmed his opinion of soothsayers. Nostradamus was pretentiously silly, Mother Shippey was worse. In any of them you could find what you looked for.

He did find one item in Nostradamus that he liked: "The Oriental shall come forth from his seat . . . he shall pass through the sky, through the waters and the snow, and he shall strike each one with his weapon."

That sounded like what the Department of Defense expected the commies to try to do to the Western Allies.

But it was also a description of every invasion that had come out of the "heartland" in the memory of mankind. Nuts!

When he got home he found himself taking down his father's Bible and turning to Revelations. He could not find anything that he could understand but he got fascinated by the recurring use of precise numbers. Presently he thumbed through the Book at random; his eye lit on: "Boast not thyself of tomorrow; for thou knowest not what a day may bring forth." He put the Book away, feeling humbled but not cheered.

The rains started the next morning. The Master Plumbers elected Miss Star Morning "Miss Sanitary Engineering" on the same day that the morticians designated her as "The Body I would Like Best to Prepare," and her option was dropped by Fragrant Features. Congress voted $1.37 to compensate Thomas Jefferson Meeks for losses incurred while an emergency postman for the Christmas rush of 1936, approved the appointment of five lieutenant generals and one ambassador and adjourned in eight minutes. The fire extinguishers in a midwest orphanage turned out to be filled with air. The chancellor of the leading football institution sponsored a fund to send peace messages and vitamins to the Politburo. The stock market slumped nineteen points and the tickers ran two hours late. Wichita, Kansas, remained flooded while Phoenix, Arizona, cut off drinking water to areas outside city limits. And Potiphar Breen found that he had left his raincoat at Meade Barstow's rooming house.

He phoned her landlady, but Mrs. Megeath turned him over to Meade. "What are you doing home on a Friday?" he demanded.

"The theater manager laid me off. Now you'll have to marry me."

"You can't afford me. Meade—seriously, baby, what happened?"

"I was ready to leave the dump anyway. For the last six weeks the popcorn machine has been carrying the place. Today I sat through *I Was A Teen-Age Beatnik* twice. Nothing to do."

"I'll be along."

"Eleven minutes?"

"It's raining. Twenty—with luck."

It was more nearly sixty. Santa Monica Boulevard was a navigable stream; Sunset Boulevard was a subway jam. When he tried to ford the streams leading to Mrs. Megeath's house, he found that changing tires with the wheel wedged against a storm drain presented problems.

"Potty! You look like a drowned rat."

"I'll live." But presently he found himself wrapped in a blanket robe belonging to the late Mr. Megeath and sipping hot cocoa while Mrs. Megeath dried his clothing in the kitchen.

"Meade . . . I'm 'at liberty,' too."

"Huh? You quit your job?"

"Not exactly. Old Man Wiley and I have been having differences of opinion about my answers for months—too much 'Jackpot factor' in the figures I give him to turn over to clients. Not that I call it that, but he has felt that I was unduly pessimistic."

"But you were right!"

"Since when has being right endeared a man to his boss? But that wasn't why he fired me; that was just the excuse. He wants a man willing to back up the Know-Nothing program with scientific double-talk. And I wouldn't join." He went to the window. "It's raining harder."

"But they haven't got any program."

"I know that."

"Potty, you should have joined. It doesn't mean anything—I joined three months ago."

"The hell you did!"

She shrugged. "You pay your dollar and you turn up for two meetings and they leave you alone. It kept my job for another three months. What of it?"

"Uh, well—I'm sorry you did it; that's all. Forget it. Meade, the water is over the curbs out there."

"You had better stay here overnight."

"Mmm . . . I don't like to leave 'Entropy' parked out in this stuff all night. Meade?"

"Yes, Potty?"

"We're both out of jobs. How would you like to duck north into the Mojave and find a dry spot?"

"I'd love it. But look, Potty—is this a proposal, or just a proposition?"

"Don't pull that 'either-or' stuff on me. It's just a suggestion for a vacation. Do you want to take a chaperone?"

"No."

"Then pack a bag."

"Right away. But look, Potiphar—pack a bag *how?* Are you trying to tell me it's *time to jump?*"

He faced her, then looked back at the window. "I don't know," he said slowly, "but this rain might go on quite a while. Don't take anything you don't have to have—but don't leave anything behind you can't get along without."

He repossessed his clothing from Mrs. Megeath while Meade was upstairs. She came down dressed in slacks and carrying two large bags; under one arm was a battered and rakish Teddy bear. "This is Winnie."

"Winnie the Pooh?"

"No, Winnie Churchill. When I feel bad he promises me 'blood, toil, tears, and sweat'; then I feel better. You said to bring anything I couldn't do without?" She looked at him anxiously.

"Right." He took the bags. Mrs. Megeath had seemed satisfied with his explanation that they were going to visit his (mythical) aunt in Bakersfield before looking for jobs; nevertheless she embarrassed him by kissing him good-by and telling him to "take care of my little girl."

Santa Monica Boulevard was blocked off from use. While stalled in traffic in Beverly Hills he fiddled with the car radio, getting squawks and crackling noises, then finally one station nearby: "—in effect," a harsh, high, staccato voice was saying, "the Kremlin has given us till sundown to get out of town. This is your New York Reporter, who thinks that in days like these every American must personally keep his powder dry. And now for a word from—" Breen switched it off and glanced at her face. "Don't worry," he said. "They've been talking that way for years."

"You think they are bluffing?"

"I didn't say that. I said, 'don't worry.'"

But his own packing, with her help, was clearly on a "Survival Kit" basis—canned goods, all his warm clothing, a sporting rifle he had not fired in over two years, a first-aid kit and the contents of his medicine chest. He dumped the stuff from his desk into a carton, shoved it into the back seat along with cans and books and coats and covered the plunder with all the blankets in the house. They went back up the rickety stairs for a last check.

"Potty—where's your chart?"

"Rolled up on the back seat shelf. I guess that's all—hey, wait a minute!" He went to a shelf over his desk and began taking down small, sober-looking magazines. "I dern near left behind my file of *The Western Astronomer* and of the *Proceedings of the Variable Star Association*."

"Why take them?"

"Huh? I must be nearly a year behind on both of them. Now maybe I'll have time to read."

"Hmm . . . Potty, watching you read professional journals is not my notion of a vacation."

"Quiet, woman! You took Winnie; I take these."

She shut up and helped him. He cast a longing eye at his electric calculator but decided it was too much like the White Knight's mouse trap. He could get by with his slide rule.

As the car splashed out into the street she said, "Potty, how are you fixed for cash?"

"Huh? Okay, I guess."

"I mean, leaving while the banks are closed and everything." She held up her purse. "Here's my bank. It isn't much, but we can use it."

He smiled and patted her knee. "Stout fellow! I'm sitting on my bank; I started turning everything to cash about the first of the year."

"Oh. I closed out my bank account right after we met."

"You did? You must have taken my maunderings seriously."

"I always take you seriously."

Mint Canyon was a five-mile-an-hour nightmare, with visibility limited to the tail lights of the truck ahead. When they stopped for coffee at Halfway, they confirmed what seemed evident: Cajon Pass was closed and long-haul traffic for Route 66 was being detoured through the secondary pass. At long, long last they reached the Victorville cutoff and lost some of the traffic—a good thing, as the windshield wiper on his side had quit working and they were driving by the committee system. Just short of Lancaster she said suddenly, "Potty, is this buggy equipped with a snorkel?"

"Nope."

"Then we had better stop. But I see a light off the road."

The light was an auto court. Meade settled the matter of economy versus convention by signing the book herself; they were placed in one cabin. He saw that it had twin beds and let the matter ride. Meade went to bed with her Teddy bear without even asking to be kissed goodnight. It was already gray, wet dawn.

They got up in the late afternoon and decided to stay over one more night, then push north toward Bakersfield. A high pressure area was alleged to be moving south, crowding the warm, wet mass that smothered Southern California. They wanted to get into it. Breen had the wiper repaired and bought two new tires to replace his ruined spare, added some camping items to his cargo, and bought for Meade a .32 automatic, a lady's social-purposes gun; he gave it to her somewhat sheepishly.

"What's this for?"

"Well, you're carrying quite a bit of cash."

"Oh. I thought maybe I was to use it to fight you off."

"Now, Meade—"

"Never mind. Thanks, Potty."

They had finished supper and were packing the car with their afternoon's purchases when the quake struck. Five inches of rain in twenty-four hours, more than three billion tons of mass suddenly loaded on a fault already overstrained, all cut loose in one subsonic, stomach-twisting rumble.

Meade sat down on the wet ground very suddenly; Breen stayed upright by dancing like a logroller. When the ground quieted down somewhat, thirty seconds later, he helped her up. "You all right?"

"My slacks are soaked." She added pettishly, "But, Potty, it never quakes in wet weather. *Never*."

"It did this time."

"But—"

"Keep quiet, can't you?" He opened the car door and switched on the radio, waited impatiently for it to warm up. Shortly he was searching the entire dial. "Not a confounded Los Angeles station on the air!"

"Maybe the shock busted one of your tubes?"

"Pipe down." He passed a squeal and dialed back to it:

"—your Sunshine Station in Riverside, California. Keep tuned to this station for the latest developments. It is as of now impossible to tell the size of the disaster. The Colorado River aqueduct is broken; nothing is known of the extent of the damage nor how long it will take to repair it. So far as we know the Owens River Valley aqueduct may be intact, but all persons in the Los Angeles area are advised to conserve water. My personal advice is to stick your washtubs out into this rain; it can't last forever. If we had time, we'd play *Cool Water,* just to give you the idea. I now read from the standard disaster instructions, quote: 'Boil all water. Remain quietly in your homes and do not panic. Stay off the highways. Cooperate with the police and render—' Joe! Joe! Catch that phone! '—render aid where necessary. Do not use the telephone except for—' Flash! an unconfirmed report from Long Beach states that the Wilmington and San Pedro waterfront is under five feet of water. I repeat, this is unconfirmed. Here's a message from the commanding general, March Field: 'official, all military personnel will report—' "

Breen switched it off. "Get in the car."

"Where are we going?"

"North."

"We've paid for the cabin. Should we—"

"Get in!"

He stopped in the town, managed to buy six five-gallon-tins and a jeep tank. He filled them with gasoline and packed them with blankets in the back seat, topping off the mess with a dozen cans of oil. Then they were rolling.

"What are we doing, Potiphar?"

"I want to get west on the valley highway."

"Any particular place west?"

"I think so. We'll see. You work the radio, but keep an eye on the road, too. That gas back there makes me nervous."

Through the town of Mojave and northwest on 466 into the Tehachapi Mountains—Reception was poor in the pass but what Meade could pick up confirmed the first impression—worse than the quake of '06, worse than San Francisco, Managua, and Long Beach taken together.

When they got down out of the mountains it was clearing locally; a few stars appeared. Breen swung left off the highway and ducked south of Bakersfield by the county road, reached the Route 99 superhighway just south of Greenfield. It was, as he had feared, already jammed with refugees; he was forced to go along with the flow for a couple of miles before he could cut west at Greenfield toward Taft. They stopped on the western outskirts of the town and ate at an all-night truckers' joint.

They were about to climb back into the car when there was suddenly "sunrise" due south. The rosy light swelled almost instantaneously, filled the sky, and died; where it had been a red-and-purple pillar of cloud was mounting, mounting—spreading to a mushroom top.

Breen stared at it, glanced at his watch, then said harshly, "Get in the car."

"Potty—that was . . . that was—"

"That was—that used to be—Los Angeles. Get in the car!"

He simply drove for several minutes. Meade seemed to be in a state of shock, unable to speak. When the sound reached them he again glanced at his watch. "Six minutes and nineteen seconds. That's about right."

"Potty—*we should have brought Mrs. Megeath.*"

"How was I to know?" he said angrily. "Anyhow, you can't transplant an old tree. If she got it, she never knew it."

"Oh, I hope so!"

"Forget it; straighten out and fly right. We're going to have all we can do to take care of ourselves. Take the flashlight and check the map. I want to turn north at Taft and over toward the coast."

"Yes, Potiphar."

"And try the radio."

She quieted down and did as she was told. The radio gave nothing, not even the Riverside station; the whole broadcast range was covered by a curious static, like rain on a window. He slowed down as they approached Taft, let her spot the turn north onto the state road, and turned into it. Almost at once a figure jumped out into the road in front of them, waved his arms violently. Breen tromped on the brake.

The man came up on the left side of the car, rapped on the window; Breen ran the glass down. Then he stared stupidly at the gun in the man's left hand. "Out of the car," the stranger said sharply. "I've got to have it." He reached inside with his right hand, groped for the door lever.

Meade reached across Breen, stuck her little lady's gun in the man's face, pulled the trigger. Breen could feel the flash on his own face, never noticed the report. The man looked puzzled, with a neat, not-yet-bloody hole in his upper lip—then slowly sagged away from the car.

"Drive on!" Meade said in a high voice.

Breen caught his breath. "Good girl—"

"Drive on! *Get rolling!*"

They followed the state road through Los Padres National Forest, stopping once to fill the tank from their cans. They turned off onto a dirt road. Meade kept trying the radio, got San Francisco once but it was too jammed with static to read. Then she got Salt Lake City, faint but clear: "—since there are no reports of anything passing our radar screen the Kansas City bomb must be assumed to have been planted rather than delivered. This is a tentative theory but—" They passed into a deep cut and lost the rest.

When the squawk box again came to life it was a new voice: "Conelrad," said a crisp voice, "coming to you over the combined networks. The rumor that Los Angeles has been hit by an atom bomb is totally unfounded. It is true that the western metropolis has suffered a severe earthquake shock but that is all. Government officials and the Red Cross are on the spot to care for the victims, but—and I repeat—there has *been no atomic bombing.* So relax and stay in your homes. Such wild rumors can damage the United States quite as much as enemy's bombs. Stay off the highways and listen for—" Breen snapped it off.

"Somebody," he said bitterly, "has again decided that 'Mama knows best.' They won't tell us any bad news."

"Potiphar," Meade said sharply, "that *was* an atom bomb . . . wasn't it?"

"It was. And now we don't know whether it was just Los Angeles— and Kansas City—or all the big cities in the country. All we know is that they are lying to us."

"Maybe I can get another station?"

"The hell with it." He concentrated on driving. The road was very bad.

As it began to get light she said, "Potty—do you know where we're going? Are we just keeping out of cities?"

"I think I do. If I'm not lost." He stared around them. "Nope, it's all right. See that hill up forward with the triple gendarmes on its profile?"

"Gendarmes?"

"Big rock pillars. That's a sure landmark. I'm looking for a private road now. It leads to a hunting lodge belonging to two of my friends— an old ranch house actually, but as a ranch it didn't pay."

"Oh. They won't mind us using it?"

He shrugged. "If they show up, we'll ask them. If they show up. They lived in Los Angeles, Meade."

"Oh. Yes, I guess so."

The private road had once been a poor grade of wagon trail; now it was almost impassable. But they finally topped a hogback from which they could see almost to the Pacific, then dropped down into a sheltered bowl where the cabin was. "All out, girl. End of the line."

Meade sighed. "It looks heavenly."

"Think you can rustle breakfast while I unload? There's probably wood in the shed. Or can you manage a wood range?"

"Just try me."

Two hours later Breen was standing on the hogback, smoking a cigarette, and staring off down to the west. He wondered if that was a mushroom cloud up San Francisco way? Probably his imagination, he decided, in view of the distance. Certainly there was nothing to be seen to the south.

Meade came out of the cabin. "Potty!"

"Up here."

She joined him, took his hand, and smiled, then snitched his cigarette and took a deep drag. She expelled it and said, "I know it's sinful of me, but I feel more peaceful than I have in months and months."

"I know."

"Did you see the canned goods in that pantry? We could pull through a hard winter here."

"We might have to."

"I suppose. I wish we had a cow."

"What would you do with a cow?"

"I used to milk four cows before I caught the school bus, every morning. I can butcher a hog, too."

"I'll try to find one."

"You do and I'll manage to smoke it." She yawned. "I'm suddenly terribly sleepy."

"So am I. And small wonder."

"Let's go to bed."

"Uh, yes. Meade?"

"Yes, Potty?"

"We may be here quite a while. You know that, don't you?"

"Yes, Potty."

"In fact it might be smart to stay put until those curves all start turning up again. They will, you know."

"Yes. I had figured that out."

He hesitated, then went on, "Meade . . . will you marry me?"

"Yes." She moved up to him.

After a time he pushed her gently away and said, "My dear, my very dear, uh—we could drive down and find a minister in some little town?"

She looked at him steadily. "That wouldn't be very bright, would it? I mean, nobody knows we're here and that's the way we want it. And besides, your car might not make it back up that road."

"No, it wouldn't be very bright. But I want to do the right thing."

"It's all right, Potty. It's *all right*."

"Well, then . . . kneel down here with me. We'll say them together."

"Yes, Potiphar." She knelt and he took her hand. He closed his eyes and prayed wordlessly.

When he opened them he said, "What's the matter?"

"Uh, the gravel hurts my knees."

"We'll stand up, then."

"No. Look, Potty, why don't we just go in the house and say them there?"

"Huh? Hell's bells, woman, we might forget to say them entirely. Now repeat after me: I, Potiphar, take thee, Meade—"

"Yes, Potiphar. I, Meade, take thee, Potiphar—"

CHAPTER THREE

"OFFICIAL: STATIONS WITHIN RANGE RELAY TWICE. EXECUTIVE BULLETIN NUMBER NINE—ROAD LAWS PREVIOUSLY PUBLISHED HAVE BEEN IGNORED IN MANY INSTANCES. PATROLS ARE ORDERED TO SHOOT WITHOUT WARNING AND PROVOST MARSHALS ARE DIRECTED TO USE DEATH PENALTY FOR UNAUTHORIZED POSSESSION OF GASOLINE. B.W. AND RADIATION QUARANTINE REGULATIONS PREVIOUSLY ISSUED WILL BE RIGIDLY ENFORCED. LONG LIVE THE UNITED STATES! HARLEY J. NEAL, LIEUTENANT GENERAL, ACTING CHIEF OF GOVERNMENT. ALL STATIONS RELAY TWICE."

"THIS IS THE FREE RADIO AMERICA RELAY NETWORK. PASS THIS ALONG, BOYS! GOVERNOR BRANDLEY WAS SWORN IN TODAY AS PRESIDENT BY ACTING CHIEF JUSTICE ROBERTS UNDER THE RULE-OF-SUCCESSION. THE PRESIDENT NAMED THOMAS DEWEY AS SECRETARY OF STATE AND PAUL DOUGLAS AS SECRETARY OF DEFENSE. HIS SECOND OFFICIAL ACT WAS TO STRIP THE RENEGADE NEAL OF RANK AND TO DIRECT HIS ARREST BY ANY CITIZEN OR OFFICIAL. MORE LATER. PASS THE WORD ALONG.

"HELLO, CQ, CQ, CQ. THIS IS W5KMR, FREEPORT. QRR, QRR! ANYBODY READ ME? ANYBODY? WE'RE DYING LIKE FLIES DOWN HERE. WHAT'S HAPPENED? STARTS WITH FEVER AND A BURNING THIRST BUT YOU CAN'T SWALLOW. WE NEED HELP. ANYBODY READ ME? HELLO, CQ 75, CQ 75 THIS IS W5 KILO METRO ROMEO CALLING QRR AND CQ 75. BY FOR SOMEBODY. . . . ANYBODY!!!"

"THIS IS THE LORD'S TIME, SPONSORED BY SWAN'S ELIXIR, THE TONIC THAT MAKES WAITING FOR THE KINGDOM OF GOD WORTHWHILE. YOU ARE ABOUT TO HEAR A MESSAGE OF CHEER FROM JUDGE BROOMFIELD, ANOINTED VICAR OF THE KINGDOM ON EARTH. BUT FIRST A BULLETIN: SEND YOUR CONTRIBUTIONS TO 'MESSIAH,' CLINT, TEXAS. DON'T TRY TO MAIL THEM: SEND THEM BY A KINGDOM MESSENGER OR BY SOME PILGRIM JOURNEYING THIS WAY. AND NOW THE TABERNACLE CHOIR FOLLOWED BY THE VOICE OF THE VICAR ON EARTH—"

"—THE FIRST SYMPTOM IS LITTLE RED SPOTS IN THE ARMPITS. THEY ITCH. PUT 'EM TO BED AT ONCE AND KEEP 'EM COVERED UP WARM. THEN GO SCRUB YOURSELF AND WEAR A MASK: WE DON'T KNOW YET HOW YOU CATCH IT. PASS IT ALONG, ED."

"—NO NEW LANDINGS REPORTED ANYWHERE ON THIS CONTINENT. THE PARATROOPERS WHO ESCAPED THE ORIGINAL SLAUGHTER ARE THOUGHT TO BE HIDING OUT IN THE POCONOS. SHOOT—BUT BE CAREFUL; IT MIGHT BE AUNT TESSIE. OFF AND CLEAR, UNTIL NOON TOMORROW—"

The curves were turning up again. There was no longer doubt in Breen's mind about that. It might not even be necessary to stay up here in the Sierra Madres through the winter—though he rather thought they would. He had picked their spot to keep them west of the fallout; it would be silly to be mowed down by the tail of a dying epidemic, or be shot by a nervous vigilante, when a few months' wait would take care of everything.

Besides, he had chopped all that firewood. He looked at his calloused hands—he had done all that work and, by George, he was going to enjoy the benefits!

He was headed out to the hogback to wait for sunset and do an hour's reading; he glanced at his car as he passed it, thinking that he would like to try the radio. He suppressed the yen; two thirds of his reserve gasoline was gone already just from keeping the battery charged for the radio—and here it was only December. He really ought to cut it down to twice a week. But it meant a lot to catch the noon bulletin of Free America and then twiddle the dial a few minutes to see what else he could pick up.

But for the past three days Free America had not been on the air—solar static maybe, or perhaps just a power failure. But that rumor that President Brandley had been assassinated—while it hadn't come from the Free radio . . . and it hadn't been denied by them, either, which was a good sign. Still, it worried him.

And that other story that lost Atlantis had pushed up during the quake period and that the Azores were now a little continent—almost certainly a hang-over of the "silly season"—but it would be nice to hear a follow-up.

Rather sheepishly he let his feet carry him to the car. It wasn't fair to listen when Meade wasn't around. He warmed it up, slowly spun the dial, once around and back. Not a peep at full gain, nothing but a terrible amount of static. Served him right.

He climbed the hogback, sat down on the bench he had dragged up there—their "memorial bench," sacred to the memory of the time

Meade had hurt her knees on the gravel—sat down and sighed. His lean belly was stuffed with venison and corn fritters; he lacked only tobacco to make him completely happy. The evening cloud colors were spectacularly beautiful and the weather was extremely balmy for December; both, he thought, caused by volcanic dust, with perhaps an assist from atom bombs.

Surprising how fast things went to pieces when they started to skid! And surprising how quickly they were going back together, judging by the signs. A curve reaches trough and then starts right back up. World War III was the shortest big war on record—forty cities gone, counting Moscow and the other slave cities as well as the American ones—and then *whoosh!* neither side fit to fight. Of course, the fact that both sides had thrown their ICBMs over the pole through the most freakish arctic weather since Peary invented the place had a lot to do with it, he supposed. It was amazing that any of the Russian paratroop transports had gotten through at all.

He sighed and pulled the November 1951 copy of the *Western Astronomer* out of his pocket. Where was he? Oh, *yes, Some Notes on the Stability of G-Type Stars with Especial Reference to Sol*, by A. G. M. Dynkowski, Lenin Institute, translated by Heinrich Ley, F. R. A. S. Good boy, Ski—sound mathematician. Very clever application of harmonic series and tightly reasoned. He started to thumb for his place when he noticed a footnote that he had missed. Dynkowski's own name carried down to it: "This monograph was denounced by *Pravda* as romantic reaction-ariism shortly after it was published. Professor Dynkowski has been unreported since and must be presumed to be liquidated."

The poor geek! Well, he probably would have been atomized by now anyway, along with the goons who did him in. He wondered if they really had gotten all the Russki paratroopers? Well, he had killed his quota; if he hadn't gotten that doe within a quarter mile of the cabin and headed right back, Meade would have had a bad time. He had shot them in the back, the swine! and buried them beyond the woodpile—and then it had seemed a shame to skin and eat an innocent deer while those lice got decent burial.

Aside from mathematics, just two things worth doing—kill a man and love a woman. He had done both; he was rich.

He settled down to some solid pleasure. Dynkowski was a treat. Of course, it was old stuff that a G-type star, such as the sun, was potentially unstable; a G-O star could explode, slide right off the Russell diagram, and end up as a white dwarf. But no one before Dynkowski had defined the exact conditions for such a catastrophe, nor had anyone else devised mathematical means of diagnosing the instability and describing its progress.

He looked up to rest his eyes from the fine print and saw that the sun was obscured by a thin low cloud—one of those unusual conditions where the filtering effect is just right to permit a man to view the sun clearly with the naked eye. Probably volcanic dust in the air, he decided, acting almost like smoked glass.

He looked again. Either he had spots before his eyes or that was one fancy big sun spot. He had heard of being able to see them with the naked eye, but it had never happened to him. He longed for a telescope.

He blinked. Yep, it was still there, upper right. A *big* spot—no wonder the car radio sounded like a Hitler speech.

He turned back and continued on to the end of the article, being anxious to finish before the light failed. At first his mood was sheerest intellectual pleasure at the man's tight mathematical reasoning. A 3% imbalance in the solar constant—yes, that was standard stuff; the sun would *nova* with that much change. But Dynkowski went further; by means of a novel mathematical operator which he had dubbed "yokes" he bracketed the period in a star's history when this could happen and tied it down further with secondary, tertiary, and quaternary yokes, showing exactly the time of highest probablility. Beautiful! Dynkowski even assigned dates to the extreme limit of his primary yoke, as a good statistician should.

But, as he went back and reviewed the equations, his mood changed from intellectual to personal. Dynkowski was not talking about just any G-O star; in the latter part he meant old Sol himself, Breen's personal sun, the big boy out there with the oversized freckle on his face.

That was one hell of a big freckle! It was a hole you could chuck Jupiter into and not make a splash. He could see it very clearly now.

Everybody talks about "when the stars grow old and the sun grows cold"—but it's an impersonal concept, like one's own death. Breen started thinking about it very personally. How long would it take, from the instant the imbalance was triggered until the expanding wave front engulfed earth? The mechanics couldn't be solved without a calculator even though they were implicit in the equations in front of him. Half an hour, for a horseback guess, from incitement until the earth went *phutt!*

It hit him with gentle melancholy. No more? Never again? Colorado on a cool morning . . . the Boston Post road with autumn wood smoke tanging the air . . . Bucks county bursting in the spring. The wet smells of the Fulton Fish Market—no, that was gone already. Coffee at the *Morning Call*. No more wild strawberries on a hillside in Jersey, hot and sweet as lips. Dawn in the South Pacific with the light airs cool velvet under your shirt and never a sound but the chuckling of the water against the sides of the old rust bucket—what was her name? That was a long time ago—the S.S. *Mary Brewster.*

No more moon if the earth was gone. Stars—but no one to look at them.

He looked back at the dates bracketing Dynkowski's probability yoke. "Thine Alabaster Cities gleam, undimmed by—"

He suddenly felt the need for Meade and stood up.

She was coming out to meet him. "Hello, Potty! Safe to come in now—I've finished the dishes."

"I should help."

"You do the man's work; I'll do the woman's work. That's fair." She shaded her eyes. "What a sunset! We ought to have volcanoes blowing their tops every year."

"Sit down and we'll watch it."

She sat beside him and he took her hand. "Notice the sun spot? You can see it with your naked eye."

She stared. "Is that a sun spot? It looks as if somebody had taken a bite out of it."

He squinted his eyes at it again. Damned if it didn't look bigger!

Meade shivered. "I'm chilly. Put your arm around me." He did so with his free arm, continuing to hold hands with the other. It *was* bigger—the thing was growing.

What good is the race of man? Monkeys, he thought, monkeys with a spot of poetry in them, cluttering and wasting a second-string planet near a third-string star. But sometimes they finish in style.

She snuggled to him. "Keep me warm."

"It will be warmer soon. I mean I'll keep you warm."

"Dear Potty."

She looked up. "Potty—something funny is happening to the sunset."

"No darling—to the sun."

"I'm frightened."

"I'm here, dear."

He glanced down at the journal, still open beside him. He did not need to add up the two figures and divide by two to reach the answer. Instead he clutched fiercely at her hand, knowing with an unexpected and overpowering burst of sorrow that his was.

PROJECT NIGHTMARE

Amazing Stories, May 1953

"FOUR'S YOUR POINT. Roll 'em!"

"Anybody want a side bet on double deuces?"

No one answered; the old soldier rattled dice in a glass, pitched them against the washroom wall. One turned up a deuce; the other spun. Somebody yelled, "It's going to five! Come, Phoebe!"

It stopped—a two. The old soldier said, "I told you not to play with me. Anybody want cigarette money?"

"Pick it up, Pop. We don't—oh, oh! 'Ten*shun!*'"

In the door stood a civilian, a colonel, and a captain. The civilian said, "Give the money back. Two-Gun."

"Okay, Prof." The old soldier extracted two singles. "That much is mine."

"Stop!" objected the captain. "I'll impound that for evidence. Now, you men—"

The colonel stopped him. "Mick. Forget that you're adjutant. Private Andrews, come along." He went out; the others followed. They hurried through the enlisted men's club, out into desert sunshine and across the quadrangle.

The civilian said, "Two-Gun, what the deuce!"

"Shucks, Prof, I was just practicing."

"Why don't you practice against Grandma Wilkins?"

The soldier snorted. "Do I look silly?"

The colonel put in, "You're keeping a crowd of generals and V.I.P.s waiting. That isn't bright."

"Colonel Hammond, I was told to wait in the club."

"But not in its washroom. Step it up!"

They went inside headquarters to a hall where guards checked their passes before letting them in. A civilian was speaking: "—and that's the story of the history-making experiments at Duke University. Doctor Reynolds is back; he will conduct the demonstrations."

The officers sat down in the rear; Dr. Reynolds went to the speaker's table. Private Andrews sat down with a group set apart from the high brass and distinguished civilians of the audience. A character who looked like a professional gambler—and was—sat next to two beautiful redheads, identical twins. A fourteen-year-old Negro boy slumped in the next chair; he seemed asleep. Beyond him a most wide-awake person, Mrs. Anna Wilkins, tatted and looked around. In the second row were college students and a drab middle-aged man.

The table held a chuck-a-luck cage, packs of cards, scratch pads, a Geiger counter, a lead carrying case. Reynolds leaned on it and said, "Extra-Sensory Perception, or E.S.P., is a tag for little-known phenomena—telepathy, clairvoyance, clair-audience, precognition, telekinesis. They exist; we can measure them; we know that some people are thus gifted. But we don't know how they work. The British, in India during World War One, found that secrets were being stolen by telepathy." Seeing doubt in their faces Reynolds added, "It is conceivable that a spy five hundred miles away is now 'listening in'—and picking your brains of top-secret data."

Doubt was more evident. A four-star Air Force general said, "One moment, Doctor—if true, what can we do to stop it?"

"Nothing."

"That's no answer. A lead-lined room?"

"We've tried that, General. No effect."

"Jamming with high frequencies? Or whatever 'brain waves' are?"

"Possibly, though I doubt it. If E.S.P. becomes militarily important you may have to operate with all facts known. Back to our program: These ladies and gentlemen are powerfully gifted in telekinesis, the ability to control matter at a distance. Tomorrow's experiment may not succeed, but we hope to convince the doubting Thomases"—he smiled at a man in the rear—"that it is worth trying."

The man he looked at stood up. "General Hanby!"

An Army major general looked around. "Yes, Doctor Withers?"

"I asked to be excused. My desk is loaded with urgent work—and these games have nothing to do with me."

The commanding general started to assert himself; the four-star visitor put a hand on his sleeve. "Doctor Withers, my desk in Washington is piled high, but I am here because the President sent me. Will you please stay? I want a skeptical check on my judgment."

Withers sat down, still angry. Reynolds continued: "We will start with E.S.P. rather than telekinesis—which is a bit different, anyhow." He turned to one of the redheads. "Jane, will you come here?"

The girl answered, "I'm Joan. Sure."

"All right—Joan. General LaMott, will you draw something on this scratch pad?"

The four-star flyer cocked an eyebrow. "Anything?"

"Not too complicated."

"Right, Doctor." He thought, then began a cartoon of a girl, grinned and added a pop-eyed wolf. Shortly he looked up. "Okay?"

Joan had kept busy with another pad; Reynolds took hers to the general. The sketches were alike—except that Joan had added four stars to the wolf's shoulders. The general looked at her; she looked demure. "I'm convinced," he said drily. "What next?"

"That could be clairvoyance or telepathy," Reynolds lectured. "We will now show direct telepathy." He called the second twin to him, then said, "Doctor Withers, will you help us?"

Withers still looked surly. "With what?"

"The same thing—but Jane will watch over your shoulder while Joan tries to reproduce what you draw. Make it something harder."

"Well . . . okay." He took the pad, began sketching a radio circuit while Jane watched. He signed it with a "Clem," the radioman's cartoon of the little fellow peering over a fence.

"That's fine!" said Reynolds. "Finished, Joan?"

"Yes, Doctor." He fetched her pad; the diagram was correct—but Joan had added to "Clem" a wink.

Reynolds interrupted awed comment with, "I will skip card demonstrations and turn to telekinesis. Has anyone a pair of dice?" No one volunteered; he went on, "We have some supplied by your physics department. This chuck-a-luck cage is signed and sealed by them and so is this package." He broke it open, spilled out a dozen dice. "Two-Gun, how about some naturals?"

"I'll try, Prof."

"General LaMott, please select a pair and put them in this cup."

The general complied and handed the cup to Andrews. "What are you going to roll, soldier?"

"Would a sixty-five suit the General?"

"If you can."

"Would the General care to put up a five spot, to make it interesting?" He waited, wide-eyed and innocent.

LaMott grinned. "You're faded, soldier." He peeled out a five; Andrews covered it, rattled the cup and rolled. One die stopped on the bills—a five. The other bounced against a chair—a six.

"Let it ride, sir?"

"I'm not a sucker twice. Show us some naturals."

"As you say, sir." Two-Gun picked up the money, then rolled 6-1, 5-2, 4-3, and back again. He rolled several 6-1s, then got snake eyes. He tried again, got acey-deucey. He faced the little old lady. "Ma'am," he said, "if you want to roll, why don't you get down here and do the work?"

"Why, Mr. Andrews!"

Reynolds said hastily, "You'll get your turn, Mrs. Wilkins."

"I don't know what you gentlemen are talking about." She resumed tatting.

Colonel Hammond sat down by the redheads. "You're the January Twins—aren't you?"

"Our public!" one answered delightedly.

"The name is 'Brown,' " said the other.

" 'Brown,' " he agreed, "but how about a show for the boys?"

"Dr. Reynolds wouldn't like it," the first said dutifully.

"I'll handle him. We don't get USO; security regulations are too strict. How about it, Joan?"

"I'm Jane. Okay, if you fix it with Prof."

"Good girls!" He went back to where Grandma Wilkins was demonstrating selection—showers of sixes in the chuck-a-luck cage. She was still tatting. Dr. Withers watched glumly. Hammond said, "Well, Doc?"

"These things are disturbing," Withers admitted, "but it's on the molar level—nothing affecting the elementary particles."

"How about those sketches?"

"I'm a physicist, not a psychologist. But the basic particles—electrons, neutrons, protons—can't be affected except with apparatus designed in accordance with the laws of radioactivity!"

Dr. Reynolds was in earshot; at Withers' remark he said, "Thank you, Mrs. Wilkins. Now, ladies and gentlemen, another experiment. Norman!"

The colored boy opened his eyes. "Yeah, Prof?"

"Up here. And the team from your physics laboratory, please. Has anyone a radium-dial watch?"

Staff technicians hooked the Geiger counter through an amplifier so that normal background radioactivity was heard as occasional clicks, then placed a radium-dial watch close to the counter tube; the clicks changed to hail-storm volume. "Lights out, please," directed Reynolds.

The boy said, "Now, Prof?"

"Wait, Norman. Can everyone see the watch?" The silence was broken only by the rattle of the amplifier, counting radioactivity of the glowing figures. "Now, Norman!"

The shining figures quenched out; the noise died to sparse clicks.

The same group was in a blockhouse miles out in the desert; more miles beyond was the bomb proving site; facing it was a periscope window set in concrete and glazed with solid feet of laminated filter glass.

Dr. Reynolds was talking with Major General Hanby. A naval captain took reports via earphones and speaker horn; he turned to the C.O. "Planes on station, sir."

"Thanks, Dick."

The horn growled, "Station Charlie to Control; we fixed it."

The navy man said to Hanby, "All stations ready, range clear."

"Pick up the count."

"All stations, stand by to resume count at minus seventeen minutes. Time station, pick up the count. This is a live run. Repeat, this is a live run."

Hanby said to Reynolds, "Distance makes no difference?"

"We could work from Salt Lake City once my colleagues knew the setup." He glanced down. "My watch must have stopped."

"Always feels that way. Remember the metronome on the first Bikini test? It nearly drove me nuts."

"I can imagine. Um, General, some of my people are high-strung. Suppose I *ad lib?*"

Hanby smiled grimly. "We always have a pacifier for visitors. Doctor Withers, ready with your curtain raiser?"

The chief physicist was bending over a group of instruments; he looked tired. "Not today," he answered in a flat voice. "Satterlee will make it."

Satterlee came forward and grinned at the brass and V.I.P.'s and at Reynolds' operators. "I've been saving a joke for an audience that can't walk out. But first—" He picked up a polished metal sphere and looked at the E.S.P. adepts. "You saw a ball like this on your tour this morning. That one was plutonium; it's still out there waiting to go *bang!* in about . . . eleven minutes. This is merely steel—unless someone has made a mistake. That would be a joke—we'd laugh ourselves to bits!"

He got no laughs, went on: "But it doesn't weigh enough; we're safe. This dummy has been prepared so that Dr. Reynolds' people will have an image to help them concentrate. It looks no more like an atom bomb than I look like Stalin, but it represents—if it were plutonium— what we atom tinkerers call a 'subcritical mass.' Since the spy trials everybody knows how an atom bomb works. Plutonium gives off neutrons at a constant rate. If the mass is small, most of them escape to the outside. But if it is large enough, or a critical mass, enough are absorbed by other nuclei to start a chain reaction. The trick is to assemble a critical mass quickly—then run for your life! This happens in microseconds; I can't be specific without upsetting the security officer.

"Today we will find out if the mind can change the rate of neutron emission in plutonium. By theories sound enough to have destroyed two Japanese cities, the emission of any particular neutron is pure chance, but the total emission is as invariable as the stars in their courses. Otherwise it would be impossible to make atom bombs.

"By standard theory, theory that works, that subcritical mass out there is no more likely to explode than a pumpkin. Our test group will try to change that. They will concentrate, try to increase the probability of neutrons' escaping, and thus set off that sphere as an atom bomb."

"Doctor Satterlee?" asked a vice admiral with wings. "Do you think it can be done?"

"*Absolutely not!*" Satterlee turned to the adepts. "No offense intended, folks."

"Five minutes!" announced the navy captain.

Satterlee nodded to Reynolds. "Take over. And good luck."

Mrs. Wilkins spoke up. "Just a moment, young man. These 'neuter' things. I—"

"Neutrons, madam."

"That's what I said. I don't quite understand. I suppose that sort of thing comes in high school, but I only finished eighth grade. I'm sorry."

Satterlee looked sorry, too, but he tried. "—and each of these nuclei is potentially able to spit out one of these little neutrons. In that sphere out there"—he held up the dummy—"There are, say, five thousand billion trillion nuclei, each one—"

"My, that's quite a lot, isn't it?"

"Madam, it certainly is. Now—"

"*Two minutes!*"

Reynolds interrupted. "Mrs. Wilkins, don't worry. Concentrate on that metal ball out there and think about those neutrons, each one ready to come out. When I give the word, I want you all—you especially, Norman—to think about that ball, spitting sparks like a watch dial. Try for more sparks. Simply try. If you fail, no one will blame you. Don't get tense."

Mrs. Wilkins nodded. "I'll try." She put her tatting down and got a faraway look.

At once they were blinded by unbelievable radiance bursting through the massive filter. It beat on them, then died away.

The naval captain said, "What the hell!" Someone screamed, "It's gone, it's gone!"

The speaker brayed: "Fission at minus one minute thirty-seven seconds. Control, what went wrong. It looks like a hydrogen—"

The concussion wave hit and all sounds were smothered. Lights went out, emergency lighting clicked on. The blockhouse heaved like a boat in a heavy sea. Their eyes were still dazzled, their ears assaulted by cannonading afternoise, and physicists were elbowing flag officers at the port, when an anguished soprano cut through the din. "Oh, *dear!*"

Reynolds snapped, "What's the matter, Grandma? You all right?"

"Me? Oh, yes, yes—but I'm so sorry. I didn't mean to do it."

"Do what?"

"I was just feeling it out, thinking about all those little bitty neuters, ready to spit. But I didn't mean to make it go off—not till you told us to."

"Oh." Reynolds turned to the rest. "Anyone else jump the gun?"

No one admitted it. Mrs. Wilkins said timidly, "I'm sorry, Doctor. Have they got another one? I'll be more careful."

Reynolds and Withers were seated in the officers' mess with coffee in front of them; the physicist paid no attention to his. His eyes glittered and his face twitched. "No limits! Calculations show over *ninety per cent* conversion of mass to energy. You know what that *means?* If we assume—no, never mind. Just say that we could make every bomb the size of a pea. No tamper. No control circuits. Nothing but . . ." He paused. "Delivery would be fast, small jets—just a pilot, a weaponeer, and one of your 'operators.' No limit to the number of bombs. No nation on earth could—"

"Take it easy," said Reynolds. "We've got only a few telekinesis operators. You wouldn't risk them in a plane."

"But—"

"You don't need to. Show them the bombs, give them photos of the targets, hook them by radio to the weaponeer. That spreads them thin. And we'll test for more sensitive people. My figures show about one in eighteen hundred."

" 'Spread them thin,' " repeated Withers. "Mrs. Wilkins could handle dozens of bombs, one after another—couldn't she?"

"I suppose so. We'll test."

"We will indeed!" Withers noticed his coffee, gulped it. "Forgive me, Doctor; I'm punchy. I've had to revise too many opinions."

"I know. I was a behaviorist."

Captain Mikeler came in, looked around and came over. "The General wants you both," he said softly. "Hurry."

They were ushered into a guarded office. Major General Hanby was with General LaMott and Vice Admiral Keithley; they looked grim. Hanby handed them message flimsies. Reynolds saw the stamp TOP SECRET and handed his back. "General, I'm not cleared for this."

"Shut up and read it."

Reynolds skipped the number groups: "—(PARAPHRASED) RUSSIAN EMBASSY TODAY HANDED STATE ULTIMATUM: DEMANDS USA CONVERT TO 'PEOPLE'S REPUBLIC' UNDER POLITICAL COMMISSARS TO BE ASSIGNED BY USSR. MILITARY ASSURANCES DEMANDED. NOTE CLAIMS MAJOR US CITIES (LIST SEPARATE) ARE MINED WITH ATOMIC BOMBS WHICH THEY THREATEN TO SET OFF BY RADIO IF TERMS ARE NOT MET BY SIXTEEN HUNDRED FRIDAY EST."

Reynolds reread it—"SIXTEEN HUNDRED FRIDAY"—two P.M. day after tomorrow, local time. Our cities booby-trapped with A-bombs? Could they do that? He realized that LaMott was speaking. "We must assume that the threat is real. Our free organization makes it an obvious line of attack."

The admiral said, "They may be bluffing."

The air general shook his head. "They know the President won't surrender. We can't assume that Ivan is stupid."

Reynolds wondered why he was being allowed to hear this. LaMott looked at him. "Admiral Keithley and I leave for Washington at once. I have delayed to ask you this: your people set off an atom bomb. *Can they keep bombs from going off?*"

Reynolds felt his time sense stretch as if he had all year to think about Grandma Wilkins, Norman, his other paranormals. "Yes," he answered.

LaMott stood up. "Your job, Hanby. Coming, Admiral?"

"Wait!" protested Reynolds. "Give me one bomb and Mrs. Wilkins—and I'll sit on it. But how many cities? Twenty? Thirty?"

"Thirty-eight."

"Thirty-eight bombs—or more. Where are they? What do they look like? How long will this go on? It's impossible."

"Of course—but do it anyhow. Or try. Hanby, tell them we're on our way, will you?"

"Certainly, General."

"Good-by, Doctor. Or so long, rather."

Reynolds suddenly realized that these two were going back to "sit" on one of the bombs, to continue their duties until it killed them. He said quickly, "We'll try. We'll certainly try."

Thirty-eight cities . . . forty-three hours . . . and seventeen adepts. Others were listed in years of research, but they were scattered through forty-one states. In a dictatorship secret police would locate them at once, deliver them at supersonic speeds. But this was America.

Find them! Get them here! *Fast!* Hanby assigned Colonel Hammond to turn Reynolds' wishes into orders and directed his security officer to delegate his duties, get on the phone and use his acquaintance with the F.B.I., and other security officers, and through them with local police, to cut red tape and *find those paranormals.* Find them, convince them, bring pressure, start them winging toward the proving ground. By sundown, twenty-three had been found, eleven had been convinced or coerced, two had arrived. Hanby phoned Reynolds, caught him eating a sandwich standing up. "Hanby speaking. The President just phoned."

"The President?"

"LaMott got in to see him. He's dubious, but he's authorized an all-out try, short of slowing down conventional defense. One of his assistants left National Airport by jet plane half an hour ago to come here and help. Things will move faster."

But it did not speed things up, as the Russian broadcast was even then being beamed, making the crisis public; the President went on the air thirty minutes later. Reynolds did not hear him; he was busy. Twenty people to save twenty cities—and a world. But how? He was sure that Mrs. Wilkins could smother any A-bomb she had seen; he hoped the others could. But a hidden bomb in a far-off city—find it mentally, think about it, quench it, not for the microsecond it took to set one off, but for the billions of microseconds it might take to uncover it—was it possible?

What would help? Certain drugs—caffeine, benzedrine. They must have quiet, too. He turned to Hammond. "I want a room and bath for each one."

"You've got that."

"No, we're doubled up, with semi-private baths."

Hammond shrugged. "Can do. It means booting out some brass."

"Keep the kitchen manned. They must not sleep, but they'll have to eat. Fresh coffee all the time and cokes and tea—anything they want. Can you put the room phones through a private switchboard?"

"Okay. What else?"

"I don't know. We'll talk to them."

They all knew of the Russian broadcast, but not what was being planned; they met his words with uneasy silence. Reynolds turned to Andrews. "Well, Two-Gun?"

"Big bite to chew, Prof."

"Yes. Can you chew it?"

"Have to, I reckon."

"Norman?"

"Gee, Boss! How can I when I can't see 'em?"

"Mrs. Wilkins couldn't see that bomb this morning. You can't see radioactivity on a watch dial; it's too small. You just see the dial and think about it. Well?"

The Negro lad scowled. "Think of a shiny ball in a city somewhere?"

"Yes. No, wait—Colonel Hammond, they need a visual image and it won't be that. There are atom bombs here—they must *see* one."

Hammond frowned. "An American bomb meant for dropping or firing won't look like a Russian bomb rigged for placement and radio triggering."

"What will they look like?"

"G-2 ought to know. I hope. We'll get some sort of picture. A three-dimensional mock-up, too. I'd better find Withers and the General." He left.

Mrs. Wilkins said briskly, "Doctor, I'll watch Washington, D.C."

"Yes, Mrs. Wilkins. You're the only one who has been tested, even in reverse. So you guard Washington; it's of prime importance."

"No, no, that's not why. It's the city I can *see* best."

Andrews said, "She's got something, Prof. I pick Seattle."

By midnight Reynolds had his charges, twenty-six by now, tucked away in the officers' club. Hammond and he took turns at a switchboard rigged in the upper hall. The watch would not start until shortly before deadline. Fatigue reduced paranormal powers, sometimes to zero; Reynolds hoped that they were getting one last night of sleep.

A microphone had been installed in each room; a selector switch let them listen in. Reynolds disliked this but Hammond argued, "Sure, it's an invasion of privacy. So is being blown up by an A-bomb." He dialed the switch. "Hear that? Our boy Norman is sawing wood." He moved it again. "Private 'Two-Gun' is still stirring. We can't let them sleep, once it starts, so we have to spy on them."

"I suppose so."

Withers came upstairs. "Anything more you need?"

"I guess not," answered Reynolds. "How about the bomb mock-up?"

"Before morning."

"How authentic is it?"

"Hard to say. Their agents probably rigged firing circuits from radio parts bought right here; the circuits could vary a lot. But the business part—well, we're using real plutonium."

"Good. We'll show it to them after breakfast."

Two-Gun's door opened. "Howdy, Colonel. Prof—it's there."

"What is?"

"The bomb. Under Seattle. I can feel it."

"Where is it?"

"It's down—it *feels* down. And it feels wet, somehow. Would they put it in the Sound?"

Hammond jumped up. "In the harbor—and shower the city with radioactive water!" He was ringing as he spoke. "Get me General Hanby!"

"Morrison here," a voice answered. "What is it, Hammond?"

"The Seattle bomb—have them dredge for it. It's in the Sound, or somewhere under water."

"Eh? How do you know?"

"One of Reynolds' magicians. Do it!" He cut off.

Andrews said worriedly, "Prof, I can't *see* it—I'm not a 'seeing-eye.' Why don't you get one? Say that little Mrs. Brentano?"

"Oh, my God! Clairvoyants—we need them, too."

Withers said, "Eh, Doctor? Do you think—"

"No, I don't, or I would have thought of it. How do they search for bombs? What instruments?"

"Instruments? A bomb in its shielding doesn't even affect a Geiger counter. You have to open things and look."

"How long will that take? Say for New York!"

Hammond said, "Shut up! Reynolds, where are these clairvoyants?"

Reynolds chewed his lip. "They're scarce."

"Scarcer than us dice rollers," added Two-Gun. "But get that Brentano kid. She found keys I had lost digging a ditch. Buried three feet deep—and me searching my quarters."

"Yes, yes, Mrs. Brentano." Reynolds pulled out a notebook.

Hammond reached for the switchboard. "Morrison? Stand by for more names—and even more urgent than the others."

More urgent but harder to find; the Panic was on. The President urged everyone to keep cool and stay home, whereupon thirty million people stampeded. The ticker in the P.I.O. office typed the story: "NEW YORK NY—TO CLEAR JAM CAUSED BY WRECKS IN OUTBOUND TUBE THE INBOUND TUBE OF HOLLAND TUNNEL HAS BEEN REVERSED. POLICE HAVE STOPPED TRYING TO PREVENT EVACUATION. BULLDOZERS WORKING TO RE-OPEN TRIBOROUGH BRIDGE, BLADES SHOVING WRECKED CARS AND HUMAN HAMBURGER. WEEHAWKEN FERRY DISASTER CONFIRMED: NO PASSENGER LIST YET—FLASH—GEORGE WASHINGTON BRIDGE GAVE WAY AT 0353 EST, WHETHER FROM OVERLOAD OR SABOTAGE NOT KNOWN. MORE MORE MORE—FLASH—

It was repeated everywhere. The Denver-Colorado Springs highway had one hundred thirty-five deaths by midnight, then reports stopped. A DC-7 at Burbank ploughed into a mob which had broken through the barrier. The Baltimore-Washington highway was clogged both ways; Memorial Bridge was out of service. The five outlets from Los Angeles were solid with creeping cars. At four A.M. EST the President declared martial law; the order had no immediate effect.

By morning Reynolds had thirty-one adepts assigned to twenty-four cities. He had a stomach-churning ordeal before deciding to let them work only cities known to them. The gambler, Even-Money Karsch, had settled it: "Doc, I know when I'm hot. Minneapolis *has* to be mine." Reynolds gave in, even though one of his students had just arrived from there; he put them both on it and prayed that at least one would be "hot." Two clairvoyants arrived; one, a blind news-dealer from Chicago, was put to searching there; the other, a carnie mentalist, was given the list and told to find bombs wherever she could. Mrs. Brentano had remarried and moved; Norfolk was being combed for her.

At one fifteen P.M., forty-five minutes before deadline, they were in their rooms, each with maps and aerial views of his city, each with photos of the mocked-up bomb. The club was clear of residents; the few normals needed to coddle the paranormals kept careful quiet. Roads nearby were blocked; air traffic was warned away. Everything was turned toward providing an atmosphere in which forty-two people could sit still and *think*.

At the switchboard were Hammond, Reynolds, and Gordon McClintock, the President's assistant. Reynolds glanced up. "What time is it?"

"One thirty-seven," rasped Hammond. "Twenty-three minutes."

"One thirty-eight," disagreed McClintock. "Reynolds, how about Detroit? You *can't* leave it unguarded."

"Whom can I use? Each is guarding the city he knows best."

"Those twin girls— I heard them mention Detroit."

"They've played everywhere. But Pittsburgh is their home."

"Switch one of them to Detroit."

Reynolds thought of telling him to go to Detroit himself. "They work together. You want to get them upset and lose both cities?"

Instead of answering McClintock said, "And who's watching Cleveland?"

"Norman Johnson. He lives there and he's our second strongest operator."

They were interrupted by voices downstairs. A man came up, carrying a bag, and spotted Reynolds. "Oh, hello, Doctor. What is this? I'm on top priority work—tank production—when the F.B.I. grabs me. You are responsible?"

"Yes. Come with me." McClintock started to speak, but Reynolds led the man away. "Mr. Nelson, did you bring your family?"

"No, they're still in Detroit. Had I known—"

"Please! Listen carefully." He explained, pointed out a map of

Detroit in the room to which they went, showed him pictures of the simulated bomb. "You understand?"

Nelson's jaw muscles were jumping. "It seems impossible."

"It *is* possible. You've got to think about that bomb—or bombs. Get in touch, squeeze them, keep them from going off. You'll have to stay awake."

Nelson breathed gustily. "I'll stay awake."

"That phone will get you anything you want. Good luck."

He passed the room occupied by the blind clairvoyant; the door was open. "Harry, it's Prof. Getting anything?"

The man turned to the voice. "It's in the Loop. I could walk to it if I were there. A six-story building."

"That's the best you can do?"

"Tell them to try the attic. I get warm when I go up."

"Right away!" He rushed back, saw that Hanby had arrived. Swiftly he keyed the communications office. "Reynolds speaking. The Chicago bomb is in a six-story building in the Loop area, probably in the attic. No—that's all. G'by!"

Hanby started to speak; Reynolds shook his head and looked at his watch. Silently the General picked up the phone. "This is the commanding officer. Have any flash sent here." He put the phone down and stared at his watch.

For fifteen endless minutes they stood silent. The General broke it by taking the phone and saying, "Hanby. Anything?"

"No, General. Washington is on the wire."

"Eh? You say Washington?"

"Yes, sir. Here's the General, Mr. Secretary."

Hanby sighed. "Hanby speaking, Mr. Secretary. You're all right? Washington . . . is all right?" .

They could hear the relayed voice. "Certainly certainly. We're past the deadline. But I wanted to tell you: Radio Moscow is telling the world that our cities are in flames."

Hanby hesitated. "None of them are?"

"Certainly not. I've a talker hooked in to GHQ, which has an open line to every city listed. All safe. I don't know whether your freak people did any good but, one way or another, it was a false—" The line went dead.

Hanby's face went dead with it. He jiggled the phone. "I've been cut off!"

"Not here, General—at the other end. Just a moment."

They waited. Presently the operator said, "Sorry, sir. I can't get them to answer."

"Keep trying!"

It was slightly over a minute—it merely seemed longer—when the operator said, "Here's your party, sir."

"That you, Hanby?" came the voice. "I suppose we'll have phone trouble just as we had last time. Now, about these ESP people: while we are grateful and all that, nevertheless I suggest that nothing be released to the papers. Might be misinterpreted."

"Oh. Is that an order, Mr. Secretary?"

"Oh, no, no! But have such things routed through my office."

"Yes, sir." He cradled the phone.

McClintock said, "You shouldn't have rung off, General. I'd like to know whether the Chief wants this business continued."

"Suppose we talk about it on the way back to my office." The General urged him away, turned and gave Reynolds a solemn wink.

Trays were placed outside the doors at six o'clock; most of them sent for coffee during the evening. Mrs. Wilkins ordered tea; she kept her door open and chatted with anyone who passed. Harry the newsboy was searching Milwaukee; no answer had been received from his tip about Chicago. Mrs. Ekstein, or "Princess Cathay" as she was billed, had reported a "feeling" about a house trailer in Denver and was now poring over a map of New Orleans. With the passing of the deadline panic abated; communications were improving. The American people were telling each other that they had known that those damned commies were bluffing.

Hammond and Reynolds sent for more coffee at three A.M.; Reynolds' hand trembled as he poured. Hammond said, "You haven't slept for two nights. Get over on that divan."

"Neither have you."

"I'll sleep when you wake up."

"I *can't* sleep. I'm worrying about what'll happen when *they* get sleepy." He gestured at the line of doors.

"So am I."

At seven A.M. Two-Gun came out. "Prof, they got it. The bomb. It's gone. Like closing your hand on nothing."

Hammond grabbed the phone. "Get me Seattle—the F.B.I. office."

While they waited, Two-Gun said, "What now, Prof?"

Reynolds tried to think. "Maybe you should rest."

"Not until this is over. Who's got Toledo? I know that burg."

"Uh . . . young Barnes."

Hammond was connected; he identified himself, asked the question. He put the phone down gently. "They *did* get it," he whispered. "It was in the lake."

"I told you it was wet," agreed Two-Gun. "Now, about Toledo—"

"Well . . . tell me when you've got it and we'll let Barnes rest."

McClintock rushed in at seven thirty-five, followed by Hanby. "Doctor Reynolds! Colonel Hammond!"

"*Sh!* Quiet! You'll disturb them."

McClintock said in a lower voice, "Yes, surely—I was excited. This is important. They located a bomb in Seattle and—"

"Yes. Private Andrews told us."

"Huh? How did *he* know?"

"Never mind," Hanby intervened. "The point is, they found the bomb already triggered. Now we *know* that your people are protecting the cities."

"Was there any doubt?"

"Well . . . yes."

"But there isn't now," McClintock added. "I must take over." He bent over the board. "Communications? Put that White House line through here."

"Just what," Reynolds said slowly, "do you mean by 'take over'?"

"Eh? Why, take charge on behalf of the President. Make sure these people don't let down an instant!"

"But what do you propose to *do?*"

Hanby said hastily, "Nothing, Doctor. We'll just keep in touch with Washington from here."

They continued the vigil together; Reynolds spent the time hating McClintock's guts. He started to take coffee, then decided on another benzedrine tablet instead. He hoped his people were taking enough of it—and not too much. They all had it, except Grandma Wilkins, who wouldn't touch it. He wanted to check with them but knew that he could not—each bomb was bound only by a thread of thought; a split-split second of diversion might be enough.

The outside light flashed; Hanby took the call. "Congress has recessed," he announced, "and the President is handing the Soviet Union a counter ultimatum; locate and disarm any bombs or be bombed in return." The light flashed again; Hanby answered. His face lit up. "Two more found," he told them. "One in Chicago, right where your man said; the other in Camden."

"Camden? How?"

"They rounded up the known Communists, of course. This laddie was brought back there for questioning. He didn't like that; he knew that he was being held less than a mile from the bomb. Who is on Camden?"

"Mr. Dimwiddy."

"The elderly man with the bunions?"

"That's right—retired postman. General, do we assume that there is only one bomb per city?"

McClintock answered, "Of course not! These people must—"

Hanby cut in, "Central Intelligence is assuming so, except for New York and Washington. If they had more bombs here, they would have added more cities."

Reynolds left to take Dimwiddy off watch. McClintock, he fumed, did not realize that people were flesh and blood.

Dimwiddy was unsurprised. "A while ago the pressure let up, then—well, I'm afraid I dozed. I had a terrible feeling that I had let it go off, then I knew it hadn't." Reynolds told him to rest, then be ready to help out elsewhere. They settled on Philadelphia; Dimwiddy had once lived there.

The watch continued. Mrs. Ekstein came up with three hits, but no answers came back; Reynolds still had to keep those cities covered. She then complained that her "sight" had gone; Reynolds went to her room and told her to nap, not wishing to consult McClintock.

Luncheon trays came and went. Reynolds continued worrying over how to arrange his operators to let them rest. Forty-three people and thirty-five cities—if only he had two for every city! Maybe any of them could watch any city? No, he could not chance it.

Barnes woke up and took back Toledo; that left Two-Gun free. Should he let him take Cleveland? Norman had had no relief and Two-Gun had once been through it, on a train. The colored boy was amazing but rather hysterical, whereas Two-Gun—well, Reynolds felt that Two-Gun would last, even through a week of no sleep.

No! He couldn't trust Cleveland to a man who had merely passed through it. But with Dimwiddy on Philadelphia, when Mary Gifford woke he could put her on Houston and that would let Hank sleep before shifting him to Indianapolis and that would let him—

A chess game, with all pawns queens and no mistakes allowed.

McClintock was twiddling the selector switch, listening in. Suddenly he snapped, "Someone is asleep!"

Reynolds checked the number.

"Of course, that's the twins' room; they take turns. You may hear snores in 21 and 30 and 8 and 19. It's okay; they're off watch."

"Well, all right." McClintock seemed annoyed.

Reynolds bent back to his list. Shortly McClintock snorted, "Who's in room 12?"

"Uh? Wait—that's Norman Johnson, Cleveland."

"You mean he's on watch?"

"Yes." Reynolds could hear the boy's asthmatic breathing, felt relieved.

"He's asleep!"

"No, he's not."

But McClintock was rushing down the corridor. Reynolds took after him; Hammond and Hanby followed. Reynolds caught up as McClintock burst into room 12. Norman was sprawled in a chair, eyes closed in his habitual attitude. McClintock rushed up, slapped him. "Wake up!"

Reynolds grabbed McClintock. "You bloody fool!"

Norman opened his eyes, then burst into tears. "It's *gone!*"

"Steady, Norman. It's all right."

"No, no! It's gone—and my mammy's gone with it!"

McClintock snapped, "Concentrate, boy! Get back on it!"

Reynolds turned on him. "Get out. Get out before I punch you."

Hanby and Hammond were in the door; the General cut in with a hoarse whisper, "Pipe down, Doctor, bring the boy."

Back at the board the outside light was flashing. Hanby took the call while Reynolds tried to quiet the boy. Hanby listened gravely, then said, "He's right. Cleveland just got it."

McClintock snapped, "He went to sleep. He ought to be shot."

"Shut up," said Hanby.

"But—"

Reynolds said, "any others, General?"

"Why would there be?"

"All this racket. It may have disturbed a dozen of them."

"Oh, we'll see." He called Washington again. Presently he sighed. "No, just Cleveland. We were . . . lucky."

"General," McClintock insisted, "he was asleep."

Hanby looked at him. "Sir, you may be the President's deputy but you yourself have no military authority. Off my post."

"But I am directed by the President to—"

"Off my post, sir! Go back to Washington. *Or to Cleveland.*"

McClintock looked dumbfounded. Hanby added, "You're worse than bad—you're a fool."

"The President will hear of this."

"Blunder again and the President won't live that long. Get out."

By nightfall the situation was rapidly getting worse. Twenty-seven cities were still threatened and Reynolds was losing operators faster than bombs were being found. Even-Money Karsch would not relieve when awakened. "See that?" he said, rolling dice. "Cold as a well-digger's feet. I'm through." After that Reynolds tested each one who was about to relieve, found that some were tired beyond the power of short sleep to restore them—they were "cold."

By midnight there were eighteen operators for nineteen cities. The twins had fearfully split up; it had worked. Mrs. Wilkins was holding both Washington and Baltimore; she had taken Baltimore when he had no one to relieve there.

But now he had no one for relief anywhere and three operators—Nelson, Two-Gun and Grandma Wilkins—had had no rest. He was too fagged to worry; he simply knew that whenever one of them reached his limit, the United States would lose a city. The panic had resumed after the bombing of Cleveland; roads again were choked. The disorder made harder the search for bombs. But there was nothing he could do.

Mrs. Ekstein still complained about her sight but kept at it. Harry the newsboy had had no luck with Milwaukee, but there was no use shifting him; other cities were "dark" to him. During the night Mrs. Ekstein pointed to the bomb in Houston. It was, she said, in a box underground. A coffin? Yes, there was a headstone; she was unable to read the name.

Thus, many recent dead in Houston were disturbed. But it was nine Sunday morning before Reynolds went to tell Mary Gifford that she could rest—or relieve for Wilmington, if she felt up to it. He found her collapsed and lifted her onto the bed, wondering if she had known the Houston bomb was found.

Eleven cities now and eight people. Grandma Wilkins held four cities. No one else had been able to double up. Reynolds thought dully that it was a miracle that they had been able to last at all; it surpassed enormously the best test performance.

Hammond looked up as he returned. "Make any changes?"

"No. The Gifford kid is through. We'll lose half a dozen cities before this is over."

"Some of them must be damn near empty by now."

"I hope so. Any more bombs found?"

"Not yet. How do you feel, Doc?"

"Three weeks dead." Reynolds sat down wearily. He was wondering if he should wake some of those sleeping and test them again when he heard a noise below; he went to the stairwell.

Up came an M.P. captain. "They said to bring her here."

Reynolds looked at the woman with him. "Dorothy Brentano!"

"Dorothy Smith now."

He controlled his trembling and explained what was required. She nodded. "I figured that out on the plane. Got a pencil? Take this: St. Louis—a river warehouse with a sign reading 'Bartlett & Sons, Jobbers.' Look in the loft. And Houston—no, they got that one. Baltimore—it's in a ship at the docks, the S.S. *Gold Coast*. What other cities? I've wasted time feeling around where there was nothing to find."

Reynolds was already shouting for Washington to answer.

Grandma Wilkins was last to be relieved; Dorothy located one in the Potomac—and Mrs. Wilkins told her sharply to keep trying. There were four bombs in Washington, which Mrs. Wilkins had known all along. Dorothy found them in eleven minutes.

Three hours later Reynolds showed up in the club messroom, not having been able to sleep. Several of his people were eating and listening to the radio blast about our raid on Russia. He gave it a wide berth; they could blast Omsk and Tomsk and Minsk and Pinsk; today he didn't care. He was sipping milk and thinking that he would never drink coffee again when Captain Mikeler bent over his table.

"The General wants you. Hurry!"

"Why?"

"I said, 'Hurry!' Where's Grandma Wilkins—oh—see her. Who is Mrs. Dorothy Smith?"

Reynolds looked around. "She's with Mrs. Wilkins."

Mikeler rushed them to Hanby's office. Hanby merely said, "Sit over there. And you ladies, too. Stay in focus."

Reynolds found himself looking into a television screen at the President of the United States. He looked as weary as Reynolds felt, but he turned on his smile. "You are Doctor Reynolds?"

"Yes, Mr. President!"

"These ladies are Mrs. Wilkins and Mrs. Smith?"

"Yes, sir."

The President said quietly, "You three and your colleagues will be thanked by the Republic. And by me, for myself. But that must wait. Mrs. Smith, there are more bombs—in Russia. Could your strange gift find them there?"

"Why, I don't—I can try!"

"Mrs. Wilkins, could you set off those Russian bombs while they are still far away?"

Incredibly, she was still bright-eyed and chipper. "Why, Mr. President!"

"Can you?"

She got a far-away look. "Dorothy and I had better have a quiet room somewhere. And I'd like a pot of tea. A large pot."

SKY LIFT

Imagination, November 1953

"ALL TORCH PILOTS! Report to the Commodore!" The call echoed through Earth Satellite Station.

Joe Appleby flipped off the shower to listen. "You don't mean me," he said happily, "I'm on leave—but I'd better shove before you change your mind."

He dressed and hurried along a passageway. He was in the outer ring of the Station; its slow revolution, a giant wheel in the sky, produced gravity-like force against his feet. As he reached his room the loud-speakers repeated, "All torch pilots, report to the Commodore," then added, "Lieutenant Appleby, report to the Commodore." Appleby uttered a rude monosyllable.

The Commodore's office was crowded. All present wore the torch, except a flight surgeon and Commodore Berrio himself, who wore the jets of a rocketship pilot. Berrio glanced up and went on talking: "—the situation. If we are to save Proserpina Station, an emergency run must be made out to Pluto. Any questions?"

No one spoke. Appleby wanted to, but did not wish to remind Berrio that he had been late. "Very well," Berrio went on. "Gentlemen, it's a job for torch pilots. I must ask for volunteers."

Good! thought Appleby. Let the eager lads volunteer and then adjourn. He decided that he might still catch the next shuttle to Earth. The Commodore continued, "Volunteers please remain. The rest are dismissed."

Excellent, Appleby decided. Don't rush for the door, me lad. Be dignified—sneak out between two taller men.

No one left. Joe Appleby felt swindled but lacked the nerve to start the exodus. The Commodore said soberly, "Thank you, gentlemen. Will you wait in the wardroom, please?" Muttering, Appleby left with the crowd. He wanted to go out to Pluto someday—sure!—but not now, not with Earthside leave papers in his pocket.

He held a torcher's contempt for the vast distance itself. Older pilots thought of interplanetary trips with a rocket-man's bias, in terms of years—trips that a torch ship with steady acceleration covered in days.

By the orbits that a rocketship must use the round trip to Jupiter takes over five years; Saturn is twice as far, Uranus twice again, Neptune still farther. No rocketship ever attempted Pluto; a round trip would take more than ninety years. But torch ships had won a foothold even there: Proserpina Station—cryology laboratory, cosmic radiation station, parallax observatory, physics laboratory, all in one quintuple dome against the unspeakable cold.

Nearly four billion miles from Proserpina Station Appleby followed a classmate into the wardroom. "Hey, Jerry," he said, "tell me what it is I seem to have volunteered for?"

Jerry Price looked around. "Oh, it's late Joe Appleby. Okay, buy me a drink."

A radiogram had come from Proserpina, Jerry told him, reporting an epidemic: "Larkin's disease." Appleby whistled. Larkin's disease was a mutated virus, possibly of Martian origin; a victim's red-cell count fell rapidly, soon he was dead. The only treatment was massive transfusions while the disease ran its course. "So, m'boy, somebody has to trot out to Pluto with a blood bank."

Appleby frowned. "My pappy warned me. 'Joe,' he said, 'keep your mouth shut and never volunteer.' "

Jerry grinned. "We didn't exactly volunteer."

"How long is the boost? Eighteen days or so? I've got social obligations Earthside."

"Eighteen days at one-g—but this will be higher. They are running out of blood donors."

"How high? A *g-and-a-half?*"

Price shook his head. "I'd guess two gravities."

"Two g's!"

"What's hard about that? Men have lived through a lot more."

"Sure, for a short pull-out—not for days on end. Two g's strains your heart if you stand up."

"Don't moan, they won't pick you—I'm more the hero type. While you're on leave, think of me out in those lonely wastes, a grim-jawed angel of mercy. Buy me another drink."

Appleby decided that Jerry was right; with only two pilots needed he stood a good chance of catching the next Earth shuttle. He got out his little black book and was picking phone numbers when a messenger arrived. "Lieutenant Appleby, sir?" Joe admitted it.

"The-Commodore's-compliments-and-will-you-report-at-once,-sir?"

"On my way." Joe caught Jerry's eye. "Who is what type?"

Jerry said, "Shall I take care of your social obligations?"

"Not likely!"

"I was afraid not. Good luck, boy."

With Commodore Berrio was the flight surgeon and an older lieutenant. Berrio said, "Sit down, Appleby. You know Lieutenant Kleuger? He's your skipper. You will be co-pilot."

"Very good, sir."

"Appleby, Mr. Kleuger is the most experienced torch pilot available. You were picked because medical records show you have exceptional tolerance for acceleration. This is a high-boost trip."

"How high, sir?"

Berrio hesitated. "Three and one-half gravities."

Three and a half *g*'s! That wasn't a boost—that was a pull-out. Joe heard the surgeon protest, "I'm sorry, sir, but three gravities is all I can approve."

Berrio frowned. "Legally, it's up to the captain. But three hundred lives depend on it."

Kleuger said, "Doctor, let's see that curve." The surgeon slid a paper across the desk; Kleuger moved it so that Joe could see it. "Here's the scoop, Appleby—"

A curve started high, dropped very slowly, made a sudden "knee" and dropped rapidly. The surgeon put his finger on the "knee." "Here," he said soberly, "is where the donors are suffering from loss of blood as much as the patients. After that it's hopeless, without a new source of blood."

"How did you get this curve?" Joe asked.

"It's the empirical equation of Larkin's disease applied to two hundred eighty-nine people."

Appleby noted vertical lines each marked with an acceleration and a time. Far to the right was one marked: "1 *g*—18 days." That was the standard trip; it would arrive after the epidemic had burned out. Two gravities cut it to twelve days seventeen hours; even so, half the colony would be dead. Three *g*'s was better but still bad. He could see why the Commodore wanted them to risk three-and-a-half kicks; that line touched the "knee," at nine days fifteen hours. That way they could save almost everybody . . . but, oh, brother!

The time advantage dropped off by inverse squares. Eighteen days required one gravity, so nine days took four, while four-and-a-half days required a fantastic sixteen gravities. But someone had drawn a line at "16 *g*—4.5 days." "Hey! This plot must be for a robot-torch—that's the ticket! Is there one available?"

Berrio said gently, "Yes. But what are its chances?"

Joe shut up. Even between the inner planets robots often went astray. In four-billion-odd miles the chance that one could hit close enough to be caught by radio control was slim. "We'll try," Berrio promised. "If it succeeds, I'll call you at once." He looked at Kleuger. "Captain, time is short. I must have your decision."

Kleuger turned to the surgeon. "Doctor, why not another half gravity? I recall a report on a chimpanzee who was centrifuged at high *g* for an amazingly long time."

"A chimpanzee is not a man."

Joe blurted out, "How much did this chimp stand, Surgeon?"

"Three and a quarter gravities for twenty-seven days."

"He *did?* What shape was he in when the test ended?"

"He wasn't," the doctor grunted.

Kleuger looked at the graph, glanced at Joe, then said to the Commodore, "The boost will be at three and one-half gravities, sir."

Berrio merely said, "Very well, sir. Hurry over to sick bay. You haven't much time."

Forty-seven minutes later they were being packed into the scout torchship *Salamander*. She was in orbit close by; Joe, Kleuger, and their handlers came by tube linking the hub of the Station to her airlock. Joe was weak and dopy from a thorough washing-out plus a dozen treatments and injections. A good thing, he thought, that light-off would be automatic.

The ship was built for high boost; controls were over the pilots' tanks, where they could be fingered without lifting a hand. The flight surgeon and an assistant fitted Kleuger into one tank while two medical technicians arranged Joe in his. One of them asked, "Underwear smooth? No wrinkles?"

"I guess."

"I'll check." He did so, then arranged fittings necessary to a man who must remain in one position for days. "The nipple left of your mouth is water; the two on your right are glucose and bouillon."

"No solids?"

The surgeon turned in the air and answered, "You don't need any, you won't want any, and you mustn't have any. And be careful in swallowing."

"I've boosted before."

"Sure, sure. But be careful."

Each tank was like an oversized bathtub filled with a liquid denser than water. The top was covered by a rubbery sheet, gasketed at the edges; during boost each man would float with the sheet conforming to his body. The *Salamander* being still in free orbit, everything was weightless and the sheet now served to keep the fluid from floating out. The attendants centered Appleby against the sheet and fastened him with sticky tape, then placed his own acceleration collar, tailored to him, behind his head. The surgeon came over and inspected. "You okay?"

"Sure."

"Mind that swallowing." He added, "Okay, Captain. Permission to leave your ship, sir?"

"Certainly. Thank you, Surgeon."

"Good luck." He left with the technicians.

The room had no ports and needed none. The area in front of Joe's face was filled with screens, instruments, radar, and data displays; near his forehead was his eyepiece for the coelostat. A light blinked green as the passenger tube broke its anchors; Kleuger caught Joe's eye in a mirror mounted opposite them. "Report, Mister."

"Minus seven minutes oh four. Tracking. Torch warm and idle. Green for light-off."

"Stand by while I check orientation." Kleuger's eyes disappeared into his coelostat eyepiece. Presently he said, "Check me, Joe."

"Aye aye, sir." Joe twisted a knob and his eyepiece swung down. He found three star images brought together perfectly in the cross hairs. "Couldn't be better, Skipper."

"Ask for clearance."

"Salamander to Control—clearance requested to Proserpina. Automatic light-off on tape. All green."

"Control to Salamander. You are cleared. Good luck!"

"Cleared, Skipper. Minus three. . . . *Double oh!*" Joe thought morosely that he should be half way to Earth now. Why the hell did the military always get stuck with these succor-&-rescue jobs?

When the counter flashed the last thirty seconds he forgot his foregone leave. The lust to travel possessed him. To go, no matter where, anywhere . . . go! He smiled as the torch lit off.

Then weight hit him.

At three and one-half gravities he weighed six hundred and thirty pounds. It felt as if a load of sand had landed on him, squeezing his chest, making him helpless, forcing his head against his collar. He strove to relax, to let the supporting liquid hold him together. It was all right to tighten up for a pull-out, but for a long boost one must relax. He breathed shallowly and slowly; the air was pure oxygen, little lung action was needed. But he labored just to breathe. He could feel his heart struggling to pump blood grown heavy through squeezed vessels. This is awful! he admitted. I'm not sure I can take it. He had once had four *g* for nine minutes but he had forgotten how bad it was.

"Joe! *Joe!*"

He opened his eyes and tried to shake his head. "Yes, Skipper." He looked for Kleuger in the mirror; the pilot's face was sagging and drawn, pulled into the mirthless grin of high acceleration.

"Check orientation!"

Joe let his arms float as he worked controls with leaden fingers. "Dead on, Skipper."

"Very well. Call Luna."

Earth Station was blanketed by their torch but the Moon was on their bow. Appleby called Luna tracking center and received their data on the departure plus data relayed from Earth Station. He called figures and times to Kleuger, who fed them into the computer. Joe then found that he had forgotten, while working, his unbearable weight. It felt worse than ever. His neck ached and he suspected that there was a wrinkle under his left calf. He wiggled in the tank to smooth it, but it made it worse. "How's she look, Skipper?"

"Okay. You're relieved, Joe. I'll take first watch."

"Right, Skipper." He tried to rest—as if a man could when buried under sandbags. His bones ached and the wrinkle became a nagging nuisance. The pain in his neck got worse; apparently he had wrenched it at light-off. He turned his head, but there were just two positions—bad and worse. Closing his eyes, he attempted to sleep. Ten minutes later he was wider awake than ever, his mind on three things, the lump in his neck, the irritation under his leg, and the squeezing weight.

Look, bud, he told himself, this is a long boost. Take it easy, or adrenalin exhaustion will get you. As the book says, *The ideal pilot is relaxed and unworried. Sanguine in temperament, he never borrows trouble.* Why, you chair-warming so-and-so! Were *you* at three and a half g's when you wrote that twaddle?

Cut it out, boy! He turned his mind to his favorite subject—girls, bless their hearts. Such self-hypnosis he had used to pass many a lonely million miles. Presently he realized wryly that his phantom harem had failed him. He could not conjure them up, so he banished them and spent his time being miserable.

He awoke in a sweat. His last dream had been a nightmare that he was headed out to Pluto at an impossibly high boost.

My God! So he was!

The pressure seemed worse. When he moved his head there was a stabbing pain down his side. He was panting and sweat was pouring off. It ran into his eyes; he tried to wipe them, found that his arm did not respond and that his fingertips were numb. He inched his arm across his body and dabbed at his eyes; it did not help.

He stared at the elapsed time dial of the integrating accelerograph and tried to remember when he was due on watch. It took a while to understand that six and a half hours had passed since light-off. He then realized with a jerk that it was long past time to relieve the watch. Kleuger's face in the mirror was still split in the grin of high *g*; his eyes were closed. "Skipper!" Joe shouted. Kleuger did not stir. Joe felt for the alarm button, thought better of it. Let the poor goop sleep!

But somebody had to feed the hogs—better get the clouds out of his brain. The accelerometer showed three and a half exactly; the torch dials were all in operating range; the radiometer showed leakage less than ten percent of danger level.

The integrating accelerograph displayed elapsed time, velocity, and distance, in dead-reckoning for empty space. Under these windows were three more which showed the same by the precomputed tape controlling the torch; by comparing, Joe could tell how results matched predictions. The torch had been lit off for less than seven hours, speed was nearly two million miles per hour and they were over six million miles out. A third display corrected these figures for the Sun's field, but Joe ignored this; near Earth's orbit the Sun pulls only one two-thousandth of a gravity—a gnat's whisker, allowed for in precomputation. Joe merely noted that tape and D.R. agreed; he wanted an outside check.

Both Earth and Moon now being blanketed by the same cone of disturbance, he twisted knobs until their radar beacon beamed toward Mars and let it pulse the signal meaning "Where am I?" He did not wait for answer; Mars was eighteen minutes away by radio. He turned instead to the coelostat. The triple image had wandered slightly but the error was too small to correct.

He dictated what he had done into the log, whereupon he felt worse. His ribs hurt, each breath carried the stab of pleurisy. His hands and feet felt "pins-and-needles" from scanty circulation. He wiggled them, which produced crawling sensations and wearied him. So he held still and watched the speed soar. It increased seventy-seven miles per hour every second, more than a quarter million miles per hour every hour. For once he envied rocketship pilots; they took forever to get anywhere but they got there in comfort.

Without the torch, men would never have ventured much past Mars. $E = Mc^2$, mass is energy, and a pound of sand equals fifteen billion horsepower-hours. An atomic rocketship uses but a fraction of one percent of that energy, whereas the new torchers used better than eighty percent. The conversion chamber of a torch was a tiny sun; particles expelled from it approached the speed of light.

Appleby was proud to be a torcher, but not at the moment. The crick had grown into a splitting headache, he wanted to bend his knees and could not, and he was nauseated from the load on his stomach. Kleuger seemed able to sleep through it, damn his eyes! How did they expect a man to *stand* this? Only eight hours and already he felt done in, bushed—how could he last nine days?

Later—time was beginning to be uncertain—some indefinite time later he heard his name called. "Joe! *Joe!*"

Couldn't a man die in peace? His eyes wandered around, found the mirror; he struggled to focus. "Joe! You've got to relieve me—I'm groggy."

"Aye aye, sir."

"Make a check, Joe. I'm too goofed up to do it."

"I already did, sir."

"*Huh?* When?"

Joe's eyes swam around to the elapsed-time dial. He closed one eye to read it. "Uh, about six hours ago."

"What? *What time is it?*"

Joe didn't answer. He wished peevishly that Kleuger would go away. Kleuger added soberly, "I must have blacked out, kid. What's the situation?" Presently he insisted, "Answer me, Mister."

"Huh? Oh, we're all right—down the groove. Skipper, is my left leg twisted? I can't see it."

"Eh? Oh, never mind your leg! What were the figures?"

"What figures?"

" 'What figures?' Snap out of it, Mister! You're on duty."

A fine one to talk, Joe thought fretfully. If that's how he's going to act, I'll just close my eyes and ignore him.

Kleuger repeated, "The figures, Mister."

"Huh? Oh, play 'em off the log if you're so damned eager!" He expected a blast at that, but none came. When next he opened his eyes Kleuger's eyes were closed. He couldn't recall whether the Skipper had played his figures back or not—nor whether he had logged them. He decided that it was time for another check but he was dreadfully thirsty; he needed a drink first. He drank carefully but still got a drop down his windpipe. A coughing spasm hurt him all over and left him so weak that he had to rest.

He pulled himself together and scanned the dials. Twelve hours and—No, wait a minute! One *day* and twelve hours—that *couldn't* be right. But their speed was over ten million miles per hour and their distance more than ninety million miles from Earth; they were beyond the orbit of Mars. "Skipper! Hey! Lieutenant Kleuger!"

Kleuger's face was a grinning mask. In dull panic Joe tried to find their situation. The coelostat showed them balanced; either the ship had wobbled back, or Kleuger had corrected it. Or had he himself? He decided to run over the log and see. Fumbling among buttons he found the one to rewind the log.

Since he didn't remember to stop it the wire ran all the way back to light-off, then played back, zipping through silent stretches and slowing for speech. He listened to his record of the first check, then found that Phobos Station, Mars, had answered with a favorable report—to which a voice added, *"Where's the fire?"*

Yes, Kleuger had corrected balance hours earlier. The wire hurried through a blank spot, slowed again—Kleuger had dictated a letter to someone; it was unfinished and incoherent. Once Kleuger had stopped to shout, *"Joe! Joe!"* and Joe heard himself answer, *"Oh shut up!"* He had no memory of it.

There was something he should do but he was too tired to think and he hurt all over—except his legs, he couldn't feel them. He shut his eyes and tried not to think. When he opened them the elapsed time was turning three days; he closed them and leaked tears.

A bell rang endlessly; he became aware that it was the general alarm, but he felt no interest other than a need to stop it. It was hard to find the switch, his fingers were numb. But he managed it and was about to rest from the effort, when he heard Kleuger call him. "Joe!"

"Huh?"

"Joe—don't go back to sleep or I'll turn the alarm on again. You hear me?"

"Yeah—" So Kleuger had done that—why, damn him!

"Joe, I've got to talk to you. I can't stand any more."

" 'Any more' what?"

"High boost. I can't take any more—it's killing me."

"Oh, rats!" Turn on that loud bell, would he?

"I'm dying, Joe. I can't see—my eyes are shot. Joe, I've got to shut down the boost. I've got to."

"Well, what's stopping you?" Joe answered irritably.

"Don't you see, Joe? You've got to back me up. We tried and we couldn't. We'll both log it. Then it'll be all right."

"Log what?"

"Eh? Dammit, Joe, pay attention. I can't talk much. You've got to say—to say that the strain became unendurable and you advised me to shut down. I'll confirm it and it will be all right." His labored whisper was barely audible.

Joe couldn't figure out what Kleuger meant. He couldn't remember why Kleuger had put them in high boost anyhow. *"Hurry, Joe."*

There he went, nagging him! Wake him up and then nag him—to hell with him. "Oh, go back to sleep!" He dozed off and was again jerked awake by the alarm. This time he knew where the switch was and flipped it quickly. Kleuger switched it on again, Joe turned it off. Kleuger quit trying and Joe passed out.

He came awake in free fall. He was still realizing the ecstasy of being weightless when he managed to reorient; he was in the *Salamander,* headed for Pluto. Had they reached the end of the run? No, the dial said four days and some hours. Had the tape broken? The autopilot gone haywire? He then recalled the last time he had been awake.

Kleuger had shut off the torch!

The stretched grin was gone from Kleuger's face, the features seemed slack and old. Joe called out, "Captain! Captain Kleuger!" Kleuger's eyes fluttered and lips moved but Joe heard nothing. He slithered out of the tank, moved in front of Kleuger, floated there. "Captain, can you hear me?"

The lips whispered, "I had to, boy. I saved us. Can you get us back, Joe?" His eyes opened but did not track.

"Captain, listen to me. I've got to light off again."

"Huh? No, Joe, no!"

"I've got to."

"*No!* That's an order, Mister."

Appleby stared, then with a judo chop caught the sick man on the jaw. Kleuger's head bobbed loosely. Joe pulled himself between the tanks, located a three-position switch, turned it from "Pilot & Co-Pilot" to "Co-Pilot Only"; Kleuger's controls were now dead. He glanced at Kleuger, saw that his head was not square in his collar, so he taped him properly into place, then got back in his tank. He settled his head and fumbled for the switch that would put the autopilot back on tape. There was some reason why they must finish this run—but for the life of him he could not remember why. He squeezed the switch and weight pinned him down.

He was awakened by a dizzy feeling added to the pressure. It went on for seconds, he retched futilely. When the motion stopped he peered at the dials. The *Salamander* had just completed the somersault from acceleration to deceleration. They had come half way, about, eighteen hundred million miles; their speed was over three million miles per hour and beginning to drop. Joe felt that he should report it to the skipper—he had no recollection of any trouble with him. "Skipper! Hey!" Kleuger did not move. Joe called again, then resorted to the alarm.

The clangor woke, not Kleuger, but Joe's memory. He shut it off, feeling soul sick. Topping his physical misery was shame and loss and panic as he recalled the shabby facts. He felt that he ought to log it but could not decide what to say. Beaten and ever lower in mind he gave up and tried to rest.

He woke later with something gnawing at his mind . . . something he should do for the Captain . . . something about a cargo robot—

That was it! If the robot-torch had reached Pluto, they could quit! Let's see—elapsed-time from light-off was over five days. Yes, if it ever got there, then—

He ran the wire back, listened for a recorded message. It was there: *"Earth Station to Salamander—Extremely sorry to report that robot failed rendezvous. We are depending on you.—Berrio."*

Tears of weakness and disappointment sped down his cheeks, pulled along by three and one-half gravities.

It was on the eighth day that Joe realized that Kleuger was dead. It was not the stench—he was unable to tell that from his own ripe body odors. Nor was it that the Captain had not roused since flip-over; Joe's time sense was so fogged that he did not realize this. But he had dreamt that Kleuger was shouting for him to get up, to stand up—"Hurry up, Joe!" But the weight pressed him down.

So sharp was the dream that Joe tried to answer after he woke up. Then he looked for Kleuger in the mirror. Kleuger's face was much the same, but he knew with sick horror that the captain was dead. Nevertheless he tried to arouse him with the alarm. Presently he gave up; his fingers were purple and he could feel nothing below his waist; he wondered if he were dying and hoped that he was. He slipped into that lethargy which had become his normal state.

He did not become conscious when, after more than nine days, the autopilot quenched the torch. Awareness found him floating in midroom, having somehow squirmed out of his station. He felt deliciously lazy and quite hungry; the latter eventually brought him awake.

His surroundings put past events somewhat into place. He pulled himself to his tank and examined the dials. Good grief!—it had been two hours since the ship had gone into free fall. The plan called for approach to be computed before the tape ran out, corrected on entering free fall, a new tape cut and fed in without delay, then let the autopilot make the approach. He had done nothing and wasted two hours.

He slid between tank and controls, discovering then that his legs were paralyzed. No matter—legs weren't needed in free fall, nor in the tank. His hands did not behave well, but he could use them. He was stunned when he found Kleuger's body, but steadied down and got to work. He had no idea where he was; Pluto might be millions of miles away, or almost in his lap—perhaps they had spotted him and were already sending approach data. He decided to check the wire.

He found their messages at once:

"Proserpina to Salamander—Thank God you are coming. Here are

your elements at quench out—": followed by time reference, range-and-bearing figures, and doppler data.

And again: *"Here are later and better figures, Salamander—hurry!"*

And finally, only a few minutes before: *"Salamander, why the delay in light-off? Is your computer broken down? Shall we compute a ballistic for you?"*

The idea that anyone but a torcher could work a torch ballistic did not sink in. He tried to work fast, but his hands bothered him—he punched wrong numbers and had to correct them. It took him a half hour to realize that the trouble was not just his fingers. Ballistics, a subject as easy for him as checkers, was confused in his mind.

He could not work the ballistic.

"Salamander to Proserpina—Request ballistic for approach into parking orbit around Pluto."

The answer came so quickly that he knew that they had not waited for his okay. With ponderous care he cut the tape and fed it into the autopilot. It was then that he noticed the boost . . . four point oh three.

Four gravities for the approach—

He had assumed that the approach would be a normal one—and so it might have been if he had not wasted three hours.

But it wasn't fair! It was too much to expect. He cursed childishly as he settled himself, fitted the collar, and squeezed the button that turned control to the autopilot. He had a few minutes of waiting time; he spent it muttering peevishly. They could have figured him a better ballistic—hell, he should have figured it. They were always pushing him around. Good old Joe, anybody's punching bag! That so-and-so Kleuger over there, grinning like a fool and leaving the work for him—if Kleuger hadn't been so confounded eager—

Acceleration hit him and he blacked out.

When the shuttle came up to meet him, they found one man dead, one nearly dead, and the cargo of whole blood.

The supply ship brought pilots for the *Salamander* and fetched Appleby home. He stayed in sick bay until ordered to Luna for treatment; on being detached he reported to Berrio, escorted by the flight surgeon. The Commodore let him know brusquely that he had done a fine job, a damn' fine job! The interview ended and the surgeon helped Joe to stand; instead of leaving Joe said, "Uh, Commodore?"

"Yes, son?"

"Uh, there's one thing I don't understand, uh, what I don't understand is, uh, this: why do I have to go, uh, to the geriatrics clinic at Luna City? That's for old people, uh? That's what I've always understood—the way I understand it. Sir?"

The surgeon cut in, "I told you, Joe. They have the very best physiotherapy. We got special permission for you."

Joe looked perplexed. "Is that right, sir? I feel funny, going to an old folks', uh, hospital?"

"That's right, son."

Joe grinned sheepishly. "Okay, sir, uh, if you say so."

They started to leave. "Doctor—stay a moment. Messenger, help Mr. Appleby."

"Joe, can you make it?"

"Uh, sure! My legs are lots better—see?" He went out, leaning on the messenger.

Berrio said, "Doctor, tell me straight: will Joe get well?"

"No, sir."

"Will he get better?"

"Some, perhaps. Lunar gravity makes it easy to get the most out of what a man has left."

"But will his mind clear up?"

The doctor hesitated. "It's this way, sir. Heavy acceleration is a speeded-up aging process. Tissues break down, capillaries rupture, the heart does many times its proper work. And there is hypoxia, from failure to deliver enough oxygen to the brain."

The Commodore struck his desk an angry blow. The surgeon said gently, "Don't take it so hard, sir."

"Damn it, man—think of the way he was. Just a kid, all bounce and vinegar—now look at him! He's an old man—senile."

"Look at it this way," urged the surgeon, "you expended one man, but you saved two hundred and seventy."

" 'Expended one man'? If you mean Kleuger, he gets a medal and his wife gets a pension. That's the best any of us can expect. I wasn't thinking of Kleuger."

"Neither was I," answered the surgeon.

A TENDERFOOT IN SPACE

Boys' Life, May–July 1958

❖

CHAPTER ONE

"HEEL, NIXIE," THE boy said softly, "and keep quiet."

The little mongrel took position left and rear of his boy, waited. He could feel that Charlie was upset and he wanted to know why—but an order from Charlie could not be questioned.

The boy tried to see whether or not the policeman was noticing them. He felt light-headed—neither he nor his dog had eaten that day. They had stopped in front of this supermarket, not to buy for the boy had no money left, but because of a "BOY WANTED" sign in the window.

It was then that he had noticed the reflection of the policeman in the glass.

The boy hesitated, trying to collect his cloudy thoughts. Should he go inside and ask for the job? Or should he saunter past the policeman? Pretend to be just out for a walk?

The boy decided to go on, get out of sight. He signalled the dog to stay close and turned away from the window. Nixie came along, tail high. He did not care where they went as long as he was with Charlie. Charlie had belonged to him as far back as he could remember, he could imagine no other condition. In fact Nixie would not have lived past his tenth day had not Charlie fallen in love with him; Nixie had been the least attractive of an unfortunate litter; his mother was Champion Lady Diana of Ojai—his father was unknown.

But Nixie was not aware that a neighbor boy had begged his life from his first owners. His philosophy was simple: enough to eat, enough sleep, and the rest of his time spent playing with Charlie. This present outing had been Charlie's idea, but any outing was welcome. The shortage of food was a nuisance but Nixie automatically forgave Charlie such errors—after all, boys will be boys and a wise dog accepted the fact. The only thing that troubled him was that Charlie did not have the happy heart which was a proper part of all hikes.

As they moved past the man in the blue uniform, Nixie felt the man's interest in them, sniffed his odor, but could find no real unfriendliness in it. But Charlie was nervous, alert, so Nixie kept his own attention high.

The man in uniform said, "Just a moment, son—"

Charlie stopped, Nixie stopped. "You speaking to me, officer?"

"Yes. What's your dog's name?"

Nixie felt Charlie's sudden terror, got ready to attack. He had never yet had to bite anyone for his boy—but he was instantly ready. The hair between his shoulder blades stood up.

Charlie answered, "Uh . . . his name is 'Spot.' "

"So?" The stranger said sharply, "Nixie!"

Nixie had been keeping his eyes elsewhere, in order not to distract his ears, his nose, and the inner sense with which he touched people's feelings. But he was so startled at hearing this stranger call him by name that he turned his head and looked at him.

"His name is 'Spot,' is it?" the policeman said quietly. "And mine is Santa Claus. But you're Charlie Vaughn and you're going home." He spoke into his helmet phone: "Nelson, reporting a pickup on that Vaughn missing-persons flier. Send a car. I'm in front of the new supermarket."

Nixie had trouble sorting out Charlie's feelings; they were both sad and glad. The stranger's feelings were slightly happy but mostly nothing; Nixie decided to wait and see. He enjoyed the ride in the police car, as he always enjoyed rides, but Charlie did not, which spoiled it a little.

They were taken to the local Justice of the Peace. "You're Charles Vaughn?"

Nixie's boy felt unhappy and said nothing.

"Speak up, son," insisted the old man. "If you aren't, then you must have stolen that dog." He read from a paper "—accompanied by a small brown mongrel, male, well trained, responds to the name 'Nixie.' Well?"

Nixie's boy answered faintly, "I'm Charlie Vaughn."

"That's better. You'll stay here until your parents pick you up." The judge frowned. "I can't understand your running away. Your folks are emigrating to Venus, aren't they?"

"Yes, sir."

"You're the first boy I ever met who didn't want to make the Big Jump." He pointed to a pin on the boy's lapel. "And I thought Scouts were trustworthy. Not to mention obedient. What got into you, son? Are you scared of the Big Jump? 'A Scout is Brave.' That doesn't mean you don't have to be scared—everybody is at times. 'Brave' simply means you don't run even if you *are* scared."

"I'm not scared," Charlie said stubbornly. "I *want* to go to Venus."

"Then why run away when your family is about to leave?"

Nixie felt such a burst of warm happy-sadness from Charlie that he licked his hand. "Because Nixie can't go!"

"Oh." The judge looked at boy and dog. "I'm sorry, son. That problem is beyond my jurisdiction." He drummed his desk top. "Charlie . . . will you promise, Scout's honor, not to run away again until your parents show up?"

"Uh . . . yes, sir."

"Okay. Joe, take them to my place. Tell my wife she had better see how recently they've had anything to eat."

The trip home was long. Nixie enjoyed it, even though Charlie's father was happy-angry and his mother was happy-sad and Charlie himself was happy-sad-worried. When Nixie was home he checked quickly through each room, making sure that all was in order and that there were no new smells. Then he returned to Charlie.

The feelings had changed. Mr. Vaughn was angry, Mrs. Vaughn was sad, Charlie himself gave out such bitter stubbornness that Nixie went to him, jumped onto his lap, and tried to lick his face. Charlie settled Nixie beside him, started digging fingers into the loose skin back of Nixie's neck. Nixie quieted at once, satisfied that he and his boy could face together whatever it was—but it distressed him that the other two were not happy. Charlie belonged to him; they belonged to Charlie; things were better when they were happy, too.

Mr. Vaughn said, "Go to bed, young man, and sleep on it. I'll speak with you again tomorrow."

"Yes, sir. Good night, sir."

"Kiss your mother goodnight. One thing more—Do I need to lock doors to be sure you will be here in the morning?"

"No, sir."

Nixie got on the foot of the bed as usual, tromped out a space, laid his tail over his nose, and started to go to sleep. But his boy was not sleeping; his sadness was taking the distressing form of heaves and sobs. So Nixie got up, went to the other end of the bed and licked away tears—then let himself be pulled into Charlie's arms and tears applied directly to his neck. It was not comfortable and too hot, besides being taboo. But it was worth enduring as Charlie started to quiet down, presently went to sleep.

Nixie waited, gave him a lick on the face to check his sleeping, then moved to his end of the bed.

Mrs. Vaughn said to Mr. Vaughn, "Charles, isn't there *anything* we can do for the boy?"

"Confound it, Nora. We're getting to Venus with too little money as it is. If anything goes wrong, we'll be dependent on charity."

"But we *do* have a little spare cash."

"Too little. Do you think I haven't considered it? Why, the fare for that worthless dog would be almost as much as it is for Charlie himself! Out of the question! So why nag me? Do you think I enjoy this decision?"

"No, dear." Mrs. Vaughn pondered. "How much does Nixie weigh? I . . . well, I think I could reduce ten more pounds if I really tried."

"What? Do you want to arrive on Venus a living skeleton? You've reduced all the doctor advises, and so have I."

"Well . . . I thought that if somehow, among us, we could squeeze out Nixie's weight—it's not as if he were a St. Bernard!—we could swap it against what we weighed for our tickets."

Mr. Vaughn shook his head unhappily. "They don't do it that way."

"You told me yourself that weight was everything. You even got rid of your chess set."

"We could afford thirty pounds of chess sets, or china, or cheese, where we can't afford thirty pounds of dog."

"I don't see why not."

"Let me explain. Surely, it's weight; it's always weight in a space ship. But it isn't just my hundred and sixty pounds, or your hundred and twenty, not Charlie's hundred and ten. We're not dead weight; we have to eat and drink and breathe air and have room to move—that last takes more weight because it takes more ship weight to hold a live person than it does for an equal weight in the cargo hold. For a human being there is a complicated formula—hull weight equal to twice the passenger's weight, plus the number of days in space times four pounds. It takes a hundred and forty-six days to get to Venus—so it means that the calculated weight for each of us amounts to six hundred and sixteen pounds before they even figure in our actual weights. But for a dog the rate is even higher—five pounds per day instead of four."

"That seems unfair. Surely a little dog can't eat as much as a man? Why, Nixie's food costs hardly anything."

Her husband snorted. "Nixie eats his own rations and half of what goes on Charlie's plate. However, it's not only the fact that a dog does eat more for his weight, but also they don't reprocess waste with a dog, not even for hydroponics."

"Why not? Oh, I know what you mean. But it seems silly."

"The passengers wouldn't like it. Never mind; the rule is: five pounds per day for dogs. Do you know what that makes Nixie's fare? Over three thousand dollars!"

"My goodness!"

"My ticket comes to thirty-eight hundred dollars and some, you get by for thirty-four hundred, and Charlie's fare is thirty-three hundred—yet that confounded mongrel dog, which we couldn't sell for his veterinary bills, would cost three thousand dollars. If we had that to spare—which we haven't—the humane thing would be to adopt some orphan, spend the money on him, and thereby give him a chance on an uncrowded planet . . . not waste it on a dog. Confound it!—a year from now Charlie will have forgotten this dog."

"I wonder."

"He will. When I was a kid, I had to give up dogs—more than once they died, or something. I got over it. Charlie has to make up his mind whether to give Nixie away . . . or have him put to sleep." He chewed his lip. "We'll get him a pup on Venus."

"It won't be Nixie."

"He can name it Nixie. He'll love it as much."

"But—Charles, how is it there are dogs on Venus if it's so dreadfully expensive to get them there?"

"Eh? I think the first exploring parties used them to scout. In any case they're always shipping animals to Venus; our own ship is taking a load of milch cows."

"That must be terribly expensive."

"Yes and no. They ship them in sleep-freeze of course, and a lot of them never revive. But they cut their losses by butchering the dead ones and selling the meat at fancy prices to the colonists. Then the ones that live have calves and eventually it pays off." He stood up. "Nora, let's go to bed. It's sad—but our boy is going to have to make a man's decision. Give the mutt away, or have him put to sleep."

"Yes, dear." She sighed. "I'm coming."

Nixie was in his usual place at breakfast—lying beside Charlie's chair, accepting tidbits without calling attention to himself. He had learned long ago the rules of the dining room: no barking, no whining, no begging for food, no paws on laps, else the pets of his pet would make difficulties. Nixie was satisfied. He had learned as a puppy to take the world as it was, cheerful over its good points, patient with its minor shortcomings. Shoes were not to be chewed, people were not to be jumped on, most strangers must be allowed to approach the house (subject, of course, to strict scrutiny and constant alertness)—a few simple rules and everyone was happy. Live and let live.

He was aware that his boy was not happy even this beautiful morning. But he had explored this feeling carefully, touching his boy's mind with gentle care by means of his canine sense for feelings, and had decided, from his superior maturity, that the mood would wear off. Boys were sometimes sad and a wise dog was resigned to it.

Mr. Vaughn finished his coffee, put his napkin aside. "Well, young man?"

Charlie did not answer. Nixie felt the sadness in Charlie change suddenly to a feeling more aggressive and much stronger but no better. He pricked up his ears and waited.

"Chuck," his father said, "last night I gave you a choice. Have you made up your mind?"

"Yes, Dad." Charlie's voice was very low.

"Eh? Then tell me."

Charlie looked at the tablecloth. "You and Mother go to Venus. Nixie and I are staying here."

Nixie could feel anger welling up in the man . . . felt him control it. "You're figuring on running away again?"

"No, sir," Charlie answered stubbornly. "You can sign me over to the state school."

"Charlie!" It was Charlie's mother who spoke. Nixie tried to sort out the rush of emotions impinging on him.

"Yes," his father said at last, "I could use your passage money to pay the state for your first three years or so, and agree to pay your support until you are eighteen. But I shan't."

"Huh? Why not, Dad?"

"Because, old-fashioned as it sounds, I am head of this family. I am responsible for it—and not just food, shelter, and clothing, but its total welfare. Until you are old enough to take care of yourself I mean to keep an eye on you. One of the prerogatives which go with my responsibility is deciding where the family shall live. I have a better job offered me on Venus than I could ever hope for here, so I'm going to Venus—and my family goes with me." He drummed on the table, hesitated. "I think your chances are better on a pioneer planet, too—but, when you are of age, if you think otherwise, I'll pay your fare back to Earth. But you go with us. Understand?"

Charlie nodded, his face glum.

"Very well. I'm amazed that you apparently care more for that dog than you do for your mother—and myself. But—"

"It isn't that, Dad. Nixie needs—"

"Quiet. I don't suppose you realize it, but I tried to figure this out— I'm not taking your dog away from you out of meanness. If I could afford it, I'd buy the hound a ticket. But something your mother said last night brought up a third possibility."

Charlie looked up suddenly, and so did Nixie, wondering why the surge of hope in his boy.

"I can't buy Nixie a ticket . . . but it's possible to ship him as freight."

"Huh? Why, sure, Dad! Oh, I know he'd have to be caged up—but I'd go down and feed him every day and pet him and tell him it was all right and—"

"Slow down! I don't mean that. All I can afford is to have him shipped the way animals are always shipped in space ships . . . in sleep-freeze."

Charlie's mouth hung open. He managed to say, "But that's—"

"That's dangerous. As near as I remember, it's about fifty-fifty whether he wakes up at the other end. But if you want to risk it—well, perhaps it's better than giving him away to strangers, and I'm sure you would prefer it to taking him down to the vet's and having him put to sleep."

Charlie did not answer. Nixie felt such a storm of conflicting emotions in Charlie that the dog violated dining room rules; he raised up and licked the boy's hand.

Charlie grabbed the dog's ear. "All right, Dad," he said gruffly. "We'll risk it—if that's the only way Nixie and I can still be partners."

Nixie did not enjoy the last few days before leaving; they held too many changes. Any proper dog likes excitement, but home is for peace and quiet. Things should be orderly there—food and water always in the same place, newspapers to fetch at certain hours, milkmen to supervise at regular times, furniture all in its proper place. But during that week all was change—nothing on time, nothing in order. Strange men came into the house (always a matter for suspicion), and he, Nixie, was not even allowed to protest, much less give them the what-for they had coming.

He was assured by Charlie and Mrs. Vaughn that it was "all right" and he had to accept it, even though it obviously was not all right. His knowledge of English was accurate for a few dozen words but there was no way to explain to him that almost everything owned by the Vaughn family was being sold, or thrown away . . . nor would it have reassured him. Some things in life were permanent; he had never doubted that the Vaughn home was first among these certainties.

By the night before they left, the rooms were bare except for beds. Nixie trotted around the house, sniffing places where familiar objects had been, asking his nose to tell him that his eyes deceived him, whining at the results. Even more upsetting than physical change was emotional change, a heady and not entirely happy excitement which he could feel in all three of his people.

There was a better time that evening, as Nixie was allowed to go to Scout meeting. Nixie always went on hikes and had formerly attended all meetings. But he now attended only outdoor meetings since an incident the previous winter—Nixie felt that too much fuss had been made about it . . . just some spilled cocoa and a few broken cups and anyhow it had been that cat's fault.

But this meeting he was allowed to attend because it was Charlie's last Scout meeting on Earth. Nixie was not aware of that but he greatly enjoyed the privilege, especially as the meeting was followed by a party at which Nixie became comfortably stuffed with hot dogs and pop. Scoutmaster McIntosh presented Charlie with a letter of withdrawal, certifying his status and merit badges and asking his admission into any troop on Venus. Nixie joined happily in the applause, trying to outbark the clapping.

Then the Scoutmaster said, "Okay, Rip."

Rip was senior patrol leader. He got up and said, "Quiet, fellows. Hold it, you crazy savages! Charlie, I don't have to tell you that we're all sorry to see you go . . . but we hope you have a swell time on Venus and now and then send a postcard to Troop Twenty-Eight and tell us about it—we'll post 'em on the bulletin board. Anyhow, we wanted to get you a going-away present. But Mr. McIntosh pointed out that you were on a very strict weight allowance and practically anything would either cost you more to take with you than we had paid for it, or maybe you couldn't take it at all, which wouldn't be much of a present.

"But it finally occurred to us that we could do one thing. Nixie—"

Nixie's ears pricked. Charlie said softly, "Steady, boy."

"Nixie has been with us almost as long as you have. He's been around, poking his cold nose into things, longer than any of the tenderfeet, and longer even than some of the second class. So we decided he ought to have his own letter of withdrawal, so that the troop you join on Venus will know that Nixie is a Scout in good standing. Give it to him, Kenny."

The scribe passed over the letter. It was phrased like Charlie's letter, save that it named "Nixie Vaughn, Tenderfoot Scout" and diplomatically omitted the subject of merit badges. It was signed by the scribe, the scoutmaster, and the patrol leaders and countersigned by every member of the troop. Charlie showed it to Nixie, who sniffed it. Everybody applauded, so Nixie joined happily in applauding himself.

"One more thing," added Rip. "Now that Nixie is officially a Scout, he has to have his badge. So send him front and center."

Charlie did so. They had worked their way through the Dog Care merit badge together while Nixie was a pup, all feet and floppy ears; it had made Nixie a much more acceptable member of the Vaughn family. But the rudimentary dog training required for the merit badge had stirred Charlie's interest; they had gone on to Dog Obedience School together and Nixie had progressed from easy spoken commands to more difficult silent hand signals.

Charlie used them now. At his signal Nixie trotted forward, sat stiffly at attention, front paws neatly drooped in front of his chest, while Rip fastened the tenderfoot badge to his collar, then Nixie raised his right paw in salute and gave one short bark, all to hand signals.

The applause was loud and Nixie trembled with eagerness to join it. But Charlie signalled "hold & quiet," so Nixie remained silently poised in salute until the clapping died away. He returned to heel just as silently, though quivering with excitement. The purpose of the ceremony may not have been clear to him—if so, he was not the first tenderfoot Scout to be a little confused. But it was perfectly clear that he was the center of attention and was being approved of by his friends; it was a high point in his life.

But all in all there had been too much excitement for a dog in one week; the trip to White Sands, shut up in a travel case and away from Charlie, was the last straw. When Charlie came to claim him at the baggage room of White Sands Airport, his relief was so great that he had a puppyish accident, and was bitterly ashamed.

He quieted down on the drive from airport to spaceport, then was disquieted again when he was taken into a room which reminded him of his unpleasant trips to the veterinary—the smells, the white-coated figure, the bare table where a dog had to hold still and be hurt. He stopped dead.

"Come, Nixie!" Charlie said firmly. "None of that, boy. Up!"

Nixie gave a little sigh, advanced and jumped onto the examination table, stood docile but trembling.

"Have him lie down," the man in the white smock said. "I've got to get the needle into the large vein in his foreleg."

Nixie did so on Charlie's command, then lay tremblingly quiet while his left foreleg was shaved in a patch and sterilized. Charlie put a hand on Nixie's shoulder blades and soothed him while the veterinary surgeon probed for the vein. Nixie bared his teeth once but did not growl, even though the fear in the boy's mind was beating on him, making him just as afraid.

Suddenly the drug reached his brain and he slumped limp.

Charlie's fear surged to a peak but Nixie did not feel it. Nixie's tough little spirit had gone somewhere else, out of touch with his friend, out of space and time—wherever it is that the "I" within a man or a dog goes when the body wrapping it is unconscious.

Charlie said shrilly, "Is he all right?"

"Eh? Of course."

"Uh . . . I thought he had died."

"Want to listen to his heart beat?"

"Uh, no—if you say he's all right. Then he's going to be okay? He'll live through it?"

The doctor glanced at Charlie's father, back at the boy, let his eyes rest on Charlie's lapel. "Star Scout, eh?"

"Uh, yes, sir."

"Going on to Eagle?"

"Well . . . I'm going to try, sir."

"Good. Look, son. If I put your dog over on that shelf, in a couple of hours he'll be sleeping normally and by tomorrow he won't even know he was out. But if I take him back to the chill room and start him on the cycle—" He shrugged. "Well, I've put eighty head of cattle under today. If forty percent are revived, it's a good shipment. I do my best."

Charlie looked grey. The surgeon looked at Mr. Vaughn, back at the boy. "Son, I know a man who's looking for a dog for his kids. Say the word and you won't have to worry about whether this pooch's system will recover from a shock it was never intended to take."

Mr. Vaughn said, "Well, son?"

Charlie stood mute, in an agony of indecision. At last Mr. Vaughn said sharply, "Chuck, we've got just twenty minutes before we must check in with Emigration. Well? What's your answer?"

Charlie did not seem to hear. Timidly he put out one hand, barely touched the still form with the staring, unseeing eyes. Then he snatched his hand back and squeaked, "*No!* We're going to Venus—*both* of us!"—turned and ran out of the room.

The veterinary spread his hands helplessly. "I tried."

"I know you did, Doctor," Mr. Vaughn answered gravely. "Thank you."

The Vaughns took the usual emigrant routing: winged shuttle rocket to the inner satellite station, ugly wingless ferry rocket to the outer station, transshipment there to the great globular cargo liner *Hesperus*. The jumps and changes took two days; they stayed in the deepspace ship for twenty-one tedious weeks, falling in half-elliptical orbit from Earth down to Venus. The time was fixed, an inescapable consequence of the law of gravity and the sizes and shapes of the two planetary orbits.

At first Charlie was terribly excited. The terrific high-gravity boost to break away from Earth's mighty grasp was as much of a shocker as he had hoped; six gravities *is* shocking, even to those used to it. When the shuttle rocket went into free fall a few minutes later, utter weightlessness was as distressing, confusing—and exciting—as he had hoped. It was so upsetting that he would have lost his lunch had he not been injected with anti-nausea drug.

Earth, seen from space, looked as it had looked in color-stereo pictures, but he found that the real thing is as vastly more satisfying as a hamburger is better than a picture of one. In the outer satellite station, someone pointed out to him the famous Captain Nordhoff, just back from Pluto. Charlie recognized those stern, lined features, familiar from TV and news pictures, and realized with odd surprise that the hero was a man, like everyone else. He decided to be a spaceman and famous explorer himself.

S. S. *Hesperus* was a disappointment. It "blasted" away from the outer station with a gentle shove, one-tenth gravity, instead of the soul-satisfying, bone-grinding, ear-shattering blast with which the shuttle had left Earth. Also, despite its enormous size, it was terribly crowded. After the Captain had his ship in orbit to intercept Venus five months later, he placed spin on his ship to give his passengers artificial weight—which took from Charlie the pleasant new feeling of weightlessness which he had come to enjoy.

He was bored silly in five days—and there were five months of it ahead. He shared a cramped room with his father and mother and slept in a hammock swung "nightly" (the ship used Greenwich time) between their bunks. Hammock in place, there was no room in the cubicle; even with it stowed, only one person could dress at a time. The only recreation space was the messrooms and they were always crowded. There was one view port in his part of the ship. At first it was popular, but after a few days even the kids didn't bother, for the view was always the same: stars, and more stars.

By order of the Captain, passengers could sign up for a "sightseeing tour." Charlie's chance came when they were two weeks out—a climb through accessible parts of the ship, a quick look into the power room, a longer look at the hydroponics gardens which provided fresh air and part of their food, and a ten-second glimpse through the door of the Holy of Holies, the control room, all accompanied by a lecture from a bored junior officer. It was over in two hours and Charlie was again limited to his own, very crowded part of the ship.

Up forward there were privileged passengers, who had staterooms as roomy as those of the officers and who enjoyed the luxury of the officers' lounge. Charlie did not find out that they were aboard for almost a month, but when he did, he was righteously indignant.

His father set him straight. "They paid for it."

"Huh? But we paid, too. Why should they get—"

"They paid for luxury. Those first-class passengers each paid about three times what your ticket cost, or mine. We got the emigrant rate—transportation and food and a place to sleep."

"I don't think it's fair."

Mr. Vaughn shrugged. "Why should we have something we haven't paid for?"

"Uh, . . . well, Dad, why should they be able to pay for luxuries we can't afford?"

"A good question. Philosophers ever since Aristotle have struggled with that one. Maybe you'll tell me, someday."

"Huh? What do you mean, Dad?"

"Don't say 'Huh.' Chuck, I'm taking you to a brand-new planet. If you try, you can probably get rich. Then maybe you can tell me why a man with money can command luxuries that poor people can't."

"But we aren't poor!"

"No, we are not. But we aren't rich either. Maybe you've got the drive to get rich. One thing is sure: on Venus the opportunities are all around you. Never mind—how about a game before dinner?"

Charlie still resented being shut out of the nicest parts of the ship—he had never felt like a second-class anything (citizen, or passenger) before in his life; the feeling was not pleasant. He decided to get rich on Venus. He would make the biggest uranium strike in history; then he would ride first class between Venus and Earth whenever he felt like it—that would teach those stuck-up snobs!

He then remembered he had already decided to be a famous spaceman.

Well, he would do both. Someday he would own a space line . . . and one of the ships would be his private yacht. But by the time the *Hesperus* reached the halfway point he no longer thought about it.

The emigrants saw little of the ship's crew, but Charlie got acquainted with Slim, the emigrants' cook. Slim was called so for the reason that cooks usually are; he sampled his own wares all day long and was pear shaped.

Like all space ships, the *Hesperus* was undermanned except for astrogators and engineers—why hire a cook's helper when the space can be sold to a passenger? It was cheaper to pay high wages to a cook who could perform production-line miracles without a helper. And Slim could.

But he could use a helper. Charlie's merit badge in cooking plus a willingness to do as he was told made him Slim's favorite volunteer assistant. Charlie got from it something to do with his time, sandwiches and snacks whenever he wanted them, and lots of knowledgeable conversation. Slim had not been to college but his curiosity had never dried up; he had read everything worth reading in several ship's libraries and had kept his eyes open dirtside on every inhabited planet in the Solar System.

"Slim, what's it like on Venus?"

"Mmm . . . pretty much like the books say. Rainy. Hot. Not too bad at Borealis, where you'll land."

"Yes—but what's it *like*?"

"Why not wait and see? Give that stew a stir . . . and switch on the shortwaver. Did you know that they used to figure that Venus couldn't be lived on?"

"Huh? No, I didn't."

" 'struth. Back in the days when we didn't have space flight, scientists were certain that Venus didn't have either oxygen nor water. They figured it was a desert, with sand storms and no air you could breathe. Proved it, all by scientific logic."

"But how could they make such a mistake? I mean, obviously, with clouds all over it and—"

"The clouds didn't show water vapor, not through a spectroscope they didn't. Showed lots of carbon dioxide, though, and by the science of the last century they figured they had proved that Venus couldn't support life."

"Funny sort of science! I guess they were pretty ignorant in those days."

"Don't go running down our grandfathers. If it weren't for them, you and I would be squatting in a cave, scratching fleas. No, Bub, they were pretty sharp; they just didn't have all the facts. We've got more facts, but that doesn't make us smarter. Put them biscuits over here. The way I see it, it just goes to show that the only way to tell what's in a stew is to eat it . . . and even then you aren't always sure. Venus turned out to be a very nice place. For ducks. If there were any ducks there. Which there ain't."

"Do you like Venus?"

"I like any place I don't have to stay in too long. Okay, let's feed the hungry mob."

The food in the *Hesperus* was as good as the living accommodations were bad. This was partly Slim's genius, but was also the fact that food in a space ship costs by its weight; what it had cost Earthside matters little compared with the expense of lifting it off Earth. The choicest steaks cost the spaceline owners little more than the same weight of rice—and any steaks left over could be sold at high prices to colonists weary for a taste of Earth food. So the emigrants ate as well as the first class passengers, even though not with fine service and fancy surroundings. When Slim was ready he opened a shutter in the galley partition and Charlie dealt out the wonderful viands like chow in a Scout camp to passengers queued up with plates. Charlie enjoyed this chore. It made him feel like a member of the crew, a spaceman himself.

Charlie almost managed not to worry about Nixie, having told himself that there was nothing to worry about. They were a month past midpoint, with Venus only six weeks away before he discussed it with Slim. "Look, Slim, you know a lot about such things. Nixie'll make it all right . . . won't he?"

"Hand me that paddle. Mmm . . . don't know as I ever ran across a dog in space before. Cats now . . . cats belong in space. They're clean and neat and help to keep down mice and rats."

"I don't like cats."

"Ever lived with a cat? No, I see you haven't. How can you have the gall not to like something you don't know anything about? Wait till you've lived with a cat, then tell me what you think. Until then . . . well, who told you you were entitled to an opinion?"

"Huh? Why, everybody is entitled to his own opinion!"

"Nonsense, Bub. Nobody is entitled to an opinion about something he is ignorant of. If the Captain told me how to bake a cake, I would politely suggest that he not stick his nose into my trade . . . contrariwise, I never tell him how to plot an orbit to Mars."

"Slim, you're changing the subject. How about Nixie? He's going to be all right . . . isn't he?"

"As I was saying, I don't have opinions about things I don't know. Happens I don't know dogs. Never had one as a kid; I was raised in a big city. Since then I've been in space. No dogs."

"Darn it, Slim!—you're being evasive. You know about sleep-freeze. I know you do."

Slim sighed. "Kid, you're going to die someday and so am I. And so is your pup. It's the one thing we can't avoid. Why, the ship's reactor could blow up and none of us would know what hit us till they started fitting us with haloes. So why fret about whether your dog comes out of sleep-freeze? Either he does and you've worried unnecessarily . . . or he doesn't and there's nothing you can do about it."

"So you don't think he will?"

"I didn't say that. I said it was foolish to worry."

But Charlie did worry; the talk with Slim brought it to the top of his mind, worried him more and more as the day got closer. The last month seemed longer to him than the four dreary months that had preceded it.

As for Nixie, time meant nothing to him. Suspended between life and death, he was not truly in the *Hesperus* at all, but somewhere else, outside of time. It was merely his shaggy little carcass that lay, stored like a ham, in the frozen hold of the ship.

Eventually the Captain slowed his ship, matched her with Venus and set her in a parking orbit alongside Venus's single satellite station. After transshipment and maddening delay the Vaughns were taken down in the winged shuttle *Cupid* into the clouds of Venus and landed at the north pole colony, Borealis.

For Charlie there was a still more maddening delay: cargo (which included Nixie) was unloaded after passengers and took many days because the mighty *Hesperus* held so much more than the little *Cupid*. He could not even go over to the freight sheds to inquire about Nixie as immigrants were held at the reception center for quarantine. Each one had received many shots during the five-month trip to innoculate them against the hazards of Venus; now they found that they must wait not only on most careful physical examination and observation to make sure that they were not bringing Earth diseases in with them but also to receive more shots not available aboard ship. Charlie spent the days with sore arms and gnawing anxiety.

So far he had had one glimpse outdoors—a permanently cloudy sky which never got dark and was never very bright. Borealis is at Venus's north pole and the axis of the planet is nearly erect; the unseen Sun circled the horizon, never rising nor setting by more than a few degrees. The colony lived in eternal twilight.

The lessened gravity, nine-tenths that of Earth, Charlie did not notice even though he knew he should. It had been five months since he had felt Earth gravity and the *Hesperus* had maintained only one-third gravity in that outer part, where spin was most felt. Consequently Charlie felt heavier than seemed right, rather than lighter—his feet had forgotten full weight.

Nor did he notice the heavy concentration (about 2%) of carbon dioxide in the air, on which Venus's mighty jungles depended. It had once been believed that so much carbon dioxide, breathed regularly, would kill a man, but long before space flight, around 1950, experiments had shown that even a higher concentration had no bad effects. Charlie simply didn't notice it.

All in all, he might have been waiting in a dreary, barracks-like building in some tropical port on Earth. He did not see much of his father, who was busy by telephone and by germproof conference cage, conferring with his new employers and arranging for quarters, nor did he see much of his mother; Mrs. Vaughn had found the long trip difficult and was spending most of her time lying down.

Nine days after their arrival Charlie was sitting in the recreation room of the reception center, disconsolately reading a book he had already read on Earth. His father came in. "Come along."

"Huh? What's up?"

"They're going to try to revive your dog. You want to be there, don't you? Or maybe you'd rather not? I can go . . . and come back and tell you what happened."

Charlie gulped. "I want to be there. Let's go."

The room was like the one back at White Sands where Nixie had been put to sleep, except that in place of the table there was a cage-like contraption with glass sides. A man was making adjustments on a complex apparatus which stood next to the glass box and was connected to it. He looked up. "Yes? We're busy."

"My name is Vaughn and this is my son Charlie. He's the owner of the dog."

The man frowned. "Didn't you get my message? I'm Doctor Zecker, by the way. You're too soon; we're just bringing the dog up to temperature."

Mr. Vaughn said, "Wait here, Charlie," crossed the room and spoke in a low voice to Zecker.

Zecker shook his head. "Better wait outside."

Mr. Vaughn again spoke quietly; Dr. Zecker answered, "You don't understand. I don't even have proper equipment—I've had to adapt the force breather we use for hospital monkeys. It was never meant for a dog."

They argued in whispers for a few moments. They were interrupted by an amplified voice from outside the room: "Ready with ninety-seven-X, Doctor—that's the dog."

Zecker called back, "Bring it in!"—then went on to Mr. Vaughn, "All right—keep him out of the way. Though I still say he would be better off outside." He turned, paid them no further attention.

Two men came in, carrying a large tray. Something quiet and not very large was heaped on it, covered by dull blue cloth. Charlie whispered, "Is that Nixie?"

"I think so," his father answered in a low voice. "Keep quiet and watch."

"Can't I *see* him?"

"Stay where you are and don't say a word—else the doctor will make you leave."

Once inside, the team moved quickly and without speaking, as if this were something rehearsed again and again, something that must be done with great speed and perfect precision. One of them opened the glass box; the other placed the tray inside, uncovered its burden. It was Nixie, limp and apparently dead. Charlie caught his breath.

One assistant moved the little body forward, fitted a collar around its neck, closed down a partition like a guillotine, jerked his hands out of the way as the other assistant slammed the glass door through which they had put the dog in, quickly sealed it. Now Nixie was shut tight in a glass coffin, his head lying outside the end partition, his body inside. "Cycle!"

Even as he said it, the first assistant slapped a switch and fixed his eyes on the instrument board and Doctor Zecker thrust both arms into long rubber gloves passing through the glass, which allowed his hands to be inside with Nixie's body. With rapid, sure motions he picked up a hypodermic needle, already waiting inside, shoved it deep into the dog's side.

"Force breathing established."

"No heart action, Doctor!"

The reports came one on top of the other, Zecker looked up at the dials, looked back at the dog and cursed. He grabbed another needle. This one he entered gently, depressed the plunger most carefully, with his eyes on the dials.

"Fibrillation."

"I can see!" he answered snappishly, put down the hypo and began to massage the dog in time with the ebb and surge of the "iron lung."

And Nixie lifted his head and cried.

It was more than an hour before Dr. Zecker let Charlie take the dog away. During most of this time the cage was open and Nixie was breathing on his own, but with the apparatus still in place, ready to start again if his heart or lungs should falter in their newly relearned trick of keeping him alive. But during this waiting time Charlie was allowed to stand beside him, touch him, sooth and pet him to keep him quiet.

At last the doctor picked up Nixie and put him in Charlie's arms. "Okay, take him. But keep him quiet; I don't want him running around for the next ten hours. But not too quiet, don't let him sleep."

"Why not, Doctor?" asked Mr. Vaughn.

"Because sometimes, when you think they've made it, they just lie down and quit—as if they had had a taste of death and found they liked it. This pooch has had a near squeak—we have only seven minutes to restore blood supply to the brain. Any longer than that . . . well, the brain is permanently damaged and you might as well put it out of its misery."

"You think you made it in time?"

"Do you think," Zecker answered angrily, "that I would let you take the dog if I hadn't?"

"Sorry."

"Just keep him quiet, but not too quiet. Keep him awake."

Charlie answered solemnly, "I will, Doctor. Nixie's going to be all right—I know he is."

Charlie stayed awake all night long, talking to Nixie, petting him, keeping him quiet but not asleep. Neither one of his parents tried to get him to go to bed.

CHAPTER TWO

Nixie liked Venus. It was filled with a thousand new smells, all worth investigating, countless new sounds, each of which had to be catalogued. As official guardian of the Vaughn family and of Charlie in particular, it was his duty and pleasure to examine each new phenomenon, decide whether or not it was safe for his people; he set about it happily.

It is doubtful that he realized that he had traveled other than that first lap in the traveling case to White Sands. He took up his new routine without noticing the five months clipped out of his life; he took charge of the apartment assigned to the Vaughn family, inspected it thoroughly, then nightly checked it to be sure that all was in order and safe before he tromped out his place on the foot of Charlie's bed and tucked his tail over his nose.

He was aware that this was a new place, but he was not homesick. The other home had been satisfactory and he had never dreamed of leaving it, but this new home was still better. Not only did it have Charlie—without whom no place could be home—not only did it have wonderful odors, but also he found the people more agreeable. In the past, many humans had been quite stuffy about flower beds and such trivia, but here he was almost never scolded or chased away; on the contrary people were anxious to speak to him, pet him, feed him. His popularity was based on arithmetic: Borealis had fifty-five thousand people but only eleven dogs; many colonists were homesick for man's traditional best friend. Nixie did not know this, but he had great capacity for enjoying the good things in life without worrying about why.

Mr. Vaughn found Venus satisfactory. His work for Synthetics of Venus, Ltd. was the sort of work he had done on Earth, save that he was now paid more and given more responsibility. The living quarters provided by the company were as comfortable as the house he had left back on Earth and he was unworried about the future of his family for the first time in years.

Mrs. Vaughn found Venus bearable but she was homesick much of the time.

Charlie, once he was over first the worry and then the delight of waking Nixie, found Venus interesting, less strange than he had expected, and from time to time he was homesick. But before long he was no longer homesick; Venus was home. He knew now what he wanted to be: a pioneer. When he was grown he would head south, deep into the unmapped jungle, carve out a plantation.

The jungle was the greatest single fact about Venus. The colony lived on the bountiful produce of the jungle. The land on which Borealis sat, buildings and spaceport, had been torn away from the hungry jungle only by flaming it dead, stabilizing the muck with gel-forming chemicals, and poisoning the land thus claimed—then flaming, cutting, or poisoning any hardy survivor that pushed its green nose up through the captured soil.

The Vaughn family lived in a large apartment building which sat on land newly captured. Facing their front door, a mere hundred feet away across scorched and poisoned soil, a great shaggy dark-green wall loomed higher than the buffer space between. But the mindless jungle never gave up. The vines, attracted by light—their lives were spent competing for light energy—felt their way into the open space, tried to fill it. They grew with incredible speed. One day after breakfast Mr. Vaughn tried to go out his own front door, found his way hampered. While they had slept a vine had grown across the hundred-foot belt, supporting itself by tendrils against the dead soil, and had started up the front of the building.

The police patrol of the city were armed with flame guns and spent most of their time cutting back such hardy intruders. While they had power to enforce the law, they rarely made an arrest. Borealis was a city almost free of crime; the humans were too busy fighting nature in the raw to require much attention from policemen.

But the jungle was friend as well as enemy. Its lusty life offered food for millions and billions of humans in place of the few thousands already on Venus. Under the jungle lay beds of peat, still farther down were thick coal seems representing millions of years of lush jungle growth, and pools of oil waiting to be tapped. Aerial survey by jetcopter in the volcanic regions promised uranium and thorium when man could cut his way through and get at it. The planet offered unlimited wealth. But it did not offer it to sissies.

Charlie quickly bumped his nose into one respect in which Venus was not for sissies. His father placed him in school, he was assigned to a grade taught by Mr. deSoto. The school room was not attractive— "grim" was the word Charlie used, but he was not surprised, as most buildings in Borealis were unattractive, being constructed either of spongy logs or of lignin panels made from jungle growth.

But the school itself was "grim." Charlie had been humiliated by being placed one grade lower than he had expected; now he found that the lessons were stiff and that Mr. deSoto did not have the talent or perhaps the wish to make them fun. Resentfully, Charlie loafed.

After three weeks Mr. deSoto kept him in after school. "Charlie, what's wrong?"

"Huh? I mean, 'Sir?' "

"You know what I mean. You've been in my class nearly a month. You haven't learned anything. Don't you want to?"

"What? Why, sure I do."

" 'Surely' in that usage, not 'sure.' Very well, so you want to learn; why haven't you?"

Charlie stood silent. He wanted to tell Mr. deSoto what a swell place Horace Mann Junior High School had been, with its teams and its band and its student plays and its student council (this crazy school didn't even *have* a student council!), and its study projects picked by the kids themselves, and the Spring Outburst and Sneak Day . . . and— oh, shucks!

But Mr. deSoto was speaking. "Where did you last go to school, Charlie?"

Charlie stared. Didn't the teacher even bother to read his transcript? But he told him and added, "I was a year farther along there. I guess I'm bored, having to repeat."

"I think you are, too, but I don't agree that you are repeating. They had an eighteen-year law there, didn't they?"

"Sir?"

"You were required to attend school until you were eighteen Earth-years old?"

"Oh, that! Sure. I mean 'surely.' Everybody goes to school until he's eighteen. That's to 'discourage juvenile delinquency,' " he quoted.

"I wonder. Nobody ever flunked, I suppose."

"Sir?"

"Failed. Nobody ever got tossed out of school or left back for failing his studies?"

"Of course not, Mr. deSoto. You have to keep age groups together, or they don't develop socially as they should."

"Who told you that?"

"Why, everybody knows that. I've been hearing that ever since I was in kindergarten. That's what education is for—social development."

Mr. deSoto leaned back, rubbed his nose. Presently he said slowly, "Charlie, this isn't that kind of a school at all."

Charlie waited. He was annoyed at not being invited to sit down and was wondering what would happen if he sat down anyway.

"In the first place we don't have the eighteen-year rule. You can quit school today. You know how to read. Your handwriting is sloppy but it will do. You are quick in arithmetic. You can't spell worth a hoot, but that's your misfortune; the city fathers don't care whether you learn to spell or not. You've got all the education the City of Borealis feels obliged to give you. If you want to take a flame gun and start carving out your chunk of the jungle, nobody is standing in your way. I can write a note to the Board of Education, telling them that Charles Vaughn, Jr. has gone as far as he ever will. You needn't come back tomorrow."

Charlie gulped. He had never heard of anyone being dropped from school for anything less than a knife fight. It was unthinkable—what would his folks say?

"On the other hand," Mr. deSoto went on, "Venus needs educated citizens. We'll keep anybody as long as they keep learning. The city will even send you back to Earth for advanced training if you are worth it, because we need scientists and engineers . . . and more teachers. But this is a struggling new community and it doesn't have a penny to waste on kids who won't study. We *do* flunk them in this school. If you don't study, we'll lop you off so fast you'll think you've been trimmed with a flame gun. We're not running the sort of overgrown kindergarten you were in. It's up to you. Buckle down and learn . . . or get out. So go home and talk it over with your folks."

Charlie was stunned. "Uh . . . Mr. deSoto? Are you going to talk to my father?"

"What? Heavens, no! You are their responsibility, not mine. I don't care what you do. That's all. Go home."

Charlie went home, slowly. He did not talk it over with his parents. Instead he went back to school and studied. In a few weeks he discovered that even algebra could be interesting . . . and that old Frozen Face was an interesting teacher when Charlie had studied hard enough to know what the man was talking about.

Mr. deSoto never mentioned the matter again.

Getting back in the Scouts was more fun but even Scouting held surprises. Mr. Qu'an, Scoutmaster of Troop Four, welcomed him heartily. "Glad to have you, Chuck. It makes me feel good when a

Scout among the new citizens comes forward and says he wants to pick up the Scouting trail again." He looked over the letter Charlie had brought with him. "A good record—Star Scout at your age. Keep at it and you'll be a Double Star . . . both Earth and Venus."

"You mean," Charlie said slowly, "that I'm not a Star Scout here?"

"Eh? Not at all." Mr. Qu'an touched the badge on Charlie's jacket. "You won that fairly and a Court of Honor has certified you. You'll always be a Star Scout, just as a pilot is entitled to wear his comet after he's too old to herd a space ship. But let's be practical. Ever been out in the jungle?"

"Not yet, sir. But I always was good at woodcraft."

"Mmm . . . Ever camped in the Florida Everglades?"

"Well . . . no, sir."

"No matter. I simply wanted to point out that while the Everglades are jungle, they are an open desert compared with the jungle here. And the coral snakes and water moccasins in the Everglades are harmless little pets alongside some of the things here. Have you seen our dragonflies yet?"

"Well, a dead one, at school."

"That's the best way to see them. When you see a live one, better see it first, . . . if it's a female and ready to lay eggs."

"Uh, I know about them. If you fight them off, they won't sting."

"Which is why you had better see them first."

"Mr. Qu'an? Are they really that *big*?"

"I've seen thirty-six-inch wing spreads. What I'm trying to say, Chuck, is that a lot of men have died learning the tricks of this jungle. If you are as smart as a Star Scout is supposed to be, you won't assume that you know what these poor fellows didn't. You'll wear that badge . . . but you'll class yourself in your mind as a tenderfoot all over again, and you won't be in a hurry about promoting yourself."

Charlie swallowed it. "Yes, sir. I'll try."

"Good. We use the buddy system—you take care of your buddy and he takes care of you. I'll team you with Hans Kuppenheimer. Hans is only a Second Class Scout, but don't let that fool you. He was born here and he lives in the bush, on his father's plantation. He's the best jungle rat in the troop."

Charlie said nothing, but resolved to become a real jungle rat himself, fast. Being under the wing of a Scout who was merely second class did not appeal to him.

But Hans turned out to be easy to get along with. He was quiet, shorter but stockier than Charlie, neither unfriendly nor chummy; he

simply accepted the assignment to look after Charlie. But he startled
Charlie by answering, when asked, that he was twenty-three years old.

It left Charlie speechless long enough for him to realize that Hans,
born here, meant Venus years, each only two hundred twenty-five
Earth days. Charlie decided that Hans was about his own age, which
seemed reasonable. Time had been a subject which had confused
Charlie ever since his arrival. The Venus day was only seven minutes
different from that of Earth—he had merely had to have his wristwatch adjusted. But the day itself had not meant what it used to mean,
because day and night at the north pole of Venus looked alike, a soft
twilight.

There were only eight months in the year, exactly four weeks in
each month, and an occasional odd "Year Day" to even things off.
Worse still, the time of year didn't mean anything; there were no seasons, just one endless hot, damp summer. It was always the same time
of day, always the same time of year; only clock and calendar kept it
from being the land that time forgot. Charlie never quite got used to it.

If Nixie found the timelessness of Venus strange he never mentioned it. On Earth he had slept at night simply because Charlie did so,
and, as for seasons, he had never cared much for winter anyhow. He enjoyed getting back into the Scouts even more than Charlie had, because
he was welcome at every meeting. Some of the Scouts born on Earth
had once had dogs; now none of them had—and Nixie was at once mas-
cot of the troop. He was petted almost to exhaustion the first time Charlie brought him to a meeting, until Mr. Qu'an pointed out that the dog
had to have some peace . . . then squatted down and petted Nixie himself. " 'Nixie,' " he said musingly, "a nixie is a water sprite, isn't it?"

"Uh, I believe it does mean that," Charlie admitted, "but that isn't
how he got his name."

"So?"

"Well, I was going to name him 'Champ,' but when he was a puppy
I had to say 'Nix' to so many things he did that he got to thinking it was
his name—and then it was."

"Mmm . . . more logical than most names. And even the classical
meaning is appropriate in a wet place like this. What's this on his collar? I see . . . you've decorated him with your old tenderfoot badge."

"No, sir," Charlie corrected. "That's his badge."

"Eh?"

"Nixie is a Scout, too. The fellows in my troop back Earthside
voted him into the troop. They gave him that. So Nixie is a Scout."

Mr. Qu'an raised his eyebrows and smiled. One of the boys said,
"That's about the craziest yet. A dog can't be a Scout."

Charlie had doubts himself; nevertheless he was about to answer

OFF THE MAIN SEQUENCE

indignantly when the Scoutmaster cut smoothly in front of him. "What leads you to say that, Alf?"

"Huh? Well, gosh! It's not according to Scout regulations."

"It isn't? I admit it is a new idea, but I can't recall what rule it breaks. Who brought a Handbook tonight?" The Scribe supplied one; Mr. Qu'an passed it over to Alf Rheinhardt. "Dig in, Alf. Find the rule."

Charlie diffidently produced Nixie's letter of transfer. He had brought it, but had not given it to the Scribe. Mr. Qu'an read it, nodded and said, "Looks okay." He passed the letter along to others and said, "Well, Alf?"

"In the first place, it says here that you have to be twelve years old to join—Earth years, that is, 'cause that's where the Handbook was printed. Is that dog that old? I doubt it."

Mr. Qu'an shook his head. "If I were sitting on a Court of Honor, I'd rule that the regulation did not apply. A dog grows up faster than a boy."

"Well, if you insist on joking—and Scouting is no joke to me—that's the point: a dog can't be a Scout, because he's a *dog*."

"Scouting is no joke to me either, Alf—though I don't see any reason not to have fun as we go. But I wasn't joking. A candidate comes along with a letter of transfer, all regular and proper. Seems to me you should go mighty slow before you refuse to respect an official act of another troop. All you've said is that Nixie is a dog. Well, didn't I see somewhere—last month's *Boys' Life*, I think—that the Boy Scouts of Mars had asked one of the Martian chiefs to serve on their planetary Grand Council?"

"But that's not the same thing!"

"Nothing ever is. But if a Martian—who is certainly not a human being—can hold the highest office in Scouting, I can't see how Nixie is disqualified simply because he's a dog. Seems to me you'll have to show that he can't or won't do the things that a Tenderfoot Scout should do."

"Uh . . ." Alf grinned knowingly. "Let's hear him explain the Scout Oath."

Mr. Qu'an turned to Charlie. "Can Nixie speak English?"

"What? Why, no, sir—but he understands it pretty well."

The Scoutmaster turned back to Alf. "Then the 'handicapped' rule applies, Alf—we never insist that a Scout do something he can't do. If you were crippled or blind, we would change the rules to fit you. Nixie can't talk words . . . so if you want to quiz him about the Scout Oath, you'll have to bark. That's fair, isn't it, boys?"

The shouts of approval didn't sit well with Alf. He answered sullenly, "Well, at least he has to follow the Scout Law—*every* Scout has to do *that*."

"Yes," agreed the Scoutmaster soberly. "The Scout Law is the essence of Scouting. If you don't obey it, you aren't a Scout, no matter how many merit badges you wear. Well, Charlie? Shall we examine Nixie in Scout Law?"

Charlie bit his lip. He was sorry that he hadn't taken that badge off Nixie's collar. It was mighty nice that the fellows back home had voted Nixie into the troop . . . but with this smart Aleck trying to make something of it—Why did there always have to be one in every troop who tried to take the fun out of life?

He answered reluctantly, "All right."

"Give me the Handbook. Is Nixie trustworthy?"

"Sure he is!"

"How?"

"Well . . . he doesn't get on furniture even if you're not watching him . . . and he won't touch food unless he's told to, and uh . . ."

"I think that's enough. Is he loyal?"

"He's loyal to *me*."

"Mmm . . . good enough. Helpful?"

"Uh, there isn't a whole lot he can do, I guess. He used to fetch newspapers in—but he can't do that here. He'll fetch anything you ask him to, if he understands what it is."

" 'Friendly'—well, obviously. 'Courteous'—we'll pass him on that, seeing what he has put up with tonight. Kind?"

"He'll let a baby try to pull his tail off, or step on his face, and never snap or growl. Uh, he did used to be kind of rough on cats, but I taught him better."

"Obedient?"

"Want to see?" Charlie put him through hand signal orders, ending with standing at attention and saluting. The applause made Nixie tremble but he held it until Charlie signalled "At ease."

"Take note of that, Alf," Mr. Qu'an said drily, "next time I have to speak to you twice. 'Cheerful'—we can skip that; I'm sure his grin isn't faked. 'Thrifty'—well, we can hardly expect him to have a savings account."

"He buries bones."

"Mmm, I suppose that's the canine equivalent. Brave?"

"*I* think he is. I've seen him tackle a dog three times his size—and chase it out of our yard, too, back home—back Earthside."

"Clean?"

"Smell him. He had a bath just yesterday. And he's perfectly housebroken."

"All that is left is 'Reverent'—and I don't intend to try to discuss that with him. I rule that Nixie is at least as reverent as the rapscallions

I've heard cussing around here when they didn't think I was listening. How about it, boys? Does he pass?"

Nixie was voted into Troop Four in his tenderfoot status unanimously . . . Alfred Rheinhardt, Tenderfoot, abstaining.

After the meeting the troop treasurer buttonholed Charlie. "You want to pay your dues now, Chuck?"

"Huh? Oh, yeah, sure—I brought some money."

"Good." The other Scout accepted payment. "Here's your receipt."

"Just mark it down in your book."

"Take it. No tickee, no washee. I'm nasty about it—that's why they made me treasurer. Now about Nixie—You pay? Or do I speak to him?"

The other boy was not smiling and Charlie could not decide whether or not he was joking. He decided to play it just as soberly. "I settle for Nixie. You see, he doesn't have pockets." He dug down in his diminished resources, managed to piece out enough to pay the same amount for Nixie. "Here."

"Thanks." The treasurer handed back a shilling. "Tenderfeet get by cheaper, under Troop by-laws. But every little bit helps. You know, when I took this job, the troop was in the hole. Now we got money in the bank."

"I believe it!" Charlie agreed. He was secretly delighted at the transaction. Nixie was no longer an "Honorary Scout," he was a *Scout*—he kept the Law and his dues were paid.

Nixie's eligibility to take part in all troop doings was not questioned until the first hike thereafter. Mr. Qu'an looked troubled when Charlie showed up with him. "You had better take Nixie home. We'll wait for you."

Charlie was upset. "But, Mr. Qu'an, I thought—Well, Nixie *always* goes on hikes."

"No doubt, back Earthside. Charlie, I'm not being arbitrary. I don't want your dog to get hurt."

"He won't get hurt! He's real smart."

The Scoutmaster frowned. Hans Kuppenheimer spoke up. "I think Nixie could come along, Mr. Qu'an."

"Eh?" The Scoutmaster looked at Hans thoughtfully. "You'll have your hands full with Chuck, since it's his first time out."

Hans had a habit of saying nothing when he had nothing to say; he did so now. Mr. Qu'an persisted, "You'd have to look out for them both, you know."

Hans still kept quiet. "Well," Mr. Qu'an said doubtfully, "Nixie is a

member of the troop. If you can take care of him—and Charlie, too—
I'll let him come."

"Yes, sir."

The Scoutmaster turned away. Charlie whispered, "Thanks, Hans.
That was swell." Hans said nothing.

Hans had surprised Charlie by his first reaction to Nixie the night
Nixie had been taken into the troop. While other boys were clustering
around making much of Nixie, Hans had stayed a wary distance away.
Charlie had felt offended. Since he was assigned with Hans as a buddy
team, Charlie decided to do something about it. After the meeting he
sought out Hans. "Don't be in a hurry, Hans. I want you to get acquainted with Nixie."

The country boy still avoided the dog. "Does it bite?"

"Huh? *Nixie?* Of course not. Well, he would if you took a poke at
me. Not otherwise."

"I thought so. And suppose I gave you a friendly slap on the back.
He could kill a man, huh?"

Nixie had listened, tense and watchful. He could feel the fear in
Hans' mind; he understood, without understanding why, that his boy
was arguing with this other boy. Charlie did not seem in immediate
danger, but Nixie stayed at yellow alert.

It showed. The savage carnivores who were Nixie's remote ancestors showed in his stance and his watchful eyes. The Venus-born jungle
rat, drilled since babyhood to keep his eyes open for just such unknown
dangers, could see the carnivore—and failed to see the gentle household pet. He watched the dog carefully.

Charlie said, "Why, that's nonsense, Hans. Pat him. Rough him up
a bit. Shake hands with him. Let him learn your smell." When Hans still
did not move, Charlie asked incredulously, "Don't you *like* dogs?"

"I don't know. I've never seen one before, up close."

Charlie's jaw dropped. But Hans had spoken the simple truth.
Some town boys in the troop, immigrants like Charlie, had once owned
dogs Earthside. Others had friends among the handful of dogs in Borealis. But Hans alone, born on Venus and living outside town, knew so
little of dogs that they were as strange to him as a tiger shark would
have been.

When Charlie finally got this incredible fact firmly in his mind he
persisted even more strongly in his effort to get his team buddy acquainted with his other partner. Before Hans went home that night he
had touched the dog, patted him, even picked him up and held him.
Nixie could feel the fear go away, to be replaced by a sudden warm
feeling. So Nixie snuffled Hans and licked his chin.

Hans showed up the next day at Charlie's home. He wanted to see Nixie.

In the two weeks that followed before the hike, Nixie adopted Hans as another member of Charlie's family. Subject always to his first loyalty, he accepted the other boy, took orders from him, even worked to hand signals, which he had never done with anyone but Charlie. At first he did it to please Charlie, but in time he was doing so because it was right and proper in his doggy mind, as long as it was all right with Charlie.

The troop set out on the hike. Before they reached the jungle at the edge of town Hans said to Charlie, "Better have him heel."

"Why? He likes to run around and poke his nose into things. But he always stays in earshot. He'll come if he's called."

Hans scowled. "Suppose he can't? Maybe he goes into bush and doesn't come out. You want to lose him?"

This was a long speech for Hans. Charlie looked surprised, then called, "Nixie! Heel!"

The dog had been supervising the van; he turned and came at once to Charlie's left and rear. Hans relaxed, said, "Better," and placed himself so that the dog trotted between them.

When the jungle loomed up over them, pierced here by a road, Mr. Qu'an held up his arm and called out, "Halt! Check watches." He held up his wrist and waited; everybody else did the same.

Jock Quentin, an Explorer Scout equipped with two-way radio, spoke into his microphone, then said, "Stand by . . . oh nine eleven."

"Anybody fail to check?" continued Mr. Qu'an. "All you with polarizers, establish base line."

Hans took out an odd-looking pair of spectacles with double lenses which rotated and a sighting device which snapped out. "Try it."

"Okay." Charlie accepted them gingerly. He did not yet own a light-polarizing sighter. "Why are we going to establish base line if we're going to stay on marked roads?"

Hans did not answer and Charlie felt foolish, realizing that the time to learn how not to get lost was before you got lost. He put on the polarizers and tried to establish base line.

"Base line" was the prime meridian of Venus, the direction from Borealis of the Sun at noon. To find that direction it was necessary first to find the Sun itself (in a grey, thickly overcast sky), then, using a watch, figure where the Sun would be at noon.

That direction would be south—but *all* directions from Borealis were south; the city lay on the north pole of the planet. The mapmakers

---

used Borealis as a zero point and the direction of the Sun at noon as a base line. With the aid of transceivers, radar beacons, and radio compass, they were gradually establishing a grid of reference points for the few hundred square miles around Borealis. A similar project was going on at South Pole City. But the millions of square miles between poles were unknown country, more mysterious and incredibly vaster than any juggle on Earth. There was a saying among the Scouts that streams at the equator were "hot enough to boil eggs," but nobody knew. As yet, no ship had landed near the equator and managed to come back.

The difficulty of telling directions on Venus is very great. The stars are always invisible. Neither magnetic compasses nor gyro compasses were of any use at the poles. Nor is there moss on the north sides of trees, nor any shadows to read—Venus is not only the land that time forgot; it is also the place of no directions.

So the colonists were forced to establish new directions. From Borealis toward the Sun at noon was prime meridian, called "base line," and any direction parallel to that was "base." Back the other way was "reverse"; the two intermediate directions were "left demi" and "right demi." By counting clockwise from "base," any other direction could be named.

It was not a perfect system since it used square coordinates for a spherical surface. But it was better than nothing in a place where the old directions had turned slippery—where all directions away from the city were "south" and where east and west, instead of being straight lines, were circular.

At first, Charlie could not see why, if they were going to use four directions, they didn't call them "north," "south," "east" and "west," instead of ringing in these silly names, "base," "reverse," "right demi," and "left demi." It was not until he saw in school a map of the colony, with the old familiar directions, north, south, east, west, on it and a "base line" grid drawn on top of it that he realized that the problem was not that simple. To go east on that map you went counterclockwise on one of those little circles—but how could you tell what direction "east" was unless you knew where you were? And how could you tell how much to curve left in order to keep going east? When compasses were no good and the Sun might be in any direction, north, south, east, or west, depending on which side of the city you were on?

So he buckled down and learned the new system.

Charlie put on Hans' polarizing spectacles and looked around. He could see nothing. Light leaked around the guards of the spectacles and the glass in front of his eyes seemed opaque. He knew that he should be able to pick out the Sun, for he knew that the light from the sky, dispersed by the clouds of Venus, was polarized, made to wiggle up-and-down or sideways, instead of in all directions. He knew that these spectacles were supposed to blank out polarized light, let him see the Sun itself. But he could not see anything.

He turned slowly, blind behind the spectacles.

Hey, it was getting brighter! He swung his head back and forth, made sure he was not mistaken. "I got it!"

"False sun," Hans announced dispassionately.

"Huh?"

"You're a hundred and eighty degrees out of phase," Mr. Qu'an's voice announced. "You're looking at the reflection of the Sun. Never mind, other people have made that mistake. But it's not a mistake you can afford to make even once out in the bush . . . so keep trying."

Charlie kept on turning—darn it, these specs fit so tight that he couldn't even see his feet! There it was again! Was it false sun? Or the Sun itself? How far had he turned?

He turned until he was dizzy, seeing brightness, then darkness, several times—and realized that one brightness was brighter than that which it alternated. Finally he stopped. "I'm looking at the Sun," he announced firmly.

"Okay," Hans admitted. "Jigger with it. Fine it down."

Charlie found that he could fiddle with screw settings on the sides of the spectacles and thereby kill the brightness almost completely. He did so, while swinging his head back and forth like a radar, trying to spot the smallest gleam that he could. "That's the best I can do."

"Hold still," Hans ordered. "Uncover your right eye. Mark me."

Charlie did as ordered, found himself staring with one eye down the sighter in front of the spectacles. Hans was thirty feet away, holding his Scout staff upright. "Don't move!" Hans cautioned. "Coach me on."

"Uh . . . come right a couple of feet."

"Here?"

"I think so. Let me check." He covered his right eye again, but found that his eye, dazzled by brighter light, could no longer pick up the faint gleam he had marked. "That's the best I can do."

Hans stretched a string along the marked direction. "My turn. Note your time." He took the spectacles, quickly gave Charlie a direction, coached him into place. The two lines differed by about ten degrees.

"Figure your hour angle," Hans said and looked at his watch.

The time was nine-thirty . . . and the Sun moved fifteen degrees each hour . . . two and a half hours to noon; that's thirty-seven and a half degrees . . . and each minute on the face of his watch was six degrees, so—

Charlie was getting confused. He looked up, saw that Hans had placed his watch on the ground and was laying out base line. Hans' watch had a twenty-four hour face; he simply pointed the hour hand at the Sun and the XII spot then pointed along base line.

No mental arithmetic, no monkeying around—"Gosh, I wish I had a watch like that!"

"Don't need it," Hans answered without looking up.

"But it makes it so simple. You just—"

"Your watch is okay. Make yourself a twenty-four-hour dial out of cardboard."

"That would work? Yeah, it would! I wish I had one now."

Hans fumbled in his duffel bag. "Uh, I made you one." He handed it over without looking up—a cardboard clock face, laid out for twenty-four hours.

Charlie was almost speechless. "Gee! Nixie, look at that! Say, Hans, I don't know how to thank you."

"Don't want you and Nixie getting lost," Hans answered gruffly.

Charlie took it, aimed nine-thirty along his line, marked noon and restretched the string to match. Base line, according to his sighting, differed by ten degrees from that of Hans. In the meantime, two patrol leaders had stretched a line at right angles to base line, along where the troop was spread out. One of them moved down the line, checking angles with a protractor. Mr. Qu'an followed, checked Charlie's layout himself. "About nine degrees off," he told Charlie. "Not bad for a first try."

Charlie felt crestfallen. He knew that he and Hans could not both be right but he had had a small hope that his answer was nearer the correct one. "Uh . . . which way am I wrong?"

"Left demi. Look at Hans'—he's dead on . . . as usual." The Scoutmaster raised his voice. "All right, gang! Bush formation, route march. Flamers out, right and left. Rusty on point, Bill on drag—shake it up!"

"Heel, Nixie."

The road cut straight through the jungle. The clearing had been flamed back wider than the road so that the jungle did not arch over it. The column kept to the middle where the ground was packed by vehicles running to and from outlying plantations. The flamers on the flanks, both of them Explorer Scouts, walked close to the walls of green and occasionally used their flame guns to cut back some new encroachment of vine or tree or grass. Each time they did so, they kept moving and a scavenger gang moved out, tossed the debris back into the living forest, and quickly rejoined the column. It was everybody's business to keep the roads open; the colony depended on roads more than Ancient Rome had depended on theirs.

Presently it began to rain. No one paid attention; rain was as normal as ice in Greenland. Rain was welcome; it washed off ever-present sweat and gave an illusion of coolness.

Presently Point (Rusty Dunlop) stopped, sighted back at Drag, and shouted, "Right demi fifteen degrees!"

Drag answered, "Check!" Point continued around the slight bend in the road. They had left Borealis heading "south" of course, since no other direction was possible, but that particular south was base thirty-two degrees right demi, to which was now added fifteen degrees clockwise.

It was Point's duty to set trail, keep lookout ahead, and announce his estimate of every change in direction. It was Drag's business to have eyes in the back of his head (since even here the jungle was not without power to strike), keep count of his paces, and keep written record of all course changes and the number of paces between each—dead reckoning navigation marked down in a waterproof notebook strapped to his wrist. He was picked for his reliability and the evenness of his strides.

A dozen other boys were doing the same things, imitating both Point and Drag, and recording everything, paces, times, and course changes, in preparation for Pathfinder merit badges. Each time the troop stopped, each would again establish base direction and record it. Later, after the hike, they would attempt to map where they had been, using only their notes.

It was just practice, since the road was surveyed and mapped, but practice that could determine later whether they lived, or died miserably in the jungle. Mr. Qu'an had no intention of taking the troop, including tenderfoot town boys not yet twenty Venus years old, into unexplored jungle. But older boys, seasoned explorer Scouts did go into trackless bush; some were already marking out land they would claim and try to conquer. On their ability to proceed by dead reckoning through bush and swamp and return to where they had started depended both their lives and their future livelihoods.

Mr. Qu'an dropped back, fell in beside Charlie. "Counting paces?"
"Yes, sir."
"Where's your notebook?"
"Uh, it was getting soggy in the rain, so I put it away. I'm keeping track in my head."
"That's a fine way to wind up at South Pole. Next time, bring a waterproof one."

Charlie didn't answer. He had wanted one, as he had wanted a polarizing sighter and many other things. But the Vaughn family was still scratching for a toehold; luxuries had to wait.

Mr. Qu'an looked at Charlie. "If convenient, that is," he went on gently. "Right now I don't want you to count paces anyhow."

"Sir?"

"You can't learn everything at once, and today you can't get lost. I want you to soak up junglecraft. Hans, you two move to the flank. Give Charlie a chance to see what we're passing through. Lecture him about it . . . and for goodness' sake try to say more than two words at a time!"

"Yes, sir."

"And—" The Scoutmaster got no further; he was hailed by the boss of the scavenger gang. "Mr. Qu'an! Squint's got a screwbug!"

The man said something bitter under his breath, started to run. The two boys followed. The scavengers had been moving a large branch, freshly flamed down. Now they were clustered around one boy, who was gripping his forearm. Mr. Qu'an burst into the group, grabbed the kid by that arm without saying a word, and examined it.

He shifted his grip so that the skin was drawn tight at one spot, reached for his belt and drew a knife—dug the point into skin, and, as if he were cutting a bad spot out of an apple, excised a small chunk of flesh. Squint screwed up his face and tears came into his eyes, but he did not cry out.

The scavenger boss had his first-aid kit open. As the Scoutmaster handed his knife to a boy near him, the gang boss placed a shaker bottle in Mr. Qu'an's hand. The Scoutmaster squirted powder into the wound, accepted a pressure patch and plastered it over the cut.

Then he turned sternly to the gang boss. "Pete, why didn't you do it?"

"Squint wanted you."

"So? Squint, you know better. Next time, let the boy closest to you get it—or cut it out yourself. It could have gone in another half inch while I was getting to you. And next time be more careful where you put your hands!"

The column had halted. Point, looking back, saw Mr. Qu'an's wave, lifted his own arm and brought it down smartly. They moved on. Charlie said to Hans, "What's a screwbug?"

"Little thing, bright red. Cling underneath leaves."

"What do they do to you?"

"Burrow in. Abscess. Don't get 'em out, maybe lose an arm."

"Oh." Charlie added, "Could they get on Nixie?"

"Doubt it. 'Cept maybe his nose. Ought to check him over every chance we get. Other things, too."

They were on higher and drier ground now; the bush around them did not go up so high, was not quite as dense. Charlie peered into it, trying to sort out details, while Hans kept up what he probably felt was a lively discourse—usually one word at a time, such as: "Poison," "Physic," or "Eat those."

"Eat what?" Charlie asked, when Hans had made the last comment. He looked where Hans pointed, saw nothing looking like fruit, berries or nuts.

"That stuff. Sugar stick." Hans thrust cautiously into the brush with his staff, pushed aside a Venus nettle, and broke off a foot of brown twig. "Nixie! Get out of there! Heel!"

Charlie accepted half of it, bit cautiously when he saw Hans do so. It chewed easily. Yes, it did have a sweetish taste, about like corn syrup. Not bad!

Hans spat out pulp. "Don't swallow the cud—give you trouble."

"I wouldn't've guessed you could eat this."

"Never go hungry in the bush."

"Hans? What do you do for water? If you haven't got any?"

"Huh? Water all around you."

"Yeah, but *good* water."

"All water is good water . . . if you clean it." Hans' eyes darted around. "Find a filter ball. Chop off top and bottom. Run water through. I'll spot one, show you."

Hans found one shortly, a gross and poisonous-looking fungus. But it was some distance off the clearing and when Hans started after it, he was told gruffly by the flamer on that flank to get back from the edge and stay there. Hans shrugged. "Later."

The procession stopped in the road clearing, lunched from duffel bags. Nixie was allowed to run free, with strict instructions to stay away from the trees. Nixie didn't mind. He sampled every lunch. After a rest they went on. Occasionally they all gave way to let some plantation family, mounted on high trucks with great, low-pressure bolster wheels, roll past on the way to a Saturday night in town. The main road led past narrow tunnels cut into the bush, side roads to plantations. Late in the afternoon they passed one such; Hans hooked a thumb at it. "Home."

"Yours?"

"Half a mile in."

A couple of miles farther the troop left the road and started across country. But this was high land, fairly dry and semi-open, no more difficult than most forest back Earthside. Hans merely saw to it that Nixie stayed close at heel and cautioned Charlie, "Mind where you step . . . and if anything drops on you, brush it off quick."

They broke out shortly into a clearing, made camp, and started supper. The clearing was man-made, having been flamed down, although a green carpet had formed underfoot. The first step in making camp was to establish four corners of a rectangle, using Scout staffs; then Jock Quentin, the troop's radioman, clamped mirrors to them. After much fiddling he had a system rigged by which a powerful flashlight beam bounced around the rectangle and back into a long tube which housed a photocell; the camp was now surrounded by an invisible fence. Whenever the beam was broken an alarm would sound.

While this was going on other Scouts were lashing staffs together, three to a unit, into long poles. Rags were sopped with a sickly-sweet fluid, fastened to the ends and the poles were erected; one at each corner of the rectangle. Charlie sniffed and made a face, "What's that stuff?"

"For dragonflies. They hate it."

"I don't blame 'em!"

"Haven't seen one lately. But if they were swarming, you'd rub it on your hide and be glad of the stink."

"Hans? Is it true that a dragonfly sting can paralyze a man?"

"No."

"Huh? But they say—"

"Takes three or four stings. One sting will just do for an arm or a leg—unless it gets you in the spine."

"Oh." Charlie couldn't see much improvement.

"I was stung once," Hans added.

"You *were?* But you're still alive."

"My paw fought it off and killed it. Couldn't use my left leg for a while."

"Boy! You must be lucky."

"Unlucky, I'd say. But not unlucky as *it* was. We ate it."

"You *ate* it?"

"Sure. Mighty tasty, they are."

Charlie felt queasy. "You eat *insects?*"

Hans thought about it. "You ever eat a lobster?"

"Sure. But that's different."

"It sure is. Seen pictures of lobsters. Disgusting."

This gourmets' discussion was broken up by the Scoutmaster. "Hans! How about scaring up some oil weed?"

"Okay." Hans headed for the bush. Charlie followed and Nixie trotted after. Hans stopped. "Make him stay behind. We can't gather weed and watch him, too."

"All right."

Nixie protested, since it was his duty to guard Charlie. But once he understood that Charlie meant it and would not be swayed, he trotted back, tail in air, and supervised campmaking.

The boys went on. Charlie asked, "This clearing . . . is it the regular Scout camp?"

Hans looked surprised. "I guess so. Paw and I aren't going to set a crop till we flame it a few more times."

"You mean it's *yours?* Why didn't you say so?"

"You never asked." Presently he added, "Some planters, they don't like Scouts tromping around, maybe hurting a crop."

Oil weed was a low plant, resembling bracken. They gathered it in silence, except once when Hans brushed something off Charlie's arm. "Want to watch that."

While they were loading with weed Hans made quite a long speech: "These dragonflies, they aren't much. You hear them coming. You can fight 'em off, even with your hands, because they can't sting till they light. They won't sting anyway, except when they're swarming—then it's just females, ready to lay eggs." He added thoughtfully, "They're stupid, they don't know the eggs won't hatch in a man."

"They won't?"

"No. Not that it does the man much good; he dies anyway. But they think they're stinging a big amphibian, thing called kteela."

"I've seen pictures of kteela."

"So? Wait till you see one. But don't let it scare you. Kteela can't hurt you and they're more scared than you are—they just look fearsome." He brushed at his arm. "It's little things you got to watch."

Oil weed burned with a clear steady flame; the boys had a hot dinner and hot tea. No precautions were taken against fire; of the many hazards on Venus, fire was not one. The problem was to get anything to burn, not to avoid forest fire.

After they had eaten, one boy was examined by Mr. Qu'an in first-aid and artificial respiration. Listening, Charlie found that there was much that he must learn and unlearn; conditions were different. Then Rusty Dunlop broke out a mouth organ and they sang.

Finally Mr. Qu'an yawned and said, "Sack in, Scouts. Hard day tomorrow. Pedro, first watch—then rotate down the list."

Charlie thought he would never get to sleep. The ground underneath his waterproof was not hard, but he was not used to sleeping with lighted sky in his eyes. Besides that, he was acutely aware of strange noises in the bush around them.

He was awakened by a shout. "Dragons! Heads up, gang! Watch yourself!"

Without stopping to think, Charlie reached down, grabbed Nixie to his chest, then looked around. Several boys were pointing. Charlie looked and thought at first that he was seeing a helicopter.

Suddenly it came into perspective and he realized that it was an enormous insect . . . unbelievably huge, larger than had been seen on Earth since the Carboniferous period, a quarter of a billion years ago.

It was coming toward camp. Something about it—its wings?— made a whining buzz.

It approached the tall poles with the smelly rags, hesitated, turned away. Mr. Qu'an looked thoughtfully after it, glanced at Hans.

"They're not swarming," Hans stated positively. "Anyhow, that was a male."

"Mmm . . . No doubt you're right. Still—double guard the rest of the night, down the roster. Tenderfeet makee-learnee only." He lay down.

The troop started back the next morning—"Morning" by clock; Charlie, awakening stiff and sleepy to the same dull-bright, changeless sky, felt as if he had napped too long but not well during an afternoon. They headed back the way they had come. Once on the cleared road, Hans left Charlie and looked up the Scoutmaster. He was back shortly, grinning. "Stay over night with me? You and Nixie?"

"Gee! Is it okay? Your folks won't mind?"

"They like company. You can ride in with Paw in the morning."

"It 'ould be swell, Hans . . . but how about my folks? Uh, do you suppose Jock could raise 'em on the portable?"

"Everything's okay. Mr. Qu'an will phone 'em when the troop gets in . . . and you can call them soon as we get to my place. If they holler, I can still catch you up with the troop."

So it was settled. When they got to the little side road for the Kuppenheimer plantation Mr. Qu'an ordered them to head for the house and no monkey business. They solemnly agreed and left the troop.

The side road was a dark tunnel; Hans hurried them through it. A few hundred yards farther on they came out into cultivated fields and Hans slowed down. "That's the only bad stretch. You okay?"

"Sure."

"Let's check Nixie."

If anything had attached itself to Nixie, they could not find it and his wagging tail gave no sign of distress; they went on. Charlie looked around with interest. "What are you cropping?"

"Jungle bread on the right. Once it's established you don't have to worry about it, smothers anything else, mostly. Other side is mutated bananas. They take more care."

Shortly they came to the house, on a rise and with no growth around it—a typical Venus settler's house, long and low and built of spongy logs and native bamboo. Hans' mother greeted Charlie as if he were a neighbor boy, seen daily, and she petted Nixie. "He minds me of a hund I had in Hamburg." Then she set out banana cake and mugs of coffee that were mostly milk. Nixie had his cake on the floor.

There were several kids around, younger than Hans and looking like him. Charlie did not get them straight, as they talked even less than Hans did and hung back from Nixie—unlike their mother, they found him utterly strange. But presently, seeing how the monster behaved with Hans and with their mother, they timidly patted him. After that, Nixie was the center of attention while they continued shyly to ignore Charlie.

Hans bolted his cake, hurried out. He was back a few minutes later. "Maw, where's the flamer?"

"Paw is using it."

Hans looked blank. "Well . . . we don't have to have it. Come on, Chuck." He carried two hefty machetes, a blade in each hand; he handed one to Charlie.

"Okay." Charlie stood up. "Thanks, Mrs. Kuppenheimer—thanks a lot."

"Call me 'Maw.' "

"Hurry up, Charlie."

"Right. Say—how about that call to my folks?"

"I forgot! Maw, would you phone Mrs. Vaughn? Tell her Chuck is staying all night?"

"Yes, surely. What's your frequency, Charlie?"

"Uh, you have to call city exchange and ask them to relay."

"Jawohl. You boys run along."

They headed off through the fields. Nixie was allowed to run, which he did with glee, returning every thirty seconds or so to see that his charges had not fainted nor been kidnapped in his absence.

"Where are we going, Hans?"

Hans' eyes brightened. "To see the prettiest plantation land on Venus!"

"It's mighty pretty, no doubt about it."

"Not Paw's land. I mean *my* plantation."

"Yours?"

"Will be mine. Paw posted an option bond. When I'm old enough, I'll prove it." He hurried on.

Shortly Charlie realized that he was lost even though they were in a cultivated grove. "Hold it, Hans! Can I borrow your polarizer?"

"What for?"

"I want to establish base, that's what. I'm all mixed up."

"Base is that direction," Hans answered, pointing with his machete. "My polarizer is at the house. We don't need it."

"I just thought I ought to keep straight."

"Look, Chuck, I can't get lost around here; I was *born* on this piece."

"But I wasn't."

"Keep your eyes open; you'll learn the landmarks. We're heading that way—" Hans pointed again. "—for that big tree." Charlie looked, saw several big trees. "We cut over a ridge. Pretty soon we come to my land. Okay?"

"I guess so."

"I won't let you get lost. Look, I'll show you the bush way to establish base—polarizers are for townies." He looked around, his quick eyes picking up and discarding details. "There's one."

"One what?"

"Compass bug. Right there. Don't scare him. Back, Nixie!"

Charlie looked, discovered a small, beetle-like creature with striped wing casings. Hans went on, "When they fly, they take right off toward the Sun. Every time. Then they level off and head home—they live in nests." Hans slapped the ground beside the little creature; it took off as if jet propelled. "So the Sun is that way. What time is it?"

"Ten thirty, about."

"So where is base?"

Charlie thought about it. "Must be about there."

"Isn't that the way I pointed? Now find another compass bug. Always one around, if you look."

Charlie found one—frightened it, watched it take off in the same direction as the first. "You know, Hans," he said slowly, "bees do something like that—fly by polarized light, I mean. That's the way they get back to their hives on cloudy days. I read about it."

"Bees? Those Earth bugs that make sugar?"

"Yes. But they aren't bugs."

"Okay," Hans answered indifferently. "I'll never see one. Let's get moving."

Presently they left cultivation, started into bush. Hans required Nixie to heel. Even though they were going uphill, the bush got thicker, became dense jungle. Hans led the way, occasionally chopping an obstacle.

He stopped. "Trash!" he said bitterly.

"Trouble?"

"This is why I wanted the flamer. This bit grows pretty solid."

"Can't we chop it?"

"Take all day with a bush knife; need heat on it. Going to have to poison this whole stretch 'fore I get a road through from Paw's place to mine."

"What do we do?"

"Go around, what else?" He headed left. Charlie could not see that Hans was following any track, decided he must know his way by the contour of the ground. About half an hour later Hans paused and whispered, "Keep quiet. Make Nixie keep quiet."

"What for?" Charlie whispered back.

"Good chance you'll see kteela, if we don't scare them." He went noiselessly ahead, with the other boy and the dog on his heels. He stopped. "There."

Charlie oozed forward, looked over Hans' shoulder—found that he was looking down at a stream. He heard a splash on his right, turned his head just in time to see spreading ripples. "Did you see him?" asked Hans in a normal voice.

"No."

"Shucks, he was right *there*. A big one. Their houses are just downstream. They often fish along here. Have to keep your eyes open, Chuck." Hans looked thoughtful. "Kteela are people."

"Huh?"

"They're people. Paw thinks so. If we could just get acquainted with them, we could prove it. But they're timid. Come on—we cross here." Hans descended the bank, sat down on muddy sand by running water and started taking his shoes off. "Mind where you sit."

Charlie did the same. Bare-footed and bare-legged, Hans picked up Nixie. "I'll lead. This stretch is shallow—keep moving and don't stumble."

The water was warm and the bottom felt mucky; Charlie was glad when they reached the far side. "Get the leeches off," Hans commanded as he put Nixie down. Charlie looked down at his legs, was amazed to find half a dozen purple blobs, large as hens' eggs, clinging to him. Hans cleaned his own legs, helped Charlie make sure that he was free of the parasites. "Run your fingers between your toes. Try to get the sand fleas off as you put on your boots, too—though they don't really matter."

"Anything else in that water?" Charlie asked, much subdued.

"Oh, glass fish can bite a chunk out of you . . . but they aren't poisonous. Kteela keep this stream cleaned up. Let's go."

They went up the far side, reached a stretch that was higher and fairly dry. Charlie thought that they were probably going upstream, he could not be sure.

Hans stopped suddenly. "Dragonfly. Hear it?"

Charlie listened, heard the high, motor-like hum he had heard the night before. "There it is," Hans said quickly. "Hang onto Nixie and be ready to beat it off. I'm going to attract its attention."

Charlie felt that attracting its attention was in a class with teasing a rattlesnake, but it was too late to object; Hans was waving his arms.

The fly hesitated, veered, headed straight for him. Charlie felt a moment of dreadful anticipation—then saw Hans take one swipe with his machete. The humming stopped; the thing fluttered to the ground.

Hans was grinning. The dragonfly jerked in reflex, but it was dead, the head neatly chopped off. "Didn't waste a bit," Hans said proudly.

"Huh?"

"That's lunch. Cut some of that oil weed behind you." Hans squatted down. In three quick slices he cut off the stinger and the wings; what was left was the size of a medium lobster. Using the chrome-sharp machete as delicately as a surgeon's knife, he split the underside of the exoskeleton, gently and neatly stripped out the gut. He started to throw it away, then paused and stared at it thoughtfully.

Charlie had been watching in queasy fascination. "Trouble?"

"Egg sac is full. They're going to swarm."

"That's bad, isn't it?"

"Some. They swarm every three, four years." Hans hesitated. "We'd better skip seeing my land. Got to tell Paw, so they'll keep the kids in."

"Okay, let's get started."

"We'll eat lunch first. Ten minutes won't matter—they aren't really swarming yet, or this one wouldn't have been alone."

Charlie started to say that he wasn't interested in lunch—not this lunch—but Hans was already starting a fire.

What was left in the exoskeleton was clean milky-white meat, lean flying muscle. Hans cut out chunks, toasted them over the fire, salted them from a pocket shaker. "Have some."

"Uh, I'm not hungry."

"You're crazy in the head, too. Here, Nixie." Nixie had been waiting politely but with his nose quivering. He snapped the tidbit out of the air, gulped it down, waited still more eagerly while Hans ate the next piece.

It did smell good . . . and it looked good, when he kept his mind off the source. Charlie's mouth began to water. Hans looked up. "Change your mind?"

"Uh . . . let me taste just a bite."

It reminded Charlie of crab meat. A few minutes later the exoskeleton was stripped too clean to interest even Nixie. Charlie stood up, burped gently, and said, "Ready?"

"Yeah. Uh, Chuck, one thing I do want to show you . . . and there's a way back above it maybe quicker than the way we came."

"What is it?"

"You'll see." Hans headed off in a new direction. Charlie wondered how Hans had picked it without the aid of a compass bug.

In a few minutes they were going downhill. Hans stopped. "Hear it?"

Charlie listened, seemed to pick out a soft roar under the ever-present multiple voice of the jungle. "It's not a dragonfly?"

"Of course not. You've got ears."

"What is it?" Hans did not reply, led on. Presently they broke into a clearing, or rather a room, for the jungle closed in overhead. It enclosed a delightful, surprising waterfall; the muted roar was its song.

"Isn't that swell?"

"It sure is," Charlie agreed. "I haven't seen anything so pretty in years."

"Sure, it's pretty. But that's not the point. My land is just above. I'll put a water wheel here and have my own power." Hans led his two friends down near it, began to talk excitedly about his plans. The noise of falling water was so great that he had to shout.

So neither one of them heard it. Charlie heard Nixie bark, turned his head and saw it at the last moment. "Hans! Dragon!"

Too late—the thing nailed Hans between his shoulder blades. It laid no eggs; Charlie killed it, crushed it with his hands. But Hans had already been stung.

Charlie wiped his trembling hands on his pants and looked down at his chum. Hans had collapsed even as Charlie had killed the thing; he lay crumpled on the ground. Charlie bent over him. "Hans! Hans, answer me!"

Hans' eyelids fluttered. "Get Paw."

"Hans . . . can you stand up?"

"Sorry . . . Chuck"—then very feebly, "My fault." His eyes stayed open, but Charlie could get no more out of him.

Even in his distress Charlie's training stayed with him. He could not find Hans' pulse, so he listened for his heart . . . was rewarded and greatly relieved by a steady, strong flub-a-*dub*! . . . flub-a-*dub*! Hans looked ghastly—but apparently it was true that they just paralyzed; they didn't kill.

But what to do?

Hans had said to get his father. Sure—but how? Could he find his way to the house? Even if he could, could he lead them back here? No, he wouldn't have to—surely Mr. Kuppenheimer would know where the waterfall was that Hans meant to harness. So what he had to do was simply get back. Now let's see; they had come down the bank there—

and after they had crossed the stream—it must be this same stream; they hadn't gone over any watershed. Or had they?

Well, it had better be the same stream, else he was lost beyond hope. Back through the bush, then and across the stream—

How was he going to cut back in and hit the stream at the place where it could be forded? The bush all looked pretty much alike.

Maybe he had better go downstream along the bank until he hit it. Then cross, and if he could find a compass bug, he could strike off in the general direction of the Kuppenheimers until he came to civilization. He remembered which way base was when they had first started out; that would orient him.

Or would it? They had gone first to that place that couldn't be passed without a flamer—but where had they gone then? How many turns? Which way were they heading when they reached the place where he had not quite seen a kteela?

Well, he would just have to try. At least he could get onto the same side of the stream as the plantation.

Nixie had been sniffing at Hans' still body. Now he began to whine steadily. "Shut up, you!" Charlie snapped. "I don't want any trouble out of you, too."

Nixie shut up.

Charlie decided that he couldn't leave Hans; he would have to take him with him. He kneeled down and started wrestling Hans' limp body into a fireman's carry, while wondering miserably whether or not Hans had told his mother where they were going? Or if it would do any good if he had, since they were not where Hans had originally intended to take them.

"Heel, Nixie."

An indefinitely long time later Charlie put Hans down on the ground in a fairly open place. It had taken only a few minutes of struggle to convince him that he could not carry Hans along the bank of the stream. A man might have been able to carve his way through with a machete—but while Charlie had two machetes he could not swing them and carry Hans as well. After giving that route up, he abandoned one machete by the waterfall, thinking that Hans could find it there some other day. He was tempted to abandon both, for the one on his belt was heavy and got in his way, but he decided that he might have to have it; they had done plenty of chopping in getting here.

So he set out again, this time trying to retrace their steps through the bush, hoping to spot the places they had chopped to help him find his way.

He never spotted such a sign; the living green maze swallowed all such puny marks.

After a long time he decided to go back to the familiar waterfall—he would stay there, nurse Hans, filter water for them all, and wait. Surely Mr. Kuppenheimer would eventually think of the waterfall!

So he turned back . . . and could not find the waterfall. Not even the stream.

He walked through something. He couldn't see it, there were branches in his face. Whatever it was it clung to his legs like red-hot wires; he stumbled and almost dropped Hans getting free of it. Then his leg did not stop paining him. The fiery burning dropped off a little but a numbness crept up his right leg.

He was glad indeed to put Hans on the ground at the first fairly open place he came to. He sat down and rubbed his leg, then checked Hans—still breathing, heart still beating . . . but out like a light.

Nixie sniffed Hans again, then looked up and whined inquiringly. "I can't help it," Charlie said to him. "He's a mess. I'm a mess. You're a mess, too."

Nixie barked.

"I will, I will . . . just as soon as I can move. Don't hurry me. How would *you* like to carry him for a while?"

Charlie continued to rub his leg. The pain was going away but the numbness was worse. At last he said to Nixie, "I guess we ought to try it, pal. Wait a second while I look for a compass bug—the way I figure it, we came mostly base, so I guess we ought to try to head reverse." He glanced at his wrist to see what time it was.

His watch had stopped.

But it *couldn't* stop—it was self-winding.

Nevertheless it had. Perhaps he had banged it in the bush, perhaps . . . no matter, it had stopped. He looked for Hans' watch, thinking that its twenty-four-hour face was easier to use as a compass dial anyhow.

But Hans was not wearing his watch, nor was it in any of his pockets. Whether he had left it at the house, along with his polarizer and duffel bag, or whether it had dropped off while Charlie was carrying him, did not matter. They had no watch between them and Charlie did not know what time it was, not even approximately. It seemed to him that he had been carrying Hans, fighting this dreary bush, for a week.

So a compass bug couldn't tell him anything.

He almost felt defeated at that moment. But he rallied, telling himself that if he went downhill he was bound to find that stream . . . then he would either find the ford or the waterfall, one or the other. He hauled himself around into position to lift Hans, favoring his right leg.

He need not have bothered; his right leg was not working.

The "pins and needles" in it were almost unbearable, as if he had sat much too long in a cramped position. But they would not go away as they always had in the past; nothing he could do would make that leg obey his orders.

He lowered his head against Hans and bawled.

He became aware that Nixie was licking his face and whining. He stopped his useless blubbering and raised his head. "It's all right, fellow. Don't you worry."

But it wasn't all right. While Charlie was no jungle rat, he did know that search parties could comb the area for weeks and not find them, could pass within feet of this spot and never see them. Possibly no human being had ever been where they were now; possibly no human would reach this spot in many years to come.

If he didn't use his head now, they would never get out.

Nixie sat patiently, watching him, trusting him.

"Nixie, this is up to you now, boy. You understand me?"

Nixie whined.

"Go back to the house. Fetch! Fetch Maw. Fetch anybody. Right now! Go back to the house."

Nixie barked.

"Don't argue with me. You've got to do it. Go home! Go back and fetch somebody!"

Nixie looked dubious, trotted a few steps in the direction in which they had come, stopped and looked around inquiringly. "That's right! Keep going! Go back to the house! Fetch somebody! *Go!*"

Nixie looked sharply at him, then trotted away in a businesslike fashion.

Sometime later Charlie raised his head and shook it. Gosh! he must have gone to sleep . . . couldn't do that . . . what if another dragonfly came along . . . have to stay awake. Was Hans all right? Have to pick him up and get out of here . . . where was Nixie? "Nixie!"

No answer. That was the last straw. But he'd have to get moving anyhow—

His leg wouldn't work . . . felt funny. "Nixie! *Nixie!*"

Mrs. Kuppenheimer heard the scratching and whining at the door, wiped her hands on her apron and went to it. When she saw what was there she threw her hands up. "Lieber Gott! What happened to you?" She kneeled swiftly, picked up the little dog and put him on her clean table, bent over him, talking to him and picking leeches from him, wiping away blood. "Schrecklich!"

"What happened to him, Mama?"

"I don't know." She went on working. But Nixie jumped out of her arms, charged straight for the closed door, tried to crash his way out—unsuccessful, he leaped and clawed at it and howled.

Mrs. Kuppenheimer gathered him up and held his struggling body against her breast. "Gerta! Get Paw!"

"What's the matter with him, Mama?"

"Something dreadful has happened. *Run!*"

The Borealis council hall was filled with Scouts and older people. Hans and Charlie were seated in the front row, with Nixie on a chair between them. Hans had crutches across one knee; Charlie had a cane. Mr. Qu'an came down the aisle, saw them, and sat down as Charlie moved Nixie over to share his seat. The Scoutmaster said to Hans, "I thought you were off those things?" His glance touched the crutches.

"I am—but Maw made me bring them."

"I—" Mr. Qu'an stopped. An older man had just taken his place at a table in the front of the hall at which were seated half a dozen others.

"Quiet, please." The man waited a moment. "This Court of Honor is met in special session for awards. It is our first duty tonight—and proud pleasure—to award a life-saving medal. Will Tenderfoot Scout Nixie Vaughn please come forward?"

"*Now, Nixie!*" Charlie whispered.

Nixie jumped off the chair, trotted forward, sat at attention and saluted, trembling.

—ALL YOU ZOMBIES—

The Magazine of Fantasy & Science Fiction, March 1959

2217 TIME ZONE V (EST) 7 Nov 1970 NYC—"Pop's Place": I was polishing a brandy snifter when the Unmarried Mother came in. I noted the time—10.17 P.M. zone five or eastern time November 7th, 1970. Temporal agents always notice time & date; we must.

The Unmarried Mother was a man twenty-five years old, no taller than I am, immature features and a touchy temper. I didn't like his looks—I never had—but he was a lad I was here to recruit, he was my boy. I gave him my best barkeep's smile.

Maybe I'm too critical. He wasn't swish; his nickname came from what he always said when some nosy type asked him his line: "I'm an unmarried mother." If he felt less than murderous he would add: "—at four cents a word. I write confession stories."

If he felt nasty, he would wait for somebody to make something of it. He had a lethal style of in-fighting, like a female cop—one reason I wanted him. Not the only one.

He had a load on and his face showed that he despised people more than usual. Silently I poured a double shot of Old Underwear and left the bottle. He drank, poured another.

I wiped the bar top. "How's the 'Unmarried Mother' racket?"

His fingers tightened on the glass and he seemed about to throw it at me; I felt for the sap under the bar. In temporal manipulation you try to figure everything, but there are so many factors that you never take needless risks.

I saw him relax that tiny amount they teach you to watch for in the Bureau's training school. "Sorry," I said. "Just asking, 'How's business?' Make it 'How's the weather?'"

He looked sour. "Business is okay. I write 'em, they print 'em, I eat."

I poured myself one, leaned toward him. "Matter of fact," I said, "you write a nice stick—I've sampled a few. You have an amazingly sure touch with the woman's angle."

It was a slip I had to risk; he never admitted what pen-names he used. But he was boiled enough to pick up only the last. " 'Woman's angle!' " he repeated with a snort. "Yeah, I know the woman's angle. I should."

"So?" I said doubtfully. "Sisters?"

"No. You wouldn't believe me if I told you."

"Now, now," I answered mildly, "bartenders and psychiatrists learn that nothing is stranger than the truth. Why, son, if you heard the stories I do—well, you'd make yourself rich. Incredible."

"You don't know what 'incredible' means!"

"So? Nothing astonishes me. I've always heard worse."

He snorted again. "Want to bet the rest of the bottle?"

"I'll bet a full bottle." I placed one on the bar.

"Well—" I signaled my other bartender to handle the trade. We were at the far end, a single-stool space that I kept private by loading the bar top by it with jars of pickled eggs and other clutter. A few were at the other end watching the fights and somebody was playing the juke box—private as a bed where we were. "Okay," he began, "to start with, I'm a bastard."

"I mean it," he snapped. "My parents weren't married."

"Still no distinction," I insisted. "Neither were mine."

"When—" He stopped, gave me the first warm look I ever saw on him. "You mean that?"

"I do. A one-hundred-percent bastard. In fact," I added, "No one in my family ever marries. All bastards."

"Don't try to top me—*you're* married." He pointed at my ring.

"Oh, that." I showed it to him. "It just looks like a wedding ring; I wear it to keep women off." That ring is an antique I bought in 1985 from a fellow operative—he had fetched it from pre-Christian Crete. "The Worm Ouroboros . . . the World Snake that eats its own tail, forever without end. A symbol of the Great Paradox."

He barely glanced at it. "If you're really a bastard, you know how it feels. When I was a little girl—"

"Wups!" I said. "Did I hear you correctly?"

"Who's telling this story? When I was a little girl—Look, ever hear of Christine Jorgenson? Or Roberta Cowell?"

"Uh, sex change cases? You're trying to tell me—"

"Don't interrupt or swelp me, I won't talk. I was a foundling, left at an orphanage in Cleveland in 1945 when I was a month old. When I was a little girl, I envied kids with parents. Then, when I learned about sex—and, believe me, Pop, you learn fast in an orphanage—"

"I know."

"I made a solemn vow that any kid of mine would have both a pop and a mom. It kept me 'pure,' quite a feat in that vicinity—I had to learn to fight to manage it. Then I got older and realized I stood darned little chance of getting married—for the same reason I hadn't been adopted." He scowled. "I was horse-faced and buck-toothed, flat-chested and straight-haired."

"You don't look any worse than I do."

"Who cares how a barkeep looks? Or a writer? But people wanting to adopt pick little blue-eyed golden-haired morons. Later on, the boys want bulging breasts, a cute face, and an Oh-you-wonderful-male manner." He shrugged. "I couldn't compete. So I decided to join the W.E.N.C.H.E.S."

"Eh?"

"Women's Emergency National Corps, Hospitality & Entertainment Section, what they now call 'Space Angels'—Auxiliary Nursing Group, Extraterrestrial Legions."

I knew both terms, once I had them chronized. Although we now use still a third name; it's that elite military service corps: Women's Hospitality Order Refortifying & Encouraging Spacemen. Vocabulary shift is the worst hurdle in time-jumps—did you know that "service station" once meant a dispensary for petroleum fractions? Once on an assignment in the Churchill Era a woman said to me, "Meet me at the service station next door"—which is *not* what it sounds; a "service station" (then) wouldn't have a bed in it.

He went on: "It was when they first admitted you can't send men into space for months and years and not relieve the tension. You remember how the wowsers screamed?—that improved my chances, volunteers were scarce. A gal had to be respectable, preferably virgin (they liked to train them from scratch), above average mentally, and stable emotionally. But most volunteers were old hookers, or neurotics who would crack up ten days off Earth. So I didn't need looks; if they accepted me, they would fix my buck teeth, put a wave in my hair, teach me to walk and dance and how to listen to a man pleasingly, and everything else—plus training for the prime duties. They would even use plastic surgery if it would help—nothing too good for Our Boys.

"Best yet, they made sure you didn't get pregnant during your enlistment—and you were almost certain to marry at the end of your hitch. Same way today, A.N.G.E.L.S. marry spacers—they talk the language.

"When I was eighteen I was placed as a 'mother's helper.' This family simply wanted a cheap servant but I didn't mind as I couldn't enlist till I was twenty-one. I did housework and went to night school—pretending to continue my high school typing and shorthand but going to a charm class instead, to better my chances for enlistment.

"Then I met this city slicker with his hundred dollar bills." He scowled. "The no-good actually did have a wad of hundred dollar bills. He showed me one night, told me to help myself.

"But I didn't. I liked him. He was the first man I ever met who was nice to me without trying to take my pants off. I quit night school to see him oftener. It was the happiest time of my life.

"Then one night in the park my pants did come off."

He stopped. I said, "And then?"

"And then *nothing!* I never saw him again. He walked me home and told me he loved me—and kissed me good-night and never came back." He looked grim. "If I could find him, I'd kill him!"

"Well," I sympathized, "I know how you feel. But killing him—just for doing what comes naturally—hmm . . . Did you struggle?"

"Huh? What's that got to do with it?"

"Quite a bit. Maybe he deserves a couple of broken arms for running out on you, but—"

"He deserves worse than that! Wait till you hear. Somehow I kept anyone from suspecting and decided it was all for the best. I hadn't really loved him and probably would never love anybody—and I was more eager to join the W.E.N.C.H.E.S. than ever. I wasn't disqualified, they didn't insist on virgins. I cheered up.

"It wasn't until my skirts got tight that I realized."

"Pregnant?"

"The bastard had me higher'n a kite! Those skinflints I lived with ignored it as long as I could work—then kicked me out and the orphanage wouldn't take me back. I landed in a charity ward surrounded by other big bellies and trotted bedpans until my time came.

"One night I found myself on an operating table, with a nurse saying, 'Relax. Now breathe deeply.'

"I woke up in bed, numb from the chest down. My surgeon came in. 'How do you feel?' he says cheerfully.

" 'Like a mummy.'

" 'Naturally. You're wrapped like one and full of dope to keep you numb. You'll get well—but a Caesarian isn't a hangnail.'

" 'Caesarian?' " I said, "Doc—*did I lose the baby?*"

" 'Oh, no. Your baby's fine.'

" 'Oh. Boy or girl?'

" 'A healthy little girl. Five pounds, three ounces.'

"I relaxed. It's something, to have made a baby. I told myself I would go somewhere and tack 'Mrs.' on my name and let the kid think her papa was dead—no orphanage for *my* kid!

"But the surgeon was talking. 'Tell me, uh—' He avoided my name. '—did you ever think your glandular setup was odd?'

"I said, 'Huh? Of course not. What are you driving at?'

"He hesitated. 'I'll give you this in one dose, then a hypo to let you sleep off your jitters. You'll have 'em.'

" 'Why?' I demanded.

" 'Ever hear of that Scottish physician who was female until she was thirty-five?—then had surgery and became legally and medically a man? Got married. All okay.'

" 'What's that got to do with me?'

" 'That's what I'm saying. You're a man.'

"I tried to sit up. *'What?'*

" 'Take it easy. When I opened you, I found a mess. I sent for the Chief of Surgery while I got the baby out, then we held a consultation with you on the table—and worked for hours to salvage what we could. You had two full sets of organs, both immature, but with the female set well enough developed that you had a baby. They could never be any use to you again, so we took them out and rearranged things so that you can develop properly as a man.' He put a hand on me. 'Don't worry. You're young, your bones will readjust, we'll watch your glandular balance—and make a fine young man out of you.'

"I started to cry. 'What about my *baby*?'

" 'Well, you can't nurse her, you haven't milk enough for a kitten. If I were you, I wouldn't see her—put her up for adoption.'

" *'No!'*

"He shrugged. 'The choice is yours; you're her mother—well, her parent. But don't worry now; we'll get you well first.'

"Next day they let me see the kid and I saw her daily—trying to get used to her. I had never seen a brand-new baby and had no idea how awful they look—my daughter looked like an orange monkey. My feeling changed to cold determination to do right by her. But four weeks later that didn't mean anything."

"Eh?"

"She was snatched."

" 'Snatched?' "

The Unmarried Mother almost knocked over the bottle we had bet. "Kidnapped—stolen from the hospital nursery!" He breathed hard. "How's that for taking the last thing a man's got to live for?"

"A bad deal," I agreed. "Let's pour you another. No clues?"

"Nothing the police could trace. Somebody came to see her, claimed to be her uncle. While the nurse had her back turned, he walked out with her."

"Description?"

"Just a man, with a face-shaped face, like yours or mine." He frowned. "I think it was the baby's father. The nurse swore it was an older man but he probably used makeup. Who else would swipe my baby? Childless women pull such stunts—but whoever heard of a man doing it?"

"What happened to you then?"

"Eleven more months of that grim place and three operations. In four months I started to grow a beard; before I was out I was shaving regularly . . . and no longer doubted that I was male." He grinned wryly. "I was staring down nurses' necklines."

"Well," I said, "seems to me you came through okay. Here you are, a normal man, making good money, no real troubles. And the life of a female is not an easy one."

He glared at me. "A lot you know about it!"

"So?"

"Ever hear the expression 'a ruined woman'?"

"Mmm, years ago. Doesn't mean much today."

"I was as ruined as a woman can be; that bastard *really* ruined me—I was no longer a woman . . . and I didn't know *how* to be a man."

"Takes getting used to, I suppose."

"You have no idea. I don't mean learning how to dress, or not walking into the wrong rest room; I learned those in the hospital. But how could I *live*? What job could I get? Hell, I couldn't even drive a car. I didn't know a trade; I couldn't do manual labor—too much scar tissue, too tender.

"I hated him for having ruined me for the W.E.N.C.H.E.S., too, but I didn't know how much until I tried to join the Space Corps instead. One look at my belly and I was marked unfit for military service. The medical officer spent time on me just from curiosity; he had read about my case.

"So I changed my name and came to New York. I got by as a fry cook, then rented a typewriter and set myself up as a public stenographer—what a laugh! In four months I typed four letters and one manuscript. The manuscript was for *Real Life Tales* and a waste of paper, but the goof who wrote it, sold it. Which gave me an idea; I bought a stack of confession magazines and studied them." He looked cynical. "Now you know how I get the authentic wowan's angle on an unmarried-mother story . . . through the only version I haven't sold—the true one. Do I win the bottle?"

I pushed it toward him. I was upset myself, but there was work to do, I said, "Son, you still want to lay hands on that so-and-so?"

His eyes lighted up—a feral gleam.

"Hold it!" I said. "You wouldn't kill him?"

He chuckled nastily. "Try me."

"Take it easy. I know more about it than you think I do. I can help you. I know where he is."

He reached across the bar. *"Where is he?"*

I said softly, "Let go my shirt, sonny—or you'll land in the alley and we'll tell the cops you fainted." I showed him the sap.

He let go. "Sorry. But where is he?" He looked at me. "And how do you know so much?"

"All in good time. There are records—hospital records, orphanage records, medical records. The matron of your orphanage was Mrs. Fetherage—right? She was followed by Mrs. Gruenstein—right? Your name, as a girl, was 'Jane'—right? And you didn't tell me any of this—right?"

I had him baffled and a bit scared. "What's this? You trying to make trouble for me?"

"No indeed. I've your welfare at heart. I can put this character in your lap. You do to him as you see fit—and I guarantee that you'll get away with it. But I don't think you'll kill him. You'd be nuts to—and you aren't nuts. Not quite."

He brushed it aside. "Cut the noise. *Where is he?"*

I poured him a short one; he was drunk but anger was offsetting it. "Not so fast. I do something for you—you do something for me."

"Uh . . . what?"

"You don't like your work. What would you say to high pay, steady work, unlimited expense account, your own boss on the job, and lots of variety and adventure?"

He stared. "I'd say, 'Get those goddam reindeer off my roof!' Shove it, Pop—there's no such job."

"Okay, put it this way: I hand him to you, you settle with him, then try my job. If it's not all I claim—well, I can't hold you."

He was wavering; the last drink did it. "When d'yuh d'liver 'im?" he said thickly.

"If it's a deal—*right now!"*

He shoved out his hand. "It's a deal!"

I nodded to my assistant to watch both ends, noted the time—2300—started to duck through the gate under the bar—when the juke box blared out: *"I'm My Own Granpaw!"* The service man had orders to load it with old Americana and classics because I couldn't stomach the "music" of 1970, but I hadn't known that tape was in it. I called out, "Shut that off! Give the customer his money back." I added, "Storeroom, back in a moment," and headed there with my Unmarried Mother following.

It was down the passage across from the johns, a steel door to which no one but my day manager and myself had a key; inside was a door to an inner room to which only I had a key. We went there.

He looked blearily around at windowless walls. "Where is 'e?"

"Right away." I opened a case, the only thing in the room; it was a U.S.F.F. Co-ordinates Transformer Field Kit, series 1992, Mod. II—a beauty, no moving parts, weight twenty-three kilos fully charged, and shaped to pass as a suitcase. I had adjusted it precisely earlier that day; all I had to do was to shake the metal net which limits the transformation field.

Which I did. "Wha's that?" he demanded.

"Time machine," I said and tossed the net over us.

"Hey!" he yelled and stepped back. There is a technique to this; the net has to be thrown so that the subject will instinctively step back *onto* the metal mesh, then you close the net with both of you inside completely—else you might leave shoe soles behind or a piece of foot, or scoop up a slice of floor. But that's all the skill it takes. Some agents con a subject into the net; I tell the truth and use that instant of utter astonishment to flip the switch. Which I did.

1030-V-3 April 1963-Cleveland, Ohio-Apex Bldg.: "Hey!" he repeated. "Take this damn thing off!"

"Sorry," I apologized and did so, stuffed the net into the case, closed it. "You said you wanted to find him."

"But—You said that was a time machine!"

I pointed out a window. "Does that look like November? Or New York?" While he was gawking at new buds and spring weather, I reopened the case, took out a packet of hundred dollar bills, checked that the numbers and signatures were compatible with 1963. The Temporal Bureau doesn't care how much you spend (it costs nothing) but they don't like unnecessary anachronisms. Too many mistakes and a general court martial will exile you for a year in a nasty period, say 1974 with its strict rationing and forced labor. I never make such mistakes, the money was okay. He turned around and said, "What happened?"

"He's here. Go outside and take him. Here's expense money." I shoved it at him and added, "Settle him, then I'll pick you up."

Hundred dollar bills have a hypnotic effect on a person not used to them. He was thumbing them unbelievingly as I eased him into the hall, locked him out. The next jump was easy, a small shift in era.

1700-V-10 March, 1964-Cleveland-Apex Bldg.: There was a notice under the door saying that my lease expired next week otherwise the room looked as it had a moment before. Outside, trees were bare and snow threatened; I hurried, stopping only for contemporary money and a coat, hat and topcoat I had left there when I leased the room. I hired a car, went to the hospital. It took twenty minutes to bore the nursery attendant to the point where I could swipe the baby without being noticed; we went back to the Apex Building. This dial setting was more involved as the building did not yet exist in 1945. But I had precalculated it.

0100-V-20 Sept 1945-Cleveland-Skyview Motel: Field kit, baby, and I arrived in a motel outside town. Earlier I had registered as "Gregory Johnson, Warren, Ohio," so we arrived in a room with curtains closed, windows locked, and doors bolted, and the floor cleared to allow for waver as the machine hunts. You can get a nasty bruise from a chair where it shouldn't be—not the chair of course, but backlash from the field.

No trouble. Jane was sleeping soundly; I carried her out, put her in a grocery box on the seat of a car I had provided earlier, drove to the orphanage, put her on the steps, drove two blocks to a "service station" (the petroleum products sort) and phoned the orphanage, drove back in time to see them taking the box inside, kept going and abandoned the car near the motel—walked to it and jumped forward to the Apex Building in 1963.

2200-V-24 April 1963-Cleveland-Apex Bldg.: I had cut the time rather fine—temporal accuracy depends on span, except on return to zero. If I had it right, Jane was discovering, out in the park this balmy spring night, that she wasn't quite as "nice" a girl as she had thought. I grabbed a taxi to the home of those skinflints, had the hackie wait around a corner while I lurked in shadows.

Presently I spotted them down the street, arms around each other. He took her up on the porch and made a long job of kissing her goodnight—longer than I had thought. Then she went in and he came down the walk, turned away. I slid into step and hooked an arm in his. "That's all, son," I announced quietly. "I'm back to pick you up."

"*You!*" He gasped and caught his breath.

"Me. Now you know who *he* is—and after you think it over you'll know who *you* are . . . and if you think hard enough, you'll figure out who the baby is . . . and who *I* am."

He didn't answer, he was badly shaken. It's a shock to have it proved to you that you can't resist seducing yourself. I took him to the Apex Building and we jumped again.

❖

2300-VII-12 Aug 1985-Sub Rockies Base: I woke the duty sergeant, showed my I.D., told the sergeant to bed him down with a happy pill and recruit him in the morning. The sergeant looked sour but rank is rank, regardless of era; he did what I said—thinking no doubt, that the next time we met he might be the colonel and I the sergeant. Which can happen in our corps. "What name?" he asked.

I wrote it out. He raised his eyebrows. "Like so, eh? *Hmm*—"

"You just do your job, Sergeant." I turned to my companion. "Son, your troubles are over. You're about to start the best job a man ever held—and you'll do well. I *know.*"

"But—"

" 'But' nothing. Get a night's sleep, then look over the proposition. You'll like it."

"That you will!" agreed the sergeant. "Look at me—born in 1917—still around, still young, still enjoying life." I went back to the jump room, set everything on preselected zero.

2301-V-7 Nov 1970-NYC-"Pop's Place": I came out of the storeroom carrying a fifth of Drambuie to account for the minute I had been gone. My assistant was arguing with the customer who had been playing *"I'm My Own Granpaw!"* I said, "Oh, let him play it, then unplug it." I was very tired.

It's rough, but somebody must do it and it's very hard to recruit anyone in the later years, since the Mistake of 1972. Can you think of a better source than to pick people all fouled up where they are and give them well-paid, interesting (even though dangerous) work in a necessary cause? Everybody knows now why the Fizzle War of 1963 fizzled. The bomb with New York's number on it didn't go off, a hundred other things didn't go as planned—all arranged by the likes of me.

But not the Mistake of '72; that one is not our fault—and can't be undone; there's no paradox to resolve. A thing either is, or it isn't, now and forever amen. But there won't be another like it; an order dated "1992" takes precedence any year.

I closed five minutes early, leaving a letter in the cash register telling my day manager that I was accepting his offer, so see my lawyer as I was leaving on a long vacation. The Bureau might or might not pick up his payments, but they want things left tidy. I went to the room back of the storeroom and forward to 1993.

2200-VII-12 Jan 1993-Sub Rockies Annex-HQ Temporal DOL: I checked in with the duty officer and went to my quarters, intending to sleep for a week. I had fetched the bottle we bet (after all, I won it) and took a drink before I wrote my report. It tasted foul and I wondered why I had ever liked Old Underwear. But it was better than nothing; I don't like to be cold sober, I think too much. But I don't really hit the bottle either; other people have snakes—*I* have people.

I dictated my report: forty recruitments all okayed by the Psych Bureau—counting my own, which I knew would be okayed. I was here, wasn't I? Then I taped a request for assignment to operations; I was sick of recruiting. I dropped both in the slot and headed for bed.

My eye fell on "The By-Laws of Time," over my bed:

> Never Do Yesterday What Should be Done Tomorrow.
> If At Last You Do Succeed, Never Try Again.
> A Stitch In Time Saves Nine Billion.
> A Paradox May be Paradoctored.
> It is Earlier When You Think.
> Ancestors Are Just People.
> Even Jove Nods.

They didn't inspire me the way they had when I was a recruit; thirty subjective years of time-jumping wears you down. I undressed and when I got down to the hide I looked at my belly. A Caesarian leaves a big scar but I'm so hairy now that I don't notice it unless I look for it.

Then I glanced at the ring on my finger.

The Snake That Eats Its Own Tail, Forever and Ever . . . I *know* where *I* came from—but *where did all you zombies come from?*

I felt a headache coming on, but a headache powder is one thing I do not take. I did it once—and you all went away.

So I crawled into bed and whistled out the light.

You aren't really there at all. There isn't anybody but me—Jane—here alone in the dark.

I miss you dreadfully!

COPYRIGHT ACKNOWLEDGMENTS